Laceys of Liverpool
and
Dancing in the Dark

Laceys of Liverpool

Dancing in the Dark

Maureen Lee

ORION

Laceys of Liverpool
First published in Great Britain by Orion in 2001

Dancing in the Dark
First published in Great Britain by Orion in 1999

This omnibus edition published in 2005
by Orion Books Ltd
Orion House, 5 Upper St Martin's Lane
London WC2H 9EA

A CIP catalogue record for this book is available from the British Library.

ISBN 978-1-898800-89-7

Printed in Great Britain by
Clays Ltd, St Ives plc

Laceys of Liverpool

Prologue
CHRISTMAS 1940

The woman lay listening to the rain as it beat against the hospital windows. She and Alice hadn't picked a good night to have their babies. As had become the custom in Bootle over the last few months, there'd been an air raid, a bad one, and they'd all been moved down to the cellar. Alice's lad had been born only minutes after the All Clear, at a quarter past eleven. Her own son had arrived almost three hours later, so they'd have different birthdays. Later, there'd been an emergency. Some woman had been found in the rubble of her house about to drop her baby. Since then, things had quietened down.

In a bed opposite, her sister-in-law was fast asleep, dead to the world, like the other six women in the ward. 'Why can't *I* sleep like that?' the woman murmured fretfully. 'I can never sleep.' Her mind was always too full of plans for the future, schemes: how to get this, how to do that. How to make twenty-five bob last the whole week, including paying the rent and buying the food. Oh, how she'd love new curtains for the parlour! But new curtains, new anything, were an impossible dream.

Unless she stole something, pawned it, bought curtains with the money. She'd stolen before, her heart in her mouth, sweat trickling down the insides of her arms. The first time it was only a string of beads that looked like pearls. The price ticket said a guinea. The pawnbroker had offered a florin, which she'd accepted gratefully and bought four nice cups and saucers in Paddy's Market.

One day she'd walked all the way into town and nicked a cut-glass vase from George Henry Lee's, which she kept on the mantelpiece, though she was the only one who knew it was cut glass. Billy thought it was just a cheap old thing. The silver candlestick she'd robbed from Henderson's had paid for a nice mat in front of the parlour fireplace. Some things she kept, some she pawned. She'd become quite skilled at shoplifting. The trick was to stay calm, not rush, smile, make your way slowly to the door. Stepping outside was the worst part. If spotted, it was the time you'd be nabbed. But she'd got away with it so far.

The woman didn't care how she looked as long as it was respectable, or what she ate, but she liked pretty things for the house: curtains, crockery, cutlery, furniture. Furniture most of all. She'd give anything for a new three-piece: velveteen, dark green or plum-coloured. She licked her lips and thought about brocade cushions with fringes, one at each end of the settee, on each of the chairs.

Most of all, she'd like a nice big house to put the lovely things in. She was sick to death of living in a two-up, two-down in O'Connell Street. But if curtains were an impossible dream, then a big house was – well, out of the question. Being married to a no-hoper like Billy Lacey, she was just as likely to fly to the moon.

She shoved herself to a sitting position. The red light on the ceiling cast a sinister glow over the ward, over the prone bodies beneath the faded cotton counterpanes. 'It looks like a morgue,' she thought. Paper chains criss-crossed the room and she remembered it was Christmas Eve. 'Everyone's dead except me and that fat bitch in the corner snoring her head off.'

The clock over the door showed a quarter past four. A cup of tea should arrive soon. Alice, who already had three kids, all girls, and knew about such things, said the tea trolley came early, around five o'clock, which seemed an unearthly time to wake anyone up. In the meantime she'd go for a walk. If she lay in bed till kingdom come, she'd never go asleep.

The rain was lashing down, making the windows rattle in their frames. It drummed on the roof and she hoped Billy would keep an eye on the loose slates over the lavatory. She'd been at him to fix them for ages, but would probably end up fixing them herself. She fixed most things around the house. Her lips twisted bitterly when she thought about Billy. His brother, John, had stayed in the ozzie with Alice until an hour before their lad was born. He'd only left because the girls were being looked after by a neighbour who was scared of the raids. But Billy had left *her* on the steps outside the ozzie when she was about to have their first-born child. Off to the pub, as usual. He didn't know yet if she'd had a boy or a girl.

There was a nurse in the glass cubicle at the end of the ward where a sprig of mistletoe hung over the door. She was at a desk, head bent, writing. The new mothers were expected to remain confined to their beds for seven whole days, not even allowed to go to the lavatory, but the woman slid from under the bedclothes and crept past, opening one half of the swing doors just enough to allow her through. The nurse didn't look up.

The dimly lit corridor was empty, silent. Her bare feet made no sound on the cold floor. She crept round corners, through more doors, dodged into the lavatories when she heard footsteps coming towards her. The footsteps passed, faded, and she looked both ways before coming out, hoping it wasn't someone on their way to

3

her ward who'd notice the empty bed, though it was unlikely. The hospital was understaffed. Some nurses had joined the Forces, or gone into better-paid jobs. There were a lot of part-timers and older nurses who'd retired and come back to do their bit.

She arrived at the place that had been her destination all along: the nursery. Five rows of babies, tightly wrapped in sheets, like little mummies in their wooden cots. Most were asleep, a few grizzled, some had their eyes wide open. Like her, they couldn't sleep.

Her own baby had been whisked away because of the emergency and she'd barely seen him. Now she did, she saw he was a pale little thing. He looked sickly, she thought. There was yellow stuff in his eyes. As she stared at her sleeping child, she felt nothing. She was twenty-seven, older than Alice, and had been married longer. But she hadn't wanted a baby. The sponge soaked in vinegar she'd inserted every night, which Billy knew nothing about, hadn't worked for once.

The child couldn't possibly have come at a worse time. Just when she'd worn Billy down, ranted at him mercilessly for month after month, until he'd conceded that letting his missus get a job wasn't a sore reflection on his masculine pride. Not with a war on and women all over the country working in ways they'd never done before. Why, there were women in the Army, on the trams, delivering the post, in factories doing men's jobs.

It was a job in a factory on which the woman had set her eye, making munitions. You could earn as much as four quid a week, three times as much as Billy. And as she said to him, 'Any minute now, you'll be called up. What am I supposed to do then? Sit at home, twiddling me thumbs, living on the pittance I'll get from the Army?'

His face had paled. He was a coward, not like his

4

brother John, who'd volunteered when war broke out, but had been turned down because he was in a reserved occupation. John was a centre lathe turner, Billy a labourer. There was nothing essential about *his* menial job. John, anxious to make a contribution towards the war, had become a fire-watcher. Billy carried on as usual and haunted the pubs waiting for his call-up papers from the Army to land on the mat.

She'd only been in the munitions factory a fortnight, packing shells. It was hard work, but she liked it. If she felt tired, she thought about the pay packet she'd get on Friday, about the things she'd buy, and soon perked up. Then she discovered she was up the stick, pregnant and, stupid idiot that she was, she told the woman who worked beside her and next minute everyone knew, including the foreman, and she'd got the push.

'This is not the sort of job suitable for a woman in the family way,' the foreman said.

The woman glared through the glass at her baby. She hadn't thought what to call him. She wasn't interested. Billy wanted Maurice for some reason if they had a boy, but she had no idea if Maurice was a saint's name. Catholics were expected to call their kids after saints. Alice's girls had funny Irish names and she didn't know if they were saints either. The new kid would be called Cormac. 'No "k" at the end,' John had said, smiling. He humoured his silly, dreamy wife something rotten.

Where was Cormac? There were cards pinned to the foot of each cot with drawing pins. 'LACEY (1)' it said on the cot directly in front of her. Her own baby was 'LACEY (2)'. Alice had yet to see her little son. It had been a difficult birth and she'd been in agony the whole way through. John had been close to tears when he'd had to go home. Afterwards, with seven stitches and blind with pain, Alice had been given something to make her sleep.

Her own confinement had been painless – she wouldn't have dreamt of making a fuss had it been otherwise. She hadn't needed a single stitch. Her belly still felt slightly swollen and she hurt a bit between the legs, that was all.

Even though she didn't give a damn about babies, the woman had to admit Cormac was a bonny lad. He had dark curly hair like his dad, and he wasn't all red and shrivelled like the other babies. His big brown eyes were wide open and she could have sworn he was looking straight at her. She pressed her palms against the glass and something dead peculiar happened in her belly, a slow, curling shiver of anger. It wasn't fair: Alice had the best Lacey, now she had the best son.

From deep within the bowels of the hospital, she heard the rattle of dishes. Tea was being made, the trolley was being set. Any minute now, someone would come.

The woman opened the door of the nursery and went in.

Chapter 1
CHRISTMAS 1945

Alice Lacey sang to herself as she swept a cloud of Florrie Piper's hair into the corner of the salon. 'Away in a manger, no crib for a bed . . .' She brushed the hair on to a shovel and took it into the yard to empty in the dustbin.

'They say you can sell hair like that for a small fortune in the West End of London,' Mrs Piper yelled from under the dryer when Alice came back.

'Who to?'

'Wig makers. They're always on the lookout for a good head of hair.'

'Really,' Alice said doubtfully. The hair she'd just thrown away was more suitable for a bird's nest: dry as dust, over-permed, full of split ends and dyed the colour of soot.

'You can comb Mrs Piper out now, Alice,' Myrtle said in a slurred voice.

'About time too,' Florrie Piper said, tight-lipped. 'These curlers are giving me gyp.'

'I don't know how you stand it to be honest.' Alice switched off the dryer, and Mrs Piper heaved her large body out of the chair and went to sit in front of a pink-tinted mirror.

'We can't all have naturally wavy hair, Alice Lacey, not like you.' Florrie Piper chose to take offence. She sniffed audibly. 'You shouldn't work in a hairdresser's if you can't take what's done to the customers.'

Alice removed the net and yelped when her fingers touched a red-hot metal curler. It must be torture, sitting for half an hour with bits of burning metal pressed against your scalp. 'I'll take them out in a minute,' she muttered. 'Would you like a mince pie?'

'Well, I wouldn't say no,' Mrs Piper said graciously. She'd already had three. Food wasn't usually provided in Myrtle's Hairdressing Salon, but it was Christmas Eve. Some rather tired decorations festooned the walls and a bent tinsel star hung in the steam-covered window. There'd been sherry earlier, but the proprietor had finished off the lot by dinner time. Myrtle was as tipsy as a lord and had made a terrible mess of Mrs Fowler with the curling tongues. The waves were dead uneven. Fortunately, Mrs Fowler's sight wasn't all it should be and she refused to wear glasses. Hopefully, she wouldn't notice.

Mrs Piper had recovered her good humour. 'What are you doing for Christmas, luv?' she enquired when Alice began to remove the curlers. Her ears were a startling crimson.

'Nothing much.' Alice wrinkled her nose. 'John's mam's coming to Christmas dinner, along with his brother Billy and his wife. They've got a little boy, Maurice, exactly the same age as our Cormac. Me dad usually comes, but he's off to Ireland tonight to spend Christmas with his sister. She's not been well.'

'Your Cormac will be starting school soon, I expect.'

'In January. He was five only yesterday.'

'And how are your girls? You know, I can never remember their names.'

'Fionnuala, Orla and Maeve,' Alice said for the thousandth time in her life. 'They're at a party this avvy

8

in St James's church hall. Something to do with Sunday School. I made them a cake to take. I managed to get some dates.'

Mrs Piper eyed the remainder of the mince pies. 'Would you like another?' Alice enquired.

'I wouldn't say no,' Mrs Piper repeated. 'It would be a shame if they went to waste. You're closing early today, aren't you? I must be one of your last customers.'

'We've got a couple of trims, that's all. Here's one of 'em now.' The bell on the door gave its rather muted ring − it probably needed oiling − and Bernadette Moynihan came in. She was a vivacious young woman with an unusually voluptuous figure for someone so small. Alice smiled warmly at her best friend. 'Help yourself to a mince pie, Bernie.'

'I thought we were having sherry an' all,' Bernadette cried. 'I've been looking forward to it all day.'

'I'm afraid it's gone.' Alice glanced at Myrtle who seemed to have given up altogether on hairdressing and was staring drunkenly at her reflection in the pink mirror.

Bernadette grinned. 'She looks like a ghoul,' she whispered.

Myrtle was a tad too old for so much lipstick, eyeshadow, mascara and rouge. Now, everything was smudged and she looked like a sad, elderly clown. Her grey roots were showing and the rest of her hair had been peroxided to a yellow frizz. She made a poor advertisement for a hairdressing salon.

'Don't comb it out too much, luv,' Mrs Piper said when the curlers were removed. 'I like it left tight. It lasts longer.'

Alice loosened the curls slightly with her fingers and Mrs Piper said, 'How much is that, luv?'

'Half a crown.'

'And worth every penny!' She left, tipping Alice threepence, with her head resembling the inside of an Eccles cake.

The door closed and Alice looked from Bernadette to Myrtle who was slowly falling asleep, then back again. 'I'm not supposed to give trims, not official, like.' She usually went to Bernadette's to trim her hair, or Bernadette came to hers.

'Well, if you don't cut me hair, it doesn't look like anyone else will.' Bernadette seized a gown and tied it around her neck. 'I just want an inch off. Anyroad, Al, you've got the knack. You couldn't do it better if you were properly trained. I only came 'cos it's Christmas and I was expecting mince pies and a glass of sherry. To be sadly disappointed,' she added in a loud voice in Myrtle's direction, 'in regard to the sherry.'

Alice giggled. 'Sit down, luv. An inch you said?'

'One inch. A fraction shorter, a fraction longer, and I'll complain to the management.'

'You'll be lucky.' Alice attacked Bernadette's smooth fair hair, draped over one eye like Veronica Lake, with the scissors. 'Are you looking forward to tonight?'

Bernadette grinned. 'Ever so much. I've always liked Roy McBride. He works in Accounts. I was thrilled to pieces when he asked me out – and to a dinner dance on Christmas Eve!'

'I hope you have a lovely time.' Alice placed her hands on her friend's shoulders and they stared at each other in the mirror. 'Don't be too disappointed if he turns out like some of the others, will you, luv?'

'Like *most* of the others, you mean. All *I* want is company, all *they* want is . . . well, I can't think of a polite word for it. Men seem to think a young widow is game for anything.' Her usually cheerful face grew sober. 'Oh, Al, I don't half wish Bob hadn't been killed. I feel guilty going out with other men. I get so lonely, but not lonely enough to jump into bed with every man I meet. If only we'd had kids. At least they'd make me feel wanted.'

'I know, luv,' Alice said gently.

'We kept putting them off, kids, until we got a house. We didn't want to start a family while we were still in rooms. Then the war started, Bob was killed, and it's been horrible ever since. And I'm still living in the same rooms.'

Alice squeezed her shoulders. 'Don't forget, you're welcome round ours tomorrer if you feel like a jangle. Don't be put off 'cos it's Christmas Day.'

'I'm going to me mam's, Al, but thanks all the same.' Bernadette reached up and touched Alice's hand. 'I'm sorry, luv, for being such a moan. You've got enough problems of your own these days, what with John the way he is. It's just that you're the only person I've got to talk to.'

'Don't you dare apologise, Bernadette Moynihan. You're the only person I've told about John. Today was your turn for a moan. Next time it'll be mine.'

The final customer of the day arrived; Mrs O'Leary, with her ten-year-old daughter, Daisy, who was in Maeve's class at school and whose long, auburn ringlets were in need of a good trim. By now, Myrtle was fast asleep and snoring.

'Would you like me to do it?' an embarrassed Alice offered. 'I won't be long with Bernie.'

'Well, I haven't got much choice, have I?' Mrs O'Leary laughed. 'At least you'll probably cut it level both sides. Myrtle's usually well out. I sometimes wonder why we come. I suppose it's because it's so convenient, right at the end of the street, but I think I'll give that place in Marsh Lane a try. Each time we come

Myrtle's worse than the time before. And it's not just the drink. She's every bit as useless if she's sober. If it weren't for you, Alice, this place would have closed down years ago.'

'Hear, hear,' cried Bernadette. 'It's Al who keeps it going.'

Alice blushed, but she had a feeling of dread. If Myrtle's closed, what would she do? She'd started four years ago, just giving a hand: sweeping up, wiping down, putting women under the dryers, taking them out again, washing hair, fetching towels, putting on gowns. Lately, with Myrtle going seriously downhill in more ways than one, she'd been taking on more and more responsibility. It was impossible to work in a hairdresser's for so long without learning how it was done. Alice was quite capable of giving a shampoo and set, a Marcel or Eugene wave, a perm – the new method was so much simpler than having to plug in every curler separately, a procedure that took all of four hours – and she seemed to have a knack with scissors. It was just a question of holding them right.

She only lived in the next street. It was easy to pop home when business was slack to make the girls their tea, keep an eye on them during the holidays. She usually brought Cormac with her. An angel of a child, he'd been quite happy to lie in his pram in the kitchen, play on the pavement outside when he got older, or sit in the corner, drawing, on the days it rained. But it wasn't just the convenience, or the extra money, useful though it was. Nowadays the hairdresser's provided an escape from the tragedy her life had become since last May. For most people the end of the worst war the world had ever known was a joyful occasion, a reason to celebrate. For the Laceys it had been a nightmare.

Myrtle's was an entirely different world: a bright, cosy,

highly dramatic little world behind thick lace curtains and steamed-up windows, quite separate from the one outside. There was always something to laugh about, always a choice piece of gossip doing the rounds. The women had sorted out the war between them – it would probably have ended sooner had Winston Churchill been privy to the sound advice of Myrtle Rimmer's customers.

Most women were willing, even anxious, to open up their hearts to their hairdresser. There were some very respectable men in Bootle who'd have a fit if they knew the things Alice had been told about them. She never repeated anything, not even to Bernie.

Bernadette waited until Alice had cut Daisy O'Leary's ringlets so they were level both sides and Mrs O'Leary pronounced herself satisfied. She wished them Merry Christmas and departed.

Alice locked the door, turned the 'Open' sign to 'Closed' and between them the two women half carried, half dragged the proprietor to her flat upstairs and laid her on the bed.

'Jaysus,' Bernadette gasped. 'It don't half pong in here. She's not fit to live on her own, Al, let alone run a hairdresser's.'

The bed was unmade, the curtains still drawn. Alice covered her employer with several dirty blankets and regarded her worriedly. 'I'll pop round tomorrer after dinner, like. See if she's all right. She said something about going to a friend's for tea.'

'Has she got any relatives?' Bernadette asked.

'There's a daughter somewhere. Southampton, I think. Myrtle's husband died ages ago.' She heard someone try the salon door, but ignored it. There was a notice announcing they closed at four.

They returned downstairs. After Bernadette had gone,

Alice brushed the floor again, gave it a cursory going over with a wet mop, wiped surfaces, polished mirrors, straightened chairs, arranged the three dryers at the same angle and tied the dirty towels in a bundle ready to go to the laundry when the salon reopened after Christmas. She glanced around to see if there was anything she'd missed. Well, the lace curtain could do with mending, not to mention a good wash, the walls were badly in need of a lick of paint, and the oilcloth should be replaced before a customer caught her heel in one of the numerous frayed holes and went flying. Otherwise, everywhere looked OK. She could go home.

Instead, Alice switched off the light and sat under a dryer. Go home for what? she asked herself. The girls weren't due till five. Her dad had taken Cormac to the grotto in Stanley Road. John was finishing work at three. He'd be home by now. Alice shuddered. She didn't want to be alone with her husband.

John Lacey regarded what was left of his face in the chrome mirror over the mantelpiece. It had been a handsome face once. He wasn't a conceited man, but he'd always known that he and his brother Billy weren't at the back of the queue when the Lord handed out good looks. Both were tall, going on six feet. John's dark-brown hair was curly, Billy's straight. They had the same rich-brown eyes, the same straight nose, the same wide brow. His mam, never one to consider anyone's feelings, used to say John was the handsomer of the two. He had a firmer mouth, there was something determined about his chin. Billy's chin was weak.

Mam didn't say that now, not since her elder son had turned into a monster. John stroked the melted skin on his right cheek, touched the corner of the unnaturally angled slit of an eye. If only he hadn't gone to the aid of

14

the seaman trapped in the hold when the boiler had exploded on that merchant ship. The hold had become a furnace, the man was screaming, his overalls on fire. He emerged from the flames, a blazing phantom, hair burning, screaming for help.

The irony was he hadn't managed to save the chap. He had died within minutes, writhing in agony on the deck, everyone too terrified to touch him. Everyone except that dickhead, John Lacey, who'd dragged him out, burnt his own hands, burnt his face. The hands had mended, but not the face.

A further irony was that the war was virtually over and the accident had had nothing to do with the conflict. The firefighters were on duty at Gladstone Dock, as they had been every night over the past five years, when the boiler had gone up. They'd come through the war unscathed, all his family, his brother's family, his mam, his father-in-law. Amber Street itself hadn't been touched, not even a broken window, while numerous other streets in Bootle had been reduced to rubble. Then, in the very last week, John had lost half his face.

He stared at the grotesque reflection in the mirror. 'Fool!' he spat through crooked lips.

Where were his children – his three girls, his little son? More important, where was his wife? He remembered the girls had gone to a party. His father-in-law had Cormac. But there was no explanation for why Alice wasn't home.

'She don't fancy you no more,' he told his reflection. 'She's with another fella. He's giving her one right now, sticking it up her in the place that used to be yours.'

John groaned and turned away from the mirror. He'd never used to think like that, so coarsely, lewdly. Making love to Alice used to be the sweetest thing on earth, but

15

now he couldn't bring himself to touch her, imagining her shrinking inside, hating it.

The back door opened and his wife came in. Until last May, until a few days before the war ended, until his accident, he would have lifted her up, kissed her rosy face, stared into her misty blue eyes, told her how much he'd missed her, how much he loved her. They might have taken the opportunity, the kids being out, of going upstairs for a blissful half-hour in bed. Instead, John scowled and said gruffly, 'I tried Myrtle's door on the way home, but it were locked. That was more than half an hour ago. Where have you been, eh? With your fancy man?'

She looked at him reproachfully. 'I haven't got a fancy man, John.'

Oh, she was so lovely! She was thirty-one, though she didn't look it: tall, gawky like a schoolgirl, a bit too thin. He used to tell her she had too many elbows, she was always knocking things over. Her face was long and oval, the skin flawless, the eyes very large and very blue. They were innocent eyes, guileless. Deep within his soul, he knew she would never be unfaithful, but the new John, the John Lacey who now inhabited his body, found it just as hard to believe that such an attractive woman, a woman born to be loved, hadn't found someone else since her husband had become so repulsive.

'So, what have you been doing with yourself for the last half-hour?' he sneered.

'Tidying up. I remember hearing someone try the door when me and Bernadette were upstairs with Myrtle. She drank all the sherry and ended up incapable.' She sighed. 'I'll make some tea.'

He grabbed her shoulder when she turned to leave. 'I don't believe you.'

'There's nothing I can do about that.' She was about

to shrug his hand away. Instead, she bent her head and laid her face against it and he could feel the rich-brown hair fluttering on his fingers. The gesture touched his heart. 'I don't need a fancy man, luv,' she said softly. 'I've got you. Why don't we go upstairs for five minutes? I can get dressed in a jiffy if the latch goes.' Alice missed making love more than she could say. She didn't care about his face. For his sake, she would prefer it hadn't happened. But it *had* happened and she loved him just as much, if not more. Sadly, it was impossible to convince John of this. Anyroad, his face wasn't nearly as bad as he made out. The right side was a bit puckered, that was all. The burn had slightly affected his eye, the corner of his mouth, but he looked nothing like the monster he claimed. She reached up and stroked the puckered skin. 'I love you.'

If only he could believe her! He wanted to, so much. But he knew, he was certain, she was forcing herself to touch him. She was a good, kind woman and felt sorry for him. She was probably feeling sick inside. The tender, loving look on her face was all put on. He seized her wrist and pushed her hand away. 'I don't want your sympathy,' he said gruffly.

He truly hadn't meant to be quite so rough. He noticed her wince and rub her wrist when she went into the kitchen. Water ran, the gas was lit and John Lacey realised he had just hurt the person he loved most in the world. He looked at himself in the mirror. Sometimes he wondered if it would be better for all concerned if he did himself in.

Alice had borne three daughters within two and a half years of her marriage to John Lacey. Fionnuala was only two months old when she had fallen pregnant with Orla and Maeve had arrived when Orla was still on the breast.

Her husband realised something had to be done. Alice was barely twenty-one. At the rate they were going, they'd have a couple of dozen kids by the time she reached forty. Although strictly forbidden by the Catholic church, for the next five years, with Alice's approval, he took precautions. Then the war started and they decided to try for a son. Nine months later, Cormac was born. Four children was enough for anyone and John started to take precautions again. It was easier now, with French letters available over the counter at the chemist.

They were an exceptionally happy family. The girls were the image of their mam with the same brown hair and blue eyes. Cormac was a lovely lad, a bit pale, a bit small, rather quiet compared with his sisters. He had his mam's blue eyes, if a shade or two lighter. Apart from that, no one was quite sure whom he took after, with his straight blond hair and neatly proportioned features.

John didn't mind when his wife went to work in the hairdresser's in Opal Street. He earned enough to feed his family, keep them comfortable, but the girls were mad on clothes and it didn't seem fair that the eldest was the only one who had new things. Anyroad, Orla was a little madam and would have screamed blue murder at the idea of always having to wear her sister's hand-me-downs. Alice worked to dress her girls and she was happy at Myrtle's. And if Alice was happy, so was John.

At least that used to be the case. Now, it was the first war-free Christmas in six years. It should have been the best the Laceys had ever known, but it turned out to be the worst.

Orla had made a show of herself at the Sunday School party, Fionnuala claimed. She'd sung 'Strawberry Fair' and 'Greensleeves'. 'Though no one asked her. I felt dead embarrassed, if you must know.'

'Miss Geraghty asked who'd like to do a turn,' Orla said haughtily. 'I put me hand up, that's all.'

'Perhaps our Fionnuala didn't hear what Miss Geraghty had said,' suggested Maeve, the peacemaker.

On Christmas Day, after dinner, when everyone was in the parlour, Orla offered to sing again.

'That'd be nice, luv,' Alice said quickly, hoping a few songs might lighten the atmosphere. It had been a miserable meal and though she didn't like to admit it, not even to herself, it was all John's fault. He glowered at everyone from the head of the table, snapped at the children, was rude to his wife. Even Billy, his brother, normally the life and soul of the party, had been subdued. By the time the pudding stage was reached the conversation had dried up completely.

As soon as the food was eaten, Billy escaped to the pub. John wasn't a drinker, but he used to like the occasional pint, particularly at Christmas. This year, he'd churlishly refused. He rarely left the house, except for work, when he wore a trilby with the brim tipped to show as little as possible of his face. At Mass he sat at the back.

Cora was watching everything with a supercilious smile, as if she was enjoying seeing the Lacey family fall to pieces. Alice had never got on with her sister-in-law. Cora was so cold and reserved. She had made it obvious from the start that she didn't want to become friends. She had, possibly, softened a little since Maurice was born, but Maurice himself seemed the sole beneficiary of this slight improvement. Yet she was strict with the boy, too much so. Alice had seen the cane hanging on the wall in her sister-in-law's smart house off Merton Road, but had also witnessed the soft look in Cora's strange brown eyes, almost khaki, when they lighted on her handsome son.

Maurice was a Lacey to his bones. His gran doted on

him. Meg Lacey carried a photo in her handbag of John and Billy when they were little, and either one could have been Maurice they were so alike.

Meg had Maurice on her knee, stroking his chubby legs – she made it obvious she had no time for Cormac. 'Who's my favourite little boy in the whole world,' she cooed.

Cora didn't look too pleased. Her small, tight face was screwed in a scowl. Alice wondered what she would look like with her hair combed loose, instead of scraped back in a knot with such severity that it stretched the skin on her forehead. Except for the odd brown of her eyes, there wasn't a spot of colour in her face. Cora scorned make-up and nice clothes. Today, she wore the plain brown frock with a belt that had been her best since Alice could remember.

Orla sang 'Greensleeves' in a fine, strong voice. If there'd been the money, Alice would have sent her to singing lessons – Mrs O'Leary's Daisy went to tap-dancing classes – but then Fionnuala would have demanded lessons in something or other and it wouldn't have been fair to leave out Maeve, although her placid youngest daughter wouldn't have complained.

'Any requests?' Orla enquired pertly when she'd finished her repertoire.

'Yes, shurrup,' Fionnuala snapped. It was said so viciously that Alice was dismayed. The girls had always got on well with each other. Perhaps, because the house was so full of love, they hadn't found it necessary to compete. Lately, though, Fion, who Alice had to concede could be dead irritating at times, had become resentful of Orla, making unnecessarily spiteful remarks, like the one just now. It didn't help when Orla, eleven, started her periods and the older Fion showed no sign. Alice wondered if it was the change in atmosphere that had done it. The house may well have been full of love once, but it certainly wasn't now.

Oh, God! This was a *horrible* Christmas. Normally, she never let Cora bother her, nor the fact that John's mother made such a fuss of Maurice and entirely ignored her other grandson. Alice was fond of Maurice, but it would have been easy to get upset. Instead, she and John usually laughed about it. Other Christmases, John organised word games. He sometimes sang, usually carols, in a rather fine baritone voice. He made sure everyone had a glass of sherry and told them amusing things that had happened at work. In the past, John had even been known to make Cora laugh. Now, Alice wasn't sure what she wanted to do most, burst into tears, or scream, as two of her daughters squabbled, Maeve looked bored, Cora scowled, her mother-in-law cooed and John's face was like thunder. Only Cormac was his usual sunny self, playing quietly on the floor with a truck he'd got for Christmas. If only her dad were there! He'd see the funny side of things and they could wink at each other and make faces.

Suddenly, John grabbed Fion and Orla by the scruffs of their necks and flung them out of the room. 'If you're going to fight, then fight somewhere else,' he snarled.

Alice got up and left without a word. The girls were in the hall, holding hands, she noted approvingly, and looking shaken.

'I *hate* Dad,' Orla said spiritedly.

'Me, too,' echoed Fionnuala.

'We weren't exactly fighting.'

'It was more an argument.'

'Your dad gets easily narked these days.' She put her arms round both her girls, they were almost as tall as she was. 'You need to humour him.'

Orla sniffed. 'Can I go round Betty Mahon's house, Mam? She got Monopoly for Christmas.'

'If you want, luv.'

'Can I come?' Fionnuala said eagerly.

Orla hesitated. Why couldn't Fion find friends of her own? Not only was she getting dead fat, but she was a terrible hanger-on. She remembered her sister had also been unfairly treated by their dad. 'OK,' she said.

Alice sighed with relief when the girls left; two less people to worry about. She opened the parlour door. 'Maeve, would you like to help me make some tea, luv?'

'I *hate* Christmas,' Maeve declared in the kitchen. 'It used to be nice, but now it's awful. Will Dad ever be in a good mood again?'

'Of course, luv. He's still getting over the accident.'

'But Mam, it wasn't *our* fault he had the accident. Why is he taking it out on us?'

Alice had no idea. Maeve had inherited her mother's easygoing nature. It wasn't like her to complain. John was gradually alienating every member of his family. Only Cormac seemed sweetly oblivious to the change in his dad.

She made tea and Spam sandwiches, spread a plate with biscuits, took them into the parlour, told Maeve that, yes, it would be all right if she stayed in the back and read her new Enid Blyton book, then excused herself from the company, saying she had to go round to Myrtle's and make sure she was all right.

The acrid grey fog that had enveloped Bootle earlier in the day was beginning to fall again. On the nearby River Mersey, ships' foghorns hooted eerily. The pavements glistened with damp, reflecting the street lights in glittering yellow blurs. It was lovely to see the lights on again after five years of blackout.

Hardly anyone in Amber Street had closed their parlour curtains. Alice passed house after house where parties were going on. She had been born only a few streets away, in Garnet Street, in another cramped terrace house that opened on to the pavement, and had known most of these people all her life. They felt like family. The Fowlers were having a riotous time, doing the 'Hokey Cokey'. Their two lads had returned unharmed after years spent in the Navy. Emmie Norris had all her family there, including the twelve grandchildren. The Martins were playing cards, a whole crowd of them in paper hats, laughing their heads off.

Everywhere Alice looked people were having the time of their lives. The strains of 'Bless 'Em All' came from the Murphys', 'We'll Meet Again' from the Smiths'.

Apart from Orla, no one had sung at the Laceys'. They had pulled crackers, but hadn't bothered with the paper hats, not even the children. It just didn't seem right for some reason. For the first time Alice felt like a stranger in the street that was as familiar to her as the back of her hand, as if she no longer belonged, as if her life was no longer on the same keel as those of her friends and neighbours.

She sighed as she went through the entry into Opal Street. Myrtle's was in darkness, upstairs and down. She remembered being at school with the girl who had lived there when it had been an ordinary house. It was more than twenty years since Myrtle had moved in and it had become a hairdresser's. The wall between the parlour and the living room had been knocked down and turned into one room. Mam had taken her there to have her hair cut. Myrtle had seemed old then, going on sixty. She claimed to have worked for some posh place in London doing rich people's hair.

'Debutantes,' she boasted, 'titled personages.' No one had believed her.

Alice unlocked the door. 'Myrtle,' she shouted. There was no reply. She went up to the bedroom, where the bed was empty, still unmade. Myrtle must have gone to tea with her friend, which was a relief.

Downstairs again, she sat under the same dryer as she'd done the night before, the middle one. She was even more miserable now than she'd been then. What was to become of her, of John, of their children? How was she to convince John that she loved him? Would she continue to love him if he remained the angry, glowering, suspicious person, nothing like the man he used to be? Could you love someone who made your children unhappy? Did he love her? What had happened was awful, but as Maeve had wisely said, he had no right to take it out on his family.

'White Christmas' was being sung not far away. 'Just like the ones we used to know . . .' Not any more, we don't, Alice thought bleakly. This Christmas has been nothing like the ones we used to know. The first after Mam died had been bad enough. Dad was gutted, but he'd done his best to brighten things up for his daughter. He'd bought her a new frock, taken her to the pantomime on Boxing Day. She was eight, an only child.

Alice knew she wasn't a clever person. She hadn't a single talent she could think of. She was often tongue-tied, stuck for something to say, slow-witted. She had achieved just five things in her life: she had married John Lacey, whom all the girls at Johnson's Dye Factory had been mad about, and she'd had four beautiful children.

But if she was to get through the years to come and stay sane, she needed to do something else. Time passed so quickly. Pretty soon the girls would start getting married. There'd only be Cormac left and what if John

24

was still the same? Things at home were unbearable now and they'd be even more unbearable with the girls gone.

Yes, she had to *do* something. But what? At the moment, even her job was on the line and it wouldn't be easy getting another, not with servicemen coming home, wanting back their jobs in the factories, and women all over the place being given the sack – women used to earning a wage and unwilling to return to being housewives. Bernadette said there'd been forty-two applications when the Gas Board where she worked had advertised for a wages clerk. Most were from women who'd been in the Forces, but it was a man who'd got the job. Not that Alice was fit to be a clerk of any sort, she couldn't even add up.

'We'll not go round our John's next Christmas if things there don't improve,' Billy Lacey said as he walked home through the fog with his family. 'I'm glad you said we were having someone round to tea, luv, even if it were a lie. I couldn't have stood another minute in that house.'

'It wasn't a lie,' Cora said coolly. 'Mr Flynn's coming to tea.'

'Mr Flynn, the landlord!'

'The very same.'

Billy grimaced at the idea of another meal accompanied by stilted conversation. They were passing O'Connell Street where they used to live and which Billy much preferred to where they lived now. 'I think I'll drop in on Foxy Jones. I haven't seen him since he came out the Army. I'll be home in time for tea, luv.'

'Like hell you will,' Cora muttered as her husband, hands in pockets, whistling tunelessly, made off down the street. She wouldn't see him again until the pubs closed. Not that she cared. The less she saw of Billy the better.

'Dad!' Maurice called plaintively, but his dad ignored him.

Cora gave her son a little shake, annoyed he wanted his dad when he had her. 'I've got a bone to pick with you.'

Maurice took the words literally. 'A bone, Mam?'

'How many times have I told you not to sit on your Grannie Lacey's knee? I can't stand to see her maul you.'

The little boy felt confused. Gran had sat him on her knee. He'd had no choice in the matter. 'I'm sorry, Mam.' He apologised to his mother a hundred times a day. He was always getting things wrong, though was often mystified as to what they were.

'You will be sorry when you get home.'

His stomach curled. He knew what the words meant and could tell by the way Mam walked, very quickly, shoulders back, lips pursed, that she was going to hit him with the cane. For the rest of the way home he did his best not to cry, but the minute the front door closed he started to bawl. 'Don't hit me, Mam. Please don't hit me.'

His mother ignored his cries. 'In here,' she said imperiously, opening the door to the living room. 'Come on!' She tapped her foot impatiently.

Maurice walked slowly into the room, dragging his feet. What had he done wrong? He never knew what he'd done wrong. He was shaking with fear as his mam told him to bend over a chair and the cane swished three times against his bottom. It hurt badly. The little boy sobbed helplessly, knowing his bottom would sting for ages. He could understand being beaten if he broke windows, did something really bad, but although he tried very hard to be on his best behaviour, somehow he always managed to make Mam angry.

'You can get to bed now.'

It was too early. He hadn't had any tea. Still crying, the child made his way upstairs. In the living room his mother listened to the faltering steps. There was something very touching about the way he climbed, drawing his feet together on each stair. Her heart turned over as she imagined the sturdy little figure clutching the banister. She heard him reach the top, go into his room, then flew after him. He was sitting on the bed, knuckles pressed into his eyes.

'Maurice!' She fell on her knees, clutched him against her breast. 'Don't cry. Oh, don't cry, luv. Your mammy loves you. She loves you more than anyone in the whole wide world.'

He felt hot, his small body shuddered in her arms, his heart thumped loudly against her own. Two small arms curled around her neck. Cora held him closely as wave after wave of raw, savage emotion coursed through her veins. There was nothing, absolutely nothing on earth comparable to the love she felt for the child sobbing in her arms, clinging to her, and it was made even sweeter by the knowledge that he loved her back, unquestioningly, wholeheartedly, because she was his mother.

'Do you love your mam, son?'

'Oh, yes.'

'Shall we go down and have some tea?'

Maurice hiccuped. 'Please, Mam.'

'Would you like some Christmas cake?'

He nodded. 'Yes.'

'Let Mam carry you.' She picked him up, laughed and said, 'Lord, you're a weight. Pretty soon you'll be carrying me.'

She carried him downstairs like a baby. Maurice, more confused than ever, wondered what it was he'd done right.

★

It was three years since Cora and her family had moved from O'Connell Street to Garibaldi Road. The new house was a great improvement on the old: semi-detached, with three good bedrooms, a proper hall, small gardens front and back. There was a bathroom and separate lavatory upstairs. Even Billy, who hadn't wanted to move, appreciated having a lavvy inside.

'But we'll never be able to afford the rent on a place like that,' Billy protested. He was home on leave from the Army where he appeared to be having a whale of a time.

'It's twelve and six a week, half a crown more than we pay now.' Cora was no longer prepared to be dictated to by her husband. If Billy wanted, he could stay in O'Connell Street on his own.

'Only twelve and a tanner for a house in Garibaldi Road!'

'According to the landlord, yes.'

Billy looked dubious. 'I don't want us to move, then have that Flynn geezer shove up the rent.'

'He won't,' Cora assured him. 'I work for him, don't I? I told you. He calls himself Flynn Properties. I keep the books.'

She'd been badgering Horace Flynn for a better house for years. They couldn't afford it, but she'd take in washing, she'd do anything to get out of O'Connell Street. Then, he'd owned just over thirty properties. Now there were forty. Every few months he bought another house.

'We're good tenants, aren't we?' she'd reasoned years ago. 'We're never late with the rent.'

'No and I don't know how you manage it, not with your husband in the Army. I've had to give notice to quit to half a dozen of me tenants since their hubbies

28

were called up. What is it you get; a shilling a day, and twenty-five bob a week allowance?'

'I'm good at managing with money.'

Mr Flynn glanced around the neat parlour of O'Connell Street. He was small and tubby, shaped like a ball, with exceptionally short arms and legs. A fringe of greying hair went from ear to ear at the back of his otherwise bald head, which was covered with brown blotches, like over-large freckles. From what she could gather, he wasn't married.

'I must say you keep the place nice.' He shook his head. 'But no, Mrs Lacey. I'm not prepared to move tenants up a notch until I feel assured they're in a position to pay the increased rent.' He smiled a touch sarcastically. 'Perhaps one day, when the war's over and your husband's in a well-paid job.'

If she had to wait for Billy to get a well-paid job, she'd be in O'Connell Street until the day she died. Cora gnawed her bottom lip. She was still shoplifting. It was easier with a baby in a pram, then a toddler in a pushchair. Like before, some things she kept, some she pawned. Once, when it was winter, she'd taken a fur coat from C & A Modes, not an expensive one, it being C & A, though she'd got five quid for it from the pawn shop. But she couldn't very well tell Mr Flynn *that*.

Maurice was two, and she'd already bought the cane, hung it on the wall and had used it a few times, when once again she had a go at Horace Flynn about a house. There was a lovely one going in Garibaldi Road and she knew it was one of his because she'd seen him collect the rent. The previous tenants were two old maids in their fifties who'd gone to live in America. She asked him into the parlour to remind him how nicely it was kept.

'I've got a job,' she lied, 'serving in a shop.'

'Which shop?'

Cora thought quickly. 'Mercer's the newsagent's in Marsh Lane.'

'I'd like to see some proof; a wage slip, a letter from the manager, if you don't mind, so I'll know you can afford the rent.'

'I'll ask the manager for a letter. I don't get wage slips.' She didn't want to admit she'd lied. Next week, she'd just pay the rent and keep her gob shut. If he mentioned Mercer's she'd say she'd left.

There was silence. Mr Flynn was staring fixedly at the wall at the cane. 'What's that for?'

'Me little boy. I'm a firm believer in discipline.'

He licked his lips. 'So am I.'

Cora saw a gleam of perspiration on the round bald head, a craving in the round wet eyes. She also saw something else: a way of getting the house in Garibaldi Road. It was the way she was to use to get the lovely furniture that went in it, the reason why it was many years before she shoplifted again.

She smoothed back her hair, curled her lip disapprovingly, said sternly, 'Have you been naughty, Mr Flynn?'

He nodded eagerly. Saliva oozed from his mouth. 'Very naughty, Mrs Lacey.'

'Then we shall have to do something about it.' She unhooked the cane from the wall.

Chapter 2

For more than a month, Alice virtually ran Myrtle's on her own. The girls took turns to give a hand on Saturdays and after school. Orla complained loudly that it was dead boring and the smells made her sick, particularly the ammonia, but sixpence a week was too good to miss. Fionnuala loved it. She would have done it for nothing, because it made her feel important. Macve didn't care what she did as long as she was left to do it in peace.

Only occasionally did Myrtle put in an appearance. She looked terrible, usually wearing tatty carpet slippers, her face grey and mottled. Once she came down in her dressing gown, a filthy plaid thing without a belt. Alice turned her round and sent her back upstairs.

'She's lost her mind,' one of the customers at the time pronounced. 'I reckon it's 'cos the war's over. It was the war that kept her going. Remember when we had to bring our own towels?'

Alice smiled. 'And we made shampoo by grating soap and boiling it in water. I was reduced to using Lux soap flakes on the customers once.'

'I remember you setting me hair with sugar and water when you'd run out of setting lotion. Myrtle used to open dead early or dead late, even on Sundays, to accommodate the women working in factories, otherwise there'd never have been time for them to get their hair done. She never charged extra.' The woman sighed. 'We all pulled together then. I wouldn't want the war back, not for anything, but there was a nice friendly spirit around. People put themselves out, like Myrtle.' She jerked her head towards the stairs. 'Is anyone seeing to her, like?'

'I usually make her a bite to eat for breakfast and dinner, and her friend, Mrs Glaister, comes round every day to make her tea and put her to bed. She's written to Myrtle's daughter in Southampton to say she needs looking after permanent.'

'You'll soon be out of a job, then?'

'Looks like it.'

Olive Cousins, Myrtle's daughter, took her time coming from Southampton. It was over four weeks later, at the beginning of February, that she turned up; a sharp-faced woman in her fifties, wearing too much pink face powder and a beaver lamb coat that smelt of mothballs. Even then, she didn't go straight upstairs. Alice was in the middle of a perm and was forced to listen while she explained in a dead posh voice, that occasionally lapsed into broad Scouse, that Christmas had been so hectic she was fair worn out and had needed time to recuperate. Her son had been home from university, her daughter had not long married a doctor and his parents had come to stay – she emphasised 'university' and 'doctor', in the obvious hope Alice would be impressed. Alice was, but decided not to show it. She disliked Olive Cousins on the spot.

'Where is mother?' Olive enquired, glancing around the salon as if expecting mother to pop up from beneath a chair.

'Upstairs, in bed,' Alice replied briefly.

'Well, I don't like the look of *her*,' the recipient of the perm announced as Olive Cousins's high heels clattered up the lino-covered stairs.

She stayed for three days, eating and sleeping in a bed and breakfast place on Marsh Lane, not that anyone blamed her for that, considering the state of upstairs. On the second day she came into the salon and announced that next morning she was taking mother back with her to Southampton.

'That's nice of you,' Alice remarked, revising her opinion of the woman, but not for long. Myrtle would be going into an old people's home in a strange part of the country where none of her friends and neighbours could visit. It was, however, more convenient for her daughter.

'She couldn't possibly live with us, there isn't the room, and I can't be doing with travelling halfway across the country every time something goes wrong.'

'You'll let us have the address, won't you? Of the home, that is, so we can write to her.'

'Of course. It'll be nice for her to get letters, but I doubt if she'll be up to reading them,' Olive said brightly, as if they were discussing the weather not her mother's health. 'Now, about the salon. I'd been expecting to sell it as a going concern, but' – her lip curled – 'no one would give tuppence for a dump like this, so I've written to the company that owns the premises. The salon will close today.'

'Today!' Alice's mouth dropped open. She probably looked dead stupid. The thing was, the appointment book was full for weeks ahead, and quite a few women had booked months in advance for weddings and the like. There was a sinking feeling in her belly. She'd have to put a notice on the door.

'Today,' Olive Cousins repeated firmly. 'I don't doubt

you'd have liked more notice, but you must have seen this coming for a long time.'

'I suppose I have.'

'Of course, you could always take the place over, assuming you could afford the lease.'

'What's a lease?' Alice felt even more stupid.

'Like rent, only more long term,' Olive explained brusquely, obviously realising that if someone didn't know what a lease was it was unlikely they could afford it. 'Mother appears to have signed a new seven-year lease only last year and it still has six years to run. There was a letter upstairs from the property company asking for this year's payment and complaining about the state of the place. Me mam, I mean mother, hasn't kept it properly maintained.' She sniffed derisively. 'Instead, she's let it go to rack and ruin.'

'She hasn't exactly been well,' Alice said. 'How much is the lease?'

'A hundred and seventy-five pounds for seven years. That's cheap at the price. My hubbie's in business, so I should know. Mam, mother, paid at the rate of twenty-five pounds a year.'

Twenty-five pounds! Alice had never even *seen* twenty-five pounds. She glanced around the shabby room and imagined the walls repainted – mauve would look nice – new curtains on the windows, new oilcloth on the floor. The chairs needed upholstering, but could be patched up for now, and the dryers looked as if they'd come out of the ark, but a good polishing would bring them up a treat. She wasn't sure what came over her when she said to Olive Cousins, 'Have you posted the letter yet to the property company?'

'It's in me, *my* bag, to post as soon as I go outside.'

'Would you mind leaving it till morning? If I'm not round by nine o'clock, post it then.'

★

The wireless was on in the living room of number eight Garnet Street. Geraldo and his orchestra were playing a selection of Cole Porter songs.

'Night and day,' Danny Mitchell hummed as he ironed his favourite shirt: blue and white striped with pearl buttons. He grinned as he thought about the evening ahead. In an hour's time he would call for Phyllis Henderson, a widow in her forties. They would go to the pub, have a few drinks, Phyllis would play hard to get, but end up inviting him back to her house for a mug of cocoa and thence into her bed.

Danny had a well-deserved reputation as a ladies' man. During the ten years he'd been married to his beloved Renee and the ten years after Renee's death, when he'd had a daughter to bring up, Danny had never given another woman a second glance, but then Alice had got married and he began to sow his wild oats, if rather late.

He was fifty-one, an electrician on the docks, and as lean and fit as a man half his age, with a full head of wavy hair the same colour as his daughter's. There was nothing particularly handsome about his face, but he had a quirky smile that people found attractive and a look in his blue eyes that made women go weak at the knees. There were numerous widows and spinsters in Bootle whose main aim in life was to tie the knot with Danny Mitchell.

'Night and Day' ended. 'You were never lovelier,' Danny sang under his breath. He was thinking of Phyllis in her black satin nightie when the back door opened and his daughter came in. All thoughts of Phyllis and the evening ahead fled from his mind and he looked anxiously at the face of his only child. He was relieved to see her eyes were brighter than they'd been in a long while. Perhaps things had started to improve between her and John.

'I've brought a couple of mince pies, Dad. There was

mincemeat in a jar left over from Christmas.' She put a paper bag on the table. 'They're still warm.'

'Ta, luv. I'll have them in a minute. There's tea in the pot if you fancy a cup. Pour one for me, if you don't mind. I've only got the cuffs of this to do.' He turned the cuffs back, ready for the studs, and hung the shirt behind the door. Then he folded the badly singed blanket he used to iron on, put it away and took the iron into the yard where he left it on the step to cool, by which time Alice had poured the tea. They sat opposite each other across the table, Alice in the place where her mother used to sit.

'How's Cormac getting on at school?' Danny asked the same question every day since his grandson had started, mainly because he liked hearing the answer.

'As I said before, Dad, he's taken to reading like a duck takes to water. The teacher's ever so pleased. He was sitting up in bed looking at a book when I left.'

'Good.' He smacked his lips with satisfaction. His grandson had always lived in the shadow of his cousin, Maurice, and it was nice to know Cormac was better at something for a change. From what he could gather Maurice was only average at school.

'Our Orla wants to see you to ask about the Great War. It's something they're doing at school.'

'Tell her to come round Saturday. I'll get some cakes in.' He would never have admitted it to a soul but Orla, with her enthusiasms and quick temper, was his favourite of the girls. He was already looking forward to Saturday.

'You'll do no such thing,' Alice remonstrated. 'If you want cakes I'll make 'em for you. I'll send some round with Orla.'

At the mention of cakes, Danny remembered the mince pies. He removed one from the bag, ate it with obvious enjoyment and quickly demolished the other.

Alice regarded him suspiciously. 'Have you had anything to eat since you came home from work?'

''Course, luv,' he assured her. He could only be bothered with making himself a Piccalilli sarnie.

'I wish you'd come round to ours for your meals.'

'You've enough to do, luv, without having another mouth to feed. And I'm always there for me dinner on Sundays, aren't I?'

She reached across the table for his hand. The eyes that had seemed so bright when she came in had dulled. 'I'd sooner you were there all the time.' There was a catch in her voice. John was apt to mind his tongue in the presence of his father-in-law and it was nice to have someone on her side, someone who would never turn against her, no matter what happened.

'It wouldn't be right, Alice,' Danny said gruffly. He knew why she wanted him, as a buffer between her and her husband, but the situation in Amber Street had to be worked out between the main participants. Lately, though, he felt increasingly tempted to give John Lacey a piece of his mind. It wasn't right, him taking things out on the folks who loved him most, particularly when the folks concerned were his dearly beloved daughter and his grandchildren.

Within the space of months, Danny had seen Alice turn from a happy, tranquil young woman into a sad, listless creature who rarely smiled. Lord knew how she'd feel when the hairdressing job went, which was likely to happen any minute. At least it provided some respite from the atmosphere at home. If only he could *do* something to put things right.

Alice released his hand. 'Anyroad, Dad. I'm here on the cadge.'

'Just say the word, luv. What's mine's yours, you

know that.' He would have given his life for her and her children.

'I need some money.'

Danny didn't show his surprise, though he knew John earned reasonable wages and had never kept her short. He dug into his pocket. 'How much?'

'I need more than you'll be carrying in your pocket, Dad.'

'Me wallet's upstairs.' He got up. 'I'll fetch it.'

To his horror, she put her head in her hands and burst into tears. 'I must be daft,' she sobbed. 'I must need me head examining. I told the woman to leave the letter till tomorrer, but I couldn't get twenty-five pounds together in a month of Sundays, let alone a few hours.'

He felt himself go pale. 'Twenty-five pounds, luv? It'd take me all me time to scrape together five, and then I'd have to wait till tomorrer when I get paid. What the hell d'you need all that much for?'

'For Myrtle's. The salon's closing, it already has, but I can take over the lease if I want. It costs twenty-five pounds. Oh, Dad!' She turned and put her arms round his waist, pressing her face against his rough working shirt. 'I'd give *anything* if Myrtle's could be mine. I'm good at hairdressing, everyone ses. I'd've hated to leave, anyroad, but now, with the way things are at home . . .'

'I know, luv,' Danny said gently. His mind rapidly assessed his few possessions. What could he pawn? Nothing worth anything much, he realised. There was only the furniture, the bedding, oddments of crockery and cutlery, a few ornaments, his books. He felt guilty for having so many shirts, for not having put away a few bob a week for a rainy day. But he was a man who liked a good time, a man free with his money. His hand was always first in his pocket when it came to a round of drinks. He enjoyed buying presents for his grandchildren. He liked feminine company, perhaps a bit too much, and the various lady friends he'd had over the years hadn't come cheap. There was a ten-shilling note in his wallet upstairs. At that minute he was worth about twelve and a tanner.

'It's so horrible at night, Dad.' Alice's hands tightened round him. 'The girls go out, not that I blame them. I encourage them to. I put Cormac to bed as early as possible. He doesn't mind if I leave the light on, so there's just me and John downstairs. He won't even have the wireless on nowadays. It's as if he can't stand anything cheerful. I stay in the back kitchen as much as possible, but there's a limit to how long you can wash dishes and do a bit of baking for tomorrer, so I try to get on with some sewing. It's hopeless trying to read. I can't concentrate, knowing John's glaring at me. Oh, Dad!' she cried. 'He accuses me of having affairs. He's got this thing in his head that I'm having it off with other men. As if I would! He's the only man I've ever wanted. Now Myrtle's has gone,' she groaned. 'At least it was something to look forward to. I loved it there. It was like a fairy-tale world, all bright and shiny.'

'There, there, luv.' Dan stroked her hair. He'd definitely be having a word with John Lacey. He'd never known his daughter in such a state, as if she were at the end of her tether. He furiously tried to think of a way of getting twenty-five pounds and wondered if there was a bank he could rob and get away with it. He thought of a possible solution and his nose wrinkled with distaste. 'What about asking that Cora woman?' he said. He couldn't abide Cora Lacey.

'Cora!' Alice stopped crying and looked at him. 'It didn't cross me mind. We're not exactly friends.'

'She's never been exactly friends with anyone,' Danny

said curtly. 'But she never seems short of a few bob, though Christ knows where it comes from. Billy earns a pittance clearing bomb sites. There's no way he could afford to pay for a house in Garibaldi Road.'

'She works for the landlord, Horace Flynn,' Alice explained. 'She does his books, whatever that involves. I suppose he let her have the house as a favour.' Horace Flynn was one of the most notorious landlords in Bootle, who chucked people on to the streets without so much as the blink of a fat eyelid.

'I reckon it involves more than doing his books.'

'Oh, Dad!' She sounded shocked. 'You've got a dirty mind. I've never known anyone so strait-laced as Cora.' She put a finger thoughtfully to her chin. 'I might go round and ask her. It won't do any harm. All she can do is say no.'

'And she might say yes. Would you like me to come with you?' He entirely forgot about Phyllis Henderson.

'No, ta, Dad. It would be best if I went on me own.'

'You'd better get a move on. It's almost half past seven. Does John know where you are?'

'I said I was coming round to yours with the mince pies.' She laughed bitterly. 'He probably thinks they're for one of me secret lovers. I'll be cross-examined when I get back, particularly if I'm late.'

'Does he know about the twenty-five pounds?'

She shook her head. 'No, he might have stopped me coming if he had. John doesn't like me working no more. He wants me safely at home where I can't get up to mischief.'

Danny Mitchell swallowed an expletive. He hadn't realised things were quite so bad. 'He won't be all that pleased if Cora comes up with the cash and you start the hairdressing on your own,' he said cautiously, worried that Alice was getting into a situation that would only make things worse.

'I don't care, Dad.' Her face tightened in a way he'd never seen before. 'I'm entitled to something out of life and I'm not getting it now. I wish with all my heart John had never had the accident. I love him, I always will, but I've given up trying to make him believe it. He's impossible to live with, so I'll just have to make a life for meself outside the house.'

Danny hadn't thought his normally timid daughter capable of such determination. He nodded approvingly. 'Right thing too, luv.'

Come in,' Cora said in surprise when she opened the door and found her sister-in-law on the step.

Alice rarely came to Garibaldi Road, mainly because she was rarely asked and Cora wasn't the sort of person you dropped in on uninvited for a jangle.

'What can I do for you?' Cora asked when they were seated in the nicely furnished living room, as if she realised it wasn't a social visit and Alice had only come for a purpose for which an explanation was due.

'Where's Billy?' She didn't want John's brother blundering in.

'At the pub, where else?' Cora sneered.

Alice nodded. 'Right. I want to borrow some money,' she said bluntly. She wasn't prepared to beat about the bush, engage in chit-chat to pass the time, then tactfully come up with a request for a loan.

'Really!' Cora laughed. It must be for something of very great importance. Under normal circumstances, Alice wouldn't have asked her for the time of day, let alone money. 'What for?'

In a cool voice Alice explained about Myrtle's. 'I'll pay

41

you back the twenty-five pounds as soon as possible with a fee on top, for borrowing it, like.'

'You mean interest?'

'Do I?' Alice said, confused.

'Interest is what you pay for borrowing money.'

'Then I'll pay interest.'

'At what rate?' Cora asked, in order to confuse her sister-in-law more.

But Alice understood what Cora was up to. 'At whatever rate you say,' she replied, cool again.

The older woman smiled unpleasantly. 'Why should I loan you a penny?'

'Because you'll make a penny in return.'

Cora smiled again. Then her voice became hard. 'It would have to be a business arrangement.'

'That's all right by me,' Alice said nonchalantly. Inwardly, she was desperately trying to keep her wits about her. She didn't trust Cora Lacey as far as she could throw her and wished she had taken up Dad's offer to come with her. What on earth was a business arrangement?

'I'll lend you the twenty-five quid, but I'll draw up an agreement and we'll both sign to say we'll share the profits till the loan's paid back.'

'*Share* the profits!' Alice exlaimed. She wanted Myrtle's more than anything on earth, but sharing the profits seemed a bit rich. 'You mean half each? That hardly seems fair. It's me who'll be doing all the work.'

'OK, you have two-thirds, I'll take a third.' Cora had known Alice, dim as a Toc H lamp though she was, would be unlikely to agree to half. A third was what she'd wanted all along. It was the easiest way she'd ever come across of making money. 'I'll just go in the parlour and write it down. I won't be long.'

Alice waited on the edge of her chair. She'd done it!

Tomorrow morning Myrtle's would be hers, but she wished it hadn't been necessary to involve Cora Lacey. It left a nasty taste in the mouth. A third of the profits! She held out her hands to warm them in front of the small coke fire. It was cold in here. She shivered. The fire gave off scarcely any heat. Cora surrounded herself with nice things, but had no regard for creature comforts. No wonder Billy took himself to the pub night after night.

She knew nothing about her sister-in-law other than that her maiden name was Barraclough, her mother had died when she was born and she'd been brought up in Orrell Park by two spinster aunts, both long dead. Nothing was ever said about a father.

It was a constant wonder what she and Billy had seen in each other. Billy was hardly ever in, Cora rarely went out. In company they ignored each other. Billy seemed nervous in the presence of his cold-eyed wife, Cora contemptuous of her childish, good-natured husband.

Her legs were numb with cold. Alice got up and walked around the room to bring them back to life. She picked up a glass vase off the mantelpiece. It shone like diamonds as she turned it back and forth in the dim light. She flicked it with her fingernail and it gave off a sharp, tinkling sound, like a bell. Cut glass! How on earth could Cora afford such a thing? Where had she got the twenty-five pounds from, come to that? Off Horace Flynn?

'I reckon she does more than keep his books,' Dad had said, or something like it. Alice shivered again at the thought of fat, greasy Horace Flynn coming within a yard of her, let alone doing his books – or far more intimate things if Dad was right.

There was a child's book on the table; a colourful cardboard alphabet book with an animal beside each letter. A for Antelope. She turned to the back page: Z for Zebra. A piece of paper fell out on which had been written several simple sums: $1 + 1$, $2 + 2$, $2 + 1$. The answers had been filled in by a clumsy, childish hand. Cora must have written the sums, Maurice had filled in the answers. She must be teaching him at home.

For some reason Alice glanced at the wall where the cane usually hung. It wasn't there. She noticed it propped against the green tiled fireplace. Her stomach turned. Was Cora whipping her little boy to make him learn?

Alice suddenly longed to get away from this lovely, cold room with its expensive ornaments and return to her own comfy, warm house, where there wasn't a single ornament costing more than sixpence, but which was far preferable to here. Hang Myrtle's. Cora could keep her money and her business arrangement.

She made for the door – and remembered John who would be sitting in the chair under the window waiting for her, glowering, wanting to know where she'd been, how many men she'd allowed to touch her. The accusations were getting wilder and wilder, more and more offensive. She couldn't bring herself to tell Dad some of the things John had said. How many men had she serviced? Did they stand in line? How much had she made? Terrible accusations from the man she had thought would love her for ever. Alice suppressed a sob, just as Cora came into the room with a piece of paper torn from a writing pad.

'Sorry I was so long, but it had to be worded carefully. Just sign here where I've drawn a line of dots. I've brought the ink with me and a pen.'

'I'd like to read it first.'

'Of course,' Cora said smoothly. 'You should never put your signature to anything you've not read first.'

'I, Alice Lacey,' Alice read aloud, 'acknowledge receipt of the sum of twenty-five pounds from Cora

44

Lacey, entitling the said Cora Lacey to a third share in perpetuity of the business presently known as Myrtle's Hairdressing Salon.' She frowned. 'What does "in perpetuity" mean?'

'Till the money's paid back.'

'That's all right, then.' It wasn't often she put her signature to anything. She sat down and carefully wrote 'Alice M. Lacey' on the dotted line.

'What's the M. for?' Cora enquired.

'Mavoureen. It was me mam's name. Me dad called her Renee.'

Cora nodded. 'Well, here's your money.' She held out a small piece of paper.

Alice regarded it vacantly. 'What's that?'

'It's a cheque for twenty-five pounds.'

'But I need the money, not a cheque!' She'd only vaguely heard of cheques and had never seen one before.

'A cheque's the same as money,' Cora said with a superior smile. 'Just give it to Myrtle's daughter. She'll know what to do with it.'

Alice wanted to protest, but it would only show her ignorance. She took the cheque, thanked Cora and said she had to be getting home.

Outside the house she paused. She felt uneasy. How could a piece of paper be worth the same as twenty-five pound notes? Oh, if only she could ask John! He seemed to know everything worth knowing. Alice sighed. But the days were long gone when they could discuss things – should they have a day out in New Brighton on Sunday if the weather was fine, for instance? Or perhaps Southport, easier to get to on the electric trains that ran from Marsh Lane Station? Was it possible to squeeze another bed into the girls' room now that they were getting older? Orla constantly complained about sleeping three to a bed.

The cheque thing was bothering her. She would have gone back to Dad's, but he'd be out by now, probably with Phyllis Henderson, his latest woman. But Bernadette would know. Unlike Alice, she was clever. Although they'd started St James's Junior and Infants together, Bernadette had passed the scholarship at eleven and gone to Seafield Convent. She lived no distance away in rooms in Irlam Road. Hopefully, Bernadette would set her mind at rest. It would make her late home, but she was already late and by now John was probably doing his nut.

'Oh, well! I may as well be hung for a sheep as for a lamb.'

'Of course a cheque's all right, silly.' Bernadette laughed. She was already in her dressing gown ready for bed although it was only half past eight. Since Christmas she'd been feeling low. Roy McBride had turned out like all the other men she'd known, except for Bob, and had tried to get his hand up her skirt in the taxi on the way home from the dance on Christmas Eve. She had decided to give up on men altogether and rely on books for company.

'We get loads of cheques in the Gas Board. What's it for, anyroad?'

For the third time that night, Alice explained about Myrtle's, then described her meeting with Cora. 'She made me sign an agreement of some sort – and she wants a third of the profits, but never mind. As from tomorrow Myrtle's will be mine, that's all that matters.'

'Oh, Alice!' Bernadette looked dismayed. 'I wish you'd asked me first. I would have loaned you the money and you wouldn't have had to sign anything. I wouldn't have demanded a share of the profits, either. Just the money back when you could afford it, that's all.'

46

Alice regarded her friend, equally dismayed. 'It never entered me head you were so flush, Bernie.'

Bernadette shrugged. 'It's why Bob and I never had kids, isn't it? I stayed at work so we could save up for furniture for our house. Since he was killed I couldn't bring meself to touch a penny. It didn't seem right, buying clothes and stuff, so the money's been lying in the Post Office for years. There must be going on for forty pounds by now. You could have had the lot and used some to do up Myrtle's place a bit. It certainly needs it.'

'Oh, Bernie! I wish I'd known.'

'Tell Cora to stuff her cheque and I'll arrange to draw the money out tomorrow.'

'I can't, can I? I told you I signed an agreement.'

Bernadette looked at her doubtfully. 'What did it say?'

'I can't remember.'

'You're too trusting by a mile, do you know that, Alice Lacey? Anyroad, how about a cup of tea? Better still, a glass of sherry to toast your new business venture.'

'You make it sound very grand.' Alice smiled.

'It *is* very grand. I feel dead proud that you're my friend. Hold on, I'll just get some glasses from the kitchen.'

While she was gone, Alice glanced around the big, rather gloomy room that was at least warm. A big fire burnt in the massive fireplace. The book Bernadette had been reading was lying face down on the floor alongside an empty cup that had obviously contained cocoa. She wouldn't have wanted to be in Bernie's shoes, not for a moment, but just then she felt a certain amount of envy for her friend for being able to do as she pleased – go to bed when she liked, stay out as long as she cared to without someone breathing down her neck wanting to check up on her every single moment. She squirmed

47

guiltily when she considered how much nicer life would be without John.

Oh, Lord! Alice felt sick. According to the sideboard clock it was ten to nine. But, she reasoned, if John was worried it was his own fault. She couldn't confide in him any more, tell him about Myrtle's. Even when she got back she could tell him where she'd been, but not *why*. He would be quite likely to tear up the cheque, say he didn't want her working. Best to leave telling him till Myrtle's was actually *hers*.

'Hey! I've just thought of something.' Bernadette returned with the glasses. 'How did Cora know who to make the cheque out to?'

'I've no idea.' Alice took the cheque out of her bag and read it properly for the first time. 'It ses "Pay Flynn Properties".' She read it again, frowning. '*Flynn Properties*'?

Bernadette shrieked, 'The bitch! Myrtle's belongs to Horace Flynn. *He's* the owner of the property company that awful daughter was on about. Oh, Al! Right now, I bet Cora Lacey's laughing up her sleeve.'

Myrtle came into the salon wearing a slightly bald astrakhan coat with a brown fur collar, a dusty black hat shaped like a turban and fleece-lined ankle boots. The lace on one of the boots was undone. Alice made her sit under a dryer while she tied it. 'In case you trip over, like.' She stroked the creased, bewildered face. 'Take care, Myrtle, luv. Look after yourself, won't you? We're not half going to miss you.'

'Here, here,' echoed Florrie Piper who had just arrived for her weekly shampoo and set.

A taxi drew up outside and Olive Cousins came downstairs dragging a large, shabby suitcase. 'Gerra move on, Mam,' she snapped. She went pink. 'I mean, do hurry, Mother.' She turned to Alice. 'Good luck with the salon,' she said shortly. 'I hope you do better with the place than Mother did. I must say you could have knocked me down with a feather when you turned up this morning with that cheque.'

Mrs Glaister, Myrtle's friend, appeared. 'You forgot your handbag, luv,' she said gently. 'I've put a clean hankie inside and a quarter of mint imperials, your favourite.'

'Ta.' Myrtle smiled tremulously at everyone. 'Can I have a cup of tea?'

'No, you can't, Mother. The taxi's waiting. Say goodbye to your friends.' Olive roughly dragged the old woman to her feet. She glanced sneeringly around the room. 'It won't exactly break my heart not to see *this* place again.'

The door closed and Myrtle Rimmer left Opal Street for ever. Mrs Glaister burst into tears. 'It won't exactly break my heart not to see *her* again either. Expecting to find Myrtle had saved thousands of pounds, she was, when all she'd saved was hundreds. Mind you, she's taken every penny.'

'It wouldn't be a bad idea to make that cup of tea, Alice,' Florrie Piper said. 'Forget about me and me hair for the minute, though I wouldn't mind a cuppa meself.'

Alice hurried into the dingy back kitchen to put the kettle on, remembering that Olive Cousins had emptied the till last night, but hadn't thought to pay her. She'd worked four days for nothing. But never mind, from now on she would be paying herself. The sadness she felt for Myrtle was mixed with jubilation. She didn't care what underhand things Cora might have got up to with the cheque, nor did it matter that Horace Flynn owned the building. *She*, Alice Lacey, was now the proprietor of a hairdressing salon. Apart from her wedding day and the times she'd had the children, this was the proudest day of her life.

'That's a nasty bruise you've got on your cheek, luv,' Florrie Piper remarked when Alice came back.

Alice touched the bruise as if she had forgotten it was there. 'I walked into a door,' she explained.

'You should be more careful.' Had it been anyone else, Florrie would have taken for granted that the bruise had been administered by her feller, but everyone knew that John Lacey would never lay a finger on his wife.

He hadn't meant to hit her. He never meant to hurt her, either by word or deed. But she was out such a long time and by the time she got back he was genuinely worried and as mad as hell.

One by one the girls came in. He didn't see much of them nowadays. They seemed to spend a lot of time in other people's houses. As soon as they realised their mother wasn't there they went straight to bed. He could hear them chattering away upstairs, laughing and giggling, and he felt excluded, knowing they were avoiding him, knowing *he* was the reason why they were out so much and never brought friends home as they used to. It was the same reason why Alice put Cormac to bed so early – so the lad wouldn't witness the way his dad spoke to his mam.

John went to the bottom of the stairs and listened to his daughters fight over who would sleep in the middle, knowing Maeve would be the loser, always wanting to please. What was needed was an extra bed. It could be squeezed in somehow. A chap at work had told him you could get bunk beds and John wondered if he could make a set, or a pair, or whatever they were called. He liked working with wood, so much more natural than metal. There'd be fights over who'd sleep on top, which was reached by means of a small ladder, but he'd organise a rota. He'd talk it over with Alice.

No, he wouldn't! With a sound that was almost a sob, John Lacey sat on the bottom of the stairs and buried his monstrous face in his hands. He had forgotten, but he and Alice didn't talk any more, and it was his fault, not hers. John felt as if he'd lost control of his brain. His brain made him say things, do things, that the real John found despicable and wouldn't let him do the things he knew were right.

The clock on the sideboard chimed eight, which meant Alice had been away an hour. But she'd said she was only going round Garnet Street to see her dad! John's lip curled and hot anger welled up in his chest. He'd like to bet she was up against a wall in a back entry with some feller. In fact, he'd go round Garnet Street and check, prove beyond doubt that he'd been right in his suspicions.

'I'm just going out a minute,' he shouted upstairs.

Only Maeve deigned to answer. 'All right, Dad,' she called.

John grabbed his coat and hurried out into the gaslit streets. It took just a few minutes to reach Garnet Street and even less to establish that there was no one in Danny Mitchell's house. To make sure, he went round the back and let himself in, but the house was as dark as it was empty.

Afterwards John was never quite sure what happened to his head. There was a glorious feeling of triumph, a quickening of his heart and a shiver ran through his bones at the realisation that he'd been right all along. Now he had a genuine reason to hate her.

He returned home, sat in the chair under the window, tapping his fingers on the wooden arm, waiting for Alice, his slut of a wife, to come home.

★

51

It was half past nine when she arrived and by then he was beginning to worry that she'd left him, though common sense told him she would never leave the children – certainly not with him.

He had rarely seen her look so lovely. Any man would be suspicious if his wife came in all starry-eyed and pink-cheeked, as if she'd just won a few hundred quid on the pools. It was the way she used to look when they made love. Something must have happened to make her eyes shine like that. Whatever it was, it was nothing to do with her husband.

'I'm sorry, luv,' she said in a rush, 'but after I'd been to me dad's I decided to drop in on Bernadette because she's been feeling dead low since Christmas. We had a drop of sherry each and I seemed to lose track of the time.'

'You've been gone two and a half hours,' John said icily.

'I know, luv. As I said, I'm sorry.'

'You've been with a feller, I can tell by your face.' Why, oh why, did he so much want this to be true? It was as if he wanted to wallow in his misery, make it worse.

She sighed. 'Oh, don't be silly, John. Go round and ask Bernadette if you don't believe me.'

'Do you think I'm daft enough not to know you've fixed a story up between you?'

'Think what you like,' she said tiredly and went into the kitchen where she put the kettle on. 'Did the girls have drinks when they came in? I can still hear them talking upstairs. Perhaps they'd like a cup of cocoa.'

Had he been the sensible man that he used to be this would be the time to mention the bunk beds. Instead, the man he had become followed his wife into the kitchen and grabbed her arm. 'I want to know where

52

you've been. I want to know why you've got that look on your face. How much did you make? How much have you got in your purse?' He released her arm. She had hung her handbag on the knob of the kitchen door. It was one of those shoulder things that had become popular during the war. He undid the zip and turned it upside down. A gold enamelled compact smashed on to the tiled floor, followed by her purse, a little comb, two neatly ironed hankies, the stub of a pencil, a couple of tram tickets and a scrap of paper.

'John! Me dad bought me that compact for me twenty-first. Oh, look, the mirror's broke.' She was close to tears, kneeling down, picking up the broken bits of glass. 'That's seven years bad luck.'

'I'll get it fixed.' Jaysus! He looked like a monster – and he acted like one. Kneeling beside her, he began to put the things back in the bag. Their shoulders touched and he longed to take her in his arms, dry her tears. Dammit, he *would*. It was now or never. Things couldn't possibly go on like this. He would just have to take the risk of seeing the disgust on her face. He said humbly, 'I don't know what gets into me some . . . what's this?'

'It's a cheque,' Alice said in an odd voice. She snatched it away before he could see who it was from and all John's suspicions returned with a vengeance he could scarcely contain.

'So, you get paid by cheque, eh? It must be some posh geezer you do it with? Let's see.'

'No!' She stubbornly put the cheque behind her back. 'It's nothing to do with you.'

'Oh, so me wife can sleep around all over the place and it's nothing to do with me!' He laughed coarsely. 'Let me see that fuckin' cheque.'

Alice shuddered. He'd never sworn in the house before, not so much as a 'bloody'. She suddenly felt sick and knew it was no use keeping the cheque from him. He was stronger than she was and could easily take it off her. 'It's from Cora Lacey,' she said. 'She's loaned me twenty-five pounds for Myrtle's salon. As from tomorrer it'll be mine.'

A year ago John would have been delighted. A year ago he would have borrowed the money for her. A mate of his had borrowed from a bank to set up his own small engineering company. But now, a year later, John felt only blinding rage, accompanied by tremendous fear. He didn't want her independent, having her own business, no longer reliant on him for money. Lately he'd even resented the few bob she earned at Myrtle's. He wanted her at home. If he could, he'd have stopped her going to the shops. He raised his hand and struck her across the face, so hard that she stumbled and almost fell. She screamed, then stopped the scream abruptly, her hand over her mouth, worried the children would hear. The cheque dropped to the floor and he grabbed it.

'Are you all right, Mam?' Orla called.

'I'm fine, luv. Just knocked meself on the kitchen cupboard, that's all.' She looked at her husband. 'If you tear that up,' she said in a grating voice, 'I'll only ask Cora for another. You're not me keeper. And as from tonight, I'll not think of you as me husband either. Go on, hit me again,' she said tauntingly when he raised his fist a second time. 'Hit me all night long, but you won't stop me from having Myrtle's.'

It was the first time she had answered back and, staring at her flushed, angry face, John Lacey realised that he'd lost her. With a groan that seemed to come from the furthest depths of his being, for the second time that night he buried his face in his hands. 'I don't know what's got into me, Alice,' he whispered.

Had Alice's cheek not been hurting so badly she might

have felt sorry for him, but for ten months she'd been treading on eggshells, trying to get through to him, putting up with his rages, his moods and, worst of all, his insults, all because she loved him. Perhaps she still loved him, she didn't know, but he had gone too far. Hitting her had been the last straw. He had frightened her girls away so they were hardly ever in. Only Cormac had been spared his bitter anger. She took the cheque and left the room.

Seconds later she was back. She felt extremely powerful, as if it was her, not him, who was in control. 'I'd sooner sleep on me own from now on,' she said curtly. 'I'll kip in the parlour. You can have the bed to yourself.'

Chapter 3

On Sunday, after early Mass, Alice and the children changed into their oldest clothes. Armed with several paintbrushes, a large tin of mauve distemper, a smaller tin of white, silver polish, rags, and various cleaning fluids and powders, and leaving behind a silent, brooding John, they made their way to Myrtle's.

Even Orla, not usually willing to lend a hand, found it very exciting. 'The girls at school will be dead envious when I tell them we own a hairdresser's,' she said boastfully.

'We don't exactly own it, luv. I only lease the place,' Alice told her.

'Oh, Mam, it's just the same.'

Bernadette Moynihan arrived just as Alice was unlocking the door. She wore old slacks and her long fair hair was tucked inside a georgette scarf. She grinned. 'Just in time.'

Alice grinned back. 'Thanks for helping, Bernie.'

'I wouldn't have missed it for worlds. What shall I do first?'

'Can I start painting the walls, Mam?' Fionnuala pleaded.

'Not yet, luv. Let's get the place cleaned first including the kitchen. There's years of dirt out there and I daren't look at the lavvy in the yard. I used to feel ashamed when customers asked if they could use it. Meself, I went home and used ours whenever I felt the urge.'

Bernadette offered to clean the lavatory. 'You can't very well ask one of the girls and you need to stay here and keep an eye on things.'

'Ta, Bernie. You're a mate. There's bleach some-where.' Alice handed out various tasks. 'Fion and Orla, you wash the walls, Maeve, clean the sinks, there's a luv. Cormac . . .' She tried to think of something suitable for a five-year-old to do. Cormac looked at her expectantly, his small face puckered earnestly, his blue eyes very large. He was such an adorable little boy. Unable to resist, she picked him up and gave him a hug. 'You can wipe the leather chairs for your mammy.' The chairs weren't leather but leatherette and she was going to make enquiries about having them re-covered.

Everyone sang happily as they worked, all the old war songs: 'Run Rabbit Run', 'We'll Meet Again', 'We're Going to Hang Out the Washing on the Siegfried Line' . . .

At half past eleven they stopped for lemonade and meat paste butties. By one o'clock Maeve, who tired easily, had begun to wilt and Orla complained she was fed up to the teeth with cleaning. Cormac was kneeling on a chair playing with the big old-fashioned till that Alice had always thought entirely unnecessary in a hairdresser's. Fion was scrubbing away in the kitchen, longing to get her hands on a paintbrush. Having finished the lavatory, Bernadette was now brushing the yard. Alice had polished the dryers until they sparkled, though there was little she could do about the paint chipped off the hoods.

'When are we having our dinner?' Orla wanted to know.

'Four o'clock. I told you before it would be late today.

Go home if you want. You too, Maeve. Your grandad will be here in a minute to distemper the ceiling.'

'Oh, Mam!' Fion cried from the other room. 'I wanted to do the ceiling.'

'You can do the walls, luv. A ceiling needs an expert hand. I did our kitchen ceiling once and I ended up covered in distemper and looking like a ghost.'

Maeve went home to read a book, but Orla decided to stay when she realised Grandad was coming. They stopped and finished off the sandwiches, and Alice made tea in the amazingly clean kitchen. 'You've done a wonderful job with this stove,' she told Fion. 'It looks like new.'

'Can I do the walls now?'

'Not yet, luv,' Alice said patiently. 'But I tell you what you can do, go upstairs and look for some old sheets to spread around while the ceiling's being done. We don't want paint spilling everywhere.'

'What are you going to do about upstairs, Ally?' Bernadette enquired.

'What d'you mean?' Alice looked at her vacantly.

'Well, it's a flat, isn't it, soft girl. You can let it, make a few extra bob a week. Once it's cleaned up it'd be nice and cosy up there. It might . . .' She paused.

'It might what?'

Bernadette glanced sidelong at Fion and waited until the girl had left the room before continuing. 'It might do for the person who give you *that*!' She nodded at the bruise on her friend's cheek that was gradually turning from purple to yellow.

'Bernie!' Alice gasped, shocked to the core.

'I loved my Bob to bits, but he'd have been out the door like a shot if he'd so much as laid a finger on me.' Bernadette folded her arms and regarded her sternly. 'Say he hits you again or lashes out at one of the kids?'

'He'd never hit the kids!'

'This time last year would it have crossed your mind he'd hit you?'

'Well, no,' Alice said soberly.

'It's not right, Alice. No woman should be expected to put up with violence from her husband.'

Alice was trying to think of what to say in reply when the bell on the door gave its rusty ring and her dad came in. He climbed into a pair of greasy overalls and proceeded to paint the drab ceiling a lovely sparkling white.

Bernadette had turned bright pink and seemed to have lost the power of speech, Alice noticed with amusement – she'd had a crush on Danny Mitchell since she was eight.

At last Fion got her hands on a paintbrush and started on the walls. Alice began to rip up the tatty linoleum, aided by Cormac and Orla – a man was coming at eight o'clock in the morning to fit the lino she'd bought on tick yesterday in Stanley Road: black, with a faint cream marble effect, the sort she wouldn't have wanted in her house, but that was perfect for a hairdressers.

She'd got a length of white lace curtaining and two lampshades at the same time, which she'd put up when the distemper was dry. She felt a tingle of excitement. Everywhere was going to look dead smart when it was finished.

Bernadette and Danny came back to Amber Street for their dinner. For once, John's glowering face wasn't allowed to dampen the atmosphere during the meal. Everyone was too full of the hairdresser's and what they had achieved.

'What are you going to call it, Mam?' Maeve enquired.

'Why Myrtle's, luv. I wasn't thinking of changing the name.'

'I think you should,' said Bernadette.

Danny nodded. 'So do I.'

'Why don't you call it Alice's,' suggested Orla.

Alice thought that sounded a bit clumsy and wondered how anyone could be as stupid as she was; fancy not thinking about a new name and not realising the upstairs flat was included in the lease! 'You're as thick as two short planks, Alice Lacey,' she told herself.

'You could call it Lacey's,' said Fion.

'That has a nice ring to it.' Bernadette nodded her approval.

Danny said it sounded classy, Maeve thought it perfect, Cormac remarked it would go with the lacy curtains, Alice looked pleased, John merely scowled and Orla pulled a face, cross that Fionnuala's suggestion had been taken up, not hers.

And Fion glowed. She had actually christened a hairdresser's and felt very proud of herself.

After the table had been cleared and the dishes washed, Bernadette announced she was going home. Danny offered to walk with her as far as Irlam Road.

'There's no need.' Bernadette went all pink again. She never knew what to say to Danny Mitchell.

'Actually, there's something I wanted to ask you,' Danny said when they were outside. 'Where did that bruise come from on our Alice's face? She claimed to have walked into a door, but I'm not sure if I believe her.'

'John did it.' Bernadette had no intention of protecting John Lacey from his father-in-law's wrath. She was slightly disappointed that Danny was only walking her home because he'd wanted to ask about Alice. 'It was on

Thursday night, when Alice came back with the cheque.'

Danny swore under his breath. 'I'll be after having a word with him as soon as I get the opportunity.' Later that night, maybe. Alice had said something about going back to the hairdresser's to put up the curtains so there was a good chance John would be alone.

Thinking she was being helpful, Bernadette told him about the flat over Myrtle's. 'I said it would do for John, but Alice wouldn't hear of it.'

'Quite right, too.' He sounded even more shocked by the idea than his daughter had. 'You can't chuck a man out of his own home, no matter what he's done,' he said, outraged.

'Huh! No matter if he'd put your Alice in hospital or done the same to one of the kids?' She forgot her awe of him and lost her temper. Men! The world would be a far better place without them. There'd only been one good one and he'd been killed in the war.

'It's not the way things are done,' Danny said testily. He was beginning to wish he hadn't offered to take her home. He'd always thought her a rather quiet little thing. He wasn't used to women arguing with him. They usually agreed with his every word.

'Well, it's about time it was. Are you suggesting women are born to be punchbags?'

He was flummoxed. What could he say to that? 'I'm suggesting nothing of the kind.'

'Yes, you are. You're saying a woman can be knocked to bits and nothing should be done about it.'

'She can always leave.' He regretted the words as soon as they'd left his mouth, because the quiet little thing burst into sarcastic laughter.

'In that case, if John hits your Alice again, I'll suggest she ups with the four kids and parks herself on you.'

Both seething, they walked the rest of the way to Irlam Road in silence.

Alice finished hanging the white lace curtains and imagined the reaction of the customers tomorrow when they saw the changes that had been made to Myrtle's – she corrected herself – *Lacey's*. She must get a signwriter to change the name over the window and pushed to the back of her mind the knowledge that there'd been a time when John would willingly have done it.

There were other things she must do – buy new towels, for instance, mauve if you could get them. And she needed a clock, a little cheap one – how on earth had Myrtle managed without a clock for all those years? And she'd have price lists printed on little cards, like wedding invitations.

She rubbed her hands together excitedly. She'd have to engage an assistant, someone to do the same things she'd been taken on for herself. A woman with school-aged kids would be ideal because Fionnuala was only too willing to come and help when she finished school, as well as on Saturdays.

All the pictures of the beautiful, dead smart coiffures that Myrtle couldn't have managed in a month of Sundays had been removed from the wall so it could be painted. Alice began to put them back with the drawing pins she'd saved, along with the adverts for various shampoos, setting lotions and hairdressings – she liked the one for Rowland's Macassar Oil the best. Her arms were aching. But it wasn't just the hard work she'd put in today, but that she'd been sleeping on the settee in the parlour since Thursday and it was extremely uncomfortable, much too short and much too hard.

Things couldn't continue at home the way they were, but once again Alice refused to think about them.

Instead, she sat under the dryer and regarded Myrtle's – *Lacey's* – with satisfaction. Tomorrow it would look even nicer with the lino laid.

Across the street, well away from the street lamp, a dark figure stood watching the woman at her various tasks. He saw her sit in the centre of the three dryers, saw the way her face glowed when she glanced around the salon, which he had to concede had improved out of all proportion for the better.

John Lacey felt sick with love for the woman who was his wife, along with stirrings of anger and jealousy, never far away these days. The bloody salon had taken *his* place in Alice's heart, but then he only had himself to blame for that.

For the first time in his life he felt the urge to get drunk, to get totally inebriated, forget everything. He'd only been that drunk once before – at a mate's wedding when he was eighteen. It hadn't been a very pleasant experience, but right now the idea of forgetting everything was infinitely appealing.

Where to go to achieve this agreeable state of mind? Not a pub where he was known, or a quiet, respectable place where they'd stare at his face. One of those rowdy ale houses on the Dock Road would be ideal. They were usually packed to the gills with foreign seamen and prostitutes. No one would take a blind bit of notice of him.

John took a final look at Alice, turned up the collar of his coat, pulled his hat down over his scarred face and hurried in the direction of the Docky.

Hours later Danny Mitchell, on his way to have a stern word with his son-in-law, was still seething over the conversation he'd had with Bernadette. If she were

63

older, she'd probably have been one of them damned, stupid suffragettes, chaining herself to railings so women could have the vote.

A little worm of reason penetrated his stubborn brain. It wasn't exactly fair that women *shouldn't* have the vote. After all, whatever those fools of politicians got up to affected them just as much as it did men. And they'd been worth their weight in gold during the war. And if a man knocked a woman about, was she supposed just to stand there and let him?

Danny squirmed uncomfortably. It niggled him that the little girl who'd been his daughter's best friend for as long as he could remember had caused him to have such disturbing thoughts. He felt like a traitor to his sex and tried to concentrate on his meeting later with Phyllis Henderson. Phyllis would butter him up no end, restore his equilibrium, as it were.

To his surprise, when he entered his daughter's house the light was on, but it appeared to be empty. 'Is anyone home?' he called.

'Only me, Grandad,' Cormac shouted from upstairs.

'Surely you haven't been left all on your own!' Danny exclaimed on his way up to the boxroom where his grandson slept.

'Dad said Mam or the girls'd be back soon.' Cormac was sitting up in bed, his slightly too big wincyette pyjamas buttoned neatly to the neck. He put down the book he was reading when his grandad came in.

'Your mam'll be dead cross if she finds you all by yourself. I'll stay till someone comes.' Danny sat on the edge of the narrow bed. 'What's that you're reading, son?'

'I'm not 'xactly *reading* it, Grandad,' Cormac explained gravely. 'I'm trying to do the sums.'

Danny gaped. The lad, only five years old, was

actually studying an *arithmetic* book. His heart swelled with pride. Wait till he told Phyllis and his mates in the pub! 'Need any help, son?' he enquired, though beyond the twelve times table he needed help himself.

'What's that word?' Cormac turned the page and pointed to the heading.

'Multiplication. It means . . .'

'I know what it means, Grandad. It means "times". I didn't know how it was said. The next page is "long" something. I don't know how that's said either.'

'Long division, son.' He was beginning to think his grandson was a genius. 'Can you do all these things – the long division and the times?'

'Only with little figures,' Cormac confessed sadly.

'Can the whole class do them?' Danny asked.

Cormac shook his fair head. 'Acshully, Grandad, school's a bit fed-upping. I wish it weren't so dead easy.'

He should be moved up to a higher class, Danny thought indignantly. He'd have a word with Alice when she came in.

Not far away in Irlam Road, Bernadette Moynihan also felt indignant. To think that all these years she'd been sweet on such a rampant misogynist! Even when she'd been married to her darling Bob she had continued to find Danny Mitchell slightly disturbing.

It had started when his wife died and Danny had appeared so devastated. She was eight, same as Alice, and had resolved to marry him, take care of him, when she grew up. He was only twenty-nine and, as Bernadette grew older – became twelve, sixteen, twenty – in her eyes Danny remained the same. One of these days she'd catch up with him, he'd notice her and ask for her hand in marriage. She had spent many happy hours imagining what it would be like being Danny Mitchell's wife. This was one of the few dreams she hadn't confided to Alice, who might not care to have her best friend as a stepmother.

Then Bernadette had met Bob Moynihan and all thoughts of Danny Mitchell had fled from her mind — except when she met him in the flesh, when her knees were still inclined to grow weak and her cheeks to turn pink. She used to pray Bob wouldn't notice and he never had.

But now! Now she had completely gone off him. 'You can't chuck a man out of his own home no matter what he's done,' he'd actually said. Oh, really! She'd have flattened John Lacey with a frying pan if she'd been in Alice's shoes, then dragged him outside and had the locks changed so he couldn't get back in.

She hated men, every single one of them, and she hated Danny Mitchell the most.

At the next table a black man had pulled a girl on to his knee and was touching her breasts beneath her green jumper.

The girl laughed and pulled away. Her face was orange with powder and her mouth a vivid scarlet. She had a green bead as big as a marble dangling from each ear. 'Eh, mate. I don't usually let fellas do that for free.'

The man leered, showing large, very white teeth. 'How much you charge?'

'Five bob and I'm all yours for half an hour.'

'Where we go?'

'Outside, I'll show you where, but give us the five bob first.'

The couple left and John Lacey felt something stir in the pit of his stomach. After ten chaste months and half a dozen pints of ale, he was badly in need of a woman. In the past the idea of using a prostitute would have disgusted him, but right now perhaps it was the drink that made him consider the idea not all that repugnant.

Jaysus! Did he really intend to sink so low? Well, why not? To have set foot inside this den of iniquity wasn't the act of a man who cared how low he sank. There'd already been a fight – two men had produced knives and gone for each other. They'd been thrown out, leaving behind quite a lot of blood. The fight had been over a woman, a gaunt young woman with hollow cheeks and vacant eyes who had followed them outside.

The place was called the Arcadia and when he'd first set foot inside the large, square room with its worm-eaten pillars, the low ceiling blackened by age and smoke, it had made him think of a scene from hell. The wooden floor was scattered with sawdust, the tables long, full of stains and cigarette burns, with benches either side. It was packed, as he had expected. Noise assaulted his ears, hurt them. Men and women shouted at each other in order to be heard above the din – the women's shrill voices seemed the louder. Directly in front of him a man with a black patch over his eye swept his arm across a table and dozens of empty glasses smashed to the floor. There was the pungent odour of dirt, unwashed bodies, cheap scent. The smoke that hung in the air smelt musky and sweet – it wasn't just tobacco.

His first instinct had been to turn on his heel and leave, but he remembered he'd wanted a place where no one would know him. What did it matter where he got plastered? Two hours later he knew his first instinct had been right. He was only half drunk, he had forgotten nothing and the ale had made him feel even more depressed. The tragedy that was now his life seemed worse, more insoluble, even less bearable, than ever. In such alien surroundings he found it hard to believe he was a married man with a lovely wife and four equally lovely children.

Another thing, sex had been furthest from his mind when he came in, but now he could think of little else. He had tried to, but couldn't, take his eyes off the grotesquely painted women in their tight frocks and short skirts. He imagined doing things with them that he had never done with Alice. He thought about what the black man was doing with the girl in the green jumper and felt himself swell.

A woman slid on to the bench opposite. 'Like a spot of company, luv?' she asked in a coarse, gruff voice. She was twice his age, with hair dyed an unnatural red, almost purple, and a gaudily painted face. John's eyes were drawn to the breasts that swelled over the top of her black blouse, the nipples prominent through the thin, gauzy material. She was wearing nothing under-neath.

He shook his head, though his heart was pounding and he longed to reach out and touch the bulging breasts. 'No, thank you.'

'Just come for a gander, have you?' she sneered and went away, muttering, 'Filthy bugger.'

All it needed was courage. Men and women kept disappearing and reappearing half an hour, an hour, later. All he had to do was approach a woman – he didn't even have to say anything, just show the money and nod towards the door. But he was terrified that even these women, the lowest of the low, would turn him down because of his face. Even worse, they might take his money with the same expression of distaste on their faces that he'd seen on Alice's, though she flatly denied it.

Someone older might be less choosy. He regretted

68

sending away the woman who'd asked if he wanted company – clearly, his face didn't bother *her*. He wondered where she'd gone so he could say he'd changed his mind. His eyes searched the packed room for her red head, but she was nowhere to be seen.

Then he saw the girl. She was two tables away, sitting demurely with her hands clasped on her lap, head bent, as if she was closely studying something on the table. Her hair was long and straight, and so fair it was almost white. Even from this distance John could see the long, pale lashes surrounding a pair of large grey eyes. The girl raised her head, as if aware she was being watched, and through the crowds their faces met – the faces of the man with the melted skin and the girl who would have been pretty if it hadn't been for the ugly hare lip.

Her name was Clare he learnt after they had made love. She'd written it down because he couldn't understand the strange, gutteral sounds that came from her mouth. She had a cleft palate, no roof to her mouth. She gestured a lot, her face fierce with concentration, pointing to herself, to him. When he asked her age, she wrote 'twenty' in the air with her finger.

John liked her. He liked the fact that she never smiled, because he himself hadn't felt much like smiling in a long time. He sensed that she found life as burdensome as he did. He admired her for not painting her face or wearing revealing clothes – she had on a plain black frock and flat black shoes, no jewellery. She was very clean and her room, on the top floor of a narrow three-storey house just round the corner from the Arcadia, was neat and tidy.

He hadn't done the disgusting things he'd imagined with the other women. He made love to her as he would have done to his wife – gently, with some passion, quite satisfyingly. Other than wrapping her legs around his waist, she didn't respond, but nor did she give the impression she found the act objectionable.

When they had finished he felt as if a great load had been lifted from his shoulders. For the first time since he'd been fire-watching and that damned ship had gone up in flames, he was able to relax. He lay beside her on the bed, watching the cold moon shining through the small window. Stars twinkled in the dark sky.

'Do you want to go back to the Arcadia?' he asked after she had answered his questions as best she could and they had lain there for a while. He was stopping her from earning her living.

She shook her head and pointed to the door, indicating that he could go if he liked.

'D'you mind if I stay? I feel dead tired.'

Closing her eyes, she gave a tiny sigh, which he understood to mean she was tired too.

John reached out and touched her twisted lips with his finger. 'You're very pretty.'

There was surprise in the intelligent grey eyes when she turned towards him. She seemed to hesitate, then lifted her hand and stroked his melted cheek. He decided he could quickly get used to her painful pronunciation when she said in her awkward way, 'You're very handsome.'

Alice had been cross the night before when she came home and discovered that, unusually for him, John had gone out, which she didn't mind, but he shouldn't have left Cormac on his own.

Her dad thought he'd almost certainly gone for a drink. 'Do him good, if you ask me.'

'Yes, but he might have *said*.'

Danny left, rather late, to meet his lady friend. The

girls came home. Alice made cocoa and several rounds of toast, and they sat round the fire, giggling helplessly, telling each other silly jokes. They made so much noise that Cormac came down to see what was going on and told the unfunniest joke of all: 'Why did the chicken cross the road?'

'To get to the other side!' everyone screamed.

'Oh,' gasped Maeve, bent double with laughter. 'It's a pity Dad isn't out more often. It's much better fun without him.' She went very red and everyone fell silent as they contemplated the truth of this remark.

'Well,' Alice said eventually, 'I think it's time we went to bed. I'm fair whacked and I need to be up early tomorrer to let the man into Myrtle's with the lino.' There didn't seem much point waiting up for John. Since last Thursday they'd hardly exchanged a word.

'Lacey's,' Fionnuala reminded her.

'Oh, yes, Lacey's.'

Alice fell asleep immediately on the uncomfortable settee and was woken by the sound of clinking bottles. The milkman had arrived. She went into the living room in her nightie and felt cross again when she discovered John hadn't lit the fire as he normally did before going to work – he'd used to wake her up with a cup of tea, but those days were long gone.

She lit the fire herself, made tea, woke Cormac, then the girls. 'I'll have to be going in a minute,' she told the three sleepy faces. I'll trust you to make sure your brother eats his cornflakes and that he's properly dressed for school. He's inclined to forget his vest if you don't watch him.'

'OK, Mam,' they chorused, and she thought what lovely children they were and how nice and cheerful last night had been without their father's brooding presence.

Perhaps he'd go for a drink more often, she thought hopefully.

The linoleum had been dead cheap and the man cut it into shape in no time. 'It's not going to last all that long,' he warned, 'not in a hairdresser's with so much traffic.'

'It's only temporary,' Alice assured him, 'just to make the place look respectable until I can buy some of that inlaid stuff.'

He wished her luck, promised to recommend Lacey's to his missus and Alice tipped him sixpence.

'You've worked a miracle, Alice,' the first customer gasped when she arrived for her nine o'clock appointment. 'Mauve, white and black go together perfect.' Throughout the day, customers continued to express their astonishment at the transformation that had taken place in Myrtle's – now called Lacey's, Alice informed them. She didn't feel the least embarrassed when a few asked to use the lavatory. At least it was clean and as soon as she could she'd paint the walls.

Late in the afternoon Mrs O'Leary popped her head round the door to ask if their Daisy could possibly be squeezed in for a trim. She regarded the salon with amazement. 'It looks lovely and bright, like a grotto. After Christmas Eve, I swore I'd never set foot in here again, but now I'm glad Gloria's in Marsh Lane were too busy to take us. Our Daisy's got a concert tomorrer night and she needs a trim dead urgent.'

Daisy tossed her auburn curls. 'I'm an elf,' she announced.

'I'm afraid you'll have to wait a bit.' Alice was halfway through a perm, and there was a customer under a dryer who would shortly need combing out. She was doing the work of two women and felt worn out.

'You look puffed,' Mrs O'Leary remarked as she sat down. 'What you need is an assistant.'

'I know. I keep meaning to put a notice in the winder, but I've been too busy all day to write it out.'

'I'd apply meself, but our Kevin's only five – he started school with your Cormac – and I'm not prepared to let him and Daisy wander the streets until you close, and on Saturdays an' all. Me neighbour's got Kevin at the moment, but I couldn't ask her every day.' She pulled a face. 'I could do with the money. The cost of Daisy's dancing class went up in January and her costumes cost a mint. Me husband claims we can't afford it and keeps threatening to make her stop. The thing is, the dancing teacher ses she's got talent.' She chucked Daisy under the chin. 'You want to go on the stage when you grow up, don't you, luv?'

'Oh, *yes*, Mam,' Daisy concurred.

'Mmm,' Alice said thoughtfully. Mrs O'Leary was always nicely dressed, and she had a warm smile and a pleasant manner. She used to get on Myrtle's nerves, boasting incessantly about Daisy and her dancing, but Alice could do much worse for an assistant. She said, 'Actually, the job would only be during school hours. Our Fion's helping out the rest of the time. In fact, she should be here any minute. Ah, here she is now.'

Fionnuala burst into the salon, eager to start work properly as a hairdresser. She pouted when her mother told her to sweep the floor. 'Oh, *Mam!*'

'Just get on with it, luv. You're not ready to give a perm just yet.' She turned to Mrs O'Leary. 'What do you say, about the job, that is?'

'I'd *luv* it,' the woman said breathlessly. 'When can I start?'

'Tomorrer wouldn't be too soon.'

'Tomorrer it is. Me name's Patsy, by the way. You

73

can't very well call me Mrs O'Leary and me call you Alice.'

I might as well be invisible, John Lacey thought sardonically when he arrived home from work and realised no one had noticed he'd been out all night. As far as his family were concerned he didn't exist.

He'd spent the night with Clare, feeling guilty, but at the same time hoping Alice would worry herself sick – he'd worried himself enough over her. He had concocted a story – he'd met a mate, drunk too much, gone back to his house and fallen asleep. But the story wasn't necessary. All Alice did was rattle on and on about hairdressing and the marvellous day she'd had, and you'd think Fionnuala had given Queen Elizabeth herself a shampoo and set from the way she spoke, when all she'd done was wash some woman's hair.

'I'm going out,' he said in a surly voice after he'd finished his tea.

'Have a nice time, luv,' Alice said brightly.

John saw Orla wink joyfully at her sisters as he left the room and longed to turn round, tell his family how much he loved them, make everything better. But it was too late. They hated him. He'd passed the point of no return.

Cormac had followed him into the hall and John wondered if the divil now possessed his soul. How could he have thought his little lad could hate anyone, let alone his father?

'Got ten out of ten for me sums today, Dad. I've brought the book home to show you.'

Tears stung his eyes as he sat on the stairs and lifted Cormac on to his knee. 'Let's have a dekko, son.'

'They're add up and take away.'

'So I see. Gosh, that's dead neat writing.'

'The teacher said it's the best in the class.'

He stroked Cormac's soft cheek. 'I bet she did, son.'

Alice poked her head round the door. 'I was wondering if you'd gone or not. I didn't hear the door slam.'

John put Cormac down and reached for his coat. 'I'm going now. By the way,' he said gruffly, 'you have the bed from now on. I'll use the settee.'

The Docky was always busy. The offices of the shipping merchants, the importers and exporters, were closed and there was less traffic than during the day. But at seven o'clock the pavements were still full of seamen and sailors of myriad nationalities. Behind the high walls of the docks activity could be heard – the shouts and thuds as ships that could have come from anywhere in the world were being loaded or offloaded in the bright glare of floodlights.

Particles of ice were being blown crazily about, this way and that, by the bitter wind that blew in from the Mersey. John could hear the water slushing noisily against the walls of the docks. He drew up his scarf around his neck.

He arrived at the Arcadia, where two small children, a boy and a girl, were cuddled against each other on the steps outside, shivering in their thin clothes. He gave them a penny each.

'Thanks, mister,' the boy said with remarkable cheer-fulness.

Clare was sitting at the same table as the night before, her back to him. John's heart lifted and he began to push his way through the crowded room. He'd been looking forward to this moment all day, a day when he'd felt at ease with himself for the first time in months. He slid on to the bench beside her. 'Hello, there.'

She frowned. At first he thought she was annoyed with him for coming until he recognised the frown was one of disbelief. Her cheeks went pink and he realised she was pleased and flattered that he was back.

She nodded furiously. 'Hello.' She hesitated, as she had done the night before, then reached for his hand. 'Glad,' she whispered. 'Glad you're here.' And then she smiled and the smile made her look almost beautiful.

John smiled back and thought what a miracle it was that he had met a woman who was as damaged as himself and that they could make each other smile.

Cora Lacey came into the salon at the end of Alice's first week. The hairdresser's was just about to close. Fionnuala was cleaning the sinks and Cormac was kneeling on a chair in front of the big till ringing up numbers.

'Had a busy week?' Cora enquired.

'I've been run off me feet if you must know.' Alice collapsed under a dryer. 'Thank the Lord it's Sat'day. I've just sent our Orla and Maeve round for fish and chips. I haven't the strength to make the tea.'

'Good,' Cora said with satisfaction. It meant the takings must be considerable. 'Shove over, son.' She gave Cormac a little nudge with her hip and he reluctantly climbed off the chair. 'Is this all there is?' She glanced suspiciously at her sister-in-law. 'Not a single note?'

'The notes are at home,' Alice explained. 'I empty the till each night, don't I? And I hardly ever take notes, anyroad, except for perms and I didn't do one today.'

'Then I'll come back to the house with you to collect me share.'

Fionnuala had stopped work to listen. She glared at her aunt whom she had never liked. 'What's she on about, Mam?'

'It's none of your business, luv.'

76

'Why is she taking money out the till? It's *our* salon.'

'Your Auntie Cora put money into the business,' Alice explained patiently. Her eldest daughter usually managed to test her patience sorely. 'She's entitled to some of the profit.'

'But there won't be profit for weeks and weeks, Mam,' Fion exclaimed. 'You said so only the other day, what with the price of paint and everything.'

'Yes, but . . .' Alice paused. Fion was right. The cost of improvements shouldn't just be borne by her, but shared with Cora, too. And the wages – she wondered if she was entitled to claim a wage for herself? Oh, Lord! She must be the stupidest woman in the world for not having grasped the blatantly obvious.

She swallowed hard – Cora always made her feel dead nervous – and said in a firm voice, 'I'm afraid you can't just come in and help yourself. I need to work things out first, what comes in and what goes out, like.'

'And what exactly goes out apart from the price of a few tins of paint?' Cora wanted to know. She had been expecting to go home with a few quid in her pocket and was annoyed at being thwarted.

Alice was about to reel off the things she'd bought and those she intended buying, when Fionnuala said aggressively, 'She said she'd write them down, didn't she? It's *our* hairdresser's. We don't have to answer to you for everything we buy.'

'Shush, luv.' Alice squeezed her daughter's arm.

The door opened and Orla and Maeve came in, each carrying a parcel of fish and chips wrapped in greasy newspaper.

'Shall we take them home and put them in the oven, Mam?' Maeve enquired.

'Please, luv. We'll be there in a minute.'

Orla's bright, curious eyes went from her mother to

her aunt, then to her sister's red, angry face. 'What's going on?'

'There's nothing going on, luv. Just get them fish and chips home before they turn cold.'

'We'll wait for you.' Orla and Maeve came into the salon and stood alongside their mother. Cormac bent his head against his mam's hip and Alice idly began to stroke the soft fair hair.

Faced with the girls' hostile eyes, it dawned on Cora that she wasn't going to find their gormless mother the easy touch she'd expected. She also felt disturbed at being presented with such a united front, conscious she had no one on her side. She wished she'd brought Maurice so she could stroke his hair the way Alice was stroking Cormac's and she wouldn't look so very much alone.

'I'll be in Monday for a statement,' she muttered.

'It might not be ready by then.' Fionnuala smirked. She was thoroughly enjoying protecting Mam from the horrible Cora. It was *her* who had reminded Mam the hairdresser's wouldn't show a profit for ages, *she* who had given it its name. She felt annoyed and very unappreciated when Mam tugged her sleeve and told her again to 'shush'.

'I'll have the statement ready for Monday,' Alice promised.

She had been born, Clare informed him, when her mother was forty-seven. By then her three brothers were in their twenties; all married, all living in different parts of the country. They rarely came home. Her parents' marriage had broken down years before. John was astonished to learn her father had been, possibly still was, a solicitor's clerk.

'My mother said she only had me because he raped

78

her. She hated me right from the start.' She conveyed this in a mixture of gestures, facial expressions, sounds and the pad on which she wrote. Her full name was Clare Frances Carlson. 'They were ashamed of people knowing I was their daughter.'

She'd been sent to a special boarding school, returning home at fourteen when her education was complete. Within months she had run away – she came from Widnes – but couldn't think of a job someone like her could do apart from cleaning. Even then, 'People don't like this.' She pointed to her mouth, then wrote, 'They think I'm an imbecile.'

'You're anything but.' John took her hands in his. She was a very clever young woman – he wouldn't have known how to spell imbecile. There were books on the sideboard, pencil drawings on the walls that he was surprised to learn she'd done herself. They were mostly of the Dock Road, which could be seen from the window – the traffic, the teeming pavements, the funnels of ships protruding from behind the dock walls. A few were sketches of the crowded interior of the Arcadia that she'd done from memory.

Her short life story was told without a shred of self-pity. She hadn't drifted into prostitution, no one had coerced her. She just heard it went on and it seemed a good way for someone like her to make a living. She didn't like it, but she didn't hate it either.

'Surely there were other things that you could have done,' John said, conscious of a note of reproof in his voice.

'What would you have done if you'd been born with your face like that?' she scribbled, underlining the 'born'.

For some reason he seized the pencil. 'Hidden from the world,' he wrote.

'That's what I'm doing in my way,' she wrote back.

'You deserve better,' he wrote in turn. He'd never been greedy for money. A few extra bob a week wouldn't have come amiss for the odd luxury, but as a skilled tradesman he earned slightly more than the average man. There'd always been enough to keep his family comfortably warm and fed, and the bit Alice got from hairdressing was merely the icing on the cake. But he longed to take Clare away from this run-down house full of tarts, find her somewhere respectable to live, support her, so that she could come off the game and belong to him alone.

But without money none of these things was possible. It gnawed at his gut, knowing that before he came, or after he'd gone, she was in the Arcadia touting for customers, yet he had no right to ask her to stop. He couldn't have afforded to see her more than once or twice a week, had she not refused to let him pay after the first night.

'I said you're different. We're friends,' she wrote, turning away the five shillings he offered. She was a curious mixture of hardness and innocence.

He thought 'friends' described their relationship perfectly. They were friends drawn together by adversity and loneliness. At the back of his mind there was always the awareness that a year ago he wouldn't have dreamt of going near the Arcadia or sleeping with a prostitute. He had told Clare he was married, but still worried that he was using her. Having broken through her hard shell, he was taking advantage of the soft, generous woman inside. He worried that he might hurt her, let her down, that she would become too dependent on him. If things ever improved between him and Alice, for instance . . . But – he sighed – things never would, particularly now that she was so deeply involved with that damned hairdresser's.

The nightly visits to the pub were doing John the world of good. Alice only wished he'd gone before. He was nicer to the girls, and after tea he'd put Cormac on his knee and discuss the things he'd done that day at school. He'd even deigned to speak to his wife in a civil manner, suggesting he build bunk beds for the middle bedroom.

'The girls are getting too big for three in a bed,' he said and actually smiled.

Alice opened her mouth to say that Maeve had been sleeping with her since she'd occupied the double bed, but quickly closed it. 'Them bunk beds sound the gear, luv,' she said warmly. 'The girls will be dead pleased.'

'I'll get the wood this weekend.'

'John!' She laid her hand on his arm and was dismayed when he quickly moved away as if disgusted by her touch. She regarded him sadly, thinking how much she'd once loved him, then felt even more dismayed at the realisation she didn't love him now. He had spurned her too often. He had driven her away.

'What?'

Alice sighed. 'Oh, nothing.'

Chapter 4
CHRISTMAS 1951

'Who'd like another mince pie?' Alice cried.

'Me!'

'Apart from you, Fionnuala Lacey. I thought it was your intention to lose a few pounds. Any minute now and you'll need a bigger overall.' The overalls were lilac nylon – 'lilac' sounded so much nicer than 'mauve', Alice thought, more tasteful.

'Oh, *Mam*!'

Alice virtually danced across the room to pass the plate beneath the noses of the three women under the dryers. They each took one.

'You look happy, luv,' Mrs Curran remarked. 'Did you make these yourself?'

'I was up till midnight baking,' Alice said cheerfully. 'It's home-made mincemeat too. I managed to get a pound of sultanas in Costigan's. I think it's disgusting. The war's been over six whole years and the country's still on rations. Do you fancy a drop of sherry with the pie?'

'Ta all the same, luv, but no. Drink plays havoc with me gallstones. I wouldn't mind a cup of tea, though.'

'Fion, make Mrs Curran a cup of tea, please.'

'On the Empire, she was,' Patsy O'Leary was saying as she combed out Mrs Glaister's wet hair ready for Alice to set. 'All the dancing schools in Liverpool took part, but our Daisy was the star of the show. Wasn't she, Alice?'

'Oh, yes,' Alice dutifully lied.

Fionnuala looked at her mother and winked. Alice must have been asked the same question a hundred times since the concert last week. Daisy had been good, but a few other girls and one or two boys had been better.

'Poor Myrtle, she wouldn't recognise this place if she saw it now,' Mrs Glaister said sadly.

'Do you ever hear from her, luv?'

'No. I always send a Christmas card, but I haven't had one back for years. I still miss her, even after all this time. She was a good friend, Myrtle.' Mrs Glaister's old eyes grew watery. 'I reckon she must have passed on.' She crossed herself.

'It happens to us all,' Patsy O'Leary commented.

'Fion,' Alice called, 'put a gown on Mrs Evans. I'll be ready for her soon.'

'Come on, Mrs Evans, luv,' Fionnuala said in a sickly, sugary voice, and proceeded to help the woman, who was barely fifty and as fit as a fiddle, to her feet, and shove her arms inside the sleeves of the lilac gown as if she hadn't the strength to lift the arms herself.

'I can manage on me own, thanks,' Mrs Evans snapped.

It was Alice's turn to wink at Patsy. Fionnuala persisted in treating anyone over forty as if they had one foot in the grave. She would help women down to the lavatory in the yard, wait for them outside and help them back again. Even when asked by one woman, admittedly elderly, but resentful at being fussed over, if she was waiting to wipe her arse, it hadn't prevented Fionnuala from assuming that most of her mother's customers were helpless invalids. Still, Alice thought, her heart was in the right place.

Alice went over to a chair facing the mirror and laid

her hands on Mrs Evans's shoulders. 'What is it you want, luv? Explain to me again.'

'Frosting. Just the tips of me hair bleached. I would have thought you'd have heard of frosting, Mrs Lacey,' the woman said sniffily, 'you being a hairdresser, like.'

'Of course I've heard of frosting. I get *Vogue* every month to keep up with the latest styles and products, don't I? I just wasn't sure if you knew what it was.' Bleached ends wouldn't suit someone as dark as Edna Evans. But then, the customer was always right and if she wanted to end up looking dead stupid it was up to her.

'I wouldn't have asked for it if I didn't know what it was.'

'Just making sure, luv,' Alice said serenely. Some customers could be really difficult.

'You're obviously very busy,' Edna Evans said grudgingly.

'I've had to turn customers away. We've been booked solid for weeks, but then Christmas Eve is always busy. Patsy's only helping today as a special favour.'

The door opened, the bell chimed sweetly and Bernadette Moynihan came in. 'Oh, it's like a little oasis in here,' she sang. 'It's dead gloomy outside. The lights in the window look the gear, Al. Lovely and bright.'

'They actually spell "Lacey's". It took me ages to do. Patsy,' she called, 'would you comb out Mrs Curran, then put a gown on Bernie and wet her hair.'

'I'm here for a Peter Pan cut, Al. It doesn't need wetting.'

'I read the other day that hair cuts better if it's wet. I thought I'd experiment on you.'

'Oh, ta! Friendship can have its limits, Alice Lacey. If you spoil me hair, I'll never speak to you again.'

The dryers gradually emptied. Edna Evans went away looking as if she'd been sprinkled with icing sugar,

84

tipping Alice sixpence, so *she* must be pleased. Mrs Glaister seemed reluctant to leave the warm, brightly lit salon with its silver decorations and coloured lights. Feeling sorry for the old woman, knowing that after five years she still missed Myrtle, Alice suggested she stay and have another glass of sherry. The salon would be closing in half an hour.

'And there's still a few mince pies left, luv. Help yourself. Fion, start cleaning the sinks, there's a good girl. Patsy, you can go if you want. Thanks for coming.'

Patsy O'Leary wished everyone Merry Christmas and went home. Mrs Glaister realised her time was up when Alice turned the 'Open' sign to 'Closed'. Fionnuala went to tidy the kitchen and Bernadette examined the Peter Pan cut in the mirror. It was a big step, going from very long to very short in the space of a few minutes. Her neck felt cold, she complained. Alice gave her a towel to keep it warm.

There were footsteps on the stairs and a stocky young woman with a vivid, smiling face entered the salon. She wore a warm tweed coat and a knitted mohair tam-o'-shanter. 'I'm off now, Mrs Lacey.'

'Miss Caddick!' Alice kissed the woman on the cheek. 'Have a lovely Christmas and I hope the wedding goes really well. Good luck for the future.'

'Same to you, Mrs Lacey. I couldn't have wished for a nicer landlady. I've just given upstairs a good clean, ready for the new tenant.'

'Ta, luv. I wish you were getting married in Bootle. I'd have come to the church for a look.'

'If I was getting married in Bootle, you'd have been invited, Mrs Lacey, but Durham's a long way to ask someone to come.' She shouted, ''Bye, Fionnuala,' bestowed a glittering smile on Bernadette and left.

'So, you've got to find a new tenant for upstairs,' Bernie said.

'I've already got one. The teacher taking over Miss Caddick's class at St James's is taking over the flat as well. Nell Greene, her name is, with an "e" on the end. I take it she's a "miss". She comes from London.'

'What's she like?'

'Dunno, I haven't seen her. It was all arranged by letter.'

Bernadette worriedly regarded her hair. 'Does this look too boyish? And I don't like the look of me ears.'

'Peter Pan was a boy, so it's bound to. As for your ears, I'll give them a trim if you like.'

'You say the nicest things. Albert'll have a fit tonight when he sees it. We're going to Reece's to a dance.'

'Albert Eley hasn't got the strength to have a fit. And I'm surprised he can dance, if you must know.'

Bernadette pretended to look angry, then her face collapsed in a loud sigh. 'He'll probably not even notice me hair or me new dress. He's a good dancer, though. He had lessons in some place in Spellow Lane.'

'Tap-dancing? Like Daisy O'Leary?'

''Course not, idiot.' She giggled. 'Ballroom dancing. He went with his mam.'

'I don't know what you see in him,' Alice said bluntly. Albert Eley was a bachelor of forty who lived in Byron Street with his mother. He was the most uninteresting man she had ever known.

Bernie shrugged. 'He's company. At least he's never tried anything on.'

'Only because he wouldn't know how. Seriously, Bernie. You're only thirty-seven, you're still dead pretty. There must be loads of men out there who'd be an improvement on Albert Eley.'

'Until I met Albert, I never came across a single one

who didn't want to jump into bed with me within the first five minutes. He's easy to be with, very polite, free with his money. The only thing that gets me down is him going on and on about his bloody mother. It's mam this and mam that until I could scream.' Bernie giggled. 'Anyroad, *you're* only thirty-seven and still dead pretty. There's a few men around who'd be an improvement on John Lacey.'

'Shush!' Alice put her finger to her lips and nodded towards the kitchen where her daughter could be heard washing dishes. 'Me and John get on fine nowadays.'

'Not all that fine,' Bernie said in a hoarse whisper. 'He still sleeps in the parlour. The kids must have guessed there's something up by now.'

'They think it's his back, he ricked it and he has to sleep on his own.'

'A likely story!'

'It *is* a story, Bernie, and as long as the kids believe it, that's all that matters. Anyroad, it doesn't bother me, not much. I've got used to it by now.' She gave her friend a little shove. 'Stop trying to make me miserable. I love having me own salon. I'm dead happy, even if things aren't exactly perfect at home. Now shove off and make yourself beautiful for Albert. Oh, and by the way, when you come to Christmas dinner tomorrer, try not to rile me dad. All you two ever do is argue.'

Bernadette opened the door. 'Tell him not to rile me,' she said pertly before closing it.

'Phew!' Alice locked the door and collapsed in a chair. 'It's been a day and a half, today has. Have you nearly finished, Fion?' she called. 'It's time us two went home.'

'I've only got to dry the dishes, Mam.'

'Just leave them on the draining board to dry themselves.'

Someone tried the door. 'We're closed,' Alice

shouted, but the person banged on the glass. 'Oh, Lord,' she groaned. 'It's only your Auntie Cora.'

'Tell her to sod off, Mam.'

'Don't be silly, luv.'

'I've just come to wish you Merry Christmas and discuss the lease,' Cora said when Alice reluctantly let her in. Her light skin was becoming sallow and her colourless hair was scraped back in its usual sparse bun. She wore an unflattering camel coat.

'Merry Christmas, Cora,' Alice said coldly. 'What about the lease?' The seven-year lease expired at the end of the month and was due to be renewed. No doubt Cora had come on Horace Flynn's behalf to announce the cost of a new one.

'It's going up,' Cora said.

'I expected it would.' It seemed only fair.

'A new seven-year lease will be fourteen hundred pounds.' The small eyes gleamed with pleasure. She clearly enjoyed being the purveyor of such grim news.

'Fourteen hundred!' Alice gasped. 'I can't afford that much, Cora! The rates went up earlier this year and the last electricity bill made me eyes pop.'

'You'll just have to cut down on expenses,' Cora said. 'Get rid of that assistant, for one.'

'Not our Fion!'

'No, the other one. That Patsy woman. You haven't needed her since Fionnuala's been full-time.'

'I couldn't possibly. She needs the money. Her husband's dead mean and she's desperate for their Daisy to go on the stage.'

'There's no room for sentiment in business, Alice.'

'There is in mine,' Alice cried. 'There's no way I'd get rid of Patsy. Anyroad, we're often in need of three pairs of hands.'

88

Cora shrugged her narrow shoulders. 'Take it or leave it – the lease, that is.'

'We'll leave it, thanks all the same,' said a voice. Fionnuala came in from the kitchen. Cora shrank back. She wouldn't have come if she'd known the girl was there. While she could wrap her gutless wonder of a mother around her little finger, she was nervous of Fionnuala who somehow always seemed to get the better of her. It was Fionnuala who, years ago, had demanded a copy of the agreement that her stupid mam had signed and pointed out Cora was only entitled to a third share of 'the business presently known as Myrtle's Hairdressing Salon', so wasn't due a penny from the upstairs flat: it was Fionnuala who made sure Cora bore her share of every single expense incurred by Lacey's, down to things like lavatory paper and hairpins and even the tea the customers drank. Fionnuala had laughed like a drain when Cora tried to suggest that tips were part of the takings.

However, even Fionnuala couldn't claim that 'in perpetuity' didn't mean just that. In perpetuity. For all time. For ever.

'But I asked you at the time, and you said "till the money's paid back",' a shocked Alice had said, years ago, when she thought she had repaid the twenty-five pounds with interest.

'I did no such thing.' Cora had contrived to look indignant. 'I assumed anyone in their right mind would know what "in perpetuity" meant. I didn't just give you a loan. I invested in the business. A third of it's mine. It ses so on the agreement.'

'You're not half an idiot, Mam,' Fionnuala had groaned and Cora couldn't help but silently agree.

Now, Fionnuala looked contemptuously away from her aunt towards her mother. 'Mam, someone said the other day that Gloria's in Marsh Lane is closing down. That agreement you signed was for Myrtle's. If we moved somewhere else it would be null and void.'

Null and void! Alice wondered where her daughter had got such a grand phrase from. 'That's right,' she said to Cora.

Cora's lip curled. Fionnuala wasn't quite as clever as she thought. 'That's funny,' she said. 'Mr Flynn holds the freehold of Gloria's and he's never mentioned anything about it closing down.'

Fionnuala was only momentarily taken aback. Her eyes flickered slightly. 'Then maybe I heard wrong, but we could still move somewhere else.'

'What, and lose all your custom?' Cora sneered. 'Don't forget, if you upped and left, this place could still be let to another hairdresser. It doesn't have to close down.'

'Oh, no!' Alice flung her arms around a dryer. 'I wouldn't want anyone else to have Lacey's.'

'Well, there you are, then.' Cora smacked her lips. 'As I said, you'll just have to cut down on expenses. It's much too warm in here, fr'instance, and you don't need so many lights on, not now you're closed. Get rid of that Patsy woman and stop being so free with the cups of tea.' She eyed the single mince pie left on a plate and the remains of the sherry. 'I bet women don't get given stuff like that when they get their hair done in Mayfair.'

Fionnuala almost exploded with rage. 'How dare you tell us how to run our business?'

'Shush, luv. Goodnight, Cora,' Alice said with false brightness. 'I'll tell you after Christmas whether I'll take up the new lease or not. It needs some deciding, like.'

'Honestly, Mam,' Fion groaned after her aunt had gone. 'You were dead stupid signing that bloody agreement.'

'Horace Flynn could still put up the lease whether I'd signed the agreement or not.'

'Yes, but we could *afford* it if we didn't have to give Cora such a big chunk of what we earn.'

'Hmm,' Alice said thoughtfully. Her dad still maintained Cora did more for the landlord than keep his books. Alice wouldn't have touched him with a bargepole, but there were more ways than one to get round a man like Horace Flynn.

Next day all the Laceys, along with Bernadette Moynihan and Danny Mitchell, sat down to Christmas dinner in the parlour of the house in Amber Street. It was a happy, festive occasion, occasionally hilarious. Bernadette and Danny pretended to be nice to each other – they'd even bought each other presents – a loud check scarf and a frilly pinafore.

From the head of the table, John Lacey beamed proudly at his family. The girls, once so similar, had acquired their own, singular features as they approached adulthood. Orla was dead pretty, the spitting image of her mother. A real heartbreaker, she already had a steady boyfriend of whom John disapproved. She'd got herself a job with the *Crosby Star*. At first, all she'd done was run messages and the like while she learnt shorthand and typing at night school. Now she was taking letters and had her own desk and typewriter. She was going to be a reporter one day, she said boastfully. 'With a big London paper.'

Maeve seemed to have stopped growing at the age of twelve. Small, dainty, quietly self-assured, she worked at Bootle General Hospital in Derby Road, just skivvying to be blunt, but with the intention of training to be a proper nurse when she was old enough.

He sometimes worried about his eldest daughter,

Fionnuala, who, at only eighteen, had become matronly stout and didn't appear to have a friend in the world. She was an awkward, graceless girl, tactless – always saying the wrong thing – and over-effusive when there was no need. Perhaps it wasn't good for her to work with her mother, mixing with women two, three, four times her age and not a lad in sight.

And Cormac! John beamed most proudly of all upon his son, eleven the day before yesterday and certain to pass the scholarship next year and go to St Mary's grammar school. He used to worry that his lad, so quiet and studious, his head always buried in a book, would be bullied at school, particularly when he'd been moved up a class and put with children a year his senior. But Cormac, with his sweet smile and gentle face, never made a show of his cleverness, never bragged. And he was good at games, not so much footie, but his slight, fragile frame could move like the wind. If the school played rugby he'd be a star.

'John, Bernie would like some more wine.' Alice smiled. 'You were in a little world of your own just then.'

'Sorry, Bernie.' John refilled her glass. 'Alice was right. I was miles away.'

Alice! His wife had ripened over the years. No longer gawky, her movements were confident, self-assured. And she was growing more and more confident by the day. He felt proud of Alice too. He hadn't thought she'd had it in her to run her own business. But, he thought drily, perhaps he'd driven her to it. She'd been given the choice of Myrtle's or staying at home and, like any sane, sensible person, she'd chosen Myrtle's. He watched her, flushed and lovely, blue eyes sparkling animatedly as she discussed hairstyles with Bernadette. She had her own hair in something called a French pleat, which he didn't like – it made her look sophisticated, a bit hard, he thought.

'Not so much, luv.' Alice put her hand on Fionnuala's arm as she was about to take a third helping of Christmas pudding.

Did he still love her? John wondered. Probably. Probably just as much as he'd ever done. But now he felt they belonged to two different worlds – the world of the damaged and the world of the perfectly formed. He smiled to himself. And ne'er the twain shall meet!

The meal finished, the table was cleared and they played cards – Cormac could wipe the floor with everyone at poker.

At four o'clock John announced he was going out. 'To the yard. I'd like to get a bit of painting done so it'll be dry by tomorrer. I've got this urgent order, see.'

'But it's Christmas Day, luv,' Alice wailed. 'And surely you're not working Boxing Day as well?'

'I can't let these people down, Alice. It's the first time I've actually had an order from a big shop.'

'And it's dark, John. You should have done it this morning if it's all that important. It's blowing a gale out there.'

'I didn't want to miss seeing the kids open their presents. I'll probably go for a drink later, so I'll be late home.'

She fussed around, tying his scarf round his neck, buttoning his coat, and he tried not to show his impatience. Across the room his father-in-law was eying him suspiciously. He was so used to clandestine assignations himself that he automatically assumed John was off on a similar mission.

Alice came with him to the door, bemoaning the fact that he had to go all the way to Seaforth. 'I'm surprised you couldn't have found a more suitable place much nearer home in Bootle.'

'I tried,' John said and closed the door.

When Alice returned to the parlour, Bernie and Danny were in the middle of an argument. Why had he bought her a pinny? Bernie wanted to know. Had he done it deliberately to emphasise a woman's place was in the kitchen?

Danny winked. 'I might have.'

'Well, it won't work. I'll never wear it.'

'I'll not wear that jazzy scarf. I don't know what made you think I had such dead awful taste.'

'You,' Bernadette said furiously, 'are the most maddening man in the whole world.'

'And you're the most abominatable woman.'

Bernadette wrinkled her nose haughtily. 'It's abominable, actually.'

Danny chuckled. 'Whatever it is, you're it, particularly with that hairstyle. It makes you look like a convict.'

The girls and Cormac were listening with interest to the inevitable squabble between Grandad and Mam's best friend. They found them highly entertaining. 'Why don't you two like each other?' Maeve wanted to know.

'It's a long story, luv.' Danny shook his head resignedly.

'They're only *pretending* not to like each other,' Cormac wisely said. 'They like each other really.'

'Don't be so ridiculous, luv.' Bernadette blushed beetroot red. Danny found something tremendously interesting on the back of his left thumb, and Alice stared at her father and her friend, flabbergasted.

'It's time for tea, Mam,' Fionnuala reminded her.

'Oh, yes.' Alice came down to earth. 'Mind everyone while I set the table.' They had guests coming – Orla's boyfriend, Micky Lavin, and two girls from the hospital, friends of Maeve.

While she prepared the sarnies, Alice tried to discern how she would feel if Cormac, clever little chap, were right. She'd always known Bernie was keen on her dad – not that she'd ever mentioned it – but it hadn't crossed her mind the feeling was reciprocated. Danny was twenty-one years older than her friend, but still a vital, attractive man, a bit like Clark Gable, though not quite so tall and less broad – much preferable to the lacklustre Albert Eley. She'd not minded Danny's never-ending stream of women in the past, because she'd always known they weren't serious. But Bernie, only the same age as herself! Would she take her own place in her father's heart?

Oh, what did it matter? Alice laughed out loud. They were two of the people she loved most in the world and it would be the gear to see them happy together. She began to plan what she would wear for the wedding.

It must have been a ten-force gale. John had to battle his way through the streets on his way to Seaforth.

These days, Alice wasn't the only Lacey with her own business. Five years ago John had built bunk beds for his girls, which had become the subject of much interest. In an area of mainly small houses and generally large families, space was always at a premium. The Murphys down the street were the first to ask if John could spare the time to make them a set of bunk beds, or two sets if he had even more time.

John had obliged and the Murphys had insisted on paying, not only for the wood, but for his labour. Before long, orders for beds stretched ahead for months. Then he made a bed for himself in the parlour, because sleeping on the old settee was crucifying for a chap as tall as he was. It was a very simple design and he managed to upholster it himself – a settee, with a seat that pulled forward and a back that slid down to make a double bed.

With many a parlour used to accommodate growing children, ageing grandads and grannies, spinster aunts and lonely uncles, even married sons and daughters, John Lacey's folding beds quickly became as popular as the bunk beds.

Instead of months, he was deluged with orders that would have taken years to complete. It seemed only sensible to give up regular employment and concentrate on making furniture.

He had rented a yard, an old dairy, and there was more than one reason why he'd chosen Seaforth, so far away from Bootle. It wasn't only because he wanted to avoid the neighbours and his family dropping in for a chat, preventing him from getting on with his work.

The wind was less fierce within the shelter of the narrow streets of Seaforth. The yard was on the corner of Benton Street and Crozier Terrace, the latter a cul-de-sac. Next door was the shop that used to be the actual dairy where milk and eggs had been sold. It had been empty for years.

John undid the padlock on the double gates. There was no sign yet announcing the name of the company inside, but the heading on the order books and invoices he'd had printed was B.E.D.S. It had been Fionnuala's suggestion and he thought the capital letters and full stops gave the name a certain authority – much better than just 'Beds'.

There was another padlock on the two-storey building inside the yard that had once housed the dairyman's horse. John used the top floor as an office and kept the finished furniture downstairs. He climbed the ladder, turned on the light and removed a paper carrier bag from beneath the table he used as a desk. Then he locked the stable, locked the yard gates and hurried away. He had no intention of doing a mite of work on Christmas Day.

The bag in his hand, John walked quickly along Crozier Terrace, his eyes fixed on the end house where light gleamed through the flowered curtains. The houses were even smaller than those in Amber Street, with only two bedrooms and no hall – the front door opened straight from the parlour.

The key already in his hand, John inserted it in the lock and went inside. The aroma of roasting chicken greeted him and music, which he had heard from outside – something classical and very grand.

Clare immediately rose from the chair in front of a roaring fire. The other chair was empty, waiting for him. She held a tiny baby in her arms. Another child, about two, with white-blond hair like his mother, was playing with bricks on the floor. He leapt to his feet.

'Dad!' He flung his arms round John's legs.

John's eyes met smiling grey ones across the room. 'Merry Christmas, Mrs Lacey.' He held up the bag. 'Prezzies.'

Meg Lacey had been round for her Christmas dinner. Billy had gone missing the minute the meal was over and Cora did her utmost to encourage his mother to follow suit – Mrs Lacey still insisted on mauling Maurice, something which made Cora's stomach curl.

'I think I'll pop round and see me friend, Ena. Her husband only died last July, so it's her first Christmas on her own. You don't mind, do you, luv?' Meg seemed as anxious to escape as Cora was to see her go. 'I'd call round our John's, but that Danny Mitchell will be there. I can't stand that man, forever making eyes at me.'

You'll be lucky, Cora thought cynically. Danny

Mitchell liked his women glamorous – he wouldn't be seen dead with a plump, grey-haired sixty-year-old like Meg Lacey. For women interested in such things, she supposed Danny Mitchell was dead attractive.

Only one man interested Cora and it wasn't Danny Mitchell. It wasn't her husband either. Not long after Maurice was born she'd begun putting Billy off: pretending to be asleep, claiming a headache, not going to bed until he was snoring fit to bust. She'd always had trouble sleeping, was usually awake at the crack of dawn, and up by the time Billy stirred himself and got ideas. She could only assume he paid for it if he needed it, or had a girlfriend. Either way, she didn't care as long as he left her alone.

His brother, John, though, was a different kettle of fish. She'd always considered him the best of the Lacey brothers and would have much preferred him to Billy, but since the accident, she'd felt even more drawn to the man with the destroyed face. She visualised touching the puckered red skin, being kissed by the twisted mouth, when she'd always thought kissing disgusting and the thing that was done in bed beyond the pale. But now, when she imagined doing it with John Lacey, there was a fluttery feeling in her belly that she'd never had before.

She didn't see much of him these days, only the times he came to visit Billy. He would nod at her curtly and not say a word. Cora was no longer welcome in Amber Street, hadn't been for years, not even at Christmas.

It's not fair, she thought. Alice was desperate for that twenty-five pounds. If it weren't for me, she'd never have got that bloody hairdresser's. Why should *I* take the blame just because she was too thick to understand a perfectly straightforward business agreement?

Cora was never usually in need of company. She enjoyed being alone, plotting and planning, thinking of things she'd like for the house. But it was Christmas Day, Billy was out, Meg had gone, Maurice was in his bedroom, where he'd been sent to avoid his grandma's mauling hands, and the house seemed much too quiet. It didn't seem right that it should be so itchily silent, not on Christmas Day. Horace Flynn was coming to tea, and she remembered what would inevitably happen afterwards once Maurice was in bed and gave an involuntary shudder, though she didn't usually let it bother her.

In Amber Street they'd probably be playing cards by now, or them parlour games she'd always considered stupid. But she wouldn't have minded being there right now, part of the noise and bustle.

There *was* something she could do to become part of it. She could go round Amber Street with the paper Alice had signed and tear it up, throw it on the fire, redeem herself in everyone's eyes, even Fionnuala's, whose loathing for her aunt was palpable.

Cora felt an odd, unexpected pang at the thought of Alice's warm smile welcoming her back into the fold. She fetched the agreement from the elegant bureau in the parlour. The words 'in perpetuity' seemed to stand out from the rest. She *had* told Alice a lie, misled her. But Alice was too trusting by a mile. Anyone with half a brain would have double-checked before putting their signature to a legal document.

Why should I tear it up? she asked herself. Why should I give up a regular income just because the house is a bit quiet? It'll be all right tomorrer. Sod the Laceys, I don't give a damn whether they like me or not. A little voice insisted she did, but Cora ignored it.

She went to the bottom of the stairs and called Maurice. 'Would you like to go for a walk?' she asked when he appeared, such a handsome, strong lad, at the top of the stairs.

'OK,' he said dully. Slowly he plodded down towards his mother.

'How are you getting on with the Meccano set you got for Christmas?'

'I'm still wondering what to make, like.' Maurice couldn't understand the instructions. He had no idea what bolt went where. What he would have liked was to take the kit round to his cousin, Cormac, and ask him. Cormac would no doubt knock up a crane or a lorry in no time. But it was more than Maurice's life was worth to ask if he could go to Amber Street on Christmas Day.

'When we get back, we'll do sums together till teatime,' Cora said.

'Yes, Mam.' Maurice sighed. He dreaded to think what would happen if he didn't pass the scholarship with Cormac. He reached the hall, glanced through the door of the living room, saw the cane hanging on the wall and decided if he didn't pass he'd run away. 'Can we go down the Docky?' he asked hopefully.

Cora was about to refuse – she would have preferred Merton Road with its big, posh houses. But it was Christmas Day and Maurice looked a bit downcast. 'All right,' she said charitably. 'We'll go down the Docky.'

At half past seven Danny Mitchell went to meet his latest woman, Verna Logan, in the King's Arms, with a rather bewildered glance at Bernadette on his way out. Orla disappeared into the parlour with Micky Lavin and stern instructions from her mother to 'leave the door open, if you don't mind'.

Maeve and her friends went up to the bedroom to discuss their future nursing careers and Cormac's head was buried in the encyclopaedia he'd got for Christmas. Every now and then he would lift his head and announce some astounding fact. Toboggan was another name for a sledge; that the proper name for salt was sodium chloride; and Guy Fawkes really had existed.

'Everyone knows that,' Fionnuala said tartly in response to the last.

'*I* didn't,' said her mother.

Bernie shook her head. 'Nor me.'

Fionnuala wondered why everything that came out of her mouth sounded wrong, either the words or the way she said them. She could have said, 'Everyone knows that' and laughed, and it would have sounded quite different. Instead, it appeared as if she was belittling Cormac, something she hadn't intended. She couldn't communicate like normal people, she thought tragically. It was the reason no one liked her, why people preferred Maeve or Orla – particularly Orla, who was everyone's favourite, including Dad and Grandad, with the gift of saying the cheekiest, most outrageous things and everyone adored her. On the occasions Orla came into the salon the customers' eyes would brighten and they'd be dead flattered if she so much as remembered their names. Yet Fionnuala, who was as nice as pie, had the horrible feeling she got on their nerves.

'This is nice,' Alice remarked pouring out a fifth, or it might have been sixth, glass of sherry. 'D'you want filling up, Bernie?'

'No, ta. I'll never find me way home at the rate I'm going.'

'I'll make some tea and sarnies in a minute.'

Bernie didn't answer. Instead, she stared into the fire. 'They're only *pretending* not to like each other,' Cormac had said earlier. 'They like each other really.'

Was it possible, was it truly possible, that she was still attracted to Danny Mitchell after he'd revealed himself as such an out-and-out misogynist? Was it possible that Cormac was right and Danny was attracted to *her*?

Well, he had another think coming if he thought she'd have anything to do with a man who'd give a woman a pinny for Christmas because he considered her place was in the kitchen. Oh, Lord! She'd had too much to drink, because all of a sudden she was imagining herself *in* Danny's kitchen, wearing the bloody pinny, making his bloody tea. Jaysus! *She was wearing nothing BUT the pinny*, and Danny was stroking her bottom and telling her she was beautiful. Bernadette moaned with delight.

'Are you all right, luv?' a concerned Alice enquired. 'I hope you're not going to be sick.'

'I'm fine,' Bernie replied in a choked voice.

In the parlour, Micky Lavin was trying to force his hand up Orla's jumper.

'No,' Orla said firmly. He could touch her breasts outside the jumper, but not in.

'Oh, come on,' Micky said coaxingly. He was nineteen, dead gorgeous, with jet-black curly hair, wickedly dirty eyes and a sexy mouth. Had the door not been open, Orla might easily have succumbed.

Micky transferred his hand to her knee and it began to creep up her skirt.

'Stop it.' She slapped the hand away. 'Why can't you just kiss me like a normal man?'

'Normal!' Micky laughed. He had lovely teeth, large and very white. 'You don't know the meaning of normal.'

'I'm not sure I want to if it means all this silly fumbling about.'

'Silly!' He laughed again.

'If you're just going to echo every word I say, then you can go home,' Orla snapped, knowing he wouldn't.

'All right, then. I'll just kiss you.'

At the touch of his lips, Orla's head began to swim and she couldn't bring herself to stop him when his hand returned to her breasts, *inside* her jumper, because it was so incredibly nice.

'Let's get married,' Micky said hoarsely when they came up for air. 'I know you're only seventeen, but your dad'll let you, won't he?'

'That's something you'll never know, Micky Lavin, because I've no intention of asking me dad any such thing. I don't want to get married, not yet. Ask me again in another ten years.' It wasn't the first time he'd proposed. He was never put off by her repeated refusal, but would ask again a few weeks later. Perhaps he was trying to wear her down, which could be easily done if he kissed her and stroked her breasts for much longer. Orla pushed him away and jumped to her feet. 'I think I can hear me mam making tea.'

She had the horrible feeling she was in love with Micky Lavin with his wicked eyes and sexy mouth. If so, she was determined to resist it. Only the other day at work the editor, Bertie Craig, had said she had an aptitude for writing racy little news items and thinking up suitable headlines. He had complimented her on her shortand and suggested that, in the very near future, she might be sent to cover council meetings.

Orla badly wanted to be a reporter like Rosalind Russell in *His Girl Friday.* She longed to leave the narrow confines of Amber Street, of Bootle, and move to London. She would live in a smart little flat somewhere dead posh and report on big criminal trials – even murders – or be sent to interview royalty and famous film stars.

Micky Lavin, who was an apprentice something or other in a foundry in Hawthorn Road, didn't feature anywhere in the plans Orla had for this exciting and fascinating future.

★

On Boxing Day, Alice put on the cornflower-blue frock she'd bought especially for Christmas. It had a satin bow at the neck and a long, straight skirt. She buckled the stiff wide belt as tight as it would go. Yesterday's gale had lessened, but it was still cold. Even so, Alice decided to wear a navy-blue boxy jacket rather than her winter coat and high-heeled shoes instead of boots. She carefully made up her face and coiled her hair into a French pleat.

'Where are you going all dolled up to the nines?' Fionnuala enquired when her mother came downstairs.

'Never you mind.'

'Can I come with you?'

'Sorry, luv, but this is something I've got to do on me own. What are you doing here, anyroad? You should have gone to the pantomime with Grandad and our Cormac.'

'The seats were already booked, weren't they?' Grandad had asked weeks ago if she'd like to go to the pantomime, but Fionnuala thought it a drippy thing for a girl of eighteen to do on Boxing Day. She had imagined something far more interesting would turn up. Except it hadn't and now she was about to be left all on her own – Maeve had gone with her friends to see Joan Fontaine in *From This Day Forward*, Dad was working and Orla was out somewhere with Micky Lavin. This last fact caused Fionnuala considerable heartache. She had always envied Orla – her slim figure and her confident manner – but nothing like as much as she envied her having Micky Lavin for a boyfriend. Fionnuala desperately wanted a boyfriend, any boyfriend, but to have someone as handsome and desirable as Micky Lavin panting after her seemed little short of heaven.

The rotund figure of Horace Flynn came to the door wearing a crumpled shirt without a collar and baggy trousers supported by a pair of frayed braces. He didn't look well, his face a sickly grey and slightly moist. He regarded the visitor with shrewd, hostile eyes.

'Hello, there,' Alice said in her sweetest voice and with her sweetest smile. 'I wanted to see you about something. I'm Alice Lacey, from the hairdresser's in Opal Street,' she went on when the landlord looked at her vacantly, which wasn't surprising, as they'd never spoken before and she only knew him by sight. He stood to one side and nodded down the hallway, which she took as a signal to come in, though she had the feeling that if it hadn't been so cold he would have left her to have her say at the door.

The large house in Stanley Road was more comfortably furnished than she would have expected from a man living on his own. He led her into a room at the back overlooking a white-painted yard. A fire burnt brightly in the black-leaded grate, in front of which two plush upholstered armchairs were set at an angle either side. The black wooden dresser was full of hand-painted plates, various items of brassware, an assortment of china vases and pretty figurines. A wireless was on, not very loud, and Nelson Eddy was singing 'September Song'.

'D'you mind if I sit down?' As she was nodded towards a chair, Alice began to wonder if he'd lost his voice. He sat his corpulent frame in the chair opposite.

'Seeing as it's Christmas, I thought I'd bring you a few bits and bobs to eat, like, knowing you lived on your own.' She put two paper bags on the table. 'There's a few mince pies and a piece of Christmas cake there, as well as a steak and kidney pudding, which'll need a bit of warming up. I made them all meself.' Her voice faltered in the face of the man's still hostile expression. This was going to be harder than she'd thought. It was said that the way to a man's heart was through his stomach and, as

Horace Flynn's stomach was such a notable part of him, she had hoped to soften him up with food.

He spoke at last. 'What d'you want?' he grunted. People only came to see Horace Flynn if they wanted something. Although Alice didn't realise it, he was quite appreciative of the food. He'd been offered many things over the years in lieu of rent – women's bodies, expensive ornaments: most of the stuff on the dresser had come by way of hard-up tenants – but no one had ever thought to suggest a good meal.

And this woman wasn't the plaintive, wheedling sort of creature he usually came across. She was extremely attractive, well-dressed, with her own successful business. He was well aware how much the property in Opal Street had improved since she'd taken over the lease.

'It's hot in here. D'you mind if I take me coat off?'

He shook his head, furtively taking in her slim waist and the way her skirt rode up when she crossed her trim ankles.

'It's about the lease for the hairdresser's,' she said. 'To be blunt, I can't afford it. I expected it to go up, naturally, but not from a hundred and twenty-five pounds to fourteen hundred. The salon can't stand it. I mean, it's no good squeezing things till the pips squeak, if there's no pips left to squeeze.' Alice winced. That last bit sounded dead stupid.

Horace blinked. He was a greedy man, he was cruel and heartless, but he wasn't a fool. It wasn't good business to demand more than the market could stand. And, unlike a house which could go overnight, if a shop was vacated it could stand empty for months, if not years. He had told Cora to increase the lease to seven hundred pounds. Who did the little tart think she was, going against his wishes, demanding double! He recognised a family feud, remembering this woman was Cora's sister-in-law. Was Cora trying to put her out of business?

Apparently not, otherwise she'd be cutting off her nose to spite her face, because the woman said, 'I might, only might, be able to afford it,' she continued in her sweet, lilting voice, 'if me sister-in-law didn't take such a large share of the profits.' She rolled her eyes and laughed girlishly. 'Silly me! I was dead ignorant in those days. I signed this agreement I didn't understand and now I'm beholden to Cora.'

Horace had the uncomfortable and alarming feeling that he'd been done. He needed Cora, but he wouldn't have trusted her as far as he could throw her. She'd never mentioned she had a share in Lacey's hairdressing salon and he wondered if *he* would have seen the extra money she was asking off this rather nice woman who worked hard running her own business and had thought to bring him food. With her smiling face and sparkling eyes, she had brought a breath of fresh air into an otherwise dull and lonely Boxing Day.

On the wireless, Dooley Wilson began to sing 'As Time Goes By'. 'I love this song,' Alice cried. 'Did you see the picture, *Casablanca*? I went to see it with me husband. It was the last . . .' She paused. It was the last picture she and John had seen together before he'd had the accident. She remembered they'd walked home, hand in hand. 'You must remember this,' John had sung. It was rarely she thought about John now. She'd grown used to their loveless relationship. The fact that they were friends seemed enough, but the song had brought back tender memories and her eyes filled with tears.

'Oh, gosh, you must think me an idiot.' She jumped to her feet and struggled into her coat. 'I'm sorry, Mr Flynn, to have forced meself on you, right in the middle of Christmas too. It was thoughtless and rude. I'll go home and leave you in peace. Forget about the lease. I'll pay it somehow, even if it means sacking one of me staff. Thanks for your time.'

She was already in the hall when he called, 'Mrs Lacey!' She went back. He was still sitting in the chair, his back to her. 'A hundred pounds a year will do.'

'What?'

'A hundred pounds a year for seven years. I'll bring the papers round meself in the new year.'

She gasped with delight. 'Thank you very much, Mr Flynn. It's much appreciated. When you come, I'll make you a nice cup of tea.'

Outside, Alice undid the belt that was killing her and let out a long, slow breath. She'd done it! He'd halved the cost of the lease. She felt quite shameless, recalling the way she'd rolled her eyes, fluttered her lashes, even showed a bit of leg. She fished in her bag for a hankie and rubbed her wet cheeks. The tears, though, had been real.

Chapter 5

The door of the salon opened and a man's voice with a cut-glass accent said cheerfully, 'Hello, there!'

Men rarely set foot inside Lacey's. Occasionally one might come to make an appointment for his wife, usually scarpering pretty sharpish at the sight of so many strange-looking women, like characters out of a Buck Rogers science fiction picture.

'Good morning.' Alice went over to the appointment book.

'Are you Mrs Lacey?'

'I am.' She thought it wasn't fair that a man should have such lovely hair. It appeared to have been spun from pure gold and was in bountiful curls all over his head. He had warm brown eyes, a perfectly straight nose and pink lips that could only be described as pretty. He wore corduroy trousers and a thick hand-knitted jumper. A colourful striped scarf was thrown carelessly round his neck. He looked about twenty-five. Fionnuala was staring at him, mouth hanging open, as if any minute she'd start to drool. 'What can I do for you?' Alice asked.

'I'm Neil Greene. By tonight I hope to be living in your upstairs flat.'

'Neil!' Alice exclaimed, flustered. 'I thought your name was Nell. I was expecting a woman.'

'I'm so sorry, it's my frightful writing. I'm afraid you've got a man. I hope you don't mind. My car's outside, loaded to the gills with all my stuff. Is it all right to start bringing it in?' He beamed at the assembled customers who were regarding him, wide-eyed. 'How do you do, ladies?'

Embarrassed, the three women under the dryers patted the thick net-covered curlers as if trying to make them disappear. Mrs Slattery, in front of the sink with her head covered in blue paste, was trying to slide down the chair out of sight.

'Of course you can bring it in.' Alice nodded, still dazed.

Fionnuala darted forward. 'Would you like a hand?'

'How terribly kind.' He smiled angelically as he unwound the scarf to reveal a slender white neck. 'But only if you can be spared.'

'I can, can't I, Mam?' Fionnuala pleaded.

'Yes, luv, but not for long.'

'Well, isn't he a regular Prince Charming!' one woman remarked when the door closed.

'He looks like a right pansy to me,' said another, Mrs Nutting, whom Alice had never much liked.

'I wish my hair were that colour.' Mrs Slattery sighed. 'And doesn't he talk nice? Dead posh.'

'More like he's got a plum in his gob,' sneered Mrs Nutting.

'I thought he'd be a woman,' Alice gasped.

'I reckon he almost is.'

'What's he here for, Alice?'

'He'll be teaching at St James's, the infants.'

Fionnuala returned, carrying a box of gramophone records, Neil Greene behind with two large suitcases. 'Don't worry, I haven't brought the kitchen sink,' he sang.

'Can we have a gramophone, Mam?'

'Perhaps, one day.'

'Isn't it time this tint was washed off, Alice?' Mrs Slattery said.

'Oh, yes. Sorry, luv. I'm a bit taken aback, if you must know. It looked just like Nell on the letter.'

'I wonder if he's related to that film star, Richard Greene? He's dead handsome too, though he's dark, not fair. Have you ever seen him, Alice?'

'No. Me and John didn't get to the pictures much when the kids were little. Nowadays we both seem to be working all the hours God sends.' She had to pretend things were normal, that they would have gone to the pictures had they had the time.

'I suppose one day soon you'll decide Amber Street's not good enough and you'll be off somewhere more select. You could easily afford it with all the money that must be rolling in.'

'I wouldn't dream of it, Mrs Nutting,' Alice said stiffly. 'Amber Street is quite select enough, thank you. It's where I live and it's where I'll die. We're having the wash-house turned into a bathroom, so we won't have to go outside to the lavvy no more. That's enough for me.'

'Oh, well, it's nice to know the money for me shampoo and set is contributing towards an indoor lavvy for the Laceys. I'll sleep better tonight, knowing that.'

Alice was amazed that the horrible woman managed to sleep at all and that her nasty mind didn't keep her wide awake all night long. She kept the thought to herself, sometimes difficult with customers who were particularly unpleasant.

'He's so *handsome*,' Fionnuala said dreamily over tea. 'A bit like the Angel Gabriel. There's not a single film star who comes near him. And you'll never guess what he did when I finished helping him move in. He only *kissed me hand*!'

'Honest!' Maeve looked impressed, but Orla, at whom the words were directed, seemed miles away.

'He's got a gramophone,' Fionnuala continued, willing her sister to listen, 'loads of records and hundreds of books.'

It was Cormac's turn to look impressed. 'What about?'

'Oh, all sorts of things. Too many to remember. He said I can borrow them, though, whenever I like.'

'Would he let me borrow some too?'

'I'll ask him if you like.' Fion gave a superior smile. 'We're already friends. Aren't we, Mam?'

'Well, yes, luv. I suppose you are.' The new upstairs tenant seemed determined to be friends with everyone.

'He asked if he could call me "Fion" and I said yes, and when I called him Mr Greene he said to call him Neil, even though he's a teacher.'

Orla came to life. 'I should think so too,' she said indignantly. 'He's not *your* teacher, so you're equal. Why should he expect to be called mister by someone your age? You're not a child.'

'I call Mr Flynn Mr Flynn,' Fionnuala said lamely.

'Yes, but Mr Flynn's *old*. How old is this Neil?'

'Twenty-seven, he told me.'

'*There* then,' Orla said, as if this proved her point. 'And I don't like the name Neil.'

Fionnuala went red. 'Well, I don't like Micky.'

'I don't care.'

'Neither do I.'

'Girls!' Alice said tiredly. 'Please can we have our tea in peace?'

'Then tell our Orla to leave me alone,' Fionnuala said sulkily.

'Orla, stop being so sarcastic with your sister.'

'Was I being sarcastic?' Orla looked around the table with pretend innocence, but no one answered.

Once the meal was over and the table cleared, Cormac started on his homework. He seemed able to concentrate no matter how loud the noise around him. Fion washed the dishes and Maeve dried them. Alice started to make pastry for a mincemeat and onion pie for tomorrow.

Micky Lavin called for Orla. They were going for a walk, which Alice considered a mad thing to do in the depths of an icy winter, but then she and John had done the same sort of silly things when they were courting. Young people in love wanted only to be with each other. The weather, no matter how awful, didn't matter.

Alice rolled out the pastry and hoped things weren't serious between Orla and Micky. He was a nice lad, considering his background: the middle child of a family of nine, whose dad was hardly ever in work and whose mam could only be described as a slattern – never seen without a pinny, even at the shops. The eldest lad was currently in jail for thieving. Coming from such a family, Micky had done well for himself, somehow managing to become an apprentice welder.

Even so, Alice wanted someone better for her daughter – for all her daughters, come to that. She wondered if it was possible something might develop between Fion and Neil Greene, but thought it most unlikely. Once his presence became known, every young single woman in Bootle would be setting her cap at him, as well as some of the married ones.

She put the pastry in the meat safe to keep cool. Fion appeared in a tweed coat and a headscarf, and announced she was going to confession.

'You only went on Friday. What awful sins have you committed that you need to confess again so soon?'

'None, Mam. I just feel like going to church.'

'Don't stay out too long, luv. It's awful cold outside.' It seemed pathetic that all a girl of Fion's age had to do was go to church.

Maeve, who was on early shift at the hospital and had to be up at the crack of dawn, went to bed early with a book. Alice offered to bring her up a cup of cocoa shortly. Cormac finished his homework and also went to bed, in his case armed with an encyclopaedia.

At last Alice was left alone. She turned on the wireless – there was a play on soon. There'd be no sign of John till all hours. She was usually in bed by the time he came home. That horrible Mrs Nutting had been talking through her hat, going on about all the money rolling in. After allowing for the overheads, Alice took little more than she'd have done in a factory and John made a surprisingly small amount considering all the hours he put in. Still, he was generous with what he did get, witness the planned new bathroom.

Sometimes Alice felt guilty, sitting in a nice warm house with her feet up, listening to the wireless or reading, knowing John was hard at work in the yard. If only he'd got a place somewhere closer she'd have popped round evenings with a flask of tea and a nice warm pie. As it was, she hardly saw him. Her face grew sad. Their marriage had become a travesty, a joke. They treated each other with friendly politeness.

The play started and she turned up the sound. She'd sooner not think about John and the way things were now.

'I love you, Orla,' Micky whispered. 'When I'm at work, all I think about is you. I can't get you out me mind. It's driving me up the wall.'

And I love you, Orla wanted to say. I feel exactly the

same. I can't wait for you to kiss me. I think about you all the time.

However, Orla said none of these things. She didn't want him to know she found him so disturbing. Instead, she said, 'I don't like it in this entry, Micky. It's dark and dirty, and smells of wee-wee.'

'Where else can we go?' Micky said helplessly.

'Why can't we just walk?'

'I'm tired of walking. I'm desperate to kiss you. Would your mam let us use the parlour, do you think?'

'What for?' Orla asked tartly.

'You know what for.'

'I feel uncomfortable in our parlour, knowing me mam's just on the other side of the wall.'

'We could do harmless things like kiss.'

'I hope you're not suggesting we could do less harmless things elsewhere?'

Unexpectedly, Micky began to walk away. 'I wouldn't dream of it,' he said coldly.

She watched the boyish, not very tall figure recede along the entry. The lights from the rear of the houses either side shone on his black hair, his broad shoulders. Even from the back he looked dead handsome. She knew he was hurt because she refused to take him seriously. Something twisted in her heart and she found herself shaking, as strange sensations she had never felt before swept through her body.

'Micky!' she called when he was about to turn the corner. 'Oh, Micky!'

'Orla!'

They ran to meet each other. Micky swept her up in his arms, kissed her, swung her around, kissed her again, undid her coat, grabbed her waist. His hands pushed under her jumper and she could feel them hard on her ribs through the thin material of her petticoat.

'Micky,' she breathed rapturously when his thumbs touched her nipples. Somehow, straps were moved, her bra undone and Orla groaned in delight when her breasts were exposed to Micky's seeking hands.

Oh, my God, she was wetting herself! And Micky was pulling up her skirt, stroking the bare flesh at the top of her legs, feeling inside her pants.

Orla could never quite remember exactly what happened next, only that it was mind-shatteringly thrilling and quite wonderful. Afterwards they walked back to Amber Street, Micky's arm round her shoulders, hers round his waist. She was still shaking and felt extremely odd, as if she'd entered a different world from the one she used to live in. She'd left the house a girl and returned a woman.

At the door, Micky said huskily, 'We're made for each other, Orla. We've got to get married now.'

'Did you have a nice walk, luv?' Alice enquired when her daughter came in.

'OK,' Orla said in a bored voice. 'I think I'll make meself a cup of cocoa and take it to bed. I've got a busy day tomorrer.' She was being sent on her very first assignment – some person off the wireless, whom admittedly she'd never heard of, was coming to Water-loo to open a shop.

'Mind you don't disturb Maeve. She's got an even busier one.'

'I won't, Mam.' As Orla waited for the kettle to boil she made up her mind that, after tonight, she would never see Micky Lavin again. It was too dangerous.

It was Cora's birthday, not that anyone knew or cared except herself. Billy had forgotten, as usual. Alice used to send a pretty card – 'From John and Alice, the girls and Cormac' it always said. Cora missed the cards, but they'd stopped five years before, along with the invitations to Christmas dinner and other events, like birthday parties.

Since Christmas, Cora had been in a terrible state. For one thing, the least important as it happened, she was fed up with the house – there was a limit to how nice it could be made to look and she felt she'd reached it. What she would like more than anything was to start afresh in a different house, this time bigger – a detached one in a wider road with trees. She wouldn't mind moving as far afield as Waterloo or Crosby. Months ago, Horace Flynn had acquired a lovely bungalow right on the shore in Blundellsands. The elderly widower he'd bought it from was a penny short of a shilling and had let it go dead cheap. Horace was having the place done up before he let it.

Cora had intended demanding it for herself in return for services rendered and would have done if it hadn't been for her sister-in-law. Because of her, going behind her back, telling tales, she'd lost favour with the fat, greasy slob of a landlord. Cora's blood boiled when she thought about it. Her hands twitched, as if she'd like to get them round her sister-in-law's neck and squeeze. She'd only seen Horace once since Boxing Day and then he'd torn her off a strip.

'How dare you countermand my orders?' he'd demanded. She'd never seen him look so cross. 'Did you intend keeping the extra money for yourself?'

'Of course not,' Cora insisted, though she had been wondering if she could get away with it. It would have depended on whether Alice paid by cheque or with cash.

'Have you done anything like this before?' His little round eyes flashed angrily.

'I only did it the once,' she said humbly. 'Only because it was personal.'

'Ah, yes, that reminds me. Why didn't you tell me the hairdresser's partially belongs to you?'

'I didn't think it mattered, if you must know.'

'Of course it matters,' he snapped impatiently. 'It was clearly your intention to cause your sister-in-law some harm. You made the mistake of letting your emotions cloud your judgement.' He left, saying he intended going very carefully through the books to make sure he hadn't been done. It was a pity, but he didn't trust her any more.

Since then, he hadn't given her any more work, nor dropped in for a spot of titillation and to give her the five quid that always followed. Even worse, one day she'd seen him coming out of Lacey's hairdresser's, so had kept watch and seen him twice again.

It was a good job she had the money from the hairdresser's, because all of a sudden she found herself paying the full rent for Garibaldi Road, which she could never have afforded on the pitiful amount Billy earned.

It was vital she get back in with Horace Flynn. He wasn't particularly old, only in his fifties, but he was a sick man – you could tell by his unhealthy colour. There was something wrong with his heart. It didn't beat proper. She wouldn't be a bit surprised if he dropped dead any minute. In fact, she often hoped he would, because he hadn't a close relative in the world, just some far-off cousins in Ireland. They'd actually talked about it once.

'I don't like the idea of some person or persons I've never met benefiting from all my hard work when I pass on,' he'd said.

'Surely you know someone closer you could leave it to,' Cora had said innocently, knowing there was only her.

'Hmm.' He'd eyed her speculatively. 'In that case I would have to make a will.'

Since then, whenever she went to his house and he wasn't looking, she'd searched for a will, but if he'd made one it must have been left with his solicitor, because she never found it.

'I'm sorry, luv, but she's gone to the pictures,' Alice said to the distraught young man outside.

'Again!' Micky Lavin said wildly. He ran his fingers through his black hair, as if about to tear it out. 'She went to the pictures last night. I stood outside the Palace in Marsh Lane until the picture finished, but I didn't see her come out.'

'She didn't go to the Palace last night, she went to the Rio in Fazackerly with some girl from work. I'm not sure where she's gone tonight,' she added, in case Micky stood outside again.

'Can I come in and wait?' His bottom lip quivered like a child's.

'I was just about to go to bed, luv,' Alice lied. 'It's not really convenient.'

'I'll sit on the step, then, till she comes.'

'I'm not sure if she'll come in the back way or the front.'

'I'll do me best to keep an eye on both.'

Alice felt dreadful as she closed the door on his desperate, unhappy face. She went to the bottom of the stairs and called, 'Orla?'

'Yes, Mam?'

'That's the last lie I'm telling Micky Lavin on your behalf. He's a nice lad and he's obviously mad about you. If you don't want to see him again, then tell him so to his face. D'you hear me, our Orla?'

'Yes, Mam.' In the bedroom, Orla buried her face in

the pillow so no one would hear her cry. It had been awful listening to Micky's anguished voice. She tried not to imagine him walking down Amber Street, as miserable as sin — as miserable as she felt herself, if the truth be known. It was all she could do not to rush out of the house and call him back. But look what had happened when she'd called him back the other night! Jaysus! It had been out of this world, totally wonderful. She ached for it to happen again.

But, she reminded herself, she wasn't the sort of girl who made love in back entries. She was going to *be* someone one day, someone dead important. Why, only yesterday Bertie Craig had suggested she practise her shortand, make it faster, so that she could become a verbatim reporter.

'When you're interviewing a politician, say, it helps if you can take down every word. If he later denies he said a certain thing, you can flourish your notebook and prove he did.'

A politician! One of these days Orla Lacey might actually interview a politician, beside which marrying Micky Lavin came a very poor second.

Oh, but if only she could get him out of her mind!

'I didn't realise until yesterday that you were the mother of the genius,' said Neil Greene.

'Eh?' It was Saturday and the salon had just closed. Alice was transferring the takings to her handbag to tot up later.

Neil had obviously been shopping in town. He was carrying several Lewis's and Owen Owen's carrier bags. 'Cormac Lacey, he's your son, right?' He raised his perfect eyebrows.

Alice swelled with pride. She nodded. 'He is so.'

'Going to pass the scholarship with flying colours, so I

understand. They're always talking about him in the common room. I knew you had a son at St James's, but I thought it was the other Lacey, Maurice. He has the look of Fion.'

'Maurice is me nephew. We don't know who Cormac takes after.'

Fionnuala emerged from the back where she was washing cups, eager to bathe in some of her brother's reflected glory. Alice felt slightly irritated by the look on her face, like a sad little puppy waiting to be noticed by its lord and master. Fion was useless on Saturdays, on edge waiting for Neil to pop in and out.

'Ah, Fion!' Neil's smile was wonderful to behold. The customers claimed it made them go weak at the knees. 'I've bought you a present.' He rooted through one of the bags and took out a little red box.

Fionnuala almost collapsed with gratitude before she even knew what the present was. 'Oh, ta,' she gasped. She opened the box and took out a large silver brooch in the shape of an 'F'. 'It's lovely,' she breathed. 'Oh, and it's got a little diamond in.' She clasped the brooch against her chest. 'I'll treasure it all me life,' she said shakily.

'I'm afraid the diamond isn't real. It's called a zircon.' Neil beamed as he handed Alice a green box. 'And one for you. It's an "A".'

'Thank you very much.' Alice deliberately didn't look at her daughter's face, knowing that she would be shattered that Neil hadn't bought a present just for her.

'That's by way of an apology,' Neil said.

'Apology for what?'

'For not putting "Mister" on my letters, for inadvertently letting you think I was a woman. With the flat, situated as it is over a hairdresser's, you might have preferred having a female of the species upstairs. You showed admirable restraint when I turned out to be the wrong sex.' He grinned. 'Another person might have given me a good bollocking and told me to take my bags elsewhere. I just hope I don't disturb the customers too much when I come in and out.'

Alice assured him he was no bother and he went upstairs. 'That was nice of him, wasn't it?' she said warmly to Fion. 'And he must think a lot of you, buying you a brooch as well as me. I mean, if it's by way of apology like he ses, there was no need to include you, was there?'

Fionnuala's face brightened – she was very easily pleased, Alice thought sadly.

'Not really, Mam.' Fion couldn't wait to show the brooch to Orla who didn't have a boyfriend at the moment, having gone completely mad and ditched that gorgeous Micky Lavin.

She'd had to tell him to his face eventually. She'd taken him into the parlour because she didn't trust herself in a place where he could take her in his arms and touch her the way he'd done before. They'd only end up doing that crazy, wonderful thing again and she'd be lost.

Oh, his expression when she told him! She would never forget it – shocked, disbelieving, close to tears. His eyes were black with despair.

'But I love you,' he'd said, as if this were the end of the matter.

'Well, I don't love you,' Orla said spiritedly.

'You do! Of course you do. You know you do. I can tell. What we did together was magic. Wasn't it, Orla?' He shook her arm. 'Wasn't it?'

She looked straight into his eyes. 'No,' she said. 'It was all right, that's all. I quite enjoyed it.'

'You're lying. You thought it was magic, same as me.'

Orla shrugged and longed for him to go, get out of the house, out of her life, for ever. She folded her arms and wished him goodnight.

'And that's it, then?'

'That's it.'

'So it's tara?'

'Tara, Micky.'

'You've broken me heart,' he said in a cracked voice.

'It'll soon mend,' she said carelessly.

The front door slammed. Arms still folded, Orla began to rock backwards and forwards on the settee. Tears dropped on to her knees, her skirt, made wet patches on her shoes and the floor around them.

It was Cormac who found her, rocking like a maniac and flooding the parlour with her tears. 'Why have you told Micky to go away when you want him to stay?' he wanted to know, which only made Orla cry even more. Her alarmed mother came in, did her best to soothe her, then sent her to bed with cocoa and a couple of Aspro.

That was weeks and weeks ago, and Orla still couldn't forget Micky's face, though now she hated it. She hated every single thing about Micky Lavin.

His face was in front of her now, staring at her from the sheet of paper in the typewriter. She resisted the urge to pull the paper out, rip it to shreds, because the face would only appear again when she put more paper in.

Another woman worked with her in the small office, Edie Jones, Bertie Craig's secretary. Edie and Orla didn't get on. The older woman seemed to resent the younger one being such a favourite of her boss.

'What's the matter with you?' Edie asked as Orla sat scowling at the typewriter.

'There's nothing the matter with me,' Orla snapped.

'Then why do you look as if you've lost a pound and found a sixpence?'

'Perhaps I have, that's why.'

Edie shrugged. 'I was only asking.'

Orla wondered what her reaction would be if she shouted, 'I think I'm pregnant, *that's* what's the matter. I bloody well think I'm bloody pregnant. And I don't want to be. I don't want to be bloody pregnant more than anything in the world. I *hate* Micky Lavin. Men are supposed to take precautions, wear things. But Micky didn't and now I'm bloody well pregnant.'

'Are you sure you're all right, Orla?' Edie sounded worried. 'Now you look as if you're about to burst into tears.'

'Wouldn't you if you'd lost a pound and only found a sixpence in its place?'

'I'm only trying to help, dear.'

Perhaps it was the 'dear' that made Orla start to weep. 'I'm sorry for being rude,' she sobbed. 'There *is* something wrong, but I can't possibly tell you what it is.'

'Why don't you go home? I'll tell Bertie you weren't feeling well. He'll understand.'

'I think I will. Ta, Edie.'

She wandered along Liverpool Road towards Bootle. She'd missed two periods, which had never happened before. She was definitely up the stick, had a bun in the oven, as some people crudely put it. Approaching Seaforth, she passed a doctor's surgery and contemplated going inside and asking the doctor to examine her. But she looked so young and wasn't wearing a wedding ring. What would the doctor say?

Orla had never cared particularly what people thought, but having a baby without a husband was just about the most shocking thing a girl could do. There was a girl in Opal Street who'd done it. That was ten years ago and the girl was now a woman, but it was still talked about as if it were only yesterday. The baby had been sent to an orphanage.

'*Mine won't.*' Orla clutched her stomach. It was no use asking a doctor, because she knew in her bones that there was a tiny baby curled up in there waiting to be born. She also knew that she had to keep it, that to have it taken away would be wrong. And if she didn't want her baby growing up with the stigma of having an unmarried mother, the equivalent of having a sign saying 'bastard' hung round its neck, then she would have to marry Micky Lavin. Furthermore, she was only seventeen and needed her parents' permission, so she would have to tell Mam and Dad.

A young woman approached, pushing a large, shabby pram. The baby inside was shrieking, as if it was being severely tortured. 'Oh, for Christ's sake, shut your gob,' the woman said in a despairing voice as she passed by.

Orla turned and watched her walk away, bent and weary. 'That will be me in a year's time,' she thought with horror. 'I'd sooner be like them.'

She glanced across the road at two girls, slightly older than she was, strolling along arm in arm, talking animatedly. They were smartly dressed in tweed costumes and little felt hats. One carried a big grey lizard handbag that Orla badly coveted. The girls were everything that she had one day planned to be herself.

Horace Flynn had taken to dropping in at the hairdresser's at least once a week. 'Just to see how things are going, Mrs Lacey,' he would say.

'Things are going fine, Mr Flynn. Thanks for asking.'

'He's got a crush on you,' announced Fionnuala. 'What on earth did you do on Boxing Day when you went round to ask about the lease?'

'I just fluttered me eyelashes a bit, that's all,' Alice replied uneasily.

'If you'd fluttered them some more, we might have got the lease for nothing.'

'Oh, Fion, don't!' Alice squirmed. 'Anyroad, it's your fault he comes so often. There's no need to make quite such a desperate fuss of him, taking him into the kitchen, plying him with cups of tea.'

'I feel sorry for him. He's got sickly skin. He probably comes because we're the only people in the world who are nice to him. Everyone else hates his guts.'

'With good reason, luv. He's a horrible man.'

'Horrible or not, I prefer having him on our side rather than Auntie Cora's.'

'There's no need to talk about sides, Fion. There isn't a war on.'

'Oh, yes, there is,' Fionnuala said darkly. 'We're on one side, Cora's on the other. One of these days we're going to win.'

These days, John Lacey considered the world darn near perfect. He rarely thought about his face. It had happened, there was no going back. He felt no guilt about having two families. It had been a question of survival and Clare had given him the ability to live with himself.

At six o'clock he locked the yard and went down Crozier Terrace to the end house where he let himself in. Robby came running towards him from the kitchen, demanding to be picked up. John hoisted the little boy on to his shoulder.

'Been for walk in park, Dad,' he gurgled. 'Lisa cried all day. She's growing tooths. Did I cry when I was growing tooths?'

'All the time,' John assured him. 'Hello, luv.'

Clare emerged from the kitchen looking slightly harassed. She wore a gingham pinny over a plain brown frock. Her long fair hair was pinned back with a slide. She rolled her eyes towards the stairs and made a guttural sound, which John immediately understood. His daughter, Lisa, was upstairs, asleep for once.

'Been getting you down, luv?'

She made a face and nodded furiously, then suddenly smiled, folding both him and their son in her slim arms. 'But happy,' she said. 'Very happy. Tea ready.'

He had learnt to read the expressions on her face, translate the strangled sounds that came from her mouth into proper English. 'Good.' He smacked his lips. 'I'm starving, and I think I can smell liver and onions.'

She nodded again and he followed her into the tiny kitchen where the table was set for three. As they ate, John wondered if he had ever felt so blissfully contented during the first years with Alice and remembered that he had. The memory disturbed him. He was doing a terrible thing, betraying his wife and their four children with a woman who had once been a prostitute.

Clare lightly touched the back of his hand with her finger. 'You all right?'

'Yes.'

She seemed able to read his mind as easily as he understood her awkward speech and facial expressions. On the pad she always kept beside her she wrote, 'Conscience?' There were some words she didn't even attempt.

'I'm afraid so.'

'Go home early,' she wrote. 'See your family.' She shook her head. 'I don't mind.'

'You're a saint.'

Her eyes sparkled. 'I'm anything but.'

'I'll see how I feel.' He knew he wouldn't go home

early to the house where nowadays he felt like a stranger. Alice had adapted very easily to his absence, he thought cynically. She never reproached him for being being away so often. His girls showed no sign of missing him. Only Cormac seemed to mind his dad not being there, a fact that caused John some heartache.

Still, there was nothing to be done. It was a question of survival, he reminded himself for the umpteenth time. He glanced around the table, at Clare, at his white-blond other son. A small cry came from upstairs, and he and Clare smiled at each other. She went upstairs to fetch Lisa. In six months' time there would be another baby.

This was his family now. These were the people who accepted him for what he was, what he had become. One of these days he would abandon the other family altogether – once the girls were married and Cormac was old enough to understand. Alice would be all right. She had the hairdresser's to keep her busy.

It was midnight when John rose from the bed he shared with Clare, got dressed and returned to Amber Street. To his surprise, Alice came into the hall to meet him. He'd never known her stay up so late before.

'Something's happened,' she said.

He noticed her eyes were red with weeping. 'Are the kids all right?' he asked, alarmed.

'Sort of. Can we talk?'

'Of course.'

She led the way into the living room. There was a teapot with a striped cosy on the table, two cups and saucers, sugar in a bowl, milk. He felt slightly guilty. She must have been waiting a long time for him to come.

'What's up?' His heart was beating rapidly in his chest.

'It's our Orla, she's in the club.' She poured tea and handed him a cup.

'Pregnant?' The cup jerked in his hand and tea slopped into the saucer.

'Pregnant,' Alice confirmed.

'The little bitch! I'll bloody kill her . . .' He rose to go upstairs and drag his daughter out of bed, shake her till her teeth rattled.

'John! Leave her. You'll only wake Fion and Maeve, and they don't know yet. Orla only told me tonight.'

He hadn't realised people actually did see red when they were angry. 'Is it that Micky chap?'

'Yes, and it was only the once. She hasn't seen him in weeks.'

'It only needs the once,' John spat. 'You should have kept a closer eye on her.'

'Oh, so it's my fault!' Alice laughed incredulously. 'You're hardly ever here, but it's *my* fault if our daughter falls for a baby. What was I supposed to do, follow her and Micky wherever they went?'

He knew she was right, but wasn't prepared to admit it. 'Did she know the facts of life?' he growled.

'Yes, she did, as it happens. I told all three of them at the same time. I trust you'll do the same with Cormac,' she added pointedly. 'Assuming you can find the time. Look,' she said reasonably, 'why can't we discuss this like civilised people? Things have to be done, said.'

'Such as?'

'We have to go round the Lavins, all three of us; you, me and Orla, talk it over with Micky's family. He hasn't been told, but Orla's convinced he'll marry her. The thing is, he's only nineteen and an apprentice welder. He earns peanuts. What are they going to live on?'

'He should have thought about that before he poked my daughter.'

Alice winced at the coarse expression. '*Our* daughter,' she said firmly. 'And it's the present we have to deal with, not the past. Orla thinks he'll give up the apprenticeship and get a proper job – he's a decent lad, John, no matter what you think. That means he'll just end up a labourer like your Billy. They need supporting for the next couple of years until he's finished his training. I wondered, could we put them up in our parlour?' Putting aside the rather unfortunate circumstances, Alice quite fancied having a baby in the house.

He was completely taken aback. 'What!'

'Our parlour, John.'

'What about me?'

'You can sleep upstairs. I'll sleep with the girls. There'll be an empty bed.'

'I'll do no such thing,' he gasped, outraged. 'Why should we have to put ourselves out because Orla's behaved like a little whore?'

'John!' Her eyes widened in shock. 'That's a terrible thing to say.'

'It's a terrible thing she's done.' He couldn't adjust to the fact that the prettiest of his girls, his favourite, had actually let a man touch her in that way. It was disgusting. 'Where did it happen?' he asked, almost choking on the words.

'I don't know, do I? I didn't ask. But whatever she's done, John, she's still *ours*. We've got to stand by her. Now, about the parlour . . .'

'She's not having the parlour,' he said brutally. 'If this house had twice as many rooms, I wouldn't have her, or that Micky, under me roof. She's made her bed, let her lie on it.'

'I see.' Alice's voice was cold. 'You know, John, when that fire burnt your face, it burnt something else an' all. It sounds a bit daft to say it burnt your heart, but that's what it seems like. There's not a drop of charity left in your body. You're as hard as bloody nails. It's not fair. You've no right to behave like this with your family.'

His wife and daughters all seemed part of the accident. When his face had been destroyed, something had happened to the love he felt for the people in this house, even Cormac. It had been damaged, perverted in some way, riddled with suspicion. He had changed from Dr Jekyll into Mr Hyde.

He wanted shot of them. They were no longer his concern, more like an intrusion into his present happiness. He felt like fleeing Amber Street there and then. He longed for Crozier Terrace, for Clare and his other family with whom he felt completely at ease.

He stood abruptly. 'I'm going to bed.'

'Will you come with us to the Lavins tomorrer night?'

'No! I'll sign the necessary forms so she can get married and off me back, but Orla can rot in hell for all I care.' He couldn't believe he'd just said that. He stopped at the door, turned to say he hadn't meant it. He was confused. He always felt confused in Amber Street. But Alice had picked up the cups and was taking them into the kitchen, and he couldn't be bothered calling her back.

The following evening Orla went on her own to Micky's house in Chaucer Street to tell him he would shortly become a father. Alice followed an hour later, apprehensive and nervous, worried the Lavins would react as badly as John had and there'd be a scene. She was surprised to find Micky had already told his mam and dad and they were delighted at the news.

She was taken into the shabby parlour, which had obviously been given a quick dusting because there were still smears of dirt left on the sideboard. A broken orange box burnt in the grate. To her further surprise the room contained one of them new-fangled television things, which she later learnt had fallen off the back of a lorry – one of the Lavin lads just happened to be there at the time.

'They'll be wed with our blessing,' Mrs Lavin said grandly. 'Won't they, Ted? We can have the do afterwards in the Chaucer Arms – our Kathleen works there as a barmaid.'

'I doubt if Orla will want much of a do. Will you, luv?'

'No, Mam.' Orla was sitting as far away from Micky as she could in the small space provided by the parlour. She looked pale and subdued, as if they were planning her funeral rather than her wedding. Micky was watching her anxiously. He was crazy about her, Alice realised, and a lump came to her throat. Were two lives about to be destroyed by this marriage? Three, if you counted the unborn child. Last night she had suggested Orla forget about Micky and go away to have the baby.

'And what would happen to it?' Orla asked thinly.

'It would have to be adopted.'

Orla shook her head. 'No, Mam. That would be dead irresponsible. I'd feel terrible for the rest of me life.'

'So would I, if the truth be known. I couldn't stand the thought of me first grandchild being brought up by strangers.'

One of the younger Lavins was being despatched to buy a bottle of sherry so a toast could be drunk to the about-to-be-married couple. Mrs Lavin wondered aloud if it was too late to go round St James's church that night and post the bans: 'So they can get spliced at the earliest, like.'

Alice found herself warming to the good-natured, red-faced woman, with her kind, generous manner and her equally kind husband. She felt deeply touched when the subject of where the young couple would live was raised and Mr Lavin said instantly, 'They can sleep in the parlour. We don't want our Micky giving up his apprenticeship and we wouldn't ask a penny off him, would we, luv? Not when he's got a wife and a kiddy on the way.'

Mrs Lavin's plump, worn face creased into a broad smile. 'The good Lord always seems to provide sufficient food for the table. At least, so I've found.'

It was so different from John's attitude the night before. 'John and I will help out, of course,' Alice said, feeling obliged to include her husband in the offer.

'They'll get by,' Mrs Lavin said placidly.

Orla uttered a strangled cry and fled from the room.

They got married, Orla Lacey and Micky Lavin, on the first Monday in March. The Nuptial Mass was at ten o'clock. Although the bans had been called for the last three weeks, few onlookers turned up at the church at such an early hour. There were no wedding cars to attract attention, no bouquets or buttonholes, no brides-maids.

In place of the bride's father, who had unfortunately been struck down a few days before with a severe bout of flu – or so Alice told the extravagantly sympathetic Lavins – Danny Mitchell gave his granddaughter away. Lacey's hairdresser's was closed for the day. Maeve was on afternoon shift at the hospital, so had no need to ask for time off. Cormac, who found the whole situation completely baffling, stayed away from school. He'd thought people only got married because they made each other happy, but all Orla did was snap people's heads off every time they spoke, particularly Micky's.

Bernadette Moynihan took the morning off to be with her friend on such a stressful day.

'I'd imagined having a great big bash when the kids got married,' Alice confessed tearfully as she got ready. 'Y'know, picking the bride's and bridesmaids' dresses, ordering flowers and the cake, arranging a nice reception with a sit-down meal. But this is going to be awful and John not being there only makes it worse.'

'What's Orla doing about her job?' Bernie asked.

'She's given in her notice. She had no choice, did she? Any minute now she'll start to show.'

Orla looked like death in the simple blue suit her mother had bought. She held a white prayer book in her white-gloved hands. Throughout the ceremony, Micky couldn't take his troubled eyes away from her stony face.

'She's going to make his life hell.' Alice's heart sank. This was a nightmare of a wedding.

Chapter 6

'The letter came this morning to say he'd passed, which means he'll be off to St Mary's grammar school in September. You should see the list of things we've got to buy!' Alice laughed and made a face. 'He was a bit put out to find he's got to wear a cap, but he's going to keep it in his blazer pocket till he gets to school.' Blazer! She never dreamt she'd have a son who'd wear a blazer.

'I suppose it's nice to have some good news for a change,' said Mrs White who came once a month for a shampoo and set. 'Your Cormac passing the scholarship makes up a bit for Orla.'

'What exactly do you mean by that?' Alice enquired in an icy voice.

'Well . . .' Mrs White must have been put off by Alice's tone. 'Nothing, really.'

'We're all very happy for Orla, if you must know. Micky Lavin is a fine lad who'll make a good husband. And we're dead pleased about the baby.'

'Yes, but . . .'

'But what?'

'She's so young to be a mother,' Mrs White said lamely.

'She's seventeen. I was only a year older when I had our Fionnuala.'

'You're fastening the curlers too tight, Mrs Lacey.

Would you mind undoing the last two and rolling them up a bit looser.'

Alice sniffed. 'Sorry.'

'I understand you're about to expand.' Mrs White must have decided this was safer ground. Alice Lacey was a brilliant hairdresser, the best in Bootle, and it wouldn't do to annoy her. She was relieved to be rewarded with a smile.

'Yes, I'm taking on a trained assistant, if you can call that expanding: Doreen Morrison, only part-time. She used to work in this exclusive salon in town till she retired.'

'She's old, then?'

'Only fifty. She retired because of a heart complaint, but feels she can manage four afternoons a week and Sat'days. She only lives down Cowper Street, so she won't have that big journey into town.'

The salon was getting busier. Women were coming from further and further afield, and Alice was often booked solid for weeks ahead. As well as taking on an assistant, she had felt obliged to have a telephone installed.

She placed a net over Mrs White's curlers, tucking two large cotton wool pads inside to cover her ears, sat her under the dryer, then went into the kitchen to make herself a cup of tea, leaving Fion in charge. Though not for long – there was a trim arriving any minute, followed by a tint, and Mrs Nutting would shortly need combing out.

It was a lovely, hot August day. The schools had broken up a fortnight ago – Cormac had gone to Seaforth sands with his mates and stern instruction only to paddle, not swim. Alice took her tea into the backyard to drink, glad to escape from the salon for a few minutes and not just because it was so warm in there.

The trouble with Bootle, which she loved with all her heart, was that everybody knew everybody else's business. She was sick to the teeth with women making remarks about Orla, who'd only been married five months, but was already as big as a house. The baby was due at the end of next month and she wondered, grimly, what people would have to say *then*.

It was annoying that Mrs White had taken some of the sheen off Cormac's achievement – she must go round and tell Orla as soon as the salon closed. It might cheer her up a bit.

Only might! Alice sighed. Orla was behaving as if the world had ended, giving poor Micky a terrible time. His mam, whose patience seemed inexhaustible, was full of sympathy.

'I was out of sorts when I was having a couple of mine. She'll be all right by the time the baby comes.'

Somehow Alice doubted it. Being confined to the Lavins' cramped, noisy parlour with a baby to look after was likely to make Orla even worse. What was it that film star, Jimmy Durante always said? 'You ain't seen nothing yet!'

If only she could afford to rent them a little house! Hopefully, once Doreen Morrison started, the profits would go up and she'd ask Horace Flynn if he had a place going.

There were all sorts of 'if onlys'. If only John earned a bit more from the business. Instead, he gave her less housekeeping than when he'd been working as a turner. He was always vague when he handed over the money, muttering about needing new tools, more stock, increasing overheads. If it hadn't been for the hairdresser's, Alice wouldn't have been able to manage. She would, though, insist John contribute towards the cost of

Cormac's uniform and all the other stuff required – she remembered there was a tennis racquet on the list.

'When will I see Dad so I can tell him?' Cormac had asked that morning when the letter came.

Alice pursed her lips, angry that John was never there when something nice happened – or something bad, like that business with Orla, with whom he had cut off contact altogether. 'I dunno, luv. Not till Sat'day, probably.' It mightn't even be then. They seemed to be seeing less and less of him, even at weekends. 'I'll wait up late and give him the news,' she promised.

'Can I come down if I'm still awake?'

'Of course, luv.'

There was yet another 'if only'. If only she hadn't been so stupid as to sign away a third of the business to Cora! It was galling to think that the money her sister-in-law took every week would have been enough to pay the rent on three, or even four, small houses.

'Mam!' Fion yelled. 'Geraldine O'Brien's here for her trim.'

'Coming, luv.'

Maurice Lacey had had nothing to eat or drink all day, having been confined to his room ever since the letter had come to say he'd failed the scholarship. Now he reckoned it was nearly teatime, and he was starving hungry and aching for a drink.

'You're bloody thick, you are,' Mam had screeched. 'Get up to your room, I'll punish you later. I daren't do it now, else I might kill you I'm so bloody mad. I thought you'd be dead clever like your dad.'

This was a very strange remark, as Mam usually claimed his dad was as thick as two short planks. He wondered if Cormac had passed and would like to bet he

138

had. He'd also like to bet that Auntie Alice wouldn't have made a huge big scene if Cormac had failed. He felt envious of Cormac, having Auntie Alice for a mam. She didn't hug him and squeeze him and kiss him, the way his own mam did, but nor did she hit him either – there was no sign of a cane in Amber Street.

For the first time in his eleven years, Maurice was struck with the thought that life wasn't fair. There'd been nearly forty children in his class, but only a few had been expected to pass the scholarship. Were all those others who'd failed shut in a dark bedroom with the threat of the cane hanging over their heads? They were more likely playing football in the street or in the park, or had gone to the shore, like Cormac. Why was he always treated differently from everyone else?

'It's not fair!' A ball of misery rose in his parched throat, where it stuck and he couldn't swallow. He badly wanted to cry because he felt so unhappy.

The front door slammed, indicating his mam had gone out. Maurice tried his own door, but it was locked from the outside. He glanced out of the window, where the sun was shining brightly enough to split the flags, and felt a longing for fresh air, the company of his mates from school. He was rarely allowed out on his own.

In a garden behind he could hear the sound of children playing and through the trees he spied a swing. They actually had a swing of their own!

His heart in his mouth, he slid open the window, climbed out on to the kitchen roof, then shinned down the drainpipe to the ground.

He was free! There'd be hell to pay when Mam got back and found him gone, but right now Maurice didn't care. He'd always done his best to be good. He was never naughty, never got into trouble, never answered back. He'd tried with all his might to pass the scholar-ship. It wasn't his fault that the questions were too hard. Anyroad, his brain had gone numb. He couldn't think.

Without any idea where he was going, Maurice began to run. If he went to North Park he'd be sure to find someone to play with. Instead, some ten minutes later, he found himself outside Auntie Alice's hairdresser's. He wanted to see her pretty, kind face light up in surprise when he went in. She was fond of him, he could tell. He'd only been in the hairdresser's a few times, but he liked it very much. It was a cheerful place and everybody there seemed happy.

He opened the door and a bell chimed. His cousin, Fion, was brushing the floor and another lady was washing another lady's hair. There was no sign of his aunt.

'Hello, luv,' Fion exclaimed. 'Is your mam with you?'

Maurice shook his head. He liked Fion, who was inclined to make a fuss of him, but it was her mam he wanted.

'You look hot. Would you like a glass of cherryade?' Fion enquired. 'We've got some in the kitchen.'

'Yes, *please*!'

'I'll get it you in a minute, as soon as I've finished this floor. Me mam's in the yard, having a quick breather. It's been like a Turkish bath in here today. Fortunately, we'll be closing soon. Why don't you go and say hello.'

Maurice trotted down the salon, through the kitchen and into the yard, where Auntie Alice was sitting on a chair. Her face was a bit sad, he thought, but brightened considerably when she saw him.

'Hello, Maurice, luv.' She beamed. 'Are you out on your own? That makes a change.'

He had no idea what came over him, because all of a sudden he'd thrown himself at his aunt and she'd dragged him on to her knee, and he was sobbing his heart out, and she was stroking his face and saying, 'There, there, luv. Tell your Auntie Alice what's wrong.'

'I've failed the scholarship,' he bawled. 'Me mam shut me in me room and tonight she's going to kill me.'

'Oh, she is, is she!' his aunt said in an ominous voice.

'I didn't mean to fail. I tried dead hard, honest.'

'I'm sure you did, luv. The best anyone can do is try.'

'I'm dead stupid.' He sobbed.

'If everyone who failed the scholarship was stupid, then the world would grind to a halt,' his aunt said wisely. 'None of our girls passed, nor did I, nor your Uncle John. Neither did your mam, come to that. Anyroad, you're good at other things – footy, for instance. You're a much better player than our Cormac.'

'I suppose so,' Maurice conceded with a hiccup.

'And you're dead handsome.' She ran her fingers through his dark curls. 'I bet you'll break lots of hearts when you grow up, by which time you'll find yourself good at all sorts of things. Me, now, I used to think I was as daft as a brush, until I discovered I was good at doing women's hair.' She hugged him very tight. 'Now, don't you ever call yourself stupid again, do you hear?'

The bell went on the door and his aunt said, 'That's probably me final customer. All she wants is a trim. You can keep me company in the salon for a while, then I'll take you home.'

He pressed himself against her. 'I don't want to go home!'

'I'm afraid you'll have to, luv, otherwise your mam will call out the bobbies and I'll be charged with kidnapping.'

'I'm hungry, Auntie.'

'In that case I'll give you your tea, *then* I'll take you home.'

It's not right, Cora,' Alice said. 'To deprive an eleven-year-old of food and drink all day just because he didn't pass a silly exam . . . well, it's just not right.'

'It's none of your business,' Cora argued hotly. 'How I treat me son is nobody's affair but me own.'

'It *is* my affair when I become involved,' Alice replied just as hotly. 'The poor little lad was forced to come to mine for summat to eat. He drank a whole bottle of cherryade and I don't know how many glasses of water. His throat must have been as dry as a bone.'

Cora cast around for something to say in excuse, but could think of nothing. She'd thought about Maurice with mixed feelings while she'd been out at the shops. She was slightly uneasy that he hadn't been fed all day, but at the same time her blood was boiling because he'd let her down and failed the scholarship. If Cormac had passed, which seemed likely, it meant Alice Lacey had got one up on her again. She'd give Maurice a good thrashing when she got home, teach him a lesson. A little thrill ran through her when she thought about after-wards, after she had forgiven him. He would fling his arms around her neck, tell her how much he loved her and she would hold him close, so very, very close. Then they'd have a lovely tea.

She went into the greengrocer's and bought a pound of new potatoes and a pound of peas, then to Costigan's for four slices of boiled ham, but remembered she had a husband and increased the order to six. Finally she bought a large cream cake in Blackledge's, Maurice's favourite, with raspberry jam as well as cream.

She was at home, putting the things away, unaware that Maurice wasn't in his room, when there was a knock on the door and Alice Lacey was outside, looking very cross indeed and holding a sulky Maurice by the hand. Cora had always thought her sister-in-law wouldn't say boo to a goose and hadn't realised she had such a temper.

She stood in the parlour, angrily waving her arms. 'It's not right,' she kept saying. 'In fact, it's cruel.'

It was a good half-hour before a strangely inarticulate Cora got rid of her. She slammed the door and stood with her back against it, breathing deeply. With each breath her own anger mounted – anger that it was no use directing against Alice. Anyroad, it was Maurice who was the cause of her shame.

She advanced on the living room, where he'd been sent out of earshot of the shouting women, and found him standing by the window. Children were playing in the house behind and their cries carried sharply on the calm evening air, emphasising the stillness and quietness of their own house.

'Don't you dare go round that bloody hairdresser's again,' Cora said in a grating voice. 'And if I shut you in your room, you bloody stay there. Do you hear me, lad?'

'Yes,' Maurice said distantly.

'Yes, what?'

'Yes, Mam.'

'You made a right show of me today, going to see Alice, telling her you were hungry. What the hell must she think of me?'

Maurice shrugged. 'Don't know, Mam.'

She had never known him appear so indifferent to her words and it only made her more angry still. Her head throbbed and she felt dizzy with rage. Hadn't he realised what he'd *done*? Didn't he understand she had to feel better than everyone else? She *had* to. As a child, dirty and unkempt, always hungry, the continual butt of her two elderly aunts' brutality, she had vowed to herself that one day she would *be* someone. She'd hardly ever gone to school, though hadn't minded, because the other kids made fun of her ragged clothes and lack of shoes, the nits in her hair and the fact that she smelt and was useless at every single lesson.

'It won't always be like this,' she used to tell herself as she lay down to sleep in the bedroom that was bare of everything except a mattress and a few flea-ridden blankets. 'When I grow up I'll live in a palace.'

She'd seen off her aunts in the end, but the following years had been hard. She had slept on the streets for a while, because no one wanted to give a job to a girl who couldn't add up, couldn't read, who didn't even know how to behave proper.

Eventually she'd got a live-in job cleaning for a woman who owned half a dozen lodging houses.

'Did no one ever teach you how to use a knife and fork?' the woman asked on her first night – Cora was eating the food with her fingers.

She'd learnt how to use cutlery, when to say 'please' and 'thank you', to wipe her bum when she went to the lavatory, to change her clothes before they began to smell. She'd learnt also to read and write, do sums. The woman she worked for had helped. She said Cora had a quick brain. It was a shame she hadn't learnt all these things before. She would have done well at school.

When she was twenty she'd met Billy Lacey, very personable and far better-looking than the men who'd shown interest in her so far. By the time he proposed, Cora had already realised he was a loser. She far preferred his brother, John, who was the dead opposite, but apart from being polite, otherwise he showed no interest in his brother's fiancée. Still, if she married Billy she'd get her own house. For a while it didn't matter that it was in O'Connell Street.

It hadn't been long before wishy-washy Alice Mitchell appeared on the scene, hanging like a leech on to the arm of John Lacey. Apart from her aunts, Cora didn't think she'd ever hated anyone before as much as she hated Alice on the day she married John and changed her name from Mitchell to Lacey.

The urge to *be* someone, to have beautiful things, was just as strong, but stronger still was the need to be one up on Alice Lacey. Cora thought she had achieved this with her handsome, stolen son, with the house in Garibaldi Road, with the third share she had wangled in the hairdresser's, but somehow Alice always seemed to go one better.

Cora stared balefully at the son who'd let her down so badly. She reached for the cane and flexed it between her hands. Nodding towards a chair, she said curtly, 'Bend over.'

To her everlasting surprise, Maurice ignored her.

'Bend over,' Cora insisted, aware a note of hysteria had crept into her voice.

'No.' He stuffed his hands in the pockets of his grey shorts and looked at her stubbornly.

'In that case . . .' She raised the cane and whipped it against his shoulders. It must have hurt through the thin cotton of his shirt, but it was like rainwater off a duck's back as far as Maurice was concerned. Cora raised the cane again and was taken aback when he caught the end in his hand. For several awful seconds' they tussled over possession, but he was a big, strong lad for eleven, stronger than she was, and he easily won.

For a horrible moment, Cora half expected the cane to be turned on her. She cowered against the wall, arms raised protectively, but Maurice merely bent it till it broke in two. He threw the pieces on the table and stared at them for a long time, as if wondering why he'd never done it before.

'Huh!' he muttered and walked out of the room. She

assumed he was on his way upstairs to sulk in his bedroom. Instead, seconds later, the front door slammed. Cora flew down the hall and opened it.

'Where are you going?' she called shakily.

'To the park to play with me mates.'

She'd lost him! Her body froze with horror. He was the only person in the world she had ever loved, the only person who had loved her in return. She wanted him back, would do anything to get him back, but had a horrible, sickly feeling that it was too late.

And, as usual, it was all the fault of Alice Lacey.

She felt as if she'd been pregnant for ever. She could hardly walk she was so big. Maybe she was expecting quins like that woman in Canada. The bed creaked like mad every time she turned over and she turned over all night long, waking Micky, who was red-eyed with tiredness in the mornings.

But Orla didn't care. She didn't care if his eyes fell out or his head dropped off. All she cared about was herself and her predicament.

She hated Micky, whose fault it was that she was in this mess, and she hated her dad for not letting them have the parlour in Amber Street, a much nicer place to be. She hated her sisters: Fionnuala looked so superior, as if trying to say, '*I'd* never get in a mess like you,' which was probably true, as there wasn't a boy in Bootle who'd go near her, and you'd think Maeve had delivered hundreds of babies the way she kept offering advice, yet there wasn't a maternity ward in Bootle hospital.

Most of all, she hated the Lavins for . . . oh, for all sorts of reasons. There was always a row going on for one thing, or two or three rows, come to that, with people screaming at each other at the tops of their voices from rooms all over the house. She hated the way they came into the parlour to watch the bloody telly when she was trying to rest and instead she had Gilbert Harding or Barbara Kelly or Lady-stinking-Barnet bawling down her ear. She hated the fact that Mrs Lavin sent one of the kids every morning to pinch a bottle of milk off someone's step for the expectant mother, then sat, watching the same expectant mother while she drank every bloody drop, oozing bloody sympathy and acquainting her with the gory details of her own nine births.

It was horrible, sitting down to a nice meal of roast beef, or lamb chops, or chicken, to have Mr Lavin wink and say, 'You'll never guess where this came from!'

Orla had guessed months ago – well, who wouldn't! The food was stolen, it had 'fallen off the back of a lorry'. She imagined Mr Lavin running after a speeding lorry, picking up the joints of meat that were being scattered in its wake. All Mrs Lavin ever bought was vegetables. The other day there'd been a trifle, a huge thing in a fluted cardboard case.

'You'll never guess where that came from!' Mr Lavin winked.

How the hell had he managed to nick a *trifle*?

Orla groaned. If she were still working for the *Crosby Star*, she might be interviewing a politician right now, or have been sent to cover a murder.

The lovely chiming clock on the mantelpiece, which had no doubt come the same way as virtually everything else in the house, struck five o'clock. Mam would be back in Amber Street soon, and she'd go round and see her. It was the only place where she got any peace and Mam was the only person in the world whom she didn't hate. Oh, and their Cormac.

Alice was just unlocking the salon door on a drizzly morning in September when Micky Lavin skidded to a halt outside on a rusty bicycle. 'It's Orla,' he gasped. 'She's gone to the hospital. The pains started about an hour ago.'

'Oh, dear!' It meant the baby was going to be a fortnight early, or two and a half months early if people were expected to believe Orla had remained virtuous until her wedding night. People never would! She prayed the baby would be small so she could claim it was premature.

It was a terrible way to think when her daughter was about to give birth. Alice nudged the thought to one side and said anxiously to Micky, 'Is she all right?'

Micky rolled his eyes. 'Is Orla ever all right? She was screaming blue murder when I came to get you.'

'I'll look after the salon, Mam,' Fion offered. 'Patsy'll be along shortly and Doreen's in this avvy. We'll manage between us, don't worry.'

'Ta, luv.' There were times when Fion could be extremely capable. 'I'll try and ring from the nursing home, tell you what's happening, like.' To Micky she said, 'You get along back, luv. I'll catch a tram. I'll be there in no time.'

Orla was in a side ward still screaming blue murder, when her mother arrived, out of breath, excited and at the same time dreading the next few hours.

'It hurts,' Orla yelled. 'Oh, Mam, the pains hurt really, really bad.'

Alice's heart sank when she saw Mrs Lavin sitting in a chair next to the bed. She was holding Orla's hand and singing a lullaby for some reason. 'Rock-a-bye baby, on the tree top . . .'

No wonder Orla was screaming.

'Why don't you go home, Mam, and see to the brekkies,' Micky suggested, as if sensing the presence of his mother wasn't helping.

'. . . when the tree falls, the baby will stop,' Mrs Lavin crooned. 'Or is it drop? Hello, Mrs Lacey. She's having a wicked time, just like I did when I had quite a few of mine. Our Micky, though, he just popped out, like a pea from a pod.'

'*Mam!*' Orla screeched.

'I'll take over now, shall I, Mrs Lavin? You've got little 'uns to see to, not like me.'

'Well . . .' Mrs Lavin seemed reluctant to give up Orla's hand or her seat beside the bed.

'I think they only allow two visitors, Mam,' Micky said.

'Oh, I'll be off then.' Mrs Lavin left after making Micky promise to come and tell her the minute the baby arrived. 'I'll bring some flowers and a bunch of grapes,' she said generously.

'Only if she finds a lorry for them to drop off,' Orla said through clenched teeth when the door closed. 'I'm more likely to get a side of beef or a chicken already trussed.'

'Try not to talk, luv.' Micky tenderly stroked the brow of his young wife. 'Save your breath for the pains. They're called contractions,' he said to Alice as if she didn't already know. 'They get closer and closer as the time comes for the baby to be born. I read it in a book,' he said proudly, 'that I got out the library.'

Orla had got a bloke in a million, Alice thought. It would take time, he was only twenty, but if she stuck it out she'd do well with Micky Lavin.

'Shurrup, Micky,' Orla snapped. 'Oh, there's another pain coming! Oh, Mam!'

Alice became quite impatient with her daughter as the morning progressed and she continued to scream and yell. There were two other women having babies at the same time and between them they didn't make half the fuss that Orla did. Alice suspected the screams were directed at Micky in an attempt to make him feel guilty.

The labour lasted five and a half hours and Orla was whisked to the delivery ward the minute the midwife judged her ready to give birth.

Alice and Micky sat in the corridor outside and waited for the screams to start again. To their surprise, in no time at all, the door opened and the midwife appeared. 'It's a girl,' she said jubilantly. 'She's absolutely beautiful and a whole seven pounds, two ounces. I've never known such a swift and painless birth. Congratulations – Dad! Would you like to come and see your daughter?'

Micky looked wistfully at Alice. 'Now it's all over, I wonder if she'll be happy? Will she stop blaming me, do you think? I love her, Mrs Lacey. I love her more than anything on earth.'

'I know you do, luv.' Alice kissed him, but felt unable to offer a single hopeful promise for the future. Her wilful, strong-minded daughter apparently considered this rather decent young man had ruined her life for ever.

'I'll go and see her now.' Micky was scarcely gone a minute, when he came out again. 'She wants you,' he said. His eyes were bright with tears.

'Why don't you nip home and tell your mam?' Alice said.

'I'll do that.' He looked relieved to have something to do.

The midwife had been right! The new baby was beautiful, a perfectly formed little girl, not the least bit red or crumpled like some babies and already with a fine head of dark, curly hair. Her eyes were wide open and her tiny body wriggled impatiently against the tightly wrapped blanket.

'She's going to be a lively one,' her grandmother whispered. 'I suppose it's all right if I pick her up.'

As she nursed her first grandchild, Alice wished with all her heart that John were there, not the John of now, but the one she had married. This was a unique moment, the sort a woman should share with her husband. She sighed. *Her* husband seemed no longer interested in his family.

'Have you decided on a name yet?' she asked Orla. Names for the baby had been the only thing that had sparked her interest over the last months.

'Lulu,' Orla said listlessly.

Alice had never heard Lulu mentioned before and thought it awful, like a music hall turn or a silent film star. However, it seemed wise to keep her trap shut.

'Hello, Miss Lulu Lavin,' she whispered. The baby stirred in her arms and uttered a tiny cry. 'I think she might want a feed. Are you up to it, luv?'

'I'm not sure. I feel as if I've just been dragged through the mill and back again,' Orla said weakly.

'The midwife said she'd never known such a swift and painless birth.'

'How would she know?' Orla demanded in a voice that was suddenly weak no more.

Alice shrugged. 'Through experience, I guess. What was it you said to Micky to make him leave so quick?'

'I told him I didn't want to see him, that I wanted you. Frankly, I don't care if I ever see him or the Lavins again.'

'Then why did you marry the poor lad?'

Orla pouted. 'I didn't have much choice, did I?'

'You didn't have many choices,' Alice conceded, 'but you didn't *have* to marry him. Nor, I might remind you, did *he* have to marry *you*. Another chap might have run a mile, or claimed the baby wasn't his. But Micky did the honourable thing and you've made his life a misery ever since.' Oh, it was hard, speaking so sternly to her pretty, distressed daughter, who was probably expecting buckets of sympathy, not a lecture, off her mam. 'I take it the . . . er, the time you conceived, he didn't rape you, that you were just as much a willing partner as him?'

Orla blushed and didn't answer.

Alice was all set to continue with the lecture, but two nurses arrived to move the new mother to a ward and take the baby to the nursery, so she excused herself and went to look for a telephone. She rang Fion to let her know she was now an aunt.

'Nip home as soon as you've got a minute,' she said, 'and let our Maeve know. She'll be back from the General by now. She can tell Cormac when he gets home from school. Tonight, we'll all come together to visit Orla and the baby.'

Maeve wrinkled her pert little nose. 'It seems dead peculiar, having a sister who's a mother.'

'I know.' Fion nodded her head vigorously. 'Dead peculiar.'

'Have you ever done, you know, the thing Micky did with Orla to make her have the baby?'

'Lord, *no*!' Fion gasped. 'Have you?'

'What? And end up living in the Lavins' parlour with people sitting on the bed watching telly while you're trying to sleep? No, thanks, I wouldn't dream of it. You'd have to be mad.'

'Perhaps our Orla *is* mad!'

'Perhaps. Though I wouldn't mind *kissing* Micky Lavin,' Maeve said thoughtfully. 'He's a dish.'

'What's a dish?' enquired Fion, who wouldn't have minded kissing Micky Lavin either.

'Someone who's dead gorgeous. Montgomery Clift's dishy, and Frank Sinatra.'

'Neil Greene's dishier than both of them,' Fion said.

She fancied kissing Neil even more than she did Micky Lavin.

In mid-afternoon Mr and Mrs Lavin arrived at the hospital, laden with fruit and flowers, and accompanied by four of the children. Visiting time was almost over. Before a nurse could complain there were too many visitors around the bed Alice left, promising to return that night.

Outside, the morning's drizzle had become a steady downpour and she wished she'd brought an umbrella. She stood in the rain and wondered whether to go home or to the salon. She didn't feel like doing either. Her nerves were on edge after the conversation with Orla. It worried her that the girl would refuse to see sense and eventually Micky would snap. There was only so much a person could stand. So far, Micky had been dead patient. But he wasn't a saint.

If only she could talk to someone – her dad or Bernie, but they'd be at work for hours yet.

She could talk to John. He might not agree, but it was every bit as much *his* problem as it was hers. Anyroad, despite the way he'd acted with Orla, he had a right to know he'd become a grandfather. And she wouldn't wait till tonight. She'd do it now while she was in the mood, go round to the yard and see him. You never knew, his attitude might change if he could be persuaded to see Lulu, who was without doubt one of the loveliest babies ever born. It was a pity the poor child had been blessed with such a dead silly name.

Alice had only a vague idea where the yard was situated: somewhere in Seaforth not far from the playing fields. Benton Street rang a bell. For some reason John had always discouraged them from going there. She caught the tram to the terminus in Rimrose Road, walked under the railway bridge and emerged in Seaforth.

The first three people she asked had never heard of Benton Street, nor a firm called B.E.D.S. The fourth, a woman, had an idea the street was near the playing fields.

'That's right,' Alice said eagerly.

The directions were complicated. Turn right, then left, then right again at a big pub the woman couldn't remember the name of. Go half a mile down Sandy Road, turn left at a greengrocer's and Benton Street was the second turning on the right, or it might be the third.

Alice got wetter and wetter as she negotiated the complicated maze of streets. She thought about giving up, but decided she couldn't, not after having made it this far.

She was soaked to the skin by the time she turned into Benton Street and hoped John had a towel so she could dry herself. A wooden sign with B.E.D.S. painted on it was attached to a pair of tall iron gates, just round the corner in a place called Crozier Terrace, a cul-de-sac with no more than ten tiny houses either side.

Her heart sank when she tried the gates and found them locked. Surely John didn't lock himself in! Behind the gates a two-storey building had a light on upstairs. It was probably the office. Alice rattled the gates in the hope of attracting her husband's attention, but to no avail.

Disappointed, she turned away. After coming so far! She wondered where he could be. Maybe he'd gone to the timber yard for wood. Alice frowned. If that was the case, what was that smart green van doing parked inside the gates? Did it belong to John? It looked new, but he'd never mentioned having a van. She noticed a wire strung across the street attached to the top half of the building, the office. He hadn't mentioned having a telephone either.

'You'll find him at home, luv.'

'I beg your pardon?'

A woman had emerged from one of the tiny houses in Crozier Terrace. She was sensibly shielded from the rain in a plastic mac and hood. 'Mr Lacey, he's gone home to see his missus. I saw him pass me winder less than ten minutes ago.'

'You can't possibly have!' John had never been known to come home during the day. Anyroad, he'd have to go the other way, down Benton Street, not past this woman's window. There was no way out of Crozier Terrace.

'Please yourself, luv.' The woman shrugged. 'But I don't doubt the evidence of me own eyes. You'll find Mr Lacey in the end house, number twenty.'

She must be mad. Alice watched the woman walk away, then gave the gates another shake. Still no one came. She was about to walk away herself but, feeling curious, went down Crozier Terrace to number twenty. She took a step back and looked it up and down. It was a perfectly ordinary house, identical to the others, with pretty, flowered cretonne curtains. There was a vase of dried leaves in the window. The front door and the sills were painted maroon.

The woman had been talking nonsense. She couldn't possibly be right. On the other hand, how could she possibly be wrong? She'd referred to 'Mr Lacey'. She lived within spitting distance of the yard, so she must know John well. And another thing, Alice's heart began to pound painfully in her chest, it was John who insisted on maroon every time he painted the outside of their house in Amber Street. She would have preferred bottle green herself.

'His missus,' the woman had said. 'He's gone to see his missus.'

'But that's *me*,' Alice said aloud. She wondered if she should go home, *run* home, forget the house, what the woman had said, just wait for John tonight and tell him about Orla. She would never mention having been to the yard. Perhaps it would be best not to know whatever secrets might lie behind this door.

But she *had* to know. She would never rest until she did. There was still a chance that the woman had got things wrong, that it was another man who looked like John who'd passed her house. Except she'd called him Mr Lacey.

Maybe there were two Mr Laceys and they were similar!

Alice took a deep breath and knocked on the door.

After a few seconds it was opened by a young woman, heavily pregnant, with lovely soft fair hair. Through the door Alice glimpsed a simply but comfortably furnished parlour with a plain brown fitted carpet – she'd always fancied fitted carpets in her own house. There was something wrong with the young woman's face – she had a hare lip. Without it, she would have been extraordinarily pretty. A tiny girl, little more than a baby, clung to her leg and Alice felt herself go cold. The little girl could have been Orla at the same age. The young woman smiled, but didn't speak.

'John Lacey,' Alice said in a cracked voice. 'I've come to see John Lacey.'

'He's upstairs.' A little boy appeared. He had his mother's fair hair.

'Would you mind giving him a call, luv.' Alice still retained a shred of hope it was another man entirely upstairs.

'Dad!' the boy obediently yelled.

'Who is it, son?' John's voice called.

'A lady.'

There were footsteps and John came to the door. Alice, sick to her soul, was presented with the perfect picture of domesticity: the little girl, so like Orla, the boy with the fair hair, her husband, John, his arm laid casually round the shoulders of the pregnant woman.

When he saw Alice his face hardened and she glimpsed hostility in the brown eyes. He bundled his family out of sight, came outside, closed the door.

But by this time, Alice had already reached the end of Crozier Terrace and was running, racing, flying home. She didn't stop until she reached Amber Street.

Alice lay curled up in the armchair, knees pressed against her chest. There was something terrifying about her blank, staring eyes in a face that had lost all trace of colour. She looked like a ghost. Every now and then her body convulsed, as if she was about to have a fit, and the sobs that emerged fom her pale lips were strangely subdued.

A frightened Cormac had begun to cry, something he had hardly ever done when he was little. Maeve was visibly shaking.

Only Fionnuala, who could always be relied on to act sensibly in a crisis, managed to remain calm. 'What's wrong, Mam?' She shook her mother again and again. 'Mam, what's wrong?' But Alice seemed incapable of understanding, let alone providing answers.

'Perhaps our Orla's baby has died?' Maeve suggested.

'Or Orla herself?' Cormac's lip trembled.

'No,' Fion said. 'She would have told us. No, it's something different from that. She's had a terrible shock.'

Cormac managed to crawl on to his mam's knee, which he still did occasionally, despite the fact he was eleven and at grammar school. 'Mam!' He tenderly stroked her face. 'Oh, Mam!'

'Maeve,' Fion commanded, 'make a pot of tea. That might bring her round.'

Maeve hurried into the kitchen to put on the kettle. 'Should we fetch someone?' she asked when she came back.

'Who?' Fion asked simply. 'Anyroad, there's no need to fetch someone, she's got us. You know what I think we should do?'

'What?'

'Throw cold water on her. She's having a fit of some sort. I saw it once in the pictures. It's either water, or slapping her face and I don't know about you, but I couldn't bring meself to slap our mam. I prefer the water idea. She's already soaking from the rain, so it won't exactly hurt her.'

'Shall I fetch a bucketful?'

'A cup will do. *You're* the one who wants to be a nurse, Maeve Lacey. You should know about these things. Cormac, mind out the road, there's a good lad, we're going to throw a cup of water on our mam.' Fion dragged her brother off Alice's knee when he appeared not to hear.

'You do it.' Maeve handed Fion the water.

'You're going to make a hopeless nurse.' Fion took a deep breath and threw the water in her mother's face.

Alice screamed and violently shook her head for several seconds. 'Oh, my God!' she screamed again when she saw three of her children standing anxiously over her. 'What have I been saying?'

'Nothing, Mam. All you did was sort of cry.' Although relieved to see her mother all right again, Fion felt suspicious that things were being kept from her. Why should Mam be worried about what she might have said? 'Has Aunt Cora been at you over something?' she asked.

'No, luv.' Alice held out her arms and the children fell upon her. They might find out one day what their father had been up to, but they'd never hear it from her. She hugged them fiercely. 'I love you. I love you so much it hurts. Now, if someone doesn't make me a cup of tea soon, I think I'll bust.'

'The kettle's already on, Mam,' Fion and Maeve said together and disappeared into the kitchen. Cormac, with his mother all to himself, snuggled his face in her shoulder.

Alice felt dead ashamed. She had only a vague memory of being in the chair, having lost all grip on reality. There'd just been that awful feeling you had when you woke up from a horrific dream, unsure whether it was true or false. For the first time in her life the dream had turned out to be true. Perhaps her brain and her body had been fighting against the truth, praying for the dream to turn out to be just that, a dream.

John! Till the end of her days she would never forget the look on his face, as if she were a trespasser on his happiness. It would have been far preferable if he'd just walked out of Amber Street, left them. But to set up another home, with another woman, other children!

Fion and Maeve came in with tea on a tray and a plate of digestive biscuits. 'Is Orla all right?' Fion demanded.

'She's fine and the baby's lovely.' Alice realised she'd have to explain the hysteria. Now seemed the time to tell them their dad wouldn't be coming home. 'I went round the yard to tell your father about Orla and we had a big bust-up. He's not coming back.'

'But what about us?' Cormac wailed. Fion and Maeve didn't appear particularly upset.

'We never got round to discussing you, luv. I know' –

she had an idea – 'you can telephone him from the salon, arrange to meet somewhere.' She hoped John would be nice to the son he'd once loved so much, that he wouldn't regard him as a trespasser as he had done his wife. She remembered the other little boy and wondered what his name was. 'Son,' John had called him. 'Who is it, son?'

'A lady,' the child had replied.

It would be easy to cry again, but not now, not with the children there. She'd already frightened them enough. Cormac was still on her knee. She hugged him hard. He adored his dad and would miss him more than any other member of the family. Well, *this* family, she thought drily. From now on, John's other family would have him all to themselves.

'She looked so pretty, so nice,' Clare wrote quickly in her neat, precise hand. She started to weep again. 'I feel terrible. So should you,' she added, underlining the 'you'.

'I do,' John said in a heartfelt voice. He did indeed feel terrible, but he also felt very hard. He couldn't get Alice's shocked white face out of his mind, but there was no way he would let her spoil things between him and Clare.

Clare was writing again. 'We should have lived further away. It was always dangerous here.'

'We'll move as soon as possible.' He didn't want Danny Mitchell or one of the girls coming round to make a scene. They could yell at him all they liked, but he wasn't prepared to let Clare or his children be subjected to abuse, though he had a feeling Alice would keep things to herself. She'd be too ashamed and embarrassed to tell anyone, not even her dad or Bernadette.

He wondered aloud why she'd come to the yard in the first place and Clare wrote, 'Perhaps your daughter has had her baby?'

John smiled and stroked her swollen belly. If that was the case, it was possible he would become a grandfather and a father again within a single week.

'You should go to see the baby.' Clare supported the stumbling words with a movement of her hands, as if shooing him out of the house.

'I can't, not now.' He shook his head. 'Alice might be there. Anyroad, I'm not particularly interested.'

'Should be.' She nodded fiercely. 'Should be. Not right.'

'I'm the person to judge what's right or not.'

'I think we should wait a few days before we tell Orla about your dad,' Alice said when the children were ready to visit their sister. 'It's said every cloud has a silver lining, and your dad going means Orla and Micky can move into the parlour. That'll be nice, won't it, eh?'

Maeve and Cormac thought it a great idea, but Fionnuala wasn't so sure. 'Will the baby cry much?' she wanted to know.

'We'll just have to see, luv. Now, are you sure you don't mind me not coming with you? I don't feel as if me legs will carry me far tonight. Just tell Orla I'm a bit off colour, but I'll be at the front of the queue of visitors in the morning.'

'Are you sure you'll be all right on your own?' Fion asked.

Alice couldn't wait for them to go, to be on her own, to think. 'I'll be fine,' she said heartily. 'I'll be even better after a rest. Now, are you sure you've got your tram fare? Maeve, be careful how you hold them flowers, else you'll have the heads off. Cormac, put some stouter shoes on. It's still raining outside.'

She ushered them into the hall – her legs felt as heavy as lead – waved to them from the step, returned to the house, slammed the door, then let go.

'You bloody hypocrite, John Lacey!' she screamed. 'You made me life a misery, accusing me of having affairs, when all the time . . .' She aimed a kick at the skirting board and hurt her foot. 'You even called our Orla names.' What was it? A little whore. In that case, what was the women he lived with?

Unless she didn't know he was married! Perhaps he was a bigamist. If he was and if it hadn't meant she'd never be able to hold up her head in Bootle again she would have reported him to the police.

No wonder he handed over such a pitiful amount of housekeeping every week – he was buying fitted carpets for his other house, buying vans, having a telephone installed in the office. She would have loved a fitted carpet in the parlour. And it would have been nice for the whole family to have gone places at weekends in the van. When Cormac passed the scholarship, she could have rung him from the salon, not stayed up till midnight to let him know. In fact, if she'd known about the telephone she would never have discovered his double life – she would have merely rung to tell him about Orla.

Alice went into the parlour and kicked the bed that he'd slept on, then collapsed upon it, sobbing. Oh, God! It *smelt* of him. The whole house smelt of him: not just the bed, but the chairs, the very air. She had to get out of here and there was only one place she could go and think in peace, a place where there was nothing to remind her of John.

She sat in her favourite place under the middle dryer.

The nights were fast drawing in, it was almost dark. But it had been dull and miserable all day.

'It's been the worst day of me life,' Alice whispered.

Her anger had been replaced by, of all things, guilt. Guilt that he'd felt the need for another woman because his own wife hadn't been sufficiently understanding. She'd tried but, somehow, in some way, she'd let him down. Perhaps she'd been selfish, taking over the hairdresser's when he would have preferred her at home. Mind you, it had seemed dead unreasonable at the time and still felt unreasonable when she thought about it now.

The young woman at the door had had something wrong with her face, a hare lip. Perhaps he felt more comfortable with someone imperfect, like himself. But it was still no excuse for having betrayed his wife and children, for taking the coward's way out.

Alice jumped when there was the sound of a key being turned in the salon door. It turned several times before it was opened and Neil Greene said, 'It wasn't locked. Alice must have forgotten.'

He had someone with him, a woman, who was laughing helplessly. Alice wondered bleakly if she herself would ever laugh again. She prayed the light wouldn't be turned on – she'd look an idiot, sitting in the dark on her own.

'I can't see a thing,' the woman giggled.

'Just a minute,' Neil said, 'the switch is over here.'

The room was flooded with light. Neil took a startled step backwards and his companion uttered a little cry when they saw the red-faced, red-eyed, swollen-faced Alice, who remembered she hadn't combed her hair since morning and it had got soaking wet, as well as her clothes, which she hadn't changed. She must look like a tramp who'd broken in, in the hope of finding a night's shelter.

'Alice!' Neil's face was full of concern. 'Are you all right?'

'I'm fine. Our Orla had the baby and I didn't manage to get in earlier. I thought I'd come and tidy up a few bits and bobs.'

'In the dark?' Neil's companion looked considerably put out. She was smartly dressed in a grey flannel costume, yellow blouse and hat. Her hair was perfectly set in a series of stiff, artificial waves. Alice would never have allowed a customer to leave Lacey's with such unnatural-looking hair.

'I must have dozed off.' Alice stood up, too quickly. She swayed, nearly fell and had to sit down again.

Neil said, 'Jean, I think it would be best if you went home. I'll drop in at the bank at lunchtime tomorrow.'

Jean made a little moue with her mouth. 'But, darling . . .'

'Tomorrow, Jean.' Neil put his hands on her shoulders and propelled her towards the door. 'Goodnight.' The door closed and he turned to Alice. 'What on earth is wrong? You look like shit.'

'Don't swear,' Alice said automatically, then remembered he wasn't one of her children. 'I'm sorry.'

'You're quite right. Teachers shouldn't swear.' He regarded her sternly. 'Alice, will you please tell me what's the matter?'

'Put the light out.'

He switched off the light. 'Is Orla's baby all right? Is Orla herself?'

'Orla's fine, the baby's beautiful.'

'Girl or boy?'

'A girl. She's calling her Lulu.'

'That's a pretty name. Lulu Lavin, sounds like a

164

flower.' He came and sat beside her. 'Are you going to tell me now that it's dark?' His voice sounded very close, only inches from her ear.

'I can't, Neil,' she said brokenly. 'You're being very kind, but I can't tell anyone, not even me dad or me best friend. It's something truly awful.'

'A trouble shared is a trouble halved, so people say.'

'I've said it meself more than once, but I'm not sure now if it's true.'

'If it's really so awful, Alice, you should tell someone. It doesn't have to be me. You shouldn't keep it all to yourself.'

Alice said wryly, 'You sound as if you know about such things, but I can't imagine anything awful's ever happened to you.'

He was always cheerful and extraordinarily good-humoured, as if he found the world a wonderful place to be. She understood he was an excellent teacher – everyone at St James's liked him, though it was considered a mystery what he was doing there when he could have been teaching at a public school, or in a different job altogether. He'd been to university and had a Classics degree, whatever that was. He came from somewhere in Surrey and wasn't short of a few bob – one of her customers who knew about such things said his suits and shoes were handmade. His car was an MG sports.

His mam and dad were referred to as 'moms' and 'pops', and he had an elder brother called Adrian and a sister, Miranda, whose twenty-first birthday it had been in August. Instead of a party, Miranda had had a dance at which some well-known orchestra had played: Ted Heath or Ambrose or Geraldo, Alice wasn't sure. It wasn't that Neil showed off, but he sometimes talked about his private life.

It could have been embarrassing, having someone so dead posh living in the upstairs flat, but Neil hadn't an ounce of side. Alice had always felt completely at ease with her tenant. And he was always gentle with Fionnuala, whose crush on him was plain for all to see.

'What are you doing tomorrow?' he asked.

'Why, coming into the salon, like normal,' she said, surprised at the question.

'Act as if nothing dreadful has happened, laugh, smile, be your usual sunny self?'

'Well, yes, of course.'

'We all do that, Alice,' he said with a dry laugh. 'We all put on a show, no matter how we feel inside. What makes you think I'm any different?'

'I'm sorry, luv.' Alice impulsively laid her hand on his. 'I was being insensitive. It's just that you act as if you don't have a care in the world.'

'It wasn't always so. Seven years ago I wanted to kill myself.' He put his other hand on top of hers. 'If I tell you about it, will you tell me in turn why you are looking so utterly wretched? I got the fright of my life when I turned on the light. I thought the hairdresser's must be haunted.'

'I'm sorry,' Alice said abjectly. 'And I made you get rid of poor Jean.'

'Poor Jean will already have got over it.' He pulled her to her feet. 'If we're going to exchange confidences, let's go upstairs where it's comfortable and we can do it over a cup of coffee or, better still, a glass of brandy. A drink will probably do you good.'

'Give us a minute first to comb me hair.'

There were still a few pieces of furniture in the flat that had belonged to Myrtle – a sideboard, a glass-fronted china cabinet, the bedroom suite, though Alice had bought a new mattress. The two armchairs, the small table with matching chairs and the kitchen dresser were good quality second-hand.

She'd been upstairs a couple of times since Neil moved in. He had added things of his own – some exotically patterned mats that had come all the way from Persia, lots of bright pictures, a pair of table lamps that cast a rosy glow over the rather gloomy room. The china cabinet was full of books and there was a statue of an elephant on top, which Neil said was made of jade. There were more jade statues on the mantelpiece.

'It's lovely and cosy up here,' she said when he switched on the lamps.

'That was my intention. Would you like coffee or brandy? I suggest the latter.'

'That would be nice, though not too much, else it'll go to me head.'

He grinned. 'That mightn't be such a bad thing. Now, sit down, I'll get the drinks, then I'll tell you the story of my life.'

Instead of an armchair, Neil sat on the floor with his back against it, his long legs stretched out across the mat. He turned on the electric fire, not the element, just the red bulb behind the imitation coals. The room looked cosier still.

'You know I was in the Army, don't you?' he began.

Alice nodded. 'You joined in nineteen forty-two when you were eighteen.' She also knew he didn't have to join. He'd been accepted by Cambridge University and could have stayed to finish the course, by which time the war would have been over.

'What you don't know, Alice, is that I got married when I was twenty.'

'Married!' she gasped, startled. He appeared to be one of the most *un*married men she'd ever known.

Neil wagged his finger. 'Don't interrupt. I'd like to get

this over with as quickly as possible. I married my childhood sweetheart, Barbara. Babs everyone called her. She was, still is, no doubt, quite gloriously pretty. Our parents had known each other for years before we were born. Even now,' he said thoughtfully, 'I'm not sure if we ever loved each other, or it was a case of doing what was expected of us. It *seemed* like love, it *felt* like it and we were happy to go along with our parents' expectations – superbly happy, I might add.'

He stared into the fire, as if he'd forgotten Alice was there. 'We married the year before the war ended. I was stationed in Kent at the time. I got special leave – we even snatched a weekend's honeymoon at Claridge's. That's a hotel in London,' he added in case Alice had never heard of it, which she hadn't. 'Babs worked for a government department, something to do with rationing. She had a little mews cottage in Knightsbridge. From then on, it's where I spent my leave, though she claimed to feel lonely when I wasn't there.' His lips twisted. 'Now that she was a married woman, she didn't lead the wild social life she'd done before. So I used to tell my fellow officers when they were going to London, "Drop in on my Babs. She'll make you feel at home for a few hours." And they did. Would you like more brandy, Alice?'

'Not yet. Perhaps later.'

'I think I'll replenish my glass.'

He got to his feet, a tall, extremely good-looking and suddenly rather tragic young man, Alice thought, even though she didn't yet know the end of the story.

'Nine months after the wedding,' he continued when he had returned to his place on the floor, 'we were posted to France. The Brits had taken it back by then. Soon we were in Germany, on our way to Berlin. We were in Berlin on the wonderful day the war was declared over. That night we had a party in the mess. Everyone drank too much, me included. Things got wild. Then a chap I hardly knew, I'd never spoken to before, mentioned this "little tart", as he called her, who he'd slept with in London. He intended calling on her the minute he got back. Her name was Barbara Greene and she'd been recommended to him as a "good lay" – that's an American term, so I understand. The chap said he felt sorry for her poor sod of a husband. Then another chap butted in who also knew Barbara Greene – she'd taught him a few tricks he didn't know, he said.' Neil laughed bitterly. 'Before long, it seemed as if the entire bloody regiment was claiming to have slept with Babs.'

'Oh, luv!' Alice breathed. 'That's terrible. What did you do?'

'I got blind drunk. I was probably the only Englishman on earth who wanted to kill himself on such a momentous night.'

'What did you do – *after* that night?'

Neil shrugged. 'Saw out the rest of my service, got demobbed, went to see my lovely wife and told her it was over. She wasn't particularly upset. We went our separate ways. A few years ago she asked for a divorce, but I refused. We're both Catholics, you see. I don't think a divorced teacher would be acceptable to a Catholic school board.'

'So, you're still married?'

'Yes. As I have no intention of ever marrying again, what does it matter?' He shrugged once more. 'Would you like another drink now? I definitely would.'

'I wouldn't mind a little bit. You're not going to get blind drunk tonight, are you?' Alice asked anxiously.

'No.' He stretched his arms, put them behind his neck and grinned. Suddenly he looked his old self again. Alice felt relieved. 'I'm over getting plastered. I'm over Babs, if the truth be known. But I shall never get over the sense of betrayal. How could she *do* such a thing? I still ask myself that from time to time.'

'What made you become a teacher?'

'I'm not sure.' He considered the question. 'After I finished Cambridge, I felt the urge to escape from the world I'd always known, do something entirely different. I took up teaching, much to my folks' horror. They thought it a terribly middle-class thing to do. They regard themselves as very much upper-class, you see.' He looked at Alice, his eyes sparkling with merriment. 'I've never told you this, but my father is Sir Archibald Nelson Middleton-Greene.'

Alice burst out laughing. 'That's a mouthful. Am I supposed to have heard of him?'

'No. I'm pleased you're amused rather than impressed.'

'Oh, I'm impressed all right.'

'Are you feeling better?'

'Loads better.'

'Me too. I've never told anyone all that before.' He refilled her glass for the third time. 'Now it's your turn to bare your soul.'

'It doesn't feel so bad now. I mean, it's still awful, it just doesn't feel as bad inside.' She told him the story right from the beginning, about how happy she and John had been with their four lovely children, then when John had burnt his face and everything had changed. She told him the awful things he'd called her. 'Then suddenly he changed again.' He'd started staying out a lot. They hardly saw him.

'Today I went round to the yard to tell him about Orla. He'd always discouraged us from going before. You'll never believe what I found.' She described knocking on the door and it being opened by the very pregnant young woman with fair hair and a toddler attached to her knee. 'She smiled at me ever so nicely.' Then the little boy came and shouted upstairs for his daddy. 'By then, I knew it must be John, but it still knocked me for six when he appeared. And his eyes! They were dead horrible. I felt about *this* big.' Alice held up her thumb and forefinger about quarter of an inch apart. 'But do you know what gets me more than anything?'

'What, Alice?'

'It sounds daft, but she had a fitted carpet. John knew I'd always wanted a fitted carpet for the parlour. It made me realise how much he put this other family before his real one. It's as if we don't matter any more.' She sniffed. 'Oh, Lord, Neil. I think I'm going to cry again and I haven't got a hankie.'

'I'll get you one.' Neil leapt to his feet and returned with a clean, but unironed, white handkerchief. To her total astonishment he knelt beside her and began to dry her eyes, which she thought a trifle unnecessary. There didn't seem any real need to kiss them either, so that she felt her lashes flutter against his lips. It was years since John had touched her and it made her feel uncomfortable, even though it was undeniably very pleasant.

'You don't have to do this, you know,' she mumbled.

'I'm doing it because I want to, not because I have to.' Neil slid his arms around her waist. 'I've been lusting after you, Mrs Lacey, since the day I first set foot in the salon.'

'But I'm thirty-eight,' Alice gasped.

'I don't care if you're eighty-eight, you're utterly adorable.' He pulled her towards him and hugged her very tight.

'Neil.' She tried to struggle out of his arms. 'You've had too much to drink.'

'No, it's you who hasn't had enough. Stay still, Alice. I promise I won't touch you anywhere that's out of bounds.'

Alice sat stock still, knowing she should leave, but curiously reluctant to move an inch, while Neil traced her eyebrows with his finger, then her ears, her cheeks, her nose. The world had gone very quiet and, apart from the ticking of a clock somewhere, there wasn't a sound to be heard. Neil's firm finger traced her jaw and she could smell soap on his hand. John had always been a tender lover, but he'd never done anything like this. The finger moved to her lips and Alice felt as if her bones had melted inside her body. Then Neil bent forward and kissed her gently, ever so gently, on her forehead and she couldn't resist another minute. She flung her arms round his neck, feeling like a wanton woman, but not caring a bit.

Chapter 7
1956

Maeve Lacey got engaged on her twenty-first birthday. Her fiancé, Martin Adams, was a colourless, fussy young man who was a radiographer at Bootle hospital. They had been courting two years, but weren't planning to get married until Maeve was a State Registered Nurse and they had saved up a deposit for a house.

Alice was pleased that it all sounded so very sensible when compared with Orla's shotgun wedding. She remarked as much to her friend, Bernadette, who was helping prepare the food for what would be the party to end all parties that night.

'Me and Bob were sensible, and look where it got us?' Bernadette said darkly. 'Absolutely bloody nowhere.'

'Yes, but you're all right now.' Alice giggled. 'Mam!'

'Oh, shurrup.' Bernadette nudged her friend's ribs. 'Stop being so cheeky, else you might get your bottom smacked.'

Three years ago, when Alice had held a similar party on the occasion of her father's, Danny's, sixtieth birthday, Bernie had taken her courage in both hands and proposed.

'Neither of us is getting any younger,' she said to the astonished birthday boy. 'I can't stand you, Danny Mitchell. If the truth be known, you drive me wild, but at the same time I think we'd be good together. I fancy you something rotten and I know you fancy me, so don't look so outraged.'

Danny had spluttered something incomprehensible in reply.

'If you're agreeable,' Bernadette went on, 'I think we should get wed as soon as possible while we've both got a bit of life left in us. And before you accept, I should tell you I'd very much like a baby. I'm thirty-nine, so if we go at it hammer and tongs, there's still time for you to put me in the club.'

Danny had spluttered something incomprehensible again.

'Think about it,' Bernadette said kindly, patting his arm. 'Take your time, but try and let me know before the party's over, so we can announce it, like, while everyone's here.'

Four weeks later Bernadette became Mrs Danny Mitchell and stepmother to her best friend. Within a year Alice was presented with a brother, Ian, and a sister, Ruth, the year after.

Danny was rarely seen in the pub these days, only on Sundays after Mass. He was content to stay indoors with his pretty wife and two young children, and watch the new telly at night, much to the chagrin of the numerous women who'd had their eye on him.

'You've made me dad very happy,' Alice said as she rolled sausage meat into a length of puff pastry. 'And he thinks the sun shines out Ian's and Ruth's little bottoms. I never thought I'd see the day when he'd take two kids in a pushchair for a walk in North Park.'

'Well, he didn't have much alternative, did he?' Bernadette sniffed. 'I'd promised to give you a hand.' She removed a baking tray from the oven. 'How many jam tarts do you want? There's a dozen here and another dozen just on finishing.'

'Well, there's thirty coming,' Alice said thoughtfully, 'but not everyone will want a tart. I reckon that's enough.'

'What shall I do now?'

'Pipe some cream on those little jellies, then sprinkle them with hundreds and thousands. Oh, by the way, could you bring some teaspoons when you come tonight? I haven't enough to go round. And some glasses too, if you've got any.'

'Of course we've got glasses. What do you think we drink the sherry out of at Christmas – mugs?'

The two women worked in contented silence for a while, each preoccupied with her own thoughts, while the smell from the kitchen became more and more mouthwatering. Two cats sat on the backyard wall, enjoying the crisp November sunshine and hoping they might be thrown the odd sausage roll.

'Who's looking after the salon today?' Bernadette enquired. 'Sat'days are your busiest day.'

'Our Fion. She's going to manage the new branch in Marsh Lane when it opens after Christmas, did I tell you?'

'Yes.' Bernadette rolled her eyes. 'New branch! Get you, Alice Lacey.'

'To think I used to look up to you when you had that good job with the Gas Board.' Alice wrinkled her nose and looked superior. 'Now you're just a housewife and I'm about to have me own chain of hairdressers.'

'I'd hardly call two a chain.'

'It's a *little* chain.' She laughed happily. 'It seemed a shame not to take on Gloria's when I discovered it was closing down – we were overstaffed once Fion got her certificate and I couldn't possibly have got rid of Doreen to make way for her. Doreen's going to Marsh Lane with

Fion and I'm taking on another qualified assistant for meself. Patsy'll stay with me, naturally.'

'Their Daisy never got on the stage, did she?'

'No, she's married now, with two kids. Her husband's a chimney sweep if you'd believe it.'

'Well, I suppose chimney sweeps need wives the same as other men.'

'I think', Neil said, 'that I could become quite a fan of Elvis Presley.'

'He's OK,' Alice conceded. 'Our Fion's mad about him. She's got all his records. I prefer Frankie Laine meself.'

'This is a great party.' Neil put his hands on her hips and squeezed.

'Don't!' Alice said in a scandalised voice. 'Someone might come in.' They were in the kitchen in Amber Street and the party was going full swing. Elvis Presley was singing something about his blue suede shoes. 'Get out the way, Neil, while I make a pot of tea.'

'Don't you think people will have guessed by now how things are? It's been five years.'

'There's no reason for people to have guessed anything,' Alice said primly, 'and I've no intention of providing them with proof. I've got me reputation to consider and you've got your job. You'd be out on your ear if you were found having an affair with a married woman.' Like her, Neil was usually very discreet about their relationship and she wondered if he'd had too much to drink. 'Anyroad, me daughter's twenty-one today and I've got things to do,' she said brusquely. '*And* she's got engaged. Oh, hello, Cormac, luv. What can I do for you?'

'Are there any more jam tarts, Mam?'

'Sorry, luv. I thought two dozen'd be enough. There's

plenty of jellies, though, some iced fairy cakes and loads of chocolate biccies. You'll find them on the sideboard in the parlour.'

'Ta, Mam.' Cormac vanished.

'He's not going to grow very tall,' Alice said. 'Not like his dad.'

'He's only sixteen, time to grow taller,' Neil said comfortably.

Maeve came in, her face flushed with happiness. 'Are there any clean glasses, Mam?'

'There will be if you fetch some dirty ones for me to wash.'

'I'll get some. Oh, by the way, Neil. Thanks for the scent. It's lovely.'

'I didn't know whether to buy a present for your birthday, or the engagement. Perhaps I should have bought one for each.'

'The scent's perfect. I haven't begun a bottom drawer yet.'

'She seems so certain of everything,' Alice said when her daughter had gone. 'It hasn't crossed her mind that things might change, not always for the better. Mind you, I was just as certain at her age.'

'So was I.' Neil sighed. 'But it's only natural that we expect our lives to pass smoothly along without a hiccup. If we were waiting for everything to fall around our ears, as it did with you and me, we'd all go bonkers.'

Alice opened her mouth to speak, but a girl she had never seen before came in and asked for the lavatory, Maeve brought the dirty glasses, someone asked if there were any more jam tarts and a lad rushed into the yard to be sick. Alice had the worrying feeling it had been Maurice Lacey, who wasn't old enough to be drinking.

Before he disappeared Neil blew her a kiss, which she affected to ignore in case anyone was watching. She poured a glass of sherry and decided to circulate, make sure the guests were enjoying themselves.

In the living room, Fion was conversing with Horace Flynn, whom she had insisted on inviting. Apparently it was all part of the war she had declared on Cora. Alice would have preferred her daughter in the parlour where everyone was dancing. She despaired of Fion ever finding a friend, let alone a man friend – other than their revolting landlord.

Cormac was doing card tricks for an admiring audience, Micky Lavin and Bernadette among them.

She found her dad sitting on the stairs with Orla. 'The ancient and the pregnant are having a bit of peace and quiet,' Danny quipped.

Orla was in the club again with her fourth child. The girl was sorely in need of advice on birth control, but had bitten her mother's head off when she had broached the subject. Still, the family now had a nice little house in Pearl Street since Micky had finished his apprenticeship and was earning a proper wage.

'How are you feeling, luv?' Alice asked sympathetically. It must be galling for someone only twenty-two and heavily pregnant to be surrounded by people mostly the same age who were all single, childless and obviously having a good time.

'How do you think I feel?' Orla snapped. She sometimes wondered if all she had to do was be in the same room as Micky to conceive. She'd heard it was unlikely to happen if you did it standing up. Well, *they'd* done it standing up and Lulu had arrived nine months later. The rhythm system had produced Maisie, the withdrawal system Gary. After Gary, Micky had worn a French letter, but here she was, once again looking like a bloody elephant. Micky must have bought the only French letter ever made that leaked. Every time a baby was born, they forced themselves to hold fire for at least six months, otherwise there'd be children popping out twice a year. When the six months was up, they'd leap upon each other the way people dying of thirst would leap upon a glass of water, draining the glass and wanting more. It wasn't a bit fair and she was fed up with Mr Lavin joking it was about time Micky tied a knot in it.

In future they'd just have to abstain, like priests. The trouble was, she loved Micky to death, though she wouldn't have dreamt of telling him. It was torture to lie in the same bed and not touch each other. And the children were too beautiful for words. Even so, it still wasn't fair.

Nothing seemed fair to Fionnuala either. Everyone was having a great time, but she'd been stuck with Horace Flynn the whole night because there wasn't another person in the house willing to speak to him. Of course, it was her own fault for asking him, but he'd seemed grateful and flattered – Fion suspected she was the only one in Bootle who treated him like a human being. She was definitely the only woman who allowed him to pinch her bum, something he did every time he came to the hairdresser's, which was often. Fion would grit her teeth and pretend to smile. 'Ooh, Mr Smith, don't be naughty!' she would say and move out of the way.

Mam didn't realise the sacrifices she was making to keep Horace Flynn on their side – he never went round to Garibaldi Road these days. The lease would be renewed again in a year's time and Fion hoped they might get it for nothing if she continued to let him pinch her bum. She just prayed he'd never stroke it.

It was galling to think that it was *her* records being played in the front room. 'Love me tender, love me do,' Elvis Presley crooned. Yet not one of those lads had thought to ask her to dance. Didn't they realise she was a fully qualified hairdresser who would be managing her own salon after Christmas?

Oh, if only she didn't feel so *old*! Old and fat, wretched and lonely. Her youth was passing her by, had already passed. She was twenty-three, but had never been kissed by a boy, yet one of her sisters was pregnant for the fourth time and the other had just got engaged. It was even more galling to think they were both younger than she was.

It was a relief when Mr Flynn decided to go home because it was getting too hot. He courteously shook her hand and rolled out of the house on his fat little legs. Seconds later, Neil Greene came and sat beside her, and Fion suddenly didn't know what to do with her hands. He was so handsome, yet not the least bit conceited and very kind. Talking to Neil always made her feel warm inside. She often wondered if he was in love with her, but too embarrassed to say. She fluttered her eyelashes at him encouragingly, but all he talked about was mundane things like the weather and what a great party it was, and he'd like to bet she was really looking forward to being in charge of the new Lacey's in Marsh Lane.

Alice, who happened to be passing, thought with a pang how pathetic Fion looked. The poor girl would feel betrayed if she ever discovered what was going on between her and Neil.

She'd never dreamt she was the sort of woman who'd have an affair, but Neil had caught her at a particularly vulnerable time and it had turned out to be quite wonderful. She had forgotten what it felt like to be loved, to feel feminine and wanted. And it was dead exciting, pretending to work late at the salon and going up to see Neil instead. Or remembering during the evening that there was something she'd forgotten to do.

'I'll just nip round to Lacey's,' she would say, giving a mythical reason, and Neil would be waiting for her, sometimes already in bed, because Alice wasn't prepared to stay long. He wasn't a masterful lover like John. Neil was always concerned that she was enjoying herself as much as he was.

So, what harm was she doing, apart from committing a sin? She wasn't sure if it was a mortal or a venial sin and there was no way she was going to ask a priest. Anyroad, it was only temporary, though it had already gone on longer than she'd expected. Somewhere in the world, she felt convinced, there was the perfect girl for Neil, someone bright and attractive who would give him children, the sort of girl he'd gone out with before but had been too scared to get serious with in case she turned out to be like Babs. *She* was nothing like Babs, *he* was completely different from John and she suspected that was where the attraction between them lay. But one of these days Neil would meet the perfect girl and have no use for Alice any more.

Alice wasn't sure how she would feel when that day came. Devastated, she suspected. She would miss him for as long as she lived. Perhaps that's why she was always so brusque with him, always in a hurry to get back home, because she didn't want him to feel guilty when the time came for him to let her go.

John Lacey had forgotten that today his daughter, Maeve, was twenty-one. He didn't know she had got engaged, or that Orla was expecting her fourth child, that Fion was now a qualified hairdresser and that Cormac had achieved six top-grade O levels before going into the sixth form at St Mary's in September. He wouldn't have known his mother, Meg, had died, had he not read it in the paper. He had decided not to attend the funeral.

It was years since Cormac had rung the yard, asking to see his dad. John had refused, though it had hurt. Cormac had been the favourite of his children, but he felt the need to shed his first family, leave them behind, concentrate on the new.

'Would you like more tea?' Clare said stiffly.

'I wouldn't mind.' He pushed the empty cup across the table. The atmosphere was thick with bitterness and suspicion.

'Is this how you treated Alice?' Clare curled her pretty pink mouth. 'Did you accuse her of going with other men, call her a prostitute, ask how much she'd earned?'

John ignored the question. 'I'd still like to know why the hell you were so late getting home,' he growled.

'I've already told you half a dozen times. It was such a lovely evening. Instead of catching the train from Exchange Station, I walked along the Docky as far as Seaforth and caught the train to Crosby from there. I watched the sunset. Is that a crime?'

'Did you call in the Arcadia, look up some of your old customers?' he sneered.

'No, I did not. I merely enjoyed a pleasant shopping trip to town. I bought a few early Christmas presents. I had a nice time. It's a pity you had to spoil it.' Her voice was as clear and tinkling as a bell.

It was happening all over again, the same thing that had happened with Alice. It was too late now, but he desperately wished he hadn't persuaded Clare to have surgery. He had read about it in a magazine. 'What do you think?' he asked, showing her the article. At first she had been reluctant. 'I have you, I have the children, I'm quite happy as I am,' she had written on her pad. How many pads had she completed in her short life? he had wondered.

'Yes, but you hardly ever go out,' he said. 'Have it

done for the children's sake, if not for mine. They've never heard you speak, not properly. It doesn't affect them now, but it will when they grow older. Let at least one of us be perfect.' He remembered smiling.

Clare had reached out and touched his scarred face. 'What about you?'

'Nothing can be done about me, I'm afraid. The surgeon actually insisted it didn't look too bad.'

She shook her head. 'Surgeon right.' Then she wrote, 'Hardly noticeable, becoming weathered, like a tree or a house.'

The treatment had taken two years, it was more difficult for an adult. She was in and out of different hospitals as bit by bit her mouth and face were repaired with dental surgery, plastic surgery, reconstructive surgery to her palate. At first her voice had been hesitant, whispery, gradually becoming louder, clearer, more confident. She was left with a slight, attractive lisp.

Throughout the two years, during the times she was away, John had been totally supportive. He had arranged for a woman to look after Lisa and David who had yet to start school when the treatment started. He left the yard early to collect Robbie from school, make the tea. They'd been living in Crosby for years, in a large, semi-detached house not far from the shore – he could afford it; B.E.D.S. was doing extremely well.

She hadn't complained, not once, when she returned from various hospitals with her face swollen or badly bruised or in obvious pain or unable to make the slightest sound, though sometimes she looked frightened.

The time came when there was no more bruising, no more pain, no more operations. She began to say the words she'd always known, but could never say before. He'd always understood she was clever, but hadn't realised how clever until she began to talk – about politics, literature, religion, of things he didn't know about himself. She seemed to have opinions on anything and everything, as if she'd been storing them in her head, unable to express them before.

John suddenly realised she was an attractive, clever woman, with steady grey eyes, a small straight nose and a perfect, absolutely perfect, mouth. Even her hair looked different – fuller, shinier, more flattering around her face.

He must have been mad! If *he* thought her so attractive, so would other men. How stupid to have allowed, actually encouraged, her to become an object of admiration! Would he be able to trust her now that people didn't avert their eyes or regard her with an unhealthy fascination? How long would it be before she realised how lovely she was?

His brain was being split in two again, as it had been after that damned fire. He knew in his heart that Clare would never be unfaithful, just as he had known the same about Alice, but there was a different message in his head. He'd already started coming home from the yard at unexpected times to check on her. If she was out shopping, he'd wait until she came back, examining her face to make sure it didn't contain an expression that shouldn't be there. Once she'd been upstairs when he let himself in and he'd later searched the bedrooms, looking under beds and in wardrobes in case there was a man hidden there.

Clare wasn't as patient with him as Alice had been. She quickly lost her temper if he became suspicious. He wondered if her true personality was beginning to emerge, if the real Clare had been hidden until now.

'What did you buy in town?' he asked, doing his best to make his voice pleasant.

'Jumpers for Robbie and David, a woollen frock with smocking on the shoulders for Lisa. I thought I'd keep them for Christmas. I also bought a few small things for their stockings. Oh, and some more decorations. We hadn't enough last year.'

'Didn't you buy anything for yourself?'

Her eyes sparkled. She must have forgiven him for the things he'd said before. She leapt to her feet – even her movements seemed to have altered, she was more lively, more alert – and delved among the carrier bags on the floor. 'I bought myself a frock, almost a party frock. I've never had one before. I thought we could go somewhere on New Year's Eve, a dinner dance, maybe. The woman next door's always offering to babysit. I got it from Lewis's. What do you think?'

She held the frock up against her. It was black velvet, with a ruched bodice, a gently flared skirt and a scooped neck. The sleeves were long and tight, ending in a point. It was an entirely modest frock, but John felt a tightness in his chest when he visualised her wearing it. She would look a knock-out, turn every man's head.

'Oh, and I bought some high heels,' she said excitedly. 'Not very high, I'm not used to wearing them. They're black suede. See!' She slipped out of her old flat court shoes into the new ones and held out a foot for him to admire.

John could stand it no longer. 'Get them off!' he snarled. 'You're not going outside wearing them damn things, nor that frock. And we're not going to no dinner dance either. We'll stay at home on New Year's Eve like we always do.'

She looked at him with curiosity rather than anger. 'What's the matter with you? Did I have my face done for your eyes only? Am I supposed to stay indoors for the rest of my life just to please you?'

'You were quite happy to stay in before.'

'I was.' She nodded gravely. 'I was happy about

everything before, but one of the reasons you persuaded me to have the operations done was so I could go out more. Today was the first time I've gone shopping on my own and been able to ask for things without feeling a freak. Why are you so intent on spoiling everything? Would you prefer I had the treatement reversed, be made the way I was before?'

There was much truth in the last remark. It had all been his idea and now he resented the result. As ever, pride prevented him from explaining how he felt. 'I'm going to bed,' he muttered.

He had reached the door when Clare said softly, 'John.'

'What?' He turned.

She was looking at him pityingly. 'I'm grateful for everything you've done for me,' she said in the same soft voice, 'although I realise it was done solely for selfish reasons. There was a time when you wouldn't have given me a second glance, when you wouldn't have set foot inside the Arcadia. But you did and we met, and the years since have been the happiest of my life.'

She gestured towards a chair, and he returned to the room and sat down. There was a feeling in his bones that what she was about to say was of tremendous importance. His legs were unsteady.

'I've grown to love you,' she continued, 'though I suspect you've never loved me. Please don't interrupt, John,' she said imperiously when he opened his mouth to argue. 'Let me have my say. If you truly loved me you wouldn't act the way you do. You would want me to be happy, not resent me. John.' She leant on the table and stared at him intently. 'I would like us to grow old together, but I am not prepared to be bullied and made a prisoner in my own house.'

'But . . .' he began, but Clare seemed determined not to let him get a word in edgeways.

'If you continue being so suspicious, cross-questioning my every move, then I shall take the children and leave, because you are making our lives unbearable. And that's not the only reason,' she went on. 'I shall leave before you go somewhere like the Arcadia, find a woman you don't feel inferior to and end up betraying me in the same way that you betrayed Alice.'

Where was he? Cora fretted. It was two o'clock in the morning and she'd never known Maurice stay out so late before. Billy's snores rumbled through the house. The snoring had been the reason she'd given for sleeping in the spare room over the last few years. Billy hadn't seemed to mind. Sometimes she wondered why he bothered coming home. It could only be for the warm bed and hot dinners – it certainly wasn't for his wife.

And now Maurice was going the same way. He'd become a labourer, just like Billy, though she hoped, unlike Billy, he'd learn a trade: bricklaying, plastering, something. Now he was earning money of his own and she hardly saw him. Even at weekends he went to the football with his mates and didn't reappear till all hours. Sundays he did the same disappearing act after a late Mass. She suspected he haunted pubs – well, he'd been shown a good example by Billy. Only sixteen, he could have passed for twenty.

There were times when she could have cried at the way things had turned out, but she'd never been given to crying and wasn't sure if she knew how.

Feeling restless, Cora edgily circled the room, picking up the occasional ornament that had given her so much pleasure to buy, but gave no pleasure now. What point was there in the place looking nice when she was the only one who saw it? Whom was she impressing with the house in Garibaldi Road, so much superior to the one in O'Connell Street? No one except herself.

There should be people to show it off to – friends, relatives, but Cora had never had a friend and she'd seen off her only relatives, the Laceys, years ago. Maeve Lacey was twenty-one today and getting engaged at the same time. Perhaps that was where Maurice was, at the party. He continued to be friendly with Alice and her kids, despite his mam's coldly expressed disapproval.

She'd heard about the party on the grapevine. Cora shopped in Marsh Lane and found it a simple matter to keep up to date with the Laceys' affairs. She knew Alice was taking over Gloria's and that Cormac had done so well in his exams that he was likely to go to university.

The key turned in the front door and Maurice came stumbling into the hall. 'Where have you been?' Cora demanded. He looked drunk, she thought.

'A party, Mam. Had a smashing time.'

'Was it Maeve Lacey's?'

'Yeh. I'm going to save up for a gramophone, buy some records. Fion had records and they were really the gear. Elvis Presley.'

'*I'll* buy you a gramophone,' she said. It would be painful, drawing the money out of the bank, but she was often driven to buying him things in the hope of winning him back, though nothing so far as expensive as a gramophone.

She was pleased when his face brightened in gratitude, but would have appreciated a kiss. 'Ta, Mam,' he said. 'I'm off to bed. I'll sleep in tomorrer, go to midday Mass.'

'I'll bring you up a cup of tea around half-eleven,' Cora promised. She watched him go up the stairs two at a time. He was every bit as good-looking as his dad, but was turning out to be a bitter disappointment. But how was she to have known that?

It was time she went to bed herself, except she hardly slept. Her mind never felt rested, never at ease. It used to be full of plots and plans for the future, but now it was more concentrated on the resentments of the present and the past.

It would have been nice to have gone to the Laceys' party. Much better than being at home by herself, with no one to talk to and the house like a tomb. Orla was likely to drop her baby soon and there'd be another big do for the christening. Cora wouldn't have minded going, buying a new frock, even getting her hair set.

Well, she knew what had to be done if she was to get back in with the Laceys. She'd have to tear up that agreement, rip it in two in front of Alice's eyes and give her the bits. After all, the investment, if you could call it that, had been returned a thousand times. It might even result in a resumption of relations with Horace Flynn – these days he only came round to Garibaldi Road to collect the rent.

She'd do it Monday, call in the haidresser's when she went to Marsh Lane shops. She might even buy a present for Orla's baby so they'd feel obliged to ask her to the christening.

Her mind wasn't at its normal feverish pitch when she went to bed and she fell asleep with unusual speed. During the night she was woken by the familiar creak of the third-to-top stair. Either Billy or Maurice was going to the lavvy. But the lavvy was on this floor and there was no need to go downstairs. The creaking sound must have come from the landing, though she could have sworn it was the stairs.

★

'I think,' Alice announced, 'I'll nip round the salon and practise a bit with them new mesh rollers.'

'Why don't you practise at home?' enquired Fion.

'Because the rollers are at the salon. They only arrived yesterday.' Alice wished she'd thought of another excuse. On reflection, this one seemed rather weak.

'Can I come with you?' Fion said eagerly. 'I quite fancy a bouffant hairdo. They're all the rage in London.'

Alice tried to think of a reason for saying no, but couldn't. It was Sunday afternoon and, as usual, Fion was the only one in the house besides herself. Apart from two cigarette burns on the parlour carpet, the house was pristine after Maeve's party the night before.

She was about to say, 'All right, luv,' because it would have been cruel to say anything else, when Maurice Lacey came in the back way, apparently to see Fion for some odd reason, and she was able to escape.

Alice always felt as if she was entering a different world from the one she knew when she went into Neil's flat. Wedding lines had given her and John permission from the Lord to make love, but lying in Myrtle Rimmer's old bed with Neil made Alice feel another person altogether, as if she'd removed her cloak of conventionality and left it outside Neil's door.

There was something faintly indecent, yet at the same time totally delicious, about letting Neil's tongue flutter against her nipples, his hands caress her body, every single part of it. Sometimes the sensations were so intense, so amazing, that she cried out, which Neil said later when she expressed embarrassment was perfectly all right and women did it all the time.

On the Sunday after Maeve's party Alice unlocked the salon door and went inside.

'Is that you?' Neil called.

'No, it's me.' Alice laughed and ran upstairs.

She couldn't find it anywhere. In the end, Cora removed every single piece of paper from the bureau and went through them one by one, but there was no sign of the agreement Alice Lacey had signed ten years before.

Could she have put it somewhere else? No, Cora decided. The bureau in the parlour was where she kept all the paperwork – the electricity and gas bills, receipts for this and that, Maurice's vaccination card, birth certificates. Everything.

It *had* to be here somewhere. She went through the papers again, emptying envelopes in case it had been mistakenly put inside. She was frantic by the time she'd finished and it still hadn't come to light. Perhaps it had been thrown away. Every now and then she sorted out the papers, threw away the old bills, but she surely wouldn't have been so daft as to throw away that agreement, even accidentally.

Mind you, finding the paper wasn't important. All she had to do was *tell* Alice she'd torn it up, that she wouldn't be asking for her share no more – and she'd be accepted back into the Lacey clan. Today was the day she called for her cut, but today she'd tell them they could keep it, though in a nicer way than that.

Cora fetched her shopping bag from the kitchen, put on her camel coat and zip-up boots, tied a headscarf round her pale, greying hair and set off for Marsh Lane.

She did her shopping first. Outside a shop that sold baby clothes she paused and examined the window display. A matinée coat would be nice for Orla's baby, white or lemon so it would do for a boy or a girl, booties to match. She'd get them tomorrow and ask for them to be wrapped in tissue paper before they were put in the bag.

There was a funny sensation in her belly when she turned into Opal Street. She'd made a mint out of that agreement, but it had caused a lot of bad blood and she wasn't sure if it had been worth it. Alice Lacey might be out of pocket, but *she* was the one who'd suffered most.

The bell tinkled when she opened the door. The salon was getting smarter with the years. There were tiles on the floor that looked like polished wood and three gleaming black dryers with leather chairs underneath. The colour scheme had been changed from mauve to orange, though Alice referred to it as 'apricot'. Just inside the door an elegant white desk housed a telephone and the appointment book. The old sinks had been replaced with shallow cream basins on which fat, stubby taps sparkled beneath the neon strip lights.

Although it was Monday morning, the place was already busy. The dryers were all occupied and two of the sinks. That Patsy woman, whom Cora had never been able to take to, was collecting dirty cups.

Alice looked up at the sound of the bell. Her eyes went cold when she saw Cora. 'The envelope's in the left-hand desk drawer as usual,' she said shortly.

'I'd like to talk to you,' Cora said eagerly.

'I'm busy right now, as you can see.'

'*I'll* talk to her.' Fion abandoned the tint she was applying and made for the kitchen.

Cora followed. It wasn't quite what she'd planned, but she couldn't very well say what she'd come to say in front of a crowded salon. And Fion would do just as well as Alice to be told the agreement no longer stood, perhaps better. She quite looked forward to seeing the girl's face collapse when she heard the news.

A kettle simmered in the kitchen. Cora coughed importantly, 'I've come . . .' she began, but Fion interrupted.

'I know quite well why you've come. Aunt Cora, to collect the money you've been doing me mam out of for

192

years.' Fion glared at her aunt. 'You're not getting another penny off Lacey's and I'll tell you why.' She smiled unpleasantly. 'No, I won't tell you, I'll *show* you.' She produced a yellowing sheet of paper from the pocket of her overall and waved it in front of Cora's eyes. 'Recognise it? It's the agreement me mam was daft enough to sign. Now just watch, Aunt Cora.' The girl was clearly enjoying herself. She thrust the paper in the flames spurting from beneath the kettle and it immediately caught alight.

Cora watched numbly as the burning paper was thrown into the sink where it quickly became a few charred scraps. Fion turned on the tap and the scraps disappeared down the drain.

'There!' she said with a loud, satisfied sigh.

'Where did you get it from?' Cora whispered.

'I'll leave you to work that out for yourself.'

'Maurice! Maurice gave it you.' She remembered the footsteps on the stairs on Saturday night. Fion must have asked him to get it at the party, to *steal* it, actually to steal it from his own mam. Cora felt sick to her stomach. 'Can I use the lavvy?'

'You know where it is.'

'Fion,' Alice called. 'What are you doing? Mrs Finnegan's only had half her tint.'

'Coming, Mam.' Fion smiled slyly at Cora. 'Mam's going to be dead pleased, I'll bet.'

'Yes.' Cora scarcely heard. Everything had been turned upside down. Maurice had betrayed her. Her son's loyalty lay, not with her, but with Alice and her family. No one wanted her: not her husband, not her son. No one.

He was beautiful, but then all her babies had been

beautiful. Orla looked proudly down at Paul, her new son.

'He's a fine little chap,' Micky said, equally proud. 'Can I hold him for a bit?'

Orla carefully put the baby in his arms. 'I suppose your mam's spoiling the other three something rotten.'

'Well . . .' Micky grinned. 'Not quite as much as me dad. They're being stuffed with sweets that came from you know where.'

'I know exactly where. The lorry some Lavin or other always seems to be at the back of.'

'Your mam's having them all day tomorrow. She said the salon's overstaffed at the moment, so she can take time off. We're very lucky with our families, Orl.'

'I know,' Orla said soberly. 'We're dead lucky with the kids, too. Some woman had a baby just before me and it died within an hour.'

'Are we dead lucky with each other, though?' Micky glanced at her from beneath his long black lashes.

Orla hadn't thought it possible to blush in front of a man by whom you'd borne four children, but blush she did. 'I reckon so, Micky,' she said in a subdued voice. 'I reckon we're lucky all round in every possible way.'

Their lips met over the new baby and Orla felt the inevitable swirl of desire. She realised that, even if she wore an iron chastity belt, Micky would only have to sneeze and she'd get pregnant.

After he'd gone, the midwife came in. It was the same one who'd delivered Lulu five years ago. 'You're becoming quite a familiar figure in these parts,' she said with a grin. 'I see from your notes this is your fourth.'

'If you work here long enough you'll be present at me twenty-fourth,' Orla said gloomily – it was actually possible to feel happy and gloomy at the same time.

'Have you considered birth control?' the midwife said

helpfully. 'I know it says on your chart that you're a Catholic, but I hope you don't mind my saying this, the Pope's not likely to lend a hand if you have a child a year for the rest of your life.'

'We've tried birth control, but nothing works.'

'Have you heard of the Dutch cap?'

'No.'

'And there's something new, a birth control pill. It only came out last year, so I don't know much about it.'

'We'll try *anything*,' Orla said eagerly. 'Just tell me where to go.'

Chapter 8

It was surprising, but the Lacey's in Marsh Lane was attracting only a very small clientele. Business had been good at first, but had gradually petered off until the salon was doing only half the business of the one in Opal Street.

Whenever she had a spare minute, Alice went round to see if she could recognise what the problem was. She'd had the salon painted in the same warm apricot shade as the other, the same wood effect tiles laid on the floor. There were new lace curtains on the windows and strip lights fitted to the freshly painted ceiling. It looked very different, but the new decoration was a definite improvement on the old. No one could possibly have taken offence.

Yet, as the weeks passed, fewer and fewer women came. Why? Alice wondered.

She got her answer in April when the Marsh Lane Lacey's had been open for four months and Doreen Morrison handed in her notice. Doreen was in her fifties, unmarried, with platinum-blonde hair, always perfectly made up. She was never without a man friend and, years ago, had gone out with Danny Mitchell more than once. She still worked part-time, afternoons and all day Saturday.

'It's not your heart, is it, luv?' Alice said anxiously.

Doreen was a top-class hairdresser and she'd be more than sad to lose her.

'My heart's fine, Alice, it's . . .' Doreen paused.

'It's what, luv?'

The woman looked embarrassed. 'I don't like to tell you.'

'If something's wrong, Doreen, I've a right to know.'

'Well . . .' She still looked reluctant. 'Well, to tell the truth, Alice, it's your Fion. She's impossible to work with. Chrissie's also talking about handing in her notice.' Chrissie O'Connell was the junior, a helpful, friendly girl.

'What does our Fion do that makes her so impossible to work with?' Alice enquired coolly, torn between wanting to side with her child, yet knowing Doreen wouldn't leave without good reason.

'See, I knew you'd be upset. I can tell by the tone of your voice.' Doreen sounded upset herself. 'I wish I hadn't told you.'

'I'm glad you did.' Alice nodded encouragingly. 'Go on.'

'It's just that she's so rude, Alice: to me, to Chrissie, to the customers, except if they're old and then she gushes over them so much the poor dears can't stand it. It was all right when she was working alongside you. You probably didn't notice, but you kept her in line, kept laughing and apologising for her. I tried that a couple of times, but she put me firmly in me place. Told me *she* was the one in charge.' Doreen warmed to her theme, clearly having been smarting over the situation for a long time. 'There's one customer couldn't stand the dryer too hot, kept switching it down every now'n again. Fion was very short with her, told her off in no uncertain terms, and the woman's never come back again, yet she'd been coming to Gloria's for ages. If a customer asks for a one-inch trim, Fion will take off two or three because she thinks it would look better. Or she'll argue over the colour of a tint, or insist someone doesn't suit a fringe when they've had a fringe for years. I often feel – you must, too – that I know better than the customer, but you've got to be dead tactful if you suggest they try something else.'

'I see.' Alice sighed. On her visits to the salon she had noticed Fionnuala was a little brusque, but perhaps she was so used to her daughter's ways that she hadn't realised how much it would grate on other people. She had hoped making her manageress would give the girl the confidence she so obviously lacked, but clearly Fion couldn't be left to run the business into the ground. 'I'll have a word with Fion tonight,' she told Doreen. 'In the meantime, will you think twice about giving in your notice?'

'Of course I will, Alice. I never wanted to leave, it was just that Fion . . .' The woman paused and didn't continue.

'I don't suppose you feel fit enough to work full-time?' Alice said hopefully. 'I'll need someone straight away to manage the place and Katy's only twenty-one and not long qualified.' Katy Kelly was Alice's assistant.

Doreen's beautifully made-up face flushed with pleasure. 'Well, actually, Alice, I wouldn't mind. I was rather hoping you'd ask when the new branch opened. It's only across the road from where I live and it never gets hectic like it did in town. The customers are nicer too, not so demanding. They don't mind waiting a few minutes if there's the occasional rush on. There's just one thing, though, you won't be leaving Fion with me, will you? That would be dead unfair on the girl, us swopping places, like. Despite what I said, I'm quite fond of her.

Her heart's in the right place and she means well. She just doesn't know how to cope with people.'

'I'll let you have Katy. Fion can work with me so I can keep an eye on her.'

'But it's not fair!' Fion raged. 'Oh, Mam, it's not fair a bit. Doreen Morrison has never liked me. She's just making it up.'

Alice's heart went out to her gauche, bungling daughter, who was on the verge of tears. 'Fion, luv, Doreen wouldn't have gone to the extent of handing in her notice if she was just making it up. That would be cutting off her nose to spite her face. And is Chrissie making it up? Because she's thinking of leaving too. And what about the customers? Every week there's fewer and fewer. They're not staying away just to get at you, luv. You're not old enough for the responsibility yet, that's all. You make them feel uncomfortable for some reason.'

'I'm twenty-four.' Fion sniffed.

'It's all my fault.' Alice decided to put the blame on herself. 'Managing a hairdresser's was too much to ask of someone quite so young.'

But this only made things worse, because Fion said tragically, 'Our Orla's got four children and Maeve's a nurse. Running a crappy hairdresser's isn't much when compared to them and I can't even do that properly.'

'Do you really think it crappy?'

Fion laid her head on her mother's shoulder and began to cry. 'No, I loved it. It made me feel grown up and important. Oh, Mam!' she cried, 'what's wrong with me? No one likes me. Everything I say comes out wrong, unnatural, like. I can even hear it meself, this dead false voice.'

'You don't sound false to me, luv.' Alice stroked her daughter's brown hair. 'And don't forget how brilliant you were with Cora. You really knew how to put her in her place. Me, I was willing to lie down and let her tread all over me.'

'You were dead annoyed when I got Maurice to steal that agreement.'

'Well, I must admit I was upset at first, but it wasn't nearly as bad as what Cora did to me in the first place. I realised that after a while. It's nice to have all the money to ourselves.' She'd been so shocked when she heard what Fion had done that she'd actually considered letting Cora continue to have her share, but everyone – her dad and Bernadette, the children – said she was stark, raving mad even to think of such a thing. 'Anyroad, luv, as from tomorrow you'll be back in the old Lacey's with me. It'll be just like old times, won't it?'

Fion nodded forlornly. 'I suppose so.'

Alice told Neil what had happened when he commented on Fion's return to the salon. It was Thursday night and they were in bed together, having just made very satisfactory love.

'Poor kid,' Neil said sadly as he smoothed his hand over the curve of her hip. 'It must be awful to be so self-conscious.'

'The thing is, Orla, Maeve and Cormac have always been so sure of themselves, which can't have helped Fion much. It doesn't help that she eats like a horse, either. She's the same height as Orla, but her waist's at least six inches bigger.'

'When I heard about Babs, I drank like a fish for months,' Neil said thoughtfully. 'I suppose some people do the same thing with food. Fion only eats so much because she's unhappy.'

'Then what on earth can I do to make her happy?' Alice wailed.

'I've no idea.' Suddenly, Neil pinched her waist and she gave a little scream. 'The other day I was offered tickets for a dance at Bootle Town Hall. I turned them down,' he said with an exaggerated sigh, 'because the only person I wanted to take refuses to be seen in public with me. Why don't I take Fion? It might cheer her up a bit.'

Alice looked doubtful. 'Oh, I don't know, Neil. She might get ideas.'

'What sort of ideas?'

'That you're keen on her. She's definitely keen on you, I've told you so before.'

'I could say she was just doing me a favour, getting me out of a hole, because the girl I planned to take had let me down and I didn't want the tickets to go to waste. Actually, I wouldn't mind going,' he said in injured tones. 'I have no social life because of you.'

'Don't tell lies, Neil. You're always off to this and that.'

'Anyroad, about this dance – did you notice I just said "anyroad", which means I've become a genuine Liver-pudlian – shall I ask Fion or not?'

'It might cheer her up, as you say – I can take her into town and buy her a new frock – but don't build up her hopes, Neil. She's miserable enough as it is. I don't want her heart broken as well.'

Fion had virtually stopped eating altogether. She had a slice of dry toast for breakfast, nothing for dinner and more dry toast for tea, because she was determined to squeeze into a size 40 frock for the dance at Bootle Town Hall instead of the usual 42. Alice had agreed to leave it till the very last minute before buying the dress and was actually closing the salon early on the day of the dance, at two instead of four.

'I want something black and slinky,' Fion said excitedly. 'Or really, really bright red, with straps as thin as shoelaces.'

'We'll just have to see,' Alice said, looking at her sharply. 'Why are you getting so excited? It's only a dance.'

'Yes, but I'm going with Neil,' Fion replied dreamily.

'Only as a replacement for the girl he really wanted to take.' Alice hoped she didn't sound too cruel, but it seemed her worst suspicions had been confirmed – Fionnuala was behaving as if Neil had proposed marriage.

Fion said, 'I think that was only a ruse, Mam. I think Neil's always wanted to ask me out, but didn't have the nerve.'

'Neil's never struck me as being short of nerve. Anyroad, he's much too old for you.'

'Oh, Mam, don't be daft. He's only ten years older. Grandad's twenty-one years older than Bernadette and you didn't turn a hair when they got married.'

Alice wondered if she should ask Neil to withdraw the invitation, but Fion would be bitterly disappointed. But she'd be just as disappointed when she realised Neil had no intention of asking her out again. She supposed that as, either way, Fion was bound to feel let down, she might as well enjoy the dance and feel let down afterwards rather than before.

She pleaded with Neil to be gentle with her daughter and he looked at her, hurt. 'As if I'd be anything else.'

Fion felt as if she was, quite literally, walking on air. The dance was all she talked about – the clothes she would wear, what sort of shoes and that if she kept on starving herself she might manage to squeeze into a size 38. She persuaded Orla's Micky to teach her how to foxtrot and they practised in the parlour of the little house in Pearl Street. She endlessly discussed with her mother exactly how she should do her hair: in one of the new bouffant styles, or the smooth look favoured by Lauren Bacall, or piled on top of her head in little curls. Or dare she risk one of them shaggy Italian cuts like Claudia Cardinale?

'For goodness sake, Fion,' her mother said impatiently, 'it's only a dance, not a reception at Buckingham Palace.'

Mam just didn't seem to comprehend the awesome significance of Neil asking her out. Fion had long been convinced that he was attracted to her. He was always so incredibly nice, so warmly understanding. Whenever they spoke, he gave her his undivided attention and asked all sorts of questions. Of course, Neil was nice to everyone, but she could tell she held a special place in his heart. He probably hadn't asked her before because he thought Mam might disapprove or Fion might turn him down. She didn't delve too deeply into exactly why he'd asked now, but he'd asked and that was all that mattered.

It was easy to imagine a bright, starry future – marrying Neil in about a year's time – she'd be down to size 36 by then and would wear one of those wedding dresses with a three-tiered skirt and have a bouquet of white roses with trailing ribbons. Orla could be a matron of honour and Maeve a bridesmaid – gosh, she'd, actually be getting married *before* Maeve! They would live somewhere dead posh like Crosby or Blundellsands, because teachers didn't normally live in places like Amber Street, except if they were unmarried, like Neil – like Neil was *now*.

The dance was three weeks away, two weeks, then only seven days. Fion continued to starve herself. Mam made her drink a glass of milk night and morning, and said it wouldn't do her any harm to lose a few pounds, dance or no dance. Mam positively refused to get into the spirit of things.

Only twenty-four hours to go. Fion lay on the bed in her room, her face covered in a mud pack and her feet on the headboard, which made the blood rush to the head and was good for the hair or the skin or the brain. Something.

Mam shouted up the stairs, 'I'm just nipping round to the salon for a few minutes. One of the dryers is playing up. I think it needs adjusting.'

'OK, Mam,' Cormac shouted from his bedroom in the new, deep voice he'd recently acquired. He was studying for yet more exams, but never seemed to mind.

'Tara, Mam,' Fion said tightly for fear she'd crack the mud pack, which felt like concrete and still had another five minutes to go.

The five minutes seemed to take for ever. Fion went downstairs and splashed the mud off in the kitchen. She went into the living room and examined her face in the mirror over the mantelpiece, and tried to decide if her skin looked softer, clearer, healthier, firmer, all the things it had promised on the packet. She wasn't quite sure. Mam had said the mud pack was a waste of time and money because Fion already had beautiful skin.

She had nice hair, too, thick and brown. But it was a very *ordinary* brown. Perhaps if Mam used one of them Tonrinzes when she set it tomorrow morning, auburn, say, it would bring out the highlights. She wondered if Mam had auburn in stock. She'd ask the minute she came home. No, she wouldn't. She'd go round now and check and, if necessary, call in the chemist's first thing tomorrow and buy one.

There was no need for a coat, not even a cardy, on such a lovely May evening. The sun was sliding behind the roofs of the houses, a great, flaming ball, briefly turning the grey slates into sheets of gleaming gold. Fion hummed to herself as she hurried along the street and through the entry into Opal Street. She opened the door of the salon, expecting to find her mother fiddling with a dryer – she hadn't noticed one was giving trouble. She was surprised to find no sign of Mam, either in the salon or the kitchen. The back door was locked, so she wasn't in the lavvy.

Perhaps she'd decided to call on Bernadette and Grandad, or she might have gone round to Orla's. Fion checked the box of Tonrinzes, found an auburn and was about to leave, when she realised she hadn't brought a key to lock the door – and why had it been unlocked in the first place? Mam must have forgotten to lock it when she left. Never mind, Neil would do it when he came home. She assumed he was out as there wasn't the faintest sound from the flat, no gramophone, no wireless.

She was about to leave a second time when she heard a woman laugh. The woman laughed again and Fion recognised Mam's warm, rusty chuckle.

From upstairs? Fion frowned. There was nothing wrong with Mam being upstairs, but why had it been so quiet until she laughed? And there was something odd about the laugh, something *intimate*.

Fion went to the bottom of the stairs. For some reason she felt reluctant to call out, announce her presence. She crept up a few steps until her eyes were level with the landing floor and glanced through the banisters. Neil's parlour, once a bedroom, was at the front. The boxroom was now the kitchen and the bedroom overlooked the backyard.

The doors to the parlour and kitchen were wide open, the one to the bedroom firmly closed and it was from behind this door that Fion heard her mother laugh again. Then Neil said something in a tone of voice she'd never heard him use before, soft and tender, throbbing with passion.

Mam was in bed with Neil Greene!

She could never remember leaving the salon, going home, but she must have done, because she was lying on the bed again – not crying, because she would never cry again, just staring at the ceiling, cold and shivering, numb with shock. Neil was in love with Mam, not her. He'd probably invited her to the dance because he felt sorry for her. It might even have been Mam's idea, to sort of make up for being demoted, for no longer being manageress of Lacey's in Marsh Lane.

'My life is a failure,' Fion said aloud.

'Did you just say something, sis?' Cormac shouted.

'No,' she shouted back.

'A complete failure.' She was whispering now, though there was no need to whisper, because everyone knew. Doreen Morrison and Chrissie O'Connell had refused to work with her, the customers hated her, her family felt sorry for her. 'I'm useless. There's something wrong with me.'

Fion felt overwhelmed by a black cloud of hopelessness and despair. When Mam came home, she shouted that she had a headache and had gone to bed early, and no, she didn't want an aspirin, thanks.

'I think you should start eating properly again as from tomorrer,' her mother called. 'I reckon you're overdoing it.'

'Yes, Mam.'

Maeve came home from her night out with Martin and Fion pretended to be asleep. She remembered she'd planned on having Maeve as a bridesmaid and wanted to curl up in embarrassment at even thinking such a thing. What a fool she'd been! And what was going to happen tomorrow? There was no way in the world she would go to that dance with Neil, and what reason could she give for refusing? If only she hadn't gone on about it so much to everyone she knew.

There was only one thing for it, Fion decided after a while, she'd just have to leave home.

When Fion woke up it was daylight, bright and sunny, though when she looked at her watch it was only six. The house was silent. She lay watching the sun filter through the curtains and asked herself if she still wanted to leave home.

She decided she did and that she would leave now, without telling anyone, before they got up, though she'd write a note. If she told Mam first, she'd only try to talk her out of it. Anyroad, she liked the idea of giving everyone a shock. Once she'd gone, they might appreciate her a bit more. She would come back in a year's time having made her fortune. Fion visualised herself with 36-inch hips and wearing a dead smart costume – black and white check with a velvet collar. She would be nice to everyone, not a bit toffee-nosed.

Unfortunately, the family didn't possess a suitcase. She managed to squeeze her underwear and a nightdress into the leatherette shopping bag that hung behind the kitchen door, and two frocks, a cardigan and some stockings into an Owen Owen's carrier bag with a string handle. She'd just have to wear her coat, which was a pity, because the day looked as if it was going to be a scorcher. It took some time deciding which shoes to wear, because sandals would look silly with the coat and heavy shoes equally silly in hot weather. In the end she decided on the shoes and managed to squeeze a sandal into each of the bags.

What to say in the note? One of Cormac's exercise books lay on the table. Only a few pages had been used.

She tore a page out of the middle, picked up Cormac's fountain pen and sat staring at the blank paper. She wanted to write, 'I'm going because I'm dead miserable and no one loves me,' so they'd all feel guilty and sorry for the way she'd been treated. But it might be better to leave them full of admiration for her bravery and spirit of adventure. 'I'm off to see the world,' she could put. 'Don't know when I'll be back.'

Upstairs, the springs creaked on the double bed and Fion wasn't sure what got into her, because all she wrote on the paper was, 'I know about you and Neil. Tara for ever, Fion.' She folded it up and tucked it behind a statue on the mantelpiece, because if Mam found it straight away she'd only come chasing after her. Flinging her handbag over her shoulder, she picked up the bags and left by the back way, which was quieter.

A few minutes later Fion had reached Marsh Lane, already having doubts and wishing she'd left the note in a more conspicuous place. She kept looking back, praying Mam would appear and persuade her to come home. If only she had a friend in whom she could confide, who would give her some encouragement, say she was doing the right thing. Or even talk her out of it, which would be even better. But there was no one.

Except Horace Flynn! He was the only person who didn't make her feel stupid, who was always pleased to see her. It was very much out of her way, but she'd call on him and say tara.

Horace Flynn didn't welcome the knock on his door at such an unholy hour. It was barely seven. If he hadn't thought it might be the postman with a registered letter containing someone's unpaid rent – it happened occasionally – he would have ignored the knock and stayed in bed.

Wrapping his roly-poly body in a plaid dressing gown, he went downstairs and found Fionnuala Lacey outside. Had it been anyone else in the world, he would have given them the sharp edge of his tongue, slammed the door in their face, but he'd always had a soft spot for Fionnuala, though even she wasn't exactly welcome at such an early hour.

'I'm running away from home,' the girl said breathlessly. 'I've come to say tara.'

The landlord was a lonely man, entirely friendless until he'd struck up a sort of relationship with this unsophisticated and rather naïve young woman. He felt hugely flattered that she'd come out of her way to say goodbye and stood aside to let her in. 'I'm very sorry to hear it,' he said, which was true. 'Would you like a cup of tea?'

'I'd love one. There wasn't time at home. I had to leave before anyone got up, see.'

'Is there any particular reason why you're running away from home?'

Fion followed him down the hall into the nicely furnished living room. She couldn't very well tell him about Mam and Neil. 'I'm twenty-four,' she said. 'I thought it was about time. I'm going to have lots of adventures.'

'I hope you do,' said Horace Flynn, who'd left Ireland forty years before in search of adventure and ended up a landlord whom no one liked. He noticed Fion's two inadequate bags. 'Would you like a suitcase?'

'If you've got one to spare. Call it borrowing. I'll bring it back one day.'

'Keep it. I doubt if I'll ever need it.' Horace put the kettle on and went upstairs. He returned with a leather case with straps, which someone had once given him in lieu of rent.

Fion looked pleased. 'That's big enough to take me

coat. I'll change me shoes, if you don't mind, put me sandals on.'

'Go ahead.' The kettle boiled. Horace made the tea and returned with two dainty cups and saucers on a tray. 'Do you take sugar?'

'I did till a few weeks ago. I don't now.'

'I thought there was a big dance tonight? You were buying a frock this afternoon, getting your hair done. You seemed to be looking forward to it, if I remember right.'

'I was, but I'm not now.' Fion shrugged nonchalantly. She was kneeling on the floor, folding her clothes inside the case, trying not to let him see her underwear in case it inspired him to pinch her bottom.

Horace sighed. 'I'll miss you.'

'I'll miss you too.'

It was worth being dragged so early out of bed for that. 'Have you got enough money?' Horace was astonished to hear the words come from his lips.

'Yes, thanks. I've got twelve pounds. It's me birthday money. I mean, it's what I've been saving up to buy presents.'

'That won't go far – where are you going, London?'

'I hadn't thought about it. I suppose London seems the obvious place.' People didn't run away to Birmingham or Manchester or Leeds.

'Just a minute.' Horace went into the parlour and opened the strong box which he kept hidden inside an antique commode. He removed twenty pounds, returned to the other room and handed the money to Fion.

She blushed scarlet. 'I can't take all that! It wouldn't be right.'

'It wouldn't be wrong either. If you like, look upon it as a loan. Once you're on your feet, you can pay me back. You don't want to come running home with your tail between your legs because you're out of money, do you?'

'No.'

Horace had the feeling that she didn't want to run away, that she wouldn't have minded being talked out of it. He felt tempted to dissuade her, because he would have preferred her to stay, but was prevented by a feeling of unselfishness that surprised him. He glanced at her fresh, innocent, unhappy face. It would do her good. She'd make proper friends, learn to be independent, find herself.

'Good luck,' he said.

Fion gulped down the remainder of her tea and got to her feet. 'I'd better get going.'

'You'll find plenty of cheap bed and breakfast hotels around Euston Station. They usually have the prices in the window. It would be best to stay there until you find somewhere permanent to live. Don't speak to any strange men,' he added warningly, suddenly concerned that the station would be teeming with men waiting for young girls like her to prey on, offering somewhere 'safe' to live.

'I won't. Thank you, Mr Flynn.'

He picked up the suitcase and took it to the door. 'Good luck again.'

'I'll send you a card as soon as I'm settled.'

'I'd appreciate that. I shall worry about you.'

'I know about you and Neil. Tara for ever, Fion.'

Alice's heart thumped painfully when she read the note that had been left on the mantelpiece. It was the first thing she'd noticed when she came downstairs.

How did Fion know? It could only be that she'd come

to the salon last night and heard Neil and her upstairs. She remembered thinking she'd heard a noise.

'I'm sure the salon door just closed,' she'd said.

'As long as it didn't open,' Neil had replied lazily. 'Come here! It's been a good five minutes since I've kissed you.'

She'd let him kiss her, forgotten about the noise. Until now. Poor, poor Fion! She'd be heartbroken. Alice, overwhelmed with guilt, was desperately trying to think of the best way of dealing with the situation when it dawned on her that Fion had written 'Tara for ever'.

She went to the bottom of the stairs. 'Fion!' she called, hardly able to breathe as she waited for an answer.

It was Maeve who shouted back. 'She's not here. She woke me up at the crack of dawn creeping about. That wardrobe door creaks like mad, Mam. It needs oiling.'

'Oh, my God!'

'What's up, Mam?' Cormac had woken.

'It's our Fion. I think she's run away.'

But she wouldn't run away for long, Alice told herself, not Fion. Fion was too clinging. She needed her family far more than the others. She wouldn't know how to manage on her own. Alice would like to bet she'd be back before the day was out – it might even be within a few hours, because she hadn't the nerve to go too far. Why, she might even be wandering around North Park at this very moment, already thinking about coming home.

When she did, she would have to be told what had happened between Neil and her mother as tactfully and as gently as humanly possible and then hope they would be able to keep the secret between the three of them.

Alice tried not to worry too much as the hours passed and still Fion didn't come home.

★

The hotel was called St Jude's, merely a large terraced house amid a long row of identical properties. It was spotless, but cleanliness was its only good point, unless you counted the strong smell of disinfectant that pervaded every nook and corner. Fion had never seen such a miserable room as the one in which she had just unpacked her case, transferring the clothes on to wire hangers in the wardrobe. A bottle-green candlewick quilt with bare patches covered the double bed and the heavy curtains were the same gloomy colour. The walls were possibly gloomier, a pale, muddy brown. There wasn't a single picture or ornament, just a dressing table and tallboy, that didn't match each other or the wardrobe. The floor covering was cheap and shiny, and boasted a faded rug beside the bed. She hadn't exactly been expecting luxury for 12/6d a night, but this was soulless, infintely depressing and suprisingly cold, considering it was such a lovely warm day outside.

'I'll go home tomorrer,' she said to herself. 'I've made me point, staying away a whole night.' She would give Mr Flynn his twenty pounds and his suitcase back.

When she arrived at Euston, she had contemplated catching the same train back, but something had prevented her, she wasn't sure what. Shame, perhaps, at the idea of running away and returning home the same day. Orla would laugh her head off, Maeve would disapprove, even Cormac would be cross with her for upsetting Mam. And poor Mam was probably doing her nut. She shouldn't have mentioned Neil in that note. After all, your mother having an affair wasn't a justifiable reason for leaving home. Neil was only being kind, asking her to the dance. And Mam had offered to do her hair and buy her a new dress. She was even closing the salon two hours early so they'd have time to shop.

Fion looked at her watch: seven o'clock. She'd taken

213

ages wandering around, trying to pluck up courage to enter a hotel, and had chosen this one because it was called after a saint, though she'd never heard of Jude and he mightn't even be a Catholic saint. Then she'd taken just as long sitting on the bed and trying to pluck up more courage to go out. It was twelve hours, almost to the dot, since she'd walked out of Amber Street. She shivered, feeling very odd and out of place in this miserable, anonymous room.

It was too early to go to bed because she wouldn't fall asleep for hours. She glanced from the bed to the door and decided she couldn't possibly stay in, not on such a beautiful evening. She'd have a wash first, but remembered she'd forgotten to bring soap and a towel, a hairbrush, lipstick, her toothbrush.

Fortunately there was a linen towel as stiff as cardboard folded over the sink and a tiny slab of yellow soap. Fion splashed her face, and rubbed her finger on the soap and cleaned her teeth. It tasted dreadful. After changing into one of her frocks, she ran her fingers through her hair, collected her bag and left to explore London.

There was a notice behind the front door announcing, THIS DOOR WILL BE LOCKED AT 10.30 p.m. Fion was about to leave, when the door marked RECEPTION opened and the woman who'd taken her money poked out her head.

'Have you read the notice?' she demanded.

'Yes, thank you.' She was a horrible woman, all sharp corners, even on her face.

'Well, just make sure you remember. I don't open the door to no one after half past ten.'

'I'll remember,' Fion said politely, wondering what on earth she was doing in this strange city, being spoken to by a strange woman as if she were a piece of dirt, when she could have been at home. She must be mad.

Outside, a huge, glittering sun hung low in the sky.

This was the same sun that was setting on Amber Street the day before when she'd been on her way to the salon. Things had changed so much since then.

Fion made her way back to Euston Station, then wandered along Euston Road, which was busy with traffic, though there were few pedestrians. She came to a road full of shops, all closed, naturally, though there were more people around. It was called Tottenham Court Road, she noticed as she crossed towards it, and it was very long.

At the end she reached a busy junction where a man was selling newspapers, shouting in what could have been a foreign language for all the sense it made. There was a cinema with a large queue outside, several cafés and a stall offering souvenirs of London: mugs and tea towels and replicas of London buses. People were pouring up steps from the bowels of the earth. Fion rounded a corner and found herself in Oxford Street.

She'd heard of Oxford Street. She must be in the very epicentre of London. Regent Street was probably not far away and Piccadilly Circus. Returning to the kiosk, she bought a map of London, despite it being a waste of money. After all, she was going home tomorrow. She noticed the film on at the cinema was *War and Peace* with Henry Fonda and Audrey Hepburn, which she'd planned on going to see with Mam when it came to Liverpool.

There was a self-service café at the top of Oxford Street. Fion went in for something to eat and to study the map – she must have lost pounds today, all she'd had was Horace Flynn's tea.

After she'd devoured two ham sandwiches and drunk a pot of tea, she found Piccadilly Circus on the map and began to wander towards it, pausing frequently to stare at the beautiful clothes in the very expensive shops. Regent Street was particularly grand and even more expensive.

The sun was setting lower now, casting sharp black shadows across the street, and the pavements were crowded with pedestrians, some wearing evening dress, obviously off to nightclubs or cocktail parties or theatres, or wherever people went in London on Saturday nights. As she passed a place called the Café Royal, a big, black car drew up and two women alighted, both wearing long satin frocks and smelling richly of perfume. One woman had a white fur cloak draped round her shoulders, which Fion thought was showing off a bit, as it was far too warm a night for furs.

She found she had arrived at Piccadilly Circus, which was drenched in golden sunshine and throbbing with life. The steps around the statue of Eros were crowded and neon lights flashed palely in the evening sunshine. Fion glimpsed a Boots chemists, still surprisingly open. She went in and bought the toiletries she'd forgotten to bring, which made a big hole in her money. Then she dodged through the traffic towards Eros, climbed a few steps, and sat down between an elderly couple with a small dog and a young man with a haversack at his feet. The dog, on a lead, came waddling towards her. She stroked it and the couple smiled. 'He won't bite,' the woman said. 'Lovely evening, isn't it?'

'Lovely,' Fion agreed and found herself smiling broadly for no reason, conscious of a strange mechanism behind her eyes making them sparkle brilliantly. She gasped and excitement coursed through her body like an electric shock, accompanied by a feeling of enormous triumph. Maeve might well be a nurse and Orla have four children, but neither had ever made it to London on their own. No one she knew had sat on the steps of Eros on Saturday night, breathing in the heady atmosphere, the *foreignness* of it all.

The young man beside her thrust a bar of chocolate in her direction. Fion took a square and muttered her thanks. It was dark and tasted bitter. It turned out the young man, like the chocolate, came from Belgium. He spoke only a few words of English and Fion didn't know a word of French, so communication was limited, though very pleasant. He left after a while, saying something about a youth hostel. Fion remembered she had to be back at the hotel by half-ten. Somewhat reluctantly, she started back. She'd probably walked further than she'd thought and had better give herself at least an hour. According to the map, the steps leading down to the bowels of the earth that she'd passed several times were stations on the London Underground. The system looked very complicated and this wasn't the time to try it out for the first time.

She would disentangle the workings of the Underground tomorrow and hoped it would be a nice day to explore the further wonders of London.

Fion entirely forgot that tomorrow she had made up her mind to go home.

While Fion was on her way back to the hotel, in Liverpool in the flat above Lacey's hairdressing salon Alice and Neil Greene were having an argument, something that didn't happen often. They usually got on exceptionally well. Had things gone as planned, Neil and Fion would have been at the dance by now.

They were in the parlour, fully dressed, sitting separately on each side of the empty fireplace. Alice had flatly refused to go to bed. She'd come for one reason only, to tell Neil their relationship must end.

'Just because Fion found out?' His jaw sagged.

'No, of course, not,' Alice snapped. 'Well, yes, in a way, I suppose it is. If Fion found out, then so can other people. I'm surprised we've gone a whole five years without anyone finding out before.' The trouble was, time had flashed by. It was half a decade since she'd confronted her husband in Crozier Terrace and discovered he was leading two lives, yet it felt like only yesterday. 'She must have heard us, Fion, last night when we were upstairs. Remember I said I thought I heard the door close?'

'Hmm.' Neil stared at the ceiling, then said casually, 'Why don't we get married?'

'Oh, don't be stupid, Neil,' Alice said more brutally than she intended. 'In case you haven't noticed, you've already got a wife and I've got a husband.'

'Babs regularly asks me to divorce her. You could divorce your husband; you've got enough grounds.'

'Oh, yes, and have me dirty linen washed all over Bootle. I'd look a right fool, wouldn't I? Me husband sets up house with another woman, has another family. What would people think?'

Neil said gently, 'Is that all that matters to you, Alice? Your reputation, what people think? Surely happiness, yours and mine, comes first?'

'I wouldn't be happy, knowing people were laughing at me behind me back,' Alice replied. 'And what about me kids? I've never told them what their dad got up to. They think he just left home, full stop. I'd sooner they never knew. They've already been hurt enough, particularly Cormac.'

'In other words there's no hope for us.' His face looked very drawn all of a sudden. 'I suppose it's no use asking you to come away with me so we can live together somewhere else?'

'No use at all, Neil. I belong here, with me family.'

'Have you ever loved me? You've said it enough times.'

'I *do* love you, Neil.' But not enough to get divorced. Even if the divorce went through without a public scandal, she wasn't the type of woman who got rid of her husband. She'd married John for better or for worse. They were joined together in the eyes of God for ever and a day. 'Oh, luv,' she said, more gently now, 'I shouldn't have let it go on for so long. I've been wasting your time, preventing you from meeting someone else. Even if there was nothing to stop us, I would never marry you, Neil. You're too young, I'm too old and I could never bring meself to meet your family, not with me speaking the way I do. I'd like you to marry someone young enough to give you children. Mind you, if word got round you were getting divorced, you'd lose your job. You work in a Catholic school, remember.'

Neil almost laughed. 'I suppose that means I'm stuck with Babs for the rest of my life.'

'Unless you get another, different kind of job, I suppose it does.'

'So, this is the end?'

'No, luv, it's just the beginning. It's been very nice, but we've been wasting each other's time all this while.'

'I certainly haven't been wasting *my* time and I would have described it as more than just nice,' he said drily.

'Oh, Neil, so would I!' Alice ran across the room and threw herself on to his knee. 'It's been truly wonderful, I'll never forget you, but all good things have to come to an end.'

He kissed her softly. 'Not necessarily, my darling.'

'This good thing has, Neil.'

'Do you have to sound so sensible?'

'It's about time one of us did. I'm almost glad our

Fionnuala found out. It's made me see things clearly at last.'

He began to kiss her more passionately and she couldn't find the strength to push him away – perhaps the truth was she didn't want to find it. She wished she weren't so sensible, so religious, so cautious, that she could find the courage to live with him openly and not give a damn about being respectable and what anyone thought. Or that she were harder, like John, able to leave the people she loved behind without a second thought.

But she was none of these things. She was Alice Lacey, who had four children, who lived in Amber Street, Bootle and owned her own hairdressers'. Somehow Alice knew she would never escape these simple facts, because deep down in her heart she didn't want to. She was her own jailer, bound by conventions she would never break. Even her love for Neil, which was far greater than she had ever admitted either to him or to herself, wasn't enough to change her.

He was carrying her into the bedroom and she didn't protest.

'We didn't know last night we would never make love again,' he whispered, 'and I'd like the last time to be special. Promise you'll never forget me, Alice.'

'I promise,' she cried.

It was an hour later when Alice crept out of the flat, leaving behind a shattered lover and some part of herself.

She prayed he'd soon see sense, realise he was wasting his time with a woman who wasn't willing to be seen with him in public, a woman who could never marry him, bear his children.

Oh, but she would never forget him, Alice thought as she hurried home, fighting back the tears.

She increased her pace. Neil wasn't the only person

who made her want to cry. There'd been no sign of Fion all day. Perhaps she was home by now . . .

But when Alice got back to Amber Street, Fion wasn't there. A worried Orla was, as well as Maeve and Martin, who'd been to the pictures and come back early just in case Fion had shown up.

The only person seemingly unconcerned was Cormac. 'She'll be all right,' he'd said earlier. 'Our Fion will manage better on her own than any one of us.'

'What makes you say that, son?' Alice asked curiously.

'Because she's unhappy, not like us. She's searching for something we've already found. Of course, she might come back today or tomorrow, but if she manages to stick it out for longer, then I doubt if we'll see her in a long time.'

Which didn't exactly cheer Alice up on top of everything else.

Chapter 9

The girl who served Fion's breakfast next morning was a distinct improvement on the woman she'd met the previous night. 'How would you like your bacon, darlin'?' she enquired, smiling sweetly, when she removed the cornflake bowl. She was about eighteen, not exactly pretty, but with big, velvety brown eyes. Her brown hair was badly cut, as if she'd hacked it off herself.

'Well, I don't like it crisp.'

'Neither do I. I'll do it medium, shall I? I won't be a jiffy.'

The dining room was every bit as miserable as the bedroom, possibly worse, with a depressing painting of a frantic-looking stag in the middle of a forest hanging above the blocked-up grate. There were only five other people there: a middle-aged couple, two Chinese girls and an elderly man who wished her good morning when she entered.

Fion sat in the window and ordered cornflakes, bacon and egg, and a pot of tea. Having this admittedly small control over her life gave her a heady feeling of adult responsibility.

The girl arrived with a slice of pink bacon, a neatly fried egg and half a tomato on a plate, as well as a rack with four triangular slices of toast. There was a saucer containing pats of butter and a small bowl of marmalade already on the table.

'Thank you, that looks lovely.'

'Let's hope it tastes as nice as it looks.'

'It did,' Fion said when the girl came to collect her plate. By now, only the elderly man remained, having finished eating and smoking a cigarette. 'Taste as nice as it looked, that is. Do you make the meals as well as wait on tables?' It seemed a lot for one person to do, especially one so young.

'Only on Sundays, when there's not usually many guests. Are you on holiday?'

Fion wasn't sure why she was there. 'I'm going sightseeing today,' she said, which didn't really answer the question. 'I thought I'd start off at Marble Arch and walk through Hyde Park.'

'Well, you've picked a smashing day for it. I hope you see all you want to see. Oh, by the way, Mrs Flowers wants to know if you're staying another night. She said you only paid for the one.'

Mrs Flowers seemed a most unsuitable name for the sharp-cornered woman. 'That's right, I wasn't sure. I'll definitely be staying another night. I'll knock on Reception and pay on me way out, if that's all right.'

'That'll be just fine.'

It genuinely was a smashing day, Fion thought outside, just as the girl had said. For some reason she could smell blossom, though there was no sign of any trees. At Euston Station she bought a guidebook – more waste of money if she didn't intend to stay – then located the entrance to the tube.

She felt quite proud, after buying a ticket, of being able to negotiate her way to Marble Arch, emerging in sunshine that seemed to have got brighter during the short journey underground.

Large crowds were gathered just inside the park and

she noticed several men perched on boxes loudly sounding off about all sorts of things – according to the guidebook, this was Speakers' Corner. One man appeared to be arguing that the world was flat. Fion listened for a few minutes and decided he was daft. She was about to explore the vast greenness of Hyde Park, when at the edge of the crowd she noticed a woman speaker surrounded by about a dozen men, all heckling so ferociously that the poor woman could scarcely be heard above the chorus of insults being thrown in her direction.

'And why shouldn't women be paid at the same rate as men?' the woman wanted to know in a dead posh voice. 'Equal pay for equal work. It's already happening in the public sector, the NHS, the Gas and Electricity Boards, the Civil Service, so why not in the private sector too? It makes sense if you think about it.'

'Rubbish!' yelled a man. '*I've* just thought about it and it makes no sense to me.'

'Women are the weaker sex. They can only manage half the output of a man,' another man yelled.

'Now it's *you* who's talking rubbish,' the woman countered. She didn't seem the least bothered by her voluble and antagonistic audience. She was very tall, with intense black eyes and greying hair. 'During the war, women did the work of men. They worked on lathes and milling machines, they riveted, they welded . . .'

'They screwed,' one man interjected to gales of male laughter.

'They drove lorries and tractors,' the woman continued as if she hadn't heard, 'dug fields, planted corn, joined the Army, the Navy and the Air Force, worked in field hospitals, delivered post . . .'

'Took off their knickers,' the same man shouted and was greeted with more hearty laughter.

'Why don't you take *yours* off, luv? Give us an eyeful.'

'She's nothing but a bloody lesbian. I bet she only shows herself to other women.'

Fionnuala, at the back of the crowd, was aware of the same hot feeling inside her head that she'd had when Cora Lacey tried to bully Mam. 'You're worse than animals, youse lot,' she screamed. 'If it weren't for women, not one of you would be here. Men like you ought to be strangled at birth. You're not fit to live, not one of you. Haven't you heard of free speech? It's what we fought for during the war, but you're not willing to listen to a word you don't agree with.'

The men had turned from the speaker and were regarding Fion with glazed eyes. 'Now, you look here . . .' One took a threatening step towards her, but Fion took an even more threatening step towards *him*.

'Don't like it, do you?' she sneered. 'Don't like it when someone insults *you*. You're lily-livered cowards, that's why.'

'If you were a bloke, I'd give you a punch on the nose.'

'Oh, yeah! Just because me opinion's different from yours?'

The men began to drift away, having lost interest, or perhaps they preferred their own rude heckling to being verbally assailed by a woman, particularly one so young with a Liverpool accent.

'Well, you were a great help, I must say,' the speaker remarked when the men had gone and she was surrounded by just Fion and fresh air. 'It's best to have an audience, even if they're an unpleasant lot, than to have no audience at all. I might have got through to at least one of them.'

'I'm sorry.' Until then, Fion had been feeling very

proud of herself, expecting the woman to welcome support from a member of the same sex.

'That's all right.' The woman grinned cheerfully. 'I know you meant well but, in future, try to structure your thoughts, make pertinent points, don't just come out with mouthfuls of invective. It doesn't get us anywhere. By "us", I mean women.'

'I'm sorry,' Fion repeated.

'That's all right. I'll just have to start again. Here, take a leaflet, so next time you let off steam you'll have the facts at your disposal.'

Fion wandered away. When she looked back, the woman was once again surrounded by a small group of men, several of whom were already shaking their fists.

She tried not to let the incident spoil her day, though every now and then she would find herself thinking up more insulting things she wished she'd said and tried to structure the insults into pertinent points. She read the leaflet, which had been issued by the Equal Pay Campaign.

The park was gradually becoming fuller. People had come to sunbathe, to fish, talk, watch their children play, to sit and lean against a tree and read the Sunday paper, or just stroll across the emerald-green grass on what was undoubtedly a glorious morning.

After studying the map, Fion realised she was now in Kensington Gardens and there should be a café around somewhere. She was longing for a cup of tea, after which she'd go to the Natural History Museum, then catch the tube to the Tower of London. Tonight she'd have a meal in Lyons Corner House, which she'd noticed by Marble Arch, then go to see *War and Peace* in the cinema at the top of Tottenham Court Road.

Late in the afternoon she remembered it was Sunday and, for the first time in her life, she hadn't been to Mass.

She caught the tube to Westminster Cathedral and went to Benediction instead. It didn't make up for Mass, but would do just for today.

The room in St Jude's was beginning to look a bit like home. On the dressing table there were a hairbrush, a lipstick and a *Woman's Own* with a picture of Princess Margaret on the front: toothbrush, paste and a pink flannel on the sink, and that day's pants hanging underneath to dry. On the bedside table the guidebook and map were waiting for her to study when she got into bed, so she could decide where to go tomorrow.

It was strange, but she had felt much lonelier in Liverpool, living within the bosom of her closely knit family, than she did in this anonymous city where she didn't know a soul. It was as if she was no longer her mother's daughter, no longer sister to Orla and Maeve. She badly missed Cormac because he was the only person who'd never done or said anything that made her feel bad about herself.

Before opening the guidebook Fion counted her money. She hadn't touched Mr Flynn's twenty pounds, but the twelve pounds she'd saved for presents had almost gone. Twelve pounds! In only two days! At this rate there'd be no money left by the end of the week. And what was she supposed to do then?

There were two obvious answers: return to Liverpool, or obtain more money, and the only way to do that was to get a job. Fion found it a tiny bit disturbing that she much preferred the second answer to the first.

'I'm sorry, Missus,' the police sergeant said portentously, 'but your daughter's an adult. She can leave home if she wants. You can't expect us to go chasing after a woman of twenty-four. Under eighteen, yes. Over eighteen, folks can do as they please and it's no one's business but their own.'

'But she's only a very *young* twenty-four. She's never even been to the pictures by herself.'

'She's still twenty-four. And she didn't just disappear into thin air, did she? You say she left a note. Have you got it with you?'

'No.' Alice had only shown the note to Neil.

'Did it say where she was going?'

Alice sighed. 'No.'

'Well, it would seem she doesn't want you to know.' The policeman suddenly softened. 'Try not to worry, Missus. She'll soon realise which side her bread is buttered and come back.'

'Let's hope so,' Alice muttered as she left the station.

Fion had been gone almost a week. Alice would have worried more had not Cormac been so convinced she was all right. As it was, she felt guilt-stricken that she'd allowed Neil to ask the poor girl out, build up her hopes, then have them dashed so cruelly. Fion was such an impressionable girl. How must she have felt when she heard her mother and Neil together? She must have come round to the salon for some reason and it could only be to do with the dance the following night. She'd been so excited, *too* excited.

Her other daughters shared their mother's guilt, particularly Orla. 'I should have been nicer to her,' she wailed. 'I was horrible most of the time, yet I felt dead sorry for her.'

'Perhaps she left because she didn't want people feeling sorry for her,' Cormac suggested.

'*I* dropped her like a hot brick when I met Martin,' Maeve moaned. 'We always went to the pictures together on Sunday nights, but we haven't gone for months.'

'It was wrong of me to have made her manageress of the new salon, then just snatch the job away. I should have thought before I acted. She was far too young.' Then there was the business with Neil, which she couldn't reveal. Alice wondered what Fion was doing right now, on Friday night, six days after she had so abruptly left. Whatever it was, wherever *she* was, the poor girl was bound to be alone and as miserable as sin.

Fion was in a pub, the Golden Lamb on Pentonville Road, with Elsa, Elsa's dad, Colin, and Elsa's grandma, Ruby. The pub was bursting at the seams, there was sawdust on the floor, a spittoon in the corner and most of the customers were already sociably drunk. Hidden from view, a pianist was thumping out 'Somewhere Over the Rainbow', his or her foot stuck firmly on the loud pedal.

Elsa was the girl who served the breakfasts in St Jude's – and cleaned the rooms and made the beds, Fion discovered after she'd been there a few days.

'I need to find somewhere to live,' she had confessed to Elsa a few days ago when the money from Horace Flynn was reduced to half. 'Do you know of anywhere?'

They had already started to chat while the breakfast tables were being cleared. She had told Elsa that she'd left home, not run away, which sounded a bit silly at her age.

The hotel was almost full, mainly with commercial travellers – one had given Fion a folding clothes brush and a window leather.

'I'll ask around, darlin',' Elsa promised. 'Do you want lodgings or a place where you look after yourself?'

'Which is cheapest?'

'Lodgings. You get breakfast and an evening meal for an all-in price.'

'Lodgings, then. I prefer the other, but I'll wait till I'm settled in a job.'

'What sort of job?'

'I'm not sure.' Fion made a face. 'Any sort of job as long as it's not hairdressing.'

'Elsa, dear!' Mrs Flowers called from the kitchen. She was always very nice to Elsa. At first, Fion had been surprised, until she realised Elsa was an exceptionally hard worker and very reliable.

'See you tomorrow,' the girl said.

Fion drained the teapot, put the two remaining triangles of toast in her bag to eat later and set off for another day of sightseeing. She wouldn't spend a single penny she didn't have to, so the remaining money would last as long as possible. It meant no more pictures, which was a pity, as she'd be stuck for something to do at night. Yesterday, she'd seen *Seven Brides for Seven Brothers* and fallen in love with Howard Keel, the day before . . . *And God Created Woman* with Brigitte Bardot.

The weather was still fine and the busy London streets were flooded with sunshine. Fion mingled with tourists and shoppers, with office and shop workers, and felt extraordinarily happy. At one o'clock she went to Piccadilly Circus, bought coffee in a cardboard cup and sat on the steps of Eros, eating the toast and feeling on top of the world.

In the Golden Lamb Ruby Littlemore enquired, 'How's the digs, darlin'?' Ruby was mildly drunk on Guinness. She had jet-black, tightly permed hair, purple-painted lips and too much mascara. She was young to be Elsa's grandma, fifty-seven, but then Colin, Elsa's dad, was only thirty-eight and looked young enough to be her brother.

'Not so bad,' said Fion. 'The room's a bit small and nowhere's very clean, and I got tripe and onions for me tea, which I can't stand. Mrs Napier looked a bit put out when I asked her not to give it me again, as if she doesn't know how to cook anything else.'

'She'll think of something,' Ruby said. 'Blimey, you don't need more than one set of brains to come up with sausage and mash. Are you hungry, darlin'?' she asked in a concerned voice. 'Come back to ours later and I'll knock you up a plate of something.'

'Thanks, but I bought a meat and potato pie on the way.' It had been absolutely delicious.

'Come round tomorrer for your dinner, anyway. Sat'days, I usually make a stew with all the leftovers. Elsa doesn't work Sat'days. I don't know if she told you.'

'Yes, she's taking me to Camden Market to buy some dead cheap clothes. I didn't bring enough with me. We're going dancing at the Hammersmith Palais tomorrer night. I'm cutting her hair before. And I'd like to come to dinner, ta.' A midday meal wasn't included in the thirty-five shillings a week Mrs Napier charged.

'Elsa ses you're starting work Monday.' Colin Littlemore, sitting on Fion's other side, couldn't possibly be described as handsome. He was desperately thin, with brown, haunted eyes, hollow cheeks and a soft, curvy mouth. Nevertheless, Fion thought him enormously attractive, far more so than Neil Greene, who hadn't an ounce of character in his face. She thought it odd that she hadn't noticed that before. During the war, Colin had been taken prisoner by the Japanese and put to work building a railway. He had managed to stay alive, but returned home an invalid, unable to work, his health in ruins. There was something wrong with his lungs, he couldn't breathe properly and could only eat the tiniest of meals. He was sitting with an untouched glass of orange juice in front of him. His wife, Elsa's mother, had been killed during the war when the factory in which she worked was bombed.

231

Fion said, 'I saw a notice outside a factory just along the road. It said "Packers Wanted". It's called Pentonville Medical Supplies. I just walked in and they took me on straight away. I start Monday,' she finished proudly. She had a job and somewhere to live in London, and it was as if Liverpool and her family had never existed.

Colin wrinkled his thin nose. 'That company pays terrible rates.'

'Four and six an hour, but I don't care as long as it keeps me going.'

'You *should* care. The labourer's worthy of his hire. I knew a bloke who worked there once. He said they refused to recognise a union.'

Fion wasn't interested in unions. No one had ever talked about unions or politics at home, mainly about hairdressing. She was reminded of the leaflet she'd been given in Hyde Park, which was still in her bag. She took it out and showed it to Colin.

'Quite right, too,' he said after he'd read it. 'Equal pay for equal work; it makes sense.'

'That's what the woman said who gave it me. I suppose it does when you think about it; make sense, that is. Anyroad, I got really mad with the men who were trying to shout her down. I shouted them down instead.'

Colin smiled his gentle, boyish smile. 'Good for you, darlin'. If more people lost their tempers when they thought something was unfair, then the world would be a much better place.' He raised an eyebrow. 'What if Pentonville Medical Supplies are paying men more for doing the same job as women?'

'Oh, gosh! I hadn't thought of that. I suppose I'll get mad, like I did in Hyde Park.'

'Let's hope so.' He suddenly got to his feet. 'I'll have to go.' His voice was suddenly hoarse. 'This smoke don't do me lungs no favours.' The smoke was rising towards the ceiling in white, wavy layers.

'I wouldn't mind an early night. I've had a busy week and I'm dead tired. I'll come with you – that's if you don't mind.'

'It'll be a pleasure, darlin'.'

'I'll just say goodnight to Elsa.'

The pianist was playing 'We'll Meet Again', when Fion and Colin Littlemore left the Golden Lamb and began to stroll down Pentonville Road. He was hardly as tall as her and as slight as a shadow. The tiny terraced house where he lived with his mother and his daughter was two streets along. Fion's digs were down a street almost opposite.

It seemed entirely natural for Fion to link her arm in his thin one. She thought how nice and uncomplaining he was, compared with her own father who'd made the whole family suffer for the injury he'd received during the war, finally doing a bunk and completely disappearing out of their lives.

They walked in companionable silence until arriving at the street where Colin lived. 'Would you like me to come in and make you a cup of tea?' Fion asked.

'I'd appreciate that, darlin'.' Colin patted her hand. He didn't think he'd ever met anyone so vulnerably innocent as Fionnuala Lacey. He remembered reading once that newly born chicks attached themselves to the first human being they clapped eyes on because they didn't have a mother. Fion had left home and attached herself in the same way to Elsa, then to Elsa's family, because she felt friendless and unbearably lonely. At the same time, he reckoned that if circumstances called for it, she could be quite tough.

'I'll send me mam a card tomorrer,' Fion said as they turned the corner. 'She's probably dead worried.'

'She's more likely climbing the walls.'

'I won't give her me address, though. I'll just say I'm all right.'

'That'll put her mind at rest. Actually, darlin',' he panted, 'I think I'll have to sit on the step a minute, get me breath back, before I go in the house.'

Fion sat on the step beside him. 'Is there anything I can do? Rub your back, or something?'

'No, but you can go in and put the kettle on. Here's the key.'

'Ta.'

He heard her run down the hall, anxious to help, then the rush of water in the kitchen, and thought she would make a good, caring mother – and a wonderful wife. With someone like Fion Lacey at his side, a man could conquer the world.

Colin smiled, then gave a little sigh. If only he were younger and in better health . . .

The young woman emerged from the art college into the grey drizzle of the late October day. She carried a large folder, the sides tied together with tape, underneath her arm. In her black and white striped slacks and baggy red jumper, and with her fair hair loose about her face, she looked like a teenager, but the man concealed in the doorway further down Hope Street knew that she was thirty and had three children, all old enough to be at school.

It was for this reason, to collect the children on time, that she was walking so swiftly and purposefully. He knew, because he had watched before, that she would walk all the way to Exchange Station rather than catch a bus somewhere more convenient like Skelhorne Street. A bus could get caught up in traffic and she might be late. She was a conscientious mother to her children.

More students came out of the college. One, a young man in his twenties, saw the young woman hurrying away. His face broke into a smile as he ran to catch her up. The woman smiled back, but didn't pause in her stride. The watching man shrank into the doorway when they passed on the other side.

What were they talking about? Would the chap accompany her all the way to the station? They might even catch the train together. The man in the doorway took a deep, shuddering breath. He smelt danger.

Clare and the young man parted on the corner of Lime Street and he went to catch the train to Rock Ferry. She wondered if John was still watching. Had he followed her this far? Or was he racing back to the factory in the van preparing for tonight's interrogation, starting with, 'Did you talk to anyone today?'

'Of course,' she would say. 'I couldn't very well spend the entire day at art school without speaking to a soul.'

'What about on the way home?'

As he'd seen her with Peter White, she'd have to concede that she had indeed spoken to someone on the way home. It was no good trying to laugh the questions away, because he would just persist and persist until he got an answer, even if it was an answer he didn't want.

'Yes, I spoke to someone on the way home. His name is Peter White, he lives in Rock Ferry and he's twenty-one. His mam and dad are Quakers. Anything else? Would you like his chest measurements? What he has for breakfast? How often he has his hair cut?'

But she wouldn't say all those things, because she'd done it before and John had called her 'insolent' and hit her. She would answer the question simply and leave it at that.

Passing St George's Hall, two men whistled at her

approach. She felt, rather than saw, them both turn and watch her walk away, and was aware of letting her hips swing more widely. It was more than a year since she'd had the operation and her perfectly mended face still gave her a thrill of delight when she caught sight of her reflection in a shop window or an unexpected mirror.

She would always be grateful to John, but he seemed to want more than gratitude and she didn't know what it was — to cocoon her from life, to hide her away out of sight of other human beings. It had been like a red rag to a bull when she said she wanted to go to art school because she'd longed to learn to draw — properly, not the scrawly, amateur things she'd done before.

John had done his utmost to stop her: threatened, bullied, refused to give her the money for the fees. Hit her!

'It's either art school or I'll get a job,' Clare said coldly. 'I'm not staying in the house by myself for the rest of my life.' She was bored out of her mind, full of unusual energy, the urge to explore, get to know people. But it was as if she'd escaped from the prison of her deformity and found herself in another, private, prison with John the warder.

'Meet anyone today?' John asked casually that night when she came downstairs after reading the children their story.

'I meet all sorts of people all day long.'

'I meant anyone special, that is.'

'I don't know what you mean by "special".' She knew she was being awkward, but 'special' seemed a strange word to use. Perhaps it was the only one he could think of to describe the short walk she'd taken with Peter White.

She could tell he was struggling to think of another way to pose the question and felt sick to her soul at the

idea of having to relate in detail the entirely in...
things she'd said to Peter. She wondered what ...
reaction would be if he knew Peter had asked her out!
Imagine telling him *that*!

'I'm going to bed.' She got up abruptly. 'I feel very
tired.' It was only half past eight and she resented having
to go so early, but it was the only way to escape further
interrogation. She would have liked to practise her
drawing.

'I'll be up in a minute. I'm fair worn out too.'

Don't hurry, she wanted to say. Please don't hurry.
These days, she couldn't stand him touching her. His
eager, exploring fingers made her stomach turn. There
was something so *possessive* about the way he made love.
He made her feel like a thing, not a person.

This can't go on, Clare thought as she pulled the
bedclothes around her shoulders. I can't put up with this
much longer. I *won't* put up with it. She'd cast out on
her own before and would do it again, though this time
she wouldn't be on her own but would have three
children. She thought of disappearing to another country, Canada or Australia, but the children had Lacey on
their birth certificates and she didn't have wedding lines
to prove she was their mother. John's authority would be
required before they would be given passports and he
mustn't know they were leaving. She had the uneasy
feeling he might kill her if he found out.

She would finish the art course first so it would be
easier to get a job. And she would need money.
Fortunately, John was generous with the housekeeping.
She'd start putting a few pounds aside each week. It
would take a while, but she already felt better, knowing
there was a future in which John Lacey no longer
figured. She would be free.

'Our Fion? Oh, she's living in London,' Alice announced gaily. 'She went weeks ago. She's having the time of her life.'

'Is she working in a hairdresser's?' the customer enquired.

Patsy O'Leary answered: 'Yes, in this dead posh place in Knightsbridge, not far from Harrods, as it happens.' Patsy was innocently relaying the lie Alice had told her to explain Fion's sudden disappearence.

Alice went into the kitchen and the customer winked at Patsy. 'I suppose she'll be back in six or seven months and the population of the world will have increased by one.'

'Oh, no,' Patsy said, annoyed. 'Not Fionnuala. She's not a bit like that.'

The woman looked suitably chastened and changed the subject to one close to Patsy's heart. 'How's your Daisy's Marilyn?

'Oh, she's fine. You'll never believe this, but she's only nine months old and already walking . . .'

As Patsy had predicted, the customer didn't believe a single word.

Orla only had to mention once to her father-in-law that she would very much like a typewriter for him to arrive at the house in Pearl Street within a week, bearing an old, battered Royal. He winked. 'You'll never guess where this came from!'

'Oh, yes I do.' Orla had known where it would come from when she'd asked him to get it. The backs of lorries proved a useful source of supply whenever they needed something they couldn't afford. Lulu's new bike had come the same way and several other of the children's toys.

'It works OK,' Bert said. 'I've tried it. Managed to

type me own name, though it took a good ten minutes. Where would you like it, luv?'

'In the parlour. Thanks, Bert.'

'Any time, luv. All you have to do is ask.'

Orla was about to joke she wouldn't have minded a mink coat, but held her tongue in case one appeared.

'Now, you look here,' she said sternly to the children that night. 'This is not a toy to be played with. This is *mine*. Do you understand that?' She spelt the word out carefully. 'M – I – N – E. It belongs to your mum.'

'Can you get toy ones?' Lulu wanted to know.

'I'm not sure. I'll ask Grandad.'

'What's it for, luv?' Micky asked when he came home. Maisie and Gary were attached to his legs, and he was holding baby Paul in his arms. Lulu, her arms resting on the table, was taking far too much thoughtful interest in the typewriter.

'To make pastry with.' Orla rolled her eyes. 'What the hell d'you think it's for, Micky Lavin? It's to type on, you great oaf. People used to send little items of local news to the *Crosby Star* and I thought I'd do the same, as well as to the *Bootle Times*. I could even try and write articles. I wouldn't make much from it, but every little helps.'

'We're not short of money, are we?' Micky looked alarmed. Every week he handed over every penny of his wages and Orla gave him five bob back for himself. Otherwise, the housekeeping was a mystery to him.

'We're all right. Not exactly flush, so a bit extra's useful. It means we might be able to afford a holiday. In a caravan, say, somewhere like Southport.'

Micky's dark eyes brightened. 'That would be the gear.'

'Wouldn't it!' Their glances met and Orla's insides did

a somersault, though there was nothing remotely romantic about a caravan holiday in Southport. By now, Orla had expected to be living in Mayfair, interviewing famous people for a top newspaper or magazine. Instead, she was stuck in a little house in Bootle with a husband and four children. She didn't know if she was happy or not.

The children, Micky and Orla collapsed together on to the settee and hugged each other lavishly. Orla wasn't sure if this was happiness, but it would do for now.

Alice was in the throes of buying the lease on a hairdresser's in Strand Road that was closing down.

'Why do you do it, Mam?' Orla asked curiously. She had come round to see her mother one Sunday afternoon. Micky had taken the children to North Park and she felt bored on her own.

'Do what, luv?'

'Keep buying new hairdressers?'

'For goodness sake, Orla. I took over Myrtle's fourteen years ago. There's only been Marsh Lane since then.'

'You might soon have one in Strand Road. That'll be three.'

Alice shrugged. 'I'm not sure why. It's not the money. I suppose I find it exciting. Anyroad, our Fion's gone, and by this time next year Maeve will be married and Cormac at university. I need something to keep me busy, fill up me life, as it were.'

'Oh, Mam!' Orla cried. 'That sounds really sad.'

'Sometimes I feel really sad.' Alice glanced around the room which still had the same furniture that Orla remembered from her childhood. 'I sometimes wonder how things would have gone if your dad were still at home. If only he hadn't had that accident.'

'I'm fed up hearing about the stupid accident,' Orla said hotly. 'Anyroad, it wasn't that that mucked everything up. It was the way he behaved afterwards. There was a girl at school whose dad lost both legs in the war, but he didn't take it out on his family. People are funny . . .' Orla paused.

'Funny in what way, Orla?'

'Things happen and it brings out the worst in people, or it brings out the best. If Dad hadn't burnt his face, we would never have known he was capable of behaving the way he did, or that you were capable of running three hairdressers.'

Alice sighed wistfully. 'We were so happy until that ship went up in flames. From then on, the world just fell apart.'

Orla hurled herself across the room and knelt beside her mother. She slid her arms around her waist and laid her head upon her knee. 'No, it didn't, Mam. You kept the world together for us. We were still happy, despite Dad – and even more happy after he'd gone.'

'You never know people, do you? I thought I knew everything there was to know about your dad.'

'Sometimes people turn out nicer than you'd expect,' Orla said encouragingly. She felt worried, it was most unlike her mother to be so despondent. 'Look at Horace Flynn. He brought you flowers the other day.'

'I know, he still comes round the salon. He misses Fion. They were friends, though I can't think why.'

Because they were two misfits together, Orla thought, but didn't say. 'Our Fion was always very kind,' she lied. Fion could be a bitch when she was in the mood.

'I wish she'd write,' Alice said fretfully. 'Oh, I know she sends cards from London, but they never say anything much. I want to know if she's happy, where she's living so I can write back. I want to know how she *is!*'

Two more years were to pass before Alice received news of her daughter. It arrived in a letter from Neil Greene and was dated November 1960.

Dear Alice,

I know we agreed not to write to each other, but something has happened I thought you'd like to know. Firstly – this is not the 'something' – my divorce from Babs came through the other day. You may not think this relevant but it is, because to celebrate my brother, Adrian, who incidentally became a fully fledged MP following last year's election, invited me to tea at the House of Commons.

I arrived at the House at about five thirty and wondered why there was such a commotion going on. It seemed as if hundreds of women, though it was probably only a few dozen, were gathered outside carrying placards, all shouting and screaming abuse at everyone in sight apart from themselves.

'A Woman's Right to Choose', the placards said, or 'Whose Body Is It Anyway?'. I remembered Adrian saying a Private Member's Bill to legalise abortion was being discussed that day. Although fully in sympathy with the Bill – unlike Adrian, who opposed it – my heart sank a little at the thought of fighting my way through a crowd of such vociferous females. It sank even further when one of the women grabbed me and I thought I was about to be attacked, or at least debagged and subjected to something shameful and possibly degrading.

But no! 'Hello, Neil,' the woman said. It took some time before I recognised it was Fionnuala. She looks wonderful, Alice. Very slim, taller somehow, long wild hair, rosy cheeks and lovely bright, bright eyes.

It was impossible to say much in such circumstances and I shall always regret not suggesting we meet some other time, but then I have always been a bit slow-witted. I managed to ask what she was doing. 'I'm a union organiser,' she said, which I found quite staggering as I can't recall her being interested in politics. I was about to ask where she was living when we were both swept away by the crowds and lost sight of each other.

Fion may have made contact with you by now and you know all this but, in case not, I thought I'd write and let you know she looks fine and you have nothing to worry about.

As for me, I miss Bootle terribly. It was where I felt at home. One day I shall return, I swear it. I miss teaching, too, but it was unfair of me to continue to deny Babs a divorce, and divorce and teaching in a Catholic school were incompatible. I'm working in the City, doing something frightfully dull and frightfully unimportant in Insurance – having a father with a title and a brother in Parliament can work wonders when you're seeking a job. I'm seeing a woman called Heather, divorced like me. We sort of like each other.

An old colleague from St James's continues to send me the *Bootle Times* each week, so I keep myself abreast of what goes on. Congratulations on the new salon – I saw the advert announcing the opening and tried to imagine exactly where in Strand Road it is. How does it feel to have three?

I also saw the news about Maurice Lacey. He seemed a nice boy, though not exactly bright. It came as a shock to read he'd been sent to prison. What was it? Breaking and entering – a newsagent's, if I remember rightly.

I closely study the Birth, Marriages and Deaths

columns. I have been holding my breath, but there has been no mention of Orla under the first, though I noticed the announcement of Maeve's wedding under the second and saw the picture the following week. Was Martin as nervous as he looked? I see Horace Flynn has died. Such a strange man! I trust his properties haven't fallen into the hands of someone who will cause problems for you with leases.

My colleague told me Cormac was accepted at Cambridge. You must feel inordinately proud.

Well, I think that's all, so goodbye, my dearest Alice. You are rarely far from my thoughts.

Your glum and rather lonely friend,

Neil.

She found Neil's letter upsetting and wished they had never become lovers, just remained good friends. Then they could have remained friends when Neil moved away. Alice missed having someone to confide in, even if it were only by letter. These days, Bernadette was completely wrapped up in Danny and the children. Although she and Alice were the same age, Bernadette had had babies when Alice already had grandchildren and seemed to be growing younger as Alice grew older.

Even worse, although she was relieved to hear that Fion was safe and well, it shocked her to the core to learn she had actually been outside the House of Commons waving a placard in support of abortion. Alice was possibly more opposed to abortion than to divorce and the idea of one of her daughters promoting legalised murder filled her with revulsion. Still, no matter what Fion had been up to, she longed for her to come home.

December came, Cormac arrived from Cambridge and she put the contents of the letter out of her mind to concentrate on her son.

Cormac was twenty. He had never grown tall like his father, but had filled out a little. His shoulders were neither broad nor narrow, but they looked strong and the tops of his arms were surprisingly muscled – he'd played tennis all summer, both at Cambridge and, during the holidays, on the courts in North Park, and the long hours spent outdoors had turned his pale skin a lovely golden brown. His hair, a mite too long in Alice's opinion, hung over his forehead in a casual quiff, streaked with white by the sun. He kept pushing it out of his eyes with a brown hand. He looked sophisticated, but at the same time his face still retained the guileless, trusting expression he'd had when he was a little boy. Even then, no one had tried to take advantage of Cormac. He was genuinely liked by everyone and everyone seemed to want him to like them in return.

Alice had been worried university would change her son, that he would grow ashamed of Amber Street and his family. But university had done nothing of the kind. Cormac was proud of his roots. He'd spent weekends in other chaps' houses and they were big, cold morgues of places, where he said he'd hate to live all the time. Most of the chaps had spent their childhoods in boarding schools, which sounded dead horrible and which he would have hated even more. He still talked with a Liverpool accent, possibly not quite so pronounced as before.

Of course, other graduates made fun of the way he spoke, but he didn't give a damn. 'I tell them I'm working class and proud of it, and make fun of the way *they* speak – they call their folks Mater and Pater.' He said he was pleased to be home among normal people.

Working class or not, Cormac must have been popular in view of the number of Christmas cards that arrived for him from all over the country, even more than last year.

On Boxing Day he'd been invited to a drinks party in a chap's house in Chester. He might go, or he might not, he wasn't sure.

The young woman came into the salon a few days before Christmas. Alice and her assistants were at their busiest and the windows were blurred with steam. Alice looked up briefly, then turned away. Patsy was seeing to her. Then Alice looked again and wondered where she had seen the young woman before. It was the hair, more than anything, that looked familiar: very fair, very smooth, silky. Perhaps the woman had been to the salon before, though she didn't often forget a customer and this one was quite outstandingly pretty.

'Alice,' Patsy called. 'Someone would like a word with you.'

'Half a mo.' Alice was combing out Florrie Piper, still a regular customer and still insistent that her hair be dyed the colour of soot, even though she was gone seventy.

'Leave me be, luv,' said Florrie. 'I don't mind waiting a few minutes and admiring the decorations. And it's lovely and warm in here.'

'Ta, Florrie.' Alice went over to the newcomer who wore a smart double-breasted navy coat with a half-belt at the back and navy boots. 'How can I help you, luv?'

'Mrs Lacey? I'd like to speak to you in private.' The request was made so brusquely, without a 'please', that Alice blinked.

'Well, there's only the kitchen.'

'That'll do.'

Alice was aware of Patsy's curious eyes following as they walked through the salon. She felt just as curious herself. 'What's this all about?' she enquired when they were in the privacy of the kitchen.

'I'm leaving John.'

'I beg your pardon?'

'I'm leaving John, your husband. I'm going today. I shall pick the children up from school in an hour's time, then catch a train somewhere far away. I shan't tell you where because I don't want John to know.'

Alice's head reeled. She swayed, reached for a chair and sat down before her legs gave way. She felt confused and very old. 'What's all this got to do with me?' She could hear the tremor in her voice.

'I thought someone should know because he's bound to be very upset and I shall worry about him.'

'I don't understand. Who *are* you?' The woman looked much older close up, at least thirty. Alice remembered where she'd seen her before. '*You're* the girl from Crozier Terrace! You've got a nerve, coming here. There's some women who'd tear your eyes out.' She stared at the face, which had gone very pink. 'I thought you had . . .'

The girl tossed her head. 'I had a hare lip, but it's been fixed and ever since John has made my life unbearable. I wasn't prepared to put up with it any longer. It's taken ages to get the money together, find a place for us to live, get a job. But now I've done it and I'm leaving today. I knew, somehow, you wouldn't tear my eyes out from things John's said. I got the impression your marriage was over long before he met me.'

'Perhaps it was.' Alice was beginning to get her wits back. 'Just let me get this straight,' she said carefully. 'You're walking out, but it makes you feel guilty, so you've decided to plonk the responsibility for what you're doing in *my* lap?'

The woman's face went pinker. 'I suppose I have.'

'That's very nice of you, I must say. What makes you think I give a damn what happens to John?'

'Is there another chair?'

'No.'

'The thing is' – she leaned against the sink – 'in a way, I still love him. I feel terrible for what I'm about to do. I imagine him coming home tonight, finding us gone.' She twisted uneasily. 'He'll be devastated.'

'And you think me turning up with buckets of sympathy will make him feel less devastated?' Alice laughed in disbelief. 'I never want anything to do with him again.'

'I thought you might possibly care.'

'Well, I don't. And if you love him all that much, then why are you walking out?'

'Because I think one day I might hate him.' She stared at the older woman almost angrily. 'Surely you understand? I love him because I know how kind and gentle he can be. He's wonderful with the children.' She pointed to her lovely face. 'John was responsible for this. It's changed my life, but the trouble is it changed him too. He became a different person. He couldn't bear me out of his sight. Did he ever hit you?'

'Just the once.' It all sounded very familiar. Alice frowned. 'Has he hit you?'

'Rather more than just the once.'

Patsy stuck her head round the door, her ears almost visibly flapping. 'Your next customer's here, Alice, and Florrie's still waiting to be finished off.'

'I'll have to go.' Alice got to her feet. Her legs still felt as if they were filled with jelly.

'I hope I haven't upset you.'

'Of course you've upset me. Who wouldn't be upset under the circumstances? All *right*, Patsy, I'll be out in a minute.' Patsy disappeared with obvious reluctance. 'I tell you what, I'll ask me dad to go round and see John, make sure he's all right. I'm not prepared to go near him.' It meant she'd have to tell Dad what had happened, that John had got himself another family, that he hadn't just walked out. Neil was the only person who knew the real truth. 'Are you still living in Crozier Terrace?'

'No, we moved ages ago. We're in Crosby now, 8 Rainford Road. Thank you. I appreciate you being so nice about this.'

'I don't feel a bit nice,' Alice said drily. 'Out of interest, what's your name?'

'Clare Coulson.' She paused at the kitchen door. 'Goodbye, Alice.'

'Good luck, Clare.'

Danny Mitchell didn't think he'd ever been asked to carry out a task that filled him with such revulsion. If he arrived at Rainford Road and found John Lacey with a rope and about to hang himself, his first instinct would have been to help him tie the knot. But it was a long time since Alice had asked for his help, possibly too long. Danny was uncomfortably aware that he had neglected his daughter, so wrapped up had he been in his young wife and their children. Alice hadn't exactly lost her dad and her best friend when Danny married Bernadette, but as good as. Neither was available for her in the way they'd been before.

His heart was full of loathing for his son-in-law. Alice had explained to him and Bernadette the real reason why the marriage had broken down.

'Oh, luv! You should have told us all this a long while ago,' Bernadette cried. She looked anguishedly at Danny and he could see his own guilt reflected in her eyes.

'I felt ashamed,' Alice said simply. 'I didn't want anyone to know.'

'It's nothing to be ashamed of.' Danny's voice was gruff. 'John's the one who should be ashamed. He brings misery on everyone he touches.'

'Anyroad, Dad. This girl, this Clare Coulson, she's worried about him.'

'She's got a nerve!' Danny and Bernadette said together.

'Actually, I quite liked her. She's got spunk, which is more than I ever had. I just sat back and let things happen.'

'You say he actually hit her?'

'Yes, Dad.'

'I'll sort him out,' Danny said grimly.

'No one wants you to sort him out, luv,' Bernadette put in. 'You're just going to make sure he's all right, that's all, like Alice promised.'

'I'd like to sort him out with me fists.'

'John's years younger than you, Danny Mitchell. I don't want you coming back here with a black eye and a broken nose. Forget your fists and use your mouth instead.'

'Yes, luv,' Danny said meekly.

Danny had barely taken his finger off the bell when the door opened and he didn't think he'd ever seen a look of such naked misery on a face when John saw who it was. He'd clearly been expecting someone else.

'Can I come in a minute?'

John seemed to collect himself. He shrugged and stood to one side. 'If you must. I can only spare you a minute. I've got things to do.'

The business must be doing all right, Danny thought as he walked down the spacious carpeted hall into a large, charming room, which had clearly benefited from a woman's touch. There were vases of rushes, bowls of dried flowers, a cosy blue moquette three-piece, rugs and numerous pictures on the walls. Danny tried to take everything in without making it too obvious, knowing

Bernadette would subject him to the third degree when he got home. Perhaps it was because he knew the circumstances, but the room had a sad, deserted air, as if all the life had gone out of it. The fire was a mountain of grey ash with only the occasional glowing coal. It felt very cold.

'What can I do for you, Danny?' John stood, legs apart, in front of the fireplace. He didn't ask the visitor to sit down. Danny sensed he was coiled as tightly as a spring. It wouldn't take much to make this man explode. He longed to be at home in his own comfortable little house with his comfortable little wife.

'I'll come straight to the point,' Danny said bluntly. 'I'm only here for one reason, to make sure you're all right. Once you've assured me that you are, then I'll be off.'

John frowned slightly. 'Is there any reason why I shouldn't be all right?'

'I understand someone walked out on you today, someone called Clare. She came round and asked Alice to see to you, as it were.' Danny glowered. 'I don't appreciate our Alice being dragged into your affairs after all this time. I thought we'd done with you once and for all.'

The man's face had gone a dark, ugly red. 'Clare came to see you?'

'She came to see Alice.'

'She left a note. She didn't mention Alice. When the doorbell went I thought she'd . . .'

'Come back for another beating? I doubt it, John. I doubt if you'll see that girl again.'

'She actually told . . .' He turned away, put his hands on the mantelpiece, stared into the fire. Danny wondered if he was ashamed, embarrassed, or just angry. 'Did

251

she say where she was going? She took the children. I'm worried . . .'

'No, she didn't. If she had, I wouldn't tell you. I don't have much time for men who hit their women.'

'I didn't mean to hit her.'

Danny gestured impatiently. He wasn't interested in anything John Lacey might have to say. All he wanted to know was how the man was bearing up before he made his departure.

Perhaps John had read his thoughts, because he turned round and said coldly, 'I can't think why Clare went to see Alice. I was a bit surprised, that's all, when I came home tonight and found she and the kids had gone. We haven't exactly been getting on in a long time. It'll feel strange for a while without the children, but even that has its compensations. They were dead noisy and I've always liked a quiet life.'

He was lying, it was obvious, but Danny didn't care. He'd asked and the man claimed to be all right. His task was done. 'I'll be off, then.'

'I'll see you out.'

'Don't bother. I'll make me own way. Tara, John.'

The front door closed. John Lacey fell to his knees on the rug in front of the fire. His mouth opened in a silent scream and he beat the floor with his fists. He wanted to roll up in a ball of pain.

Clare had gone, the children. He knew in his heart he would never see them again. He had driven them away, just as he drove everyone away. He prayed to God to make him die.

Minutes later, or it might have been hours, when God seemed unprepared to answer his prayer and John hadn't the courage to take matters into his own hands, he got to his feet and went round the house gathering together a few possessions, which he threw in the back of the van parked outside.

The landlord could have his house back, as well as everything in it. From now on he'd live in the office at the yard. From now on nothing mattered any more.

Chapter 10

Cora bought the *Liverpool Echo* especially. She opened it as soon as she got home and searched for Twenty-Firsts.

'LACEY, Cormac John. Many Happy Returns, son, on your twenty-first. With all my love, Mum,' she read.

There were three more entries for Cormac: from Maeve and Martin, from Orla and Micky and the children, and the last from Grandad, Bernadette, Ian and Ruth: 'Congratulations to a fine young man on reaching his majority.'

There would be no entries tomorrow for Maurice Lacey. Anyone who knew him would have laughed, because Maurice was in Walton jail.

Oh, the shame of it! Since the court case Cora had hardly left the house. She did the shopping Strand Road way where she wasn't known, rather than in Marsh Lane.

She still didn't know what had got into Maurice. He'd lost his job – he was 'unpunctual', according to his boss. Cora had considered it fortunate that he'd been called up to do his National Service almost straight away. It would do him good, teach him the discipline that Cora had failed to do. But the minute he came out he'd started hanging around with a girl, Pamela Conway, who had a reputation for being no better than she ought to be. It was Pamela's brothers who'd led Maurice astray, of that Cora was convinced. They were much older than him, with convictions for breaking and entering behind them. One had threatened a shopkeeper with a knife and wasn't long out of jail himself.

They'd *used* Maurice. He was a soft lad, easily led. He'd broken a window to get into the shop and it hadn't entered his daft head that someone might hear and call the bobbies. They were waiting for him when he came out, laden with boxes of cigarettes and baccy, almost certainly for the Conways to sell in the pubs at half price. He refused to clat on them. Cora suspected he was frightened.

For once, Billy had been in when the bobbies arrived and requested they come to the station, where he'd leapt at Maurice and had almost throttled him by the time he was pulled off. He wanted nothing more to do with him, he said. But when had Billy had anything much to do with his wife and son?

She recalled her own criminal past, though she'd been too clever to get caught. Perhaps thieving was inherited, like the same coloured eyes and hair. But if that was the case, Cormac . . .

Sometimes she forgot what the truth was.

By now, Cormac would be home from university for Christmas and there was bound to be a birthday do somewhere tonight – Alice threw parties at the drop of a hat.

Restless, Cora wandered round the house, touching things. It wasn't fair. Nothing was fair. Nothing had gone the way she'd expected. Horace Flynn had popped his clogs last year, but hadn't left her a thing. The chap who came to collect the rent said a nephew back in Ireland, a priest, had inherited the lot and wanted everything left the same. All the chap did was collect the leases and the rents, and send cheques to some church in County Antrim. When Cora asked why Horace's big house in Stanley Road remained empty, he knew nothing about it.

She wondered if Cormac's do would be held at home or whether Alice had booked somewhere bigger, seeing as how it was a twenty-first. Wherever it was, she wouldn't mind going and waiting outside so she could take a peek, see who was there – if she could do it without being noticed, that is.

They'd probably know in the Strand Road salon – she looked inside whenever she passed. It was always busy, but she'd never once seen Alice there. It looked a posh place, much bigger than the Laceys' in Opal Street and Marsh Lane. But she couldn't just barge in asking questions, she'd have to have something done to her hair. She'd get a trim, though she usually cut it herself, and give a false name. It wouldn't do to say she was a Lacey.

The thought cheered her up somewhat. It gave her a reason for getting out of the house. She'd go now.

Cora went into the hall and lifted her camel coat off a hook. It was twelve years old, but good quality and she wouldn't have dreamt of buying another until it wore out. She pushed her small feet into a pair of stout suede boots that were even older than the coat, then tied a scarf round her head. For some women, appearance was everything, but Cora didn't give a damn. She fastened the buttons in front of the full-length mirror. She was fifty-one and looked neither younger nor older. Not a soul in the world would have given her a second glance.

The woman in Lacey's who was doing her hair was called Enid. Cora would suit it shorter, she said. It would give it more texture and she'd look like June Allyson. 'She's a film star,' she went on in response to Cora's puzzled look. 'She was in *Little Women* and *Executive Suite*.'

'I don't get to the pictures much.'

'Don't you, luv? Me, I go at least three times a week.'

Cora said she'd prefer to stick to just an inch off, thanks all the same. She was about to add sourly that she had more important things to do with her time than go to the pictures three times a week, but remembered she wanted to pump the woman for information. This proved easy when she mentioned she was an old friend of Alice whom she hadn't seen in years. 'How's her kids getting on? Four she had, didn't she? Three girls and a boy – he was almost exactly the same age as me own lad.'

'In that case your lad must be round twenty-one, like Cormac. It's his birthday today. He's a smashing lad – I sent him a silver key meself. We're all going to his party tonight.'

'And where would that be?'

'You know Hilton's Restaurant on Stanley Road? Well, it's in the room above. There's at least fifty of us going. Alice has invited all the staff and Cormac has asked some friends from school and university. Did you know he's at Cambridge, luv? He's taking Chemistry, if you'll believe.' The woman couldn't have sounded prouder had Cormac been her own son. 'After he's got his degree, he's going to stay and get more letters after his name. When he leaves he'll be called doctor.'

Cora waited until eight o'clock before stationing herself across the road from Hilton's, a large restaurant well known as a venue for wedding receptions and parties. It was situated on the corner of busy Stanley Road and Greening Street. The double-fronted downstairs was in darkness. She could hear the noise of the party upstairs, the music and the chatter, the laughing and the singing, from all this way away, despite the passing trams and other traffic.

Why was she doing this, cowering in a doorway on a freezing cold night in December, listening to other people enjoying themselves? Because this night had been stolen from her, she told herself. This night should be *hers*. It should be *her* throwing the party for Cormac.

She waited a good hour, huddled inside her coat, stamping her feet, her gaze fixed hypnotically on the lighted upstairs windows opposite. There was no way she'd see a thing from here and she wanted to know what was going on. Spots of ice blew against her face as she crossed over and went down Greening Street to the side door of the restaurant where people had been going in. Hopping from one foot to the other, she stood hesitantly outside before pushing the door open, though she didn't go in. Narrow stairs led upwards and the noise here was deafening, a whooping and stamping of feet, as if people were doing some strange sort of dance. Cora had never been to a dance.

Dare she go in? Sneak upstairs, just peer through the door, so she didn't feel totally excluded from Cormac's twenty-first?

Well, even if she was discovered, she was unlikely to be chucked out on her ear. Alice would never be rude. Fion would have been, except she wasn't there. The woman in the salon said she was still living in London.

Cora crept upstairs, making not a sound in her crèpe-soled boots. To her left at the top there was a Ladies and a Gents, a kitchen and a door marked 'Office'. The whoops and stamping came from behind the door to her right.

Someone – it was Bernadette Mitchell – was coming out of the kitchen carrying a birthday cake with the candles already lit, too concerned with watching her feet in case she tripped over to notice Cora, who shot into the Ladies, heart thumping.

The music and the stamping suddenly stopped. There was utter silence for a minute, then 'Happy birthday to you, Happy birthday to you, Happy birthday, dear Cormac . . .'

They loved him. Everyone loved Cormac.

Cormac, Maurice. Maurice, Cormac. The names chased each other around Cora's brain. She'd thought she was doing a good thing all them years ago, but she'd done a bad one. If only she'd left things as they were, it would be Alice with a lad in Walton jail, not her. If only she could go back twenty-one years and put everything right.

The Ladies was a large room that doubled as a cloakroom. Two sides of the walls were full of coats, and there were two lavatories. Cora went inside one and closed the door. She pulled down the seat to sit on. They were singing 'For he's a jolly good fellow' now. Alice was probably hanging on to his arm, looking gormless. She didn't deserve Cormac for a son.

Oh, it wasn't *fair*!

There was a sudden rush of women into the Ladies. They kept trying Cora's door. 'Who's in there?' someone said. 'They've been ages.'

A few minutes later there was a knock. 'Are you all right?' It was that bloody Patsy woman who worked for Alice.

'Yes,' Cora replied gruffly.

The Ladies emptied. The music started again, quieter now, romantic music. She imagined the lights turned low and everyone dancing, and wondered if Cormac had a girlfriend with him.

Not long afterwards the women returned to collect their coats. The party must be over. From their conversation, they'd had a dead good time. After about fifteen minutes of bustle there was silence. Alice hadn't been in for her coat, Cora would have recognised her voice. Unlatching the door, she came out to find only a handful of coats left on the hooks and wondered if she could make it from the lavatory to the stairs without being seen, otherwise she might end up being locked in the building all night.

There was no one in the kitchen. Cora had reached the top of the stairs and was about to creep down as quietly as she'd come, when she noticed the door to the big room was open and there was still music, very faint, so faint that it was almost drowned out by the noise of the traffic outside.

She paused. At the far end, Orla and Maeve were dancing with their husbands: that no-mark Micky Lavin and the one who had a good job at the hospital, Martin. Danny and Bernadette were standing by a radiogram, sifting through records. Cora edged closer until Alice came into view. She wore a lovely bottle-green dress with a fluted hem and was sprawled on a chair, legs stretched out in front, clearly worn out. But Cora didn't think she'd ever seen such a look of perfect contentment on a face before. Alice quite literally glowed. Her face seemed to be exuding darts of electricity and Cora felt her own face prickle, as if from tiny electric shocks. Her sister-in-law was experiencing the happiness that was *her* due, the happiness that had been denied her all these years.

She edged closer, her eyes searching for Cormac. He appeared, inch by inch, bending over Alice. He wore black trousers and a white shirt that looked too big for him, she thought. It was all bunched up round the waist where it was tucked inside a narrow belt. He might have started off the evening with a tie, but wasn't wearing one now. The collar of the shirt was open, emphasising his slender neck. Cora's heart missed a beat. He looked dead handsome. He and Alice were laughing together about something. The whole scene looked like a painting of Happy Families. Then Cormac suddenly reached out and stroked Alice's hair.

Something snapped in the watching woman. Her head felt as if it was full of smoke: thick, black smoke, that swirled around and got hotter and hotter.

By now, Maurice would have kipped down in his cell. 'Lights Out' would have been called. Everywhere smelt of pee, he claimed. The food was awful. After a few months, Cora had stopped going to see him. She didn't know what to say and the other visitors were scum. She felt ashamed, mixing with them. She wasn't sure if she wanted Maurice back home. She wasn't sure if she loved him any more.

This was her son, her lad, the fruit of her womb, this fair-haired, clever, extremely dashing young man.

'Drat!' Alice had kicked something over. A glass of wine. The liquid spilled like blood on to the polished floor.

'I'll get a cloth from the kitchen.' Cormac began to hurry towards the door, towards Cora, the son towards his mother. God must have arranged for that glass to be knocked over.

Cora backed up so that she was in the kitchen when Cormac came in. He jumped, startled. 'Aunt Cora! I didn't know you were here. Why don't you go in the big room with me mam?'

She fixed her eyes squarely on his neat, good-looking face. 'You're mine,' she said in a deep, passionate voice that she didn't know she possessed.

'I beg your pardon?' Cormac said courteously.

'I said, you're *mine*,' she continued in the same

unnatural voice. 'The night you were born, I swapped you round for Maurice. I went for a walk in the hospital. Everyone was asleep, 'cept me. When I came to the nursery, Maurice was in the cot marked Lacey 1, and you were in Lacey 2. I changed you round.'

Cormac was actually smiling. 'Don't talk rubbish, Aunt Cora. I don't like to be rude, but I've never heard such ridiculous nonsense.'

'It's not nonsense, luv. It's true,' Cora insisted hoarsely.

He laughed. 'Things like that aren't allowed to happen in hospitals.'

'They happened that night. There was a raid. It was like hell on earth, women and babies all over the place: in the cellar one minute, in the wards the next.' Cora clutched his arm, but he shrugged her away.

'This is going beyond a joke.' His voice had become icy cold. 'I'm sorry about Maurice being in prison, Aunt Cora, but it doesn't mean you have to spoil *my* twenty-first for me.'

He thought she was saying things out of spite! 'Oh, luv,' she cried. She reached for him, but he moved away with an expression of distaste. 'I don't want to spoil anything, I just thought it was time you knew the truth. I told you, it was bedlam in the hospital, nurses rushing around like lunatics. There was this emergency. Alice wasn't shown her baby till next morning, when they gave her you 'stead of Maurice. It's not your twenty-first till tomorrer. It's Maurice who's twenty-one today.'

It seemed as if the reference to the birthdays, trivial in comparison with the other things she'd said, had sewn a seed of doubt in Cormac's mind. He went as white as a sheet. 'Just supposing,' he said carefully, 'just supposing there's a grain of truth in what you've said, what on earth would possess you to do such a wicked thing?'

Cora smiled slyly. 'Because I thought Maurice looked the better bet, but it turned out I was wrong.'

'Jaysus!'

She felt slightly uneasy at the sight of his gentle face contorted with horror and disgust. Perhaps she should have approached it differently, or at least thought things through before she opened her big mouth. Perhaps it would have been best if she'd told Alice first. Alice knew the way things had been that night and would have been easier to convince.

'Cormac!' Alice shouted. 'Where's that cloth?'

'Won't be a minute, Mam.' His face had cleared, become devoid of expression. 'I don't believe you. You're just making trouble, something you're very good at, going by past experience.'

'Just take a look at yourself in the mirror, son,' Cora said softly. She'd upset him badly, which was only to be expected. She felt a surge of sympathy that made her body ache, but no way was she going to deny that what she'd said was true. She'd already suffered enough for that one silly mistake. 'It's never crossed anyone's mind to notice, but you're the spitting image of me, your mam – the same shaped face, the same little hands.' Alice had long, thin hands, John's were broad. She held out her own hands, spreading the small fingers, regarding them impassively. 'See, son.'

For the first time in Cormac's life his legendary calm deserted him. 'Don't you dare call me "son". I'm not your son. I'd sooner die than be your son. I want nothing to do with you.' He could hardly speak. The words came out thickly, as if his tongue had got too big for his mouth.

Cora chewed her bottom lip. She didn't like seeing her boy in such a state, but what had she expected? For him to throw himself into her arms? All this must have come as a terrible shock. 'Why don't we get Alice out here?' she suggested.

'Does Mam *know*?'

'No, but it's about time she did.' She thought Cormac was about to hit her. He reared over her, pushed his face in hers. 'Don't you *dare* breathe a word about this to me mam, d'you hear? It would kill her. I don't want anyone else to know. Do you hear me, Aunt Cora. *I don't want anyone else to know.*'

'But,' Cora began, disappointed, because she wanted the whole world to know that *this* was her son: Maurice, the jail bird, belonged to someone else.

Then Cormac put his small white hands round Cora's scraggy neck and began to squeeze. 'If you tell another soul, Aunt Cora, so help me, I'll kill you. I swear it. No matter where I am, I'll come back and kill you stone dead.'

She was gagging. 'Leave go, son. I won't tell a soul.'

He removed his hands. 'You'd better not,' he said threateningly. 'And don't, don't ever call me son again.'

With a sense of perverse pride, Cora realised that soft, gentle Cormac, who everyone thought wouldn't have hurt a fly, who had never been heard to raise his voice in anger, meant every word. She herself had killed, a long time ago, two people. A chip off the old block, she thought. He's his mammy's son, that's for sure. She sighed happily. Cormac knew the truth and that was all that mattered. One of these days he'd come round and learn to love his mam.

Cormac went into the Gents and stared at himself in the mirror. Within the space of a few minutes the bottom had dropped out of his world. He hadn't realised how swiftly life could change, that you could be completely happy one minute, in the depths of despair the next.

He had never liked Aunt Cora. She gave him the jitters. There was something unhinged about her. As he grew older, he'd become convinced that she was mad and, if she truly was his mother, then he, Cormac, could easily become mad himself. He hadn't, for instance, considered himself remotely capable of murder, yet minutes ago he'd grabbed a woman by the throat with the intention of strangling her. He wondered if he would have done it if there hadn't been other people around.

By some obscene coincidence her name could actually be made from the letters of his: Cormac, Cora, as if, inadvertently, there'd been a connection between them all along.

The idea that everything that had happened so far in his life was due entirely to the quirk of a crazy woman wandering around a hospital in the dead of night made his stomach curl with horror. It was enough to make anyone lose his mind.

On the other hand he supposed he was lucky. It could have been *him*, not Maurice, brought up in the house in Garibaldi Road with a cane hanging on the wall.

Poor Maurice! Cormac shuddered.

He no longer felt sure who he was, whom he belonged to, which family was his. He told himself that Aunt Cora was talking rubbish, as he'd first thought, except that the person staring back at him from the mirror had the cold eyes and the nothing face of his detested aunt. The eyes were a different colour, that was all.

Oh, God! Why hadn't he noticed before? Why hadn't anyone? Until now, he'd always considered himself at least averagely good-looking, but the face in the mirror looked like that of a corpse.

'We don't know who on earth he takes after,' Mam said when people remarked Cormac was nothing like the rest of the family. No one had noticed the remarkable resemblance between the woman who now claimed to be his mother and himself. He would never, never be able to get his head round the fact that Alice wasn't his mam.

There was a knock on the door. 'Cormac, are you all right, son? I hope you haven't made yourself sick with all that beer. Oh, by the way, I've got a cloth meself.'

'I'm all right.' He couldn't bring himself to say 'Mam', he just couldn't. 'I'll be out in a minute,' he called.

Chapter 11
1965

Cormac lay flat on his back within a circle of brittle corn. He stared at the sky through the corn tunnel that grew narrower and narrower until the top seemed no bigger than his eye. The flattened plants beneath him stuck sharply into his body through his thin Indian top and flared cotton pants, though they didn't hurt. His arms were spread as wide as they would go and his hands were hidden within the yellow stalks. The tips of his fingers touched those of Wally on one side and Frank the Yank, snoring his head off, on the other.

He imagined himself a bird passing overhead and seeing himself and his friends spread out like a row of little paper men.

'Why is the sun red?' Wally murmured.

'I don't know,' Cormac answered. 'Why is everywhere so hot?'

'Because the sun is so red, man. It's on fire.'

'I need a drink.' Cormac sat up and experimentally touched his bare toes. The fact that he was physically capable of such an act meant he was badly in need of a joint as well as a drink so that his senses would become sufficiently blurred.

He got to his feet and staggered towards a luridly painted coach that was parked in the corner of a field in Suffolk, Sussex or Surrey, he couldn't remember which. He knew they were on their way to play at a pop festival in Norwich, which would start the day after tomorrow. The farmer whose field they were on was so far unaware he had trespassers. If he noticed before they left that night, they would be turfed off sharpish with the aid of a couple of savage dogs, a shotgun, or possibly both.

Inside, the coach buzzed with flies. When bought, it had already been converted into a mobile home with six bunks, three each side, as close as shelves, a tiny sink and a table at the rear with fitted, plastic-covered benches. Behind a screen a chemical lavatory remained unused because no one was prepared to empty it and there was a tiny fridge that no longer worked. The windows had been painted over to provide privacy, apart from the one in the roof, which wouldn't open. The sun scorched through the glass like a blowtorch, turning the cramped space into an oven.

Cormac could hardly breathe in the suffocating heat. He opened the fridge and remembered it was broken when he came face to face with half a mouldy tomato. Nothing came out when he turned on the tap over the sink – the water tank must be empty. He searched everywhere, in the cupboard under the sink, under bunks, under the clothes that littered the bunks, but could find nothing except a few empty beer bottles that yielded not a drop when he attempted to drain them. In the process he knocked over a guitar, which fell to the floor with a hollow boom and he noticed one of the strings was broken.

Then he recalled that the girls had gone into the village to buy supplies: Tanya and Pol, but his memory was hazy as to the time they'd gone. It could have been five minutes ago or five hours.

Jaysus, the smell in here was foul. Someone had been sick the night before and everywhere reeked of vomit. Perhaps that was what attracted the flies. There was another smell, quite strong, and Cormac realised it was paint. The fiery sun was burning the paint off the outside of the coach.

He'd die if he didn't have a drink soon. Perhaps a joint would lessen his thirst. He remembered a joint was one of the reasons he was there and reached under the pillow on his bunk for the battered Golden Virginia tin in which he kept his stuff.

'Hello, friends,' he said affectionately to the contents of the tin: a packet of red Rizla papers and a book of matches nestling within a bed of tobacco and, most important, a lump of hash that felt warm. He spread the tobacco on a paper and shredded a portion of the hash with his fingernail so that it was evenly spread, then put back the remainder carefully. He lit the spliff, took a long, deep puff, then went out and sat in the shade of the coach, his back against it. It didn't feel even vaguely cool, but at least he was out of the sun.

'Hi, man.' Wally appeared. 'Is there anything to drink in there?'

Cormac shook his head. 'Not a drop, man.'

'Where's Tanya and Pol?'

'Gone somewhere. Where's Frank?'

'Asleep.'

'Shouldn't someone wake him? He'll get sunburn.' Did you get sunburn or catch it?

'I suppose someone should.' Wally must have decided it wasn't going to be him. He sat beside Cormac and gestured towards the joint. Cormac handed it to him. They shared everything, including the girls. Cormac and Wally had shared each other, only the once, but had decided it wasn't for them.

Frank the Yank provided most of the money. His pa had sent him abroad to escape the Vietnam draft and wherever they went, Frank only had to find a Lloyds bank and produce his passport, and massive amounts of cash would be handed over. It was Frank who'd bought the coach and they'd painted it together. The others signed on the dole if they stayed somewhere long enough, but that didn't happen often.

A pleasant fog had formed inside Cormac's head. He was no longer thirsty. This hazy sensation of wanting nothing, needing nothing, was something Cormac wished to retain for the rest of his life. His ambition was to get from one day to the next in the deepest possible daze without actually becoming unconscious – unconsciousness appealed, but was impractical.

The girls returned, loaded with shopping. Cormac feebly raised a hand in greeting. Pol smiled, but Tanya eyed them balefully.

'You're stoned,' she said accusingly. 'I bet you haven't cleaned up inside.' Tanya was tall, breathtakingly beautiful and extremely bad-tempered for most of the time. She wore a full-length flowered skirt and a skimpy T-shirt. Her mother was a famous model.

'Cleaned up inside?' Cormac and Wally said more or less together. They looked at each other. It was the first they'd heard of it.

'It stinks in there. It wasn't Pol or me who was sick. You promised you'd clean it.'

'Did we?'

'I'll do it.' Pol was short and slight, and merely pretty. She had crisp brown curly hair and a heart-shaped face. In her limp, shapeless cotton frock, she looked no more than sixteen, though she was twenty-one, three years younger than Cormac. 'As my horrible mother used to say, "If you want something done properly, then do it yourself".'

'Alice used to say something like that.' Cormac grinned.

'Where's Frank?' Tanya demanded.

'Asleep,' Wally said.

'In there?' She pointed to the coach.

'No, over yonder,' Wally said poetically and gave a vague wave in the direction of the field.

'Tsk, tsk. He'll get sunburnt.' Tanya marched away, her back rigid, like a schoolmistress. Cormac supposed that someone had to keep them in order. He was glad Tanya was around. And Pol. Particularly Pol.

'I'll put these away.' Pol staggered as she picked up one of the bags laden with shopping.

Cormac's innate courtesy came to the fore and he stumbled to his feet. 'I'll give you a hand with those.'

'Ta, Cormac. Phew, what a smell!' Pol gasped when they were inside the coach. She tripped over the guitar and it slid along the floor until it stopped under the table with a thump. 'We need to find a launderette and wash the sleeping bags. There's bound to be one in Ipswich, and they're usually open till late. I'll chuck everything outside for now.' With that, she began to grab the sleeping bags and the scattered clothes, and to throw them out of the door. The worst of the smell went with them.

Where on earth did she get the energy from? Cormac wondered. He himself would have found it a simple matter to wallow in filth for the rest of his life rather than wash a sheet. 'Is that where we are, Ipswich?' He'd only vaguely heard of the place before.

'About five miles away. Are you thirsty?' She was putting the food away under the sink.

'I think I might well be.'

'Would you like some lemonade?'

'That would be most acceptable.'

'Sit down, then, and I'll pour you some.'

'Thank you, Pol,' Cormac said gravely.

'When we stop in Ipswich to do the washing, it wouldn't hurt if you washed your hair, Cormac. It's getting quite matted. You could do it in a Gents toilet.'

'I like it matted.' Cormac touched the hair that went halfway down his back. It felt greasy and unusually thick.

Pol shrugged, easygoing. 'Please yourself.'

'I'll wash me hair for *you*.' He liked Pol very much, perhaps a bit too much. He was beginning to resent having to share her with Wally and Frank. Perhaps they should find another girl and split into three separate couples. 'I think I love you, Pol,' he said seriously.

'Oh, Cormac! You're too stoned to think most of the time.' She looked at him curiously. 'Why do you do it? I mean, I like a spliff myself, but you seem to be on a permanent high.'

'It's a long story, Pol. Something happened.' Cormac spoke slowly, carefully enunciating the words, hoping they made sense. 'One day, no, one minute, everything was perfect, next minute it was shit.'

'What was it that happened?'

'I discovered I wasn't the person I'd always thought meself to be.'

Pol looked impressed. 'That sounds deeply disturbing, Cormac.'

'Intensely deeply.' Cormac was about to reach for her, pull her on to a bunk, when Wally fell into the coach, following by Frank, who was being led by an irritable Tanya. Frank's face and arms were as bright red as his hair and slightly puffy.

'I'm all right, man,' he protested. 'Stop making a fuss.'

'You won't feel all right tomorrow. You'll be as sick as a dog. Is there calamine lotion in the first aid box, Pol?' It was Tanya's idea to have a first aid box, and Cormac had to concede it came in useful from time to time.

'I don't think so, no.'

'Then I suggest we leave now, straight away,' Tanya said briskly. 'We'll call in Ipswich, do the washing, fill the water tank, buy some calamine lotion. Are any of you three fit to drive?'

Cormac occasionally drove, even though he'd never had a lesson. 'I'm ferfectly pit,' he announced.

'Oh, yeh!' Tanya glared at Wally who had collapsed on the floor. Frank had started to shiver violently for some reason. 'It looks as if I'll have to drive myself. One of these days we'll be stopped by the police and I haven't got a proper licence.'

The surface of the large field had baked as hard as clay. It was impossible to imagine the soil having been soft enough for the huge tyres of tractors to have made such perfect moulds – they made comfortable seats, Cormac discovered, just wide and deep enough for his bottom to fit.

Pol sat between his legs, leaning against him. His hands lay limply on her lap. They sprawled at the very edge of the field, where they could hardly see the group playing beneath an awning that fluttered not an inch on such a windless day. The music stopped and there was a smattering of applause from the crowds that dotted the field like confetti. The audience included many children, most of them naked. A few of the women were bare to the waist. The numerous dogs seemed to have been trained to defecate and piss as frequently as possible.

Today, Pol wore a different frock, just as shapeless. He nuzzled her hair, which smelt of soap. His own hair, beautifully clean, was wondrous to behold: clouds of pale-blond locks held together at the back with an elastic band.

'Where do you come from, Pol?' he asked. She'd probably told him before, but he'd forgotten.

'Lancashire, same as you. Blackpool.'

'I went to Blackpool once. There was something called the Golden Mile.' He'd gone on the big wheel with Fion and Orla. Maeve had been too scared. Grandad had been there. It was before he'd married Bernadette.

'You should see the Blackpool Lights in a few weeks' time, they're terrific.'

'Shall we go together?'

'No chance, Cormac. I might meet my mother.'

'Would that be so awful?'

'Awfully awful. She's a bitch.'

'So's mine.' Cormac shuddered.

'I thought you said your mother was lovely.' She turned her face towards him and he kissed her nose. 'You're always on about Alice.'

'Alice isn't my mother, she just thinks she is.'

'Oh, Cormac, you don't half talk rubbish. Were you adopted or something?'

'No, I was given away at birth.'

'Who by, a bad fairy?'

'Well, yes, as it happens. Very bad.'

'You're something of a mystery, do you know that, Cormac?'

'I'm a mystery to meself,' Cormac said darkly.

'Are we playing here tomorrow?'

'I doubt it, not if Frank's still laid low with sunburn. And I think one of the guitars is broken.' The Nobodys were usually the first on the bill, hired to keep folks amused while they looked for somewhere to sit, or searched for their seats if the concert was indoors. Frank and Wally played guitar not very well. The only decent musician was Tanya who was brilliant with the fiddle.

Pol had a sweet, high voice and Cormac could rattle a tambourine as well as anyone. He was the group's manager-cum-roadie. At least, he was when he remembered. The Nobodys were unusual in that they recognised their limitations and weren't interested in either fame or money. It was just something to do, giving occasional point to their otherwise meaningless lives.

'I think I'll go back to the van, bathe poor Frank's head, or something,' Pol said.

'I'll come with you,' Cormac said with alacrity. He didn't want her alone with Frank, who might not be one hundred per cent incapacitated by the sunburn.

'There's no need, Cormac.'

'This group are shit and I need a rest.'

'What from? You've been sitting in that rut virtually all day.'

'I need a rest from sitting in this rut.'

Vehicles were parked nose to tail along the narrow country lane: buses, caravanettes, lorries, large vans, small vans, ambulances with the word 'Ambulance' painted out, the occasional car. According to the radio, it was the same for miles around. The police had decided to let the festival go ahead rather than turn hundreds of vehicles away. It would cause less hassle. On the radio, several local residents had huffed and puffed, and said it was disgraceful. Why weren't these people at work? How dare they descend on a peaceful, law-abiding community and create havoc? Pubs, restaurants, one or two garages, had signs outside, 'No Festival Goers'. The Nobodys were out of water again and it was impossible to get more.

'My skin won't let me move, man,' Frank complained bitterly when Pol and Cormac climbed into the coach. He was poised stiffly on a bench, elbows on the table, wearing only a pair of shorts with a pattern of butterflies.

The skin on his upper half was less livid, but still looked painful. His red hair looked crisp, as if it had been fried. 'My chest hurts when I breathe.'

'Shall I douse you in calamine?'

'Please, Pol.'

Cormac reached under the pillow for his stuff and began to roll a joint. The first puff brought on a sensation of enormous lethargy. He lay down and within seconds was asleep.

It was dusk when he awoke, slightly cooler. He could hear music thumping away in the distance. The spliff had burnt a perfect round hole in the nylon sleeping bag, but there was still half left. He was searching for the matches when he noticed Frank and Pol squeezed together on the bunk opposite, both asleep. Pol was naked, her small, perfect body glistening with perspiration, and Frank's shorts were around his knees. His red skin was splattered with pink calamine.

Cormac groaned. He'd come back with Pol to keep an eye on her, yet she and Frank had made love directly in front of his closed eyes. They badly needed another girl, someone for Frank. Wally could have Tanya, Cormac would have Pol.

Another girl! He made his unsteady way outside and began to walk in the direction of the music to look for another girl. Dusk was falling. There were lights on in some of the vehicles and he could hear the clink of dishes. The smell of food made him feel nauseous, though he'd had nothing to eat all day and possibly yesterday, for all he knew. A police car came zooming down the lane, blue light flashing. Cormac pushed a small child and an exceptionally hairy dog to safety. The child cried and the dog growled ungratefully.

Cormac had no idea why he should cry as he walked towards the music. He wasn't even conscious of crying until one of the great, bulbous tears pouring down his face landed on his bare foot and he thought it was raining. He looked up into the clear, dusky blue sky and realised he was crying and the rain was a tear. He was thinking about Pol and Alice and Grandad and his sisters, about Amber Street, about Bootle, Lacey's hairdressers, the schools he'd gone to, the friends he'd made. He thought about university and the fact that he hadn't gone back to finish his degree, about Alice's face when he told her. He thought about Cora Lacey.

'Here, look where you're going, luv.'

He'd collided with a woman coming from the opposite direction, leading two children by the hand.

'I'm sorry.' Cormac wept. 'So sorry.'

'It's not the end of the world, luv,' the woman said kindly.

Still crying, Cormac walked on, when a voice said incredulously, 'Is that you, Cormac?'

He turned. The woman with the children had stopped and was looking at him, her face as incredulous as her voice. She was tall, well built, but shapely and her long, wild hair was tied in a knot on top of her head. She wore a black T-shirt with a white CND sign on the front and narrow black pants. She was, unfortunately, too old for Frank, about thirty, and there was no room for the children in the coach.

'I'm Cormac, yes,' he conceded in a whisper.

'It's Fion, luv. Fionnuala, your sister.'

'Fion!' Cormac had never, in all his life, been so pleased to see anyone. He stopped crying, grabbed his sister and showered her face with kisses. She hugged him tightly in return and rubbed his back, as if he were a baby. One of the children, the boy, tried to pull her away.

'It's all right, Colin. This is Cormac, your uncle. Oh,

277

Cormac, you look bloody awful. Are you sick or something? C'mon, luv, we're only along here.'

The children ran ahead, stopping outside a smart white caravanette. Fion, holding Cormac firmly by the arm as if worried he'd run away, opened the door and pushed him through. Inside, the vehicle was cheerful and scrupulously tidy. Red gingham frills framed the tiny windows and there was a matching cloth on the table, as well as a small bowl of roses. The miniature stainless steel sink sparkled and a red carpet graced the floor. There wasn't a dish or an item of dirty washing in sight.

The grip of his sister's hand on Cormac's arm made him feel as if he had suddenly been plugged back into the normal world and the scene of domestic neatness reminded him of a time when he had known nothing else, when it had been a simple matter to get washed, wear clean clothes, brush his teeth, sit down to proper meals.

'Blimey, Cormac, you don't half pong,' Fion said bluntly. 'Have a wash, there's a good lad, while I make some tea. I'll find you a clean T-shirt in a minute. This is Colin and Bonnie, by the way. He's nearly five, she's nearly four. Say hello to your Uncle Cormac, kids, then get into your pyjamas. It's nearly time for bed.'

Bonnie pushed herself boldly forward. 'Hello, Uncle Cormac.' The boy hung back and sucked his finger.

'Hello, kids,' Cormac said, doing his best to sound like a proper grown-up uncle. 'Where's their dad?' he said to Fion.

'Dead. He died two years ago. His name was Colin too.'

'Oh, hell! I'm sorry.'

'So am I,' Fion said matter-of-factly. 'I loved him more than words can say, but he'd been in a Japanese prisoner of war camp and was dying when I met him.

When we got married we never thought he'd last six whole years, but he did and they were the best years of me life.' She gestured towards him with soap and a towel. 'Take your shirt off, luv, and chuck it away before you stink the place out. Are you hungry?'

'I wouldn't mind some bread and butter.'

'I think we can manage that.'

Cormac had never had a favourite sister, but had always felt more drawn to Fionnuala than he had to loud, aggressive Orla and quietly confident Maeve. There had been something very vulnerable about tactless, hopeless Fion, forever putting her foot in it, saying the wrong thing. To find his wretched self plucked off a country lane in Norfolk by the sister he hadn't seen in years and put down in this neat, cool place, where there was fresh water, healthily smelling soap, roses on the table and a kettle boiling for tea, was little short of a miracle.

'What are you doing here?' Fion asked while he was getting washed. The children watched with interest as they changed into their pyjamas.

'I belong to a group, the Nobodys. We're on tomorrow's programme, but Frank's too ill to play.'

'Never heard of you.'

'Nobody ever has, hence the name.'

'Mummy, he hasn't cleaned behind his ears.'

Fion grinned. 'Bonnie says to clean behind your ears, Cormac.'

'Sorry, Bonnie.'

'And under your arms.'

'Yes, Bonnie.' Cormac was beginning to feel vaguely happy.

In quick succession Fion opened a tin of beans, shoved toast under a grill, poured water on the pot. Within minutes the children were sitting down to beans on toast, and Cormac was drinking a mug of scalding tea and wearing a T-shirt with Amnesty 61 on the back. There seemed to be plenty of provisions. A loaf appeared, a plastic butter dish, a tin of cocoa, a bottle of milk, a packet of biscuits — custard creams. Cormac couldn't remember having seen such a rich assortment of food in years.

'Is the van yours?' he asked.

'No, it's hired. We're on holiday, on our way to Scotland. Some of my friends were coming here, so I thought I'd make a detour and let the children see what a rock concert's all about. Bonnie thought it great, but Colin hated it, didn't you, luv?' Colin had yet to open his mouth and merely nodded. Fion ruffled his hair and for some reason the gesture made Cormac want to cry again.

'Me and Colin,' Fion continued, 'big Colin, that is, though he wasn't all that big as it happens, went touring every year. It's the cheapest way of seeing the country. We didn't come last year, so it's our first holiday since he died.'

'Did you ever get near Liverpool on one of your tours, sis?' Cormac said mildly. 'Alice gets dead upset whenever your name's mentioned. She misses you. We all do.'

Fion glanced at the children who had eaten the beans on toast, drunk their cocoa and were now munching biscuits, listening avidly to the conversation between their mother and their newly discovered uncle. 'Come on, you two, bed.' She clapped her hands. 'I'll leave the light on and you can take the biscuits with you as a treat, seeing as how we're on holiday, like. Mind a minute, Cormac, there's a good lad.'

She folded down the leaves of the table, which was surrounded on three sides by thickly cushioned benches

covered with red moquette, with storage spaces underneath. Several items of bedding were removed and laid
on two of the benches. The children obediently lay
down and Colin immediately began to suck his thumb.
Then Fion produced two folding stools out of thin air
and took them outside, round to the back of the van, out
of the way of any traffic that might go speeding past. It
was almost dark by now and the air was slightly cooler.

'They don't usually go so willingly to bed, but they're
dead tired. Colin's quiet because the holiday reminds
him of when his dad was alive. He still misses big Colin
something rotten. It doesn't bother Bonnie, she can
hardly remember him. Would you like some orange
juice, Cormac? It's lovely and cold.'

'I'd love some.'

'Won't be a mo.'

Cormac glanced in the direction of the field where the
concert was being held. By now, it was almost dark and
searchlights criss-crossed the sky. Through the interven-
ing hedges he glimpsed a blur of coloured lights and the
thumping music could be clearly heard. It was a familiar
number played by a familiar group whose name he
couldn't remember.

Fion was back with two glasses and a carton of juice.
'Here you are, luv.'

'Ta.'

She sat on the stool, their arms touching. 'You asked
why I've never been home, Cormac. The thing is, I
don't rightly know. I've sent cards from time to time so
Mam would know I was all right, like. I didn't give me
address in case someone came and tried to persuade me
to go back. A year later, when I married Colin, it seemed
too late, too embarrassing, to let anyone know and the
longer it went on the more embarrassing it got.'

'Alice wouldn't have felt embarrassed.'

'I know,' she said abjectly. 'I *should* write, break the ice, as it were, because I'll be coming home to Liverpool soon. Ruby, Colin's mother, died last month and Elsa – she's his daughter from his first marriage – married a soldier and went to live in Germany.' She sighed. 'So there's nothing to keep me in London any more. Me neighbours are lovely, but it's not the same as having your own flesh and blood around. I'd like the children to have a grandma, aunts and uncles, cousins. Colin's due to start school at Christmas and it'd be best for him to start in Liverpool, rather than have him change in a few months' time.'

'There's plenty of room for the three of you in Amber Street, sis.'

'Oh, I've already got a house,' Fion said suprisingly. 'Remember Horace Flynn? He left me his house in Stanley Road. He was the only one who knew I was leaving. I wrote and told him where I lived when I sent back this twenty quid he loaned me and he promised never to tell Mam. We wrote to each other often – he sent a present when me and Colin got married. The house has been rented out for years. It seemed like fate when I got a letter from the tenants giving a month's notice the same week Ruby died. Anyroad . . .' She refilled his glass with juice. 'How is everyone? Has our Maeve had any children yet? Has Orla had more? How are Grandad and Bernadette?' Her voice dropped, became husky. 'And how is our mam, Cormac? I've missed her, you know, every bit as much as she's missed me.'

Cormac didn't doubt it. He knew how easy it was to love someone to distraction, yet treat them with terrible cruelty. At this very moment he was breaking Alice's heart, but his own heart was cold and he didn't care. 'Maeve and Martin haven't had children so far,' he said.

'They're too wrapped up in their house in Waterloo. Orla still only has the four – they're growing up, Lulu's already a teenager. Grandad's retired. He's seventy-two, but as fit as a fiddle, and Bernadette and the kids are just fine.'

'And Mam?'

'How do you think, sis?' Cormac shooed away the dog whose life he'd saved and that had repaid him with a growl. 'You walked out seven years ago and haven't been seen since and her only son has more or less resigned from the human race.'

'Hmm.' Fion gripped her knees. 'I never visualised you becoming a hippy, Cormac. I've always imagined you working in a laboratory, mixing noxious liquids, or whatever it is you do in laboratories, having left university loaded with honours and distinctions. You did, didn't you?' she said anxiously when Cormac pulled a face.

'I didn't finish my degree, Fion. I didn't go back for the last two terms. Alice did her nut. I just missed having to do National Service, I'm pleased to say, otherwise I would have had to register as a conscientious objector.'

'Why do you keep calling her Alice, Cormac? She's our mam.'

He'd love to tell someone, share the knowledge that had been gnawing away at his soul for three and a half years.

'Why, Cormac?' Fion persisted.

'If I tell you, will you promise never to repeat it to a living soul?'

'Cross my heart.'

Cormac took a deep breath. His head felt lighter as he began to relate the story of his twenty-first birthday party, finding Aunt Cora in the kitchen, the terrible things she'd said. 'I can't describe how I felt afterwards.

283

My feet no longer felt as if they were on firm ground. I felt unreal, like a ghost. Living in Amber Street was a great big lie. I couldn't talk to Alice any more. I didn't know what to say, and what I did say sounded stiff and unnatural.' He shook himself, as if trying to rid himself of the memory of that dreadful period. 'I knew it was a waste of time going back to university; my brain seemed to have frozen solid and refused to work. The only place that I could stand was the Cavern, where I was able to drown in the music, it was so loud and I didn't have to think. It was there I met an old mate from St Mary's who was trying to get a pop group together to rival the Beatles. I joined as general dogsbody and chief tambourine player. I've been on the road with different groups ever since. I'm afraid none has come even remotely close to rivalling the Beatles.'

'No other group ever will.' Fion rocked back and forth on the stool. She didn't look as shocked as Cormac had expected. She said, slowly and thoughtfully, 'If I were you, Cormac, I wouldn't believe Cora. I reckon she's jealous, that's all, what with you doing so well and their Maurice being in prison – I met Neil Greene once in London and he told me. She was always trying to stir things up. Look at what she did to Mam with that agreement thing.'

'But, Fion,' Cormac wailed. 'I look so much like her. No one's ever noticed before. When you think about it, it's obvious she's my mother.'

Fion regarded him in the light falling through the window of the caravanette. 'I don't see a resemblance meself. You're probably just imagining it.'

Cormac shivered. 'I can't stand the thought of her being me mother. I have nightmares about it.' He often dreamed of how it might have happened, of Cora slithering through the sleeping hospital, arriving at the nursery, changing him over with Maurice. 'Maurice looked a better bet,' she'd said.

'If I were you,' Fion said again, 'I wouldn't take any notice of Cora. I'd try and pretend she never told you all that stuff.' She linked her arm in his. 'I'll never think of you as anything other than me brother, Cormac, and I know Orla and Maeve feel the same. Grandad thought the sun shone out of your arse. And Mam – you're not being very fair on Mam, luv.'

'Could you forget if it were you it had happened to?'

'No, but I'd want someone to talk to me the way I'm talking to you. It's almost quarter of a century since you were born and whatever happened that night isn't important any more. It's what's happened since that matters.' She gave him a little shake. 'You're Mam's son, our brother, Colin's and Bonnie's uncle.'

'But say if I'm not, Fion?'

'You *are*,' Fion said confidently. 'I remember the day Mam brought you home from hospital. You felt like me brother then, every bit as much as you do now. We all laid claim to you, Cormac. You're *ours*.'

Cormac was beginning to feel as if there was a way out of the morass in which he had been wallowing for so long. If he could just hold on to the fact that what Cora said didn't matter after all this time, that it was how things were *now* that was important. 'What about Uncle Billy,' he said, 'and Maurice?'

'I doubt if Uncle Billy gave a damn who Cora brought home from the hospital. As for Maurice . . .' She paused.

'I owe him a debt worth more than a kingdom,' Cormac said softly.

'*You* don't owe him a thing. If it's all true, not that for a moment I think it is, then I suppose it's hard luck on Maurice.' She wrinkled her nose. 'Well, worse than hard luck, having Cora for a mam.'

'Particularly instead of Alice. He would have grown up a different person altogether in Amber Street. He wouldn't have gone to prison for a start.'

'You can't say that for certain.'

'Yes, I can,' Cormac assured her.

'What's he doing now?'

'Living in the flat over the hairdresser's, where Neil used to live. Cora chucked him out.'

'She's mad,' Fion said flatly. 'She's not likely to say anything about this to Mam, is she? That would really put the cat among the pigeons.'

'I doubt it. I told her if she did I'd kill her. I meant it, Fion. It makes me wonder if one day I might go mad too.'

'Don't be silly. You're the sanest person I've ever known.'

'Once maybe, not now.'

'I'm going to tell *you* a secret, then I'll make us some tea and sandwiches.' Fion regarded him slyly. 'You'll never guess, but Mam was having an affair with Neil Greene. It was the reason I left home. I heard them in bed together and it made me feel such a fool.'

Cormac smiled. 'I already knew that, sis. You couldn't help but notice the way her eyes went all starry when she announced she was "popping round" to Opal Street for some reason. They were even starrier when she came back.'

'Jaysus, Cormac Lacey! Nothing escaped your gimlet eyes.'

Fion went to make the sandwiches. Cormac leant against the back of the van, suddenly conscious of the music in the distance. He'd forgotten where he was. The lane was busy. Children were being brought home from the concert and latecomers were on their way towards it. Two girls, conventionally dressed, rode by on bicycles –

he'd like to bet the young people of the area weren't as opposed to the festival as their elders.

The sky above was as clear as sapphire with a twinkling of stars and a perfectly round moon, but at the edges, just above the horizon, black clouds were banked, looking as impenetrable as mountains. This effect of nature, both impressive and oppressive, made Cormac feel very small, insignificant, in the great scheme of things. Looked at one way, the bombshell that had been dropped on the night of his twenty-first seemed trivial, not worth bothering about.

He wouldn't have minded a spliff, but his stuff was under his pillow in the coach and he didn't feel like going back, not yet. Anyroad, Fion might not approve of spliffs. He was grateful to his sister for bringing him down to earth, showing him there was a future.

As soon as he could, without letting down his friends, he would extricate himself and Pol from the life they were leading – from the life they were *wasting* – and . . .

Cormac paused in his reverie. Two young men were walking past, bare to the waist, supporting a girl between them. In their free hands the men wielded bottles of the local cider, a lethal concoction. The girl stumbled. The men roughly hoisted her upright. One squeezed her bottom through the thin cotton frock that looked ominously familiar.

Pol! She rarely drank. Half a bottle of that lethal brew and she'd be senseless. It was possible she was being taken back to the coach for her own safety, but somehow Cormac doubted it. He leapt to his feet. He had to rescue Pol.

It meant that when Fion emerged from the van with tea and sandwiches, her brother had gone.

★

287

It might have continued for ever and a day: the spliffs, the drink, missing gigs, driving nowhere, doing nothing, had it not been that Pol discovered she was pregnant.

'I can get the bread together for an abortion,' Frank said when they sat round the table for a conference. Everyone had been on tenterhooks waiting for Pol to start her period, but she'd missed two and was definitely pregnant. They wore a motley assortment of coats and jackets because it was November, and no one had any idea how to keep the coach warm, apart from using an oil heater, which brought on Wally's asthma. Being on the road had its disadvantages in winter. 'Abortion's legal in this country, isn't it?'

No one knew.

'I don't want an abortion whether it's legal or not,' Pol said defiantly. 'I want my baby.' She laid her hands on her stomach, as if she could already feel its shape inside.

'Don't be foolish,' Tanya snapped. 'This is no life for a baby.' A baby would clutter up their already cluttered lives. Tanya was very conventional. Cormac sometimes wondered if she was only there to annoy her family and had the firm intention of returning home when she felt she'd annoyed them long enough.

'I'll go away,' Pol said. 'I'll find a place to live, a bedsit, probably in London. The state will support me. I mean, us.'

'Who's the father?' Wally asked.

'I don't know, do I? It's either you, you, or you.' Pol nodded one by one at the three men.

'I'm afraid I can't offer monetary support, Pol.'

'No one's asked you to, Wally.'

'I'll buy the pram and the diapers and stuff, honey.'

'Thank you, Frank.'

'Come back to Liverpool and live with me, Pol,' Cormac said, wincing as he massaged the wrist that had been broken months ago when he'd rescued Pol from the two louts who turned out not to be taking her back to the coach, but to their own ex-Post Office van. The plaster had only been removed last week.

Everyone looked at him in surprise, including Pol. 'Hey, man. Isn't that a bit heavy?' Wally murmured.

'Live with you, Cormac?' Pol's grey eyes smiled into his. 'Why, I'd like that very much.'

'Oh, well, that's settled,' Tanya said, as if they'd just decided which pub to go to. 'Would anyone like a cup of tea?'

Chapter 12

Billy Lacey strolled along the Dock Road, a woman on his arm whose name he couldn't remember. It was August and still very hot, despite the lateness of the hour – at that moment Cormac Lacey was sitting in a remote Norfolk lane with his sister, Fionnuala.

The Docky wasn't nearly so busy as it had been when Billy was a lad and he'd come with his brother, John, to look at the ships. There was hardly any traffic, hardly any ships to look at. Even the smells had gone: the musky aroma of spices, coffee, perfumed teas and the strange, dusty smell that turned out to be carpets. He considered it a poor show that such a vital, throbbing part of Liverpool was being allowed to waste away and die. Only the moon, swinging freely – Billy was drunk – in the navy-blue sky and the soaring brick walls of the docks, the giant gates, remained the same.

Despite the jowlly cheeks and the monstrous beer gut that had long ago cancelled out his waist, leaving his trousers somewhat perilously supported by a narrow leather belt, at fifty-four, Billy was still a fine figure of a man, with his thick, dark hair and broad shoulders. A cheap suit adorned his burly body, the jacket hanging open because it wouldn't meet round his swollen belly. Yet he carried himself well. Not a few female eyes were cast in his direction as he swaggered along, linking the arm of his anonymous companion. She was taking him home for a nightcap. Billy wasn't sure which he was most looking forward to, the drink or what was to follow.

'Have you got a missus?' enquired the woman who was leading him towards the longed-for nightcap and her bed.

'She's left me,' Billy lied. For years now, possibly since the day after the wedding, he'd wished Cora would leave. He would have left himself, except he couldn't be bothered looking for somewhere else to live. Anyroad, he'd have to cook his own food, make his own bed, do his own washing. It was comfortable in Garibaldi Road, if nothing else. He and Cora hardly talked, but he wouldn't mind if she never opened her mouth again for the rest of her life. It was sad about Maurice: first jail, then leaving home, but Billy had never really felt that Maurice was his son. He belonged to Cora, who spoiled the poor lad rotten when she wasn't thrashing him with that bloody cane. He'd probably ended up dead confused. Billy knew he should have put a stop to it, but he'd never been much of a match for his wife.

He had no idea why he'd married her, Cora. He must have been pissed when they met, pissed when he proposed and pissed the day they got married – he could never actually remember saying 'I do', though his mam claimed he'd behaved impeccably at the wedding. Still, it had been done and it was a long time ago now. Billy had quite enjoyed his life, Cora or no Cora. He still did. Another woman mightn't have let him do as he pleased, be so glad to see the back of him. Mind you, it would have been nice to have had a few more bob in his pocket. As it was, Cora took scarcely a penny off him, but he still had to rely on finding some poor woman like the one on his arm, desperate for company, poor cow, to keep his belly primed nightly with ale. He had no idea where Cora got the cash from to keep things going and had never bothered to enquire.

'Are we nearly there, luv?' he asked.

'Yes, Billy. It's just round the next corner.'

The pubs had not long ago called time, otherwise there was no way Billy would have been out in the open, breathing in the fresh, warm air. They were approaching the Arcadia, a pub with such a wicked reputation that even Billy had never dared enter its doors, despite intimate knowledge of most of the ale houses in Bootle. A man and woman came out, arguing furiously. At least the woman was furious, the man appeared to be drunk, but not the boozy, mild sort of drunk that Billy knew. This geezer was paralytic. You could have cut off parts of his body and he wouldn't have known. The woman gave him a shove. 'You're bloody useless, you are,' she sneered. 'I'm giving you a wide berth in future.'

The man collapsed on to his knees, wobbled, then crumpled into the gutter. His eyes, staring upwards, were glazed, unseeing. His face looked as if it had been made of stone.

'Here, mate, let's give you a hand,' Billy said sympathetically. He leant down, put his hands under the man's armpits and hoisted him to his feet. 'Jaysus, you're as light as a feather.'

The man's head hung down, like a scarecrow's, as if he too needed a pole to keep it straight. It wasn't until they were face to face that Billy realised that the man he was supporting was his brother, John, whom he hadn't seen in years.

'Don't tell anyone I'm here,' John said to Cora next morning.

'Not if you don't want me to, luv.'

Cora was in her element. This was the man she had

desired all her adult life and now she had him under her roof, at her mercy, you might say.

She had never seen anyone so thin. No wonder Billy had been able to walk all the way from the Docky with his brother over his shoulder like a sack of coal. Last night they had conversed, she and Billy, for the first time in ages.

'Look who I found!' Billy said when she opened the door, him being unable to use his key, like. 'It's our John. I found him collapsed in the Docky.'

Billy looked upset. If things had been different he might have loved his wife and son, but his brother had been the only person he'd ever felt real affection for. 'I'm taking him upstairs, to Maurice's room,' he said gruffly. He stared defiantly at his wife, as if expecting her to object, but Cora flew ahead to put clean, aired linen on the bed and open the window of the stuffy, unused room.

'He hasn't a pick on him,' Billy said with unexpected tenderness when he laid John down. 'Is there a spare pair of pyjamas?'

'I'll get some.' When Cora came back, Billy was stripping John of his clothes. He looked as if he might object when Cora started to help, but must have decided two pairs of hands were better than one. John moaned once or twice as his clothes were removed and he was lifted into a pair of far too big pyjamas. Cora tucked the bedclothes around his waist.

'What shall we do now, Billy?'

'Leave him be. Let him sleep it off. He's as drunk as David's sow. He'll have a head on him in the morning.'

'He needs building up, Billy. He needs to stay in bed a week and be fed proper. He looks as if he's been neglecting himself something awful.'

'Do you mind if he stays?'

Cora shook her head vigorously. 'I always liked your John. Alice hadn't enough patience with him after the accident. I'm not surprised he left. Where's he been living?'

'I've no idea.'

'I wonder if he's still got that business of his?'

'I don't know, luv. I wrote to him twice at that place in Seaforth, didn't I? But he didn't answer. Mind you, that was years ago.'

They went to bed in their separate rooms. During the night Cora, even less able to sleep than usual, got up and went to look at their guest. The curtains had been left open to allow fresh air through the window and the room was brightly bathed in moonlight. She knelt beside the bed and gently stroked the damaged cheek, which by now was scarcely noticeable. The skin was no longer red and one side of the thin, sombre face was merely slightly more wrinkled than the other. Once he had more meat on him, it would be even less obvious.

Cora breathed a kiss on the thin lips of the man she had always wanted, then went through his pockets, the jacket first. He had three pounds, ten shillings in a wallet, along with a photograph of a fair-haired girl and a separate one of three young children, none of whom she recognised. There were some grubby business cards, including several for B.E.D.S. In another pocket she found a packet of ciggies, a lighter, a dirty hankie, a bunch of keys. His trouser pockets held nothing but change. She rubbed the material between her thumb and forefinger: good quality, but it smelt sour and was badly in need of dry-cleaning.

John was still asleep when his brother went to work next morning. Cora kept popping her head round the door, but it wasn't until midday that she found him staring vacantly at the ceiling. His head, his arms, lying loosely on the covers, were in exactly the same position as the night before, as if he hadn't the strength or will to move them. His eyes turned fractionally when Cora went in, but showed no surprise. He didn't appear particularly bothered where he found himself.

'I was wondering where I was,' he whispered. 'How did I get here?'

'Your Billy found you on the Docky and carried you all the way back. Would you like a cup of tea, luv?'

'I think I might, thank you, Cora.'

She put extra milk in the tea so it wasn't too hot, and had to support his head with one hand and hold the cup for him with the other. It gave her a feeling of intense satisfaction to have John Lacey so dependent on her.

When he'd finished he said, 'Don't tell anyone I'm here.'

'Not if you don't want me too, luv,' Cora assured him.

That afternoon she made him bread and milk, and fed it to him with a spoon. By the time Billy came home he was sitting up, propped against a heap of pillows, smoking a cigarette.

'I didn't know you smoked, mate,' Billy remarked.

John shrugged. 'I started years ago.'

'How are you feeling?'

'Exhausted,' John said thinly.

'What were you doing in the Arcadia, mate? It's a dump.' Billy regarded his older brother with concern. He'd missed John badly since he'd left Alice and had been hurt when his letters hadn't been answered. He found it upsetting to see this once strong, vital man lying like a shadow in the bed. Billy had been raised with the dictum 'Why can't you be more like your brother' constantly in his ear. Mam had made no bones about the fact she liked John best, that she was proud of him, whereas Billy was the family black sheep, the failure. Now it seemed their positions had been reversed and it made Billy feel uncomfortable.

'I can't remember going to the Arcadia,' John confessed. 'In fact, I can't remember anything much about yesterday.'

'Been on a bender, eh!'

'One bender too many, I'm afraid.'

Billy chuckled, though there was nothing to laugh about. He put his hand over his brother's thin one, slightly embarrassed. 'What's up, mate? How did you get yourself in such a state? You look like shit.'

'I feel like shit.' John took a long puff on the ciggie. 'Things happened, Billy. Things I'd sooner not talk about.'

'Whatever you say. Where are you living these days? What's happened to that company of yours?'

'I still do a bit of business – I've been living in the office for quite some time.'

'I'd've come and seen you if I'd known.'

John gave a curt nod of appreciation, but Billy had the odd feeling he wouldn't have been welcome and the even odder feeling that he wasn't particularly welcome now, that John would much prefer to be alone.

'You're looking well, though, Billy,' John said with an obvious effort. 'There's enough fat on you for both of us.'

Billy patted his monstrous stomach. 'It's the ale.'

'You always had a weakness for the ale.' John's mouth curved drily. 'I didn't have any weaknesses, did I? I was the perfect husband, the perfect father, a good provider for me family. Then this happened' – he pointed to his face – 'and I turned out to be weaker than most men. Another bloke would have taken it in his stride and got on with things. I let it ruin me life instead. Nothing's been the same since.'

'It was a brave thing you did that day, John.' Billy had had little experience with conversations of this sort. There was a break in his voice when he said, 'There's hardly another man in the world who would have tried to save that sailor. You should have got a medal.'

'They offered me a medal, but I turned it down, just like, in a way, I turned Alice down, as well as me children. I was determined to suffer and I wanted everyone to suffer with me.'

'Perhaps there's time to put things right yet. Alice is still on her own.'

John didn't answer. Cora came in with a bowl of home-made soup and announced Billy's tea was ready downstairs.

Cora was disappointed when John insisted on feeding himself. She sat on the bed, watching. 'There's jelly and custard for pudding,' she said when he'd finished.

'Maybe later. Thank you, Cora. You and Billy are being very kind. Where's Maurice, by the way? Isn't this his bed I'm in?'

He mustn't have known Maurice had been in jail. Cora wasn't about to tell him now. 'He wanted his independence. He's got his own place. It's in Opal Street, over Lacey's, as it happens.'

Later, Billy came back upstairs and Cora went down. For the first time in years, Billy didn't go to the pub. John softened slightly and the brothers reminisced, reminding each other of things that had happened when they were children. Billy had the most to say, his voice was the loudest. His laughter boomed through the normally silent house, awakening it.

Cora sat with the television on, but the sound turned down, listening, planning tomorrow's menu and the other things she'd do. She'd get John's suit cleaned – his shirt and underclothes were already washed and ironed, his tie sponged. She'd ask if he'd like some books from the library. Unlike his brother, John Lacey had always been a reading man.

John couldn't possibly have been looked after more tenderly and efficiently. 'You should have been a nurse, Cora,' he said when, after seven days of cosseting and being fed bland though nourishing meals, he felt up to coming downstairs for his tea.

It was possibly the first time in Cora's life that she had blushed. 'You just needed a bit of building up, like,' she mumbled. 'You'd let yourself go.'

'I've been letting meself go for years.'

'There's no need for it any more,' Cora assured him eagerly. 'You can stay with us for always. There's plenty of room.' It would be one in the eye for Alice when she discovered her husband was living in Garibaldi Road. Cora had promised not to breathe a word, but it was bound to get out some time.

'We'll just have to see,' John said, lighting a ciggie.

A few days later John announced he felt like a walk. Cora accompanied him round the block, proudly linking his arm. By now, August had turned into September and the air felt cooler. The flowers in the gardens smelt as sweetly as wine. She sniffed appreciatively. Normally, she never noticed such things.

'I enjoyed that,' he said when they got back to the house. 'I might go again tomorrow, further afield.'

'I'll come with you.'

'That would be nice.' His face was filling out, his suit already fitted better. He looked dead handsome, she thought. He had yet to smile, but John Lacey was a dignified, serious man, not much given to laughing and smiling. She wished there were a way of getting shot of Billy, so there'd be just the two of them left in the house.

She bought John a shirt because he only had the one and Billy's swam on him. It had a striped body and a white collar. 'The man in Burton's said it's the latest fashion.'

'Cora! You've made me feel dead embarrassed.' She could tell, though, that he was pleased. It was probably a long time since a woman had made a fuss of him, got him a prezzie.

'This is very smart. I'll wear it tonight.'

'Let me iron the creases out first.'

Billy said John looked like a stockbroker or a solicitor in the shirt and addressed him as 'Sir', while they ate their tea. When the meal was over John announced he was going out. There was someone he wanted to see.

Cora's blood turned to ice. She knew for certain he was going to see Alice and her heart seethed with jealousy. Something told her he intended asking Alice if she would have him back.

'Will you be long?' she asked when he was ready to leave, hair combed, freshly shaved, wearing the shirt *she'd* bought.

'I've no idea, Cora.'

Alice was sitting with her feet on a stool. She'd had a busy day, but then all her days were busy. It was something of an anticlimax to enter the unnaturally quiet house. The emptiness always reminded her of her two missing children. Where was Fion? she wondered fretfully. Why didn't she come home, if only to visit? And she worried constantly about Cormac. At least she saw him from time to time, but something had happened to him that she didn't understand. He appeared with-drawn, almost sullen, yet he was a lad who'd always looked upon the world with such obvious delight.

She hadn't been home long when, much to her relief, the back door opened and Bernadette yelled, 'It's me.'

'Put the kettle on while you're out there,' Alice yelled back. 'How's me dad and the kids?' she asked when her friend plonked herself in an armchair with a deep sigh.

'Everyone's fine. How's yourself?'

'A bit bored, if the truth be known. I quite fancy some excitement.'

'How about the pics? Danny's given me the night off. We could go into town. Henry Fonda's on at the Odeon. I could *eat* Henry Fonda.'

'Oh, we all know the things you'd like to do to Henry Fonda, but when I said excitement I meant something a bit more personal, not watching Henry Fonda having all the excitement.'

'Well, I'm afraid, Ally, that it's the pics or nothing.'

'I suppose the pics are better than nothing,' Alice grumbled. The kettle whistled in the kitchen. 'You can make that tea while I get changed. I won't be a mo.'

Alice had changed into a green linen costume with a fitted jacket and pleated skirt and was brushing her hair when the knock sounded on the door.

'I'll get it,' Bernadette shouted.

There was a long silence. Alice was about to ask 'Who is it?' when Bernadette came into the bedroom. Her face was white.

'It's John,' she said.

'John who?'

'John Lacey, daft girl. Your husband. I'll be getting along home.'

'Don't go, Bernie!' Alice cried, but Bernadette mutely shook her head and ran downstairs. Alice stared at her own white face in the mirror for several seconds before going downstairs herself, holding tightly to the rail to support her trembling legs.

John was standing in the living room. He looked fit enough, she thought, though showed every one of his fifty-six years. He'd also lost a bit too much weight. She would have had to look at him twice if she'd met him in the street before recognising him as the man who was still her husband.

He inclined his head. 'Hello, luv.'

'Hello, John.' She would have preferred it if he hadn't called her 'luv'. It didn't seem right after they hadn't seen each other for so long a time. 'Sit down,' she said politely. 'How are you?'

'Ta, luv.' He sat in his old place under the window. 'I've felt better, but I've felt worse, too. I've been living the last few weeks at our Billy's.'

'I didn't know.' Her voice was very cool — and perfectly steady, she noted with relief. She didn't want him to know how badly she was shaking inside. She prayed she looked as calm as he appeared to be.

'You've hardly changed a bit,' he said.

Alice squirmed uncomfortably when she saw the obvious admiration in his eyes. She didn't reply.

'How are the kids?' he asked.

'Fine. Fion's in London. I'm not quite sure where Cormac is right now. He travels a lot, like. Maeve's married and Orla has four kids, two boys and two girls.' She remembered it was the day Lulu was born that she'd discovered he'd got himself another woman and a brand-new family.

'I suppose our Cormac's in a dead good job. I take it he went to university?'

The 'our' Cormac was another mistake. 'He decided not to in the end,' Alice said coldly. If his father had been around he might have been able to talk his son into completing the last two terms. 'He went into the music business instead. He's in a group that plays all over the country.'

He didn't ask what the group was called, what Fion was doing in London, where did Orla and Maeve live. Alice sensed he'd come for a purpose and it wasn't to know how his family were.

'Would you like some tea? Bernadette made some just before you came.'

'Please, luv.'

She went into the kitchen, poured the tea and wished he'd stop calling her 'luv'. It was getting on her nerves.

'You've got the place looking nice, luv,' he said when she came back. 'All this furniture's new, isn't it? I remember you going on about how much you wanted a fitted carpet.' His eyes swept approvingly around the room. 'Hairdressing must pay well.'

'I've got three salons now.' She resented being reminded of the days when she'd been dependent on him. 'I'm able to buy me own carpets.'

John gnawed his bottom lip. He glanced at her covertly. The coolness of her tone must have got through to him. 'I suppose you're wondering why I'm here?'

'It had crossed me mind.'

'Well, luv, I won't beat about the bush. I'll be totally honest with you. Do you mind if I smoke?'

Wordlessly, Alice fetched an ashtray, though the request surprised her. In the past he'd always claimed smoking was a complete waste of money: 'You may as well set light to a ten-bob note every week or so.' She noticed he'd lost some of his composure. His hands were unsteady as he lit the cigarette.

'The truth is, luv,' he said in a rush, 'I've been going

302

further and further downhill over the last few years until a few weeks ago when I hit rock bottom. I don't want to stay at our Billy's for ever.' He paused. 'I was wondering if you'd mind if I came back home?'

Alice folded her arms over her chest, pressing them against herself so hard that it hurt. At least he'd been honest, as he'd promised. He didn't want to come back because he loved her or he'd missed her, or he wanted to be near his children. He wanted to return because he'd reached rock bottom and had nowhere else to go.

'It's bloody miserable on your own, luv,' he said forlornly.

'I already know that, John. I've been on me own for thirteen years.'

'Well, it'll be nice to have a man around the house for a change,' he said with an attempt at jocularity.

She looked at him directly. 'Not if the man is you. Am I so pathetic that you think *any* man will do for me? Including one who walked out on me for a younger woman and wouldn't be here if that woman hadn't walked out on *him*!'

'It was nothing like you think with Clare. I wouldn't have had anything to do with her if it hadn't been for me accident.'

'Your accident!' Alice laughed bitterly. 'Oh, we all know about your bloody accident. I'm surprised you didn't put a notice in the papers and announce it to the world. You'd think you were the only person who'd ever been hurt. In turn, you hurt everyone who loved you. I'll not forget when you moved in permanently with Clare. Cormac kept ringing the yard. He wanted his dad, but you'd have nothing to do with him. You were dead cruel, John. Cruel and selfish. People don't go that way because they've had an accident. It must have been there always. You just hadn't shown it before.'

'I'm sorry, Alice.' His body had gone limp. He lit another cigarette from the stub of the first and seemed to have trouble making contact.

'So you should be,' Alice said brutally, then immediately regretted it. 'Look,' she said more kindly. 'There's nothing to stop you coming round now and then for a cup of tea. I could arrange for Maeve and Orla to be here.'

'I doubt if they'd want to see me.'

On reflection, Alice doubted it too. 'You could still come round. I could make you a meal.'

'Do you really want me to?'

She couldn't meet his eyes because she could think of few things she wanted less. Until that night she hadn't realised he meant so little to her, that she actually disliked him. 'Of course,' she said.

It was John's turn to laugh. 'I think I get the picture. Perhaps I should have said I wanted to come back because I love you.'

'It wouldn't have made any difference. And it wouldn't have been true.'

'Oh, yes, it would, Alice. I *do* love you. I've never loved anyone else the way I love you.' His face collapsed. He was almost crying and it was horrible seeing a man like John Lacey so close to tears. He dropped the cigarette. The glowing end fell on his shirt, and she leapt to her feet and knocked it away before it burnt a hole, then picked up the ciggie off the carpet. She was still holding it when John grabbed her legs and laid his head against her stomach. 'I do love you, Alice.' He sobbed. 'I can't go on living the way I am.'

She pushed him away, wanting to cry herself. 'But I don't love you, John.' She only wished she did. Then she would have been happy to take him back.

He collapsed into the chair. 'What am I to do?' he asked pitifully. 'Where am I to go?'

'Home.'

'I haven't got a home.'

'Back to your Billy's, then.'

'I can't stay there for ever. You know how much I've always loathed Cora.'

Alice had reached the point where *she* had begun to feel cruel and selfish. 'I'll find you a home, a little house somewhere,' she said desperately. 'I'll give you the money for the furniture if you're short.'

It was a genuine offer, made because she felt genuinely sorry for him, but it immediately brought her husband to his senses. His face turned to stone. 'Do you really think I'd take money off a woman?'

'I'm offering to help, John, that's all.'

'I don't want your help, or your sympathy.'

'What else do you expect when you start crying?'

He got to his feet. 'I have the distinct feeling I've made a fool of meself. I think I'll go now.'

'John.' She put her hand on his arm, but he shrugged her away. Alice had a sense of déjà vu. In the past, he'd done the same thing when she'd been trying to reach him and had been rewarded with the same churlish rejection.

'Goodnight, Alice.'

Alice shut her eyes until the front door closed. She didn't open them until she heard someone coming in the back way.

Seconds later her dad barged in, livid with anger. 'Is he still here?' he demanded.

'No, Dad. He's gone.'

'What did he want?'

'To come back.'

'The nerve of the bugger. I hope you told him to go

. . . to go . . .' Danny paused, trying to think of a way of putting it without using an unacceptable expletive. 'To go and jump in the lake.'

'I just said no, Dad.'

'He's upset you, hasn't he? I can tell by your face.'

'Oh, Dad,' Alice cried. 'He seemed so *tragic*. I feel sorry for him. What's going to happen to him now?'

'That's no longer any of your concern, girl. You're too soft, you are. If John Lacey's tragic, then it's his own fault. He's already put you through enough. Come on, luv.' He put an arm round her shoulders. 'Come back to ours and have a cup of tea, then you can go to the pictures with Bernadette. Even better, go somewhere and have a nice meal and a jangle.'

Alice willingly allowed herself to be led away. Anything would be better than being left with her own thoughts. She just wished she didn't have the horrible feeling that she'd let John down.

If only you could relive certain scenes in your life and do them differently! He should have been more controlled with Alice, more practical. He shouldn't have broken down, made himself look pathetic. Perhaps he should have asked more questions about the children, then approached the subject of him coming home more casually, skirting round it, like, as if the idea had just come to him. As it was, he'd made a terrible show of himself. His flesh crawled, thinking about it.

She'd looked so lovely, too: fresh and young, elegant in that green costume. She'd changed, though, since they used to live together. She'd never have said the things then that she'd said tonight – 'Do you think *any* man will do me?' – as if he was just a piece of shit.

In Marsh Lane, John paused outside an off-licence and realised how much he needed a drink. A sup of liquor hadn't passed his lips since the night Billy had carried him home from the Docky. He'd sworn never to get in such a state again, but now he felt like getting smashed rotten. He went into the shop and bought a bottle of whisky, the cheapest there. Outside, he stopped in the first doorway, unscrewed the top, put the bottle to his lips and swallowed deeply. The alcohol seemed warmly familiar as it poured down his throat and he immediately felt better, more in charge of himself.

He walked towards Garibaldi Road, only slightly unsteady on his feet, anger mounting. Who did Alice think she was? Had she forgotten that they were still man and wife, that he had rights? It could be she had no lawful right to turn him away. It could be that the house in Amber Street was still legally his. It was *his* name that used to be on the rent book. He might go and see a solicitor tomorrow.

Cora opened the door as he was struggling with the key. 'I'll give you a key if you like, luv.' She nodded at the one in his hand. 'That must be for somewhere else.'

'Sorry.' He frowned at the key. It was for the padlock on the gates of the yard.

'You weren't gone long,' Cora said, slyly pleased. There'd obviously been no great reconciliation.

'Where's Billy?' John lurched into the hall.

'He went out not long after you. Why don't you come and watch telly till he comes home?'

'I'd sooner go to bed early, if you don't mind. I feel very tired.'

'Anything you like, luv.'

Cora could smell the drink on him. As he went unsteadily upstairs, she saw the whisky bottle protruding from the pocket of his jacket. Alice must have turned him down.

What John didn't realise was that the woman who was

perfect for him was directly under his nose – herself. They thought the same black thoughts, they looked darkly upon life, they didn't suffer fools gladly, they took great risks.

For the next two hours she sat in front of the empty grate, hands clasped on her lap, unmoving. Billy came in and wanted to know if John was home, and she told him he was in bed, but didn't mention the whisky.

'I think I'll turn in meself,' Billy announced, yawning.

Within minutes she could hear him snoring. And still Cora sat, shoulders tense, arms stiff, hands held together tightly, like a knot in a rope. Dare she show John, that very night, how exactly right they would be for each other? Billy wouldn't hear. The house could fall down around Billy's ears, but you'd still have to shake his arm to wake him.

Dare she?

She'd known he was for her the very second she'd set eyes on him. She felt certain something had passed between them. But he wasn't the sort of man who'd steal his brother's girl. He'd pretended to ignore her, but she could tell he wanted her as much as she wanted him. Alice, wishy-washy, gormless Alice Mitchell, was merely a substitute for the woman he really loved.

Cora went upstairs and changed into her best nightie. It was blue, that brushed-nylon stuff, and she'd got it in a sale in T. J. Hughes's. She undid her bun and combed her greying hair loose around her shoulders. There was scent somewhere, Californian Poppy, that Alice had given her for Christmas in the days when she'd been made welcome in Amber Street. She found the tiny bottle in a drawer under her stockings and dabbed some behind her ears.

Then she crept along the landing to the room where John Lacey slept.

He lay sprawled on the bed in his vest and underpants, his suit and the shirt she had bought him thrown carelessly on the floor. On the bedside table the whisky bottle was three-quarters empty and the clean ashtray she'd provided earlier overflowed with butts. The smell of smoke, of whisky fumes, only increased Cora's desire. She leant over the bed and started to touch him.

'Darling!' John reached for her and began to stroke her body through the scratchy nightdress. Cora pulled it over her head, leaving herself entirely exposed to him, giving herself, touching him as he touched her. Her body arched and shuddered with pleasure beneath his exploring hands. Then he thrust himself inside her and she had to hold back a shriek as a feeling, impossible to describe, began to grow and grow in her gut, like a firework, sizzling away, getting brighter and brighter, louder and louder, as it prepared to explode in a shower of stars and sparks.

Then the explosion came and her body, from head to toe, was encased in a silent scream of ecstacy. Cora had been waiting all her life for this day, for this hour, for this single minute.

She fell back on the bed, blissfully exhausted. John grunted, collapsed beside her and immediately fell asleep, but she didn't care. She snuggled against him and put her arm round his waist.

'That was nice, luv. It was never that way with your Billy,' she whispered. 'Later on, we'll do it again. We'll do it again and again for the rest of our lives. We're soulmates, you and me. I bet I could tell you things and you wouldn't be the least bit shocked.' She looked at his face, wondering if he could hear. 'I've never breathed a word about this to a soul, but I killed two people once. They were me aunties, Kate and Maud. You see, luv, me mam wasn't married when she had me and she died right after I was born. I never knew who me dad was. Kate and Maud, they took me in, but they didn't like me. Oh, no, they didn't like me a bit. I was a "badge of shame", they said. They treated me worse than an animal, fed me scraps, hit me and kicked me whenever they felt like it. I got hardly any learning. I never even learnt how to be happy, like. So, you know what I did?'

She paused, half expecting him to say, 'What, luv?' but there was no answer. 'I murdered them. I set fire to the house we lived in. I waited in the backyard till I heard them scream, then I waited till the screaming stopped, then I ran away. Sometimes, in the dead of night, I can still hear them screams. I can even smell the fire. It's the reason I can never sleep.' Cora sighed. 'Are you comfy, luv?' She adjusted the pillow beneath his head, pulled the sheet over them both. 'You have a nice rest, now, and when you wake up I'll make you feel dead happy again.'

Cora had never known what it was to relax, for her body to feel rested, her soul to be at peace, her brain to feel as light as air, and free for once of the thoughts and memories that plagued her. Before long, although it was the last thing she intended, she, too, was fast asleep.

The palest of grey light was creeping through the window when John Lacey woke. The birds in the garden had just begun to sing. For a few seconds he felt disorientated.

He recognised the lampshade hanging above him and remembered he was at Billy's. It took several more seconds before he realised there was someone in bed with him: a woman. For one mad moment he thought it might be Alice. He'd been to see her the night before. But the hair just visible in the still dusky shadows of the morning was the wrong colour. Anyroad, Alice had turned him down and he'd bought a bottle of whisky.

He'd obviously gone somewhere, met a woman and couldn't remember a thing about it – it had happened before. He must have been plastered out of his mind to have brought her back to his brother's house.

Jaysus! He was longing for a fag. As soon as he'd smoked it, he'd get rid of his companion of the night as quietly as possible. Gingerly he eased himself out of bed. The ciggies were on the bedside table. He lit one, breathed in deeply, then noticed the blue nightdress thrown over the foot of the bed.

His reflexes must be working dead slow this morning, because it took John quite a while to realise the significance of this. There was only one person the nightdress could belong to.

Cora! He stumbled backwards, horrified. Cora Lacey was lying in his bed, naked. They must have . . .

Christ! He wanted to be sick. Something stirred in his sluggish brain, a memory, of hands touching him, of him touching back. He could remember them making love – and that it had actually felt good. He gagged. He had to get out of here.

Frantically he picked up his clothes, the ciggies, the remainder of the whisky and carried them on to the landing, where he clumsily got dressed, thrusting his foot into the wrong trouser leg, buttoning up his shirt all crooked. As he did so other memories returned, of a voice in his ear talking about murder, about burning people alive in their beds, listening to their screams.

Outside, a fine grey mist hung in the air and he could feel the moisture on his face as he walked towards Seaforth, towards the place that had been his home since Clare had left with their children.

Every now and then he stopped and took a mouthful of whisky. If he drank enough for long enough it might drown out the memory of last night.

By the time he reached the yard the whisky had gone and he could hardly walk. He flung the empty bottle into the gutter, where it smashed into a thousand brilliant shards. It took some time to fit the key into the padlock on the gates, more time to unlock the door of the two-storey building that was a store room, an office and the place where he lived – there was little use for an office these days. B.E.D.S. was all washed up. He'd been neglecting the firm for years. He owed money for the materials going rotten in the yard.

Somehow he managed to climb the stairs, where he collapsed on the filthy bed and immediately lit a ciggie.

The place stank, but he couldn't be bothered getting up and opening a window. He couldn't remember when it had last been cleaned. For years, now, he had let himself wallow in his misery, in the dirt of his surroundings. He had let B.E.D.S. collapse around his ears.

It never ceased to amaze him that a man as sensible as he'd always considered himself had made such a total and completely unnecessary mess of his life, culminating in last night's misadventure with Cora. He squirmed at the memory and wondered if he'd just imagined the things she'd said. Was his brother's wife a murderer?

In a minute he'd look for something to drink. He'd drink himself completely senseless, so he wouldn't be able to think. There were times, like the night Billy had found him on the Docky, when his mind was nothing but a blank.

The fag had burnt so low he could feel the heat on his lips. He spat it out and reached for another. The effort of stretching made his head swirl crazily and John didn't mind a bit when he found himself sinking into welcome unconsciousness.

The stub of the cigarette had landed on the bed, rolled under the pillow. John Lacey was too far gone to notice when the pillow began to smoulder.

Chapter 13

The police were still trying to trace the relatives of John Lacey, the man whose charred body had been found after the fire in the timber yard had been extinguished, when Fionnuala Littlemore returned to Liverpool with her children.

It was Sunday afternoon, and Fion came in the back way just as Alice was preparing a salad for Maeve and Martin who were expected later for tea.

'Hello, Mam,' Fion said, as casually as if she'd been gone five minutes, not several years.

'Fion!' Alice dropped a slice of ham on the floor. 'Oh, Fion, luv. It's good to see you.' She flung her arms round her eldest daughter, stroked her face. 'How are you, luv? Where have you been? And who are these?' Only then did Alice become aware of the children.

'This is Colin and this is Bonnie, and we've been living in London. Say hello to your grandma, kids.'

'They're yours?' Alice dropped more ham.

'Very much mine, Mam. And before you ask, their dad, me husband that is, died two years ago.'

'Oh, luv!' Alice burst into tears for the son-in-law she'd never met and hadn't even known existed. 'Oh, they're lovely children,' she said tearfully. 'Let's take a look at you.' She knelt down and examined Colin's face. 'You must take after your dad, because you're nothing like our family. And you' – she turned to Bonnie – 'are the image of your mam.'

Both judgements seemed to please the children inordinately. Alice forgot the salad and took them into the living room.

Fion immediately made herself at home. 'I'll put the kettle on, Mam. I'm dying for a cuppa.'

'I wouldn't say no to a cuppa either.' Alice drew her new grandchildren on to her knee. They went willingly. 'You're prettier than Ruby,' Bonnie said.

'Who's Ruby?'

'Ruby was their other grandma,' Fion said as she came in. 'She was much older than you. She died a few months ago. That's why we're back home.'

She'd come home for good! Alice did her best not to feel glad that the unknown Ruby had died, otherwise Fion, who'd clearly not acquired an ounce of tact in her absence, would still be in London. Her daughter had acquired one thing, though – confidence. Alice watched as Fion unzipped a small travelling bag and began to root swiftly and efficiently through the contents. She seemed very sure of herself. She was slimmer and had grown her hair, which was gathered in an untidy knot on top of her head. Long wavy tendrils had escaped and trailed over her neck and ears. Her outfit was a bit peculiar: black slacks and a thin black jumper under a brightly coloured patchwork waistcoat. Neil Greene, who'd met her in London, said she worked for a union.

'Oh, it's good to see you, Fion,' Alice cried. 'You look wonderful.' Her mind went back to the day Fion, her first child, had been born. She'd arrived two weeks late, after a long, tiresome labour, very early in the morning. At almost nine pounds, she was the biggest of Alice's babies – and the biggest in the maternity home, she remembered. John had been so proud. She recalled him taking his daughter in his arms, looking down at her, his eyes filled with love. It had never crossed her mind that one day that love would disappear.

'It's good to see you, Mam,' Fion said practically. 'And you don't look so bad yourself.'

'Where's your luggage, luv? You won't last long out of that small bag.'

'I've got more than luggage, Mam. I've got furniture. It's coming in a van tomorrow.'

Alice felt alarmed. 'But there isn't the room here for furniture, Fion.'

'I know that.' Fion snorted. 'I'm not an idiot. The furniture's going to me house on Stanley Road.'

'You've got a house!'

'It's Horace Flynn's old house that he left me in his will.'

'Bloody hell!' exclaimed Alice, who usually managed not to swear if children were present. 'Who'd have thought it, eh? Wonders will never cease.'

'Is our Orla still living in Pearl Street?'

'Yes, luv,' Alice said weakly, still trying to come to terms with the incredible fact that Horace Flynn's house in Stanley Road now belonged to Fion. 'Maeve's in Waterloo. Her and Martin are coming to tea.'

'I'll go round and see Orla in a minute. I'll leave the kids with you, if you don't mind.'

'As if I'd mind being left with these two little darlings,' Alice cried, hugging the children to her. 'Ask Orla and everyone back to tea. I'll take Colin and Bonnie round me dad's and see if Bernadette can lend us some food. Oh, I can't remember when I last felt so happy.' Fion's return more than made up for John's recent visit, the memory of which still haunted her.

To make things even better Fion had news of Cormac. 'I think he might soon be back as well.'

'Did he say what was wrong?' Alice asked anxiously. 'I think something must have happened at university to make him not want to go back. He was doing so well, too.'

'He didn't say anything, Mam. Perhaps he'd been studying so much his brain got tired. I've heard it can happen.'

Alice sighed blissfully. 'I can't wait to have him home. It'll be just like old times, all four of you here. And these two little 'uns will make it absolutely perfect.'

'Oh, so you saw fit to show your face again, Fion Lacey.' Orla's face was cold when she opened the door to find her sister on the step. 'You know, Mam was dead upset when you walked out.'

'She was dead upset when Micky Lavin put you up the stick,' Fion said, grinning. 'So I reckon we're even when it comes to upsetting Mam. And it's Fion Littlemore, if you don't mind. I'm a mother now of two small children.'

Orla's cold expression vanished and she grinned back. 'It's great to have you home, sis. You look marvellous. Our Maeve's become a real pain since she got married. All she talks about is her bloody house.'

'It's good to *be* home, Orla. Now, are you going to let me in, or must I stand on this doorstep for ever?'

An impromptu party took place at the Laceys' that night. Danny Mitchell went to the off-licence and returned laden with wine, beer and crisps. Bernadette quickly made two dozen sausage rolls. Orla, never an expert in the kitchen, coaxed Lulu into making a tray of fairy cakes. Maeve was telephoned and asked to bring whatever was available.

'I bought a tin of iced biscuits for Christmas the other

day. I'll fetch them and anything else I can find,' Maeve promised. 'Tell our Fion I can't wait to see her.'

'Jaysus! She's become so *efficient*!' Orla groaned. 'Who in their right mind buys biscuits for Christmas in September?'

'Our Maeve does, obviously. It's no worse than someone with four children not being able to rustle up a fairy cake.'

'You've not changed, Fion. You were always one to call a spade a spade.'

'I could never understand why anyone would want to call a spade anything else. Are my Elvis records still around, Mam?'

'They're in the parlour, luv. You'll find Cormac's there too. He was fond of Gerry and the Pacemakers and Herman's Hermits – and the Beatles, of course.'

It's quite like old times, Alice thought as she prepared a mountain of sandwiches and listened to her daughters bicker. But there was no spite behind it now. Fion wasn't jealous of Orla any more. She felt her equal.

Eight o'clock. Most of the adults were slightly tipsy. Colin and Bonnie were upstairs, tired after the long journey from London, fast asleep in their mother's old room. The other children were in the parlour playing something that seemed to require a great deal of noise.

The weather had changed. The long Indian summer had ended late that afternoon when the sun abruptly disappeared and the sky became a solid mass of black, leaden clouds. Thunder rumbled in the distance, lightning flashed. Every now and then there would be a splattering of rain against the windows. A downpour was expected any minute.

In Amber Street the lights were on and the weather

did nothing to dampen spirits. The three men were contemplating going to the pub for a pint.

'But we've got beer here,' Alice pointed out.

'It tastes different in a pub,' Danny claimed.

'What happens if it rains?' Orla wanted to know. 'I'm not pressing your best suit if it gets soaked, Micky Lavin.'

Maeve looked reproachfully at Martin. 'Fancy deserting me for a pint of beer!' the look said. Martin affected to ignore it.

'Well, will we or won't we?' Danny demanded.

Micky slapped him on the shoulder. 'I say we will.'

'Me, too.' Martin was still avoiding Maeve's accusing stare.

Lulu appeared in the doorway, her blue eyes round and slightly scared. 'There's a police car stopped outside,' she said. 'The man's just got out.'

There was a knock on the door.

Alice still felt shattered next day. 'It's all my fault,' she said hoarsely. 'If only I'd taken him back!'

'Don't be daft, Mam. If I'd come home and found him here I'd have been out the house again like a shot.'

'Don't say things like that, Fion.'

'Well, don't you go saying stupid things like it's all your fault. It's nobody's fault but his own. The police said the fire was started by a cigarette. He could have done the same thing here and it wouldn't have been just him who'd gone up in smoke, but you as well.'

Alice sighed. 'You sound awfully hard, luv.'

'I'm just being sensible, Mam,' Fion said more gently. 'Why don't you go in to work, try and forget him.'

'As if I could forget your dad! He was everything to me once.' Alice looked imploringly at her daughter. 'You'll come to the funeral, won't you, luv? I wish we could get in touch with Cormac, tell him.'

'I'll come for your sake, Mam, not his. Orla and Maeve are coming for the same reason, and Grandad and Bernadette. As for Cormac, he's lucky to be out of it. I only wish I'd left coming back another week and I'd've been out of it too.'

Billy Lacey was the only person to cry at his brother's funeral. His sobs sounded harsh and bitter across the deathly wastes of Ford Cemetery. It was a strange morning, neither warm nor cold, not quite sunny, not quite dull.

Billy's wife made no attempt to comfort him. The other mourners would have been surprised if she had. Cora's face was as strange as the morning. She gave no sign to show that she cared her brother-in-law had gone.

It was left to Maurice who, at twenty-five, could have been the double of the young John Lacey, to step forward and put his arm around the broad, heaving shoulders.

'Never mind, Dad,' Maurice mumbled awkwardly, and father and son embraced, as they had never done before.

Alice wouldn't let herself cry, because the tears would have been for herself, not John. They would have been hypocritical tears. She was sorry John had died such a horrible death, but her prime emotion was guilt that she might have stopped it.

John's daughters were there purely for their mother's sake. Alice was a stickler for appearances. It mattered to Mam what people, particularly the neighbours, thought. However, so far, none of the neighbours had guessed that the John Lacey, whose death in a fire in Seaforth was reported in the local paper, was the John Lacey who once lived in Amber Street.

Good riddance to bad rubbish, Danny Mitchell

thought as the coffin was lowered into the grave. Our Alice should be glad to see the back of him.

Bernadette Mitchell thought more or less the same.

Only one piece of paper remained that had belonged to John Lacey. All the rest had been destroyed in the fire, every scrap; the unpaid bills, the files, the audited accounts going back for years, every single letter John had ever received and the carbon copies of those he had sent, the photos of Clare and their children.

The paper that remained had been lodged in a bank. It was a deed, confirming that John had owned the freehold of the piece of land fronting the corner of Benton Street and Crozier Terrace. Alice, as the lawfully wedded wife of the deceased, was now the legal owner, so the bank informed her in a letter.

'I don't want it,' she said with a shudder when she showed the letter to her dad.

'Then get the place cleaned up. It's bound to be in a mess. And sell it,' Danny advised.

What would she do with the money? There was money piling up in the bank from the three salons, but none of her children was prepared to take a penny. Maeve and Martin had refused help with their mortgage, and Micky Lavin had been indignant when she'd offered to buy him and Orla a house. Cormac had lived happily on his grant at university and she had a feeling Fion wouldn't let her pay for Horace Flynn's old place to be done up – it was dead shabby and the plumbing made some very peculiar noises.

Why was she bothering to make all this money when there was nothing to spend it on? She was fed up with her customers wondering aloud why she was still in Amber Street, why she hadn't bought herself a nicer house in a nicer place.

'Because I'm perfectly happy where I am,' she would reply. She felt very dull and unimaginative.

Fion was looking for someone to care for the children so she could go to work. Alice could sell the salons and become a full-time grandma.

'No, I need more than that,' she told herself. 'I may well be dull and unimaginative, but I need to *be* someone, not just a mother or a grandmother, not just a wife. I need to be special in me own way.'

Since John's death, Billy Lacey had taken to calling on his sister-in-law on his way home from work. Alice was the closest link to the brother he had lost, found, and finally lost again.

He couldn't understand why John had left the house in Garibaldi Road, he said repeatedly. 'He was in bed when I came home the night before, but gone next morning, without a word of explanation. I thought he was happy there. He *seemed* happy. Cora liked having him. He could have stayed for ever as far as we were concerned.'

Alice didn't mention it was the night before that she'd turned John away. She already blamed herself enough and she didn't want the burden of Billy's blame as well.

'Have you ever been to that timber yard place?' Billy asked.

'Just the once.'

'I should have gone meself. It's not far. I shouldn't have let him sink into such a state, me own brother, like.'

'Don't reproach yourself, Billy. John knew where you lived. It was him who walked out, on all of us, including you. It was up to him to keep in touch, not for you to search him out.' Alice wished she could take her own sensible advice. She showed Billy the letter from the bank.

'Do you mind if I take a look at the place?' His face brightened. 'I'll tidy it up if you like.'

He would have been hurt if she'd turned him down. She accepted his offer with a show of gratitude, though she didn't give a damn what happened to the yard. Billy perked up considerably and decided to go round to Seaforth there and then.

'I'll call for our Maurice on the way. The two of us can do the job together.'

At least one good thing had come out of John's death: Billy and his wayward son were now reunited.

The iron-barred gate was secured with a padlock and chain. The men peered through the bars at the dismal remains of John's once thriving business. The building he had lived in had almost completely burnt away. There were no walls and only the skeleton of the roof remained, the beams silhouetted starkly against the livid evening sky – more rain looked inevitable later.

The yard itself was covered with ash and soot, mixed with other debris, including curls of black tar paper, like apple peelings, from the roof. Pools of black water reflected the angry yellow sky. The few lengths of timber stacked around the walls had been badly singed. There was a rusty van with a flat tyre.

'We'll have to get a key from somewhere to match the padlock,' Billy said.

'It'll be a job and a half, clearing this place up,' said Maurice.

'You don't mind though, do you, son? After all, it's not as if you've got anything else to do.'

'I don't mind and no, I haven't got anything else to do.' Maurice's voice was bitter. A prison record didn't help when you were looking for a job. Maurice hadn't worked since he'd come out of Walton jail, though he'd never stopped trying.

'I didn't mean it like that, son.'

'I know, Dad. I was a fool to break into that newsagent's. I only did it to impress some girl – I can't even remember her name. I know I shouldn't make excuses. I was an adult. I should've known better, but her brothers talked me into it.' Maurice laughed drily. 'They made it sound so easy.'

They began to walk back towards Bootle. 'You know,' Maurice said after a while, 'we could do something with that yard.'

'Such as?'

'I'm not sure. Remember that place I used to work, the builders' merchants? Something like that.'

'We'd need money to get started, son.' Billy jangled the coins in his pocket. They were all he had until he got paid on Friday.

'You can borrow money from the bank to start a business. Not that they'd lend it me,' Maurice said hastily. 'Not with my record. But they might lend it you. After all, we've already got the premises.'

'Who said we've got the premises. Alice wants the place sold.'

'She won't sell if we tell her our plans,' Maurice said with utter conviction. 'Not Auntie Alice. Anyroad, once we get going we'll pay rent. We might even buy the site off her one day.'

'What plans?' Billy asked, bewildered.

'The plans you and me have to start our own business. Dad.' For the second time in a week Maurice placed his arm round his father's shoulders. 'I wonder if that van goes?'

Cormac came into the salon wearing an Afghan coat that

looked as if it had been gnawed by a hungry animal, red cotton trousers and open-toed sandals, despite it being November and very cold. His long fair hair was tied back with a ribbon. He looked a sight.

Alice was torn between the joy of seeing him again and worry that her customers would recognise who he was. She rushed her once-perfect son into the kitchen. 'Fion said to expect you one day soon.' She longed to kiss and hug him, but Cormac seemed to have gone off that sort of thing. 'Are you hungry, luv? Shall we go home and I'll make you something to eat?'

'I've just eaten at Fion's, thanks.'

'You went to see Fion first?' Alice felt hurt.

'I wanted to put my stuff there.' For some reason he refused to meet her eyes. 'I'll be living at Fion's, on the top floor. I hope you don't mind.'

'Of course not.' Alice minded very much, but didn't show it. 'Your room's always there if you change your mind.'

'The thing is' – he shuffled his near-naked feet – 'I've brought a girl. We'll be living together.'

Alice swallowed and reminded herself that young people did this sort of thing nowadays. 'I hope she's nice. What's her name?'

'Pol. She's very nice. She's also pregnant.'

To Alice's surprise she burst out laughing and at the same time thanked God he hadn't expected to live in Amber Street with his pregnant girlfriend. 'What else are you going to tell me, that she's got two heads?'

Cormac smiled for the first time. 'No, just one head, Mam. Fion said to come round tonight so you can meet her.'

It might have been a mistake, but he'd called her Mam, something else he avoided these days, along with the hugs and kisses.

★

Horace Flynn would have turned in his grave if he could have seen the state of his house, which hadn't seen a lick of paint in years. The few pieces of expensive furniture still remaining were covered in cigarette burns and the scars of too hot cups. Cats – Fion already had two strays – had scratched curves in the legs of the mahogany table, the six chairs that went with it and the lovely sideboard that used to house Horace's pretty ornaments.

Fion's own furniture was cheap stuff, similarly marked with years of wear and tear. Alice suspected it had been bought second-hand.

She had insisted on paying for the curtains to be cleaned – they were too thick and heavily lined to wash – because they made the rooms smell musty. 'Regard it as a prezzie,' she said to Fion. 'People usually buy each other house-warming presents.'

The long velvet parlour curtains had emerged from the cleaners in tatters. 'They were rotten,' the woman assistant announced when Alice went to collect them. 'I'm afraid we can't pay compensation.'

Alice had bought replacements, but Fion didn't notice that the curtains that went up in the parlour were different from the ones that came down. Fion seemed oblivious to her surroundings. The shabby furniture didn't bother her. Neither did the clanky, grumbling plumbing, the ancient bathroom, the tatty carpet on the stairs, the grimy ceilings, the wallpaper peeling in the corners . . .

And it wasn't just stray animals Fion had started to collect, but human beings too. Alice had no idea where she found them. The three Littlemores lived on the vast ground floor. On the floor above, in the front bedroom, a Mrs Freda Murphy spent her days knitting unwearable garments for the children.

'Where did she come from, luv?' Alice asked curiously

when Freda first turned up. Fion had scarcely been living in the place a week.

'Her son was all set to throw her out. The thing is, Mam,' Fion said indignantly, 'the rent book used to be in her name, but he persuaded her to change it.'

How had Fion *known?* Alice didn't bother to pursue the matter.

Not long afterwards the Archibalds arrived, Peter and Geoffrey, twin brothers in their thirties, who occupied the bedroom at the back. 'They've been in a mental home, poor things,' said Fion.

'Are you sure they're safe, y'know, with the children, like?' Alice asked nervously.

'There's nothing wrong with them, Mam. They went in the mental home by mistake. Anyroad, it's only temporary. The corporation have promised to find them a proper house.'

Now Cormac was moving into the top floor with a pregnant girl called Pol and there were still two bedrooms empty. Alice dreaded who might turn up next.

Yet the strange thing was that she loved being at Fion's. The fire in the living room was always lit, the shabby chairs were comfortable, tea was permanently in the pot for anyone to help themselves. The telephone rang non-stop, because Fion, who never used to have a single friend, now seemed to have dozens. Alice discovered she was a member of numerous organisations and charities, and was always in the throes of arranging fund-raising events: jumble sales, coffee mornings, parties, lectures. She had persuaded her mother to help at a Christmas bazaar early in December. A few weeks ago she had taken the children down to London for a CND march.

'What's CND?' Alice asked.

'The Campain for Nuclear Disarmament. Honestly, Mam, you're dead ignorant. All you know about is hairdressing.'

Alice humbly agreed.

She felt very nervous the night that she went to meet Cormac's pregnant girlfriend. She prayed that they would like each other and that Pol would make a suitable wife – she assumed they would get married one day – for Cormac, who was a remarkable lad and would make a wonderful husband.

Freda Murphy opened the door to Alice's knock, the long needles of her untidy knitting tucked under her arms. Two strange children were playing in the hall with Colin and Bonnie.

In the living room a woman with a black eye was talking in a high-pitched, angry voice to Fion.

'Hello, Mam,' Fion said calmly. 'This is Jenny. She's staying with us a while until the police do something about her louse of a husband. Our Cormac's upstairs with Pol. Tell them to come down in a minute; I've made some scouse.'

'You gave birth to an angel when you had that girl,' Freda remarked when Alice reappeared.

'Did I really?' She went up two flights of stairs. The top floor was merely one large room with a sloping ceiling and windows at both ends.

'Come in,' Cormac shouted in answer to her knock.

Alice took a deep breath, opened the door, and found Cormac and a young girl sitting crossed-legged on the floor, facing each other and holding hands.

'We're doing breathing exercises,' Cormac said. 'We've bought a book on what to do when you're having a baby. This is Pol, by the way. Pol, say hello to . . . to my mother.'

'Hello, Mrs Lacey,' Pol said in a breathless, childish

voice. She scrambled to her feet, a rosy-cheeked girl, with guileless eyes and curly brown hair. She wore an ankle-length cotton skirt and a coarse woven top. Her feet, like Cormac's, were bare. She looked no more than sixteen.

'Call me Alice.' They shook hands. Pol's hand was very small and limp. 'How are you feeling, luv? When's the baby due?'

'I feel fine. I haven't been sick or anything. I'm not sure when it's due.' She looked vague.

'Well, the doctor should be able to tell,' Alice said comfortably. 'He'll send you to the clinic where they'll keep an eye on you.'

Pol gave a tinkling little laugh. 'Oh, there's no need for doctors and clinics, Alice. As long as I look after myself, eat properly and do the breathing exercises I shall be OK.'

'I see.' Alice was horrified. She glanced at her son, still sitting cross-legged on the floor, eyes closed, apparently in a trance. He must approve of Pol's plans for her pregnancy. Still, she had always made a point of not interfering in her children's affairs and wasn't going to start now. 'Oh, well, but you need to book into hospital, so they'll be expecting you.'

'There's no need for that either.' Pol regarded her pityingly. 'Cormac's going to deliver the baby here.'

'He'll sew you up, will he? If you need stitches, like.'

'She won't need stitches,' Cormac said without opening his eyes. 'She'll be too relaxed to tear.'

Jaysus! Alice announced the scouse would be ready soon and escaped downstairs. The pair were crazy, out of this world.

Fion was alone, stirring pans in the old-fashioned kitchen. A cat watched with interest from its unhygenic position on the draining board. She looked up when her mother came in. 'What did you think of her?'

'She seems very nice, but awfully young.'

'She's twenty-one, older than she looks.'

'Has she told you her plans for having the baby? They're not very sensible, Fion. I'm worried.'

'She'll change her mind nearer the time.'

'Lord, I hope so. Our Cormac's a clever lad, but I'm not sure if he's up to delivering a baby.'

The Christmas bazaar was to raise funds for an orphanage in Ethiopia. Fion put Alice in charge of the bottle stall. The main prize was a bottle of whisky. Every bottle had a raffle ticket attached, the numbers ending in a nought. People bought tickets for sixpence each and if they picked one that matched the number on a bottle it was theirs.

Naturally, everyone wanted to win the whisky. The trouble was the winning ticket wasn't in the box. Fion had taken it to put in later when most of the bottles had gone.

'You can't do that!' her scandalised mother gasped.

'Of course I can, Mam. If the whisky's won right at the start, no one will want a go any more. Don't forget, it's all in a good cause.'

Alice had been hoping to enjoy herself. Instead, she felt like a criminal as she tended her colourfully decorated stall. Carols issued from a loudspeaker and their innocent message made her feel even more sinful. She was very busy, always surrounded by a crowd, and the prizes – the bottles of chop sauce, vinegar, shampoo, lemonade, mayonnaise – rapidly diminished as the afternoon progressed. The more they diminished the more the eager participants saw their chance of winning the whisky, which had started to look very lonely, not quite by itself but almost.

Where the hell was Fion? She couldn't leave the stall and look for her. Alice began to panic. Any minute, now, someone would guess the ticket for the whisky wasn't there and she'd be driven from the hall by a justifiably angry crowd. She felt conscious of her burning face, her racing heart.

'Are you all right,' said a voice. 'It's Mrs Lacey, isn't it? Fion's mum.'

She'd noticed the slightly balding man who seemed to be in charge of things. He was about her own age, casually dressed in a black polo-necked jumper and baggy corduroy pants, his craggy face deeply tanned, as if he'd spent many years abroad. He had a slow, gentle, very patient smile.

'No, I'm not all right,' Alice said in a cracked voice. 'I need our Fion urgently.'

'I'll find her for you.'

Fion arrived seconds later. Alice stared at her accusingly over the heads of the crowd surrounding the stall.

'Can I have a go, Mam?'

'I think you better had.'

Only Alice noticed the ticket already in Fion's hand when she dipped it into the box. 'If she brings it out again and claims the whisky I'll bloody kill her,' she vowed. Luckily for Fion, she withdrew a losing ticket. Not long afterwards the whisky was won by a little boy and immediately appropriated by his delighted father. Alice breathed a sigh of relief.

'Would you like a cup of tea?' The man in the black jumper was back.

'I'd give my right arm for a cup of tea, ta.'

'There's no need for such extremes.' He smiled. 'You can have one for nothing.'

Now the whisky had gone, so had all interest in winning the motley collection of bottles that remained. Alice sank on to one of the chairs against the wall behind.

The helpful man returned with two cups of tea and sat beside her. 'My name's Charlie Glover. Do I call you, "Fion's Mum" or "Mrs Lacey"?'

'I'd prefer Alice and I don't know what I would have done without you earlier. You were a great help.'

'Pleased to be of service, Ma'am.' He smiled his lovely smile. His eyes were dark-grey with little shreds of silver.

Alice wondered why she was noticing a strange man's eyes, his smile. She was fifty-one, for heaven's sake. She'd lost all interest in men years ago. 'Have you been living abroad?' she asked conversationally.

'Yes, Ethiopia. I used to run the orphanage we're raising funds for.'

'Used to?'

'I thought it was time I had a rest and a change,' he explained. 'I'm staying with my brother and his wife in Ormskirk.' His voice was deep and pleasing, and Alice detected the faint trace of a Lancashire accent. He spoke slowly, with the air of a man unused to being interrupted. 'In another three months I'm off to the Transvaal, this time to take over a hospital on the borders of Swaziland.'

'You're a doctor?'

'Yes. I work for a charity called Overseas Rescue.'

'Gosh! It all sounds very exciting.'

'It's more worthwhile than exciting.' He half smiled. 'My wife used to love it when we moved somewhere new, but she sadly died ten years ago.'

Alice put her hand on his arm. 'I'm so sorry.'

'That's kind of you. Fion told me her father died recently. You're being very brave about it.'

She felt uncomfortable. 'Me and John hadn't lived together in a long while. I was upset he died, but not devastated. Mind you' – her lips twisted wistfully – 'I would have been devastated once.'

'You obviously have good memories to look back on.' He got to his feet. 'Duty calls. I'm due to draw the raffle any minute.' To her surprise he sat down again. 'Look, are you doing anything tonight?'

'Nothing particular. I'll probably watch television,' Alice replied, taking the question literally and wondering why he seemed so pleased by her answer, why his grey eyes lit up.

'Then why don't I take you out to dinner instead?' he said eagerly. 'Somewhere in Southport would be nice.'

'Dinner!' she exclaimed, immediately flustered. 'Oh, no. No, I couldn't possibly. Thanks for asking, but no . . . excuse me. I've just seen my other daughter. Orla!' she called and almost ran over to the door that Orla had just entered by. 'What are you doing here?' she asked breathlessly.

Orla waved the notebook in her hand. 'Covering the bazaar for the paper. Have you been trying to run a four-minute mile, Mam? You're all puffed out and as red as a beetroot.'

'I've been working hard on a stall, that's all.'

'Where's our Fion? I need to know how much she raised, then I've got to interview a chap called Charlie Glover. He wants to appeal for funds for some hospital abroad.' She made a face. 'I once envisaged meself interviewing film stars and politicians, not reporting on a grotty bazaar. You know how much I'll get for this?' She waved the notebook again. 'Tuppence a line!'

'Oh, stop moaning, luv.'

Orla was jealous of Fion, with her active social life, loads of friends and part-time job at Liverpool University where she worked in the Students Union. Beside that of her sister, Orla considered her life hideously dull and uneventful, and the Lavins' house in Pearl Street poky in the extreme compared with the one in Stanley Road. 'Ta, Mam. You're all sympathy,' she said tartly.

'Tell Fion when you see her I've gone back to Stanley Road, and that I've taken Colin and Bonnie. They look dead bored. And by the way, that's Charlie Glover over there, about to draw the raffle.'

Alice was gently frying sausages when Fion arrived home, looking flushed and exhausted. 'We raised over two hundred pounds,' she said triumphantly. 'Where's the kids?'

'Watching telly. They said they were starving, so I've fed them. All I could find in the fridge was sausages, so I've done the same for us. You've got no spuds, either, only frozen chips.'

'I need to do some shopping,' Fion said vaguely. 'By the way, what did you do to poor Charlie?'

Alice nearly dropped a fork in the sausages. 'Nothing that I know of. We just chatted a bit, that's all. Why, what did he say I'd done?'

'Nothing, but he talked about you non-stop while we were packing up. He obviously fancies you dead rotten, but when I invited him back to tea and said you'd be here he claimed you wouldn't be too pleased.' She stared accusingly at her mother. 'Why on earth should he say that, Mam?'

'He asked me out and I refused.' Alice went red.

'Idiot!'

'I am not an idiot, Fion. I didn't want to get involved, that's all. I wouldn't have known what to say. I'm quite happy staying in and watching television.'

'Well, you shouldn't be.' Fion lit the gas under the

334

chip pan, already full of fat that hadn't been changed in weeks. 'You're not exactly old and Charlie's quite decent-looking for somone in his fifties. You should have grabbed the chance to enjoy yourself for a change. Our Orla agreed.' Her eyes narrowed calculatingly. 'If you'd played your cards right, you could have gone with him to the Transvaal in a few months' time.'

'What as, one of the cleaners in his bloody hospital?'

'No, as his wife. You're not half daft, Mam. He fell for you like a ton of bricks.'

Alice's heart gave a little lurch. 'Are you after getting rid of me, Fion?'

Fion laid her chin on Alice's shoulder. 'No, Mam. I just want you to be happy, do something interesting and exciting for a change. I don't like you living on your own in Amber Street. You're going nowhere fast. Why don't you tell Charlie you've changed your mind? Give him another chance; he'd leap at it.'

'He might be a Protestant.'

'For God's sake, Mam,' Fion said, exasperated. 'As if that matters at your age.'

'I'll think about it,' Alice promised, though she had no intention of doing any such thing.

That night the television was on but Alice wasn't watching. Instead, she was going over the events of the afternoon. She didn't want to leave Amber Street, let alone travel to the other side of the world. She didn't even want her humdrum life interrupted by having dinner with a man she hardly knew.

She wasn't particularly happy, but nor was she particularly sad. She just existed, went from day to day, living a life in which little happened that was exciting or remarkable. Babies were born; people died; there was an occasional juicy bit of gossip in the salon; she sometimes went to the pictures with Bernadette; her children and *their* children came to tea on Sundays. Every now and then she threw a party. She'd got used to being the proprietor of three hairdressing salons and they had long ceased to be a source of pride.

It wasn't much of a life, but it was the life she wanted.

No one thought to close the curtains when Alice Lacey held a party on Christmas Eve. From the parlour a sharp ray of yellow light fanned across the dimly lit street. There were other parties in Amber Street that night, other lights, making the unlit areas darker and more starkly defined, shadowy. It was a beautiful night, calm and tranquil, not particularly cold for the time of year. There was no moon, but the black sky was littered with stars.

The solitary figure of a woman lurked in the shadows outside the Laceys', peering through the window, dodging from one side of the glass to the other. The woman wore the same camel coat, the same clumsy fur-lined boots that she'd worn four years before when she'd spied on Cormac's twenty-first. She spied on him now, watched him lounging against the wall, looking a bit fed up, she thought.

She was disappointed in her son, who'd given up university for some reason and had actually been seen in the labour exchange, shamelessly queuing for his dole money. She didn't approve of his long hair and the way he dressed, like he'd just picked stuff out of a ragbag. The girl, Pol, was there, obviously in the club. No one knew if she and Cormac were married. By all accounts Alice kept her mouth firmly buttoned when she was asked.

In fact, Maurice looked far more presentable, in a blue check shirt and nicely pressed grey pants. He and the Pol girl seemed to be getting on like a house on fire. They'd been laughing together on the settee for almost an hour.

Cora's lips bared in a snarl when Fionnuala came into the room with a plate of sandwiches. She'd very much like to know what favours Fion Lacey had done for Horace Flynn so that he'd seen fit to leave her his lovely big house, yet hadn't thought to let *her* have a penny.

Billy was there! Billy had come into the parlour supping a can of beer. Her own husband had been invited to Alice's party and hadn't said a word – not that they normally exchanged many words. There'd just been those weeks while John was living with them. Since then the usual silence had prevailed.

John!

She hadn't cried much in her life, but she still cried when she thought about John and the future that had been denied them – the future *together*. It would always remain a mystery why he'd left Garibaldi Road so suddenly. That morning she'd woken up, felt for him, but he wasn't there! After Billy had gone to work she'd rushed around to the yard. But it was already on fire, blazing away, throwing sparks into the sky. Someone must have called the fire engine, because it arrived almost straight away. She had stayed for hours, watching the building fall to pieces, watching the flames gradually subside, watching the firemen carry out something on a stretcher.

There didn't look to be much left of John under the tarpaulin. She longed to snatch it off and kiss the burnt remains of the only man she had ever loved. Cora clenched her fists and her nails bit into the soft flesh of her palms.

A burst of laughter came from inside the house whose occupants interested her so greatly. Billy, of all people, had made a puppet out of his hand and was making it talk. She couldn't hear what it was saying, but everyone was falling about.

Fion suddenly leapt to her feet and closed the curtains, and Cora was left desolate, with nothing to see.

In the parlour Fion shuddered and said to nobody in particular, 'It's funny, but I felt as if there was someone watching us from outside.'

Chapter 14

It was April Fool's Day and the baby had taken it into its head to fool them by arriving early, though Pol had always been vague about the date. Cormac opened the window, put a tape of soothing music in the tape recorder and lit a fresh joss stick.

'Take deep breaths, Pol. Really deep now,' he instructed when the labour appeared to be reaching a climax. He sat on the edge of the bed and took several deep breaths himself to demonstrate how. 'Sing your song. "Here we go round the mulberry bush, the mulberry bush, the mulberry bush. Here we . . ."' he warbled very much out of tune.

Pol screamed.

'I didn't think it was all that bad,' Cormac joked.

Pol screamed again. There was a veil of perspiration on her brow and her body was rigid with fear.

'Push,' he commanded, determined to stay calm. 'No, don't push. Oh, where's that bloody instruction book?'

'On the table,' Pol yelled. 'Cormac, I think I need to go to hospital.'

'But we were going to do this by ourselves!'

'No, Cormac. *I* was going to do it by myself. *You* were going to help and you're not helping a bit. Ooh!' she groaned. 'I never knew you could be in such pain. Fetch your Fion. She might know what to do.'

'She's gone to a coffee morning.' Cormac felt a stir of panic. 'I'll ring for the ambulance.'

'Do it quickly, Cormac. Please!'

Two hours later Pol was delivered of a perfect baby girl weighing six pounds, two ounces. Mother and baby seemed unharmed after what had turned out to be an unexpected ordeal.

'Who does she look like?' Pol asked Cormac when he was allowed in to see her and the new baby. 'Wally, Frank the Yank, or you?'

Cormac had thought he wouldn't care, but when he stared at the little, round, scrunched-up face discovered, somewhat surprisingly, that he did. 'Me. She looks like me,' he claimed, despite the fact that the baby had red hair exactly the same shade as Frank the Yank's.

Pol touched her on her tiny ball of a chin. 'Say hello to mummy and daddy, Skylark.'

Cormac groaned. 'Oh, no, Pol. Not Skylark.' He thought they'd dispensed with Skylark. It had been Buttercup for a girl the last time they'd discussed names.

'It's a lovely name, Skylark.'

'Except this is Liverpool. It isn't full of flower people like San Francisco. Everyone will poke fun at her at school. I suggest we call her something else as well, say . . .' He said the first name that came into his head: 'Sharon! Skylark can be her second name.'

'All right, Cormac,' Pol said, easygoing to a fault.

'That girl of Cormac's, she had her baby this morning,' Billy told his son when he called in Lacey's Tyres at teatime, 'TYRES FITTED ON THE PREMISES' it said on the newly painted board outside.

Maurice drew in a quick intake of breath. 'What did she have?'

340

'A girl. A pretty little thing, according to Alice. Going to call her Sharon.'

'That's nice.'

'Business good today?' The plan was for Billy to continue going out to work until the firm was doing well enough to keep them both busy.

'Not exactly.' Maurice pulled a face. 'Two cars, that's all, and only three tyres between them.'

'Things'll improve, son,' Billy said stoutly. 'Once word gets around how cheap we are.'

'It takes time for word to get around, Dad. We need to advertise now.'

'Can't afford it, Maurice, lad. We've used up all the bank loan to buy stock and do up the yard. They're expecting us to start paying the loan back in the not too distant future.'

'I know, Dad.' Maurice glanced fearfully around the yard that had once housed B.E.D.S. The cheap retreads from Hungary were stacked in neat heaps around the wall – it hadn't exactly been cheap to buy so many. Then there was the smart hut that had been erected in place of the burnt-out building because it was essential to have an office of some sort; the telephone; the sign; the second-hand van, bought when John's old van proved beyond repair; the chicken-wire roof they'd had put up when they discovered two boys fishing over the wall for tyres with a giant hook.

He wasn't making enough to live on, let alone pay back the loan. Dad didn't realise you could go to prison for defaulting on a loan – it was *him* who'd go, not Maurice, because it was taken out in his name. He'd been getting on well with his dad since Uncle John's funeral. There hadn't been the opportunity when he was growing up to discover how kind Billy was – and he'd worked like a Trojan getting the yard ready. Over the last few months Billy's support for his son had been rock solid.

Maurice felt nausea rise, like a ball, in his throat. Everything was his fault. He'd thought all you had to do to start a business was find the premises, stock them with whatever you wanted to sell and that was it. You were made; the customers would come flocking in. Perhaps they would have if there'd been adverts in the press, or the site weren't so much out of the way. As it was, hardly anyone knew they were there. Every day Maurice felt more desperate and the feeling of nausea was never far away.

'Which hospital is Pol in?' he asked when Billy emerged from the hut with two mugs of tea.

'Liverpool Maternity. Why? Are you thinking of going to see her?'

'I might,' Maurice muttered. It was another thing that added to his misery, thinking about Pol. Maurice wasn't sure, but he had a feeling he was in love with her. They'd first met at Alice's party on Christmas Eve and he'd been unable to stop thinking about her since. He'd started going round to the house in Stanley Road on the pretence of seeing Fion, but in reality to see Pol. Something about her childish fragility struck a chord in his heart. He wanted to look after her, cherish her, keep her warm at night. He had stupid visions of them growing old together, stupid because she belonged to his cousin, Cormac. There was a saying, 'All's fair in love and war', but Maurice was fond of Cormac and couldn't bring himself to steal his girl from behind his back, always assuming Pol was willing to be stolen in the first place.

Mind you, Cormac was no longer the person he used to be. He looked a proper ponce in those daft clothes and had made no attempt to get a job. Although he hadn't been successful, at least Maurice had tried to find work. These days he didn't feel as inferior to his cousin as he used to.

'I think I'll close early tonight, Dad.' Lacey's Tyres was open twelve hours a day, from seven in the morning till seven at night.

'No,' Billy said stubbornly. 'I'd sooner we stuck to the hours it ses on the board. You sod off, son. I'll lock up.'

Alice and her daughters were just leaving the hospital when Maurice arrived bearing a meagre bunch of flowers that was all he could afford. Cormac had gone in search of tea, he was told, and baby Sharon was in the nursery.

'You can keep Pol company till the new dad comes back,' Alice suggested.

'Hello, Pol. Congratulations.' Her eyes lit up as he approached the bed, but Pol's eyes lit up for everyone. She wore a faded cotton nightie that hadn't been ironed. He wished he could have bought her something rich and silky, trimmed with lace, but not only did he not have the money, it wasn't done for men to buy nighties for other men's girls.

'Thank you, Maurice. Are those for me?' She gasped, as if he'd presented her with a magnificent bouquet of roses. 'They're lovely. What are they?'

'Dunno.'

'They're very pretty, whatever they are. I'll ask the nurse to put them in water after you've gone. How's business?'

Pol was one of the few people in whom Maurice had confided the true state of Lacey's Tyres. If anyone else asked he would reply modestly, 'Not bad.'

'Bloody awful,' he said gloomily. 'I'm worried sick, if you must know.'

'Oh, you poor thing,' she said, her blue, doll-like eyes

343

so full of sympathy that Maurice easily could have cried. He longed to bury his head in her small breasts and sob his heart out. 'Things will buck up soon, Maurice. They're bound to.'

'I hope so.' He explained about not earning enough to pay back the loan. 'It's me dad who worries me. He's the one who'll get into trouble, not me.'

'Perhaps you should expand, Maurice, sell more than tyres.' She waved her arm vaguely. 'Other bits for motor cars, fr'instance: brakes and stuff.' She patted his hand, when it should have been *him* patting *her* hand, her being the one in hospital, like.

'Gosh, Pol, I hadn't thought of that.' It was a good idea, but he hadn't the cash to buy so much as a tyre gauge. Still, she meant well. 'You're very clever, Pol,' he said admiringly.

'Me!' She laughed. 'What a lovely thing to say. Everyone usually thinks I'm very stupid.'

'You're anything but stupid,' Maurice said, meaning it sincerely.

Cormac was about to enter the ward when, through the glass panel in the swing door, he saw his cousin, Maurice, sitting beside Pol's bed. He always felt uncomfortable with Maurice, as if he had stolen from him something of incalculable value. One of these days, when Alice was dead, he might tell Maurice the truth about their parentage, something that was out of the question while Alice remained alive. He, Cormac, had lived twenty-one enjoyable years of Maurice's life, while Maurice had endured twenty-one years on *his* behalf with Cora.

Once again Cormac went to push open the door and once again he paused. Maurice was leaning on the bed, arms crossed, laughing at something Pol had said.

Unaware he was being watched, his face was naked, showing everything, hiding nothing, and Cormac real-ised with a shock that his cousin was head over heels in love with Pol.

Was he jealous? No, Cormac decided calmly, standing aside to let a nurse into the ward. What was the point of being jealous over something that couldn't be helped?

Did he mind? Cormac wasn't sure. He was in love with Pol himself. He had assumed that one day they would get married, have more children and spend the rest of their lives together, that they would be happy. It wasn't until now that it came to him that something was lacking, because he had never looked at Pol the way Maurice looked at her now, so *absolutely*. Cormac felt almost envious. Would he ever look at a woman like that?

And Pol? Sometimes he wondered if Pol would have gone just as willingly with Wally or Frank the Yank, had they asked. Pol loved everybody. She was like a kitten, happy any place where she was warm, comfortable and petted. She could just as easily be in love with Maurice as with Cormac.

He owed his cousin so much. Justice would be partially done if Maurice were allowed to steal Cormac's girl, just as Cormac had, inadvertently, stolen Maurice's mother.

A man came out of the ward and nearly hit him with the door. 'Sorry, mate,' he muttered and rolled his eyes in disgust when he noticed Cormac's rainbow knitted jumper, full of snags, his green flared trousers, dirty feet, his sandals. For the first time since he left Amber Street Cormac felt slightly ashamed of his clothes. He smiled ruefully. Alice used to keep him so neat!

It was time for another cup of tea. He'd return to the ward five minutes before the bell went to indicate visiting time was over. And from now on he'd give his girlfriend and his cousin every encouragement. He'd invite Maurice round to Fion's, then make excuses to go out, leaving him and Pol together.

After all, it was only fair.

It didn't *feel* very fair, not right now, not to Cormac. In fact, he felt quite depressed. Sniffing audibly, he wished Maurice hadn't come to the hospital, that he'd never discovered he was in love with Pol.

Lord, he'd give anything for a spliff to blunt the rawness of his misery. He had been looking forward to life with Pol and his daughter. Well, there was a one-in-three chance she was his daughter and probably no chance at all if you took into account the red hair.

The debt to Maurice had to be paid some time.

'Christ, Mam, you're not half bad-tempered lately,' Lulu said acidly. 'Every time anyone opens their mouth you bite their head off.'

'Don't you dare swear in this house!' Orla screeched.

'I hate you, Mam.' Maisie's lip curled.

'So, hate me. I don't care.'

'I hate you too.' Paul's lip wobbled. He was the most sensitive of the Lavin children.

'Join the club,' Orla snarled.

'I'm leaving home,' announced Gary. 'I'm going to live with Nana Lacey.'

'Well, don't let me stop you. Shall I pack a suitcase?'

Orla and her four children glared at each other across the breakfast table. Then Orla's face collapsed and she held out her arms. 'Oh, come here. I love you! I adore you! You are the most beautiful children in the world and I am the most horrible mother. I don't deserve you. I truly don't deserve you. I'm sorry. I'm sorry, sorry,

sorry.' She kissed their heads one by one. 'So sorry,' she whispered.

'Are you in the club, Mam?' Lulu asked. 'Nana Lavin said you might be.'

'No, luv.' Orla sobbed. 'I'm not in anything as far as I know.'

'Is it an early mennypause?' enquired Gary. 'Granny Lavin thought it might be that as well.'

'It can't be both, luv. It can only be one or the other and it's neither. It's just that your mother's been in a state with herself lately.'

'What sort of state?'

'An upside down, inside out, up in the air, down in the dumps, topsy-turvy sort of state.'

'Wow!' said Gary, impressed.

'I promise not to be bad-tempered again, least not till tonight, then you'll just have to excuse me and tell yourselves I don't mean it.'

The children went to school. Orla washed the dishes, dried them, made the beds, dusted, threw herself on to the settee in the parlour, burst into tears, cursed her husband . . .

'I *hate* you Micky Lavin,' she said aloud.

No, she didn't. She loved him. But she wished he'd try to understand just how *unhappy* she was, how unutterably and stultifyingly bored she was with life. The trouble was, putting it bluntly, Micky was too thick to understand. Micky felt exactly the opposite and was so lacking in imagination that he couldn't understand anyone feeling different. He was as happy as a sandboy. He enjoyed his lousy job without a future, he was perfectly content living in this grotty little house. Going to see Liverpool or Everton play football at weekends was the ultimate joy, particularly if they won. Micky didn't want a car, holidays abroad, flash clothes, posh furniture. He didn't mind seeing the occasional film as long as lots of people in it got killed, but as for the theatre, it belonged in an alien world, as did books that contained words of more than one syllable, anything intellectual on television, politics and newspapers that weren't littered with pictures of naked girls.

It meant they had nothing to talk about. Even sex had lost its thrall and become a tiny bit tedious with someone who was essentially a moron.

Micky had refused to let Mam buy them a house somewhere nicer with a garden for the children to play.

'Why not?' Orla screeched. She seemed to screech an awful lot these days.

'I've got my pride,' Micky said huffily.

'You weren't too proud to fill this house with stuff that had fallen off the back of a hundred bloody lorries.'

'That's different.'

'In what way is it different?'

He shuffled his feet. 'I dunno, it just is.'

She'd grown past him. He wanted to spend his life standing still, but she wanted to go forward. She would have got a proper job, but it would mean giving up the newspaper and the extra money wouldn't have been enough to make a difference. Besides, although she would have denied it till she was blue in the face, she got a thrill out of attending various pathetic functions and announcing, 'I'm from the press,' and occasionally seeing her name under the headline of a news item she'd sent in. She kept hoping the *Crosby Star* would take her back in the office so she'd be a real reporter, but there hadn't been a vacancy in ages.

This afternoon, she was interviewing some stupid ex-Everton footballer – anyone willing to take up kicking a ball up and down a field as a career *had* to be stupid. She'd only been asked because Dominic Reilly came from Pearl Street. His parents still lived in the house opposite. His mam, Sheila, had had twelve children. Orla shuddered delicately: *twelve*! Dominic, who at thirty-two was the same age as herself, had come back from Spain for the wedding of one of his numerous brothers and was returning that night. She had no idea what he'd been doing in Spain, but it was the first on the list of questions she'd prepared. At least it broke up the tedium of the day.

She went out and bought the *Guardian*, and read everything except the sport. Would that great intellectual Micky Lavin be interested in the fact that the war in Vietnam was escalating? No, he bloody wouldn't. Nor would he care that Mrs Gandhi had become Prime Minister of India, or that Great Britain had just elected a Labour government led by the vaguely dishy Harold Wilson. Orla had sent him out to vote, but he'd met a mate and gone for a game of billiards instead.

Seething, Orla rolled the paper into a ball and flung it across the room. It was time she got ready for the interview.

It was also time she had some new clothes, she thought irritably when she examined the miserly contents of her wardrobe. Except there wasn't the money.

'You'd look lovely dressed in rags,' Micky insisted when she complained.

In that case she was bound to look lovely, because there was nothing but rags hanging on the rail. Orla sulkily removed a black skirt and a white blouse that mightn't look so bad if they were ironed. She didn't just need new clothes, but a new house, a new husband, a new life.

She left her long brown hair loose, made her face up carefully and, promptly at three o'clock, knocked on the Reillys' front door. Sheila Reilly opened it. She was a pleasantly pretty woman, lumpily overweight, though anyone would be overweight if they'd had twelve children. Sheila was as old as her mother, but had children younger than Orla's. Two toddlers hung silently to her skirt who, unless Sheila had had more babies when no one was looking, were grandchildren – she had hordes.

'Hello, Orla, luv. I suppose you've come to see our Dominic.'

'If he's available, Sheila. I'm from the press.'

'I know, luv. He's expecting you, though where you'll find the quiet to talk I don't know. I've half a dozen of the grandkids here to see their Uncle Dominic.'

'We can go over to our house if you like.'

'I'm sure he'd appreciate that, if only for a bit of peace.'

Dominic came into the hall. He was casually dressed in pale blue linen slacks, a white, short-sleeved shirt and white canvas shoes. 'Hi, there. I've seen you around, but I don't think we've ever spoken before. I vaguely remember you from school.'

'We didn't move in till you'd left home. I vaguely remember you from school too.'

They shook hands. Orla hadn't realised he was quite so good-looking, quite so tall, quite so tanned. He reminded her a bit of Robert Redford, with his dark-blond wavy hair and broad build, his dazzlingly warm smile.

'Orla said you can use her house for the interview, luv.'

'That's a relief, otherwise I won't be able to hear meself think.'

They crossed the street to the Lavins'. Orla felt super conscious of Dominic's arm brushing against hers when she showed him into the parlour. She asked if he'd like a cup of tea. 'Or sherry?' There was sherry over from Christmas.

'Tea would be grand, ta.'

When she returned he was sitting on the settee, arms stretched along the back, legs crossed. A gold watch glinted on his brown wrist, muscles bulged in his arms, his waist was very slim.

Orla swallowed and looked away. She settled in a hard chair, pad on her knee, pencil poised, coughed importantly and asked her first question: 'What were you doing in Spain?'

For some reason Dominic choked on the tea. She hoped it wasn't too hot. 'Playing football,' he replied.

'They play football in Spain? I didn't realise. What part of Spain?'

'Barcelona.' His face had gone very red.

'They have stadiums there, just like in Liverpool?'

'Just like in Liverpool.' He nodded and she wondered why his brown eyes were glinting with amusement.

'And what made you go to Spain in the first place? Couldn't you get a job playing football in this country?'

He regarded her silently for several seconds. 'That's right,' he said eventually. 'I was on me uppers, if the truth be known. The offer from Barcelona was a lifeline.'

'You poor thing,' Orla said sympathetically, making a note in her pad. She glanced at him surreptitiously. He looked very odd, as if he was about to bust a gut. Perhaps he was dying to use the lavatory.

'Is this for publication?' Dominic asked.

'Of course.' Orla tossed her head importantly.

'In that case I think we'd better start the interview again, otherwise you're going to make a right fool of yourself.'

'Am I, now!' she said huffily. 'In exactly what way?'

'For one, you clearly know nothing about football.

Barcelona is one of the leading clubs in the world, with a stadium every bit as good as those in this country, if not better. For another, I was offered a hundred quid a week to play there, twice as much as I was getting with Everton. I live in a flat overlooking the Mediterranean, I drive a sports car, I have a beautiful girlfriend – though she's not as beautiful as you. All in all, I live the life of Reilly – appropriately, considering me name.' He burst out laughing and didn't stop till tears ran down his cheeks. 'Oh, Gawd!' he gasped, wiping them away with the flat of his hands. 'I haven't enjoyed meself so much in a long time. It makes a change to have a reporter feel sorry for me; they're usually so sycophantic it makes me want to puke.'

Orla felt dizzy with shame and embarrassment. If only she had condescended to tell Micky about the interview he would have filled her in on Dominic's background. 'Jaysus!' she muttered, unable to meet his eyes. 'I wish the floor would open up and swallow me.'

'I don't, because then I wouldn't be able to look at you any more.'

She found herself blushing on top of everything else and remembered he'd said something about his girlfriend not being as beautiful as she was. There was silence in the world for a while as Orla stared at her shoes and Dominic Reilly stared at *her*, and her stomach trembled in the way it had done in the early days with Micky. Then Dominic gave her a challenging look and patted the cushion beside him and Orla knew that if she responded to the challenge everything would change, even if it appeared nothing whatsoever had altered when the children came home from school and Micky from work.

The notebook and pencil fell to the floor as Orla got up and moved into Dominic's welcoming arms. After a while they went upstairs to the bed where she'd lain with Micky for almost fifteen years.

She was sorry afterwards — deeply, wholeheartedly, wretchedly sorry. Perhaps she wouldn't have felt like that if it hadn't been so wonderful. For half an hour, an hour, she'd glimpsed another world, a world of blue seas and golden sands, of beautiful clothes, good times, parties, a world in which every day was different from the day before, where exciting, unexpected things happened, as opposed to the drab, colourless world she occupied now, in which every day was the same as the next, counting Sundays when she went to church and to tea with Mam or one of her sisters, or they came to tea at hers.

Then Dominic rose from the bed, kissed her gently and went home, and the wonderful world came crashing down around her ears.

After a few minutes she went and soaked in the old-fashioned bath that had fallen off the back of a lorry, using the last of the bath salts Micky had bought her for Christmas. At the time she'd thought how little imagination he showed: he gave her bath salts, talc, cheap perfume, every year, usually Boots' own brand. She noticed a scratch on her wrist from Dominic's watch. He'd had to take it off. She'd put disinfectant on it when she got out.

The events of the afternoon hadn't made her love Micky more, she wasn't suddenly counting her blessings, appreciating what she already had. On the contrary, she would much sooner not have glimpsed that other magical world. It made the one in which she lived seem drabber, even more colourless than it had been when she woke up. There were so many things she would never know, never do, sights she would never see if she lived to be a hundred.

She was gentle with the children when they came home. Nothing that happened would ever make her love them less. Lulu was the reason she'd been stuck with Micky, but that wasn't Lulu's fault but her own.

'What's the matter?' Micky asked that night when they were watching telly – least he was watching. Orla was miles away.

'Nothing.'

'You're very quiet. It's not like you.'

'Isn't it?' She looked at him and noticed his hair was receding slightly at the temples, that he had a small paunch. He also had a hole in his sock that needed mending. 'Shall we go to bed early tonight?'

'I wouldn't say no.' He grinned and, for a moment, she saw the teenager who'd charmed her all those years ago. Perhaps if she could lose herself in him, recapture the magic of those days . . .

They went upstairs. There was a time when they would have leapt naked into bed, but now Orla put on her nightdress, Micky his pyjamas. He went to put out the light, stopped and said in a voice she'd never heard before, 'Who does this fuckin' watch belong to, Orla? And what's it doing beside our bed?'

Orla turned up in Amber Street late one Sunday night just as Alice was thinking about going to bed. Unusually for Orla, who was inclined to arrive in a flaming temper over something, she appeared pale and listless.

Alice sat her down and made her a cup of cocoa. 'What's wrong, luv?' she asked sympathetically.

Orla didn't look at her mother but stared at her shoes. 'Mam, don't get mad at me, but I've done something awful.' There was a pause. 'I've slept with someone and Micky found out.'

'Jaysus, Orla!' Alice's sympathy vanished, to be

354

replaced with anger and alarm. 'You stupid girl,' she snapped. 'Who was it?'

'It doesn't matter who it was, Mam.'

'Then why are you here? What d'you expect me to do about it?'

'Nothing, Mam,' Orla said in a subdued voice. 'I just wanted to tell someone, that's all. Micky's making me life hell.'

'I'm not surprised. Most men would if they found their wife had been sleeping around.' Alice frowned. 'He's not hit you, has he?'

'No, Mam. He just won't talk to me, that's all.'

'You can hardly blame him, luv.' Alice thought what a perfect world it could be if only human beings, including herself, could bring themselves to behave sensibly. 'When did this happen?'

'Last Monday. Micky hasn't spoken to me since. Not that I mind, to be frank, but there's a terrible atmosphere at home. The children have noticed and it's making them dead miserable.'

Alice remembered Sheila Reilly had been in Lacey's the Saturday before last having her hair done for her son, Niall's, wedding. She'd mentioned Orla was seeing Dominic, her eldest, before he went back to Spain. Alice immediately put two and two together. Micky Lavin was a nice, hard-working lad, but as dull as ditchwater and without an ounce of Dominic Reilly's glamour. She didn't approve of what her daughter had done, but could understand Orla being bowled over by a man so entirely different from her husband.

'I should never have married Micky, Mam,' Orla cried tragically. 'I wish things had been different then, the way they are now. No one's nagging our Cormac and Pol to get married.'

'No one nagged *you* to get married,' Alice reminded her.

'No, but it wasn't on in those days to have a baby out of wedlock. I felt obliged to marry Micky for Lulu's sake. If I had me time over again, I wouldn't go anywhere near an altar.' She buried her face in her hands and began to cry. 'I'm ever so unhappy, Mam. I have been for years. All those dreams I used to have are dead and I feel all dried up inside. I ache for something nice to happen, something interesting or unusual or enjoyable. I long to go out and have a good time or go on holiday abroad, somewhere like Spain. I wish we had a car so I could learn to drive, and I'd just drive and drive and drive till I came to the end of the rainbow. I wish – oh, Mam,' she sobbed. 'I wish all sorts of things.'

'I know, luv.' Alice patted her daughter's knee. She was like a beautiful wild animal trapped inside a cage, the exact opposite of her mother who gave the slightest opportunity of excitement a wide berth. 'I'll buy you a car if you like. As long as Micky doesn't mind.' She knew she was being too generous, too indulgent. After all, Orla shouldn't be rewarded for her bad behaviour. But a car would make things better for the whole family.

'Oh, *would* you, Mam?' There was something terribly pathetic about Orla's excited reaction, as if Alice had opened the door of the cage a few enticing inches. 'It would help with me job as a reporter. I could go further afield, not just stick to Bootle. And I could take the kids out weekends, to Southport and Chester and places. I'd take them on the train, except I can never afford the fares. As for Micky, I don't give a fig if he minds or not.'

'Sweetheart, I don't want to make things worse between you two.' She remembered Micky had adamantly refused to let her buy them a house and wasn't likely to take kindly to a car – he had more character than people gave him credit for.

'Oh, you won't, Mam. A car will make me happy and if I'm happy then so is Micky.'

Alice thought this an exaggeration. No doubt Orla had been happy making love with Dominic Reilly, but it hadn't exactly sent her husband into paroxysms of delight. Her main concern, though, was her daughter, who'd arrived wan and pale, and now looked happy and excited, as if she'd just been handed a million pounds.

Chapter 15
1970

The air on Easter Saturday was as heady as wine: pure and sparkling, with that exceptional clarity only evident in spring. When the Nuptial Mass was over and the bride and groom posed for photographs in St James's church-yard the sharp, fresh aroma of recently cut grass combined with the earthy smell of upturned soil, adding to the flavour of the day.

Lulu Lavin made an exceptionally pretty bride. There were appreciative murmurs from the waiting crowd when she stepped out of the grey limousine in her simple white voile frock with short sleeves and a drawstring neck. Calf-length, the hem hung in points, each decorated with a tiny rosebud. More rosebuds were threaded through her dark hair arranged earlier that morning in Grecian style by her Nana Lacey. Her shoes were white satin, flat, like a ballerina's. She looked for all the world like a nymph, as did the bridesmaids, in the palest of green: her sister, Maisie, her cousin, Bonnie, and Ruth Mitchell, great-grandpa's daughter, who was Lulu's great-aunt, though three years her junior.

From across the churchyard Orla Lavin, fiercely proud, watched her daughter while the photographs were being taken. Lulu was about to escape the narrow, suffocating streets of Bootle. In two weeks' time, after their honeymoon in Jersey – a present from Alice – Lulu and Gareth would live in his tiny one-bedroomed flat in an unfashionable part of London and Gareth would continue with his ambition to make a living as an artist, though he hadn't so far sold a single painting. The people who had seen his strange, incomprehensible pictures anticipated he never would. The couple had met on a demonstration in London that Lulu had gone to with her Aunt Fion.

Everyone, except Orla, considered it a most inauspicious start to married life: the husband not earning a bean and reliant on his eighteen-year-old wife to put food on the table.

But Orla had given her daughter every encouragement. 'Go for it, girl,' she whispered, more than once. 'Even if things fail, you've given it a try. You've had your fling. You won't spend your life thinking that you've wasted every minute, that there's a million things out there to do and you haven't done a single one.'

'Things won't fail, Mum,' Lulu had assured her, clear-eyed and full of confidence. 'I love Gareth and he loves me. I can't wait for us to be together.'

And now it was done. Lulu was Mrs Gareth Jackson and would shortly be starting on a great adventure.

'Can I have the parents of the bride and groom?' the photographer shouted.

Micky nodded curtly at Orla and they posed for several photographs with the newly married couple; with the bridesmaids; with each other; and with Gareth's widowed mother, Susan, a feisty, bizarrely dressed woman, something of an artist herself, according to Fion, with whom she'd immediately become friends.

Orla was making awkward conversation with Susan, hoping she hadn't noticed the tension between the bride's parents, when she saw the middle-aged, strikingly good-looking man lurking just round the corner of the church. He grinned when their eyes met, then stepped back, out of sight. What one earth was he doing here? she wondered fearfully. How did he know about the wedding? How the hell was she going to get rid of him, not just from the church, but from out of her life?

'I want a photie with Great-grandpa,' Lulu announced.

'Go on, luv.' Bernadette pushed Danny forward. 'It's you she wants, not me,' she insisted when Danny tried to pull her with him.

Bernadette watched the erect, silver-haired figure of her husband stand stiffly between the bride and groom. It was obvious he was making a determined effort to hold himself together and her heart filled with aching sadness. In the not too distant future she was going to lose him. He hadn't told her what was wrong. She hadn't asked. But for the last two months he'd eaten like a bird and hadn't touched the ale he'd always been so fond of. In bed at night he held her tightly in his arms, as if worried he might never hold her that way again.

Alice came up. She nodded at the wedding group. 'How is he?'

'Not so good, Ally. He was sick again this morning. I thought he'd never stop vomiting.'

'It still might not be too late for him to see a doctor.' It had become a bone of contention between the women, whether Danny should, or should not, seek medical attention.

Bernadette shook her head firmly. 'Danny's the most intelligent man I've ever known. He knows where the doctor lives, but when it comes down to it, he'd sooner die in his own way, luv, quickly and as painlessly as possible, not have long-drawn-out treatment and operations. He'd hate me and the children to see him an invalid.'

'Whatever you say, Bernie.' Alice tried not to sound

cold. She had no more wish to lose Danny than did Bernadette and she longed to interfere. She felt an outsider in the relationship between her father and her best friend.

'Your Cormac's girlfriend looks very studious,' Bernie remarked, changing the subject. 'What's her name?'

'Vicky. She's not a girlfriend, just a colleague from work. She's the one he's starting the business with.' Alice's gaze drifted from her son towards Pol and Maurice Lacey. Pol was expecting her third baby. Alice still found it shocking the way Pol had transferred her affections from Cormac to Maurice not long after baby Sharon was born, though Cormac had taken it incredibly well and there was a surprising lack of animosity between the cousins. Of course, the switch had caused no end of gossip at the time. It was hard for people of her age to get used to the way some young people behaved these days. Morals seemed to have gone out the window during the Sixties. In Alice's opinion it had started with rock'n'roll, and men growing their hair long and wearing earrings.

'As soon as they've finished the photographs I'll show you the three Lacey salons,' Cormac said to Vicky. 'We're lucky, starting off with an outlet, even though it's only small.'

'Have you discussed it with your mother yet?' Vicky enquired. She was a serious young woman wearing an ill-fitting brown costume, flat shoes and round, horn-rimmed glasses. Her dark, crisp hair was boyishly cut.

'Alice was all for it. We're an entrepreneurial family, Vic. My father had his own business. So does my cousin, Maurice. Mind you, his is just ticking over.' At that moment a beaming Maurice didn't appear concerned that he just managed to scrape a living from Lacey's Tyres.

'Why do you call your mother Alice?'

'It's just a habit I've got into,' Cormac explained.

'I've not long turned me house into a refuge for battered women,' Fion was informing Susan Jackson, the bridgegroom's mother. 'Why don't you come and take a look after the reception? You can stay the night if you like. It's a big house and there's plenty of room.'

'Don't the neighbours mind, about the refuge, that is?' Susan asked.

'Oh, yes. They're forever complaining, to me and to the corpy. I just don't take any notice.'

'Good for you. I'd love to stay the night, save rushing home on a late train. And next time you're in London you must stay with me.'

So many children, thought Maeve Adams as she watched them bent like birds searching for confetti, swinging on the railings, getting their new clothes dirty. The older children tried to look grown-up in the new gear bought specially for the wedding. By this time next year Orla could be a grandmother, yet her . . . She was thirty-five, getting on. But there were still so many things needed for the house – a bigger freezer for one – and she and Martin had always promised themselves they'd have a garage built on the side. And Martin didn't like driving a car that was more than a few years old, worried it might be unreliable. And the kitchen was getting a bit old-fashioned – she'd like plain white units for a change – and while the workmen were there, they might as well have the floor retiled; terracotta would look nice.

But none of these things would be possible if she stopped work to have babies.

Martin came over and took her hand. 'Penny for them, darling.'

'I was watching the children,' Maeve said wistfully. All

of a sudden the kitchen and a new freezer didn't seem to matter.

'We don't need children when we've got each other.'

'Don't we?'

'No, we jolly well don't,' Martin said. Perhaps he didn't mean to sound so irritable. 'I hope you're not getting broody on me, Maeve. Our lifestyle would have to change drastically if we only had my salary to live on. We'd have to go without all sorts of things.'

Maeve sighed and supposed that, to keep Martin happy, she'd have to go without children.

Orla managed to escape the guests and make her way round to the side of the church where Vernon Matthews was leaning against the wall, smoking. He threw the cigarette away when she approached and tried to take her in his arms.

She pushed him away and said angrily, 'Don't you dare touch me!'

'Worried your hubby might see?' His smile was almost a sneer.

'Naturally, but I wouldn't want you touching me if we were stranded alone together on a desert island.'

'You didn't always feel like that.'

'Well, I feel like that now.' She had been mad to sleep with him. It had happened two years after the incident with Dominic Reilly. In all that time Micky hadn't touched her — he still hadn't, though Orla had got used to it by now. But this was before she'd got used to it, when she used to drive the second-hand Mini Mam had bought deep into the countryside, singing to herself, feeling liberated. Mixed with this was a sense of gut-wrenching frustration, a longing for something even faintly interesting to happen.

After a while she got into the habit of stopping at out-of-the-way pubs for a drink of lemonade or orange juice.

It made her feel sophisticated, a woman of the world. She would get out her reporter's notebook and pretend to make notes, so people would think she was a businesswoman on her way to an important meeting.

The second time she stopped a man approached and asked to buy her a drink. Orla told him politely to get lost. A few weeks later, when she was approached again, she accepted the drink. The man turned out to be a commercial traveller who'd been on the stage in his youth. He was interesting to talk to and asked if he could see her again. Orla refused, though she had quite enjoyed the illicit excitement of the occasion. She hadn't felt like herself, but a different person altogether.

The next man who bought her a drink asked if she'd like to come upstairs with him to his room.

'You mean, you're staying here?'

'No, but I very quickly could be.'

'I'd sooner not.' Orla was beginning to feel like a character in a novel. She called herself unusual, romantic names whenever she met a man, which was happening regularly: Estella, Isabella, Madeleine, Dawn.

Micky wanted to know where she took herself every day in the car. 'Nowhere in particular,' Orla said vaguely. 'Just around. Sometimes I interview people for the paper.'

'I suppose anywhere's better than home,' Micky said nastily.

'You said it first,' Orla snapped.

They were nasty to each other most of the time. They slept in the same bed, their backs to each other. They got dressed and undressed in the bathroom.

She told Vernon Matthews her name was Greta. They met just before Christmas in a little thatched pub in Rainford that did bed and breakfasts. There were silver decorations and a lighted tree in the lounge. He was about fifty, with dark hair and dark eyes, and a Clark Gable moustache. He told her he was a representative for an engineering company and always used the pub as a base when he was in the north-west.

He also told her she was one of the most beautiful women he'd ever met. His dark eyes glistened with admiration when he said this and Orla's stomach twisted pleasantly. She felt very strange, almost drunk, though she'd only had orange juice. Afterwards, she felt convinced he'd slipped something in her drink.

Orla couldn't remember agreeing to go upstairs, but she must have, because the next thing she knew she and Vernon were lying naked on a bed together, making love. Her first thought was how to escape, but she knew it was no use trying to push away the heavy body on top of hers. She thought about screaming, but if someone came they might call the police and it could get in the papers – it was the sort of situation she was always on the lookout for herself in her role as a reporter.

Eventually, Vernon reached a noisy, gasping climax and collapsed on top of her. Orla slipped wordlessly from beneath, got partially dressed and went into the bathroom where she washed herself from tip to toe. When she came out, Vernon Matthews had emptied her bag on the bed and was going through the contents.

'How dare you!' she expostulated.

He merely laughed and picked up her driving licence. 'Orla Lavin, 11 Pearl Street, Bootle,' he read aloud. 'So you're not Greta, after all. And according to this, you're married. Does your hubbie know you spend your afternoons playing the whore?'

'I don't think that's any of your business.' She snatched the licence out of his hand.

'I could make it my business pretty damn quick.'

Orla began to push the things back in her bag. She said

threateningly, 'If you say anything to me husband he'll kill you. He might kill me first, but then he'll kill you, I promise you that.'

Vernon laughed again. 'Oh, I'm shaking in my shoes, I really am.'

He lay on the bed and watched her leave, and Orla drove back to Bootle like a maniac. It was weeks before she could bring herself to use the car again, and then it was to do some genuine reporting for the *Crosby Star*.

She thought the whole horrible experience was over and done with until three months later, when she got the first phone call.

'Hello, it's me, Vernon. Love in the afternoon, remember?'

Orla was alone in the house and the hairs prickled on her neck. 'What do you want?'

'To see you. I keep thinking of those happy hours we spent together. I can't wait for a repeat.'

'Then I'm afraid you'll have to wait for ever,' Orla said shortly. She put the phone down.

It rang again almost immediately. She left the receiver off the hook until the children came home from school.

The phone calls continued for ten days, usually in the mornings. Perhaps he had too much sense to ring when Micky was home. They stopped for three months and Orla thought she was rid of him, until they started again. He must call when he was in the Liverpool area and he only called to torment her, have some fun. Orla would be reminded of their afternoon together, which Vernon would describe in sickening detail if she held on and tried to plead with him to stop.

Sometimes he wrote letters: horrible, explicit letters that she burnt immediately, without opening, once she realised who they were from. It was awkward when

Micky was home and he picked up the post before she could get to it.

'Aren't you going to read it?' he would ask when she stuck the letter on the sideboard, unopened, waiting to be burnt.

'I'll read it later. It doesn't look important.'

One day, not long ago, she'd driven to Crosby to deliver some reports, wondering why a grey Marina stuck to her tail the whole way. When she came out, Vernon had been waiting, smiling, holding out his arms.

'You're crazy,' Orla had shrieked hysterically. 'Haven't you got a job to go to? Why won't you leave me alone? I never want to see you again.' She'd got in the Mini and driven away before he could reply, terrified, knowing she was trapped in a situation entirely of her own making and unable to think of a way out.

Now he'd had the brass cheek to turn up at her daughter's wedding, to spoil everything, at least for her. He must have seen the announcement in the *Bootle Times*.

'I'd like you to go,' she said shakily.

'And I'd like to stay.' She could tell he enjoyed getting under her skin, hearing her voice shake. 'I was wondering if I could inveigle my way into the reception.'

'I'd stop wondering if I were you. I'm not the only person who knows exactly who's been invited.'

His mouth twisted. 'That's a pity.'

'You're the one who needs the pity. You're crazy. Anybody sane would have better things to do with their time. Perhaps it wouldn't be a bad idea if I found out where you lived and told your wife what you were up to.'

'I haven't got a wife.' His eyes flickered and she knew he was lying. She felt she had got one up on him for a change, but it was useless knowing he was married. There was no way she could discover where he lived.

'Orla!' Bernadette came round the corner of the church. 'They're going to take a photie of everyone together.' She smiled at Vernon. 'Hello.'

'Hello, there,' he said charmingly. ''Bye, Orla. See you again one day soon.'

Cormac and Vicky managed a quick tour of the three Lacey's salons before sitting down to a ham salad in Hilton's Restaurant, where the reception was being held and where Cormac had celebrated his twenty-first.

'The salon in Opal Street is a bit off the beaten track, but the other two on main roads will make wonderful showcases for our products,' Vicky enthused.

Cormac grinned. 'Our products! That sounds very grand and businesslike, Vic.'

Vicky went pink, something she was apt to do very easily, particularly if Cormac was around. 'I suppose it does, for a business about to be started in my parents' garage. Still, I think grand and businesslike is what we should aim for, Cormac.'

'I think so too. And "Lacey's of Liverpool" sounds very grand indeed. You don't mind your name being left out, do you?' Cormac said anxiously.

'Not under the circumstances – and I've never liked the name Weatherspoon. If our products are associated with an already long-established hairdresser's it will help get them off the ground.'

'You talk like a business manual, Vic.'

Vicky tried to discern if there was the faintest hint of flirtatiousness in Cormac's tone, but decided there wasn't. She was nearly thirty and Cormac was the first man she had fallen in love with. Not that he knew. Not that he would *ever* know, because she would never tell him. She might have done had she been as remotely pretty as any one of his three sisters. Even his mother looked gorgeous in a lacy lilac dress and little matching hat. Vicky sighed. If Cormac so much as suspected she was in love with him he'd probably run a mile.

They'd met three years before when Cormac had started work in the research department of Brooker & Sons, a large company in St Helens where Victoria Weatherspoon had worked since she finished university with a degree in chemistry. Brooker's, a household name, were primarily the manufacturers of domestic cleansing agents: washing-up liquid, washing powder, scourer, bleach, soap. They were also famous for their baby products and produced a small range of cosmetics, including shampoos and conditioners.

For most of the three years Cormac and Vicky had done no more than pass the time of day. They had never been involved in the same research project. While Vicky concentrated on ways of making the washing-up liquid more bubbly or the scourer more ruthless, Cormac was involved in different experiments which could lead to the world being rid of every speck of dirt and every known germ.

Two and a half months ago – Vicky remembered the day precisely, it was January the fourteenth – she and Cormac happened to be working late together. He was sitting on a stool at a table at the far end of the laboratory, writing, presumably a report on his current project. Vicky was using the shaker, a piece of machinery that gripped containers and tossed them about crazily for two minutes so that the contents were thoroughly mixed.

'What's that you're doing, Vic?' Cormac enquired.

'Mixing shampoo for my mother. Sorry, is the noise getting on your nerves?'

'No. I was wondering what the smell was, that's all.' Cormac sniffed appreciatively. 'It's very nice. What is it?'

'Geranium oil.'

'Do we make geranium oil shampoo?' He put down his pen and came towards her.

Vicky felt her heart quicken. 'No. This is Brooker's basic mixture before the perfume's added. I didn't steal it, Cormac. It's been paid for, I can assure you.'

'Gracious, Vic. I wouldn't give a damn if you pinched a ten-ton container. I'm just interested in what you're doing, that's all.' He looked with surprise at the row of plastic bottles on the worktop. 'There must be enough there to last your mother the rest of her life. Sorry, Vic,' he said apologetically, putting his hand on her arm. 'I'm being dead nosy. It's just that I'm bored witless writing up a report. I was looking for a diversion, that's all. Even so, I wouldn't mind knowing what your mother's going to do with so much shampoo.'

'She sells it, Cormac. She belongs to the Women's Institute and they have a sale of work every month to raise money for charity. Aromatherapy oils have a heavenly smell. The shampoos go like hot cakes. I usually make a couple of dozen a month, using different fragrances. This time I'm using geranium, lavender, lemongrass and rosemary.' Vicky wondered if her dull, monosyllabic tone was as evident to him as it was to herself. She sounded as if she was reading the lesson at a funeral.

'Aromatherapy oils?'

'The Egyptians first used them, possibly as long ago as 3000 BC. They can be used for massage and, oh, for all sorts of things, as well as making cosmetics.'

'Hmm! Interesting.' Cormac rocked back on his heels. 'Fancy a drink when you've finished, Vic?'

Over the next few weeks they went for several more

drinks after work. Vicky could hardly believe it when he told her about his life on the road belonging to a group called the Nobodys.

'I must have smoked every known substance. We didn't know where we were most of the time.'

'I would never have guessed.' His neat good looks didn't fit in with the life he'd just described.

'What about you, Vic? What have you been up to since you left university?'

'Working in Brooker's,' she confessed, slightly ashamed.

'Ah, an upright, conscientious member of society, unlike myself.'

'I wish I'd been a bit more adventurous, if only in my job. Brooker's is so ... so ...'

'Mindnumbingly dull?' Cormac suggested, making a face, and she laughed. The more they saw each other, the more relaxed she became.

'I suppose so. I once had visions of doing something as spectacular as splitting the atom.'

'Or discovering penicillin. I know, Vic, me too.'

A few days later Cormac said, 'Is there anything unique about Brooker's shampoos, Vic?'

'No. Most shampoos contain the same basic substances: aqua, sodium laureth sulfate, cocamide, hydroxy-propyltrimonium, glycerine.'

'Wow!' Cormac looked impressed. 'Could we mix all those various chemicals ourselves?'

'I beg your pardon?'

'Could we buy the cocamide and the glycerine and the other unpronouncable chemicals and make our own shampoo?'

'Of course, Cormac.' She looked at him wonderingly. 'You mean you and me? But why should we want to?'

He answered her question with another. 'Do you want to stay at Brooker's for the rest of your life, Vic?'

'Well, no.' She had always hoped to get married and have children, and Cormac was the person she'd like to achieve this ambition with. Fortunately, they were both Catholics, so religion wouldn't be an obstacle. The only obstacle was the fact he hadn't shown the slightest interest in her as a lifelong companion. 'No, I definitely don't want to stay at Brooker's.'

'Neither do I,' he said with a heartfelt groan. 'I'll never get the sort of job I wanted when I was at Cambridge because I didn't finish the course. I was lucky Brooker's took me on, but I want more than a career trying to make bleach thicker and whites whiter. I thought we could go into business together making aromatherapy shampoo and conditioner. I was virtually brought up in a hairdresser's, so I suppose it's only natural I feel drawn to the idea. I'm not suggesting we give up work. That can wait till things catch on, which might be months or years.' He wrinkled his nose. 'It could even be never.'

Had it been anyone else but him, Vicky would have pronounced him mad and walked away. But it *was* Cormac, whom she loved and who had actually suggested they do something together. She would have preferred it to be something other than starting their own business, but it was better than nothing at all.

As the weeks went by, however, she began to catch some of his enthusiasm. They would start off with a thousand bottles each of shampoo and conditioner of several different fragrances. His mother was thrilled to bits at the idea and had promised to use them in her salons – providing they were satisfactory – and display them for sale. Vicky still lived at home in Warrington with her parents and her own mother was equally thrilled. She had offered the garage to use as a workshop.

'Daddy won't mind. He can leave the car outside,' Mrs Weatherspoon said dismissively — her mother had always worn the trousers in the Weatherspoon household.

They only needed a small amount of equipment, which was fortunate as they only had a small amount of money between them, a few hundred pounds of savings. Initially there would be a lot of tedious work to do by hand. It should be a simple matter to obtain the formula for Brooker's shampoo and conditioner, and they would change a few of the basic elements so theirs would be different.

Sample bottles were ordered, a brand name decided upon: Lacey's of Liverpool.

'It has a ring to it,' Cormac mused. 'A few years ago Liverpool was the most famous city in the galaxy. Lacey's and Liverpool go perfectly together. It's not exactly gimmicky, but it's unusual.'

'We still haven't decided what colour bottles,' Cormac reminded her at the wedding as a waitress removed their plates. The best man, a friend of Gareth's, was nervously studying the speech he had written beforehand.

'I like the opaque white ones best. White with gold lettering.'

'I'm not sure if I don't prefer the black.'

'Black's showy, white's tasteful,' Vicky said stubbornly. It wasn't often she got her own way in the enterprise.

'We could have black bottles for the man's shampoo, the sage.'

'That's a great idea.'

He smiled broadly and put his hand over hers. 'We make great business partners, don't we, Vic?'

'Oh, yes, Cormac. Great.'

★

If you ask me, Sarge,' the driver of the police car said out of the corner of his mouth, 'women whose blokes have given them a good hiding have almost certainly asked for it.'

'Shush, Morgan.'

'She can't hear, Sarge, not with that howling baby and the screaming kids.'

'D'you think they asked for it too, the children?'

'Possibly. I've boxed me own kids' ears before now. Sometimes kids – and wives – need to be shown who's boss.'

Sergeant Jerry McKeown glanced over his shoulder at the woman on the back seat who was trying to quieten the baby and soothe two small children at the same time. Her face was covered in blood. 'Have you ever blacked your wife's eye and split her lip?' he asked sarcastically.

'Well, no, Sarge. 'Course not.'

'That's what's happened to Connie Mulligan in the back. So, get a move on, Morgan. She needs a doctor quick and afterwards a place to sleep, out of danger, like.'

'The woman who runs this women's refuge is probably a right ould cow,' Morgan said derisively. 'One of them feminists, I bet, and a lesbian too. All they do is run men down and that's only because they're too ugly to catch one for their selves.'

'You're full of worldly wisdom, Morgan. That's the place, over there. I think it might be a good idea to stop and deliver our passengers safely, not just speed past and chuck 'em on to the pavement.'

'Whatever you say, Sarge.'

The car stopped. Jerry McKeown jumped out and tenderly helped the injured woman and her terrified children out of the back. 'You'll be safe here,' he assured them. The woman recoiled from his touch and didn't speak.

He vaulted up the stone steps and knocked on the front door. It was opened almost immediately by a tall women in black jeans and T-shirt. Her bountiful hair was knotted on top of her head, cascading around her face and neck in feathery tendrils. She had large, beautiful eyes, a strong nose and mouth, and he had never seen anyone look so kind, so concerned, as the woman enfolded Connie Mulligan in her lovely long arms and drew her into the house. 'Come on, luv. I've been expecting you. The police phoned to say you were on your way. There's tea made and a nice, warm room ready for you. The doctor will be here soon – it's a woman.'

She glanced at Jerry McKeown and made to close the door. 'Thank you, officer,' she said briefly.

'Can I come in, make sure she's settled?' It hadn't been his intention to go inside, but he'd quite like to get to know this woman more.

'I'm sorry, but men aren't allowed on the premises. It's a rule. I had to put me own brother out not long ago and he was forced to find a bedsit near where he works.' Another woman had appeared and was taking the injured woman and her children to the back of the house. The tall woman made to close the door again, but Jerry put his foot in the way.

'Can I have your name, please? For the records, like.'

'I thought you already had me name on your records, but never mind. It's Mrs Littlemore. Mrs Fionnuala Littlemore.'

'Ta.' Jerry McKeown returned to the car.

'You might like to know, Morgan, that the woman who runs the place isn't old, isn't a cow and definitely isn't ugly. I wasn't there long enough to establish whether or not she's a feminist.' As for Fionnuala Lacey being a lesbian, he very much hoped not.

He went back to the house early next morning wearing plain clothes. A boy of about ten, with a grave, grown-up expression, opened the door.

'I thought Mrs Lacey said men weren't allowed on the property,' Jerry remarked with a smile.

'I'm her son, so she makes an exception.' The boy didn't smile back.

'What's your name?'

'Colin.'

'Well, Colin, does your mum make an exception for your dad as well as you?'

'Me dad's dead.'

'I'm sorry about that, Colin.' Jerry had never been so pleased about anything in his whole life.

'Who is it, luv?' Fionnuala Littlemore came into the hall wearing the same clothes as the night before. 'What do you want?' she asked abruptly when she saw the policeman on the step. 'Connie's in no position to make a statement yet. Anyroad, she'll only talk to a women police officer, so you're wasting your time if you come again.'

She was looking at him, but not *at* him. She wasn't seeing him properly. If they met in the street tomorrow, she wouldn't recognise him from Adam. But Jerry had come prepared to make her notice him.

'I've brought some toys for Connie's kids. I got them last night in Tesco's. They close late Fridays.' He held out a plastic bag. 'I hope they like them.'

'I'm sure they will. Thank you very much, officer.'

'The name's Jerry.'

'Thank you, Jerry. Connie will be pleased. Well, tara. It was nice of you to come.'

'Also . . .' He stuck his foot in the door before she could close it. The bloody woman still hadn't *seen* him. 'I'd like to make a contribution towards the refuge.

You're doing a great job. I admire you. I hope you'll find this ten quid a help.'

'Oh, we will. Thank you, er, Jerry.' She took the note and tucked it in the pocket of her jeans.

'Also,' Jerry continued desperately. 'I wondered, do you ever have fund-raising events, jumble sales, like? If so, I'd be willing to give a hand.'

'Well, there's nothing planned at the moment.'

'In that case, when the bloody hell can I see you again, other than on this bloody doorstep?'

'Oh!' She blinked and took a step backwards.

She'd seen him at last!

Fion saw a very tall, broad-shouldered, rugged man in his thirties, smartly dressed in a navy-blue suit. The skin on his face was weather-beaten and his nose was slightly crooked, as if it had been broken. His lips were scarred – he either boxed or played rugby. Very short brown hair stuck up in little spikes around his crown. He was anything but handsome, but he wasn't ugly either. In fact, taking in the quirky smile and the warm brown eyes, she thought him very attractive and liked his air of dependability. She could trust this man.

'Are you married?' she asked.

It was his turn to blink. 'Divorced, no children.'

'I never go out with married men.'

'Does that mean you will, go out with me, I mean?' He couldn't believe his luck.

'Mondays are supposed to be me day off.'

'Then I'll pick you up Monday at half-seven. OK?' He removed his foot and Fionnuala Littlemore closed the door.

'I'm meeting Sammy tonight and going straight from work to the pictures, Mum,' Maisie said as she was leaving. 'Don't do me any tea.'

'And when are we going to meet this Sammy?' Orla enquired.

'I dunno, Mum. It's not as if it's serious. I'm not going to be like our Lulu and get married at eighteen. I want to have a good time first. By the way, what's wrong with Dad? He was coughing and sneezing all night long.'

'He's got a cold, luv. One of those terrible summer ones. It doesn't help working in a foundry and he wouldn't dream of taking a day off. Anyroad, have a nice time tonight.'

Gary left not long afterwards. She was glad he'd managed to avoid manual work, not that there was much future in a shoe shop, but at least it was clean. Paul, her baby, left it right till the very last minute before leaving for school where he was in his final term.

Orla breathed a sigh of relief and made a fresh pot of tea. She took it into the yard to drink because it was such a lovely July morning and wished for the millionth time they had a proper garden. It was good to be alone at last and think about the phone call she'd had last night from Cormac.

'Hey, sis. Me and Vic have just decided you'd be perfect.'

'What for?'

'For selling Lacey's of Liverpool hair products. You've got a car, you've got the personality and you wouldn't have to give up your job with the paper.'

'I might be interested, Cormac. What sort of salary are we talking about?' There was something about the tone of his voice that made her anticipate what the answer would be.

'We weren't thinking in terms of salary, Orl, just commission,' he said sweetly. 'Twenty per cent, same as Mam gets, plus your expenses, i.e. the cost of petrol.'

'Make it twenty-five per cent,' Orla said promptly.

'I'll be putting meself out a bit more than Mam. But I'm only doing it because you're me brother and I expect to be given a high-powered job one day when you're successful.'

'You'll be head of international sales, sis,' Cormac said with a chuckle. 'It's a promise.'

She would be the only sales rep because, although he and Vic were working flat out, they couldn't produce enough bottles to cater for a larger market. 'It's a bit of a chicken-and-egg situation,' Cormac said. 'We can't take orders until we turn out more and we can't turn out more till we've got the capacity to do it, though we'll have to bite the bullet soon and get some proper equipment. Me and Vic are working ourselves to a standstill turning out stuff by hand.'

A few Liverpool shops had ordered, and since reordered, quite large supplies. Mam usually sold out within days of fresh stock being delivered. An advert in *The Lady* had produced dozens of orders in the post.

Orla would be supplied with leaflets and samples. She would start with Lancashire and Cheshire, and go further afield when they'd been covered. Chemists and small supermarkets would be her main target. Big supermarkets ordered centrally and would be approached when the company felt able to cope with a large amount. 'I don't suppose expenses would cover the cost of a nice business suit?' she asked wistfully. 'I don't possess anything remotely smart, Cormac.'

'Sorry, Orl. Anyroad, you always look nice, whatever you wear.'

'Oh, yeah! That was a typical man talking.'

She would start on Monday and was already looking forward to it. Tonight she'd tell Micky, not that he'd be interested. It might prove difficult when she went far enough away to have to stay overnight, but she'd cross that bridge when she came to it. She finished the tea and went to check the pathetic contents of her wardrobe in case anything needed washing. On her way downstairs with a denim skirt and two white blouses she heard the backyard door open and footsteps in the yard. Micky must have come home, which didn't surprise her, as his cold was really bad.

To her horror, when she entered the living room by one door, Vernon Matthews was coming in by the other. He must have waited for Micky and the children to leave. He looked overdressed for the warmness of the day, in a dark suit, collar and tie, black, highly polished shoes.

'Thought I'd give you a surprise.' He smirked.

'Get out of this house immediately!' She could hardly control her rage, which was mixed with panic and a feeling of fear. There was no one in the houses on either side.

She might as well not have spoken. 'I thought we could have a little chat.' He sat in Micky's chair under the window and, although he must have known he was less than welcome, he had the air of a man who felt entirely at home in the strange surroundings. Orla, disorientated and confused, could almost believe he belonged there.

'I don't want to talk to you – *ever*!' But she had already learnt it was a waste of time trying to reason with him. He didn't listen, or he didn't want to know, or perhaps it was just another way of tormenting her, taking not a blind bit of notice of what she said.

'Oh, come on, Orla. We had a lovely talk that first time, didn't we? Followed by an experience I shall never forget. I'd very much like to do it again, in fact. Now seems an appropriate time, when there's no one around.'

Orla leant limply against the sideboard, wondering

what to do. If she ran down the hall and out of the front door, she could scream for help. Or she could dial 999 and ask for the police. Except what would she tell people: the police, whoever came to help if she screamed?

He was watching her through lowered lids, still smirking, as if he recognised her predicament. 'Have you met this man before?' was the first question she'd be asked and it would all come out, the details of the afternoon they'd spent together in the pub in Rainford. Even if she tried to deny it, how could she explain how he knew where she lived? She had no idea what would happen then, whether he would be arrested, charged. Birds' wings of panic fluttered in her chest.

'Oh, come on, Orla. What harm would it do?'

He was actually getting up, coming towards her, smiling. Orla seized a large statue of Our Lady off the sideboard, ready to strike if he so much as touched her.

'Let's go upstairs. Just for a little minute, eh?'

'I'll swing for you first.' She raised the statue but he easily caught her wrist in his hand. The statue dropped to the floor but didn't break. The birds' wings were beating madly now, painfully. He slid his other arm around her waist and tried to pull her against him, groaning. 'I've been waiting too long for this.'

Orla tried to raise her knee and thrust it in his stomach, but her legs, her body, were trapped by his weight against the sideboard. She spat in his face instead.

'What's going on here?'

Micky! Feverishly red, face glistening with perspiration, eyes black with anger and tinged with incomprehension. He must have felt too ill for work after all.

'Just trying to renew my acquaintanceship with your wife,' Vernon said lightly.

'Out!' Micky seized his collar, flung him through the

kitchen, into the yard, into the entry that ran along the back, as if Vernon had only the strength and weight of a small child. Orla had never dreamt her husband was so strong, though she realised it was a strength born of uncontrollable rage.

Micky slammed the yard door and slid the bolt. He returned inside and Orla shrank back in the face of his anger. 'How long's he been coming round?'

'He's never been before, Micky, honest,' she stammered, more terrified of him than she'd been of Vernon. Micky looked as if he could easily kill her. 'He came when I was upstairs, just walked in.'

'Then what was that about renewing his acquaintanceship with me wife?' Micky snarled.

'I met him once, more than a year ago. He's been pestering me ever since.'

'Why didn't you tell me?'

'Because . . . because . . . oh, I don't know, Micky.' She had no idea about anything any more.

'You slept with him, didn't you?' His eyes had narrowed to slits.

She hadn't the strength to deny it. She nodded.

All Micky's rage subsided in a slow hiss of breath. He sank into the chair Vernon had recently vacated and buried his face in his hands. 'I used to love you once, Orla,' he whispered.

'I *still* love you, Micky.' She had never felt such total love as she did now, staring at him, hunched in the chair in his shabby working clothes. He had started to shiver. In a minute she'd make tea, get him aspirin, put him to bed. She wouldn't take the job Cormac had offered. And she'd give up reporting, find an ordinary job in an office not far away. The car could be sold. She'd never feel fed up or bored again. Somehow, in some way, she would talk Micky round into them starting again. She had been sorry about Dominic Reilly, but at the same time was too annoyed with Micky to care that they hardly ever spoke, never made love. This time she would work on him, *make* him love her again. She felt a surge of excitement at the idea of them recovering the feelings they'd had for each other when they were teenagers, when they'd first moved to Pearl Street.

'I'll just pack a bag,' Micky said, easing himself out of the chair.

'Why?' she asked, bewildered.

'I'm leaving, that's why. Surely you don't expect me to stay after what happened today?'

'But I love you, Micky!'

He looked almost amused. 'You have a funny way of showing it, Orla.'

'I've been a terrible wife, Micky. But I learnt me lesson today.' She took hold of his hands. 'Let's start again. Remember what it used to be like? Remember the first time in the entry behind our house in Amber Street?'

He removed his hands from hers, none too gently. 'I remember. You made me life hell and you've been making me life hell ever since. You always thought yourself too good for me, didn't you?' He looked at her thoughtfully, head on one side. 'Perhaps you were, still are. All I know is, luv, that I've had enough of you. I was going to hang on till the children were a bit older, till Paul reached eighteen. Under the circumstances I'll be off today. We'll sort out the divorce later.'

Orla felt herself go cold. 'You mean there's someone else?'

'There's been someone else for two years.' He smiled gently. 'If you hadn't been so wrapped in yourself you might have noticed.'

'Who is she?'

'Just an ordinary woman without your airs and graces who makes me feel good about meself for a change.'

Orla's voice rose. 'Who is she, Micky?'

'I hope you're not going to lose your temper, luv.' Micky's voice was mild. 'It doesn't sit well, considering what's just happened. If you must know, it's Caitlin Reilly from Garnet Street who used to live across the road. Her husband was killed in an accident on the docks when they'd hardly been married a year. She's got a lad the same age as our Paul.'

'She was in our Maeve's class at school. She used to come round to our house sometimes. Her married name is Mahon.' Caitlin was a pretty, round woman, the image of Sheila, her mother. 'You've got a nerve, Micky Lavin,' Orla said hotly, 'going on about what happened today when you've been having an affair for two whole years.'

'We've both done wrong, Orla, though don't forget you were the first. I was bloody mad earlier, I admit it, but what man wouldn't be if he came home and found a strange bloke trying to rape his wife?'

Wordlessly, Orla went into the kitchen and put the kettle on. Over the years, despite the contempt she felt for Micky, the impatience, deep inside she still loved him. The fact that he no longer loved her shook her to the core. There had always been an unshaken conviction in her heart that, no matter what she did, no matter how much she riled or offended him, Micky would remain steadfastly loyal through thick and thin. She considered pleading with him to stay, coaxing him to bed so that she could show him how much she cared.

But common sense prevailed. If Micky stayed, in a few weeks' time, when she'd got over her fright that morning, she would feel discontented again and start nagging him to do things she knew he never would.

The kettle had boiled. Orla made the tea, found the aspirin and took both into the living room, where Micky was leaning against the mantelpiece, staring into the empty grate.

'I'd like you to stay,' she said. When he opened his mouth to argue, she said quickly, 'I'll leave instead. Ask Caitlin and her son to come and live here. It'll set a lot of old tongues wagging, but who cares?'

Micky's jaw dropped. 'It'd break the kids' hearts if you left, luv.'

'They'd be just as upset to lose you. Anyroad, I won't be far away. I'll find somewhere nearby to live – Mam'll put me up for now.'

'But what will you do with yourself all on your own?'

'Our Cormac's offered me a job. I was going to tell you about it tonight. I'll do me best to make something of it.'

She would put her heart and soul into the job with Lacey's of Liverpool, drive all over the country, stay away for as long as she liked, knowing her children would be safe with Caitlin Reilly.

Orla's spirits soared. She was free to do the sort of things she'd planned on doing twenty years ago before she'd met Micky Lavin.

Chapter 16

'Where are you off to today, luv?' Alice enquired.

'Bury, Rochdale, Bolton,' Orla said briskly. She wore a smart black costume and was thrusting the new leaflets Cormac had brought the night before into a briefcase, checking she had enough samples. 'I'll probably be home dead late, Mam, so don't wait up.'

'I wouldn't dream of waiting up, luv, considering the hours you keep. I don't know how you keep going to be frank.'

'Enthusiasm keeps me going, Mam: commitment, ambition. The things you felt when you started Lacey's.'

'I didn't feel any of them things, Orla. I just wanted to get out the house away from your dad.' Alice smiled. 'I'm glad you're happy, though. I thought you'd be dead miserable, breaking up with Micky, though you never stopped complaining about the poor lad since the day you married him – and before, if I remember right.'

Orla closed the briefcase with a snap. 'I miss the kids,' she said soberly. 'I miss them coming in for their tea, making cocoa at bedtime. I even miss – only a bit – doing their washing. Still, Lulu's gone and I think our Maisie's more serious about this Sammy than she'll admit. Gary was talking about joining the Navy. Soon, there'll only be Paul left.'

'And he'll have Caitlin's lad, Calum, for company.' Alice always made a point of not sounding as shocked as she felt by all this switching around, as if marriage, relationships, were just a game of musical chairs. Pol had left Cormac for Maurice Lacey, Orla had walked out on Micky and, before you could blink, Caitlin Reilly had moved in and there was talk of divorce. She knew of other respectable women whose children were divorced or living in sin. That policeman, Jerry McKeown, that Fion had taken up with, had been married before, leaving Maeve the only one of Alice's children who led a conventional married life. At least, so far!

'Are you off now, luv?'

'Yes, Mam.' Orla kissed her. 'I'll see you when I see you. D'you realise what time it is? You'll be late for work.'

'I'm taking the morning off.' Alice flushed. 'I'm having another driving lesson.'

'Good for you, Mam,' Orla sang as she slammed the door.

An increasing number of cars were appearing in Amber Street, so Alice didn't feel too ostentatious buying one herself. It was only a little car, a Citroen Ami, though she was beginning to wonder if she'd ever get the hang of the damn thing.

She was on edge, waiting for the instructor to arrive in his own car, when the telephone rang.

'Mrs Alice Lacey?' a male voice enquired.

'Speaking.'

'I'm calling regarding a Mrs Cora Lacey. She's your sister-in-law, so I understand.'

'That's right. Is something wrong?'

'You could say that, Madam. We would be obliged if you would come to Bootle Police Station straight away.'

'Why?' Alice asked irritably and immediately regretted it. Cora might have had a bad accident.

'Because the lady concerned has been apprehended and gave your name as her closest relative.'

'Apprehended! Why?'

'That will be explained at the station, Madam.'

Cora was in a cell, hunched in her camel coat as if it were a blanket, her small, sallow face expressionless. She'd been caught shoplifting, according to the desk sergeant, trying to nick two woollen vests from a shop in Strand Road. It was a first offence, so charges wouldn't be pressed, but Cora had better keep her hands to herself in future, he said warningly, else she'd find herself behind bars.

'Cora!' Alice said reproachfully when the women were alone. 'What on earth possessed you?'

'Needed vests for the winter, didn't I?' Cora shrugged her shoulders churlishly. 'Me old ones were in shreds. It must be twenty years since I last bought some.'

'I would have bought you vests, Cora.'

Cora snorted. 'Oh, you would, would you?'

'Rather than see you steal them, yes. Look, can we go home? I feel uncomfortable here.' Alice glanced at the barred window, the hard bench on which prisoners were supposed to sleep. 'I've come in a car, not mine, the driving school's. The instructor turned up for me lesson just as I was leaving. I'll just have to forget about this week's lesson.' Lord knows what the instructor would think, being asked to take her to the police station – such a nice young man too.

Cora didn't speak on the way home. Alice got out of the car when she stopped in Garibaldi Road – Cora had given her name to the police, and she felt obliged to see her safely home and find out why she had been driven to steal.

Inside the house, Cora seemed to sag. 'I'm going to the lavvy,' she numbled.

Alice realised she was far more affected by the events of the morning than she pretended. She went into the scrubbed kitchen to make tea and was shocked to find the cupboards bare: no tea, no sugar and not a drop of milk on the premises. Was Cora so skint she couldn't afford even basic food? Later, she'd buy the woman some groceries. It was years since she'd given a thought to Cora – someone had mentioned seeing her outside the church at Lulu's wedding, but that was all.

Cora came in, looking more composed. 'You can go now,' she said belligerently. 'There was no need to have come in the first place.'

Alice had no intention of going. 'Why are you so short of money that you need to go thieving? I always thought you had private means – and Billy's working.'

'The "private means", as you call them, dried up a while ago. And Billy's never given me more than a few bob a week in years.'

'Why not ask for more?'

The yellow face twisted in a scowl. 'He's hardly ever here to ask. These days, Billy spends most of his time in Browning Street with Maurice and his family. 'Stead of the ale, most of his wages go on propping up that useless business of Maurice's.'

'Then what on earth are you living on?' Alice asked, alarmed. Now that she had removed her ancient coat, Cora, always thin, looked no more than skin and bone.

'Nothing, if you must know.'

'But a person can't live on nothing, Cora,' Alice cried.

Cora turned on her angrily. 'Look, I'd appreciate it if you got out me house and minded your own business. How I manage is nowt to do with you.'

'Then why did you give the police my name?'

'Yours was the only name I could think of. I didn't want Billy or Maurice knowing, did I?' Cora swayed and would have fallen had not Alice leapt forward and caught her.

'Have you had anything to eat this morning? Come on, let's go into the other room and sit you down.'

Alice settled her sister-in-law in an armchair and fetched a glass of water. 'What you need is a cup of hot, sweet tea, but all you've got is the water. How long has this being going on, luv?'

The near-collapse seemed to have broken Cora's spirit. 'Since earlier this year, when I turned sixty,' she said in a hoarse, frightened voice. 'Apart from the few bob I get off Billy, which pays the rent, I haven't had a penny piece. The 'leccy bill's not paid, nor the gas. I can't remember when I last ate.' She looked at Alice, her strange eyes terrified. 'When they stopped me outside that shop I nearly died, imagining me name in the papers, everyone knowing.'

'There, there,' Alice soothed, but there was something not quite right about what Cora had just said. 'I thought women were entitled to a pension at sixty?'

'Oh, Alice.' Cora had begun to shake with fear. 'I've done something terrible, worse than a bit of shoplifting. The thing is, I'm scared to claim me pension. I've got the book, they sent it months ago, but I daren't take it to the post office.'

'Why on earth not, Cora?'

Cora was wringing her hands agitatedly; spittle drooled from the corner of her mouth. 'When we first moved here,' she said in the same hoarse voice, 'I found a Jacob's biscuit tin full of papers in the fireplace cupboard. Two spinsters used to live here, sisters, about fifty. They went to America during the war. I've no idea what happened afterwards, whether they came back or not. The tin was full of private things, birth certificates, like, insurance policies, some shares. I kept them, they weren't taking up much room, in case they wrote one day and asked for them back.

'Years later,' Cora went on, 'I got a letter from the government to say one of the sisters, the oldest, was due for her old age pension. They sent a form for her to sign.' She paused.

'Oh, Cora, you didn't sign it!' Alice gasped.

'I needed money. I was desperate for money. By then, there was nothing but Billy's wages coming in. I signed the woman's name and filled in something to say I was her niece and she'd given me authority to collect the money from the post office. Two years later a form came for the other sister, so I signed that too. And I cashed the insurance policies and sold the shares.'

'You could go to prison for a long time for that, Cora,' Alice said primly. 'It's called fraud.' She was shocked to the bone. Shoplifting was one thing, but this was far more serious.

Cora grabbed her arm. 'Do you think the police will check up on me, now they've got me name and address, like?'

'I doubt it. I take it you've stopped taking the pensions?'

'Months ago, when I heard about me own pension. I got frightened. I thought it would look suspicious, collecting three pensions from the post office, all at the same address.' The small hand tightened, claw-like, on Alice's arm. 'I'm worried I'll be asked for death certificates, seeing as the pensions aren't being taken any more. I'm worried someone from the government will wonder why I'm not taking me own.' Cora released Alice's arm and collapsed back in the chair. Her eyes had almost disappeared into their sockets. She looked like death. 'What am I going to do?'

'I have absolutely no idea, Cora,' Alice said coldly. She got to her feet. 'I'll be off now and buy some groceries. I'll not see you starve. And I'll give you a few bob to be getting on with.' She emptied the contents of her purse on to the coffee table. 'There's nearly three pounds there. When I come back, let's have the electricity and gas bills and I'll see they're paid. But that's as far as I'm prepared to go. If you must know, I'm thoroughly disgusted by what you just told me. I haven't a clue what advice to give. It might help if you moved to a smaller house that's cheaper to run. And I suppose you could collect your pension from a different post office.'

Alice paused at the door. 'When you feel better, I suggest you look for a job. We need a cleaner at the salons. It's either early in the morning or late at night, whichever suits best. You can let me know if you're interested when I come back with the food.'

The door closed. Cora swivelled her head and watched Alice go down the path. She turned to shut the gate.

Cow!

She had never hated anyone as much as she hated her sister-in-law at that moment. *I'm thoroughly disgusted by what you just told me.* Oh, was she, now! What did she know about being on your beam ends, not knowing where your next meal was coming from? Alice Lacey had always had it soft.

Still, there'd been no need for her to have been so understanding, Cora thought grudgingly. Oh, she'd gone on a bit, but another person might have ranted and raved, and washed their hands of Cora altogether when they heard the criminal things she'd done. There was money on the table and food on its way. She'd even offered her a job. It meant that Alice cared, even if it was done with a sickly air of being holier than thou that made Cora want to puke.

We need a cleaner at the salons.

Well, Cora had cleaned before and she'd clean again. In fact, she'd spent her whole life cleaning. She glanced round the shining, spotless room. The furniture was probably out of fashion, but it had been lovingly cared for, tenderly polished. The net curtains were the whitest in the road. Cleaning was what Cora was good at. She'd take the job because she had to live. Anyroad, soft-girl Alice would almost certainly pay more than most employers.

Cora enjoyed cleaning the three hairdressers. So there would be less chance of being seen by the neighbours she started early, at six o'clock. Each salon took just over half an hour, and she felt enormous satisfaction when she'd finished and the plastic surfaces shone, the mirrors sparkled, the sinks gleamed.

She didn't mind working on her own. She was used to it. Most of the time she preferred her own company and early in the morning, with few people around and hardly any traffic, it was easy to pretend she was the only person in the world, a situation Cora would very much have preferred. Sometimes she even sang as she worked.

Billy didn't know she was working. Billy knew nothing about her. He never had. Cora had been cleaning the salons for a fortnight when he came home one night at about half past seven. They hadn't spoken to each other in a long while and she was surprised when he came into the living room and asked if she'd make him a cup of tea.

She was about to tell him to make it himself, but

remembered he didn't ask for much, probably knowing he wouldn't get it.

'Is something wrong?' she asked. He looked on edge, jingling the coins in his pocket as if he needed something to do with his hands. His face was hot and red, and she noticed his mouth kept twitching. 'Is Maurice all right?'

He didn't answer. Cora made the tea sweet and strong, the way Alice had wanted to make it for her the day she'd been arrested for shoplifting.

'What's the matter, Billy?' she asked, putting the tea beside him on the coffee table.

'I've done something dead wicked, Cora.' Tears trickled down his fleshy cheeks. At sixty-three, he was still a good-looking man, with thick, iron-grey hair and a clear complexion. His paunch had almost disappeared since he'd come off the ale. 'I've set fire to the yard.'

Cora gasped. 'You've *what*?'

He was looking at her with round, scared eyes, like a little boy, the way Maurice had done many years ago. 'I've set fire to the yard. I suppose I must have got the idea from our John, though in his case it wasn't intentional.'

'But *why*?'

'Because it was the only way out. He was losing money hand over fist, our Maurice. He's no business-man, Cora. He was making scarcely enough to feed his family, while the overdraft got bigger and bigger, and I was the one paying it back.' He swallowed nervously. 'The writing's been on the wall a long time. Six months ago I pumped up the insurance on the premises, so now Maurice can claim he's lost his livelihood. As I said, it seemed the only way out.'

'You mean you've been planning this for six months?' Cora was impressed.

'I reckon I must have.'

'Had the fire properly taken by the time you left?'

Billy nodded. 'The smoke was black. I could see it rising over the rooftops. The fire engines came, I heard them.'

'What happens if they blame our Maurice?' Cora frowned.

'There's something happening at Sharon's school, a concert. I deliberately waited till a night when he'd have – what d'you call it, luv?'

'An alibi.'

'That's right, an alibi.'

'And what about you, Billy? Have you got an alibi?'

Billy looked at her pleadingly. 'Only if you swear I've been home with you for the last few hours.'

'Of course I will,' Cora said instantly. It was the first time Billy had done something she admired. He was smarter than she'd given him credit for. She regarded the slumped figure in the chair and gave the shoulder a little squeeze. 'Come on, Billy, cheer up. Everything's going to be all right, I can feel it. In fact, it's going to be better than before, with Maurice out of trouble and you without an overdraft to pay.' She stood. 'Shall I make you something nice for your tea, luv? Fish and chips? Or there's bacon and eggs if you prefer it. Afterwards, we can watch telly. There's some good programmes on tonight.'

'Fish and chips would go down a treat, luv.' Billy sat up and squared his shoulders. He smiled. 'I never thought you'd take it so well. You're a good sort, Cora.'

At the end of September Danny Mitchell died quietly in his sleep. Bernadette woke and found him by her side, his body as cold as ice, smiling peacefully. She allowed herself a little cry before telling Ian and Ruth. If only she'd been awake to kiss him goodbye, so that he would have felt her arms around him as he slipped from this world to the next, and she could have kept him warm for a little while longer.

Then she woke up the children and rang Alice.

At the funeral there was a stiffness between the wife of the deceased and his daughter. Alice was convinced she'd been sidelined during her father's last few months on earth, prevented from seeing him as much as she would have liked.

Bernadette had thought Alice too interfering. Danny didn't want to be nagged to see a doctor, brought tonics, asked in a maudlin voice how he felt. They had played a game between them, she, Danny and their children. The game was that he was temporarily out of sorts but would get better very soon. It meant that even when he was on his deathbed they could laugh when otherwise they might have wept. The game had continued until the night Danny died. But Alice was a spoilsport and refused to play along with them.

'He's asleep,' Bernadette would claim whenever his daughter came to see him. 'I'd sooner he wasn't disturbed.'

She didn't like doing it. Alice was her best friend, but Danny was her husband. He came first.

'We're a rapidly expanding company,' Orla informed the middle-aged, impeccably dressed manager of the small, exclusive Brighton department store. At first he'd been slightly irritated at being interrupted, but she'd soon brought him round. 'We've recently moved to a new factory in Lancashire with the very latest equipment.' This wasn't strictly true. The new factory was a dilapidated building on a run-down trading estate near St Helens and the equipment was second-hand. However, it was the case that the company was rapidly expanding. In a few weeks' time, at Christmas, two new lines were being introduced: skin freshener and cleansing lotion. Perfume was on the cards for next summer.

'I like the look of it,' the manager said. 'And I like the name too: Lacey's of Liverpool. It has a nice ring to it.'

'That's what everybody says.' Orla smiled her most dazzling smile. 'I use it meself.' She ran her fingers through her shining brown hair. 'I'm a walking advertisement for our products.'

'And an excellent advertisement, I must say.'

'Would you like me to leave some samples?' She smiled again.

'I'd sooner place an order.' The manager's answering smile was more speculative than dazzling. 'Are you free for dinner tonight?'

Orla giggled. 'Depends on how much you're going to order.'

'How about a hundred bottles of each?'

'Then I'm free for dinner.'

Cormac and Vicky would be pleased: another two hundred bottles on top of the order for two hundred and fifty she'd taken that morning, making over a thousand she'd sold during her two days on the south coast.

Orla was a first-class sales representative for Lacey's of Liverpool. Within the space of six months she had sold the company's products in virtually every city and major town in the country, charming the male managers and buyers, and flattering the women. 'You've found your niche,' Cormac had declared appreciatively. He and Vicky had taken the plunge and were working out their notices with Brooker's.

Life sometimes got a little lonely on the road, staying in shabby hotels with nothing much to do at night-time. There was always the pictures, but Orla felt even more lonely in a cinema by herself when the rest of the audience were in couples. She missed her children. Occasionally she even missed Micky, particularly his warm presence in bed beside her. But next morning she always woke up refreshed, looking forward to the day ahead and the feeling of achievement when she took a big order.

When Lacey's of Liverpool became properly established, Orla would become Head of Sales and have her own office, a secretary. She visualised having charts on the wall showing the movements of reps all over the country. And when the company became more successful still, there would be no more need for reps. Orders would automatically come flooding in on reputation alone, or so everyone hoped, and it would then be Orla's job to seek markets abroad, in Europe and the States, all over the world.

She hugged herself when she thought about travelling to America to introduce Lacey's of Liverpool's products to discerning customers there. She wasn't doing exactly what she'd planned all those years ago when she was a teenager, interviewing famous people, but this was even better. One of these days a reporter might want to interview *her*.

The manager of the Brighton department store sat unnecessarily close throughout dinner. He kept putting his hand on her thigh, or grasping her arm, and she could feel his knuckles press into her breast. Orla didn't particularly mind. In its way, it was rather thrilling. She'd let him kiss her when the evening ended, but that was all. After Vernon Matthews, kissing was as far as Orla was prepared to go.

'Would you like something to eat, Maeve?' Fion enquired.

'No, thank you.'

'Well, it's time I made the kids' tea. I'm starving meself, as it happens.'

'I'll come and help.'

The sisters went into the big shabby kitchen of Fion's house in Stanley Road. A woman was already there, furiously mashing potatoes. Sausages sizzled on the stove. A small boy was squirting washing-up liquid on the floor.

'Don't do that, Tommy, luv,' Fion said mildly. 'It'll make people slip over.'

The woman turned and slapped the child's ear, hard. 'I'm sorry, Fion. I didn't realise what the little bugger was up to.' Maeve gasped and the little boy started to howl.

Fion said, not quite so mildly, 'Olga, don't you dare let me see you hit Tommy again. You're only here because someone did the same to you. This is a refuge, for children as well as their mothers.'

'I don't know how you stand it,' Maeve said when a sullen Olga and a sobbing Tommy had gone.

'I feel as if I'm doing a bit of good.' Fion was wiping off the fat Olga had splashed all over the stove. She took a big packet of fish fingers out of the fridge.

'Doesn't your nice policeman mind?'

'Jerry? Oh, he minds a lot. He wants us to get married. I said I'd marry him as soon as I found someone to take over the refuge.'

'I couldn't stand it meself. I'd feel as if me house wasn't me own. And Martin . . .' Maeve paused.

'And Martin what?'

'Martin couldn't stand it either.'

'Speaking of Martin, won't he be home from work by now and wanting something to eat?'

'Possibly.'

'Is something wrong, Maeve?' Fion regarded her small, neat sister searchingly. Maeve hadn't been to work that day. She'd arrived at one o'clock and they'd sat talking about nothing in particular ever since. Fion had expected her to go home ages ago to make Martin's tea, but Maeve had stuck to the chair and continued with the conversation that was rapidly running out of steam, mainly because she seemed unable to concentrate on one subject for more than a few minutes. She looked on edge, kept glancing at her watch, couldn't keep still.

'Everything's fine,' Maeve said in the sort of voice that indicated everything was nothing of the sort.

The telephone rang and Maeve said, 'If that's Martin, don't tell him I'm here.'

'Why ever not, sis?'

'Just don't, that's all.'

Fion went to answer the phone and came back a few minutes later. 'It wasn't Martin, it was Mam. Martin's just phoned to ask if you were there. She said he sounded worried. I didn't say you were with me.'

Maeve didn't answer. The phone rang again. When Fion returned she said, '*That* was Martin. He sounds even more worried. What's up, sis?'

'I'm pregnant!' Maeve burst into tears. 'I had a test this morning and it was confirmed.'

'That's marvellous, luv.' Fion flung her arms round her sister. 'I'm so happy for you.'

'So am I.' Maeve wept. 'But Martin won't be happy, he'll be livid. Oh, Fion! He'll be so cross. Can I come and live with you?'

'Of course, but surely it won't come to that? Martin will be thrilled to pieces. After all, how long is it you've been married? Going on thirteen years.'

Maeve shook her head wildly. 'I told you, Martin will

be livid. He doesn't want children. He wants holidays and garages and new fridges, new cars.'

'Then it's about time he grew up and lived in the real world,' Fion said crisply. 'How did it happen? Did you forget to take your pill or something?'

'No. I *stopped* taking the pill.' Maeve sniffed and managed a tiny smile. 'I haven't taken it since Lulu's wedding. I decided I wanted a baby more than I wanted Martin.'

'Then why are you so worried about him finding out?'

'Because I still love him.' Maeve started to cry again. 'Least, I think I do.'

The phone went. It was Mam. Martin had rung a second time and was about to contact the police. 'I told him she's only a couple of hours late, but he said she hasn't been in work today. He's climbing the walls, Fion, and I'm getting a bit worried meself. This isn't a bit like our Maeve. I mean, where on earth can she be?'

'Actually, Mam, she's with me,' Fion confessed and explained the circumstances.

Mam listened in silence, then said, 'I'm pleased about the baby, but I never realised it was mainly Martin's idea they didn't have children. It'll do him good to climb the walls for a while longer. He might have come to his senses by the time he discovers where she is.'

Fion replaced the receiver soberly. How peculiar fate was, so topsy-turvy! She recalled Maeve's engagement party when she'd been stuck with Horace Flynn and everyone else seemed to be having a whale of a time. She'd felt so grateful that Neil Greene had condescended to talk to her. Yet, years later, when she'd met Neil in London he'd looked as miserable as sin and she'd wondered what she'd seen in him. Now Maeve was in a state because she was pregnant when by rights she should be on top of the world. And Orla! Gosh, she used to be so envious of Orla, who had married Micky Lavin and was everything Fion herself wanted to be. Now Orla was wandering the country like a lost soul selling crappy make-up, trying to pretend it was fantastically adventurous, when it was in fact a desperately pathetic life for a thirty-six-year-old woman to lead. Poor Orla. Poor Maeve. And poor Neil.

I never thought I'd feel sorry for a single one of them, Fion mused, let alone all three. She felt very lucky, totally fulfilled. There was hardly another thing she wanted that she could think of. Colin had been a wonderful husband and Jerry would make another.

She resolved that tonight she would suggest she and Jerry got married straight away, because it seemed silly to waste time living apart. Anyroad, there *was* something she wanted – more children. But she wasn't prepared to move into his modern flat in Litherland. It would be too cramped. Besides, she loved this house that had been bequeathed to her by Horace Flynn. She'd been the only person who'd liked him, except when he pinched her bum. Another house would have to be found for the refuge. It would be her next project and she'd put everything she had into it. Fion mentally ticked off all the things she'd have to do: badger the council for an empty property, bring the local MP on board, start fund-raising, contact the press and get them on her side.

She returned to the kitchen. Maeve had made a cup of tea and started to fry the fish fingers.

'These look nice,' she said. 'Me and Martin have never had fish fingers.'

'They're lovely with beans and tinned tomatoes. Jerry's mad on them.'

'We always have posh, three-course dinners. They take ages to cook.'

'Well, that'll stop once you've got a baby to look after.' Fion grinned.

Maeve pulled a face. 'Martin will do his nut.'

'Stuff Martin. Any man who prefers three-course meals to babies wants his bumps feeling.'

'Hmm. If I have one of these fish fingers, will it make you short?'

'Have as many as you like. There's another packet in the fridge.'

The evening wore on. There were more phone calls from a frantic Martin. The police had refused to take action. Mam phoned to say she was beginning to feel sorry for him and could Fion persuade Maeve to go home, put the poor chap out of his misery?

Fion agreed that mightn't be a bad idea. 'I think our Maeve might welcome it by now. She's a bundle of nerves. It's best to get the confrontation over and done with.'

At eight o'clock Jerry McKeown arrived – the rule 'no men on the premises' had been relaxed on his behalf. He offered to fetch Martin in a police car with the blue light flashing.

'Can I go with you?' Bonnie demanded eagerly.

'Perhaps it would be best if Maeve went,' said Fion. 'How about it, sis?'

Maeve considered this silently for a while. 'Will Jerry wait outside the house until after I've told him? Just in case I have to come back here to live if he chucks me out.'

'If there's any such suggestion as chucking out, it'll be Martin out on his ear, not you,' Jerry said darkly.

Maeve Adams had never created a fuss during her entire neat and tidy life, had never given her mam and dad, or her husband, a moment's worry. She would have been embarrassed to think she had. Maeve strongly disapproved of the way her sister, Orla, behaved – though she wouldn't have dreamt of saying so – throwing herself all over the place and complaining loudly over just about everything in sight. She had thought it dead selfish of Fion to run away to London and give her family so much heartache. Even Cormac, whom everyone considered an eminently sensible person, had had a brainstorm and refused to finish university, then gone wild for several years.

Now, not only had Maeve missed a day's work at the hospital without phoning in an excuse, but she had disappeared for several hours, causing her husband a great deal of grief. In Maeve's eyes this behaviour was on a par with that of her sisters and brother.

She didn't want to lose Martin, who would be angry when he discovered she'd stopped taking the pill without discussing it with him first. But she'd only not discussed it because she knew he wouldn't agree. Martin's priorities didn't allow for children. They were still saving to have a garage built and only the other day he had complained that the car was getting old.

'*I'm* getting old,' Maeve said to herself as the police car – without its blue light flashing – made its way to Crosby through the evening traffic. Jerry thoughtfully remained silent. 'In a few years' time I'll be too old to have babies. And I'm not prepared to go without children just so Martin can have the latest car and a garage to put it in.'

He could be as angry as he liked. Maeve folded her small hands protectively over her stomach. She would have the baby with him or without him, it was up to him to decide.

Jerry stopped outside the Adamses' immaculate modern semi, though it looked entirely different from the house Maeve had left that morning. All the lights were on, including the coach lamp outside. The front door was wide open, the car was idling in the path, headlamps on, white smoke pumping from the exhaust. Martin was about to get in the car, leaving the house open and brightly lit for any passing burglars to help themselves. Normally as neat as his wife, his hair was on end, he was tieless and had forgotten to put a coat on, despite it being a bitingly cold November night.

He turned when the police car drew up and his face seemed to collapse with horror, which turned to relief when Maeve climbed out of the passenger seat.

'Darling! Oh, my darling Maeve. I thought you were dead. I thought you'd had an accident. Are you all right? Tell me you're all right.' He stroked her arms and neck, as if expecting to find broken bones. 'Where have you been?' He suddenly frowned when he noticed the driver of the car. 'Is that Jerry? Why is he bringing you home? Maeve, what's going on?'

Maeve decided not to beat about the bush. 'I'm having a baby, Martin. If you want, I'll go straight back to our Fion's with Jerry once I've collected some clothes – that's where I've been all day.'

'You've been at Fion's! Oh, Maeve,' he said reproachfully. 'I've been out of my mind with worry.' His jaw dropped. 'Did you just say you're having a baby? How on earth did that happen?'

'The same way it happens with everyone,' Maeve said cheerfully. 'I stopped taking the pill months ago and if you don't like it, Martin, then you'll just have to lump it. As I said, I'll live with Fion.'

'Can't we discuss this indoors?'

'There's nothing to discuss.' Maeve smiled sweetly. 'I'm having a baby and that's all there is to it. Once you accept that fact and promise not to complain about the age of the car, our lack of a garage, how much you fancy a colour telly and an even more expensive holiday next year than we had last, then I'll stay. Otherwise, I'll collect me clothes and be on me way.'

Martin's relief had turned to cold annoyance. 'I never dreamt you could be so deceitful, Maeve. Having a baby should be a mutual decision, not one the wife takes for herself. I'm very disappointed with you.'

'Not half as disappointed as I am with you, Martin Adams. Mind out me way while I go and collect a few things. I'll come back for the rest tomorrow while you're at work.'

'No!' Martin grabbed her shoulder. Jerry McKeown got out of the police car and leant against it, folding his arms. He watched the couple intently. Martin gasped and let go of his wife when he realised Jerry was concerned he might hurt her. He said quietly, 'The last thing on earth I want is for you to leave, Maeve. Come inside. We can talk there.'

'I'll come, but there's nothing to talk about. I'm having a baby and the sooner you get used to the fact the better.' Maeve marched up the path.

Jerry McKeown watched them go inside. They had forgotten all about him. He got out, switched off the engine of Martin's car, locked the doors and put the keys through the letter box. He then drove back to Stanley Road and, for the umpteenth time, asked Fion to marry him and was delighted, though slightly taken aback, when she accepted straight away.

Orla was the first person Lulu and Gareth had had to dinner in their tiny London flat. Orla watched her daughter fondly as she set the little round table in the window. It reminded her of when she was little and she'd played house with Fion and Maeve. The young couple hadn't enough dishes and the ones they had were cracked. None of the cutlery matched. The chairs were odd. The room smelt of oil paints and there was a half-finished painting on an easel in the corner – Gareth couldn't afford a studio. So far, the painting consisted of several dead fish pegged, like washing, on a line.

'What will you call it?' she asked him.

'I haven't thought of a name yet.'

They sat down to a tasty chicken and mushroom casserole followed by trifle. Orla had brought a bottle of wine.

'I'd've done something more ambitious, Mum, but the cooker's useless.'

'This is lovely, Lulu,' Orla said sincerely. A candle stuck in an old wine bottle flickered in the draught. The window of the fourth-floor room overlooked a landscape of Camden roofs glistening icily in the moonlight. It was December and painfully cold. 'I never realised roofs were so many different colours,' she remarked.

'I shall paint that scene before we leave,' Gareth remarked. '*If* we leave.'

Orla looked from her daughter to her son-in-law. 'Are you thinking of moving?'

Lulu wrinkled her nose. 'We *might*, but not till after Christmas. Last week we met this chap who owns an art gallery in New York, only a titchy place, badly run-down. He thinks the Americans would go for Gareth's paintings and has promised to show half a dozen on a regular basis – you wouldn't believe the price he suggested asking, Mum.'

'I don't want to compromise my integrity,' Gareth growled.

'Painters only paint paintings in order to sell them, surely,' Orla said. 'The money you earn merely proves their worth. There's no point otherwise, unless it's just a hobby and you don't mind giving them away.'

'See,' Lulu said triumphantly. 'I knew Mum would be all for it. Gareth's worried that if he earns money he'll have sold out.'

'I'm probably more scared no one will buy my work,' Gareth confessed glumly.

Orla tried to convince him he was talking rubbish. At Lulu's age – at any age – she would have gone to New York like a shot. She didn't want her daughter to miss out on what sounded a wonderful opportunity.

After dinner, quite a few friends dropped in, bringing more wine: artists mainly, male and female, not all of them young. The lights were turned off, leaving the flickering candle and the brilliant silver moon to illuminate the shabby room, and they talked about a myriad things – art mainly, politics, the latest films, the latest shows . . .

God, how I would have loved this, Orla thought longingly. I've missed so much. I've missed everything.

It was midnight when she returned to the small hotel in Victoria. To her surprise, there were half a dozen men in the lounge and the tiny bar was still open. She bought a double whisky and the men suggested she join them. Orla thought of her small, cold room with its small, cold bed and agreed. Five of the men were reps like herself, much older. Their clothes were cheap, their laughter false, their voices much too loud. They exuded an air of faint desperation as if this wasn't the life they had envisaged twenty or thirty years before. By now, they had expected an office with their name and title on the door, their own staff, respect.

The sixth man was very different. Better dressed than the others, quietly spoken, he exuded confidence rather than desperation. Orla gathered he was an engineer working for a French tool company, calling on firms by invitation to quote for new, highly expensive machinery.

He said very little in a quiet voice with only the suggestion of an accent. The other men called him Louis. Orla was particularly intrigued because, unlike his friends, he completely ignored her. He was a small, slender man, dark-haired, thin-lipped, with a tight, unsmiling face. She hadn't felt so immediately attracted to someone since she'd first met Micky. She kept looking at him in the hope of catching his eye, but he never once glanced in her direction.

An hour and two more whiskies later, she announced she was off to bed. The other men bade her a noisy goodnight, but Louis merely stared at his highly polished shoes and didn't speak.

Chapter 17

'This room is like a fridge,' Vicky Weatherspoon muttered. 'If I were a pint of milk, I'd keep for weeks.' She glared at the ice on the metal-framed windows, wondering if it was inside or out, and rubbed her numb hands together, but they had lost all feeling.

It was useless trying to write. She threw the pen on to the desk and tucked her hands inside the sleeves of her jumper. They felt only slightly warmer.

A plumber was coming to install second-hand central heating at the end of December. He was a very cheap, highly sought-after plumber, which meant they'd had to wait months until he was free. It hadn't been so bad in October when they'd first moved in and had spent most of their time decorating the shabby, run-down building inside and out, while Mary Gregory and Robin Hughes, both eighteen and with A levels in Chemistry, were in the workshop turning out thousands of bottles of Lacey's of Liverpool shampoo and conditioner. A business had never been started on so short a shoestring, Cormac had said, laughing.

Lucky Cormac! Vicky made a face. Cormac was at that moment in a nice warm restaurant in Liverpool, lunching with a girl called Andrea Pryce, a model, who would become the face of Lacey's of Liverpool in an advertising campaign in the press, starting January. It would swallow up all the profit the company had made so far, but hopefully be worth it in the end. Andrea was startlingly pretty and ten years younger than Vicky, who wasn't only envious of Cormac being warm. Say if he fell in love with Andrea! Say if she tried to seduce him!

Vicky tried to imagine how a woman went about seducing a man, but her imagination wouldn't stretch that far. She thought miserably that Cormac was no more attracted to her now than a year ago when they'd gone into partnership. They couldn't possibly have got on better. They were friends, they went to dinner together, had even gone to a hotel in Yorkshire on a weekend business course; they sometimes shared quite intimate thoughts. The only thing missing was romance. Cormac had shown not the slightest sign of wanting to kiss her – she didn't count the triumphant kisses he planted on her cheek when they received a big order, or the hugs he gave her for the same reason. It was a sad fact that Cormac didn't regard her as a woman, but as a mate, a business partner. He would have been just as fond of her had she been a man.

Yet with each day they spent together, Vicky only loved him more. She'd tried to make herself attractive by growing her short, crisp hair longer, but was forced to cut it off when it became a halo of wire wool. Her mother warned her she looked like a clown when she tried using make-up. 'Stick to lipstick, Victoria, and then make it pale. You've got too big a mouth for such a bright red.'

Vicky blushed at the memory and wondered if Cormac had noticed her turning up for a whole week looking as if she was about to join a circus. Did he ever notice anything about her?

The new clothes had also proved a disaster. She was short and dumpy. She didn't suit flowing frocks and pleated skirts. And, 'Your legs are too sporty for high heels,' claimed her mother. By sporty, Vicky assumed she meant her overdeveloped calves. She would never know why she had acquired such heavily muscled legs when she'd been useless at games at school.

Then she'd spent a fortune on contact lenses so she could dispense with her glasses but, try as she might, she couldn't get used to the damn things.

Still, on New Year's Day Cormac's sister, Fionnuala, was getting married and Vicky had been invited to the wedding. Naturally, she and Cormac would go together. If they spent enough time in each other's company, she thought hopefully, he might get so used to her that he'd want them to get married because he couldn't visualise another woman in his life.

Cora and Billy Lacey had also received an invitation to Fion's wedding. Cora breathed a sigh of relief that she'd been accepted back into the Lacey fold. She'd buy herself a new coat and wear that diamanté brooch in the lapel that she'd nicked from Owen Owen's a long time ago. It wouldn't hurt Billy to have a new suit – he'd lost so much weight that his best one hung round him like a tent. Perhaps they could go to town on Saturday, have a meal afterwards.

There was an odd sensation in Cora's breast when she thought about going shopping with Billy. Another person would have recognised it as happiness, but Cora wasn't used to being happy and couldn't have explained what the sensation was.

After forty years of ignoring each other, she and Billy had suddenly started to get along. Billy had more or less given up the ale and most nights they spent watching telly. One night they'd even gone to the pictures to see *The Sound of Music* and enjoyed it no end – that girl, Julie something, had a lovely voice.

Money was no longer a problem since the yard had burnt down and Billy was able to keep all his wages. As expected, Alice paid far over the odds for cleaning the salons and Cora had started collecting her pension from the post office in Marsh Lane. Maurice and Billy between them had settled all Lacey's Tyres' outstanding debts with the money off the insurance and Maurice seemed much happier working as a driver for Bootle Corporation. He'd come to tea last Sunday, bringing Pol and the kids, and Cora realised she was quite fond of the lad even if he was a loser, unlike her real son who was very much on the up and up. The kids got on her nerves a bit with their noise, but she felt like a proper grandma and had actually bought them some odds and ends of clothes.

In a few weeks' time they'd be even better off. Alice Lacey was looking to buy a house and would be leaving Amber Street for ever once she'd found one. It was Billy who'd suggested him and Cora take over Amber Street from Alice who'd had the place done up dead smart. The rent was thirty bob a week cheaper than Garibaldi Road.

Cora was surprised to find she didn't mind, not much, living in the house of the woman she'd always hated. Nowadays, there wasn't all that much room for hatred in her heart.

Fionnuala Littlemore married Sergeant Jerry McKeown on the first day of January 1971. It was snowing and Fion wore a cream fitted coat over a matching dress – Jerry had offered to buy her a fur coat as a wedding present, but Fion didn't approve of animals being slaughtered for their skins.

Over ninety guests had been invited to the reception at Hilton's Restaurant. It wasn't until six o'clock that the newly married couple left for their honeymoon in London.

Alice waved them off tearfully, though she wondered why young people bothered with honeymoons any more. In her day a honeymoon was the time you got to know each other properly. There used to be all sorts of jokes about the first night. She remembered feeling dead nervous herself, but John had been a gentle, tender lover right from the start. Nowadays, the first night happened long before the honeymoon and people knew each other far better than God had intended by the time they condescended to get wed.

She returned upstairs to where the air was fuggy with cigarette smoke and several couples were dancing to a recording of 'A Whiter Shade of Pale', which was being played loud enough to be heard several streets away.

Orla came up. 'You look dead miserable, Mam. Have a drink. What would you like, sherry?'

'Just a little one, luv.'

Orla looked as if she'd already had too much to drink herself and there were four more hours to go before the reception ended. She also looked much too thin, Alice thought worriedly. Her eyes were unnaturally bright. She seemed to laugh a lot at things that weren't remotely funny. It was an unnatural life she led, particularly for a woman: on the road, staying in strange hotels in strange places. Still, it would all change in a few months' time, when she would be based in her own office in St Helens: Head of Sales.

Alice wondered if the time would ever come when she would stop worrying about her children. At least Fion was happy, the one she'd least expected to be, and Maeve was like the cat that ate the cream since she'd fallen pregnant, though Martin didn't exactly look too pleased.

Her son appeared on top of the world, the business doing so amazingly well, but Cormac had turned thirty a week ago and it was time he got married, started a family. Of course, he already had a daughter, Sharon, Pol's eldest girl, but Alice wasn't the only one who suspected Cormac had had nothing to do with the lovely red-haired child who resembled neither her mother nor her supposed father. She'd always hoped things would get serious between Cormac and Vicky, but he'd brought that model, Andrea Pryce, to the wedding. She was a nice girl, if a trifle empty-headed.

She looked for Vicky, saw her sitting alone on a chair, looking rather downcast, and went to sit beside her. 'Would you like a piece of wedding cake to take home for your mam and dad, luv?'

'That's very kind of you, thanks.'

'I'd have sent an invitation for two if I'd known you were coming on your own. You could have brought someone with you.'

'There's no one I could have brought. I thought . . .' She paused and said no more.

'Thought what, luv?'

'Nothing.' There were tears in the girl's eyes.

Alice realised that she'd thought she'd be coming with Cormac. The poor thing was almost certainly in love with him – he chose to dance past at that moment with Andrea in his arms, clearly more impressed with beauty than brains, stupid lad. 'Would you mind helping me make everyone a cup of tea, luv?'

Vicky jumped to her feet with alacrity, obviously glad to be rescued from her lonely chair.

In the kitchen, Cora was finishing washing a mountain of dishes. 'I've just put that urn thing on to make a cup of tea,' she said when she saw Alice.

'Thanks, Cora. I was about to do the same thing

meself. I think I'll use them cardboard cups, save more washing.' Alice and Vicky began to spread the cups into rows.

'I've sent Billy out to buy some sugar 'case we run short.'

Cora looked very smart in a tweed costume with a white jumper underneath. Her hair had been set that morning in the Stanley Road Lacey's. That shoplifting incident, dreadful though it was at the time, had done her the world of good, brought her to her senses. She was much more friendly nowadays, almost human.

'I was wondering,' Cora said, 'if you'll be leaving the carpets behind when you move. We've carpets of our own, naturally,' she added hurriedly, 'all fitted, but it seems daft to take them up and cut them down.'

'I'm leaving all the fixtures and fittings, curtains included.' Alice sighed. She was dreading leaving Amber Street, but circumstances and her children were forcing her out. The circumstances were that the salons were making a mint, not just from hairdressing, but she was the only stockist in Bootle of Lacey's of Liverpool products and they sold like hot cakes. She had never been so flush, yet nearly every one of her neighbours had to struggle to keep their heads above water, which made her feel dead uncomfortable.

As for the children, they'd been nagging her to buy a place of her own for years: Southport, or near the sands, Ainsdale or Formby way. When they were little she'd taken for granted she knew better than her kids, but since they'd grown up they seemed to think they knew better than *her*. Perhaps it was only natural. After all, she'd constantly tried to rearrange her dad's life, much to the chagrin of Bernadette.

It reminded her for the umpteenth time that she hadn't seen much of her friend since Danny died. There remained a stiffness between them. Bernadette was at the wedding, naturally, a pale, rather sad figure, surprisingly old, Alice thought when she'd come into the church with the children. This was the first big occasion that she'd attended as a widow.

'Excuse me, Vicky. I won't be a minute.' Impulsively, Alice went back into the reception. Bernadette was standing with a group, yet somehow looking very much alone, watching Ian and Ruth dance together. Alice was struck by how closely seventeen-year-old Ian resembled his father. Tall and lithe, he had the same appealingly wicked smile. She touched Bernadette's hand. 'He's going to be a heartbreaker one of these days, just like me dad.'

'I think he already is. I'm not sure if it's a good thing or a bad one that he looks so much like Danny.' Bernadette gave a rueful smile. 'It means I'm reminded of him a hundred times a day.'

'I reckon it's good.'

'I suppose so.'

They looked at each other. Alice wrinkled her nose. 'I'm sorry, Bernie.'

'For what?'

'For barging in when me dad was ill, trying to take control, insisting he see a doctor.'

'You only had his best interests at heart, luv. Trouble was it wasn't what Danny wanted. Perhaps I should have been a bit more tactful meself.'

Alice linked her friend's arm. 'Why don't we go to the pictures next week? We can have a meal beforehand. *Butch Cassidy and the Sundance Kid* is on at the Forum. I've been dying to see it for ages.'

'So've I.' There was an expression of relief on Bernadette's face. 'I'd love that. Ally. I'll pop in the salon and we'll arrange a time.'

'Come to tea tomorrer and we can do it then. Bring Ian and Ruth, except they'd probably find it dead boring. None of me grandchildren want to come to tea any more, not even Bonnie and she's only nine. I'll be glad when our Maeve has her baby and I'll have a little 'un again.'

Sheffield in January! Anywhere in January when it was snowing hard and freezing cold made you yearn to be somewhere else, like the South of France.

Or Spain.

Orla thought about Dominic Reilly, living in Barcelona. He'd married the girlfriend he'd said wasn't as beautiful as she was – it had been on the front page of all the papers. As soon as she could afford it she'd go on holiday to Spain. Perhaps Mam would come with her. She didn't fancy going on her own. In fact, she was fed up to the bloody teeth with being on her own and couldn't wait for April when Cormac had announced the company would go through a sort of minor relaunch and she would be working permanently in St Helens. A lot depended on how well the press campaign went with that model. If it went well, there would be no more need for her to roam the country, thank the Lord.

She trudged through the slush towards the hotel. At least it had a more-or-less decent lounge and she could sit in comfort until it was time to go to bed in an icy room with icy sheets.

The hotel also had a bar. By the end of the evening other reps would arrive, some of whom she'd be bound to know and she'd have people to talk to, make her laugh.

What a lousy day! The weather was vile, the street lamps a depressing sickly yellow, the traffic horrendous, and her car was parked miles away. Even worse, half the places she'd called in, mainly chemists, had refused to see her, even the ones where she'd made a prior appointment: people were off with colds and flu, and they were too busy.

She was beginning to hate this job. This wasn't adventure. It was no longer the least bit exciting. Maybe she was a bit run down because she seemed to have lost all her initial enthusiasm.

The hotel at last! The usual seedy establishment that looked as if it hadn't seen a lick of paint in years. Lots of plastic flowers and oatmeal paintwork. Orla hung her heavy trenchcoat on a rack in the hall. Underneath, she wore a smart black suit which no one had seen all day because this was the first chance she'd had to remove the mac. She went into the empty lounge with her briefcase. There was no fire, but an elderly radiator emitted moderate heat. The bar was in the corner and there was no one behind the tiny counter. Orla rang the bell, a woman appeared and she ordered a whisky.

'Sit down and I'll bring it over.'

'Ta.' Orla chose the armchair closest to the radiator and tucked her legs against it. The woman brought the whisky. As soon as she'd gone, Orla drank it in a single gulp. She felt in the briefcase for the half-bottle she'd bought on impulse on her walk back, the first time she'd ever done such a thing, but tonight, for some reason, she felt exceptionally depressed, what with the weather and a completely wasted day.

Refilling the glass, she drank the contents, slower now, before filling up the glass again. She wasn't trying to avoid the bar prices, just the embarrassment of reordering so quickly.

It had become a habit, starting off the evening with a couple of whiskies. They helped her forget about the present and think about the future, which looked particularly rosy when she'd had a few drinks, though she'd never had three before in such a short space of time. She drained the glass, closed her eyes and felt a pleasant warmth swill round her stomach, which reminded her how empty it was because she'd forgotten to have dinner. She'd eaten nothing since she'd left another hotel that morning – where had it been? Rotherham.

'Good evening.'

Her eyes shot open to find the sombre figure of Louis Bernet staring down at her. He wore a grey suit and a very white shirt that contrasted agreeably with his brown skin and smooth black hair. This was the second time they'd met since the night in London when she'd had dinner with Lulu and Gareth. On the last occasion they'd chatted amicably, only about trivial things. He wasn't as unfriendly as he had first seemed, more reserved, a bit shy.

'Hello.' She tried to smile.

He nodded at her empty glass. 'Would you like a drink?'

'Yes, ta.' Another drink wouldn't hurt. Not tonight, when she felt so unusually miserable.

'Whisky?'

'Please.' He'd remembered what she drank, her 'tipple', as Grandad used to say. He went over to the bar and for some reason Orla's eyes filled with tears. It must be thinking about Grandad, which made her think of Bernadette, Mam, her sisters, her children. And Micky.

Bootle seemed worlds away from this cold, crummy hotel. In Pearl Street there'd be a roaring fire in the grate, the telly would be on, the kids would be home from work desperate for their tea – and Caitlin Reilly, or whatever her name was now, would be bustling in and out of Orla's kitchen getting food ready.

Jaysus! 'What am I doing here?' Orla asked herself. 'Why did I leave?' At that moment, Pearl Street with her husband and children seemed the most desirable place on earth. 'I must be mad. I'm searching for rainbows, but you can only *see* a rainbow. You can't touch it.'

Louis Bernet returned with the drinks. He sat in the armchair next to hers. 'We seem to be the first here.'

Orla nodded and pulled herself together. She reminded herself that she was with a devastatingly attractive man. The first minute she'd set eyes on him, she'd sensed a magnetism about him. Now they were alone together and it was her opportunity to . . . to do what?

To make eyes at him over the whisky, flutter her lashes, lick her lips and pretend she was a scarlet woman? Except she wasn't a scarlet woman. She was Orla Lavin from Bootle, married, with four children whom she badly missed.

'What company do you work for?' Louis asked. He had the faintest of French accents. 'I didn't ask the time we met before.'

'Lacey's of Liverpool. It's my brother's firm. We make cosmetics. As from April, I'll have me own office back home. Would you like some samples? You can give them to your wife.'

'I haven't got a wife. Do you have a husband?'

'Sort of.' Orla paused. 'We're separated.'

'He must be mad, this husband, allowing himself to be separated from a woman like you.' His narrow lips twisted in a smile.

Orla forgot the house in Pearl Street and its occupants. She traced the rim of her glass with her finger as she'd once seen an actress do in a film, someone like Ava Gardner or Elizabeth Taylor. 'I'm not very nice,' she said seductively. 'That's why me and me husband parted.'

'I don't believe that.'

'It's true.'

'You seem exceptionally nice to me.' He moved his legs so that their knees were touching.

Orla's flesh felt as if it was on fire. A pulse throbbed in her throat. She was trying to think of an answer, when Louis said, 'Have you eaten yet?'

'I forgot to eat.'

'Would you join me for dinner here?'

'They serve meals?'

He shrugged and spread his hands, a very foreign gesture. 'Not very good meals, but edible. There aren't any restaurants nearby and it's too awful a night to go searching for one.'

'In that case I'll be pleased to join you for dinner.'

Louis was right. The meal was just about edible: badly cooked lamb, very dry roast potatoes, frozen peas. He ordered a bottle of wine to make the food go down more smoothly.

On top of the whisky, it also made Orla more than a little light-headed. She began to see the romance of the situation: two virtual strangers, stranded in a third-rate hotel, snow whipping against the windows. All that was needed was some haunting music.

During the meal he told her about himself. He'd been born in a little village north of Paris. His parents had a smallholding. The village was very dull, nothing ever happened. He'd been taken on by a local engineering firm to train as a draughtsman. At twenty-one, he'd gone to work in Paris. He kissed his fingers and threw the kiss into the air. 'Ah, Paris!' He pronounced it Paree. 'Paris is *très* beautiful. Very, very beautiful. And so full of life. It has everything a man – or woman – can possibly want.'

'I'd love to go there,' Orla breathed.

His brown eyes smiled into hers. 'I'll show it to you if you like.'

'I *would* like.'

'In the spring?'

She felt dizzy. 'Yes, in the spring.' She'd never met anyone like him before. He seemed so grown-up and sophisticated compared with the other men she'd known, particularly Micky, who was a child by comparison.

No one else had come into the dining room by the time they finished the meal. They returned to the lounge where an elderly couple had bagged their armchairs by the radiator. Otherwise the room was empty. The other reps must have wisely stayed in town and found bars with a bit more life in them. The clock showed half past nine – the last few hours had raced by.

Louis took her elbow. 'Would you like another drink?'

'A whisky and soda,' she replied, though she'd already drunk far too much. 'Just a little one.' She swayed and almost fell into an armchair.

'One more drink and I think we should go to bed.' He regarded her challengingly, eyebrows raised.

'If you say so,' she said demurely. Every nerve in her body felt alive. She couldn't possibly sleep on her own after tonight. A memory returned, of the night in a Bootle entry when she'd first made love with Micky. She had the same feeling now, of wanting to be touched all over, but this time by Louis Bernet.

Orla quickly drank the whisky. Louis held out his hand and helped her to her feet. She wondered if he felt the same pounding excitement as she did. She could hardly stand and it wasn't all to do with the amount of alcohol she'd drunk.

Her room was on the third floor. They took the lift,

where they kissed for the first time and Orla felt a rush of raw desire when she felt him pressed against her.

In the corridor she stumbled and Louis grabbed her arm. He supported her as far as her room where, to her surprise, he paused. There was a look of what might have been irritation on his face. 'I didn't realise you'd drunk enough to get in this state and I find drunken women rather unappealing. Tonight you'd go to bed with any man who asked.'

'That's not true!' Orla cried. She didn't want to be alone. She couldn't stand it, not tonight. 'I don't usually make a habit of this sort of thing. I'm only doing it because it's you.' There was a sob in her voice. She unlocked the door, put her hands round his neck and drew him into the chilly room. Snow was whirling crazily against the windows and the traffic outside was muted. 'I'm more tired than drunk, but not too tired to . . .' She paused, blushing. '. . . To make love with you.'

Perhaps it was the blush that convinced him she was, at least partially, telling the truth. He sighed and said huskily, 'You're also extremely beautiful – and very hard to resist.'

'Please don't try.' She removed the jacket of her black suit. The blouse underneath was blue and very frilly.

He came over and took her in his arms, buried his head in her shoulder. She could feel his lips through the thin material of the blouse. Then he began to undo the buttons, so slowly and deliberately that she wanted to scream at him to hurry. He slid the blouse off her shoulders, his hands warm on her skin as he pushed her down on to the bed and her head swam. He took off his jacket and kissed between her breasts, then pulled down the straps of her underskirt and bra so that she was exposed to him. She felt both vulnerable and wanton as she took his head in her hands and directed his lips on to her right nipple. He sucked greedily, kneading the flesh around with his fingers. Then he transferred to the other breast and Orla moaned.

Suddenly he released her and lay back on the pillow, all passion apparently spent.

'What's the matter?' Orla asked, bewildered.

'Nothing. Let me hold you, come here.' He slid an arm round her shoulders and put the other across her waist.

Orla began to touch him, but he caught her hand and held it tightly. 'Let us lie still a minute, *chérie*,' he said softly.

'But why?' What had she done wrong? It can't have been anything all that bad, because he was being so gentle with her. But it was very mysterious all the same.

'Because there are times when it is good to stop and think, just stay quiet for a while.'

She began to catch his mood, her own passion having vanished with his, and relaxed against him. He was still almost fully dressed and he felt warm and comfortable.

'Do you ever get lonely, Orla?' His voice was little more than a whisper.

'Lately I feel lonely all the time,' she said with a sigh.

'Me, also. All the time. But unlike you, I have no family to return to.'

'You poor thing!'

'I am very much a poor thing. I have spent the last ten years travelling across Europe, searching for something I have yet to find.'

'Love?'

He nodded. 'Love, possibly. Happiness, maybe. Who knows what? It might be God. And what are you searching for, *chérie*?'

'I'm not searching for anything. I'm just doing me job.'

'No, you're searching, like me. I could see it in your eyes.' He laughed quietly. 'I've seen the same expression in my own, that's how I know. You weren't satisfied with what you had. It's why you left your husband and children. After a while, the searching can become very tedious.'

'I suppose it can.' She wondered what he was getting at. Was he leading up to something? He had turned out to be a very strange man. She liked him more now than she did before, even if she couldn't understand him.

The hotel was exceptionally silent and it would have been easy to believe they were the only two people in it. Apart from the traffic, there wasn't another sound to be heard.

'You are a lovely woman, Orla.' He caressed her face and touched her hair with his lips. 'I like you very much. I think I could very easily fall in love with you if given half a chance. You pretend to be so sophisticated, but you're not. You're vulnerable, like a child. I shouldn't have asked you to come to bed with me. I was taking advantage of your need, not for sex, but for something else: romance perhaps, which is a very different thing. I feel ashamed, but I only did it because, like you, I didn't want to spend the night alone.'

'Why are you saying all this, Louis?' Orla whispered. 'Why didn't you take advantage? What stopped you? Was it something I did?'

'No, I just wanted to say these things before I told you. I want you to realise how hopeless your search is, so you'll understand you're not missing anything when you go back home to your family.'

'Told me what? And I can't go home till Saturday, and then it's only for the weekend.'

'I think you should go now. You see, *chérie*, you have a lump in your left breast, a large one. Now is the time for you to return to the people you love – and the people who love you.'

All she wanted was for him to leave. She appreciated being told so kindly, if rather strangely, about the lump – another man might have noticed, made love and said nothing. But now she knew and all she wanted was to be with her mam.

Louis understood how she felt. He helped her pack and took her in his car to where hers was parked. It was still snowing.

'I meant it about Paris,' he said when he had put her things in the boot and came round to the driver's side to say goodbye. Orla rolled down the window. 'I hope and pray it might still happen. Here's my card in case you feel like getting in touch when you're better.'

'Thank you. Thank you for everything, Louis.'

As she was driving out of the car park, Orla threw the card out of the window, then closed it.

The journey to Liverpool was a nightmare. Snow kept sticking to the windscreen. The wipers were useless. Lorries thundered past, spraying her with slush. She couldn't see. The car kept skidding on the icy surface, but she managed to steady it. She wasn't sure if she cared if the car crashed or not. Would her children, her family, find it easier to cope with her death in an accident rather than a long, slow death from cancer? She reminded herself that the lump might be benign and, even if it wasn't, you could have treatment. Patsy O'Leary, who worked for mam, had had breast cancer and recovered. She'd had a breast removed. But Patsy was nearly sixty. Orla was only thirty-seven and to lose a breast would be the end of everything.

'This is a funny time to come home, luv,' Mam said

when Orla came in just as she was making the first cup of tea of the day. 'It's only just gone seven and I'm not long up. Don't tell me you've driven all night in this weather? No wonder you look exhausted.'

Mam looked so welcoming and comfortable in her candlewick dressing gown, her greying hair all mussed. Orla burst into tears. 'Will you come to the doctor's with me later, Mam. I'm too frightened to go on me own.'

A week later and tests showed that the lump was malignant. And there was a smaller lump in the right breast that was malignant too. Orla was advised to have a double mastectomy.

'Oh, Mam!' she screamed in the hospital when the doctor conveyed the terrible news.

'I wish it was me, luv,' Alice whispered. 'Oh, dear God, I wish it was me.'

'You can wear a padded bra,' Fion said practically later that night when the family gathered together in Amber Street for a conference. 'No one will know.'

'*I'll* know,' Orla yelled. 'I'll be deformed for the rest of me life.'

'Orla, you'll still be as beautiful as ever,' Cormac assured her. 'After the operation you can carry on with the job exactly as planned, with your own office in St Helens.'

'I'll be as ugly as sin. And you can stuff the job, Cormac. I don't want it.'

'I'll pray for you, Sis,' Maeve said softly. 'I'll pray every minute of every day, I promise.'

'It's too late for prayers.' Orla wept. 'It's happened. Anyroad, I don't believe in prayers. They don't work. I used to pray for all sorts of things, but I never got them.'

Instead, she'd got a husband in a million and four lovely children, Alice thought sadly. Enough to make most women happy, but Orla had always wanted the impossible.

'I imagined one day I'd get married again, but no man will ever want me now.'

Cormac shuddered and turned away. How would he feel about Andrea if both her breasts had been removed?

Alice glanced at her other daughters. Fion made a face and Maeve shrugged. No one quite knew what to say.

'Jerry, I want a baby. I want to conceive tonight,' Fion told her new husband when they got into bed.

'I'll do me best, darling. I'm already trying hard, but I'll try twice as hard if you like. Anyroad, why the urgency all of a sudden?'

'I'm not sure.' It was something to do with Orla, something stupid, as if a new life growing inside her would act as protection against what was happening to her sister. Or perhaps it was a wish to grab at things that mattered before it was too late. 'Just a minute.'

'Where are you off to?' Jerry enquired patiently when Fion got out of bed.

'I'm going to kneel the way we used to do when we were little and say a proper prayer for our Orla.' At the end of the prayer, Fion slipped in a little one for herself. 'Please God, please make me conceive tonight.'

'How's Orla?' Martin enquired stiffly when Maeve came home. He was sitting in the lounge with a typed letter on his knee.

'In a state, as you can imagine. I'd be in a state meself if I was in the same position. She's having an operation next week.'

'I'm sorry to hear that. Oh, by the way . . .' He waved the letter, 'This is from that double-glazing firm who contacted us last year. Remember we said we might be

429

interested in the spring? I rang and told them it's off because my wife has given up work. Another thing, I think the clutch might be going on the car. We really need a new one – car, that is – but I suppose we'll just have to do with a new clutch instead.' He sniffed disdainfully.

'Did you tell the double-glazing firm exactly why I'd given up work?' Maeve enquired. 'That I'm having a baby in three months' time?'

'It was none of their business.'

'Nor is the fact I've given up work. I suspect you didn't tell them that at all. It's just another little dig at me for getting pregnant without your permission. You'd sooner have double glazing and a new car than a baby.' Maeve's usually serene face darkened with anger. Normally she was patient with him, but tonight, thinking about Orla, she wasn't in the mood. Her voice rose. 'You've got your priorities all wrong, Martin.' If he didn't buck up his ideas, there'd soon be another divorce in the Lacey family.

Orla opened her eyes. A familiar face was bending over the hospital bed. A kiss brushed against her lips. 'Micky!'

'Hello, sweetheart. How are you feeling?'

'Still a bit dopey. You look well.' She'd forgotten how handsome he was, even if his dark hair was slightly thinner and his face had filled out somewhat.

'You probably won't believe me, but so do you. A bit pale, that's all.' He stroked her cheek. 'Do you mind me coming to see you?'

'Of course not. For a moment I thought you were here because I'd had a baby. Doesn't Caitlin what's-her-name mind you coming?'

'Caitlin left a while ago, Orla. She couldn't compete.'

'Against who?'

christening, won't you, Mum?' She squeezed her mother's wrist, as if daring her to say no.

'In New York, luv?'

'It costs the earth to have a baby in America. I'll have it here, in Liverpool.'

'Then I'll be at the christening, luv. I promise.'

The house was besieged by visitors: family, friends, neighbours. Orla had passed the point of thinking she would get better, that there was hope. It made things easier for the visitors, not having to pretend. She imagined being the star of a terribly moving drama that would make a fantastic film – Vanessa Redgrave would be marvellous in her part.

Once she had got over the trauma of the operation, she felt well enough to go out, though she tired easily. She bought a stiff padded bra and filled it with cotton wool, so no one would guess she had no breasts when she went with Micky to the pictures and to the theatre when a couple of tickets managed to flutter off a lorry. After two visits to the hospital for radiotherapy, she decided not to go again. It made her feel washed out and she knew it was a waste of time.

The actual act of dying Orla tried not to think about. Only in the dead of night, lying in the double bed with Micky asleep beside her and the glimmer of the street lamps peeping through the gap in the curtains, would she let herself visualise closing her eyes for the very last time on the people she loved most dearly. She would never see them again. She would be gone from their lives for ever. They would miss her, grieve for her, but after a while they would have no alternative but to get on with their own lives and it would be as if she had never existed.

Sometimes she would start to cry, waking up Micky, who would take her in his arms and she would sob that she didn't want to die, to leave him and the children. But what could Micky say except, 'Shush, luv. There, there, sweetheart, don't cry.' He never said, 'Everything's going to be all right,' because they both knew it wasn't.

Micky was a saint for taking her back. When she thought about her moods and tantrums in the past, the bad-tempered scenes that were all her fault, she felt ashamed and embarrassed.

'I was horrible to you, wasn't I?' she said one night when the children had gone to bed and they were sitting on the settee in the parlour having just watched an old Humphrey Bogart film on television.

'You certainly were,' he agreed.

'I'm sorry,' she said penitently. 'I decided the other night that you're a saint for putting up with me for so long.'

He smiled ruefully. 'I'd sooner have married you, luv, than any other woman on earth. I just wish I'd been able to make you happy.'

'No one could have made me happy. I wanted too much.' She linked his arm. 'But you're making me happy now, Micky. I feel wonderful, being home. I remember thinking, it was the night in Sheffield, just before I came back, about how much I was missing Pearl Street and me family. I longed so much to be here I felt an ache in me heart.' The encounter with Louis Bernet she kept to herself. She'd told everyone she'd noticed the lump when she was having a bath. 'Though I'm worried about the children. It's not good for them, watching their mother die in front of their eyes. Our Maisie hardly ever goes out these days – I remember I used to nag her for never being in – and Gary's put off joining the Navy until . . . well, you know. Poor Paul's forever on the verge of tears. He's more sensitive than the others. As for

434

Lulu, I daren't think what her phone bill will be like. She calls every other day.'

'We can't shield them from reality, Orla, luv.'

'I suppose not.' She chuckled. 'I'll be a grandma, won't I? If I live long enough. It's strange, because our Fion, who's a year older than me, has just announced she's in the club and Maeve's only got another six weeks to go. I wish . . .'

'Wish what, luv?'

'Oh, nothing.'

Later, in bed, Orla said, 'I've been thinking, Micky.'

'I thought as much, you've been dead quiet.'

'I'd like a baby too.'

Micky gasped. 'Don't talk daft, luv. You can't guarantee . . . That's a stupid idea, Orla.'

'You were going to say I can't guarantee I'll be alive in nine months' time, but I will be, Micky, I swear it. I'll *keep* meself alive to see Maeve's and Fion's babies born, as well as me granddaughter and me own baby.'

'That would be dead irresponsible,' Micky said, outraged. 'Who'd look after it, for one thing?'

'Everybody,' Orla said promptly. 'Mam would and me sisters would, and your mam and dad would. And you would, Micky, as well as our children. It would be the dearest loved baby in the world.'

Orla coaxed and cajoled for the next half-hour, but Micky remained implacable. But still Orla persisted, giving all the positive reasons she could think of for having a baby. 'It would make me so happy, Micky. I wouldn't feel as if I was dying if I had a baby growing inside me. It would be like knowing me soul would be passed on to me child.'

'That's nonsense, Orla.'

After another half-hour of persuasion, Micky said reluctantly, 'Let's see what the doctor has to say.'

'No. The doctor will advise against it. I know he will.'

'There!' Micky said triumphantly, as if this proved his point.

'The doctor can't do anything else. If he said "go ahead" and things went wrong, he'd be open to blame.'

'So, you concede things can go wrong.'

'Things won't go wrong, but the doctor can't be sure of that. He'll advise against it to protect his back.'

'You might not conceive.'

'If I don't, I don't. But I'd like to try.' She began to touch him. 'Please, Micky,' she whispered. 'Anyroad, I'm not the delicate invalid you seem to think, not yet, and I feel like making love.'

'All right,' he said in a choked voice, 'we'll make love tomorrer – after I've bought some French letters. As for a baby, I'd prefer you thought about it for a bit longer than a few hours. We'll talk about it again next week. Oh, don't stop, luv. Don't stop. I've been dying for you to do that ever since you came home.'

Chapter 18

Bernadette Mitchell looked up in surprise one morning when her best friend came storming through the backyard into kitchen.

'You'll never guess what our Orla's gone and done,' Alice raged. 'She's only got herself pregnant. I've never known anything so irresponsible in all me life. If circumstances were different, I've have torn her off a strip a mile wide. As it was, I felt obliged to keep me mouth shut.'

'You'd think Micky would have been more careful,' Bernadette gasped, equally shocked.

'Orla wouldn't have let herself get in the club if she hadn't have wanted to – she learnt birth control the hard way, didn't she? She could always wrap poor Micky twice around her little finger. I'd like to bet it's all her idea.'

'It's a funny idea to have, Ally.'

'Well, you know Orla. She always has to be different. *She* can't just die like ordinary people.' Alice clapped her hand to her mouth. 'Jaysus, Bernie, that was a terrible thing to say. It's just that I'm so upset. And you know what she said, our Orla? "It will be like being born and dying at the same time, Mam." Oh!' Alice burst into tears. 'It's so sad, I could cry for the rest of me life.'

'What does the doctor at the hospital have to say?'

'She hasn't told him yet. I reckon he'll have a blue fit.'

'They might make her get rid of it.'

'Over my dead body, they will. It's a daft thing Orla's done, but it's done, and that's all there is to it. There's no going back. Is that kettle on for tea, Bernie? If I don't have a cuppa soon, I'll faint. Kids!' Alice sniffed and dried her eyes. 'They worry you sick when they're little and you think it'll stop when they grow up, except it gets worse. There's something dead funny going on between our Maeve and Martin, and Cormac's been moping around like a lovesick rabbit ever since that Andrea girl went back to London. Then there's Orla . . . I sometimes wish I'd never had children, I really do.'

'No, you don't, Ally. We women would be lost without our kids. Here's your tea. Let's take it into the other room. Shouldn't you be at the salon?'

'No, I should be at me new house in Birkdale measuring for curtains. I'm signing the final contract on Friday.' Alice sighed. 'Oh, Bernie. I hate signing things. Remember that bloody agreement Cora had me sign? Ever since, when I've signed anything I've been worried what I'm letting meself in for.'

'I wish it were me signing for a lovely bungalow overlooking Birkdale golf course,' Bernadette said wistfully.

'I wish it were you too. I'm dreading it, me. Anyroad, only toffs play golf. I'd sooner look out over Anfield football ground or Goodison Park.' Orla's news had put her in a bad mood and she was exaggerating. The bungalow was beautiful, with large, luscious gardens front and back, a lounge big enough to hold a dance in, two bedrooms and a dream kitchen. Alice had gasped in admiration when she saw the cream fitted units, matching tiled walls, the plum-coloured floor. There was a pine table almost as big as her present kitchen. The fridge, cooker and automatic washing machine were being left by the vendors, an elderly couple off to live in Spain.

Mind you, she still felt as if she had been badgered into moving by the children. It didn't help, either, when she casually mentioned to Billy Lacey she was only *thinking* of moving and he'd leapt on the idea of taking over her old house. In a weak moment she'd agreed it would be a good idea, though she felt certain Cora wouldn't. Unfortunately, Cora had, and both her and Billy had been in and out of the place like yo-yos ever since wanting to know what she was leaving behind. She wouldn't need a van to move. The few things Cora and Billy hadn't collared would fit in the boot of the car.

'Have you ever been in love, Vic?'

'Yes, Cormac. Very deeply in love.'

'Was it reciprocated?'

Vicky shook her head. 'No.'

'The chap must be a fool.'

'He's a complete idiot.'

'You're a prize, Vic. You'd make some man a wonderful wife.'

'You're drunk, Cormac. In your present state you'd make some woman a lousy husband.'

Cormac stared gloomily into his beer. He wasn't drunk, just mildly inebriated, but Vicky was still fed up with him. They'd come for a drink after work because he claimed he couldn't bear to be alone and all he'd done, for the umpteenth time, was ask questions about Andrea. Why hadn't she phoned? Why was she never in when he phoned her?

How was Vicky supposed to know? She was glad the affair had ground to a halt when Andrea had gone back to London – she took it for granted it had been a *proper* affair from the sickening way they mauled each other when they thought no one was looking. Now there was talk of using Andrea again when they promoted their perfume, Tender, in the spring. After all, Andrea was the face of Lacey's of Liverpool. It would be daft to have a different face, or so Cormac claimed, sensibly as it happened.

Vicky was dreading it because she knew the affair would start all over again. She had no idea whether Andrea was as smitten with Cormac as he was with her, but she was the sort of girl who probably liked having a man dancing constantly in attendance. No doubt she'd been thrilled to bits to find a good-looking single male available when she'd come to Liverpool for the press campaign.

'Do you think I should go down to London and look for her?' Cormac asked.

'Whatever you like, Cormac. I can't possibly pass an opinion.'

'Why not?'

'Because it's none of my business, is it? You must do what you think is best.'

'You're a lot of help, I must say. I haven't a clue what's best.'

Vicky scowled and quickly changed it to a smile – she looked plain at the best of times. She'd look hideous if she scowled. 'If I were in your position, I'd go to London.'

'There!' Cormac looked delighted. 'I knew you'd come up with an answer. I'll go tomorrow after we've seen that rep about the boxes.' They were contemplating selling their products in sets, covered with cellophane in pretty cardboard boxes.

'Glad to be of help,' Vicky said and immediately regretted sounding so sour.

He turned up next morning in his only suit to go to

see Andrea: light-grey flannel with a blue shirt and navy tie. At midday, after they'd placed an order for boxes and the rep had gone, they went together out to his car.

'Will you be able to manage on your own?' he asked cheerfully and Vicky wondered if he'd give up the idea of Andrea and London if she said she couldn't.

She preferred not to find out. Anyway, she'd been left by herself loads of times before. 'I won't be on my own, will I?' Since Christmas, Lacey's of Liverpool had taken on four more staff. There was a secretary, to type the letters and answer the phone, in an elegant reception office by the door; a young man for the newly formed packaging department; two women for the large room now referred to as the workshop. 'I thought I might go and see your Orla tonight, take her some samples of Tender.'

He kissed her chastely on the forehead. 'Give her my love if you do.'

'I will, Cormac. Have a nice time.'

She watched him leave with tears in her eyes. In a few hours' time he might well be holding Andrea in his arms. Tonight, they would go to bed together. It hurt so much, just thinking about it, that she got a pain in her chest and wondered if her heart was breaking into a million little pieces.

While Cormac was driving down to London, his sister, Orla, was being examined by an astounded doctor who had just been informed that she was pregnant. Across the room a nurse glared at her, shocked and angry.

'An accident, I assume,' the doctor said coldly. 'You should have been more careful in your condition. I'll arrange for a termination straight away.'

'It wasn't an accident,' Orla said cheerfully. 'It was

deliberate. And I don't want a termination, I want the baby, if that's all right with you.'

The doctor gasped, the nurse snorted. 'Since you ask, it's not all right,' the doctor snapped. 'It's one of the most stupid things I've ever heard. To be blunt, Mrs Lavin, you're dying. You might not live long enough to bring the baby to full term. Having a child in your condition is quite mad.'

'I *am* mad,' Orla agreed. 'And I will live long enough for me baby to be born. I *will*. I swear it.' She grinned. 'Though I might not breastfeed.'

The nurse rudely butted in, 'And who'll look after it?'

'The whole of Bootle.'

'What brought this on, pray?' the doctor enquired while the nurse tut-tutted. 'The wish to have a child under such dire circumstances.'

'Well, both me sisters are expecting, as well as me eldest daughter. I didn't want to be left out. Besides . . .' Orla paused.

'Besides what?' the doctor prompted.

'Normally, I wouldn't have dreamt of having another baby. But things aren't normal, are they? I'll be bringing a child into the world that wouldn't have been born otherwise. It seems to be a fruitful thing to do with me last few months on earth.'

The doctor's face broke into an unexpected smile. 'That's rather tortured reasoning, Mrs Lavin. Even so, I admire your spirit. I'll have your notes transferred to the maternity hospital straight away where my friend, Dr Abrahams, will look after you from now on. I'll ask him to keep me informed of your progress. You can be assured he will do all he can to see you have a healthy baby.' He went over to the desk and behind his back Orla stuck out her tongue at the nurse.

★

Alice opened the door to the house in Pearl Street in answer to Vicky's knock. 'Hello, luv. Come in. Orla will be pleased to see you.'

Vicky gasped when she was ushered into the parlour. 'I didn't realise you were having a party.' Every chair was occupied and there were people sitting on the floor. The light was switched off and dozens of candles and night lights burnt steadily on the mantelpiece. The flames flickered wildly from a sudden draught. There was music, very subdued, from a record player in the corner: Frank Sinatra singing 'Pennies from Heaven'. Voices came from the living room, the rattle of dishes from the kitchen.

'It's not a party,' Alice said. 'It's often like this. You must come more, luv. The world and his wife are welcome as far as Orla is concerned.'

'Vicky!' Orla shouted from across the room. Her cheeks were flushed, her eyes brighter than the candles. She looked more alive than anyone else in the room, in a white satin kimono, vividly patterned, and high-heeled red shoes. Her face was heavily made up and she wore too much jewellery. 'Give us a kiss. Everyone who comes has to give me a kiss. What would you like to drink? Micky, someone, get Vicky a drink.'

'I'd like a glass of white wine, please,' Vicky said to the young man who was Cormac's cousin. His name was Maurice, she remembered. She went over and kissed Orla on the cheek. 'I've brought you some samples of our new perfume. It's called Tender.'

'Tender is the night,' Orla crooned. 'Let's try some.' She unscrewed the tiny bottle and dabbed behind her ears. The heady scent of spring flowers mingled with the smell of melting wax. 'Oh, it's the gear. You and Cormac will be millionaires one day.'

'You've given me an idea for our next one. It's going

to be more musky than this, for evenings. We could call this one Tender Mornings and the other Tender Nights. It would probably be best if we brought them out together.'

As was her way, Vicky melted into the background and found Maurice by the door with her wine. Fion was smiling up at her from the settee. She patted the arm. 'Sit down, Vic.'

'Thank you,' Vicky whispered. 'Who are all these people?'

'Laceys, mostly. Don't forget, there's fourteen of us altogether, seventeen with Bernadette and her kids, and twenty-five if you include Uncle Billy's lot. Some people are neighbours, some are friends from school.' Fion laughed. 'When I was young I could never understand why our Orla was so popular. She was horrible to everyone as far as I could see, yet they all liked her. I used to be as nice as pie, but no one liked me a bit.'

'I'm sure that's not true.'

'It is. It might still be true for all I know. The thing is, I don't care any more.'

'You'd never think Orla was . . .' Vicky blushed. She'd been about to say something very tactless.

'Dying?' Fion supplied. 'Oh, it's all right. You can say it quite openly. We all do. Orla doesn't mind. You've heard of people who make a drama out of a crisis, well that's what Orla's doing with knobs on. The sicker she gets, the more dramatic the crisis will get. She's even got her stage make-up on, see! In a few months' time we'll all be gathered round her bed waving candles and singing hymns, and she'll be smiling at us angelically from the pillow. She's enjoying herself no end.' Fion's voice changed, became softer. 'I don't half admire her. I didn't realise how much I loved her till the last few weeks. She's got more character in her little finger than most

444

people have in their whole body. Did you know she's expecting a baby?'

'Yes, Cormac said. It's incredible news. And you are too − congratulations.'

'Ta. Can you feel it?'

'The baby?'

'No, the atmosphere. The whole house is throbbing with emotion. It's almost tangible. Every now and then I have to catch me breath.'

'Yes, I think I can, feel it, that is.' But she wasn't part of it. Vicky felt more like an observer than a participant in the tragic, enchanted events taking place in the tiny house in Pearl Street. She wished with all her heart she were a Lacey and these people would belong to her and she to them.

Cormac stared up at the third-floor window of the house in Camden. It was an elegant house, slightly shabby, situated on a busy road full of traffic on its way to and from the centre of London. The curtains on the window that so attracted his attention were tightly drawn against the brilliant sunshine of a lovely May morning. Perhaps Andrea was still asleep after her night out with her brute of a boyfriend. Perhaps they were *both* still asleep.

He'd looked like a brute to Cormac. His name was Alex and he had a remarkably heavy build for a banker, as well as a coarse face, a rasping voice and a plummy accent. He'd hated him on the spot.

Worst of all, Andrea hadn't been the least bit pleased to see him. She'd actually been reluctant to let him in, turning her face away when he tried to kiss her − he'd arrived in London late afternoon the day before and had driven straight to her flat. Alex had yet to make an appearance.

'I didn't answer your letters because I didn't want to,'

she said coldly. She wore tight black trousers and a long silky blouse. Her perfect feet were bare, the toenails painted crimson. 'Anyway, I've been away for most of the time since Christmas, in the States doing a fashion shoot. We went all over the place. I didn't find your letters till I got back last week. Did you need to send so many?'

'I thought we were in love,' Cormac stammered. 'I thought . . .' He stared at her lovely cold face. 'Weren't we?'

'You may have been, darling. I certainly wasn't.'

'But you said . . .'

'People say all sorts of things in the heat of passion. They don't have to mean them.'

'*I* did.'

Her expression softened slightly. 'I'm afraid *I* didn't, Cormac. I thought we were just having a nice little affair to pass the time. I won't deny that I enjoyed it. But it meant nothing.' Her smooth brow puckered in a frown. 'I could have sworn you felt the same, darling. You didn't give the impression of being madly in love.'

A key had turned in the door, and a figure in a pinstriped suit carrying a bowler hat, a brolly, and a briefcase lumbered in: Alex.

'Who's this?' he said suspiciously – and rudely, Cormac thought.

'Remember that little job I did a few months ago for a company called Lacey's of Liverpool?' Andrea trilled. 'Well, this is Cormac Lacey. Cormac, meet my boy-friend, Alex Everett.'

'How do you do,' Cormac said courteously as he shook hands with a reluctant Alex who didn't speak. 'Let me know, won't you, Andrea, if you'd like to do the job again? As I said, we're launching the perfume in June.'

'I'm sure I would, Cormac.'

'Why doesn't he get in touch with the agency?' Alex growled.

'Don't be such a sourpuss, darling. It's only natural he should approach me personally. I was best friends with Cormac and his partner, Vicky. Wasn't I, Cormac?'

'The very best,' Cormac agreed.

He'd left the flat, thought about driving back to Liverpool straight away, but felt too tired, so booked into a hotel nearby. He lay in bed for ages, staring impassively at the ceiling, feeling curiously empty, trying to discern what was wrong with him. Dawn was breaking by the time he fell asleep. Even so, he woke little more than an hour later, too early for breakfast. He left immediately to come and stare at Andrea's window.

Something in him was missing, a chemical in his brain maybe, because Andrea was right. He hadn't been in love with her. He'd realised almost straight away, as soon as he'd left the flat, expecting to be heartbroken, but finding he didn't care. He'd *thought* he was in love. He'd badly wanted to be. It was what men and women did: fall in love, get married, have children. The same thing had happened with Pol with whom he'd expected to spend the rest of his life, yet hadn't minded too much handing over to his cousin, Maurice.

Andrea was a shallow human being, he told himself, and if he hadn't been so anxiously looking for a soulmate he wouldn't have allowed himself to be so easily taken in.

Why was he gazing at the window of this shallow human being who could well appear any minute accompanied by her brutish banker boyfriend in his bowler hat?

Cormac had no idea. It was as if he expected the window, glinting so brightly in the sunshine, to send him back an answer, tell him what was missing.

The thing had gone, the link that was missing, the night of his twenty-first when Aunt Cora had informed him Alice wasn't his mam. He hadn't been able to love anyone since then. There was a coldness in his heart. He wasn't sure who he was any more, where he came from, precisely where he stood in the world.

If only Vicky were there and he could tell her how he felt. He could talk to Vicky about anything on earth in a way he'd never talked to anyone else. He'd never discussed what Aunt Cora had told him because he'd never felt the need. But he felt the need now. Vicky would tell him what was was wrong with him. She had answers, solutions, for every problem on earth. He urgently wanted Vicky and it would take hours to get back to St Helens when they could speak. In which case he'd telephone. There was a call box in the lobby of the hotel where he'd stayed.

Cormac ran like the wind back to the hotel. In the lobby he emptied his pockets of change and arranged the coins in little piles on the box: pennies, sixpences, shillings. He was about to dial the factory when he remembered it wasn't yet eight o'clock and Vicky would still be at home.

'Hello.' Her voice was quietly efficient when she answered.

'Vicky, it's Cormac.' The words tumbled over each other. 'I need to talk. I'm in a terrible state, Vic. There's something wrong.'

'Cormac! Have you had an accident or something? Is Andrea all right? Are you still in London?'

'No to the first question, yes to the others. Oh, damn! This thing needs more coins already. Hold on a mo.'

'Give me the number and I'll ring back,' Vicky said crisply. 'A long-distance call will eat money as fast as you speak.'

Cormac shoved a pile of pennies in the box, reeled off the number, put down the receiver and snatched it up again a few seconds later when it rang.

'You know you asked once why I called Alice Alice?' he said immediately, sinking down on to a black plastic chair. The long leaves of a pot plant brushed against his cheek.

'I remember, Cormac. And you're calling now, a whole year later, all the way from London, to tell me why?'

'Because she isn't me mother. Aunt Cora is. I was born the same night as Maurice and she swapped us over in the hospital.' His voice rose to a wail. 'Oh, Vic! I don't know who I am. Least I do, but I'm not the person I want to be, the person I always thought I was. I'm someone else entirely.'

There was silence from the other end of the line for quite a while as Vicky took in this startling fact. 'Don't be silly, Cormac,' she said eventually. 'You're Cormac Lacey and you always have been. You belong to Alice. They put you in her arms in the hospital and she took you home and brought you up. As far as Alice is concerned, you're her son.'

'And as far as Auntie Cora is concerned I'm *her* son.'

There was another pause, then Vicky said in a strangely puzzled voice, 'But you can't be.'

'Yes, I can, Vic. Somehow, I believed Cora when she said she switched me and Maurice around. It's the sort of thing she would do.' Cormac shuddered. 'She's evil.' And she was his mother!

Then Vicky said in what Cormac called her 'school-mistressy' voice, 'I'm surprised at you, Cormac. You're supposed to be so clever. How could you not know such a basic fact?'

'What are you talking about? What basic fact?'

'That a brown-eyed couple can't have blue-eyed children. It's something to do with genes. I thought it was something everyone knew. Your Uncle Billy has brown eyes and so does your Aunt Cora – I remember noticing what a strange brown they were at your Fion's wedding.'

'Not everyone's got a mind like an encyclopaedia, Vic,' Cormac snapped. 'People can't be expected to know everything.' He gulped. 'Does that mean . . .?'

'It means that if it's true your aunt swapped you round with Maurice, you weren't actually her baby to swap in the first place.'

'Then whose baby am I?' Cormac shrieked. A man had come into the lobby with a suitcase and was staring at him strangely.

'Maybe the nurses got confused and put the two Lacey babies in the wrong cots in the first place,' Vicky said sensibly. 'Cora merely put you back in the right one.'

'I'd love to believe that, Vic. Except – Mam told us this loads of times – it was hell on earth in the hospital the night I was born. There was an air raid and everyone was moved down into the cellar and back again. A woman was brought in who'd been found in the wreckage of her house about to give birth. I could belong to any bloody one.'

The man with the suitcase clearly thought he was sharing the lobby with a lunatic. He hurried into the dining room.

'Oh, Cormac, don't think about it now. Come home. But drive carefully. We'll talk about it tonight over dinner.'

'All right, Vic.' His voice trembled. 'I can't wait to see you.'

'Nor me you, Cormac.'

He replaced the receiver. Vicky had created more

questions than answers, but he felt better after talking to her. In fact, he felt better all round. He sniffed. The smell of fried bacon came from the dining room and he suddenly felt very hungry. Mistakes had been made when he was born, but what did it matter after such a long time? And perhaps, you never knew, Cora had put him in the right cot after all. If so, he had much to thank her for. After he'd eaten he'd give Mam a ring; he still had plenty of change. They'd hardly spoken since she'd gone to live in Birkdale in her posh new house. Then he'd go home to Vicky.

It made Alice feel dead peculiar to get out of bed, pull back the curtains, and be met with nothing but the sight of her own back garden and miles and miles of sky. Apart from the birds, there wasn't a sound to be heard. She'd been used to coming face to face with a row of tightly packed houses across the street, hearing the clink of milk bottles, cars, voices as people went to work.

Every morning she found herself leaving earlier and earlier for the hairdresser's, coming home later and later. Pretty soon she'd be sleeping there! What would it be like in the winter? She dreaded to think.

She missed having friends in the same street or the next one, the library and the post office being just round the corner, as well as every sort of shop a person could possibly need. Instead, she had to drive everywhere, even to Mass.

Bernadette claimed she wasn't giving the bungalow a chance. She came to visit and ran her fingers along the cream worktop, looked out of the window at the pretty garden where Ruth and Ian were playing, and said, 'It's beautiful here, Ally. You'll soon get used to it.'

'I suppose so, Bernie. I'm trying hard.' She sniffed. Bernadette was the only person who knew she hadn't settled in. 'What have Cora and Billy done to me old house?'

'I don't know, luv, and I'm not likely to, am I? I can't see them asking me inside.' She regarded Alice sternly. 'The trouble with you, Alice Lacey, is you've made a ton of money but don't know how to enjoy it.'

Alice sighed. 'I'd give it away, except no one will take it. Only Orla let me buy her a car.'

'Talking of Orla, how is she? I haven't seen her for a day or so.'

'Driving everybody mad, including Micky, though he loves it. I wouldn't have thought it possible for a woman in Orla's state to get on so many people's nerves.'

Maeve Adams felt the first twinge of what might have been a contraction soon after breakfast. Martin had just gone to work. She glanced at her watch, calmly made a cup of tea and waited for the next twinge. It came half an hour later and was stronger than the first. The baby was on its way!

Glancing at her watch again, she washed the dishes and was just making the beds when a wave of pain passed through her tummy that couldn't possibly be described as a twinge.

She cautiously made her way downstairs, took the suitcase, already packed, out of the understairs cupboard and, in quick succession, rang for a taxi, the hospital in Southport to say she was coming, Martin at work to tell him he was about to become a father – should he be interested, that was – then her mother at the hairdresser's. Finally she rang her sisters to let them know that the first of the four Lacey babies due to arrive that year was already on its way.

'Good luck, sis,' Orla sang. 'As for me, I do believe me bump's starting to show a bit.'

In the taxi, she took deep breaths all the way. The driver assured her he'd once delivered a baby on the back seat, so there was no need to worry if it came early. Maeve worried all the same. The contractions were getting closer and more painful with each mile.

'You look very calm.' The nurse smiled when she walked into the hospital, the taxi driver coming behind with her case.

'Well, I don't like to make a fuss.'

The labour was swift and very painful, but still Maeve didn't make a fuss. She just gritted her teeth, took more deep breaths and got on with it. Her little boy was born within the hour. He weighed eight pounds, three ounces.

'He's beautiful,' said the midwife.

'All babies are beautiful,' Maeve said serenely. 'Can I hold him? I've been waiting nearly thirty-six years for this.'

'Only for a minute, dear. We've got to get you sewn up. You need at least three stitches.'

Maeve was propped against the pillow, her baby wrapped in a sheet and placed in her arms. He felt big and warm. He was real. He was a real, live baby, with real hands and feet and perfect little fingers, a snub nose, a tiny rosebud mouth, hardly any hair and sleepy blue eyes. And he could move. He could wave his hands and wriggle his body. He could make a noise, the sweetest sound she had ever heard, a squeaky croak. And he was hers! Maeve Adams was a mother at last. Her calm deserted her and she burst into tears, just as Martin walked into the delivery room, slightly dishevelled, his tie crooked and his usually neat hair on end.

He stood at the foot of the bed, looked at her, then at the baby. 'So, you've done it,' he said in a voice devoid of expression.

'Yes, I've done it, Martin. This is our son. I thought we might call him Christopher.' Maeve wiped her eyes with the corner of the baby's sheet. 'Isn't he beautiful?'

Martin edged closer. 'He's got no hair.'

'Lots of babies are born without hair. It'll soon grow. Would you like to hold him?'

'I'm not sure. I might drop him.' He came closer still. 'He doesn't look like either of us.'

'There's plenty of time,' Maeve said placidly. 'I thought he looked a little bit like Grandad.'

'He's got my mother's mouth.' Martin suddenly sat on the edge of the bed and gathered his wife and his new son in his arms. 'Oh, Maeve, I'm so *scared*,' he said hoarsely. 'I'm scared you'll love him more than me, that he'll take my place in your heart. I'm scared to love him myself in case he dies, babies do sometimes. What if he's unhappy at school, gets bullied? What if he goes off the rails when he gets older, the way your cousin, Maurice, did? Or he runs away like Fion? How must your mother feel about Orla? We're going to worry about him for the rest of our lives and I don't think I can cope.' He began to cry. 'We were so happy before, darling. Why did you have to spoil everything by having a baby?'

'*I* wasn't happy, Martin, and I suspect you weren't either. No, don't argue.' She put her hand over his mouth when he opened it to speak. 'We cared about such trivial things. Our baby's *real*. Oh, yes, he'll be a worry, but the world would come to an end if everyone stopped having babies because they were scared of the future. If your parents and mine had felt like that, neither of us would have been born. As to loving him more than you, I'll love him differently, that's all. You'll find the same.'

The door opened, the midwife came in and clapped her hands. 'Would you mind waiting outside, Mr

Adams. I'm about to sew your wife back together. I'll take baby into the nursery and you can admire him through the window. There are more visitors outside who can't wait to see this lovely little chap.'

Alice was in the corridor with Bernadette and Fion. A few minutes later Orla and Micky arrived, Orla proudly displaying her bump. Then Martin's parents, and later on his sister and his niece. Cormac came with Vicky. By then, Maeve had been wheeled into a ward, exhausted but extremely pleased with herself.

Martin felt dazed as he was hugged and kissed, his hand was shaken, his shoulder punched, and he was congratulated so many times he felt as if he must have done something uniquely remarkable to deserve such approbation.

The men decided there was just time enough to wet the baby's head before the pubs closed. On the way out, they passed the nursery, where Martin paused and looked at his son lying wide awake in his cot. By God, he was a magnificent baby, far superior to every other one there. He longed to pick him up and cuddle him. He caught his breath. In another week's time, Maeve would bring him home and he could pick up his son whenever he pleased.

'What it is to be a Lacey!' Vicky remarked to Cormac on the way back to St Helens in his car. 'There's always something going on. If there isn't a new baby, or several new babies, in the pipeline, then someone's getting married or a party's thrown for no reason at all as far as I can see. All my family's ever celebrated is my parents' silver wedding. We merely went to dinner on my twenty-first because there weren't enough people to make a party.'

'We have funerals too,' Cormac said soberly. 'I think there's one on the cards in the not too distant future.'

'I hope not. Your Orla looks as if she could live for ever. What's coming next? Whose baby is due first, Fion's or Orla's?'

'Neither. Lulu's due in October. At least that's when she's coming back to England. The other two are expected to make an appearance about a month later. By the way,' he said, changing gear, 'you forgot about the wedding.'

'I didn't know there was a wedding. Who's getting married?'

'I can't tell you yet because the woman hasn't agreed.'

'You mean, there might not be a wedding?'

'Not if the woman doesn't agree.'

'You're talking in circles, Cormac,' Vicky said patiently. 'Is she having trouble making up her mind?'

'No, it's more a matter of her not having been asked.'

She laughed. 'Then why doesn't the man ask her?'

'D'you think he should?'

'Of course he should, if he wants to marry her.'

'In that case, Vicky Weatherspoon, will you marry me?'

'I beg your pardon!'

'You heard, Vic.' He grabbed her knee, removing his hand immediately when they had to turn a corner. 'I want you to be my wife and I desperately hope you want me for a husband, because I can't live without you.' He looked at her sideways. 'What do you say?'

'Yes, I'll marry you, Cormac.' She was amazed her voice sounded so sensible when she really wanted to scream with delight. It was the question she'd been aching for since the day, years ago, that they'd first met. In her wildest dreams she never thought he'd ask. Now he had and she would savour the words for the rest of her life. She would have preferred the surroundings to be more romantic: a candlelit restaurant, champagne and for Cormac to have gone down on one knee. Maybe in real life that didn't often happen.

'When?' he demanded. He was grinning. He looked incredibly happy and all because Vicky Weatherspoon had said 'yes'.

'Before all the babies are due so everyone's sure to be there. Say September.'

'September it is. We'll buy an engagement ring on Saturday. What sort would you like?'

A round one, she wanted to say. Any sort of stone. In fact, a piece of string would do. 'A diamond solitaire,' she said dazedly.

'What will your folks have to say?'

'Oh, they'll be thrilled. *I'm* thrilled.' She turned to him to explain exactly how thrilled she was that they were getting married, to tell him how much she loved him, always had, always would, but something prevented her. She merely pressed her shoulder against his and said nothing. Theirs would be an unequal partnership. He looked happy, but there'd been something casual about his proposal, as if he had taken for granted what her answer would be. They were comfortable together and, on his side, there wasn't the passion he'd clearly felt for Andrea. He hadn't told her that he loved her. There was still time for that, but Vicky knew he would never love her as much as she loved him – it might embarrass him to know how much. She would have to hold back a little, stay calm, be cool, match his emotion with her own.

Despite this, Vicky's heart throbbed with a dazed, exultant happiness. Before the year was out she would be Mrs Cormac Lacey and, whatever the circumstances were, she couldn't wait.

Chapter 19

The three sisters had never been so close. Every afternoon Fion and Maeve, with baby Christopher, would arrive in Pearl Street to sit with Orla and gossip, play cards for pennies, swap jokes – Orla had learnt some that were very near the knuckle during her time on the road. Fion laughed heartily and Maeve winced.

Micky had given the backyard a fresh coat of paint and a set of white plastic garden furniture had fallen off the inevitable lorry accompanied by a red and white striped umbrella. Baskets of flowers hung on the walls. There was a tub of hydrangeas in each corner. On sunny days the women sat outside – it was like a pavement café in Paris, Orla said once. Micky grinned foolishly before escaping to the pub for a drink, as he was inclined to do when the house was taken over by three women and a baby.

'I bet it's not a bit like Paris,' Orla said after he'd gone. 'But it pleases Micky no end to hear me say it. I'm learning to be nice, though it's a bit late in the day.'

Alice usually managed to join them for an hour and when Cormac discovered his family met every day, he came over from St Helens whenever he could, so that the five Laceys could be together – after all, time was precious. In a matter of months there would be only four of them left. They talked about the years when they'd only had each other, before husbands and children had appeared on the scene. They talked about John. Alice found it upsetting that they could remember so little of the time when everything had been perfect in the house in Amber Street, before their father had had the accident and everything had changed.

'In my mind, there was always a horrible atmosphere,' Fion claimed.

'Same here.' Maeve nodded.

'I remember hating him so much,' said Orla.

'I loved him.' Cormac made a rueful face. 'Trouble was, I always had the feeling he didn't love me back.'

'He had other things on his mind.'

'What do you mean, Mam?' asked Cormac. 'What other things?'

Alice hesitated before deciding they were old enough to know the truth, old enough for it not to hurt them any more. She told them about the day Lulu was born when she'd gone round to B.E.D.S. and found John with a new young family.

'You mean he dumped us for another lot?' Orla gasped, outraged.

'No, it wasn't you, his children, that he dumped, it was me, his wife. He found a girl as damaged as himself. But she got better and he began to treat her the same way as he'd done me, and she left him.'

'Poor dad,' Cormac said, always the softest. She was glad he was engaged to Vicky who she felt sure would never hurt him as his father had done.

It was strange that Fion, thirty-eight, but a strapping, healthy woman, was the one who suffered most during the early months of pregnancy. She was often sick, her legs swelled, she had dizzy spells, went off her food. Whereas Orla, the invalid, bloomed. Her hair was thick and glossy, her eyes star bright. Her skin had the texture of the thinnest, finest china and she had never smiled so much. The baby was growing well in her womb.

'She's a blessed baby,' Orla cooed. 'She's charmed.'

'She?' said Micky.

'Oh, it's a girl. She's another me. She's coming to take my place after I've gone.'

'No one can ever take your place, sweetheart.' Micky knelt in front of the chair and laid his face against her stomach. He felt the sharp bones of her hips under his hands and could have sworn he could hear his baby's heart beating. He wondered how he would manage to get through the next few months without completely breaking down. It was a tremendous effort always to appear composed, to look after the endless guests, engage in conversation, when he was being torn apart inside.

Orla was the only woman he'd ever wanted. He'd loved her since they were fourteen and they'd been in the same class together at school. But this love, burning, wholehearted and totally committed, hadn't been enough to make her happy. She had slept with other men. She had walked out on him. If it weren't for the cancer, she would be in an office in St Helens dreaming of even better things. She'd only returned to him and their children because she was dying.

It made him feel guilty for being so glad that she was back. For Micky, a dying Orla was better than no Orla at all and there would be nothing left for him after she had gone.

She ran her fingers through his hair. 'Cheer up, luv. Life is for enjoying, not enduring.'

'Don't say things like that.'

'Why not? It's true.' She lifted up his head, rather painfully, by the ears, and slid into his arms. 'If I'd had a bit more sense, I would have enjoyed meself more when I had the opportunity. And I'd like to think you've got a lot of years left to enjoy. I'll be keeping me eye on you, Micky Lavin, from up in heaven.'

He kissed her. 'They'll never take you in heaven, Orla. You'll be keeping an eye on me from a place much warmer than that.'

Lacey's of Liverpool perfumes were proving a great success. Tender Nights and Tender Mornings came on to the market in June. The lovely face of Andrea Pryce featured prominently in a press and television advertising campaign carried out from London. Andrea and Cormac never met again.

All the big Liverpool stores had extensive displays of the local products: Lewis's, Owen Owen's, George Henry Lee's. Cormac and Vicky were looking for a bigger factory so they could expand their range to include lipstick and face powder.

'In a few years' time we'll do an entire range of make-up,' Cormac boasted.

'How can you have aromatherapy mascara and eye-brow pencil?' Orla wanted to know.

'Don't ask awkward questions, sis. We're working on it.'

'Do you wish you were part of it, luv?' Micky asked when Cormac had gone.

'I'm having a baby, Micky, which is far more important.'

Cora Lacey helped herself to a couple of perfumes while she was cleaning the Strand Road salon, the morning one and the night one, though personally she couldn't tell the difference. They would do as a birthday present for Pol, save buying something.

Alice noticed, but tactfully kept her mouth shut. Cora

was an excellent cleaner and as long as she didn't make off with one of the dryers she didn't care.

At the end of August, six months into her pregnancy, Fion started to feel better. The feeling of constant nausea went away, along with the dizziness and the swollen legs. She ate like a horse and developed a passion for apples, which were at least healthy.

Fion, though, would have preferred to remain sick, or indeed feel much worse, if it could have prevented her sister's sudden deterioration.

Orla was rapidly losing weight, getting thinner and thinner, almost daily it seemed to concerned onlookers. She was having pain more severe than she had known humanly possible. Every nerve in her body shrieked in raw agony. It was the cancer, not the baby.

The baby was all right. The baby was fine. Dr Abrahams, who had adopted her as his special project, confirmed that her child was coming along well when Orla went to see him at the hospital.

'Would you like some painkillers?' he asked for the fourth week running.

'No, doctor.' Orla shook her head violently. 'I'll not forget what Thalidomide did to unborn babies. There's no way I'm taking so much as an aspirin in case it harms me little girl. I'd sooner have pains than tablets, any day.'

'You're a very brave woman, Mrs Lavin.'

'No, I'm not, doctor. I'm a realist. Anyroad, I've learnt that, if I notch meself up a gear, the pain goes away and I can't feel it any more.'

The doctor looked at the starry eyes in the thin face. 'You're a very remarkable woman then, Mrs Lavin. Will you allow me to say that?'

'I've always wanted to be remarkable at something, doctor. I'm glad to have managed it at last.'

★

Micky's sole reason for existing was to take care of Orla. The children felt the same. They came straight home from work every night to sit with their mam and hold her hand, to fetch and carry, to bring her anything on earth she wanted.

To please them, to make them feel needed, to make up for the hurt that she had caused them, she asked for a daily newspaper and made a show of reading it, requested cups of tea and glasses of lemonade she didn't feel like drinking. Maisie massaged her feet which she found extremely irritating. She pretended an interest in football, which she loathed, but Micky and the boys were passionate about it. It meant they could watch the — far too many — matches on the telly without feeling they should be watching something on another channel that Orla would in fact have found ten times more interesting.

September, and the weather was sunny, gently warm. The trees in North Park began to shed their russet leaves and the flowers in the Lavins' backyard bent their heads and died. The big petal balls on the hydrangeas turned brown. Pretty soon they would become brittle. Next spring they would have to be pruned to make way for new blossoms.

Orla sat on a white plastic chair, knowing she would never see this happen. But her baby would. She laid her hands on her stomach. The baby had been very still this morning. She felt a moment of fear, closed her eyes, concentrated hard and directed all the goodness left in her emaciated body on to the baby, now fully formed in her womb. Her little daughter gave her an almighty kick. Orla gasped with pain and relief.

The other pain she'd learnt to live with. It didn't matter any more. She'd stepped outside it.

★

Alice woke up every morning in the silent bedroom of her silent house with a deep sense of foreboding. The next few months would be nightmarish. What would Christmas be like with one of her children gone for ever? She also felt unreasonably depressed that Cormac, her baby, was getting married, which she might not have done if it hadn't been for Orla. There was a saying: 'A daughter is a daughter for the rest of her life. A son is a son until he takes a wife.' She was losing two children. She wouldn't be needed any more. It only emphasised the fact that she was on her own. The future seemed very bleak.

Then she would get up, pull herself together and prepare for the day ahead. She never let anyone, not even Bernadette, know how low she felt.

Lulu Jackson came back from America a few days before the wedding. Gareth was to fly over nearer the time the baby – Alice's first great-grandchild – was expected the following month. Alice picked her up from Manchester airport, took her to Pearl Street to see her mother, then to the bungalow where she was to stay. There was plenty of room and she was glad of the company.

'I like your frock, luv,' she remarked. Lulu wore a spectacular yellow garment lavishly trimmed with lace with its own little lace bolero.

'It's Indian and it's not really a maternity dress. I can wear it afterwards. I brought one for Mum in cream. I thought she might like to wear it to the wedding. Oh, and I've got you a scarf, Gran. There's this lovely Indian shop right by where we live in Greenwich Village.'

As soon as they'd eaten, Lulu asked if she'd mind if she returned straight to Pearl Street. 'I'd like to spend the evening with Mum. She looks well, doesn't she? Far better than I expected. A bit thin, that's all.'

'Your mam always manages to put on a show, Lulu. And I wouldn't build up your hopes too much that she'll be at the wedding. It's not exactly close, way over the other side of Warrington. Apart from the hospital, she hasn't been outside the house in months.'

Lulu's pretty blue eyes filled with tears. 'She was always bursting with life, me mum. She was the only person who encouraged me to marry Gareth. Everyone else thought marrying an artist was daft. And she thought going to New York was a great idea.'

'She saw you doing the things she'd wanted to do herself,' Alice said sadly. 'Anyroad, luv, come on. I was intending to spend the evening at Pearl Street meself. You'll find the house bursting at the seams.'

It was raining steadily on the Saturday of the wedding. The sky was a miserable grey, heavy with clouds, and there wasn't the faintest sign of blue.

Lulu emerged from her room in an even more magnificent frock than the one she'd arrived in: tangerine silk with an embroidered bodice and long, loose sleeves. Her hat was merely a circle of velvet trimmed with net.

'You make me feel very drab,' Alice remarked as she glanced in the hall mirror at her plain blue suit and conventional flowered hat.

'You look lovely, Gran. But then I can never remember a time when you didn't.'

The young woman and the much older one kissed lovingly. Alice smiled. 'That's a nice thing to say, but I can't help noticing me hair's as grey as the sky outside.'

'You *still* look lovely. I hope I look as beautiful when I've got grey hair.'

'Flattery will get you everywhere, Lulu. I'll be changing me will in your favour as soon as I get back.

We'd better be off. The coach is due in Marsh Lane at half past ten and I've promised to show meself in the hairdresser's before we leave.'

A coach had been hired for the bridegroom's guests. The men were pleased. They wouldn't need their cars so could drink as much as they liked.

Alice parked outside the Lavins', where the door was wide open, despite the rain. She waved at Fion and Jerry who were just about to go inside – Fion looked big enough to be carrying half a dozen babies.

'Tell your mam I've nipped round Opal Street. I'll be back in a minute,' she said to Lulu. 'Pass us that umbrella out the glove compartment, there's a luv.'

'My, don't you look a sight for sore eyes,' Patsy O'Leary gushed when Alice entered the salon. Patsy was silver-haired now. Her daughter, Daisy, with the long, gleaming ringlets, had never gone near the stage when she grew up. Nowadays Patsy boasted endlessly about her grandchildren, all of whom were exceptionally talented in their various ways, or so she claimed. She had never ceased to get on Alice's nerves, but she had grown fond of the woman who had worked for her for more than a quarter of a century.

She nodded at her other staff and promised to bring them a piece of wedding cake on Monday. They were mostly new. How many staff had she had over the years? How many customers? How many heads of hair had been permed, shampooed and set, trimmed, dyed a different colour?

'Oh, someone rang about the upstairs flat,' Patsy said. 'A man. I don't know where he heard about it. I told him it wasn't available yet. It had to be decorated.'

'I must get someone in to do it,' Alice murmured. 'I've been meaning to for ages.' Since the last tenant left in July.

'Well, you've had other things on your mind, haven't you?'

'Actually, in here could do with a coat of paint at the same time.' She glanced at the walls, where the paint was peeling off in places. 'I hadn't noticed before. I'm usually too busy working.' It worried her that she was letting the place fall to pieces around her ears, the way Myrtle Rimmer had done, and another, younger woman would end up taking it over, bringing it back to scratch. She suddenly laughed.

'What's so funny?' asked one of the customers.

'Nothing. I was just having a flight of fancy, rather a morbid one.'

'This is no time to be morbid,' Patsy admonished. 'Your only son's getting married today.'

'So he is. I'd better be going.'

Orla was wearing the cream dress Lulu had brought from America. The thin material lay over the bulge in her stomach and Alice felt concern for the tiny child curled up inside the tissue flesh, the fragile bones.

For once, Orla looked very down. Apart from Micky, Alice was the only other person there. Everyone else must be waiting in the coach. 'I wish I was coming, Mam.'

'So do I, Orla, luv.'

'We're going to have a fine ould time,' Micky said heartily, though Alice sensed a strain of desperation in his voice. 'On our own for a change, nice and quiet. There's a match on the telly this avvy.'

'Did you see the children, Mam? *Our* children. Didn't our Lulu look a treat in that frock? It's funny to think I'll be a grandma soon. And Maisie's wearing a mini-dress – I hope Vicky's family aren't too disgusted. It hardly covers her behind.' Orla's mouth twisted and Alice realised she was trying to laugh. 'It's just the sort of frock

467

I'd have worn meself at her age. And the lads, they had new suits – I bet you can guess where they came from. They looked dead handsome. Oh, I'm so proud of me kids, Mam.'

'And I'm proud of mine, particularly this one.' She stroked her daughter's face. 'You know Cormac and Vicky are coming to say goodbye before they leave for their honeymoon, don't you? Vicky's keeping her wedding dress on so you can see her in all her glory – are you listening, luv?'

Orla's eyes seemed to be floating backwards into her head. Alice touched her arm, frightened, and the eyes flickered and fixed on her mother's face. 'Yes, Vicky's coming. Have a nice time, Mam. I'll see you later.'

'She's been doing that all morning,' Micky said worriedly as he showed Alice out. 'Drifting away, as it were, not hearing.'

Alice hesitated by the door. 'Perhaps it would be best if I stayed.'

'Cormac will only cancel the wedding if you don't turn up. Go and have a nice time, like Orla said.'

She managed to stay dry-eyed throughout the entire ceremony, mainly because Mrs Weatherspoon, who looked so fierce and capable when she marched into church, made a desperate show of herself, sobbing helplessly, getting louder and louder, until the noise resembled a banshee's wail. The guests on the bride-groom's side began to smile, the children giggled and the noise woke up six-month-old Christopher, who started to howl. Cormac could hardly keep a straight face and the bride's shoulders heaved.

Alice was glad that what she had expected to be a touching occasion had turned into something resembling a pantomime or farce. She wasn't exactly in the mood for tears, particularly her own.

The light mood continued throughout the afternoon at the reception, held in a modern, rather featureless hotel. Even a shamefaced Mrs Weatherspoon was able to see the funny side of things. 'I don't know what came over me,' she said to Alice. 'I really hadn't expected to cry.'

'I expected to cry buckets, but I think it's the first wedding I've been to when I haven't shed a tear.'

The best man, Maurice Lacey, made a far better speech than anyone thought him capable of.

Cora watched him, feeling unexpectedly proud. Maurice would never be a success like Cormac, but he'd become a solid citizen, with a lovely family, a nice house in Browning Street and a reasonably well-paid job with prospects of promotion. Pol had obviously decided a long while ago that he was a better bet than Cormac, and Pol was prettier than that Vicky by a mile. Vicky had a face like the back of a bus. It was said that all brides managed to look beautiful on their wedding day, but Vicky proved an exception to the rule. Cora wouldn't have fancied having her for a daughter-in-law.

Alice was pleased to see Orla's children enjoying themselves. It would do them good to have a break, forget the tragedy they had been witnessing for so many months.

At five o'clock, Cormac came over. 'Vicky and I are leaving in a minute, Mam. We're going to Orla's first. Vicky will get changed upstairs, then we'll be off to the airport and Majorca.'

'I'll come with you, if you don't mind,' Alice said with alacrity – she was pleased that Cormac had begun to address her as 'Mam' again lately. She could never understand why he'd stopped.

'Why don't you stay and enjoy the reception? It's going on till all hours and everyone's having a whale of a time.'

'I think Micky might like some company back in Pearl Street. Orla didn't seem quite herself this morning. I'll just say goodbye to Mr and Mrs Weatherspoon.'

On the way to Bootle, Vicky sat in the back of the car, where her massive brocade crinoline dress with long puffed sleeves could be more easily accommodated. Personally, Alice thought she would have suited something much plainer so she didn't look too much like the cake but, naturally, no one had asked for her opinion.

It was still raining steadily when the car drew up in Pearl Street – it hadn't stopped all day. Alice jumped out and knocked on the door of number eleven and was surprised when no one answered. She was about to go round the back when Sheila Reilly came out of her house across the street.

'Alice. I've been keeping a lookout for you. I'm sorry, luv, but your Orla went into a coma early this avvy. Micky rang for an ambulance and she was taken to the maternity hospital. He said to tell you the minute you came back.'

'Ta, Sheila. I'll go straight away.' Alice was already on her way to her own car, which she had left parked outside the house that morning.

'Would you like a cup of tea first?' Sheila called. 'Steady your nerves, like.'

'No, thank you.'

Cormac was standing on the pavement. 'What's up, Mam?'

In a trembling voice she explained the situation. 'You go off on your honeymoon, luv. Vicky will just have to get changed in the Ladies at the airport.'

'I'll do no such thing,' Vicky said. She had rolled

down the car window and was listening. 'Cormac, drive Alice to the hospital. It doesn't matter about us.'

'Get in, Mam,' Cormac said in a voice that brooked no argument and Alice did as she was told.

Micky was walking up and down the hospital corridor like a wild man. He looked as if he had, quite literally, been trying to tear out his hair. His eyes were mad with grief and Alice wondered if he'd lost his reason.

Mr and Mrs Lavin were there, Mrs Lavin sobbing uncontrollably. Alice immediately assumed the worst. Her body seemed to seize up, she could hardly speak.

'What's happened?' she croaked.

'Orla's having a Caesarean at this very minute,' Micky said raggedly. 'They don't hold out much hope for the baby. As for Orla, they think this is the end.'

'Aah!' The cry came from her very soul. Orla had invested every shred of herself into this baby. If it died, it would all have been in vain.

Cormac had been searching for somewhere to park. He came rushing up with Vicky, still in her bridal gown. Mr Lavin explained the situation and went to fetch everyone cups of tea.

They had to wait over an hour for news, though it felt more like twenty. No one spoke. It was almost seven o'clock before a nurse appeared. Alice searched her face, trying to discern from her expression if the news was good or bad. She didn't look particularly grave.

'The baby has arrived safely,' she announced and there was a concerted sigh of relief. 'It's a girl and she appears to be in surprisingly good shape, though she's only tiny, barely three pounds. She's gone straight into an incubator. Her dad can see her later on, but no one else, I'm afraid. As far as the mother is concerned, I'm sorry to say there's no change.'

Micky made no sound. He hid his face in his hands for several seconds. When he removed them his face was pale, but he was himself again. His eyes were normal. 'Orla will be pleased about the baby,' he said. For the first time he seemed to notice Cormac and Vicky. 'Isn't it time you two were on your way?'

'We'd sooner stay.' Vicky's dress rustled as she went over and embraced him and Alice thought she'd make a fine Lacey. She was pleased and proud the girl was now a member of the family.

'And I'd sooner you went,' Micky growled. 'If Orla was asked for her opinion, she'd say the same.'

'I think so too,' Alice put in. 'There's enough of us here.'

'Would you like me to ring the reception, tell the children?' Cormac asked.

'No, leave the kids be.' Micky shook his head. 'Let them enjoy themselves as long as possible. They'll know soon enough. Tara, Cormac. Tara, Vicky. Good luck.'

The newly married couple left, albeit reluctantly. Cormac said he'd telephone as soon as they reached Majorca.

Mr Lavin left to fetch more tea. A young woman walked past in a dressing gown, heavily pregnant. 'I'm just going for a walk,' she said, 'to try and bring it on. It stopped coming the minute we got here.'

Another nurse arrived and said Micky could see his new daughter. He came back after only a few minutes. 'She's so tiny,' he said gruffly, holding out his hands about twelve inches apart. 'Pretty, like a doll, with lots of fair hair.'

Mrs Lavin began to cry again. Voices and footsteps could be heard approaching and Orla's children came hurrying round the corner, their faces anxious, their eyes bright with fear.

'How's Mum?'

'Can we see her?'

'Has she had the baby?'

'Are you all right, Dad? You should have told us.'

They crowded round their father. Micky hugged them one by one and tried to answer their questions. It seemed to Alice that he'd aged since morning, when she could have sworn he didn't have a stoop. His features were blurred. He looked middle-aged. For some reason she remembered the desperate young man who'd called at the house in Amber Street all those years ago asking for Orla who was hiding upstairs and Alice was obliged to tell him lies, send him packing, though she'd tried to do it kindly.

She left the group, feeling in the way. No one had taken a blind bit of notice of her, which she found quite understandable. No doubt Fion and Maeve would arrive shortly – they'd probably taken the children home first. She found a padded bench in a quiet corridor by the closed X-ray department where she sat, feeling extremely alone, wondering how John would have felt if he were there, knowing his favourite daughter was dying. Well, once she'd been his favourite. Perhaps another daughter had taken her place, just as another woman had taken hers.

'Alice! We've been looking for you everywhere.'

It was Billy Lacey accompanied by Cora. He sat beside her and put his arm round her shoulders. 'Are you all right, luv? You look dead lonely all by yourself.'

'I'm fine.' Alice sniffed. 'Just felt like a bit of peace and quiet.'

'I don't blame you. That Mrs Lavin doesn't half go on.'

Cora sat opposite. She saw Alice grit her teeth, as if determined not to cry, unlike that other woman, Micky's mam, who was making a terrible scene, not helping things a bit. It struck her that Alice had never made a scene, not even when John had left. She'd just gritted her teeth, like she'd done now, and got on with things. When you thought about it, John Lacey hadn't been much of a catch, not compared with Billy who'd stuck by his wife through thick and thin. It had taken a long time for the penny to drop, but Cora realised she'd married the right brother after all. As for Cormac, Alice was welcome to him and his ugly missus. She'd prefer Maurice and Pol any day.

Thinking about it, Cora couldn't remember anything that Alice had done to spite her. In fact, she'd only tried to help. It was Alice who'd collected her from the police station that time, then given her a job even after she'd heard about the pensions Cora had been fraudulently collecting all them years.

There was a funny sensation in her stomach as she leaned over and patted Alice on the knee. 'Everything's going to be all right, luv,' she said consolingly, even though she knew, and Alice and Billy knew, that it wasn't.

Then Billy stood up and slapped his thigh. 'Come on, ould girl. We'd better start making tracks. It's still raining cats and dogs outside and I don't know if there's any buses running at this time of night.'

Cora stood up and linked his arm, and they went home together to Bootle.

During the long night that followed the relatives were allowed to see the patient once, a few at a time. Alice went in with Fion and Maeve.

Orla was lying peacefully still, long, dark lashes resting on her white cheeks, lips curved in a slight smile. Fion gasped. 'I've never seen her look so beautiful!'

474

'She looks about sixteen,' Maeve whispered.

Alice said nothing. She bent and kissed the cold, smiling lips, and wondered if she would ever kiss them again.

In a hotel room in Majorca, which smelt of strangely scented blossoms and chloride from the pool below, and where the blue, luminous water of the Mediterranean could be seen from the balcony, Cormac put down the phone. 'No change.' He sighed. 'There are times when I wish I smoked. I have a feeling a cigarette would be a great help at the moment.'

'It would also be very bad for you,' Vicky said primly.

'I've heard there are people around who say the same thing about sex.'

'Oh!' Vicky looked nonplussed. She was sitting up in bed with nothing on, a sheet chastely covering her breasts – she'd only been a married woman for a matter of hours and nudity took some getting used to. 'Oh, they can't possibly be right about sex.'

Cormac grinned. 'If those people are so very wrong – about sex, that is – then I assume it would be OK if we did it again.'

She blushed. 'It would be OK as far as I'm concerned.'

'As we are the only two people whose opinion matters, I suggest we do it immediately, though it will be necessary for you to remove that sheet.'

Vicky removed the sheet.

The hospital was very quiet. Occasionally a baby cried, there were footsteps in other corridors far away. Outside the room where Orla lay, her husband, her children, her sisters and her mother hardly spoke, and when they did it was in subdued murmurs. Mr and Mrs Lavin had gone home long ago.

Fion felt ashamed of how much she longed to be at home, under her own roof, with Jerry's warm body in bed beside her and the kids safely asleep not far away. They weren't the sort of couple who lived in each other's pockets, but she badly missed her husband right now. She squeezed the hand of Maeve, sitting beside her.

Maeve must have been having the same thoughts. 'You really appreciate your own family in situations like this,' she whispered. 'I shall never feel irritated again if Martin changes Christopher's nappy wrongly or complains about the car.' He still did occasionally.

'We're ever so lucky, sis.' Fion sighed. 'We've got everything.'

'I know, but it's a pity it takes a tragedy to make us realise it.'

Sunday afternoon, and Micky and Alice were persuaded to go home and rest. Jerry drove them. It was still raining heavily and the clouds were even greyer than they'd been the day before. Jerry stopped at the end of Pearl Street, where Micky got out, and Alice said quickly, 'I think I'll go and see Bernadette before she leaves for the hospital. She sent a message to say she was going this avvy.'

'Are you sure? I'll take you home if you prefer. It's no trouble.'

'It's kind of you, Jerry, luv. But I prefer Bootle to Birkdale at the moment. Anyroad, me own car's around here somewhere.' She couldn't possibly go back to her smart bungalow at a time like this, even though she would have liked to get rid of her hat, collect a mac and change her suit for something more comfortable. She got out of the car, kissed Micky and almost ran, not to Bernadette's, but to the dark, silent salon in Opal Street, where she let herself in and sat under the middle dryer – something she hadn't done in years.

She hadn't realised she was quite so tired. Almost immediately, she fell awkwardly asleep, a sleep full of horrible dreams, which she couldn't remember when she woke up, but she knew her mind had been preoccupied with things unpleasant.

Jaysus! Would the rain never stop! She could see nothing, not even her watch, because by now it was completely dark, but the downpour sounded even heavier, as if the rain was bouncing off the pavements.

It would have been better to have gone to Bernadette's, where she could have slept in a proper bed, had something decent to eat, not be stuck here with nothing but her own miserable thoughts to keep her company.

Mind you, what other thoughts could you expect to have at a time like this? Alice found herself dredging up every single memory she could of Orla. Orla being born, walking for the first time, saying her first word, her first day at school – she'd come home and informed her mother she was the prettiest in the class, as well as the cleverest.

'Arrogant little madam.' Danny chuckled when he was told – she'd been her grandad's favourite, as well as John's. Alice had never had a favourite. She loved all her children the same and would have felt just as devastated had any one of them been in hospital in a coma.

'Oh, I feel so *sad*!' The sadness rolled up into a ball at the back of her throat. In a minute she'd make a cup of tea – except there'd be no milk. At weekends Patsy usually took home what was over in case it went sour.

Perhaps it wouldn't be a bad idea to turn the light on, go round to Bernie's who might be home again by now. She was only making it worse, sitting by herself in the pitch dark, longing for a drink. She was about to heave herself out of the chair when the key turned in the lock and someone came in. She held her breath. It was a man, she could just make out his bulky form against the window.

He reached for the light, turned it on and uttered a startled cry when he saw her. 'Alice! I am feeling a definite sense of déjà vu.'

'Who are you?' For some reason, she didn't feel the least bit frightened.

'Have I changed so much?' the man said dejectedly.

She stared at him. He wore a well-cut tweed suit and looked about fifty. Once he had been handsome, still was in a way, but his face was deeply lined, his expression careworn. Iron-grey hair, slightly receding and wet from the rain, was combed back from his forehead in little waves. He was smiling and it was a nice smile that involved his entire face, including his very blue eyes, which were dancing merrily in her direction. Despite everything that was happening in her life, despite the fact that she didn't recognise the man from Adam and he had just walked uninvited into her salon, that somehow he had a key, Alice smiled back.

'I remember doing precisely the same thing,' the man said. 'Coming in, finding you in the dark – oh, it must be twenty years ago. You gave me a fright then. Mind you, this time I deserve it.'

'Neil!' She stared at him in disbelief. Suddenly he looked achingly familiar and she couldn't understand why she hadn't known him straight away.

'Whew! Recognition at last. How are you, my dear Alice? If you knew how many times I have longed for this moment you would be deeply flattered.' He came and sat beside her.

'How did you get in?' she stammered. 'Well, I know

478

how you got in. I mean, how did you get the key? No one's supposed to have it.'

He dangled the key in front of her eyes. It was attached to a St Christopher medal keyring that she remembered well. 'This is my original key. I forgot to give it back and have kept it all these years. I was hoping it would fit, that you hadn't had the lock changed, because I wanted to see the flat. I intended sneaking in and out so no one would know I'd been, but you seem to make a habit of sitting under a dryer in the dark.'

'What if there'd been someone living upstairs?'

'I knew there wasn't,' he said surprisingly. 'I heard from a friend in Bootle that the flat was vacant, but when I phoned I was told it was badly in need of decoration. I wanted to see exactly how bad it was in case I could manage it myself.'

'Patsy said someone had phoned.' Alice frowned. 'Have you taken up painting and decorating?'

'Only of the upstairs flat.' His smile faded. 'Things haven't gone exactly well for me over the last few years, Alice. In fact, nothing's gone well since I left Liverpool all those years ago. I suddenly decided I'd like a little bolt-hole to hide in when I felt particularly low. And what better place than the one where I spent the happiest years of my life.'

They'd been happy years for her too. Looking back, the time they'd spent together seemed unreal. The flat had also been her bolt-hole, a place where she'd felt able to leave all her troubles outside and relax in Neil's arms. It felt like a million years ago.

'Would you mind having me as your upstairs tenant a second time?' he was saying. 'It would only be for occasional weekends.'

'I don't think I would mind that at all, Neil,' she said, and wondered if she was still dreaming and, if so, how much of the past had been a dream and how much had actually happened. At what point in her life would she wake up?

He smiled at her delightedly. 'Well, now that's settled, enough about me. What about you, Alice. How are Cormac and the girls and your multitude of grandchildren? How many do you have now?'

'Seven,' she said automatically. 'No, eight.' She'd forgotten about the tiny girl who'd been born the night before. Her eyes filled with tears when she thought about Orla, whom, incredibly, she'd almost forgotten since Neil had arrived. Just as she had done the other time he found her in the dark, Alice started to cry. She told him about Orla, the baby in the incubator, the wedding yesterday. Time fell away, the years merged to nothing, as he held her hand, patted her cheek and agreed that it was all quite unbearably sad, but that one day, a long time off, it would be bearable again, incredible though that might seem right now.

'God works in mysterious ways that I don't pretend to understand,' he said.

'Me neither.' She sighed. 'What time is it?'

'Just gone nine.'

She must have been asleep for hours. Her neck ached from having been in an uncomfortable position and she had pins and needles in her legs. 'I'd better be getting back to the hospital.'

'Can I come with you?'

'Oh, yes, please'. She didn't care if it sounded too eager, she just wanted him there. She didn't care about anything much at the moment. It didn't matter that she was fifty-seven and he was ten years younger. It didn't matter if they got back together again though she had a feeling it was what he wanted. Nor did it matter if they didn't. It would be nice to have him in the upstairs flat again, but if it all fell through, that didn't matter either.

Nothing mattered except the moment, now, when she was about to return to the hospital to see her child who would shortly die.

She got tiredly to her feet and went over to the window. The street lights were reflected, wobbling slightly, in the wet pavements. 'It's stopped raining,' she remarked. 'The stars are out.' She noticed that Neil's bones creaked as he came to stand beside her. Together, they watched the stars.

Then one star, more vivid than the others, left its mates and shot across the sky. Alice turned off the light so she could observe more clearly the bright, twinkling point passing over the earth, soaring silently towards who knew where. She pointed. 'See that one! It must be a shooting star.'

'I can't see anything.' Neil shook his head.

Alice knew then that Orla was dead and, for the Laceys, nothing would ever be the same again. The star had been her daughter's final flamboyant gesture to the world.

She held her breath. One day, very soon, she would go abroad, to a place that Orla would have enjoyed. She would go by herself, but she wouldn't feel lonely, because Orla would be with her in her heart. She'd like that.

'I hope Micky was with her when she passed away,' she murmured softly. 'Or at least I hope he saw the star.'

For Yvette Goulden

I am grateful to the authors of the following books which were of great assistance when writing *Dancing in the Dark*. *The Admiralty Regrets* by C. E. T. Warren and James Benson, published by White Lion Publishers, provided a thorough and detailed description of the *Thetis* tragedy. David M. Whale's fascinating series, *Lost Villages of Liverpool*, published by T. Stephenson & Sons, told me all I needed to know about old Toxteth.

Prologue

It always began with the sound of the footsteps, the soft, slithering footsteps on the stairs, the unshod feet in their well-darned socks lifting steadily from one step to the next. He wasn't the sort of man to wear slippers. Listening, I would picture him in my mind's eye, just his feet, coming up the narrow beige carpet with the red border, the cheapest you could buy, worn away to threads in the middle and secured to the stairs with triangular-shaped varnished rods that slid into bronze brackets at the side. I saw everything very, very clearly, in precise detail.

Even on the nights when there were no footsteps, I never went asleep before Mam came home from work at ten o'clock. Then I would feel relatively safe, but not completely. Mam had never been able to offer much protection. But even he must have realised that a child's screams at dead of night might have alerted someone; a neighbour, a passer-by.

I still dream about it frequently, always the footsteps, never the violence, the terror that was to come. Because in my dreams I am not there when he enters the room. My bed is empty. Yet I can see him, as though an invisible me is present, the tall figure of my father, an expression on his dark, handsome face and in his dark eyes that I could never quite fathom. Was it excitement? Anticipation? Behind the glitter of the main emotion, whatever it might have been, I sensed something else, mysterious, sad, as if deep within him he regretted what he was about to do. But he couldn't help it. The excitement, the anticipation, gripped him like a drug, stifling any other, kinder, feelings he might have had.

In my dream I would watch him slowly undo his belt

I

buckle, hear its tiny click, the feathery smooth sound the leather made as he pulled it through the loops of his trousers until it dangled from his hand like a snake.

Then he would reach down to drag me out of bed, but this was a dream *and I wasn't there!*

Oh, the look on his face then! I savoured it. I felt triumphant.

At this point, I usually woke up bathed in perspiration, my heart beating fiercely, still triumphant, but at the same time slightly sick.

I'd escaped!

Sometimes, though, the dream continued, just as life had continued in the days when the dream wasn't a dream but real.

I knew that when he came back from the pub, always drunk, he would scratch around downstairs, poking here and there, in the dirty washing, through the toys, searching for something that would give him an excuse to let rip with a thrashing. He liked to have an excuse. He'd find the mark of a felt-tipped pen on a tablecloth that Mam hadn't had time to wash, paint dropped on a frock at school, the arm off a doll, or toys not put away properly. Anything could trigger the sound of those slithering footsteps on the stairs.

There were other nights, the best ones, when he would fall asleep in the chair — according to Mam, he worked hard — or he might watch television. Looking back, my memory softened slightly by time, this probably happened more often than I used to think.

In the extended dream I still wasn't there, but now my little sister was in the other bed, and it was she who bore the brunt of our father's anger, or frustration, or excitement, or self-loathing, or whatever it was that made him want to beat the life out of his wife and children, so that his dark shadow lay heavily over our house, even when he wasn't there.

There would be no feeling of triumph when I woke up, just desolation and despair. Would the dreams never end? Would I ever forget? For the rest of my life, would I, Millie Cameron, never stop wishing that I was invisible?

Millie

I

The sun spilled under the curtains, seeping on to the polished window-sill like thick cream. The wine bottle that Trudy had painted and given me for Christmas dazzled, a brilliant flame of light.

Sunday!

I sat up and stretched my arms. I was free to do whatsoever I pleased. In the bed beside me, James grunted and turned over. I slid carefully from under the bedclothes so as not to disturb him, put on a towelling robe and went into the living room, closing the door quietly behind me.

With a sigh of satisfaction at the thought that it was all mine and mine alone, I surveyed the room, its dark pink walls and off-white upholstered sofa, old pine furniture and glass-shaded lamps. Then, I switched on the computer and the television and reversed the answering-machine. In the kitchen, I paused momentarily to admire the effect of the sun on the Aztec-patterned tiles before filling the kettle. Back in the living room, I opened the door to the balcony and stepped outside.

What a glorious day, unseasonably hot for late September. The roses bordering the communal garden were overblown red and yellow cabbages, the dew-drenched grass glistened like wet silk. In the furthest corner, the biggest tree had already begun to shed its tiny, almost white leaves, which scattered the lawn like snow.

I loved my flat, but the thing I loved most was the balcony. It was tiny, just big enough for two black wrought-iron chairs and a large plant-pot in between. I knew nothing about gardening and had been thrilled when the squiggly green things I'd been given last spring had turned out to be geraniums. I enjoyed sitting outside early in the morning with a cup of tea, savouring the salty Liverpool air; the river Mersey was less than a mile away. Occasionally, just before bed on warm evenings, I would sit with the light from the living room falling on to the darkness of the garden, reliving the day.

Most of the curtains in the three-storey block of flats that ran at right angles to my own were still drawn. I glanced at my watch – just gone seven. From the corner of my eye, I became aware of activity in a kitchen on the ground floor. The old lady who lived there was opening a window. I kept my head turned away. If she saw me looking she would wave, I would feel obliged to wave back, and one day I might find myself invited in for coffee, which I would hate. I was glad I'd managed to get a top-floor corner flat. It meant I was cut off from the other residents.

The kettle clicked and I went to make the tea. There was a political programme on television, so I switched it off and turned up the sound on the answering-machine. I nearly turned it down again when I heard my mother's voice. A shadow fell over the day when I remembered it was the last Sunday of the month; my family would be expecting me for lunch.

'. . . this is the third time I've called, Millicent,' my mother was saying shrilly. 'Don't you ever listen to that machine of yours? Ring back straight away, there's bad news. And I don't see why I should always have to remind you about dinner . . .'

I groaned. I could tell from the tone of my mother's voice that the news wasn't seriously bad. Possibly Scotty had been on one of his regular sexual rampages and other dog owners had complained, or Declan, my brother, had lost his twentieth job.

Just as I was about to take my tea on to the balcony, the bedroom door opened and James came out. He wore a pair of dark blue boxer shorts and his straw blond hair was tousled. He grinned. 'Hi!'

'Hi, yourself.' I eyed his tanned body enviously and wished I could turn such a lovely golden brown in the sun.

'Been up long?'

'Fifteen, twenty minutes. It's a lovely day.'

'The best.' He enveloped me in his muscular arms and nuzzled my neck. 'Know what today is?'

'Sunday?'

'True, but it's also our anniversary. It's a year today since we met.' He kissed me softly on the lips. 'I went into a wine bar in Castle Street and there was this gorgeous leggy ash-blonde with the most amazing green eyes – who was that guy you were with? I knew him slightly – that's how I managed to get introduced.'

'I forget.' I felt uneasy. Remembering anniversaries seemed a sign of . . . well, that the relationship *meant* something, when we had always maintained stoutly that it didn't.

'Rodney!' he said triumphantly. 'Rod. I met him at a Young Conservatives' do.'

I moved out of his arms and went to the computer. 'I didn't think you were interested in politics.'

'I'm not, but Pa maintains it's good for business. He makes lots of useful contacts in the Party. Is there more tea?'

'The pot's full. Don't forget to put the cosy back on.'

He saluted. 'No, ma'am.'

When he came back, I was seated at my desk. He stood behind me, his arm resting lightly on my shoulder. 'This your report?'

'Uh-huh.' I pressed the mouse and the words rolled down the screen. I read them quickly. Despite night school and the subsequent A level in English, I worried that my terrible education might be obvious when I wrote at length. I hoped I hadn't split any infinitives or put an apostrophe in the wrong place.

7

'You've spelt "feasible" wrong,' James said. 'It's "-ible" not "-able".'

'I did that bit when I was tired. I probably wasn't thinking straight.' He'd gone to one of the best public schools in the country, followed by a good university.

'Shall we go somewhere special for lunch to celebrate? How about that new place in Formby?'

'Sorry, duty calls. Today I'm lunching with my parents.' I wished I had a more pleasant excuse.

'Of course, the last Sunday . . .' To my irritation, he knelt down and twisted the chair round until we were facing each other. 'When am I going to meet your folks?'

'What point is there in you meeting them?' I said coldly.

'You've met mine.'

'You invited me, I didn't ask.' I disliked going to see his family in the converted, centuries-old farmhouse in its own grounds three miles from Southport. I felt out of place, uncomfortably aware of the stark contrast between it and my own family's home on a council estate in Kirkby. His mother, with her expensive clothes and beautifully coiffured hair, was always patronising. His father was polite, but in the main ignored me. A businessman to the core, he spent most of the time on the phone or ensconced in his study plying fellow businessmen with drink. Phillip Atherton owned three garages on Merseyside, which sold high-class sports cars to 'fools who've got more money than sense', according to my own father. Atherton's rarely dealt in cars worth less than twenty thousand pounds. James was nominally in charge of the Southport garage, but his father kept a close eye on all three.

The phone went. James was still kneeling, his arms around my waist. After three rings, the answering-machine came on, with the sound still turned up. My mother again. 'Millicent. You've not been out all night, surely. Why don't you call back?'

8

James's eyes sparkled. 'Millicent! I thought it was Mildred.'

'I would have hated being Mildred even more.' I got up quickly to pick up the receiver. I didn't want him hearing any more of the whining voice with its strong, adenoidal Liverpool accent, one of the reasons I'd told my mother never to call me at the office. 'Hello, Mum.'

'There you are!' She sounded relieved. 'Can we expect to see you today?'

'Of course.'

'Sometimes I worry you'll forget.'

I rolled my eyes. 'As if!'

'Don't be sarcastic, Millicent. After all, it's only once a month you visit. You'd never think you only lived a few miles away in Blundellsands. Mrs Mole's Sybil comes every week from Manchester to see her mam.'

'Perhaps Mrs Mole's Sybil's got nothing else to do.'

'You might like to know she's got two kids and a husband.' There was a pause. 'You've become awfully hard, luv.'

'Don't be silly, Mum.' With an effort, I made my voice softer. Mum set great store by the regular family gatherings now that only Declan was left at home. 'What's the bad news?' I enquired.

'Eh? Oh, I nearly forgot. Your auntie Flo's dead. The poor old soul was knocked down by a car or something. But the thing is, luv,' her voice throbbed with indignation, 'she was already six feet under by the time some woman rang to let your gran know.'

'Why should Gran care? She had nothing to do with Flo.' Auntie Flo had, in fact, been a great-aunt, and the black sheep of the family, I had no idea why. Gran never mentioned her name. It was only when Auntie Sally had died ten years ago that I first set eyes on Flo, at the funeral. She was the youngest of the three Clancy sisters, then in her sixties, had never married, and seemed to me an exceptionally mild old woman.

'Blood's thicker than water,' my mother said mean-inglessly.

'What did Auntie Flo do that was so awful?' I asked curiously.

'I think there was a row, but I've no idea what it was about. Your gran would never talk about it.'

I was about to ring off, when Mum said, 'Have you been to Mass?'

To save an argument, I told her I was going to the eleven o'clock. I had no intention of going to Mass.

I replaced the receiver and looked at James. There was a strange, intense expression in his light blue eyes, and I realised he'd been watching me like that throughout the entire conversation with my mother. 'You're very beautiful,' he said.

'You're not so bad yourself.' I tried to sound jokey. Something about his expression disturbed me.

'You know, marriage isn't such a bad thing.'

Alarm bells sounded in my head. Was this a round-about way of proposing? 'That's not what you've said before.'

'I've changed my mind.'

'Well, I haven't.' He came towards me, but I avoided him by going on to the balcony. 'I've tried it before, remember?'

James was standing just inside the window. 'You didn't keep his name. Were things really so awful?'

'I didn't want his name once we were no longer a couple. And it wasn't awful with Gary, just deadly dull.'

'It wouldn't be dull with me.'

So it *was* a proposal. I stuffed my hands in my dressing-gown pockets to hide my agitation and sat down. Why did he have to spoil things? We'd made it plain to each other from the start that there was to be no commitment. I liked him – no, more than that, I was very fond of him. He was good to be with, extraordinarily handsome in a rugged open-air way. We got on famously, always had loads to talk about, and were great together in bed. But I

10

didn't want to spend the rest of my life with him or with anybody else. I'd struggled hard to get where I was and wanted to get further, without having a husband questioning my every decision, interfering.

I remembered Gary's astonishment when I said I wanted to take an A level. We'd been married two years. 'What on earth d'you want that for?' I recalled his round pleasant face, his round moist eyes. We'd first gone out together at school and had married at eighteen. I'd realised, far too late, that he'd been my escape route from home.

Why did I want an A level? Perhaps to prove to myself that I wasn't as stupid as my teachers had claimed, for self-respect, to gain the enjoyment from books that I'd only briefly experienced before my father had put a brutal stop to it.

'I'd like to get a better job,' is what I said to Gary. I was bored rigid working at Peterssen's packing chocolates. 'I'd like to learn to type as well, use a computer.'

Gary had laughed. 'What good will all that stuff be when we have kids?'

We were living in Kirkby with his widowed mother, not far from my parents. Although we'd put our name down for a council house, one would not be forthcoming until we had a family – not just one child but two or three. I visualised the future, trailing to the shops with a baby, more kids hanging on to the pram, getting a part-time job in another factory because Gary's wages as a storeman would never be enough to live on. It was why we'd never even considered buying a place of our own.

Two years later we were divorced. A bewildered Gary wanted to know what he'd done wrong. 'Nothing,' I told him. I regretted hurting him, but he was devoid of ambition, content to spend the rest of his life in a dead-end job wondering where the next penny would come from.

My father was disgusted, my mother horrified: a Catholic, getting divorced! Even so, Mum did her utmost to persuade me to come back home. My younger sister, Trudy, had found her own escape route via Colin Daley and had also married at eighteen, though Colin had been a better bet than Gary. After ten years they were still happily together.

Wild horses couldn't have dragged me back to Kirkby and my family. Instead, I rented a bedsit. I had my English A level by then, and until I bought my flat, nothing in life had given me more pleasure than the certificate to say I'd achieved a grade C. Armed with a dictionary, I'd *made* myself read the books I'd been set, struggled for hours to understand them in the bedroom at my mother-in-law's, while downstairs Gary watched football and game-shows on television. It seemed no time before the words started to make sense, as if I'd always known them, as if they'd been stored in my head waiting to be used. I shall never forget the day I finished reading *Pride and Prejudice*. I'd understood it. I'd enjoyed it. It was like discovering you could sing or play the piano.

Once settled in the bedsit, I took courses in typing and computing at night school, left Peterssen's, and began to wonder if it had all been worth it as I drifted from one dead-end office job to another – until three years ago, when I became a receptionist/typist with Stock Masterton, an estate agent's in the city centre. Of course, I had to tell George Masterton I'd worked in a factory until I was twenty-four, but he had been impressed. 'Ah, a self-made woman. I like that.'

George and I hit it off immediately. I was promoted to 'property negotiator'. Me! Now George was contemplating opening a branch in Woolton, a relatively middle-class area of Liverpool, and I was determined to be appointed manager, which was why I was writing the report. I'd driven round Woolton, taking in the number of superior properties, the roads of substantial semi-detacheds, the terraced period cottages that could be hyped and sold for a bomb. I'd noted how often the buses ran to town, listed the schools, the supermarkets . . . The report would help George make up his mind and show him how keen I was to have the job.

It was through Stock Masterton that I'd found my flat. The builders had gone bankrupt and the units were being sold for a song, which was unfair on the people already there who'd paid thousands more but the bank wanted its money and wasn't prepared to wait.

'I've not done bad for someone not quite thirty,' I murmured to myself. 'I've got my own place, a job with prospects and a car. I earn twice as much as Gary.'

No, I'd not done badly at all.

Yet I wasn't happy.

I leaned on the iron rail and rested my chin on my arms. Somewhere deep within I felt a deadness, and I wondered if I would ever be happy. There were times when I felt like a skater going across the thinnest of ice. It was bound to crack some time, and I would disappear for ever into the freezing, murky water beneath. I shook myself. It was too lovely a morning for such morbid thoughts.

I'd forgotten about James. He appeared on the balcony tucking a black shirt into his jeans. Even in casual clothes, he always looked crisp, neat, tidy. I turned away when he fastened the buckle of his wide leather belt.

He frowned. 'What's the matter?'

'Nothing. Why?'

'You shuddered. Have you gone off me all of a sudden?'

'Don't be silly!' I laughed.

James sat in the other chair. I swung up my bare feet so they rested between his legs and wriggled my toes.

'Cor!' he gasped.

'Don't look like that. People will realise what I'm doing.'

'Would you like to do it inside where no one can see?'

'In a minute. I want to take a shower.'

He smacked his lips. 'I'll take it with you.'

'You've just got dressed!'

'I can get undressed pretty damn quick.' He looked at me quizzically. 'Does this mean I'm forgiven?'

'For what?' I was being deliberately vague.

'For proposing. I'd forgotten you modern women take an offer of marriage as an insult.' He took my feet in his hands. I was conscious of how large and warm and comforting they felt. 'As an alternative, how about if I moved in with you?'

I tried to pull away my feet, but he held them firmly. 'The flat's only small,' I muttered. 'There's only one bedroom.'

'I wasn't contemplating occupying the other if there were two.'

No! I valued my privacy as much as my independence. I didn't want someone suggesting it was time I went to bed or asking why I was late home – and did I really want the living room painted such a dark pink? I wished I could start the day again and stop him proposing. I had been quite enjoying things as they were.

James put my feet down carefully on the balcony floor. 'Between us we could get somewhere bigger.'

'You've changed the rules,' I said.

He sighed. 'I know, but it's not the rules that have changed, it's me. I think I'm in love with you, Millie Cameron. In fact, I know I am.' He tried to catch my eyes. 'I take it the feeling isn't reciprocated?'

I bit my lip and shook my head. James turned away and I contemplated his perfect profile: straight nose, broad mouth, pale, stubby lashes. His hair lay in a flattering corn-coloured quiff on his broad, tanned forehead. He didn't look as if it was the end of the world that I'd turned him down. According to his mother, who never failed to mention it, there'd been an army of girls before me. How many had he fallen in love with? On reflection, I didn't know him all that well. True, we talked a lot, but never about anything serious; the conversation rarely strayed from films, plays, mutual acquaintances and clothes. Oh, and football. I sensed he was shallow and also rather weak, always anxious still to do his father's bidding, even though he, too, was twenty-nine. I felt irritated again that he'd spoiled things: I didn't want to give him up. Nor did I want to hurt him, but I couldn't be expected to fall in love with him just because he had decided he was in love with me.

'Perhaps we can talk about it some other time?' I ventured. In a year, two years, ten.

He closed his eyes briefly and gave a sigh of relief. 'I was worried you might dump me.'

'I wouldn't dream of it!' I jumped to my feet and ran inside. James followed. Outside the bathroom, I removed my dressing-gown and posed tauntingly before opening the door and going in. I stepped into the shower and turned on the water. It felt freezing . . . but it had warmed up nicely by the time James drew the curtain back and joined me.

2

'Hello, luv. You look pale.'

'Hi, Mum.' I made a kissing noise two inches from my mother's plump, sagging cheek. Whenever I turned up in Kirkby, she claimed I looked pale or tired or on the verge of coming down with something.

'Say hello to your dad. He's in the garden with his tomaters.'

My father – I couldn't even *think* of him as Dad – had always been a keen if unimaginative gardener. Dutifully, I opened the kitchen door and called, 'Hello.'

The greenhouse was just beyond the neat lawn, the door open. 'Hello there, luv.' My father was inside, a cigarette hanging from his bottom lip. His dark, sombre expression brightened at the sound of my voice. He threw away the cigarette, wiped his hands on the hips of his trousers and came inside. 'How's the estate-agency business?'

'Okay.' I managed to keep the loathing out of my voice. He told everyone I was a property negotiator. Nowadays he claimed to be proud of his girls. 'Where's Declan?'

'Gone to the pub.' Mum couldn't have looked more harassed if she had been preparing a meal for royalty. She took a casserole out of the oven, then put it back. 'What have I done with the spuds? Oh, I know, they're in the top oven. Declan's promised to be back by one.'

'Will the grub be ready on time, luv?'

'Yes, Norman. Oh, yes.' Mum jumped at her husband's apparently mild question, though it was years since he'd beaten her. 'It'll be ready the minute our Trudy and Declan come.'

'Good. I'll have another ciggie while I'm waiting.' He disappeared into the lounge.

'Why don't you have a talk with your dad and I'll get on with this?' Mum said, as she stirred something in a pan.

As if I would! She'd always tried to pretend we were a perfectly normal family. 'I'd sooner stay and talk to you.'

She flushed with pleasure. 'What have you been up to lately?'

I shrugged. 'Nothing much. Went to a club last night, the theatre on Wednesday. I'm going out to dinner to-night.'

'With that James chap?'

'Yes,' I said shortly. I regretted telling them about James. It was when Declan had jokingly remarked he was thinking of trading in his bike for a Ferrari that I'd told him about Atherton Cars where several could be had. The following Sunday, my father had driven over to Southport to take a look and I was terrified that one day he'd introduce himself to James.

Mum was poised anxiously over the ancient cooker, which had been there when we moved into the council

16

house in 1969. I was three and Trudy just a baby; Declan
and Alison had yet to arrive. These days, Mum wasn't just
stout but shapelessly stout. Her shabby skirt, with no
waist to fix on, was down at the front and up at the rear,
revealing the backs of her surprisingly well-shaped but
heavily veined legs. I always thought it would have been
better if they had grown fat with the rest of her. As it was,
she looked like some sort of strange insect: a huge, round
body stuck on pins. Her worried, good-natured face was
colourless, her skin the texture of putty. The once beautiful hair, the same ash-blonde as her children's, she cut
herself with no regard for fashion. She wore no makeup,
hadn't for years, as if she was going out of her way to
make herself unattractive, or perhaps she just didn't care
any more. She was fifty-five but looked ten years older.

Yet she'd been so lovely! I recalled the wedding photo
on the mantelpiece in the lounge, the bride tall, willowy
and girlish, the fitted lace dress clinging to her slim,
perfect figure, though her face was wistful, rather sad, as
if she'd been able to see into the future and knew what
fate had in store for her. Her hair was long and straight,
gleaming in the sunshine of her wedding day, turning
under slightly at the ends as mine and Trudy's did. Declan
and Alison had curly hair. None of us had taken after our
father, with his swarthy good looks and bitter chocolate
eyes. Perhaps that's why he'd never liked us much; four
children and not one in his image.

The back door opened and my brother came in. 'Hi,
Sis. Long time no see.' He aimed a pretend punch at my
stomach and I aimed one back. 'That's a nice frock. Dark
colours suit you.' He fingered the material. 'What would
you call that green?'

Declan had always been interested in his sisters'
clothes, which infuriated our father who called him a
cissy, and had done his brutal best to make a man out of
him.

'Olive, I think. It was terribly cheap.'

' "It was terribly cheap!" ' Declan repeated, with an

17

impish grin. 'You don't half talk posh these days, Mill. I'd be ashamed to take you to the pub.'

A shout came from the lounge. 'Is that you, Declan?'

'Yes, Dad.'

'You're only just in time,' the voice said pointedly.

Declan winked at me. He was twenty, a tall, lanky boy with a sensitive face and an infectious smile, always cheerful. He was currently working as a labourer on a demolition site, which seemed an entirely unsuitable job for someone who looked as if a feather would knock him down. I often wondered why he still lived at home and assumed it was for Mum's sake. He shouted, 'Scotty met this smashing bitch. I had a job getting him home. I forgot to take his lead.'

'Where is Scotty?'

'In the garden.'

I went outside to say hello to the little black dog that vaguely resembled a Scotch terrier. 'You're an oversexed ruffian.' I laughed as the rough hairy body bounced up and down to greet me.

A car stopped outside, and seconds later two small children came hurtling down the side of the house. I picked up Scotty and held him like a shield as Melanie and Jake launched themselves at me.

'Leave your aunt Millie alone!' Trudy shouted. 'I've told you before, she doesn't like kids.' She beamed. 'Hi, Sis. I've painted you another bottle.'

'Hi, Trude. I'd love another bottle. Hello, Colin.'

Colin Daley was a stocky, quiet man, who worked long into the night six days a week in his one-man engineering company. He was doing well: he and Trudy had already sold their first house and bought a bigger one in Orrell Park. I sensed he didn't like me much. He'd got on well with Gary and perhaps he thought I neglected my family, left too much to Trudy. During the week, she often came over to Kirkby with the children. He nodded in my direction. 'Hello, there.'

'Do you really not like kids?' Jake enquired gravely.

18

He was six, two years older than his sister, a happy little boy with Colin's blue eyes. Both Trudy's children were happy – she'd made sure of that.

'I like you two,' I lied. As kids went they weren't bad, but talking to them got on my nerves. I hugged Scotty, who was licking my ear. I would have had a dog of my own if I hadn't spent so much time at work.

Jake looked at me doubtfully. 'Honest?'

'Cross my heart.'

We all went indoors. Mum shrieked, 'C'mon, you little rascals, and give your gran a hug.' The children allowed themselves to be kissed, then they cried, 'Where's Grandad?'

'In the lounge.'

Mum looked wistful as Melanie and Jake whooped their way into the other room. She said, 'They've got a thing about their grandad.'

'I know.' It was strange that Trudy's children adored the man who'd once nearly killed their mother. She still bore a scar from his belt buckle above her left eyebrow.

When I went in Trudy was standing in the lounge, hovering near her children who were sitting on their grandad's knee. I noticed her eyes flicker to the big hands, one resting on each child's waist. We looked at each other in mutual understanding.

As usual, the meal was revolting. The mound of mashed potatoes, watery cabbage and stewing steak on my plate made me feel nauseous. 'I'll never eat all this, Mum,' I protested. 'I asked you not to give me much.'

'You look as if you need a decent meal, luv. There's a nice apple charlotte for afters.'

'It's a sin to waste good food,' my father said jovially.

I caught Trudy's eye and Declan hid a grin. The final Sunday of the month was a day for catching eyes and making faces. Odd phrases brought back bitter memories: 'It's a sin to waste good food,' was not said so lightly in those days.

On the surface, it was a civilised gathering, occasionally merry, a family united for Sunday lunch, except for Alison, of course. But I always felt on tenterhooks, as if I were watching someone blowing up a balloon, bigger and bigger until it was about to burst. Perhaps it was just me. Perhaps no one else remembered how Colin detested his father-in-law, how nervous Mum was, what Sunday dinner used to be like when we were little. Even now, I was still terrified that I would drop food on the tablecloth and that a nicotine-stained hand would reach across and slap my face, so hard that tears would come to my eyes, even though I'd sworn at an early age never to let him see me cry.

The conversation had turned to Auntie Flo. 'We were friendly for a while before I married your dad,' Mum said. 'I went to her flat in Toxteth a few times, though your gran never knew.' She turned to me. 'Actually, Millicent, that's where you come in.'

'What's Auntie Flo got to do with me?'

'Your gran wants her place cleared before the rent runs out, otherwise the landlord might chuck everything away.'

'Why ask me?' I could think of few less welcome things to do than clear out the belongings of an old lady I hadn't known. 'Why not you or Gran or Trudy? What about that woman you mentioned, the one who rang?'

Mum looked hurt. 'It's not much to ask, luv. I can't do it because . . .' she paused uncomfortably '. . . well, your dad's not very keen on the idea. Gran's too upset, she's taken Flo's death hard. Anyroad, she never goes out nowadays.'

'And Trudy's already got enough to do,' Colin growled.

'As for the woman who rang, she's just someone who lives upstairs. We don't want a stranger going through Auntie Flo's precious things, do we?'

'What precious things?' I noticed my father's fists clench. I reminded myself that he could do nothing to

20

me now. I could say what I liked. 'I don't know what she did for a living, but I can't imagine Auntie Flo having acquired many precious things.'

'She worked in a launderette till she retired.' For a moment, Mum looked nonplussed. Then she went on eagerly, 'But there'll be papers, luv, letters perhaps, odds and ends of jewellery your gran would like. The clothes can go to one of those charity shops, Oxfam. I'm sure you'll find someone to take the furniture, and if there's anything nice, I wouldn't mind it meself. Declan knows a lad who has a van.'

I tried to think of a way of getting out of it. My mother was looking at me pleadingly, her pasty face slightly moist. *She* would probably thoroughly enjoy going through the flat, but Dad had put his foot down for some reason, not that he'd ever needed a reason in the past. The mere fact that Mum *wanted* to do something was enough. Maybe I could get it done in a few hours if I went armed with several cardboard boxes. I had one last try. 'I've always avoided Toxteth like the plague. It's full of drugs and crime. People get murdered there, shot.'

Mum looked concerned. 'Oh, well, if that's —' she began, but my father butted in, 'Your auntie Flo lived there for over fifty years without coming to any harm.'

It seemed I had no choice. 'Oh, all right,' I said reluctantly. 'When's the rent due?'

'I've no idea.' Mum looked relieved. 'The woman upstairs will know. Mrs Smith, her name is, Charmian Smith.'

'Don't forget to give me the address before I go.'

'I won't, luv. I'll ring and tell Gran later. She'll be pleased.'

After the meal was over and the dishes washed, Trudy produced the bottle she'd painted for me. It was exquisite, an empty wine bottle transformed into a work of art. The glass was covered with roses and dark green leaves edged with gold.

'It's beautiful!' I breathed, holding it up to the light.

'I'm not sure where to put it. The other one's in the bedroom.'

'I'll do you another,' Trudy offered. 'I'm running out of people to give them to.'

'I suggested she have a stall in a craft market,' Colin said proudly. 'I could look after the kids if it was a Sunday.'

I waved the bottle in support. 'That's a great idea, Trude. You'd pay ten pounds for this in a shop.'

'Millicent.' Mum came sidling up. 'Have you got much to do this afternoon?'

I was immediately wary. 'I'm in the middle of a report.'

'It's just I'd like to go and see Alison.'

'Can't you go yourself?' The only reason she'd learned to drive was so she could visit Alison in the home.

'There's something wrong with the car. Your dad promised to get it fixed but he never got round to it.'

He'd probably not got round to it deliberately. He would prefer to think his youngest child didn't exist. 'Sorry, Mum. As I said, I've got this report to write.'

'We'll take you, luv.' Colin must have overheard. 'It's a couple of weeks since we saw Alison.'

Mum looked grateful. 'That's nice of you, Colin, but there's nothing for Melanie and Jake to do. They get fed up within the first five minutes.'

'You can leave the kids here with me,' my father offered.

'No, thanks,' Trudy said, much too quickly.

'I'll take them for a walk once we get there, and you and Trudy can stay with Alison,' Colin said.

In the midst of this discussion, I went upstairs to the lavatory. The bathroom, like everywhere else in the house, reeked of poverty, the linoleum cracked and crumbling, the plastic curtains faded. I was well into my teens before I discovered we were relatively well-off – or should have been. My father's wages as a toolmaker were high, but the family saw little of the money. He'd been a betting man all his life and a consistent loser.

As usual, I couldn't wait to be back in my own place. I felt guilty for refusing to visit Alison, pity for my mother, angry that the pity made me turn up for the monthly get-togethers then guilty again, knowing that I would get out of coming if I could. When Stock Masterton had begun to open on Sundays, I'd hoped that would provide a good excuse, but George, a workaholic, insisted on looking after the office himself with the help of a part-timer.

After saying goodbye, I went outside to the car. Several boys were playing football in the road, and someone had written 'Fuck off' in black felt pen on the side of my yellow Polo. I was rubbing it off with my handkerchief when Trudy came out with the children. She ushered them into the back of the family's old Sierra and came over to me. 'Thank the Lord that's over for another month.'

'You can say that again!'

'I can't get me head round this kindly old grandfather shit.' Absent-mindedly she rubbed the scar over her left eyebrow.

'I suppose we should be thankful for small mercies.'

Trudy regarded me keenly. 'You okay, Sis? You look a bit pale.'

'Mum said that. I'm fine, been working hard, that's all.' I eyed the car. I'd got most of it off and what was left wasn't legible. 'Look, Sis, I'm sorry about Alison,' I said in a rush, 'but I really have got work to do.'

Trudy pressed my arm. She glanced at the house where we'd grown up. 'I feel as if I'd like to drive away and never have to see another member of me family again, but we're trapped, aren't we? I don't know if I could bear it without Colin.'

As I started the car, I noticed that the house opposite had been boarded up, although children had broken down the door and were playing in the hallway. There was a rusty car without wheels in the front garden. As I drove away, the sun seemed to darken, although there wasn't a cloud to be seen. Unexpectedly, I felt overwhelmed by a sense of alienation. Where do I belong? I wondered, frightened. Not here, please not here! Yet I'd been born in a tower block less than a mile from this spot, where nowadays Gran lived like a prisoner: Martha Colquitt rarely left home since she'd been mugged for her pension five years ago. My own flat in Blundellsands was a pretence, more like a stage set than a proper home, and I was a fake. I couldn't understand what James saw in me, or why George Masterton was my friend. I was putting on an act, I wasn't real.

And what would James think if he met my slovenly mother and chain-smoking father, and if I told him about my brutal childhood? What would he say if he knew I had a sister with severe learning difficulties who'd been in a home since she was three, safely out of my father's way? A scene flashed through my mind, of my father slapping Alison, knocking her pretty little face first one way then the other, trying to make her stop saying that same word over and over again. 'Slippers,' Alison would mutter, in her dull monotone. 'Slippers, slippers, slippers.' She said it still, when agitated, although she was seventeen now.

Even if I were in love with James, we could never marry, not with all the family baggage I had in tow. I reminded myself that I didn't want to get married again, that I wasn't capable of falling in love. I belonged nowhere and to nobody.

Nevertheless, I had an urgent desire to see James. He was calling for me at seven. I looked forward to losing myself in empty talk, good food, wine. He would bring me home and we would make love and all that business with my family would be forgotten, until the time came for me to go again. Except, that is, for the dreams, from which I would never escape.

3

It wasn't until Thursday that I managed to get to Toxteth. James had tickets for a jazz concert at the Philharmonic Hall on Monday night, which I had forgotten about. Tuesday, I'd promised to go to dinner with Diana Riddick, a colleague from the office whom I'd never particularly got on with, but then few people did. Diana was thirty-five, single, and lived with her elderly father, who was a 'pain', she claimed, particularly now that his health was failing. She was a small, slight woman, permanently discontented, with a garishly painted face, a degree in land and property management, and an eye on the position of manager of the Woolton office. She didn't realise that I nursed the same ambition and when we were alone together she openly discussed it. I'd suspected she had an ulterior motive in inviting me that evening and it turned out she wanted to pump me about George's plans.

'Has he ever talked to you about it?' she asked, over the Italian meal. There were red and white gingham cloths on the tables and candles in green bottles dripping wax. The walls were hung with plastic vines.

'Hardly ever,' I replied truthfully.

'I bet you anything he gives the job to Oliver.' She pouted. Oliver Brett, solid and dependable, was the assistant manager, in charge when George was away, which was rare.

'I doubt it. Oliver's nice, but he's proved more than once he couldn't handle the responsibility.' I sipped my wine. On nights like this, Kirkby seemed a million miles away. 'Remember last Christmas when he rang George in the Seychelles to ask his advice?'

'Hmm!' Diana looked dubious. 'Yes, but he's a man. The world is prejudiced in favour of men. I shall be very cross if it's Tweedledum or Tweedledee.'

'That's most unlikely.' I laughed. Apart from June,

who'd taken my old job as receptionist, the only other permanent members of staff were two young men in their mid-twenties, Darren and Elliot, startlingly alike in looks and manner, which accounted for their nicknames. Both were too immature for promotion. 'George has never struck me as being prejudiced against women,' I added.

'I might do a survey of Woolton, see how the land lies.' Diana's rather heavy eyebrows drew together in a frown and the discontented lines between her eyes deepened further. 'I'll type up some notes for George.'

'What a good idea,' I murmured. I hadn't added to my own report since last week.

It was late on Wednesday when I returned to the office in Castle Street. I'd taken a couple, the Naughtons, to see a property in Lydiate. It was the sixth house they'd viewed. As usual, they walked round several times, wondering aloud whether their present furniture would fit, asking if I would measure the windows so they could check if the curtains they had now would do. George insisted that keys were returned, no matter how late, and it was almost eight when I hung them on the rack. George was still working in his glass-partitioned office and Oliver was about to go home. His good-natured face creased into a smile as he said, 'Goodnight.'

I was wondering if there was time to drive to Blundellsands, collect the cardboard boxes I'd acquired from a supermarket, return to town and start on Auntie Flo's flat. I couldn't bring the car to work with boxes on the back seat when I had to take clients to view.

Before I'd made up my mind George came out of his cubicle. 'Millie! Please say you're not doing anything special tonight. I'm longing for a drink and desperately in need of company.'

'I'm not, doing anything special that is.' I would have said the same whatever the case. At the moment it was essential to keep in George's good books.

We went to a wine bar, the one where I'd met James.

George ordered a roast-beef sandwich and a bottle of Chablis. I refused anything to eat. 'You should get some food down you.' He patted my hand in a fatherly way. 'You look pale.'

'That's what everyone keeps telling me. I'll wear blusher tomorrow.'

'You mean rouge. My old mother used to go to town with the rouge.' His mother had died only a year ago and he missed her badly, just as he missed the children his ex-wife and her new husband had taken to live in France. He was alone, hated it, and buried himself in work to compensate. George Masterton was fifty, tall and thin to the point of emaciation although he ate like a horse. He wore expensive suits that hung badly from his narrow, stooped shoulders. Despite this, he had an air of drooping elegance, enhanced by his deceptively laid-back, languid manner. Only those who knew him well were aware that behind the lazy charm George was an irascible, unpredictable man, who suffered from severe bouts of depression and panic attacks.

'Why the desperate need for company?' I asked lightly. I always felt at my oddest with George, as if one day he would see what a fake I was, and never speak to me again.

'Oh, I dunno.' He shrugged. 'It was Annabel's birthday on Monday. She was sixteen. Thought about whizzing over to France on Eurostar but told myself Stock Masterton would collapse without me. Really, I was scared I wouldn't be welcome. I'm supposed to be having her and Bill for Christmas, but I shan't be at all surprised if they don't come.'

It was my turn to pat his hand. 'I bet Annabel would have been thrilled to see you. As for Christmas, it's months off. Try not to start worrying yet.'

'Families, eh!' He chuckled. 'They're a pain in the arse when you've got them, and a pain when they're not there. Diana calls her old dad everything but now he's ill she's terrified he'll die. Poor chap, it sounds like cancer. Anyway, how's your lot over in Kirkby?'

'Same as usual.' I told him about Auntie Flo's flat, and he said bring the boxes in tomorrow and put them in the stationery cupboard until I found time to go. He asked where the flat was.

'Toxteth, William Square. I don't know round there all that well.'

His sandwich arrived. Between mouthfuls, he explained that William Square had once been very beautiful. 'They're five-storeyed properties, including the basement where the skivvies used to work. Lovely stately houses, massive pillars, intricate wrought-iron balconies like bloody lace, bay windows at least twelve feet high. It's where the nobs used to live at the turn of the century, though it's gone seriously downhill since the war.' He paused over the last of the sandwich. 'Sure you'll be safe? Wasn't there a chap shot in that area a few weeks ago?'

'I'll go in daylight. Trouble is, finding the time. Things keep coming up.'

George grinned. 'Such as me demanding your company! Sorry about that. Look, take tomorrow afternoon off. I'd feel happier about you going then. Don't forget to take your mobile and you can call for help if you get in trouble.'

'For goodness sake, George, you'd think I was going to a war zone!'

'Toxteth's been compared to one before now. As far as I'm concerned, it's as bad as Bosnia used to be.'

At two o'clock on a brilliantly sunny afternoon, William Square still looked beautiful when I drove in. I found an empty parking space some distance past the house I wanted, number one, and sat in the car for several minutes, taking in the big, gracious houses on all four sides. On close inspection, they appeared anything but beautiful. The elaborate stucco decorating the fronts had dropped off leaving bare patches like sores. Most of the front doors were a mass of peeling paint, and some houses

28

to echo the colour of the shawl. It was the sort of thing I might have done myself.

I walked slowly down the room, which ran the length of the house. Halfway along, two massive beams had been built into the walls to support an equally massive lintel, all painted black, and covered with little brass plaques. An elderly gas fire was fitted in the green-tiled fireplace, and on each side of it, more cupboards reached to the ceiling, one of which I opened. Every shelf was stuffed to capacity: clothes, crockery, books, bedding, more ornaments stored in boxes . . .

'I can't do this all on my own,' I said aloud. I had no idea where to start, and I would need more like a hundred cardboard boxes than ten.

A window at the far end overlooked a tiny yard, which was level with the rear of the flat. It contained a wooden bench, a table and plant-holders full of limp pansies. The wall had been painted almost the same pink as my lounge – another indication that Auntie Flo and I had shared similar taste. The woman upstairs had said I was like Flo, and I wondered if there was a photograph somewhere.

I turned and surveyed the room, and supposed that, in its way, it had charm. Very little matched, yet everything seemed to gel together nicely. There was a large brown plush settee and a matching chair with crocheted patch-work covers on the backs and arms. Obviously Flo hadn't believed in leaving an inch of space bare. There were numerous pictures and several tiny tables, all with bowls of silk flowers. Linoleum, with a pattern of blue and red tiles, covered the floor, and there was a handmade rag rug on the hearth. A large-screen television stood next to an up-to-date music centre, a record visible on the turntable beneath the smoky plastic lid.

If only it wasn't so cold! On the hearth next to the fire I saw a box of matches. I struck one, shoved it between the bars and turned the knob at the side. There was a mini explosion and the gas jets roared briefly before settling down into a steady flame.

I held out my hands to warm them and remembered I'd been looking for a photo of Flo. After a while, I got up and moved round the room again until I found some on a gate-leg table, which had been folded to its narrowest against the wall. The photos, about a dozen in all, were spread each side of a glass jar of anemones.

The first was a coloured snap of two women taken in what looked like a fairground. I recognised Flo from Auntie Sally's funeral. Despite her age, it was obvious that she'd once been pretty. She was smiling at the camera, a calm, sweet smile. Her companion wore a leopardskin coat and black leggings, and her hair was a violent unnatural red. I turned the photo over: 'Me and Bel at Blackpool Lights, October 1993'.

There was a picture of Auntie Sally's wartime wedding, which I'd seen before at Gran's. The bride, in her pin-striped suit and white felt hat, looked like a character out of *Guys and Dolls*. Another wedding photo, the couple in Army uniform. Despite the unflattering clothes, the woman was startlingly lovely. On the back was written, 'Bel & Bob's wedding, December, 1940'. Flo and Bel must have been friends all their lives.

I found two more photos of Bel getting married; 'Bel & Ivor's wedding, 1945,' in what looked like a foreign setting, and 'Bel & Edward's wedding, 1974' showed a glamorous Bel with a decrepit-looking old man.

At last I held a picture of a young Flo, a snapshot turning white at the edges. It was taken outside a ramshackle building with 'Fritz's Laundry' above the door. A man in a dark suit and wire-rimmed glasses – Fritz? – stood in the middle of six women all wearing aprons and turbans. Flo was recognisable immediately because she was so like me, except that she was smiling and I had never smiled like that in all my life. She looked about eighteen, and seemed to be bursting with happiness, you could see it in her eyes, her dimples, and the curve of her lovely wide mouth.

As I replaced the silver-framed photo on the table, I

sighed. More than half a century spanned the images of my great-aunt, the one in Blackpool, the other outside Fritz's Laundry, yet little seemed to have happened over the years to make her expression change.

I was turning away with the intention of getting on with what I'd come for, when I noticed a studio portrait, in sepia tones, of a woman with a baby. There was something familiar about her grim yet good-looking face. I knew nothing about babies and couldn't tell the child's age – it was a boy in an old-fashioned romper suit with a sailor collar – but he was adorable. I looked at the back, and read, 'Elsa Cameron with Norman (Martha's godson), on his first birthday, May, 1939'.

The baby was my father! His mother had died long before I was born.

I slammed the photo face down on the table. I was shivering again. I was about to kneel in front of the fire once more, when I saw the sherry on the sideboard, the modern one. My jangling nerves needed calming. In the cupboard underneath, where I looked for a glass, I found five more bottles of sherry, and several glasses hanging by their stems from a circular wooden stand. I filled a glass, drank the sherry, filled it again, took it over to the settee, and sank into the cushions. My head was buzzing. How could such a beautiful child grow up to become such a *monster?*

The sherry took effect quickly and I began to relax. There seemed to be a sagging hole in the middle cushion of the settee into which my bottom fitted perfectly. Perhaps it was where Flo had always sat. Outside, cars drove past occasionally and I could hear children playing in the square. People walked by, heels clicking on the pavement, only their legs visible from the knees down through the small window by the door.

I put down the empty glass and promptly fell asleep.

When I woke up it was nearly half past five. There was a throbbing between my eyes, which I supposed was the result of the sherry, though it didn't feel particularly unpleasant. I would have given anything for a cup of tea or coffee and remembered I hadn't seen the kitchen yet, or the bedroom.

I got to my feet, and staggered towards the door at the back of the room, where I found myself in a little dark inner hall with a tiled floor and two more doors, left and right. The left led to a tiny Spartan kitchen with a deep porcelain sink, a cooker older than Mum's, a digitally operated microwave oven but no fridge. In the wall cupboard, behind several packets of biscuits, there was coffee and, to my relief, a jar of Coffeemate. I put a spoonful of each with water in a flowered mug and stuck it in the microwave to heat.

Whilst I was waiting, I went back to the inner hall, opened the other door, and switched on the light. The bedroom was mainly white, curtains, walls, bedspread. A pair of pink furry slippers were set neatly side by side under the bed. A large crucifix hung from the wall and there was a statue of Our Lord on the six-drawer chest, surrounded by smaller statues. The walls were covered with holy pictures: Our Lord again, Baby Jesus, the Virgin Mary, and an assortment of saints. Otherwise, the room was sparsely furnished: apart from the chest, there was only a matching wardrobe with a narrow, full-length mirror on the door, and a little cane bedside table, which held an old-fashioned alarm clock, a white-shaded lamp, and a Mills & Boon novel with an embroidered book-mark. An old brown foolscap envelope was propped against the lamp. I picked it up and put it in the pocket of my linen jacket. It might contain Flo's pension book, which would need to be cancelled.

I admired the wardrobe and the chest-of-drawers. They looked like stained oak and had been polished to satin smoothness. They'd look lovely in my flat, I thought. I wouldn't have minded the brass bedstead either. My own bedroom furniture had been bought in kits and had taken weeks to put together.

In the kitchen, the microwave beeped. I sat on the bed, which was like sitting on a cloud it felt so soft, and bounced up and down, but stopped when I caught sight of my reflection in the mirror. I saw a tall, graceful young woman who looked years younger than her age, dressed in white and pink, with long slim legs and hair that shone like silver under Auntie Flo's bedroom light. Her wide, generous mouth was turned up slightly – she'd been childishly enjoying bouncing on the bed. At school, she had been regarded as stuck up because of her straight, slightly patrician nose, but James's mother had said once, 'What fine bone structure you have, Millie. Some women would pay a plastic surgeon a fortune for cheek-bones like that.'

The young woman had forgotten to use blusher and she *did* look pale, as everyone had been saying, but it was the deadness in the green eyes that shocked me.

I took the coffee and a packet of custard creams into the lounge, switched on the television and watched *Neighbours*, then an old cowboy film on BBC2.

Just as the film was finishing, I glimpsed through the window the majestic figure of Charmian Smith descending the concrete stairs. I kicked the boxes aside and opened the door, feeling slightly uncomfortable when she gave me a warm smile, as if we were the greatest friends.

'I'd forgotten all about you until our Minola, that's me daughter, collected her kids and said there was a light on in Flo's flat. Me feller's just got home and I wondered if you'd like a bite to eat with us.' She came into the room without waiting to be asked, as if it was something she was used to doing.

'What does your daughter do?' I was astonished to learn that Charmian was grandmother to the children I'd seen earlier.

'She's learning to use a computer. It was when Jay, that's me son, went to university last year, she decided it was time she used her brain.' Charmian's brown eyes danced. 'I told her she'd regret getting married at sixteen. I said, "There's more things to life than a husband and a family, luv," but kids never listen, do they? I didn't listen to me own mam when I got married at the same age.'

'I suppose not.'

'Are you married? Y'know, I don't know your name.'

'Millie Cameron, and no, I'm not married.' I wished the woman would leave so I could get down to work. It seemed imperative suddenly that I take at least half a dozen boxes of stuff to Oxfam tomorrow. To my dismay, she sank gracefully into the armchair, her long bead earrings swinging against her gleaming neck.

'I didn't know Flo had any relatives left after her sister Sally died,' she said, 'apart from Sally's daughter who went to live in Australia. It wasn't until Bel gave me a number to ring after the funeral that I knew there was another sister.'

Bel, the woman in the photographs. '*After* the funeral?'

'That's right, Martha Colquitt. Is she your gran?' I nodded. 'I felt terrible when the poor woman burst into tears, but Bel said that was the way Flo wanted it.' Charmian glanced sadly round the room. 'I can't get used to her not being here. I used to come and see her several times a day over the last year when she was stuck indoors with her terrible headaches.'

'That was very kind of you,' I said stiffly.

'Lord, girl, it was nothing to do with kindness. It was no more than she deserved. Flo was there for me when I needed her – she got me a job in the launderette when me kids were little. It changed me life.' She leaned against the crocheted cover and, for a moment, looked as if she might cry. Then, once again, her eyes swept the room. 'It's like a museum, isn't it? Such a shame everything's got to go. People always fetched her ornaments back from their holidays.' She indicated the brass plaques on the beams. 'We brought her the key and the little dog

36

from Clacton. This was Flo's favourite, though – and mine.' She eased herself smoothly out of the chair and switched on the lamp on top of the television.

I had already noticed the cut-out parchment lamp with its wooden base and thought it tasteless. It reminded me of a cheap Christmas card: a line of laughing children dressed as they might have been in this very square a hundred years ago, fur hats, fur muffs, lace-up boots.

'I'll switch the main light off so you can see the effect once the bulb warms up,' Charmian said.

To my surprise, the shade slowly began to revolve. I hadn't realised there was another behind it that turned in the opposite direction. The children passed a toyshop, a sweetshop, a church, a Christmas tree decorated with coloured lights. Shadows flitted across the ceiling of the long, low room. Hazy, almost lifesize figures passed over my head.

'Tom brought her that from Austria of all places.'

I felt almost hypnotised by the moving lamp. 'Tom?'

'Flo's friend. She loved sitting watching her lamp and listening to her record. The lamp was still on when I came down the day they found her dead in the park. Did you know she got run over?'

'My mother said.'

'They never found who did it. Oh dear!' Now Charmian did begin to cry. 'I don't half miss her. I hate the thought of her dying all alone.'

'I'm terribly sorry.' I went over and awkwardly touched the woman's arm. I hadn't the faintest notion how you were supposed to comfort a stranger. Perhaps another person, someone who didn't have dead eyes, might have taken the weeping woman in their arms, but I could no more have done that than I could have sprouted wings and flown.

Charmian sniffed and wiped her eyes. 'Anyroad, I'd better go. Herbie's waiting for his tea – which reminds me, luv, would you care to join us?'

'Thanks all the same, but I'd better not. There's so

much to do.' I gestured at the room, which was exactly the same as when I'd come six hours before.

Charmian squeezed my hand. 'Perhaps next time, eh? It'll take you weeks to sort this lot out. I'd offer to help, but I couldn't bear to see Flo's lovely stuff being packed away.'

I watched her climb the steps outside. I had meant to ask when the rent was due, so that I could pay a few weeks if necessary. I hadn't realised that dusk had fallen and it was rapidly growing dark. The streetlights were on, and it was time to draw the curtains. It was then that I noticed someone standing motionless outside. I pressed my face against the glass and peered upwards. It was a girl of about sixteen, wearing a tight red mini-dress that barely covered her behind and emphasised the curves of her slight body. There was something about her stance, the way she leaned against the railings, one foot slightly in front of the other, the way she held her cigarette, left hand supporting the right elbow, that made me guess immediately what she was. I pressed my face the other way, and saw two more girls outside the house next door.

'Oh, lord!' I felt scared. Perhaps I should let someone know where I was – James or my mother – but I couldn't recall seeing a phone in the flat and, despite what George had said, I'd left my mobile in the office. As soon as I'd had another cup of coffee, I'd go home and come back on Sunday to start packing.

The kitchen was like a fridge. No wonder Flo didn't have one – she didn't need it. I returned, shivering, to the settee, my hands wrapped round a mug of coffee. It was odd, but the room seemed even more cosy and charming now I knew about the girl outside. I no longer felt scared, but safe and secure, as if there was no chance of coming to any harm inside Auntie Flo's four walls.

I became aware of something stiff against my hip and remembered the envelope that I'd found in the bedroom. It didn't contain a pension book, but several newspaper cuttings, yellow and crisp with age, held together with a paper clip. They'd mainly been taken from the *Liverpool Daily Post* and the *Echo*. I looked at the top one for a date – Friday, 2 June 1939 – then skimmed through the words underneath.

THETIS TRAPPED UNDERWATER was the main headline, followed by a sub-heading. *Submarine Fails to Resurface in Liverpool Bay – Admiralty Assures Relatives All Those On Board Will Be Rescued.*

I turned to the next cutting dated the following day. *Hope Fading For Men Trapped On The Thetis. Stunned Relatives Wait Outside Cammell Laird Offices in Birkenhead.* The news had been worse when the *Echo* came out that afternoon: *Hope Virtually Abandoned for 99 men on Thetis*, and by Sunday, *All Hope Abandoned* . . .

Why had Flo kept them?

On the television, the lamp swirled and the children did their Christmas shopping. I found myself waiting for a girl in a red coat and brown fur bonnet to come round. She was waving at someone, but the someone never appeared.

Flo had sat in this very spot hundreds, no, thousands of times, watching the girl in red, listening to her record. Curious, I went over to the record player and studied the controls. I pressed Play, and beneath the plastic lid, the arm lifted and swung across to the record.

There was crackling, then the strains of a vaguely familiar tune filled the room, silent until then except for the hiss of the gas fire. After a while, a man's voice, also vaguely familiar, began to sing. He'd been in a film on television recently – Bing Crosby. 'Dancing in the dark,' a voice like melting chocolate crooned.

What had Flo Clancy done to make her the black sheep of the family? Why had Gran refused to mention her name? Bel, Flo's old friend, had asked Charmian Smith to ring Gran *after* the funeral because 'that's the way Flo wanted it'. What had happened between the sisters to make them dislike each other so much? And

39

why had Flo kept cuttings of a submarine disaster beside her bed?

I would almost certainly never know the truth about Auntie Flo, but what did it matter? As the lamp slowly turned and dark shadows swept the ceiling of the room and the music reached a crescendo, filling every nook and corner, I took a long, deep breath and allowed myself to be sucked into the enchantment of it all. A quite unexpected thing had happened, something quite wonderful. I had never felt so much at peace with myself before.

Flo

I

Flo Clancy opened her eyes, saw that the fingers on the brass alarm clock on the tallboy were pointing to half past seven, and nearly screamed. She'd be late for work! She was about to leap out of bed when she remembered it was Whit Monday and she could lie in.

Whew! She peeped over the covers at her sisters, both fast asleep in the double bed only a few feet away. Martha would have done her nut if she'd been woken early. Flo pursed her lips and blew gently at Sally who was sleeping on the outside, but Sal's brown eyelashes merely flickered before she turned over, dead to the world.

But Flo was wide awake and it was a sin to stay in bed on such a lovely morning. She sat up carefully – the springs of the single bed creaked like blazes – and stretched her arms. The sun streamed through the thin curtains making the roses on the floorcloth seem almost real. She poked her feet out and wriggled her white toes. As usual, the bedclothes were a mess – her sisters refused to sleep with her, claiming she fidgeted non-stop the whole night long.

Shall I get up and risk disturbing our Martha? Flo mused. She'd have to get dressed in the little space between the wardrobe and the tallboy. Since their dear dad, a railwayman, had died two years ago – struck by a train on the lines near Edge Hill station – and they'd had to take in a lodger, the girls could no longer wander round the little house in Burnett Street half dressed.

The frock Martha had worn last night when she'd gone

with Albert Colquitt, their lodger, to see Bette Davis in *The Little Foxes* was hanging outside the wardrobe. Flo glared at it. What a miserable garment, dark grey with grey buttons, more suitable for a funeral than a night out with the man you hoped to marry. She transferred her gaze to her sister's head, which could just be seen above the green eiderdown. How on earth could she sleep with her hair screwed up in a million metal curlers? And did someone of only twenty-two *really* need to smear her face with layers of cold cream so she looked as if she'd been carved out of a block of lard?

Oh dear! She was having nasty thoughts about Martha again and she loved her just as much as she loved Mam and Sally and Mr Fritz who owned the laundry where she worked. But since dear Dad died, what with Mam not feeling too well, Martha seemed to think it was her job as the eldest to be In Charge and keep her sisters in line. Not that Dad had ever been strict — he'd been a soft ould thing. Flo's eyes prickled with tears. It was still hard to get used to him not being there.

She couldn't stand being in bed a minute longer. She eased herself out and got dressed quickly in her best pink frock with white piping on the collar and the cuffs of the short puffed sleeves. That afternoon, she and Sal were off to New Brighton on the ferry.

As she crept downstairs, she could hear Mam snoring in the front bedroom. There was no sound from the parlour. Mr Colquitt must have gone to work, poor man. Flo felt for him. As a ticket inspector on the trams, he had to work on days most people had off.

In the living room, she automatically kissed the feet of the porcelain figure of Christ on the crucifix over the mantelpiece, then skipped into the back kitchen where she washed her face and cleaned her teeth. She combed her silvery blonde hair before the mirror over the sink. As an experiment, she twisted it into two long plaits and pinned them together on top of her head with a slide. Irene Dunne had worn her hair like that in a picture she'd seen recently. Flo had been meaning to try it ever since. It looked dead elegant.

She made a face at herself and was about to burst into song, when she remembered the superstition, 'Sing before breakfast, cry before tea.' Anyroad, everyone upstairs was still asleep. She'd make a pot of tea and take them a cup when she heard them stir. Martha and Sally enjoyed sitting up in bed, pillows tucked behind them, gossiping, on days they didn't have to get up for work. Unlike Flo, they both had horrible jobs: Martha was a bottle topper in Goodlad's Brewery, and Sally worked behind the counter of the butcher's on the corner of Smithdown Road and Tunstall Street.

Oh, but it was difficult not to sing on such a glorious day. The sun must be splitting the flags outside, and the whitewashed walls in the backyard dazzled so brightly it hurt her eyes to look. Flo filled the kettle, put it on the hob over the fire in the living room, releasing the flue so the embers from the night before began to sizzle and glow, and decided to dance instead. She took a deep breath and was twirling across the room like a ballerina, when she came to a sudden halt in the arms of their lodger.

'Mr Colquitt! I thought you'd gone.' Flo felt as if she'd blushed right down to her toes. He was wearing his regulation navy blue uniform with red piping, and grinning from ear to ear.

'I'm glad I hadn't, else I'd have missed the sight of a fairy dancing towards me to wish me good morning.'

'Good morning, Mr Colquitt,' Flo stammered, conscious of his arms still around her waist.

'And the same to you, Flo. How many times have I told you to call me Albert?'

'I can't remember.' To her relief, he removed his hands, came into the room and sat in the easy chair that used to be Dad's. Flo didn't mind, because she liked Mr Colquitt – Albert – though couldn't for the life of her understand why Martha was so keen on capturing for a

43

husband a widower more than twice her age. Since her best friend, Elsa, had married Eugene Cameron, Martha was terrified of being left on the shelf. Like Flo, she took after Mam's side of the family, with her slim figure, pale blonde hair and unusual green eyes, but had unfortunately inherited Dad's poor eyesight: she had worn glasses since she was nine and had never come to terms with it. She thought herself the unluckiest girl in the world, whose chances of finding a decent husband were doomed.

Martha had been setting her cap at Albert ever since he arrived on the scene. He was a tall, ungainly man with a round pot belly like a football. Although he was not handsome, his face was pleasant and his grey eyes shone with good humour. His wispy hair grew in sideboards to way below his ears, which Flo thought looked a bit daft. The main thing wrong with Albert, though, was that he didn't get his uniform cleaned often enough, so it ponged something dreadful, particularly in summer. It was ponging now, and she would have opened the window if it hadn't meant climbing on his knee.

'Would you like a bite to eat?' she enquired. Breakfast and an evening meal were supposed to be included in his rent, but he usually left too early for anyone to make breakfast, so compensated by eating a thundering great tea when he came home.

'I wouldn't say no to a couple of slices of toast, and is that water boiling for tea?'

'It is so.' Flo cut two slices of bread and managed to get both on the toasting fork. She knelt in front of the fire and toasted her arm at the same time.

'You've done your hair different,' Albert said suddenly. 'It's very nice. You look like a snow princess.'

'Ta.' Flo had never mentioned it to a living soul, but she sometimes wondered if he liked her better than he did Martha, though not in a romantic way, of course. She also thought that maybe he wasn't too keen to allow pretty, bespectacled Martha Clancy to get her claws into him. He might be twice her age and smell awful, but he didn't want to get married again. Flo hoped Martha wouldn't try too hard so that he'd feel obliged to leave. His thirty bob a week made all the difference to the housekeeping nowadays. It meant they could buy scented soap and decent cuts of meat, luxuries that they could never afford otherwise. Although there were three wages coming in, women earned much less than men.

He ate his toast, drank his tea, made several more flattering remarks about her appearance, then left for work. Flo returned to the living room, poured a cup of tea, and curled up in Dad's chair. She wanted to think about Tommy O'Mara before anyone got up. If Martha was in the room, it was impossible – her sister's mere presence made Flo feel guilty. For a second, a shadow fell over her face. Tommy was married to Nancy, but he'd explained the strange circumstances to Flo's satisfaction. Next year, sooner if possible, he and Flo would be married. Her face cleared. Until the magic day occurred, it was perfectly all right to meet Tommy O'Mara twice a week outside the Mystery.

Upstairs, Mam coughed and Flo held her breath until the house was quiet again. She'd met Tommy on the Tuesday after Easter when he'd come into the laundry by the side door. Customers were supposed to use the front, which led to the office where Mr Fritz was usually behind the counter. It was a dull day, slightly chilly, but the side door was left open, except in the iciest of weather, because when all the boilers, presses and irons were working at full pelt, the laundry got hotter than a Turkish bath.

Flo was pressing sheets in the giant new electric contraption Mr Fritz had only recently bought. She was nearest to the door, wreathed in steam, only vaguely aware of someone approaching through the mist until a voice with a strong Irish accent said, 'Do you do dry-cleaning, luv?'

'Sorry, no, just laundry.' As the steam cleared, she saw

a young man with a brown suit over his arm. He wore a grey, collarless shirt and, despite the cold, the sleeves were rolled up to his armpits, showing off his strong, brown arms – there was a tattoo of a tiger on the right. A tweed cap was set jauntily on the back of his untidy brown curls. His waist was as slim as a girl's, something he must have been proud of as his baggy corduroy trousers were held up with a leather belt pulled as tight as it would go. A red hanky was tied carelessly around his neck, emphasising the devil-may-care expression on his handsome, sunburnt face.

'The nearest dry-cleaner's is Thompson's, that's along Gainsborough Road on the first corner,' she said. There was a peculiar feeling in the pit of her tummy as she watched him over the pressing machine. He was staring at her boldly, making no attempt to conceal the admiration in his dark eyes. She wanted to tear off her white turban and let him see she looked even prettier with her blonde hair loose.

'What's your name?' he asked.

Flo felt as flustered as if he'd asked to borrow a pound note. 'Flo Clancy,' she stammered.

'I'm Tommy O'Mara.'

'Are you now!' You'd think she was the only one there the way he kept his eyes locked on hers, and seemed unaware that the other five women had stopped work for a good look – Josie Driver was leering at him provocatively over the shirts she was supposed to be ironing.

'I suppose I'd better make me way round to Thompson's,' he said.

'I suppose you had.'

He winked. 'Tara, Flo.' With a swagger, he was gone.

'Tara,' Flo whispered. Her legs felt weak and her heart was thumping madly.

'Who was that?' Josie called eagerly. 'Jaysus, he could have me for sixpence!'

Before Flo could reply, Olive Knott shouted, 'His name's Tommy O'Mara. He lives in the next street to us, and before you young 'uns get too excited, you might like to know he's well and truly married.'

Flo's thumping heart sank to her boots. Married!

Mr Fritz came out of the office to ask what all the fuss was about.

'We've just had Franchot Tone, Clark Gable and Ronald Colman all rolled into one asking if we did dry-cleaning,' Olive said cuttingly.

'Why, Flo, you've gone all pink.' Mr Fritz beamed at her through his wire-rimmed spectacles. He was a plump, comfortable little man with a round face and lots of frizzy brown hair. He was wearing a brown coat overall, which meant he was about to go out in the van to deliver clean laundry and collect dirty items in return. Olive, who'd been there the longest and was vaguely considered next in command, would take over the office and answer the telephone.

'I didn't mean to,' Flo said stupidly.

'It must be nice to be young and impressionable.' He sighed gloomily, as if he already had one foot in the grave though he wasn't quite forty. For some reason, Mr Fritz was forever trying to make out he was dead miserable, when everyone knew he was the happiest man alive – and the nicest, kindest employer in the whole wide world. His surname was Austrian, a bit of a mouthful and difficult to spell, so everyone called him by his first name, Fritz, and referred to his equally plump little Irish wife, Stella, as Mrs Fritz, and their eight children – three girls and five boys – as the little Fritzes.

He departed, and the women returned to their work, happy in the knowledge that on Tuesdays he called at Sinclair's, the confectioner's, to collect the overalls and would bring them back a cream cake each.

Try as she might, Flo was unable to get Tommy O'Mara out of her mind. Twice before, she'd thought she was in love, the first time with Frank McGee, then Kevin Kelly – she'd actually let Kevin kiss her on the way home from the Rialto where they'd been to a St Patrick's Day dance – but the feelings she had for them paled to nothing when she thought about the man who'd looked at her so boldly. Was it possible she was properly in love with someone she'd exchanged scarcely more than half a dozen words with?

When they were having their tea that night Martha asked sharply, 'What's the matter with you?'

Flo emerged from the daydream in which an unmarried Tommy O'Mara had just proposed. 'Nowt!' she answered, just as sharply.

'I've asked three times if you want pudding. It's apple pie.'

'For goodness sake, Martha, leave the girl alone.' Mam was having one of her good days, which meant she resented Martha acting as if she owned the place. At other times she was too worn out and listless to open her mouth. More and more often, Flo found her in bed when she arrived home from work. Mam patted her youngest daughter's arm. 'She was in a lovely little world of her own, weren't you, luv? I could tell. Your eyes were sparkling as if you were thinking of something dead nice.'

'I was so.' Flo stuck out her tongue at Martha as she disappeared into the back kitchen.

'Can I borrow your pink frock tonight, Flo?' Sally enquired. 'I'm going to the Grand with Brian Maloney.'

'Isn't he a Protestant?' Martha shouted from the kitchen.

'I've no idea,' Sally yelled back.

Martha appeared, grim-faced, in the doorway. 'I'd sooner you didn't go out with Protestants, Sal.'

'It's none of your bloody business,' Flo said indignantly.

Mam shook her head. 'Don't swear, luv.'

Sally wriggled uncomfortably in the chair. 'We're only going to the pictures.'

'You can never tell how things develop with a feller. It's best not to get involved with a Protestant from the start.'

48

'I'll tell him I won't see him again after tonight.'

'In that case, you won't need our Flo's best frock. Go in something old. He might get ideas if you arrive all dolled up.'

Flo felt cross with both her sisters, one for being so bossy and the other for allowing herself to be bossed.

'What are you doing with yourself tonight, luv?' Mam asked.

'I thought I'd stay in and read a book — but I'll play cards with you if you like.' When Dad was alive, the two of them used to play cards for hours.

'No, ta, luv. I feel a bit tired. I might go to bed after I've had a cup of tea. I'll not bother with the apple pie, Martha.'

'I wish you'd go to the doctor's, Mam,' Flo said worriedly. Kate Clancy had never been a strong woman, and since the sudden, violent death of her beloved husband, she seemed to have lost the will to live, becoming thinner and more frail by the day.

'So do I.' Martha stroked Mam's hair, which had changed from ash-blonde to genuine silver almost overnight.

'Me, too,' echoed Sally.

But Mam screwed her thin face into the stubborn expression they'd seen many times before. 'Now, don't you girls start on that again,' she said tightly. 'I've told you, I'm not seeing a doctor. He might find something wrong with me, and there's no way I'm letting them cut me open. I'm just run down, that's all. I'll feel better when the warm weather comes.'

'Are you taking the bile beans I bought?' Martha demanded.

'They're beside me bed and I take them every morning.'

The girls glanced at each other with concern. If Mam died so soon after Dad, they didn't think they could bear it.

Mam went to bed and Sally got ready to meet Brian

Maloney. Martha made her remove her earrings before she left, as if sixpenny pearl earrings from Woolworths would drive a man so wild with desire that he'd propose on the spot and Sally would feel obliged to accept!

It was Flo's turn to wash and dry the dishes. She cleared the table, shook the white cloth in the yard, straightened the green chenille cloth underneath and folded one leaf of the table down, before putting the white cloth on again for when their lodger came home. A meal fit for a giant was in the oven keeping warm. Flo set his place: knife, fork and spoon, condiments to the right, mustard to the left. As soon as she'd finished, she sank into the armchair with the novel she was halfway through, *Shattered Love, Shattered Dreams*.

Martha came in and adjusted everything on the table as if it had been crooked. 'You've always got your head buried in a book, Flo Clancy,' she remarked.

'You moan when I go out and you moan when I stay in.' Flo made a face at her sister. 'What do you expect me to do all night? Sit and twiddle me thumbs?'

'I wasn't moaning, I was merely stating a fact.' Martha gave the table a critical glance. 'Will you look after Albert when he comes?'

'Of course.' There was nothing to be done except move the plate from the oven to the table, which Albert could no doubt manage alone if no help was available.

'I'd stay meself, but I promised to go and see Elsa Cameron. That baby's getting her down something awful. I'm sure she smacks him, yet the little lad's not even twelve months old.'

'Norman? He's a lovely baby. I wouldn't mind having him meself.'

'Nor I.' Martha shoved a hatpin into a little veiled cocked hat, then sighed as she adjusted her glasses in the mirror. She was smartly dressed, although she was only going around the corner, in a long grey skirt with a cardigan to match. The whole outfit had cost ten bob in Paddy's Market. 'Trouble is, Flo, I'm beginning to think

Elsa's not quite right in the head. She's been acting dead peculiar since Norman arrived. The other day when I turned up she was undoing her knitting, but when I asked why, she'd no idea. She mightn't be so bad if Eugene was there, but him being in the Merchant Navy, like, it means he's hardly ever home.'

'It's a terrible shame,' Flo said sincerely. Norman Cameron was Martha's godson and the most delightful baby she'd ever known. It was terrible to think he was getting his mam down. 'Can't Eugene get a different job?'

'Not with a million men already out of work,' Martha said. 'Mind you, that'll soon change if there's a war.'

'There won't be a war,' Flo said quickly. She looked at her sister, scared. 'Will there?'

'Oh, I don't know, luv. According to the papers, that Hitler's getting far too big for his boots.'

Like Mam dying, war was something best not thought about. After Martha left, Flo tried to bury herself in her book, but the man over whom the heroine was pining was a pale, insipid creature compared to Tommy O'Mara, and instead of words, she kept seeing *him* on the page: his dark, shameless eyes, his reckless face, the cheeky way he wore his cap. She reckoned it was a good job she wouldn't be seeing him again. If he'd been as knocked sideways by her as she'd been by him, he might ask her out, and although a good Catholic girl should never, never go out with a married man, Flo wasn't convinced she'd be capable of resisting Tommy O'Mara.

She *did* see him again, only two days later. He came into the laundry, this time bearing two white shirts that already looked perfectly clean. She looked up from the press and found him smiling at her intently as if she was the only woman in the world, never mind the laundry.

'I'd like these laundered, please.'

Flo had to swallow several times before she could answer. 'You need to take them round the front and Mr

Fritz will give you a ticket,' she said, in a voice that sounded as if it belonged to someone else.

He frowned. 'Does that mean I won't see you when I collect them?'

'I'm afraid not,' she said, still in someone else's voice.

He flung the shirts over his shoulder, stuck his thumbs in his belt and rocked back on his heels. 'In that case, I'll not beat about the bush. Would you like to come for a walk with me one night, Flo? We can have a bevy on the way – you're old enough to go in boozers, aren't you?'

'I'll be nineteen in May,' Flo said faintly. 'Though I've never been in a booz – a pub before.'

'Well, there's a first time for everything.' He winked. 'See you tomorrer night then, eight o'clock outside the Mystery gates, the Smithdown Road end.'

'Rightio.' She watched him leave, knowing that she'd done something terribly wrong. She felt very adult and worldly wise, as if she was much older than Sally and Martha. Tomorrow night she was going out with a married man and the thing was *she didn't care!*

'What did he want?' Olive Knott brought her down to earth with a sharp nudge in the ribs.

'He brought his shirts to the wrong place. I sent him round the front.'

Olive's brow creased worriedly. 'He didn't ask you out, did he?'

For the first time in her life Flo lied. 'No.'

'He's got his eye on you, that's plain to see. Oh, he has a way with him, there's no denying it, but it's best for nice girls like you to stay clear of men like Tommy O'Mara, Flo.'

But Flo was lost. She would have gone out with Tommy O'Mara if Olive had declared him to be the divil himself.

Friday was another dull day and there was drizzle on and off until early evening when a late sun appeared. It looked as soft as a jelly in the dusky blue sky, and its gentle rays filled the air with gold dust.

Flo felt very odd as she made her way to the Mystery. Every step that took her nearer seemed of momentous significance, as if she was walking towards her destiny, and that after tonight nothing would ever be the same again. She thought of the lie she'd told at home – that she was calling on Josie Driver who'd been off sick and Mr Fritz wanted to know how she was, which had been all she could think of when Martha demanded to know where she was going.

When she arrived Tommy was already there. He was standing outside the gates, whistling, wearing a dark blue suit that looked a bit too big, a white and blue striped shirt with a high stiff collar, and a grey tie. A slightly more respectable tweed cap was set at the same jaunty angle on the back of his curly head. The mere sight of the swaggering, audacious figure made Flo feel quite faint.

'There you are!' He smiled. 'You're late. I was worried you might have changed your mind.'

The thought had never entered her head. She smiled nervously and said, 'Hello.'

'You look nice,' he said appreciatively. 'Green suits you. It sets off your eyes. That was the first thing I noticed when I came into the laundry, those green eyes. I bet you have stacks of fellers chasing after you.'

'Not exactly,' Flo mumbled.

'In that case, the fellers round here must be mad!' When he linked her arm Flo could smell a mixture of strong tobacco and carbolic soap. She got the peculiar feeling in her tummy again as they began to stroll through the park, though the Mystery was more like a playing-field: a vast expanse of grass surrounded by trees. The Liverpool-to-London railway line ran along one side. The trees were bursting into life, ready for summer, and pale sunlight filtered through the branches, making dappled patterns on the green grass underneath.

Without any prompting, Tommy briefly told her the story of his life. He'd been born in Ireland, in the county of Limerick, and had come to Liverpool ten years ago when he was twenty. 'I've got fourteen brothers and sisters, half of 'em still at home. I send me mam a few bob when I've got it to spare.'

Flo said she thought that very generous. She asked where he worked.

'I'm a fitter at Cammell Laird's in Birkenhead,' he said boastfully. 'You should see this ship we're building at the moment. It's a T-class submarine, the *Thetis*. Guess how much it's costing?'

She confessed she had absolutely no idea.

'Three hundred thousand smackeroos!'

'Three hundred thousand!' Flo gasped. 'Is it made of gold or something?'

He laughed and squeezed her arm. 'No, but it's the very latest design. You should see the instruments in the conning tower! *And* it's got ten torpedo tubes. I don't envy any German ships that come near the *Thetis* if there's a war.'

'There won't be a war,' Flo said stubbornly.

'That's what women always say.' He chuckled.

She realised he'd omitted to tell her about one important aspect of his life – his wife. There was silence for a while, except for his whistling, as they strolled across the grass and the April sun began to disappear behind the trees.

Perhaps Tommy had read her thoughts, because he said suddenly, 'I should have told you this before, Flo. I'm married.'

'I know,' Flo said.

He raised his finely drawn eyebrows in surprise. 'Who told you?'

'A woman at work, Olive Knott. She lives in the next street to you.'

'Does she now.' He made a face. 'I'm surprised you came, knowing, like.'

54

Flo wasn't in the least surprised: she'd have come even if she'd been told he had ten wives.

They'd arrived at the other side of the Mystery and emerged into Gainsborough Road. Tommy steered her inside the first pub they came to. 'What would you like to drink?' he asked.

'I've no idea.' The only alcohol that ever crossed Flo's lips was a small glass of sherry at Christmas.

'I'll get you a port and lemon. That's what women usually like.'

The pub was crowded. Flo glanced 'round when Tommy went to be served, worried someone might recognise her, but there were no familiar faces. She noticed that quite a few women were eyeing Tommy up and down as he waited at the bar, legs crossed nonchalantly at the ankles. Without doubt he was the best-looking man there – and he was with *her!* Flo gasped at the sheer magic of it all, just as Tommy turned round and winked.

Her eyes flickered as she tried to wink back, but couldn't quite manage it. Tommy laughed at her efforts as he came over with the drinks. 'You know,' he whispered, 'you're the most beautiful girl here, Flo Clancy, perhaps the most beautiful in the whole of Liverpool. There's something special between us, isn't there? I recognised it the minute I set eyes on you. It's something that doesn't happen often between a man and a woman, but it's happened between you and me.'

Flo felt as if she wanted to cry. She also wanted to say something meaningful, but all she could think of was, 'I suppose it has.'

Tommy swallowed half his beer in one go, then returned the pint glass to the table with a thump. He took a tin of tobacco from his pocket and deftly rolled a ciggie out of the thick dark shreds that smelt of tar. He shoved the tin in Flo's direction, but she shook her head. 'It's time I explained about Nancy,' he said grandly.

'Nancy?'

'Me wife. It's not a genuine marriage, Flo, not in any respects.' He looked at her knowingly. 'I met Nancy in Spain when I was fighting in the Civil War. She's a gypsy. I won't deny I fell for her hook, line and sinker. I would have married her proper, given the opportunity, but 'stead, I did it Nancy's way.' The way he told it it sounded like the most romantic novel ever written. He and Nancy had 'plighted their troth', as he put it, at a gypsy ceremony in a wood near Barcelona. 'It means nowt in the eyes of British law or the Roman Catholic Church,' he said contemptuously. He'd been meaning to leave for a long time, and as soon as Nancy got better he'd be off like a shot. 'Then I'll be free to marry an English girl, proper, like, this time.' He clasped Flo's hand and gazed deep into her eyes. 'And you know who that'll be, don't you?'

Flo felt the blood run hot through her body. She gulped. 'What's wrong with Nancy?'

Tommy sighed. 'It's a bit embarrassing to explain, luv. It's what's called a woman's complaint. She's been to Smithdown Road ozzie and the doctors said it'll all be cleared up in about six months. I don't like to leave till she gets better,' he added virtuously.

The guilt that had been lurking in a little corner of Flo's mind about going out with a married man disappeared, along with the suspicion that he'd only told her about Nancy in case someone else did. Why, he was almost single! It seemed wise, though, not to mention him and his peculiar circumstances to her family. Martha, in particular, would never understand. She'd say nothing until they got engaged.

'I trust you'll keep what I've just said under your hat for now, luv,' Tommy said conspiratorially. 'I don't want people knowing me private business, like, till the time comes to tell them.'

'I won't breathe a word,' Flo assured him. 'I'd already decided to keep you a secret.'

'A secret! I like the idea of being the secret man in Flo

Clancy's life.' His brown eyes sparkled. 'How about another drink before we go?'

'No, ta.' The port and lemon had already gone to her head.

'I'll just have another quick pint, then we'll be off.'

It was dark when they went outside. The sky glowed hazy orange where the sun had set, but was otherwise dark blue, almost black. They wandered hand in hand through the Mystery, the noise of the traffic behind growing fainter, until nothing could be heard except their feet on the grass, the slight rustle of the trees, and Tommy's musical whistle.

'What's that tune?' Flo enquired. 'I can't quite place it.'

'"Dancing in the Dark." Have you never heard it before?'

'I couldn't remember what it was called.'

He began to sing. '"Dancing in the dark . . ." C'mon, Flo.' He grabbed her by the waist and twirled her around. Flo threw back her head and laughed. '"Dancing in the dark,"' they sang together.

They stopped when two men walked past and Flo shivered. 'I forgot to bring a cardy.'

Tommy put his arm around her shoulders. 'You don't feel cold.' He placed his hand on the back of her neck. 'You feel hot. Your neck's sweating.'

She wasn't sure if she was hot or cold. Her body felt as if it was on fire, yet she shivered again. Tommy's hand pressed harder on her neck as he began to lead her towards a tree not far away. He pushed her against the broad trunk and took her in his arms. 'I've been thinking of nothing else but this for days.'

A train roared past on the furthest side of the park, the engine puffing eerie clouds of smoke. Flo thought about Dad, who'd been knocked down on that very same railway line, but not for long: Tommy's lips were pressed against hers and she felt as if she was being sucked into a whirlpool. Her head spun and she seemed to be slipping down and down and down. She came to briefly and found herself lying on the damp grass with Tommy bent over her. He'd undone the front of her dress and his lips were seeking her breasts, his tongue tenderly touching her nipples. Flo arched her back and almost screamed because the sensation was so wonderful. She knew what was to come, she knew it was a bad thing, but she could no more have stopped him than she could have stopped the sun from rising the next morning.

Tommy was pushing up her skirt, pulling away her underthings. There was the sound of her stockings tearing and she felt his callused hand between her legs. He was groaning, murmuring over and over, 'I love you, Flo,' and she could hear other little breathless cries that she realised came from her own throat. All the while, she was running her fingers through his thick dark curls, kissing his ears, his neck . . .

He felt so *big* when he entered her, and it hurt, but the hurt soon faded and turned into something else, something that no words had been invented to describe.

It all ended in a wild, feverish explosion that left them shaken and exhausted, and with Flo convinced that the only reason she'd been born was to make love with Tommy O'Mara.

'Jaysus, Flo!' he said hoarsely. 'That was the best I've ever known.' After a while, he began to pull her clothes back on. 'Get dressed, luv, else you'll catch cold.'

Flo touched his sensually curved lips with her finger, feeling the love flow from her heart right down her arm. 'I love you, Tommy.'

'I love you, girl.'

There was the faint murmur of voices upstairs: Martha and Sally were awake. Flo leaped out of the chair to take them up a cup of tea. On the way to the back kitchen, she did a pirouette. She'd always been happy, but nowadays she was so happy she could bust – and it had all begun that night in the Mystery when she'd danced in the dark with Tommy.

She and Sally had a wonderful day in New Brighton. They went on every single ride in the fairground, even the children's ones. Sally complained afterwards she felt quite sick, though it was more likely caused by the fish and chips followed by a giant ice-cream cornet with strawberry topping. She recovered swiftly on the ferry back when they clicked with two sailors who invited them to the pictures. 'Why did you turn them down?' she grumbled, on the tram home to Wavertree.

'I didn't fancy that Peter,' Flo replied. In fact, both sailors had been quite nice, but she was meeting Tommy at eight o'clock. Even if she wasn't, she would have felt disloyal going out with another man.

'I quite fancied Jock.' Her sister sighed. Sally was neither plain nor pretty, a bit like Dad with her neat brown hair and hazel eyes. She hadn't had a date since the one with Brian Maloney, almost two months ago.

Flo felt bad about the sailors. If it hadn't been for Tommy she'd have gone like a shot. 'You gave Jock your address, Sal. He might write,' she said hopefully.

'And where are you off to?' Martha demanded that night when Flo came downstairs ready to go out.

'I'm going to see Josie.' Unknown to Josie Driver, she and Flo had become the greatest of friends since Tommy had appeared on the scene. She met Josie twice a week, Mondays and Fridays. Josie would have been surprised to learn she was thinking of becoming a nun and needed someone in whom she could confide her deepest, most intimate thoughts while coming to such a major decision.

Martha's eyes looked suspicious behind her thick glasses. 'Why do you need a red bow in your hair just to see Josie?'

'I bought the ribbon in New Brighton,' Flo replied haughtily.

59

'It looks very nice,' Albert Colquitt said, from the table where he was having his tea.

'I think so, too,' Mam concurred.

Martha gave up. 'Don't be too late.'

'Have a nice time,' Flo called, as she slammed the door. Albert had just bought a wireless and everyone was staying in to listen to a play, Mam armed with two bottles of Guinness to 'build her up', although she'd been feeling better since the weather had improved. Flo shuddered to think of her sisters sitting in the parlour on Albert's bed-settee. What a way for two young women to spend a bank-holiday evening!

'I like your bow,' said Tommy.

'I like your tie,' Flo sang.

'I like your face, your eyes, your lips. I like every single little thing about you!' He picked her up and spun her around until they both felt dizzy and fell, laughing, on to the grass, whereupon he began to kiss her passionately.

'It's still broad daylight,' Flo murmured.

'So it is.' He kissed her again and caressed her breasts.

'We might get arrested and it'd be in the *Echo*.'

'Would that matter?'

'Not to me it wouldn't,' Flo giggled, 'but me mam wouldn't be pleased and our Martha'd have a fit. Nancy wouldn't like it either.'

'Nancy would just have to lump it.' Nevertheless, he sat up and smoothed his unruly curls.

Flo had never told him she'd seen Nancy. One day when she knew he was at work she'd set out for Clement Street, off Smithdown Road. It was a respectable street of small two-up, two-down houses. The windows shone, the steps had been scrubbed that morning. Flo paused across the road opposite number eighteen.

So this was where he lived. Nancy must take pride in her house. The curtains were maroon cretonne, upstairs and down, and there were paper flowers in the parlour window. The front door and the window-sills were dark green, freshly painted. Flo's heart missed a beat – had *he* painted them? She'd never ask because she didn't want him to know she'd spied on his house.

She walked up and down the street several times, keeping a close eye on number eighteen in case Nancy came out to clean the windows or brush the step. After about half an hour, when she was about to give up, a woman carrying a shopping basket came towards her from the direction of Smithdown Road. Flo knew it was Nancy because she looked exactly like the gypsy Tommy had said she was. She was outstanding in her way, the sort of woman that would be described as handsome. Her skin was the colour of cinnamon, her eyes as black as night, and she had a big beaked nose and glossy black hair drawn back in a cushiony bun at the nape of her thin neck.

'Mercy me!' Flo muttered. She wasn't sure why, but something about the woman disturbed her. And what peculiar clothes she wore to go shopping! A flowing black skirt, red satin blouse and a brightly embroidered garment that wasn't quite a jacket and wasn't quite a shawl.

The two women passed. Flo had no idea if Nancy glanced in her direction because she kept her own eyes fixed firmly on the ground. After a few seconds, she turned and saw the colourful figure cross the road and go into number eighteen.

In the Mystery, Tommy got to his feet and reached down to pull her up. 'We'll come back later when it's dark. And then . . .' His dark eyes smouldered and Flo's tummy did a cartwheel.

'And then . . .' she whispered. Then they would come as close to heaven as it was possible to get on earth.

She told him about the sailors because she wanted to make him jealous and he duly was. 'You belong to me, Flo Clancy,' he said angrily. 'We belong to each other till the end of time.'

'I know, I know!' she cried. 'I wouldn't dream of going out with another man when I've got you.'

He looked sulky. 'I should hope not!'

In the pub, he informed her that the submarine he'd been working on, the *Thetis*, was taking its first diving exercise on Thursday. 'Some of the shipyard workers are sailing with it, but my name wasn't on the list. You get extra pay, at least ten bob.' He looked wistful. 'I would have gone for nothing.'

'Never mind.' Flo was keeping a close eye on the sky outside. She wasn't bothered about the *Thetis*. All her concentration was centred on how swiftly night would fall so they could go to the Mystery and make love.

2

The Fritz family had been to Anglesey for Whit, a regular haunt, and Mr Fritz didn't return to the laundry till Thursday when the children were due back at school. He'd bought a camera, there was one exposure left on the roll, and he wanted a snapshot taken of him with his girls. Later that morning, Mrs Fritz came bustling along to take it. It was the first of June and a perfect day for taking photographs. The weather had been brilliantly sunny all week.

The six women trooped outside, excited. 'You stand by me, Flo,' Mr Fritz hissed. 'It's an excuse to put my arm around you. I want a record of that smile. It's always been enough to dazzle the strongest eyes, but lately it's not just a smile, it's a miracle.'

Mrs Fritz stationed her plump body in the middle of the street. 'Try and get the sign in over the door, Stella,' her husband shouted, as everyone shuffled into position.

'Say cheese!' Mrs Fritz called.

'*Cheese!*'

There was a click. 'All done!'

'If it turns out all right, I'll order a copy each.' Mr Fritz squeezed Flo's waist and whispered, 'I enjoyed that.'

Flo knew he was only joking, because he adored his

sweet little wife and eight children, but she hoped no one had noticed – Josie was always complaining that Flo was Mr Fritz's favourite.

The rest of the day passed in a dream, as the days did since she'd met Tommy. She lived for Monday, lived for Friday, then lived for Monday again. They would have met more often, but he didn't like to leave Nancy while she felt so poorly.

Six o'clock came and she made her way home, still immersed in her dream, and scarcely noticed the crowd that had gathered on the corner of the street next to hers until she reached it.

'What's up?' she asked.

A woman grabbed her arm. 'There's been a terrible accident, girl. Haven't you heard?'

'What sort of accident?'

'It's some ship, a submarine called the *Thetis* – it's trapped underwater in Liverpool Bay and they can't find its position. There's over a hundred men on board.'

'Holy Mary, Mother of God!' Flo crossed herself. At first she felt relieved that Tommy hadn't been on board, but concern followed quickly for the men who were. She could think of nothing more horrific than to be trapped beneath the sea in a vessel she imagined being shaped like a big black fish. 'They'll be rescued, won't they?' she said anxiously.

An elderly man butted in. 'Of course they will, luv. I'm an ould salt meself, so I know Liverpool Bay's no more than twenty-five fathoms deep. They'll have them men up in no time.'

When she got home Mam and her sisters had already heard the bad news. Martha was wondering if they dared invade Albert's room and turn on the wireless.

'It's not been declared official yet,' Mam said. 'So far it's just rumour.'

'You mean it might not have happened?' Sally looked hopeful.

'Oh, it's happened all right.' Mam shook her head

sadly. 'Mrs Cox's nephew works in Cammell Laird where everyone knows full well there's been an accident. Women have already started to collect outside to wait for news of their men. It's just that nothing's been confirmed, so the news won't have reached the wireless.'

It wasn't until ten o'clock that the plight of the *Thetis* was conveyed to the nation by the BBC. One hundred and three men were on board, fifty of them civilians. The Admiralty assured everyone concerned that rescue ships were on their way and there was every hope the men would be saved.

'I should think so!' Flo said indignantly. 'It's only twenty-five fathoms deep.'

'How much is that in feet?' Martha asked Albert, as if men automatically knew everything. Albert confessed he had no idea.

There was a search for Dad's dictionary, which had conversion tables at the back. Twenty-five fathoms was 150 feet.

In bed that night, Flo was unable to get the trapped men out of her mind. She tossed and turned restlessly.

'Are you awake, Flo?' Sally whispered.

'Yes. I can't stop thinking of those men in the *Thetis*.'

'Me neither.'

Martha's voice surprised them because she usually slept like a log, despite the metal curlers. 'Let's say a silent prayer. Remember that one we learned at school for shipwrecked mariners?'

Eventually the sisters fell asleep, the words of the prayer on their lips.

When they woke next morning the *Thetis* came straight to mind. The weather was lovely, gloriously sunny, and it seemed incongruous and unfair that those safe on land should be blessed with such a perfect day in view of the disaster unfolding beneath the sea.

Albert had given them permission to listen to his wireless, from which they learned there'd been no developments overnight. Ships and aircraft were still trying to pinpoint the position of the stricken submarine.

On her way to work, Flo passed several groups of people gravely discussing the tragedy, which had touched the hearts of everyone in Liverpool. Twice she was asked, 'Have you heard any fresh news, luv?' All she could do was shake her head.

She bought a *Daily Herald*. Everyone in the laundry had bought a paper and the *Thetis* was the main headline on them all, as well as the sole topic of conversation all morning. Betty Bryant knew a woman who knew a woman whose cousin's husband was on board.

'I know someone on board even better than that,' Olive Knott said smugly. 'In fact, we all do. Remember that feller who brought his suit in for dry-cleaning a couple of months ago, Tommy O'Mara? He's a fitter with Cammell Laird. His poor ould wife wasn't half making a scene last night! Running up and down the street she was, screaming her head off. It took half a dozen neighbours to calm her. Mind you, Nancy O'Mara's always had a couple of screws loose.'

'But he wasn't supposed to go!' Flo's horrified words were lost in the chorus of dismay.

'Such a dead handsome feller, what a shame!'

'He was a cheeky-looking bugger, but I liked him.' Josie Driver looked close to tears.

Olive made a sour face. 'I don't wish him any harm, but Nancy'll be better off without the bugger. He drove the poor woman doo-lally with his philandering. No woman, married or single, was safe near Tommy O'Mara.'

That's not true! Flo wanted to scream that Olive was talking nonsense. Tommy may have been a bit of a blade in the past – in fact, he'd hinted so more than once – but it was only because Nancy hadn't been a proper wife in a long time. Since he'd met Flo, he wouldn't have given another woman a second glance. Oh, if only she could tell them! But why on earth was she thinking like this

65

when it didn't matter a jot what Olive thought? What mattered was that Tommy might die! If he did, Flo wanted to die, too.

In her agitation she nearly scorched a shirt. Then Betty made things worse by reading out something from the newspaper. There was only enough oxygen on board to last thirty-six hours. Once the supply dried up, the men would die from carbon-dioxide poisoning. 'It means there's not much time left.' Betty clasped her hands together as if she were praying. 'Holy Mary, Mother of God, please save those poor men!'

Then Mr Fritz came hurrying in, panting for breath. 'The *Thetis* has been spotted with its stern sticking out of the water fourteen miles from Great Ormes Head. It was on the wireless just before I left.'

'Thank the Lord!' Josie shouted. 'They're bound to save them now.'

Relief swept through Flo's body so forcefully that, for a moment, she felt sick. She swayed, and Mr Fritz snatched the gas iron from her hand. 'Are you all right, Flo?'

'I hardly slept last night. I feel a bit ragged, that's all.'

'You go home, girl, if you don't feel better soon,' he said concernedly. 'I don't want you on your feet all day if you've got problems.'

'Problems' meant he thought she had a period. Standing for ten hours in the equivalent of a steambath was hard on women who had trouble with their monthlies, and Mr Fritz was always sympathetic if someone needed a day off. Flo, however, had always sailed through hers without so much as a twinge. Apart from a week's holiday each year, she hadn't had a single day off since she'd started five years ago straight from school.

'I'll see how I feel,' she told him gratefully.

The feeling of sickness soon left her, but for the first time the noise in the laundry began to get on her nerves: the churning of the washing in the boilers, the clatter of the belt-driven wringers, the hiss of the irons. Flo knew she couldn't work all day with the sounds pressing against her brain while she remained ignorant of the fate of the *Thetis*.

At midday, she went into the office and told Mr Fritz she felt no better. 'I wouldn't mind going home, after all.' She felt slightly ashamed of how good she'd become at lying over the last two months.

He fussed around, patted her cheek, and said she didn't look anything like her usual glowing self. He even offered to take her to Burnett Street in the van.

'No, ta,' she said. 'I might walk around a bit to clear me head. I'll go to bed this avvy.'

'Good idea, Flo, I hope you feel better tomorrow.'

Several hundred men and women had congregated in front of the gates of Cammell Laird. Some of the women held babies in their arms with slightly older children clutching their skirts. Some faces were hopeful, others blank with despair. A woman she couldn't see was shouting for her man. Flo's heart sank. It would seem there hadn't been more good news.

A girl with a glorious head of red hair, about the same age as herself, was standing at the back. 'What's happening?' Flo asked.

'Four men got out through the escape hatches, otherwise nowt.' The girl's face was extraordinarily colourful: pink lips, rosy cheeks, black-lashed eyes the colour of violets, all framed in the cloud of red waves.

'But someone at work said the stern was sticking out the water,' Flo groaned. 'I'd have thought they'd have hauled it up by now.'

The girl shrugged. 'I'd have thought so, too, but they haven't.' She looked at Flo sympathetically. 'Have you got someone on board?'

Flo bit her lip. 'Me feller.'

'Aye, so's mine. Well, he's only a sort of feller.' She didn't look the least bit upset. 'I only came out of curiosity. I'm always looking for an excuse to get off

67

work. I suppose it's about time I went – I called in and said I had to see the doctor.'

'I told a lie to get away meself,' Flo confessed.

The girl made a face as if implying they were partners in a crime. 'Are you from Liverpool or Birkenhead?' She spoke in a loud, musical voice that rose and fell as if she was singing.

'Liverpool. I came on the ferry.'

'Me, too. I'll catch the next one back. Are you coming?'

'I only just got here. I'd sooner stay and see if anything happens.' Flo wished the girl didn't have to go. She rather liked her friendly, down-to-earth manner.

'I might go to the pics tonight. It'll be all about the *Thetis* on the Pathé News. Tara, then.' She clattered away on her high heels.

'Tara.' Flo sighed. If the submarine hadn't been brought up by tonight, it would be cutting things fine for those on board.

She turned her attention to the crowd. 'What I'd like to know,' a man muttered aggressively, 'is why they don't bore a hole through the hull and get everyone out that way, or at least pass in a hose of oxygen.'

Somewhere a woman was still shouting: 'What have you done with my man?' Flo edged her way through the throng.

'There's no need for that carry-on,' an elderly woman remarked acidly. 'Most of us are feared for our lads, but we're not reduced to weeping and wailing like a bloody banshee. Just look at the way she's throwing herself about an' all!'

Flo didn't answer. She had almost reached the front when she froze. Nancy O'Mara was kneeling on the ground, her hands clasped imploringly towards the closed gates of the ship-builder's. Her crow-black eyes burned unnaturally bright, as if with fever. Long strands of hair had escaped from the big bun coiled on her neck, and writhed like little snakes as she rocked to and fro. She looked almost insane with grief. Every now and then she turned her tragic face towards the men and women standing silently each side of her. 'Why?' she pleaded. 'Why, oh, why?'

Nobody answered, the faces remained impassive. They had no idea why. At that moment, there wasn't a person on earth who knew why ninety-nine human beings still remained on the stricken vessel when it was surrounded by rescue ships and the stern was visible for all to see.

Flo stood stock-still as she watched Tommy's wife throw herself back and forth on the pavement. Nancy paused to seek succour from those around her yet again. 'Why?' Then she caught sight of Flo, who stood trans-fixed as the burning eyes bored into hers, so full of hate that she felt her blood turn to ice.

Nancy knew!

With a cry that almost choked her, Flo turned and pushed her way through the crowd. She ran, faster than she'd ever run before, past the docks, the half-built ships, the vessels waiting to be loaded or unloaded. She ran until she reached the ferry, where a seaman was just about to raise the gangplank, and launched herself on to the deck. 'Just made it, luv.' He grinned.

Flo hardly heard. She climbed the stairs until she reached the top deck where she leaned on the hand-rail and stared into the calm greeny-brown waters of the Mersey. A warm breeze fanned her face, and her mind was blank, devoid of emotion or thought.

'Hello, there,' said a familiar voice. 'I thought you were going to stay and see what happened?'

'I decided not to.' Flo turned. The red-haired girl was the only person she didn't mind seeing at the moment. 'I felt too upset.'

'You shouldn't get upset over a feller.' The girl leaned on the rail beside her. She wore a smart emerald-green frock that accentuated her vividly coloured face. At any other time Flo would have felt ashamed of the shabby blouse and skirt she wore for work. 'There's plenty more where he came from. Someone with your looks will soon get fixed up again.'

'I don't want to get fixed up again,' Flo whispered. 'I'll never go out with anyone else. Never!'

'Don't tell me you're in love?' The girl sounded faintly disgusted.

Flo nodded numbly. For the first time since she'd heard the news about Tommy, she began to cry. The tears flowed freely down her cheeks and fell silently on to the smooth waters below.

'Come on, girl.' Flo felt her shoulders being painfully squeezed. 'What's your name?'

'Flo Clancy.'

'I'm Isobel MacIntyre, but everyone calls me Bel.' She gave Flo a little shake. 'Look, the ferry's about to dock. Shall we find somewhere and have a cup of tea?'

'I'd love to, but what about your job?'

'Sod me job! I'll tell them the doctor said I was run down and I needed a day off to put me feet up. Anyroad, it says almost half past two on the Liver building clock, so it's not worth going in.'

Flo couldn't help but smile through her tears. 'You're the healthiest-looking person I've ever seen.'

There was a café a short way along Water Street, almost empty after the dinner-time rush. They were about to enter, when Flo remembered she had only enough money for her tram fare home.

'Don't worry,' Bel said, when she told her. 'I'm flush so it can be my treat.'

As they drank their tea and Flo nibbled at a sticky bun, Bel informed her that she worked as a waitress at La Porte Rouge, a restaurant in Bold Street. 'That's French for the Red Door. It's dead posh and I get good tips, particularly off the fellers. Last week, I got fifteen bob altogether.'

'Just in tips! Gosh, I don't get much more than that in wages.'

Bel asked where she worked and where she lived and all about her family. Flo could tell she was trying to keep

70

her mind off the events taking place above and below the sea not too many miles away. She gladly told her all about Fritz's Laundry, about Mam and her sisters, and how they'd had to take in a lodger when Dad died. 'He's dead nice, Albert. The thing is, our Martha's determined to marry him. I can't think why, 'cos though he's nice, he's no oil painting, and he's forty-five. She wears glasses, though, and she thinks she'll never catch a feller. You should hear the way she bosses me and our Sal around, just 'cos she's the oldest,' Flo said indignantly.

'She couldn't be any worse than me auntie Mabel,' Bel said flatly. 'She's an ould cow if there ever was one.' She explained that her mam had died when she was only four and she'd been dumped on Auntie Mabel who lived in Everton Valley. 'Me dad's away at sea most of the time. I can't wait to get away meself. I'm eighteen, and the very second the war starts, I'm going to join the Army.'

'But the Army only take men!'

'Of course they don't, soft girl! They take women an' all. They're called the ATS, which stands for Auxiliary Territorial Service.'

Just then, two men came in, talking volubly, and sat at the next table. After they had given the waitress their order, they continued their conversation.

'It's bloody disgraceful!' one said angrily. 'If I had a son on board, I'd kick up a stink all the way to Parliament. Why was she allowed to dive with twice the normal complement on board? Why was the Navy so long finding her position? And I'll never understand why cutting gear hasn't been brought by now and a hole made in her stern. The men would be free if the powers-that-be had any sense of urgency.'

'If someone doesn't get their finger out pretty soon, it'll be too late,' the other man said.

'If it isn't already! That business about there being enough oxygen for thirty-six hours, I'd like to know if that takes account of the extra men as well as the crew.'

'Do you ever go dancing, Flo?' Bel asked brightly.

But Flo's mind had been distracted long enough. 'I wonder if anything's happened,' she whispered.

'Don't sound like it. But try not to lose heart, Flo. There's still hope.'

Flo gave a deep, shuddering sigh. It was strange, but she couldn't help thinking about Nancy.

'Your chap's married, isn't he?' Bel said knowingly.

'How did you guess?' Flo gasped.

'If he was a proper boyfriend, this Mr Fritz would have let you off like a shot. Instead, you had to tell a lie to get away.'

'So did you,' Flo pointed out. 'Your chap must be married, too.'

Bel made a face. 'It so happens he's not. Tuesday was only the second time I'd seen him. That's when he told me he was sailing with the *Thetis* because some other feller had been taken poorly. When I saw the headlines in this morning's papers, it seemed a good excuse for a ride on the ferry – I often go on me own. In fact, that's where I met my chap, on the Birkenhead ferry.' She pursed her red lips primly. 'I'm not the sort of girl who goes out with married men, thanks all the same. Mind you, Flo, you don't look the sort, either, particularly with you being a Catholic an' all, not like me.'

Flo felt it was important to explain the nature of her relationship with Tommy. 'My chap wasn't married proper. We were going to get married next year.' She paused, frowning. 'His wife – I mean, his sort-of-wife – was outside Cammell Laird's. You never heard such a carry-on.'

'Was she the one who was shouting?'

'That's right, Nancy. The thing is, I'm sure she recognised me.'

'Maybe she's been following you and your bloke around?'

Flo shuddered. 'Oh, don't! Tommy would have a fit at the very idea.'

'Who?'

'Tommy. Tommy O'Mara. What's your chap's name?'

Bel was scowling at the teapot as she poured more water in. Her cheeks were flaming. 'Er, Jack Smith,' she said shortly. Despite having refilled the pot, she leaped to her feet and paid the bill. Outside, she began to walk quickly, for no reason that a rather confused Flo could see, back towards the river.

They arrived at the Pier Head just as a ferry returning from New Brighton was docking. Children came running off the boat on to the landing-stage carrying buckets and spades, their hair full of sand, faces brown from the sun. Flo remembered going to New Brighton with Mam and Dad and her sisters. It seemed a hundred lifetimes ago. The area was unusually crowded for a weekday. People were staring out to sea, as if hoping to see signs of the attempts being made to rescue the ill-fated submarine. The girls wandered across to join them.

They stood for a long while in silence, until Flo said dully, 'I don't know what I'm going to do if Tommy's dead. I'll never love another man the way I loved him. If they don't fetch the *Thetis* up, me life's over.'

'I've never heard such nonsense!' Bel's expressive face conveyed a mixture of sympathy and impatience. 'No one's life's over when they're only nineteen. What about all the proper wives? Are their lives over, too? You're dead stupid you are, Flo Clancy, letting yourself get all worked up over a chap who's not worth twopence.'

The criticism was rather blunt and scathing coming from someone she'd only just met, but Flo was too upset to take offence. She began to cry again. 'How would you know what he's worth?' she sobbed. 'Tommy O'Mara's worth a million pounds to me.'

'I've never met a chap worth twopence meself,' Bel said brusquely. 'When I meet a threepenny one, I'll marry him like a shot. The trouble with you is you're dead soft. I'm as hard as nails, me. You'll never see me cry over a man, not even a threepenny one.' She seemed unable to grasp the extent of Flo's despair. 'C'mon, let's walk into town. It might take your mind off things, though we'd best steer clear of Bold Street case someone from work sees me.'

It wasn't until half past five that Flo and Bel parted. They exchanged addresses and promised to keep in touch. Flo wanted to arrive home as she usually did from work. She wouldn't tell anyone where she'd been that afternoon.

'Good heavens, Flo!' Mam remarked, when she went in. 'You're as white as a ghost and you're shivering. I hope you're not coming down with a cold. Summer colds are the worst to shake off.'

'Has anything happened?' Flo demanded abruptly.

Mam knew exactly what she meant. 'No, luv,' she said sadly. 'According to Mrs Cox, they managed to get a hawser to the hull, but it snapped and the ship sank underwater. I went to church today to say prayers with the Legion of Mary, but they don't seem to have done much good.'

Flo refused anything to eat. At Mam's insistence, she went to bed after a cup of tea. She felt uncomfortable when Martha came up later with a hot-water bottle and tucked her in. Martha wouldn't be so sympathetic if she knew the reason why her sister felt so out of sorts.

That night, she slept fitfully. Each time she woke, she was left with the memory of the same dream: she'd been wandering alone through the Mystery when an orchestra wearing full evening dress appeared before her, the sort she'd seen in films. But these were hollow, insubstantial figures – she could see right through them. They were playing 'Dancing in the Dark', and equally shadowy couples began to waltz in a circle around her. Instead of staring at each other, they gazed at Flo, unpleasant, gloating expressions on their faces. They were sneering because she was the only person without a partner. Her sense of isolation was so acute that she felt as if she was encased in a block of ice. Then the couples disappeared, the music stopped, and all that could be heard was the

74

rustle of the trees. Flo was alone with only the moon for company.

Next morning, Mam came up with a cup of tea. 'To save you asking, I just listened to the BBC and there's no news, I'm afraid.'

Flo sat up. To her amazement there was no sign of Martha and Sally, and their bed was neatly made.

'They've gone to work,' Mam explained. 'We decided not to wake you. It wouldn't hurt to have the day off, it being Saturday, like, and you'd only be there till one. I'm sure Mr Fritz won't mind – you've never been off before.'

Flo was only too willing to comply. After Mam had gone, she pulled the bedclothes over her head and sobbed her heart out. She wasn't sure what time it was when she heard a knock on the front door, followed by Mr Fritz's voice asking how she was. 'We're all worried about her. It's not like Flo to be sick.' She hoped he wouldn't say she'd been off yesterday. It seemed he didn't, because Mam came up shortly afterwards and didn't mention it.

'He's a lovely man,' she said warmly. 'I'm very fond of him. You're ever so lucky, Flo, working in such a nice place.'

By late afternoon everyone was home, including Albert. Flo got up, and after tea they all trooped into the parlour to listen to the six o'clock news. In a chilling voice the announcer read a statement: 'The Admiralty regrets that hope of saving lives in the *Thetis* must be abandoned.'

Liverpool, the entire country, was stunned. A cablegram arrived from King George VI in Canada. His mother, Queen Mary conveyed her sympathies to the grieving relatives, and Adolf Hitler sent condolences from the citizens of Germany. When this was announced in the cinema, the audience set up a chorus of boos. A fund was set up for relatives of the dead; within days it had reached thousands of pounds. The Clancy family clubbed together and managed to raise a pound between them. Albert Colquitt added another pound and promised to take it to the collection point in the town hall.

The following Tuesday was a day of mourning. Birkenhead Cenotaph was said to be a mass of wreaths. Fifteen thousand attended the service and five thousand workers marched in honour of the memory of those who had died.

While the country mourned and salvage work began on the *Thetis*, the press were asking questions. It was impossible to grasp that so many lives had been lost when only a few feet had separated the men from their rescuers. Why hadn't experienced divers been rushed to the scene? Where was the oxyacetyline gear? A tribunal was appointed to investigate.

It wasn't until November that the *Thetis* was salvaged and able to deliver her dead for proper burial. The ship was pronounced sound enough to return by sea to its place of birth in Birkenhead. At any other time, this would have been headline news, but by now the country was already in the grip of a tragedy that would result in far greater loss of life than on a single submarine. The unthinkable had happened: Great Britain was at war with Germany and immersed in the struggle to survive.

Flo Clancy drifted through the months after Tommy O'Mara died. Everyone wanted to know what had happened to her lovely smile. Mr Fritz gave her the lightest jobs, much to the chagrin of Josie Driver who turned quite nasty. Mam bought an iron tonic, which Flo took dutifully three times a day, though she knew it wouldn't do any good. Only Bel MacIntyre, whom she saw regularly, knew why Flo no longer smiled. But Bel knew only the half of it. Flo had more things than the loss of Tommy to worry about.

On the first Sunday in September, a day blessed with shimmering sunshine and an atmosphere as heady as wine, Flo sat in the parlour listening to Albert's wireless. She heard Neville Chamberlain, the Prime Minister, announce that the country was at war and wished it mattered as much to her as it did to the rest of her family. Sally had burst into tears. 'What's going to happen to Jock?' she wept.

Jock Wilson had been writing to Sally ever since Whit Monday when they'd met on the New Brighton ferry. He'd been back to Liverpool to see her whenever he could manage a few days' leave.

Albert turned off the wireless. He looked grim. Martha reached across and self-consciously took his hand. Poor Mam's face seemed to collapse before their eyes. 'Oh, I don't half wish your dad was here!' she cried.

But Flo was too concerned with her own luckless state to care. She'd scarcely noticed missing the first period, and it wasn't until July that she had become alarmed. By the time July had given way to August and there was still no sign, she realised, with increasing horror, that she was pregnant with Tommy O'Mara's child.

Millie

I

Sharp fingers of light strobed the dark ceiling of the nightclub, interlocking briefly; blue, red, green, then yellow, followed by blue again. The disc jockey's overwrought, grating voice announced a change of record, though his words could scarcely be heard above the music booming from the huge speakers on either side of him.

In the centre of the large room, which was mainly painted black, the dancers gyrated, faces blank. Only their bodies reacted to the pounding rhythm of Joey Negro's 'Can't Take it With You', the sound bouncing off the ceiling and the walls.

I could feel the noise vibrating through the plastic seat and the soles of my shoes. It throbbed through the table and up my arms. Although I hadn't danced so far, the heat felt tremendous and my neck was damp with perspiration.

Beside me, James didn't look bored exactly, but definitely fed up. He'd been like that since we met earlier, which wasn't a bit like him. I felt put out. After a stressful week, I'd been looking forward to Saturday and his relaxing company. The friends we'd come with, Julie and Gavin, had got up to dance about half an hour ago, though I could see no sign of them on the floor.

I put my mouth against James's ear and shouted, 'Enjoying yourself?'

'Oh, I'm having a wonderful time.' He spoke with a sarcasm I'd never heard before. 'Want another drink?'

I shook my head just as Julie and Gavin returned.

Gavin was an old schoolfriend of James, a massively built yet graceful man who played amateur rugby. He surreptitiously removed a piece of folded paper from the breast pocket of his silk jacket and emptied the contents on to the table. Three pink tablets rolled out.

'Eleven quid each,' he shouted. He pushed one towards James. 'Have this on me.'

'Not tonight, thanks,' James said stiffly.

'Come on, James,' Julie coaxed. She was a pretty girl with a cascade of blonde curly hair. 'You look way down in the dumps. An E will put a different perspective on things.'

'I said no, thanks.'

Gavin shrugged. 'How about you, Millie? Does Miss Morality fancy changing the habit of a lifetime and popping a pill for once?'

I was tired of explaining that refusing Ecstasy had nothing to do with morality, but that the thought of not having full control of my faculties frightened me. Before I could refuse, James said angrily, 'No, she doesn't.' He looked at me, irritated at his own impatience, because he knew I would resent his answering on my behalf. 'Aw, shit!' He groaned. 'I can't stand it here. I'm going out for some fresh air.'

'He's not himself,' I said in excuse. I collected my coat and bag and James's jacket. 'We might see you later, but don't wait.'

I pushed my way through the crowded tables and found James outside in the car park. He was already shivering without his coat. October had brought an end to the beautiful Indian summer and the temperature must have dropped twenty degrees. I handed him the jacket. 'Put this on or you'll catch cold.'

'Yes, ma'am.' He forced a smile. 'Sorry about that, but I'm getting too old for clubbing.'

I linked his arm as we strolled through the car park towards the rear of the club. I had no idea where the place was situated; over the water, somewhere between

Birkenhead and Rock Ferry. 'You'd think you were ready to collect your pension.'

'Seriously, Millie, once you reach a certain age, life has to have more to it than the non-stop pursuit of a so-called "good time". Life's got to mean something.' There was a tinge of desperation in his voice. 'Oh, hell! I'm no good at explaining. It's just that, at twenty-nine, I feel I should be doing something rather more worthwhile than prancing round a nightclub, taking happy pills.'

'Such as?' To my surprise, I found we'd reached a stretch of lumpy sand and the Mersey glinted blackly in the distance, reflecting a wobbly quarter-moon. We climbed the chain-link fence and walked towards the water.

'You'll be annoyed if I tell you.'

'I promise, on my heart, not to be.'

'I'd like us to get married and have kids,' James said flatly. 'And I'd prefer to do a job that made some sort of contribution towards society.'

Astonished, I came to a standstill on the sand. 'You'd give up the garage? What would your father have to say?' The business was to be his one day.

'Sod Pa, and sod the garage,' James said, even more astonishingly. 'I'm sick to death of selling poncy, over-powered cars to idiots like myself. The job's as worthless as my life. It's useless, *I'm* useless.' He kicked moodily at a stone. 'I took today off and went to Liverpool. There was a march, hundreds of dockers who've been turfed out by Mersey Docks and Harbour Board because they refused to sign contracts that meant worse conditions and less pay. They've been out of work a year. There were fathers and sons among them. Men like that are the salt of the earth. I feel so . . . so *inadequate* compared to them.'

We reached the water. James released my arm and stuffed his hands in his pockets. He stared into the black waves. 'I've led a charmed life, Millie. I've never had to struggle for anything. Everything I've wanted has just dropped into my lap without my needing to ask. We're very lucky, the pair of us.'

I wanted to laugh out loud and say, 'You speak for yourself! Nothing has ever dropped into *my* lap. I've worked very hard for what I've got.' But what did he know about it? I'd told him virtually nothing about myself. Instead, I muttered, almost inaudibly, 'Marriage may not be the answer, James. It sounds to me like you're going through some sort of crisis.'

'Oh, God, Millie!' He pulled me into his arms, so tightly I could hardly breathe. 'Then help me through, darling. I've been going out of my mind over the last week.'

Only a week, I thought wryly. It was only during the past two or three years that I'd vaguely begun to feel an acceptable member of the human race. I put my arms around his neck and laid my head on his shoulder, not sure what to say. A dredger, barely lit, was moving silently down the river. The music from the nightclub was a muted throb. A memory returned, as it so often did, of one of the worst beatings. Mam had been out, working evenings to make ends meet. I didn't hear him come in. I heard nothing until the slithering footsteps sounded on the stairs and my body froze with fear. *I was reading in bed with a torch!* I was six and had only just learned to read. The teacher was amazed at how quickly I'd taken to it, but books offered undreamed-of pleasures, as well as escape from grim reality. I read in the lavatory, at break-times, and in the canteen. I had no idea why my father should detest the idea of my reading. It was as if he couldn't stand his children, or his wife, getting enjoyment from something, being happy.

So I'd been ordered not to read in bed. At the sound of the footsteps, I fumbled frantically with the torch, but it wouldn't go off. My hands were clammy with terror and I dropped it on the floor. The book followed. Two little thuds that sounded like thunderclaps in the quiet house.

'I thought I told yer not ter read in bed.' His voice was low and quiet, full of menace. The words travelled the years, as if they'd been spoken only a few minutes ago.

'I'm sorry, Dad.' I quaked with fright. I could feel my insides tearing apart, the way the ground erupts in an earthquake.

'I'll give yer summat to be sorry for. Gerrout!'

But I was still frozen, terrified, under the covers. I couldn't move. He pulled them back, roughly dragged me on to the floor, and began to undo the buckle of his wide leather belt. 'Kneel down,' he ordered. 'Kneel down against the bed and pull yer nightie up.'

'I didn't mean it, Dad. I won't read again, I promise,' I wailed. This was before I vowed never to let him see me cry. In her bed on the other side of the room, our Trudy stirred. 'Whassa matter?'

'Get back ter sleep,' our father snarled.

With my face buried in the bedclothes, I began to whimper. 'I won't do it again, Dad, honest.'

'Yer can bet yer life on that, yer little bitch! Bend over further.'

My arms tightened around James's neck as I remembered and felt the blows rain down on my bare bottom for the millionth time. The hard leather cut into my soft, childish flesh and I felt blood trickle down my legs. I heard my screams of pain, my pleas for mercy. 'I won't read again, Dad, I promise.'

I never did, not for a long time. The teacher was mystified as to why words no longer meant anything to her best pupil. 'It must have been a flash in the pan,' she said.

Perhaps it was Trudy, sobbing hysterically, that made him stop or perhaps he was exhausted. I was never sure. My face was still pressed against the bed, when I heard him going downstairs, the most welcome sound on earth. 'Thank you, God!' I breathed.

I broke free of James's arms and began to walk along the sands. My heart was beating rapidly and my legs were shaking. The tide rippled in over my shoes, but I didn't notice.

James caught up and grabbed my arm. 'Darling, what's wrong? What did you just say? Thank you, God, for what?'

'Nothing.' I hadn't realised I'd spoken aloud.

'You're trembling. How can it be nothing?' He regarded me sadly. 'Why are you keeping things from me?'

'Because there are things I don't want you to know.'

'If we're to be married, we should know everything about each other.'

I put my hands over my ears to shut him – everything – out, I shouted, 'Who said we're to be married? *I* didn't. When you brought the subject up last Sunday I said I'd sooner talk about it some other time. I didn't mean a few days later.'

'Darling, your feet are getting soaked.' Before I knew what was happening, he'd picked me up in his arms and carried me back to where the sand was dry. He crouched down beside me and started to take off my wet shoes. 'We're a mixed-up pair, Millie,' he said.

'You were perfectly well adjusted when we met. If you're mixed up now, it must be my fault.'

He stroked my hair. 'That's probably true. You're driving me nuts, Millie Cameron.'

I relaxed against him. Perhaps marrying James wouldn't be such a bad thing, though I'd have to think long and hard before having children. He was so comfortable to be with, so nice. But, then, no one could have been nicer than Gary, who'd bored me silly, and presumably Dad had been as nice as pie when he was courting Mum.

He was hurt when I insisted that he leave immediately after lunch next day. 'I thought we'd be spending Sunday together,' he said forlornly.

But I was firm. 'I'm clearing out my auntie's flat. I told you about it, remember? This is my only free day.'

'Why can't I go with you?' he pleaded. 'I could help. I could carry stuff out to the car. Anyway, it isn't safe for a woman on her own round there. Isn't William Square a red-light area?'

'Don't be silly,' I said dismissively. I couldn't wait to get to Flo's flat and had no intention of taking anyone with me. Mum had telephoned on Friday night and offered to lend a hand after she'd finished in the news-agent's shop where she worked till noon. 'You could meet me off the bus in town and let me have the key – I'll leave it with the woman upstairs. As long as I'm home before your dad, he'd never know I'd been.'

'It's quite all right, Mum,' I assured her. 'I can manage on my own.' I felt as if the flat was mine.

'Are you sure, luv? Last Sunday I got the impression you didn't want to be bothered.'

'I don't know where you got that idea from,' I said innocently. 'I don't mind a bit.'

After James had gone, I dressed in jeans and sweatshirt, and was brushing my hair when the phone rang. I ignored it, and heard the answering-machine click on. It was Mum. I sat on the off-white settee with a sigh and listened to the whining voice.

'Millicent, it's Mam. Your dad and Declan are out. Are you there, luv? It's just that I got this letter yesterday from the charity that runs our Alison's home. They can only keep her till she's eighteen. Next April she'll be transferred to this adult place in Oxford. Is that far, luv? I daren't show the letter to your dad – you know how he feels about Alison – and I can't find the atlas anywhere . . .'

My mother rambled on, as if the answering-machine itself was enough to talk to. I felt tears prickle my eyes as I listened. Mum loved her youngest child to distraction. She spent any spare money saved from the housekeeping on little presents for Alison, and had never stopped pining for her lost daughter. I couldn't bear to think how she would feel if Alison was placed out of reach of her weekly visits.

Oh, if only I could get shot of my family as easily as I'd got shot of Gary! If only I could divorce them and never see them again! By now, tears were pouring down my cheeks and I couldn't stand my mother's pain another second. I stumbled across the room and picked up the receiver.

'Mam!' But she had hung up. I had neither the strength nor the courage to ring back.

I breathed a sigh of relief as I closed the door of Flo's flat behind me. It felt like coming home. There were letters on the mat. As I lit the fire I scanned through them quickly, then turned on the lamp and went into the kitchen to put the kettle on. Nothing important; circulars, a market-research survey, a reminder that the TV licence was due. I put them aside and made a cup of tea. This time, I'd brought teabags, fresh milk and sandwiches. Still dunking a teabag, I returned to the living room and sank into the middle of the settee.

After a few minutes, I got up and put on Flo's record. Listening to Bing Crosby's soothing voice, I relaxed even more. The newspaper cuttings about the lost submarine, the *Thetis*, were still on the coffee table. I'd meant to ask someone about it, but the only elderly person I knew was Gran.

For almost an hour, I breathed in the peaceful atmosphere of the room, and the tension flowed from my body. I would have been quite happy to stay there for ever, but after a while I got up and began to wander round, poking in cupboards and drawers. Flo had been only superficially tidy. One sideboard drawer was full of gloves, another full of scarves, all in a mess. Another contained balls of string, a tangle of old shoelaces, an assortment of electric plugs, and a wad of money-off coupons held together with a rusty paperclip, which were years out of date.

For some reason, I found it necessary to untangle the laces, and was concentrating hard on undoing knots and trying to find pairs when there was a knock at the door. It would be Charmian I thought, and went to answer it. An elderly woman, very thin, with a huge cloud of unnatural mahogany-coloured hair and a still lovely though deeply wrinkled face, was standing outside. She wore a fake leopardskin jacket over a purple mohair jumper and black leggings, and appeared to be in the middle of a conversation with someone.

'Can't you wear a jacket or something?' she demanded angrily. There was a mumbled reply I couldn't catch, then the woman said, 'You'll do even less business if you catch the flu.' She turned and smiled at me ruefully, revealing a set of over-large false teeth. 'That bloody Fiona! She's wearing a dress with no sleeves that barely covers her arse. She'll perish in this weather. Hello, luv.'

No one waited for an invitation into Flo's, it seemed: the woman bounced into the room with the vitality of a teenager, although she must have been well into her seventies, followed by a waft of expensive perfume. 'I'm Bel Eddison, Flo's friend,' she said loudly. 'I know who you are – Millicent Cameron. I asked Charmian to give me a ring next time you came. She was right. You're the spitting image of Flo, and it's even more obvious to me 'cos I knew her when she was a girl. It gave me quite a turn when you opened the door.'

I'd already recognised the woman from the snapshot taken in Blackpool. It felt strange shaking hands with Flo's best friend, as if I was stepping back into the past, yet Bel was very much part of the present. 'How do you do?' I murmured. 'Please call me Millie.' I don't think I had ever seen such lovely eyes before, genuine violet. They were heavily made up, though, far too much for someone so old. The purple shadow had seeped into the crêpy lids, giving the effect of cracked eggshells.

'I'm tip-top, luv. How are you?' Bel didn't wait for an answer. Instead, she put her hands on her hips and regarded the room with exaggerated surprise. 'You haven't touched a thing,' she remarked. 'I was expecting to see the place stripped bare by now.'

'I was working out a plan of action,' I said guiltily, pushing the laces back into the drawer and closing it. 'Would you like a cup of tea?' I asked, when the newcomer removed her coat and threw herself on to the settee as if she'd come to stay. The springs squeaked in protest.

'No, ta, but I wouldn't mind a glass of Flo's sherry,' she said. Not only did she speak loudly, but also very quickly, in a strong, melodic voice that gave no hint of her age. 'Me and Flo sat here getting pissed on sherry more times than you've had hot dinners.'

Flo pissed didn't quite fit the image I'd built up in my mind, and I said as much to Bel when I gave her a glass. I poured one for myself too.

'It was her only vice,' Bel said. 'That's if you could call sherry a vice. Otherwise she led the life of a saint. For a long while, she went on retreat once a month to some convent in Wales. What's these?' She picked up the newspaper cuttings. 'Oh, you found them.' She grimaced.

'They were by the bed. Why did she keep them?' I asked.

'Draw your own conclusions, luv. It should be obvious.'

'She was in love with someone and he died on the *Thetis*?' I did a quick calculation: Flo would have been nineteen at the time.

'I said, draw your own conclusions.' Bel pursed her lips. I got the impression she enjoyed being mysterious. 'I'm not confirming or denying anything. I'd be betraying Flo's memory if I told things she kept to herself all her life.' She regarded me with her bright violet eyes. 'So, you're Kate Colquitt's eldest girl?'

'You know my mother?' I said, surprised.

'I did once. She used to come and see Flo a long time ago, but not since she married your dad. She was a lovely girl, Kate Colquitt. How is she these days?'

'She's okay,' I said abruptly.

Bel wriggled contentedly on the settee. Her expressive face displayed even the most fleeting emotion. 'This is nice! I never thought I'd sup sherry in Flo's again – pass us the bottle, there's a good girl. Ta!' she said comfortably. 'I'll top your glass up, shall I? We used to do this regular every Sunday. Sometimes Charmian joined us. It's uncanny, what with Flo dead, but you looking so much like her. Actually,' she continued with a frown, 'I'm racking me brains trying to bring to mind your husband's name. Was it Harry? You'd only been married a couple of years when Sally died – can you remember me at the funeral? Sally was the only contact Flo had with your family. When she died, Flo had no way of knowing how you were all getting on.'

'I'm sorry I don't remember you. I looked out for Flo, wondering what she was like. She disappeared before anyone could speak to her.'

'And how's Harry getting on?' Bel probed.

'Actually, it was Gary. We're divorced.'

'Really!' Bel sipped her sherry, clearly interested. 'What's your position now?' She looked all set for a long jangle. I felt less annoyed than I'd expected that the afternoon I'd anticipated having to myself had been interrupted. In fact, I *wasn't* annoyed. I liked Bel: she was so cheerfully vivid and alive. I wondered if we could trade information. If I told her a few things about myself, would she provide some details about Flo?

'I've got a boyfriend,' I explained. 'His name's James Atherton and we've been going out for a year. He's twenty-nine, and his father owns three garages on Merseyside. James manages the Southport one.'

'Is it serious?' Bel enquired gravely.

'On his side, not mine.' I thought about what James had said last night on the sands outside the nightclub. 'He's been going through some sort of crisis for an entire week.'

'Poor bugger,' Bel said laconically. 'Fellers wouldn't

88

recognise a crisis if it crept up behind and threw them to the ground.'

'It's all my fault.' I wrinkled my nose.

'It shouldn't do him any harm. Men generally have it too easy in relationships with women.'

'Where did you meet Flo?' It was time she answered a few questions.

'Birkenhead, luv, a few months before the war began. She was a year older than me. She lived in Wavertree in those days.'

'Did Flo join the forces like you?'

'How did you know . . . ?' Bel began, then nodded at the photographs on the table. 'Of course, the photo of yours truly getting hitched to dear ould Bob. That was me in the ATS. No, Flo stayed working in the laundry during the war. I was posted to Egypt and it was years before I saw her again.' She glanced sadly around the room. For the first time she looked her age as her face grew sober and her eyes darkened with sadness. She appeared to be slightly drunk. 'She was such a lovely girl. You should have seen her smile – it was like a ray of sunshine, yet she buried herself in this place for most of her life. It's a dead rotten shame.'

'Would you like more sherry?' I asked. I much preferred the cheerful Bel, even if it meant her getting even drunker.

'I wouldn't say no.' She perked up. 'The bottle's nearly gone, but there'll be more in the sideboard. Flo always had half a dozen in. She said it helped with her headaches. Is there anything to eat, luv? Me stomach's rumbling something awful. I would have had summat before I left, but I never thought I'd be out so long.'

In the kitchen, I found several tins of soup in a cupboard. I opened a tin of pea and ham, poured it into two mugs and put them in the microwave to heat, then unwrapped the ham sandwiches I'd brought with me. I didn't realise I was singing until Bel shouted, 'Someone sounds happy! You've been listening to Flo's record.'

It was totally different from how I'd spent Sunday afternoons before and I wasn't doing anything that could remotely be considered exciting, yet I felt contented as I watched the red figures count down on the microwave. I wondered if Flo had bought the microwave and other things like the record player and the television on hire purchase. During my rather pathetic forays into drawers and cupboards, I hadn't come across any papers. Flo must have a pension book somewhere, possibly an insurance policy, and there were bound to be other matters that had to be dealt with; electricity and gas bills, council tax, water rates. I was being negligent in dealing with her affairs. This was the second time I'd come and the flat was no different now than it was when Flo died, except that there was less sherry and less food. As soon as Bel went, I'd get down to work, clear a few drawers or something.

I searched for a tray and discovered one in the cupboard under the sink. There was salt and pepper in pretty porcelain containers – 'A Gift from Margate'. I put everything on the tray and took it into the living room where Bel was half asleep.

'Who paid for the funeral?' I asked.

Bel came awake with a furious blinking of her thickly mascaraed lashes and immediately attacked a sandwich. 'Both me and Flo took out special funeral policies. She showed me where hers was kept and I showed her where to find mine. We used to wonder which of us would go first. Flo swore it would be her. I never said anything but I thought the same.' She made one of her outrageous faces. 'I'll have to show someone else where me policy is, won't I?'

'Haven't you got any children?'

'No, luv.' For a moment, Bel looked desolate. 'I was in the club three times but never able to bring a baby to term. Nowadays, they can do something about it, but not then.'

'I'm sorry,' I said softly. In fact, I was so sorry that a lump came to my throat.

Unexpectedly Bel smiled. 'That's all right, luv. I used to joke with Flo sometimes that we were a barren pair of bitches but, as she'd say, kids don't automatically bring happiness. Some you'd be better off without.' She went on tactlessly, 'How's that sister of yours, the sick one? I can't remember her name.'

'Alison. She's not sick, she's autistic.' I shrugged. 'She's the same as ever.'

'And what about your other sister? And you've got a brother, haven't you?'

I was being cross-questioned again, I told her about Trudy. 'As for Declan, he just drifts from job to job. He's getting nowhere.'

Bel screwed up her face in an expression of disgust. 'There's not much hope for young people nowadays.' She sipped her soup for a while, then said casually, 'How's your gran?'

I had the definite feeling that Bel had been leading up to this question from the start. 'She's fine. She was eighty in June.'

'Is she still in the same place in Kirkby?'

'Yes.'

Bel stared at her ultra-fashionable boots: lace-ups with thick soles and heels, not quite Dr Marten's, but almost. 'I don't suppose,' she said wistfully, 'you know what that row was all about?'

'What row?'

'The one all them years ago between your gran and Flo.'

'I don't know anything about it,' I said. 'We were always led to believe Flo had done something terrible, and Gran never spoke to her again.'

Bel pulled one of her peculiar faces. 'I heard it the other way round, that it was Martha who'd done wrong and Flo who'd taken umbrage. More than once she said to me, 'Bel, under no circumstances must our Martha be told if I go to meet me Maker before she does – at least not till the funeral's over,' but she'd never tell me why, although she wasn't one to keep secrets from her best friend. We knew everything about each other except for that.'

At six o'clock, Bel announced that she was going home, but changed her mind when Charmian arrived with a plate of chicken legs and a wedge of home-made fruitcake. By then I was a bit drunk and gladly opened another bottle of sherry. At half past seven we watched *Coronation Street*. It was hours later that my visitors left, and I was sorry to see them go. Charmian was natural and outgoing, with a sharp wit, and I felt completely at ease, as if I'd known them both all my life. It was as though I had inherited two good friends from Flo.

'I've had a great time today,' Bel said, with a satisfied chuckle when she was leaving. 'It's almost as if Flo's still with us. We must do this again next Sunday. I don't live far away in Maynard Street.'

I was already looking forward to it, forgetting that I was there to sort out Flo's possessions, not enjoy myself.

Charmian said, 'Our Jay's twenty-one this week, Millie, and we're having a party on Saturday. You're invited if you're free – bring a boyfriend if you've got one.'

'Of course she's got a boyfriend, a lovely girl like her!' Bel exclaimed. 'A party might be just the thing to help your James through his crisis.'

Charmian rolled her eyes. 'It's a party, not a counselling session.'

'I'll ask him, but I'm sure he's already got something arranged.' I was convinced that James would hate the idea.

The flat felt unusually still and quiet without Bel and her loud voice, though it still smelt strongly of her perfume. A police car came screeching round the corner, the flashing blue light sweeping across the room through the thin curtains. It made me realise that I'd had more glasses of sherry than I could count. If I was stopped and breathalysed, I would lose my licence, and I couldn't afford that: a car was essential to my job. I'll have to stay here tonight, I thought.

The idea of sleeping in the soft, springy bed was appealing. I made coffee, put it in the microwave and went into the bedroom to take stock. There were night-dresses in the bottom drawer of the chest. I picked out a pretty blue cotton one with short puffed sleeves and white lace trimming on the hem. A dramatic quilted black dressing-gown, patterned with swirling pink roses, was hanging behind the door, and I remembered the pink furry slippers under the bed. I undressed quickly and put on the nightie. It felt crisp and cold, but the dressing-gown was lined with something fleecy and in no time I was warm. I shoved my cold feet into Flo's slippers. Everything smelt slightly of that lovely scent from the Body Shop, Dewberry! It seemed odd, because I kept thinking of Flo as belonging to another age, not someone who frequented the Body Shop.

It didn't seem the least bit odd or unpleasant to be wearing a dead woman's clothes. In fact, it seemed as if Flo had left everything in place especially for me.

There wouldn't be time in the morning to go home and change, and George disapproved of jeans in the office. A quick glance in the wardrobe showed it to be so tightly packed with clothes that I could barely get my fingers between them. There was bound to be something I could wear.

I collected the coffee, took it into the bedroom and climbed into bed. I switched on the bedside lamp and picked up the book Flo had been reading before she died, turning to the first page. I was deeply involved when my eyes started to close, although it wasn't yet ten o'clock, hours before I usually went to bed. I turned off the lamp, slid under the bedclothes and lay in the cool darkness, vaguely aware of the saints staring down at me from the walls, and the crucifix above my head.

There were shouts in the distance, followed by a crashing sound, as if someone had broken a window. A car's brakes shrieked, there were more shouts, but I scarcely noticed. I thought about James. Perhaps I was too hard on him. I resolved to be nicer in future. My thoughts drifted briefly to Bel, but she had scarcely occupied my mind for more than a few seconds before I fell into a deep, restful and dreamless sleep.

2

'That's a charming dress,' said George. 'You look exceptionally sweet and demure this morning.'

'So do you,' I replied tartly. I always resent men considering it their prerogative to make comments on a woman's appearance. 'The dress belonged to my aunt. I stayed the night in her flat.'

George looked at me askance. 'That's a bit risky, isn't it? I hope you weren't alone.'

'I was, but seem to have survived the experience.'

The extension rang on my desk and George disappeared into his office. It was James. 'Where on earth were you last night?' he demanded crossly. 'I rang and rang and left increasingly desperate messages on your answering-machine. Then I called early this morning and you still weren't there.'

I frowned in annoyance. What right had he to know my whereabouts for twenty-four hours a day? 'I had visitors at my aunt's flat and we drank a bottle of sherry between us. It didn't seem safe to drive.'

'If I'd known what number your aunt had lived at, I'd have come to William Square in search of you.'

'If you had, I'd have been very cross,' I said coldly.

James groaned. 'Darling, I've been out of my head with worry. I thought you might have come to some harm.'

I remembered that I'd vowed to be nicer to him, so bit back another sharp reply. 'I'm perfectly all right,' I said pleasantly. 'In fact, I had the best night's sleep in years.'

Even Diana had remarked on how well I looked. 'Sparkling' was how she had put it. 'You never usually have much colour, but your cheeks today are a lovely pink.'

'Shall we meet tonight, catch a movie, have dinner? *Leaving Las Vegas* is on at the Odeon.'

'Not tonight, James. I really need to get on with some work at home. I haven't touched my report in ages.' George had muttered something earlier about having found an ideal site in Woolton for the new office. 'Perhaps Wednesday or Thursday.'

'Okay, darling.' He sighed. 'I'll call you tomorrow.'

I hadn't time to worry if I'd hurt him because the phone rang again immediately I put the receiver down. The Naughtons wished to view a house in Ormskirk; they'd received the details that morning. This time they'd make their own way there, and I arranged to meet them outside the property at two o'clock.

The phone scarcely stopped ringing for the rest of the morning. I ate lunch at my desk, and remembered my appointment with the Naughtons just in time to avoid being late. Snatching the keys off the wall, I told George I'd probably be gone for hours. 'They take for ever, wandering around discussing curtains and stuff.'

'Humour them, Millie, even if it takes all day,' George said affably. He grinned. 'I must say you look a picture in that dress.'

I stuck out my tongue at him because I knew he was teasing. Flo's dress was a pale blue and pink check with a white Peter Pan collar, long sleeves and a wide, stiff belt. The material was a mixture of wool and cotton. It fitted perfectly and didn't look in the least old-fashioned. Neither did the short pink swagger coat that had been tucked at the back of the wardrobe, though I'd had an awful job pressing out the creases with a damp tea-towel. Even Flo's narrow, size seven shoes could have been bought with me in mind: the clumpy-heeled cream slingbacks went perfectly with everything.

Until I reached the countryside, I hadn't noticed how

miserable the weather was. Mist hung over the fields, drifting in and out of the dank wet hedges. The sky was a dreary grey with blotches of black.

When I drew up outside the house the Naughtons were waiting in their car. It was a compact detached property on a small but very smart estate that had been built only five years ago.

I got out and shook hands with the rather homely middle-aged couple. Their children had left home and they were looking for something smaller and easier to clean. The trouble was, they were unwilling to give up a single item of furniture and seemed unable to visualise life without their present curtains. 'Let's hope this is it!' I smiled. They were registered with several other agents and had been viewing properties for months. 'The vendors are both at work, so we'll have the place to ourselves.'

The house was owned by schoolteachers who were moving south. It had been very untidy when I had called to take details a few days before, but I'd assumed they would tidy up when they knew prospective purchasers were coming – I'd never known a seller yet who hadn't. However, when we went in, the place was a tip. Heaps of clothes lay on the stairs to be taken up, the remains of breakfast was still on the kitchen table and there were years of ground-in dirt on the tiled floor.

'This is disgusting,' Mrs Naughton expostulated indignantly. Her husband nudged her, embarrassed, but she refused to be silenced. 'It smells!' she claimed.

After a brief glance in the lounge, which looked as if a hurricane had swept through it, Mrs Naughton refused to go upstairs. 'I dread to think what the bathroom must be like. I couldn't possibly live here.' She made for the door.

Seconds later, I found myself shaking hands again and apologising for the state of the house. They drove away, Mrs Naughton in high dudgeon, and I returned to my car. I had expected the view to take at least an hour but it had been over within a few minutes.

I drove out of the estate and was about to turn right towards Liverpool when I remembered that the St Osyth Trust, where Alison lived, was only about five miles away. On impulse, I turned left in the direction of Skelmersdale. I'd tell George the Naughtons had taken their usual lengthy time. 'I'm normally very conscientious,' I told myself virtuously. 'I rarely take time off. I'm never ill.'

It was months since I'd seen my sister. I preferred to go without Mum, who frequently made a big emotional scene, patting and kissing a mystified Alison who had no idea what all the fuss was about.

The sky was growing darker and it began to drizzle. I hated driving with the windscreen wipers on, and it was with relief that I turned off the narrow, isolated road into the circular drive of the gloomy red-brick mansion.

The big oak trees bordering the grounds at the front had shed their leaves and a gardener was leisurely raking them into little heaps on the lawn. Round the side of the house, a bonfire smouldered reluctantly. I parked in the area reserved for visitors. Perhaps because it was Monday, I appeared to be the only one there.

The heels of Flo's shoes clicked loudly on the polished wooden floor as I went over to Reception where a woman was typing. She looked up questioningly. 'Can I help you?'

'I've come to see Alison Cameron. I'm her sister.' I felt uncomfortable. The woman, Evelyn Porter, had worked there for as long as I could remember, yet she didn't recognise me because I came so rarely.

'Of course. I should have known. Alison's in the lounge. She's already got a visitor. You know the way, don't you?'

I nodded and turned to go, when Evelyn Porter said, 'I should warn you that Alison's a little upset today. We had to have the upstairs redecorated – it was in a terrible state, and the painters are in her room. Alison can't stand her precious things being disturbed and you'll find her rather agitated.'

The lounge was built on to the rear of the house, a sturdy conservatory that went its entire width, filled with brightly cushioned cane furniture. I paused before going in, praying it would be Trudy who was visiting, not Mum. Trudy's car hadn't been outside, though, and Mum couldn't fit in the bus journey to Skelmersdale between finishing work and being home in time to make my father's tea. During the week he monopolised the car – it would have been fixed quick enough when he needed it himself, assuming there'd been anything wrong in the first place.

To my pleased surprise, when I opened the door I found Declan, who was supposed to be at work, alone in the lounge with Alison. 'What on earth are you doing here?'

He stood up and hugged me. 'Hi, Sis. You're the last person I expected to see.'

We stayed in each other's arms for several seconds. It was only when I saw him that I remembered just how much I loved my little brother, though he was several inches taller than me now. 'Declan, love, you're thinner than ever,' I said. I could feel the bones protruding from his neck and shoulders, and I remembered the violence meted out to his puny body by our father. I gave him an affectionate push and turned to my sister. 'Hallo, Alison. It's Millie. I've come to see you.'

Over the last few years, Alison Cameron had grown into a beautiful young woman. She'd always been the prettiest of us three sisters, but now she was breathtaking. Her eyes were large and very green, like a luminous sea in sunlight, the lashes long and thick, several shades darker than her abundant ash-blonde hair, emphasising the creamy whiteness of her flawless skin. Her condition was only evident in the movements of her lovely body: stiff, clumsy, lacking grace.

'Hallo, hallo, hallo.' Alison flicked her long fingers in front of her eyes. 'You want to go upstairs.'

She meant, 'I'. 'I want to go upstairs.'

'Sorry, luv. You can't,' Declan said gently. 'Your room's being painted a nice new colour.'

I kissed the smooth, porcelain cheek, but Alison didn't seem aware of the gesture. 'It will look very pretty when it's done, darling. Then you can spread all your lovely things out again.' She kept her talcum powder, hairslides, toys and other odds and ends in neat rows on the bedside table and window-sill, and was always deeply distressed if anything was put in the wrong place.

'You want to go upstairs.'

'Later, darling, later.'

Alison looked at the floor, avoiding eye-contact. 'Come in thing with wheels?'

'I came in my car, yes.'

'You go in thing with wheels.'

'You've been in a car? Whose car, darling?'

'I think Trudy and Colin took her for a drive yester-day,' Declan whispered, when Alison shook herself irri-tably and began to flick her fingers again.

I had never been able to comprehend what went on in my sister's mind, although one of the doctors had once tried to explain it to Mum. It was something to do with mind blindness, the inability to perceive another person's emotions, which was why she sometimes laughed when our mother cried. Poor Mum was unable to accept that Alison wasn't laughing at *her*. My sister just wasn't aware of tears.

'Would you like to do a jigsaw puzzle, luv?' Declan suggested. 'The woman brought some in before,' he said. 'Thought they might calm her down, like.'

But Alison was looking out of the window, where a narrow line of smoke was drifting upwards from the bonfire. She had an uncanny, inexplicable ability to do the most complicated jigsaws in a fraction of the time it would have taken most people.

Declan and I looked at each other. As far as Alison was concerned, we might as well not be there.

'You know,' Declan said softly, 'I used to think me dad was responsible for the way Alison is. I thought he shook and slapped her so hard it damaged her brain. I envied her something rotten. I always hoped he'd do the same to me so I'd be sent here, too.'

'He did more than shake and slap you, Dec. He leathered the three of us regularly.'

'You had it the worst, Mill. You were the oldest, and he seemed to have it in for you more than the rest of us.'

I made a face. I seemed to have caught the habit from Bel. 'Maybe there was something about me that drove him over the edge,' I suggested lightly.

'Still, it didn't damage our brains. We all stayed quite normal.' Declan grinned. 'Least, relatively normal. Mind you,' the grin disappeared, 'there's still time for one of us to snap. I'll end up behind bars if I stay in that house much longer. I swear one day I'll kill the bastard because of the way he treats Mam. He hasn't given her any money in weeks. It used to be the horses, now it's that bloody lottery. Yet you should hear him moan if the food isn't up to scratch. He nearly hit the roof when we got a reminder for the electricity bill, as if she could pay everything out of the fifty quid a week she earns and what I hand over for me keep. He called her a lazy bitch and said it was about time she got a full-time job. If she did, there'd be hell to pay if his meals weren't ready on time.'

Declan's soft, rather feminine voice was rising, and I noticed that his hands, long and white like Alison's were gripping the arms of the chair, the knuckles taut. His gentle face was drawn and tired. I leaned back in the chair and sighed. My brother's unhappiness was painful to watch and it was to avoid that pain that I kept as far away from my family as I could. I almost wished I hadn't come or that Declan hadn't been there. 'Why don't you leave, Dec?' I pleaded. Then there'd only be Mum for me to worry about.

'As if I could leave Mam on her own with that bastard.'

'You can't stay for ever, love.'

'I'll stay as long as I have to.'

I got up and walked down the long room to the coffee machine provided for visitors. The light was on, which meant the machine was working. 'Fancy a coffee, Dec?' I called. Alison remained fascinated by the smoke.

'Please.'

'What are you doing here, anyway?' I asked, when I returned with the drinks. 'You're supposed to be at work.'

Declan recovered his good humour swiftly. His knack of making a joke of things that would have driven another person to despair was impressive. Dad's belt had broken once in the middle of a thrashing. 'Never mind, Dad,' he had said chirpily. 'I'll get you another for Christmas.'

'I lost me job.' He smiled. 'I got the sack three weeks ago.'

'Mum never said!'

He shrugged his delicate shoulders. 'That's because she doesn't know. She gets dead upset every time I get the shove. No one knows except our Trudy. I've looked for other work, Millie, honest, but I can't get anything. I've got no references because I've never held a job down long enough. The thing is, all I know is labouring and I'm not up to it.'

'Oh, Dec! What do you do with yourself all day?' I felt hurt that he had confided in Trudy and not in me. I was his sister, too. I wanted, reluctantly, to help.

'I wander the streets, go to the Job Centre, call on Trudy, then go home for six o'clock so Mam thinks I've been to work. This is the third time I've come to see Alison, but it means hitching lifts and last time I had to walk all the way back.'

'You should have told me.' I would have given him the key to my flat, where he could watch TV and help himself to food.

'I didn't think you'd be interested,' Declan said, which hurt more.

'I'll have to go soon,' I said. 'They'll be expecting me at the office. We don't seem to be doing much good here.' I made a quick decision. 'Look, I'll take you into town and you can go to the cinema – *Leaving Las Vegas* is on at the Odeon. When I finish work, we'll go back to my place for a meal. I've got pizza in the freezer.'

Declan's big green eyes sparkled. 'Great idea, Sis. I'll ring Mam and tell her I'm working late or she'll want to know how I met you. The pictures are out 'cos I'm skint. I give Mam all I get off the social, but it'll be nice to look round the shops. I haven't been to town in ages.'

It was even worse than I'd thought. 'What have you been doing for money all this time?' I asked, dismayed.

'Trudy gives me the odd few quid, but she doesn't want Colin to know what's happened. She reckons he's had enough of the Camerons.'

Despite Declan's protests that he didn't want to scrounge, I insisted he take all the money I had with me, twenty pounds.

A woman in a white overall came in to ask how Alison was. 'She doesn't want to know us today, do you, Sis?' Declan chucked his beautiful sister under the chin, but she remained as unaware of the gesture as she'd been of my kiss. 'Slippers,' she muttered. 'Slippers, slippers, slippers.'

'The builders are just packing up for the day so we can put her things back in place. They've only got the ceiling to do tomorrow. Would you mind if I took her upstairs? I think she'll feel happier once she knows everything's back to normal. Next time you come she'll be fine.'

Well, as fine as she'll ever be, I thought sadly. I watched Alison being led away, oblivious to the presence of her brother and sister.

When it came down to it, I was no good at telling blatant lies. I couldn't bring myself to tell George that the Naughtons had taken ages viewing the house when it wasn't true. 'I hope you don't mind, but I went to see my sister. She only lives a few miles away. It was a spur-of-the-moment thing.'

'The one in the home?'

'That's right.' Sometimes I forgot George knew things about me that no one outside my family did.

'No problem,' George said easily.

'I should have let you know on the mobile.'

George laughed. 'I said, no problem. You could get away with murder in that dress, Ms Millicent Cameron. What prompted your folks to call you that, by the way?'

'It's after a singer my mother liked, Millicent Martin.'

'Oh, Lord!' he groaned. 'I liked her, too. Does that show my age?'

'Very much so, George,' I said gravely, getting my own back for his comments on Flo's frock.

We grinned at each other amiably, and George said, 'I was wondering where you were. Mrs Naughton telephoned to complain to a higher authority about the state of that house. I'll give the vendors a ring tonight, suggest they tidy up, but be prepared to warn people in future, just in case.'

I hung up the keys and went over to my desk, aware of how close I'd come to blotting my copybook with George.

It was my job to prepare a list of properties to advertise in the local press and I was gathering together details to feed into the computer when I became aware that Diana, whose desk was next to mine, was crying quietly. Tweedledum and Tweedledee were out, and Oliver Brett was in George's office. June, the receptionist, was on the phone, her back to us.

'What's the matter?' I asked. The woman's eyes were red with weeping.

'It's my father. I don't know if I told you he was ill. It's cancer of the stomach. A neighbour's just called to say she found him unconscious on the kitchen floor. He's been taken to hospital.'

'Then go and see him straight away. George won't mind.'

'Why should I?' Diana looked at me mutinously. 'I've got work to do – I'm just finishing off those notes on Woolton. It could affect my prospects of promotion.'

I said nothing, but wondered where my priorities would lie in the same situation.

'Parents are a pain,' Diana said, in a hard voice. 'When they grow old, it's worse than having children.' She blew her nose, wiped her eyes, and began to cry again. 'I don't know what I'll do if Daddy dies!'

'I think you should go to the hospital.'

Diana didn't reply. She typed furiously for a while, then said, 'No. I'm too busy. I wish that bloody neighbour hadn't phoned. There comes a time when you've got to put yourself first.'

'If you say so.' I tried to ignore her as I finished off the adverts then faxed them through to the press, by which time it had gone six o'clock. I was meeting Declan in a pub in Water Street close to where I'd parked the car. When I left Diana was still typing, her brow creased in concentration, her eyes still red. I stood for a moment, looking at her and wondering what to say. Eventually, all I could think of was, 'Goodnight, Diana.'

'Night,' Diana replied, in a clipped voice.

Declan had thoroughly enjoyed the film. 'Dad would be in his element in Las Vegas,' he said, chuckling, on the way to Blundellsands.

'Only if he had a few thousand pounds to play with,' I said drily, 'and he'd probably lose that within a day.' I patted his knee. 'Try to forget about him and enjoy yourself for a change. We can watch a video later, if you like.'

'That'd be the gear, Sis.' Declan sighed blissfully as I drove into the parking area at the side of my flat. 'I feel dead honoured. I've only been here once before.' His voice rose an octave and became a squeak. 'Jaysus, look at that car! It's only a Maserati!'

A low-slung black sports car was parked against the boundary wall. It wasn't possible to see through the dark-tinted windows who was inside it, but a terrible suspicion entered my mind.

'I'd sell me soul for a car like that!' Declan murmured reverently. He leaped out of the Polo as soon as it stopped and went over to the black car with the deference of a pilgrim approaching the Pope. My suspicions were confirmed when the car door opened and James climbed out. He frequently turned up in strange cars belonging to the garage.

'Millie?' His voice contained a great deal of anger and hurt. It even sounded slightly querulous. 'Millie?' he said again.

I realised he thought that Declan was a boyfriend. He'd asked me out that night and I'd refused, saying I had work to do. Instead I was seeing someone else. I felt irritated. Why shouldn't I go out with another man if I wanted? I was cross that James had turned up uninvited. Now I would have to introduce him to Declan, and I wanted the Camerons and the Athertons kept apart for as long as possible. For ever would be even better.

'This is my brother, Declan,' I said stiffly. 'Declan, this is James.'

James's broad shoulders sagged with relief. 'Declan!' he said jovially, as he shook hands. 'I've heard a lot about you.' He was being polite: he knew nothing about my brother other than that he existed.

'Is this your car?' Declan's jaw dropped in disbelief: he had a sister who had a boyfriend who drove a Maserati.

'No, I just borrowed it for tonight. My own car is an Aston Martin.'

'Jaysus! Can I look under the bonnet? Would you mind if I sat behind the wheel, only for a minute, like?'

James was happy to oblige. He got back into the car and pulled the lever to raise the bonnet. Seconds later the pair were bent over the engine and James was explaining how things worked. I trudged upstairs, dreading the evening ahead.

I put the kettle and the oven on, and began to prepare a salad. James would probably expect to stay to dinner and fortunately the pizza was a large one. I opened a bottle of wine and drank a glass to steady my nerves. By the time James and Declan arrived, almost half an hour later, I'd drunk half the bottle and had to open another to have with the meal. I blamed Flo. It wouldn't have crossed my mind to drink alone if I hadn't come face to face with all that sherry.

The two men were getting on famously. The conversation had turned to football. 'There's a match on TV later, Liverpool versus Newcastle.' James rubbed his hands. 'You don't mind if we watch it, do you, Millie?'

'Not at all.' By now, I was terrified Declan would say something, give the game away, and the whole respectable edifice I'd built around myself would come tumbling down.

It wasn't until they had finished their meal that he revealed the smallest of my secrets. 'That was great, Sis. I haven't had such decent grub in ages.' He turned to James. 'Our mam does her best, but everything comes with mashed spuds and cabbage.' He patted his stomach. 'I'm not half glad I went to see Alison in Skem, else I wouldn't have met our Millie.'

'I thought Alison lived in Kirkby with you,' James said, puzzled.

'Oh, no. Alison's autistic. She's in a home. Hasn't Millie told you?'

'Who'd like coffee?' I said brightly. I went into the kitchen, bringing that line of conversation to an abrupt end. When I returned with the coffee, Declan had just rung home. 'I forgot to tell Mam I'm supposed to be working late. I lost me job the other week,' he explained to James, 'and I still haven't got round to telling our mam and dad.'

James looked sympathetic. 'What sort of work do you do?'

I gritted my teeth as Declan replied, 'Only labouring. I was working on this demolition site, but it seemed to be me who got demolished more often than the building.'

'You're wasted as a labourer. Why don't you take a college course like Millie did?'

To my surprise, Declan's face turned bright red. He blinked his long lashes rapidly and said, 'It's never entered me head.'

Fortunately, it was time for the match to start. I switched on the television, then the computer. I wanted to finish my report, but my brain was incapable of competing with the sound of the television and James and Declan's bellows of support alternated with groans of despair whenever Newcastle went near the Liverpool goal. I tried to read a book, gave up, and went into the kitchen where I caught up with the ironing and prayed the match wouldn't go into extra time. The minute it was over, I'd take Declan home. It was imperative that my brother and my boyfriend were separated before any more of the Camerons' dirty linen was aired.

To my dismay, James had already offered Declan a lift. I thought of the burnt-out car abandoned opposite my parents' house – hopefully James wouldn't notice in the dark – of the lads who'd still be playing outside and might not feel too charitably towards the driver of a Maserati.

'Tara, Sis.' Declan punched me lightly on the shoulder. 'It's been a smashing evening.'

'We must do it again soon. Perhaps next time there's a match, eh?' James kissed me on the lips. 'I'll call later.'

'Oh, no, you won't,' I cried as soon as I'd closed the door. I took the phone off the hook, ran a bath, and finished off the wine while I soaked in the warm, scented water. The events of the day swirled through my mind: the Naughtons and that filthy house, Alison, Declan, Diana and her father, James.

James! What was Declan saying to him? It wasn't that I

cared about him loving me less, I only cared about him – anybody – *knowing*. And when it came down to it, it was nothing to do with the house in Kirkby, or being poor, or Mum letting herself go, or Alison. It was the terror of my childhood that I wanted to keep to myself: the beatings, the fear, the sheer indignity of it all. I'd felt as if my body didn't belong to me, that it could be used by someone else whenever the whim took them. What I wanted more than anything was to put the past behind me so that the dreams would stop. I wanted to forget everything and become a person not a victim. But this would never happen while my family remained a haunting reminder, always there to ensure that the past was part of the present and, possibly, the future. The only solution would be to go far away, start a new life elsewhere – but although my mother set my teeth on edge, I loved her so much that it hurt. I could never desert her.

The water in the bath had gone cold. I climbed out, reached for a towel, and was almost dry when the doorbell rang.

'Blast!' I struggled into a bathrobe.

'I tried to call you on the car phone,' James said, as he came breezing in, 'but you seemed to be incommunicado.' He noticed the receiver was off the hook. 'Is this deliberate or accidental?'

'Deliberate,' I said irritably. 'I want some peace. I want to be left alone.' He tried to take me in his arms, but I pushed him away. 'Please, James.'

He threw himself on to the settee with a sigh. 'Why didn't you tell me all that stuff before?'

My heart missed a beat. 'What stuff?'

'You know what I mean. About Alison, and about Declan being gay.'

'Declan's not gay!' I gasped.

'Of course he is, Millie. It's obvious.'

'You're talking utter rubbish,' I said half-heartedly, remembering how Declan had blushed when James paid him a compliment. Then I remembered all sorts of other things about my brother. He was girlish, no doubt about it, but gay?

'Darling, I guessed straight away.'

I shook my reeling head. It was too much, coming after such an eventful day. 'What did you and Declan talk about on the way to Kirkby?'

'Cars, mainly, football a bit. Why?'

'I just wondered.'

'After I dropped him off, I gave some kids a ride around the block. They were very impressed with the Maserati.'

'That was nice of you.'

I made him a coffee, then insisted he went home. Before going to bed, I took three aspirins. Even so, unlike last night at Flo's, it was several hours before I eventually fell asleep, a restless, jerky sleep, full of unwelcome, unpleasant dreams.

Diana's father was kept in hospital overnight. The fall had nothing to do with his illness; he had had a dizzy spell. Next morning she said that a neighbour had offered to bring him home. 'I suppose you think I'm awful, not going myself,' she went on.

'Why should I?'

'Well, I think I'm awful. Daddy's being incredibly brave. At times, I wish he'd have a good old moan and I'd really have something to complain about. I'd feel less of a louse.' She wrinkled her nose. 'I'm all mixed up.'

'Who isn't?' I snorted.

3

James had been told bluntly that I needed time to myself, time to think. If he turned up uninvited again, I would be very cross. He agreed meekly that we wouldn't meet again until Saturday. 'Will you be very cross if I call you?' he asked, in a little-boy voice.

'Of course not, but if I'm not around I don't want anguished messages left on my answering-machine.'

'No, ma'am. Thank you very much, ma'am.'

I kissed his nose, because he was so patient and understanding. I couldn't imagine allowing a man to mess me about as much as I did him. Nor could I understand why he put up with it from someone like me.

Throughout the week, I did my utmost to get to the flat in William Square, but the estate-agency business, while not exactly booming, was picking up. On Wednesday and Thursday I was still hard at work in the office until well past seven o'clock.

On Friday night, I finished off the report and stapled together the eight pages. I decided to read through it again and give it to George on Monday: he'd begun negotiations for the empty shop, which he hoped to have open by Christmas. Even if Diana got her 'notes' in first, it would show that I was equally keen.

Afterwards, I phoned home, which I'd been meaning to do all week, and was relieved when Declan answered.

'Where's Mum?' I asked.

'Out. Dad went to the pub, so I gave her five quid of that twenty I got off you on condition she went to bingo.' He chuckled. 'She was dead chuffed.'

'Declan?'

'Yes, luv?'

'That suggestion James made, about you going to college, why don't you do it? You could learn car mechanics or something, get a job in a garage.' Unlike me, he had left school with two reasonable O levels.

'Oh, I dunno, Millie. Me dad would blow his top.'

'You're twenty, Declan. It's nothing to do with him what you do with your life.'

'That's easy for you to say. It's not you who'd face the consequences when he finds out I've given up work for college.' He sounded peevish, as if he thought I'd forgotten the way my father's powerful presence still dominated the house in Kirkby.

'You've already given up work, Declan – or, rather, work's given up on you.' He was too soft, too unselfish, not like me and Trudy, who couldn't wait to get away. He was also weak. In a strange way, the horror had made my sister and me stronger, but our father had beaten all of the stuffing out of his only son. Declan's sole ambition seemed to be to exist from day to day with as little effort as possible.

'I suppose it wouldn't hurt to make a few enquiries,' he said grudgingly. 'What I've always fancied is learning about fashion – y'know, designing dresses or material, that sort of thing.'

'In that case, go for it, Dec,' I urged, and tried to imagine what our father would say when told his son was training to be a dress designer. Even worse, how would he react if James was right and he, too, realised that Declan was gay? I would have liked to discuss it with Declan there and then, but it was up to him to out himself. Until he did, I would never breathe a word to a soul.

I had expected James to claim he'd missed me dreadfully, but when he picked me up on Saturday night he said 'I've had a great week. I've joined the SWP.'

'The what?' I felt a trifle put out, particularly when he didn't even notice my new outfit, a short black satin shirt, nor that I'd parted my hair in the middle and smoothed it back behind my ears for a change.

'The Socialist Workers' Party.'

'Good heavens, James!' I gasped. 'Isn't that a bit over the top? What's wrong with the Labour Party?'

'Everything!' he said crisply. 'This chap, Ed, said that they're all a shower of wankers. This morning I helped collect money for those dockers I told you about. I nearly brought my placard into Stock Masterton to show you.'

'I'm glad you didn't!' I hid a smile. 'Does this mean you're over your crisis?'

'I'm not sure, but for the first time in my life, I feel as if

I have some connection with the real world, real people. I've learned an awful lot this week. You wouldn't believe the tiny amount single mothers have to live on, and I never knew the National Health Service was in such a state.'

All the way into town, he reeled off statistics that most people, me included, already knew. Only a tiny percentage of the population owned a huge percentage of the country's wealth; revenue from North Sea oil had disappeared into thin air; privatisation had created hundreds of millionaires.

In the restaurant, a favourite one in the basement of a renovated warehouse, with bare brick walls and a Continental atmosphere, he didn't show his usual interest in the food. 'I went to Ed's place on Wednesday to watch a video. Did you know that in the Spanish Civil War the Communists fought on the side of the legally elected government? I'd always thought it was the other way round, that the Communists were the revolutionaries.'

I stared at him, aghast: he'd been to public school, followed by three years at university during which he'd studied history, for God's sake, and he hadn't known that! 'What does your father have to say about your miraculous conversion?' I asked. 'A couple of weeks ago, you were in the Young Conservatives.'

He frowned and looked annoyed. 'My folks think it jolly amusing. Pop said he's glad I've started to use my brain at last. My sister got involved with a group of anarchists at university, and he thinks I'll grow out of it, like Anna did.'

Anna was married with two children and lived in London. So far, we'd not met. I sipped my coffee thoughtfully. I wasn't sure if I wanted him to grow out of it. The trouble was, like his folks, I found the whole thing rather amusing. Although, no doubt, he felt sincerely about his newly found beliefs, he didn't sound sincere, more like a little boy who'd discovered a rare stamp for his collection.

'Where shall we go?' He looked at his watch. 'It's only half past ten.'

All I could think of was a club, but James reminded me he'd gone off them. 'I've just remembered,' I said, 'We're invited to a party in William Square.' It was Charmian's son's twenty-first.

'Great,' James said eagerly. 'Let's go.'

'But you'd hate it,' I laughed. 'They're not at all your sort of people.'

He looked hurt. 'What do you mean, not my sort of people? You'd think I came from a different planet. I quite fancy partying with a new crowd. Wherever we go it's always the same old faces.'

The same old middle–class professionals; bankers and farmers, stockbrokers and chaps who were something in insurance. Some of the women had careers, and those who'd given up their jobs to have children complained bitterly about the horrendous cost of employing cleaners and au pairs. I always felt out of place, just as I probably would at Charmian's. I wondered if there was anywhere I'd feel right.

'We'll go to the party if you like,' I said, but only to please James. After all, now he'd joined the SWP he'd have to get used to mixing with the hoi polloi.

Charmian looked exotic in a cerise robe with a turban wound round her majestic head. 'Lovely to see you, girl,' she murmured, and kissed me.

Rather to my own surprise, I kissed her back as I handed over the wine James had bought in the restaurant for a ludicrous price because he couldn't be bothered to search for an off-licence. I introduced him to Charmian, who seemed taken aback when he shook her hand and said, in his beautifully cultured voice, 'How lovely to meet you.'

The Smiths big living room was packed, though several couples in the middle were managing somehow to dance to the almost deafening sound of Take That's

'Relight My Fire'. I met Herbie, Charmian's husband, a mild, good-humoured man with greying hair who was circulating with a bottle of wine in each hand. 'Our Jay's around somewhere.' Charmian peered over the crowd. 'You must meet the birthday boy.' With that, she plunged into the fray.

I found a bedroom and left my coat. When I returned, there was no sign of James so I helped myself to a glass of wine and leaned against the wall, hoping Bel had been invited so that I would have someone to talk to.

A young man with a wild head of shaggy black curls and a fluffy beard came and stood beside me, his dark eyes smiling through heavy horn-rimmed glasses. 'You look like the proverbial wallflower.'

'I'm waiting for my boyfriend,' I explained.

'Fancy a dance in the meantime?'

'I wouldn't mind.' I felt rather conspicuous on my own.

He took my hand and led the way through to the dancers. There wasn't room to do anything other than shuffle round on the spot.

'Do you live round here?' I asked politely. I'd never been much good at small talk.

'Next door, basement flat. Do you still live in Kirkby?'

'You know me!' I never liked coming across people from the past.

'We were in the same class together at school. You're Millie Cameron, aren't you?'

I nodded. 'I'm at a disadvantage compared to you,' I said. 'I don't recall anyone in class with a beard.'

'I'm Peter Maxwell, in those days known as Weedy. You can't have forgotten me. I usually had a black eye, sometimes two, and an inordinate amount of cuts and bruises. The other lads used to wallop me because I was no good at games. Me mam wasn't slow at walloping me either but she didn't need a reason.'

'I remember.' He'd been a frail, pathetic little boy, the smallest in the class, smaller even than the girls. There never seemed to be a time when he wasn't crying. Rumour had it that his father had been killed during a fight outside a pub in Huyton. I envied his ability to talk about things so openly: there'd been no need for him to tell me who he was. Maybe he knew my own history. It had been no secret that Millie and Trudy Cameron's father hit his girls.

'How come you grew so big?' I asked. He was only as tall as I was, about five feet eight, but his shoulders were broad and I could sense the strength in his arms.

'Turned sixteen, left home, found work, spent all my spare time in a gym, where I grew massively, but mainly sideways.' He grinned engagingly. 'Having developed the brawn, it was time to develop the brain, so I went to university and got a degree in economics. I teach at a comprehensive a mile from here.'

'That's a tough job!' I admired him enormously, particularly his lack of hang-ups.

'It helps to have muscles like Arnold Schwarzenegger,' he conceded, 'particularly when dealing with bullies, but most kids want to learn, not cause trouble. Now, that's enough about me, Millie. What are you up to these days? If I remember rightly, you married Gary Bennett.'

'I did, yes, but we're divorced. I'm a property negotiator with Stock —'

Before I could say another word, a young woman in a red velvet trouser suit pushed through the dancers and seized his arm. 'There you are! I've been looking everywhere for you.' She dragged him away, and he turned to me, mouthing, 'Sorry.'

I was just as sorry to see him go – it had been interesting to talk to someone with a background similar to my own. I spotted James, deep in conversation with a middle-aged couple. He seemed to have forgotten about me. I felt a bit lost and made my way to the kitchen where I offered to help wash dishes. Herbie shooed me away with an indignant, 'You're here to enjoy yourself, girl.'

By now, the party had spilled out into the hall. I went

out in the hope of finding Bel, but there was no sign of her so I sat on the stairs and was immediately drawn into an argument over the acting ability, or lack of it, of John Travolta.

'He was great in *Pulp Fiction*,' a woman maintained hotly.

'He stank in *Saturday Night Fever*,' someone else said.

'That was years ago.' The woman waved her arms in disgust. 'Anyroad, no one expected him to act in *Saturday Night Fever*. It was a musical and his dancing was superb.'

The front door opened and a man came in, a tall, slim man in his twenties with a pale, hard face and brown hair drawn back in a ponytail. He wore small gold gypsy earrings and was simply dressed in jeans, white T-shirt, and black leather jacket. There was something sensual about the way he moved, smoothly and effortlessly, like a panther, that made me shiver. At the same time, his lean body was taut, on edge. Despite his hard expression, his features were gentle: a thin nose, flaring wide at the nostrils, full lips, high, moulded cheekbones. I shivered again.

The man closed the door and leaned against it. His eyes flickered over the guests congregated in the hall. I held my breath when our eyes met and his widened slightly, as if he recognised me. Then he turned away, almost contemptuously, and went into the living room.

'What do you think? What did you say your name was?' The woman who had been defending John Travolta was speaking to me.

'Millie. What do I think about what?'

'Didn't you think he was fantastic in *Get Shorty*?'

'Amazing,' I agreed, still preoccupied with the man who'd just come in.

For the next hour I barely listened as the discussion moved on to other Hollywood stars. Someone brought me another glass of wine, then James appeared, gave a thumbs-up, and vanished again. I contemplated looking for the man with the ponytail to find out who he was –

but I had left it too late: the front door opened and through the crowd I glimpsed him leaving.

At one o'clock, the party was still going strong. There were sounds of a fight from the living room, and Herbie emerged holding two young men by the scruff of the neck and flung them out of the door.

By now, I was tired of Hollywood and longed to go home. I searched for James and found him sitting on the floor with half a dozen people who were all bellowing at each other about politics. He'd removed his jacket and was drinking beer from a can. I didn't like to disturb him when he appeared to be enjoying himself so much. Nevertheless, I fancied some peace and quiet and knew exactly where I could find it.

William Square, bathed in the light of a brilliant full moon, was quiet when I went outside, though the silence was deceptive. Women, barely clothed, leaned idly against the railings, smoking and waiting for their next customer. A car crawled past, then stopped, and the driver rolled down the window. A girl in white shorts went over and spoke to him. She got in, the driver revved the engine and drove away. Two dogs roamed the pavements, casually sniffing each other. In the distance, the wail of a siren could be heard, and in the even further distance, someone screamed. A cat rubbed itself against my legs, but ran away when I bent to stroke it.

Suddenly, a police helicopter roared into the sky, like a monstrous, brilliantly lit bird. The noise was almost deafening. It really was a war zone, as George had said. I ran down the steps to Flo's flat. To my consternation, I saw that the curtains were drawn and the light was on, yet I could distinctly remember switching off the light and pulling back the curtains the last time I was there. Perhaps someone, Charmian or Bel, had decided it would be wise to make the place look lived in. But there was only one key, the one I held in my hand right now.

Cautiously I unlocked the door. It was unlikely I'd come to any harm with fifty or sixty people upstairs. I opened the inner door and gasped in surprise. The man with the ponytail was lounging on Flo's settee, his feet on the coffee table, watching the swirling lamp and listening to her record.

'Who are you? What are you doing here?' I snapped.

He turned and regarded me lazily, and I saw that his eyes were green, like mine. His face seemed softer than when I'd seen him upstairs, as if he, too, was under the spell of the blurred shadows flitting around the room and the enchanting music.

'I never thought I'd do this again,' he said. 'I came to leave me key on the mantelpiece and found Flo's place no different than it's always been.'

'Where did you get the key?'

'Off Flo, of course. Who else?' His voice was coarse, his Liverpool accent thick and nasal. He was the sort of man from whom I'd normally run a mile, and yet, and yet . . . I did my level best to hide another shiver.

'You still haven't told me who you are.'

'No, but I've told you why I'm here.' He swung his feet off the table with obvious reluctance, as if he wasn't used to being polite, and stood up. 'I was a friend of Flo's. Me name is Tom O'Mara.'

Flo

I

'Tommy O'Mara!' Martha's voice was raw with a mixture of hysteria and horror. 'You're having a baby by Tommy O'Mara! Didn't he go down on the *Thetis*?'

Flo didn't answer. Sally, sitting at the table, pale and shocked, muttered, 'That's right.'

'You mean you've been with a married man?' Martha screeched. Her face had gone puffy and her eyes were two beads of shock behind her round glasses. 'Have you no shame, girl? I'll never be able to hold up me head in Burnett Street again. We'll have to start using a different church. And they're bound to find out at work. Everybody will be laughing at me behind me back.'

'It's Flo who's having the baby, Martha, not you,' Sally said gently.

Flo was grateful that Sally appeared to be on her side or, at least, sympathetic to her plight. A few minutes ago when she had announced that she was pregnant, Martha had exploded but Mam had said quietly, 'I can't stand this,' and had gone straight upstairs, leaving Flo to Martha's rage and disgust. The statement had been made after tea deliberately, just before Albert Colquitt was due when Martha would feel bound to shut up. After Albert had been seen to, she might have calmed down a bit, but Flo knew that she would be at the receiving end of many more lashings from her sister's sharp tongue.

'It might be Flo having the baby, but it's the whole family that'll bear the shame,' Martha said cuttingly. She turned to her youngest sister, 'How could you, Flo?'

'I was in love with him,' Flo said simply. 'We were going to get wed when Nancy got better.'

'Nancy! Of course, he married that Nancy Evans, didn't he? Everyone used to call her the Welsh witch.' Martha scowled. 'What do you mean, you were going to get wed when she got better? She's never been sick, as far as I know. Anyroad, what's that got to do with it?'

As Martha was unlikely to know the intimate details of Nancy O'Mara's medical history, Flo ignored the comment, but she was disconcerted to learn that Nancy was Welsh when she was supposed to have been Spanish. In a faltering voice she said, 'He wasn't married proper to Nancy.' She didn't mention the gypsy ceremony in a wood near Barcelona because it sounded ridiculous. In her heart of hearts, she'd never truly believed it. It was too far-fetched. She wondered bleakly if Tommy had ever been to Spain, and realised that everything of which Martha accused her was true: she was a fallen woman, lacking in morals, who'd brought disgrace upon her family.

It wasn't surprising to hear Martha say that there was no question of Tommy O'Mara not being married proper to Nancy Evans, because she had been in church when the banns were called. 'He used to lodge with the family of this girl I met at Sunday school,' she said, and added spitefully, 'She said her mam couldn't wait to get shot of him because she had a terrible job getting the money off him for his bed and board.'

Sally gasped. 'Shush, Martha. There's no need for that.'

'I'm sorry,' Flo said brokenly. 'I'm so sorry.'

'There, there, Sis.' Sally slipped off the chair and put her arms around her sister, but Martha wasn't to be swayed easily by expressions of regret.

'And so you should be sorry,' she blasted. 'You realise everyone will call the kid a bastard? No one will speak to it at school. It'll be spat upon and kicked wherever it goes.'

'Martha!' Mam said sharply, from the doorway. 'That's enough.'

Flo burst into tears and ran upstairs, just as the front door opened and Albert Colquitt arrived.

A few minutes later, Sally came in and sat on the bed where Flo was lying face down, sobbing.

'You should have taken precautions, luv,' she whispered. 'I know what it's like when you're in love. It's hard to stop if things get out of hand.'

'You mean, you and Jock . . .' Flo raised her head and looked tearfully at her sister. Jock Wilson continued to descend on Liverpool whenever he could wangle a few days' leave.

Sally nodded. 'Don't tell Martha, whatever you do.'

The idea was so preposterous, that Flo actually laughed. 'As if I would!'

'She doesn't mean everything she says, you know. I don't know why she's so bitter and twisted. You'd think she was jealous that you'd been with a man.' Sally sighed. 'Poor Martha. Lord knows what she'll say when she finds out me and Jock are getting married at Christmas, if he can get away. She'd have expected to go first, being the eldest, like.'

'Sally, Oh, Sal, I'm so pleased for you.' Flo forgot her own troubles and hugged her sister. Sally made her promise to keep the news to herself: she didn't want anyone to know until it was definite.

After a while, Sally went downstairs because it was her turn to do the dishes and she didn't want Martha getting in a further twist.

Flo sat up, leaned against the headboard, and rested her hands on her swelling tummy. She'd put off breaking the dreadful news for as long as possible, but it was October, she was four and a half months' pregnant, and it was beginning to show. One or two women in the laundry had been eyeing her suspiciously, and the other day when she'd been hanging out sheets in the drying room she'd turned to find Mrs Fritz at the door, watching keenly.

Then Mrs Fritz had spent quite a long time in the office with Mr Fritz.

At first Flo had considered not telling a soul, running away and having the baby somewhere else. But she didn't want to stay away for ever and there'd be a baby to explain when she came back. Anyroad, where would she run to and how would she support herself? She had no money and wouldn't be able to get a job. She realised, sadly, that she would have to leave the laundry and it would be dreadful saying goodbye to Mr Fritz.

The door opened and Mam came in. 'I'm sorry I walked out, girl, but I couldn't stand our Martha's screaming. Perhaps it would have been best if you'd told your mam first and left me to deal with Martha.' She looked at her daughter reproachfully. 'How could you, Flo?'

'Please, Mam, don't go on at me.' Flo began to cry again at the sight of her mother's drawn face. Mam had seemed much better since the war began, as if she'd pulled herself together and was determined to see her family through the conflict to its bitter end. 'I'll leave home if you want. I never wanted to bring shame on me family.' Getting pregnant had been far from her mind when she'd lain under the trees in the Mystery with Tommy O'Mara.

'The man, this Tommy O'Mara, he should have known better. Martha says he was at least thirty. He was wrong to take advantage of a naïve young girl.' Mam pursed her lips disapprovingly.

'Oh, no, Mam,' Flo cried. 'He didn't take advantage. He loved me, and I loved him.' The lies he'd told meant nothing and neither did the promises. It was only because he was worried she might not go out with him that he'd said the things he had. 'If Tommy hadn't died, he'd have left Nancy by now and we'd be together.'

This was altogether too much for her mother. 'Don't be ridiculous, girl,' she said heatedly. 'You're talking like a scarlet woman.'

Perhaps she *was* a scarlet woman, because Flo had meant every word she said. Perhaps other couples didn't love each other as much as she and Tommy had. To appease her mother, she said meekly, 'I'm sorry.'

'Anyroad, that part's over and done with,' Mam sighed. 'What we have to deal with now are the consequences. I've had a word with Martha and Sal, and we think the best thing is for you to stay indoors until you've had the baby, then have it adopted. No one in the street will have known a thing. I'll go round and see Mr Fritz tomorrer and tell him you've been taken ill and won't be coming back. I hate to deceive him, he's such a nice feller, but what else can I do?'

'Nothing, Mam,' Flo said calmly. She was quite agreeable to the first part of the suggestion, that she stay indoors until the baby was born, but there was no way she intended giving up Tommy O'Mara's child, which was the next best thing to having Tommy himself. She wouldn't tell Mam that, otherwise there would be non-stop rows for months. Once it was born, she would move to another part of Liverpool, a place where no one knew her, but not too far for her family to come and visit. She'd say she was a widow who had lost her husband in the war, which meant there was no reason for anyone to call her child a bastard. She would support them both by taking in laundry and possibly a bit of mending Mr Fritz often declared that no one else could darn a sheet as neatly as Flo.

War had made little impact so far on the country and people had begun to refer to it as 'phoney'. Lots of lads had been called up and ships were sunk frequently, with enormous loss of life, but it all seemed very far away. There was no sign of the dreaded air-raids and food was still plentiful.

Flo passed the days knitting clothes for the baby: lacy matinée coats and bonnets, unbelievably tiny booties and mittens, and dreaming about how things would be when her child was born. Occasionally, she could hear Mam and her sisters having whispered conversations in the kitchen, and the word adoption would be mentioned. It seemed that Martha already had the matter in hand. Flo didn't bother to disillusion them – anything for a quiet life. When she wasn't knitting, she read the books that Sally got her from the library. Once a month, she wrote to Bel McIntyre, who'd joined the ATS and was stationed up in the wilds of Scotland where she was having a wonderful time. 'There's a girl for every fifteen men,' she wrote. 'But there's one chap in particular I really like. Remember I said once I'd never met a chap worth twopence? Well, I've come across one worth at least a hundred quid. His name is Bob Knox and he comes from Edinburgh like me dad.' Flo didn't mention the baby in her letters. Bel had thought her daft to become involved with a married man, and she didn't want her to know just how involved and completely daft she'd been.

Often, she wished she could go for a walk, particularly when it was sunny, and as the time crawled by, she ached to go out even in the pouring rain. The worst time was when visitors came or their lodger was at home and she had to spend hours shut in the bedroom. According to Martha, of all the people in the world, Albert Colquitt was the one who must remain most ignorant of Flo's dark secret. If he knew what sort of family he was living with he might leave, and that would be disastrous, 'seeing as you're no longer bringing in a wage.' She sniffed. Sally thought Martha was mainly worried that he wouldn't want to marry her, a goal she was still working towards with all her might.

'How do you explain that I'm never there?' asked Flo.

'He's been told you're run down, anaemic, and have to stay in bed and rest.'

'I've never felt so healthy in me life.'

She was blooming, her cheeks the colour and texture of peaches, her eyes bright, and her hair unusually thick and glossy. She wondered why she should look so well when she felt so miserable without Tommy, but perhaps it was because she couldn't wait to have the baby. Also, Mam had ordered extra milk especially for her, and Martha, for all her carping comments and sniffs of disapproval, often brought home a pound of apples and made sure there was cod-liver oil in the house, which was what Elsa Cameron had taken when she was pregnant. 'And look what a lovely baby Norman turned out to be.' Flo knew she was lucky: another family might have thrown her out on to the street.

It was on a black dreary morning in December that the Clancys' lodger discovered the secret he was never supposed to know. Mam had gone Christmas shopping and Flo was in the living room, knitting, when the key turned in the front door. It wasn't often anyone used the front door apart from Albert. She assumed Mam's shopping bags were too heavy to carry round the back, and hurried out to help. To her horror, she came face to face with Albert.

'I forgot me wallet,' he beamed, 'least I hope I did, and it's not lost. It's not just the ten-bob note I had, but there's me identity card, and some photos I'd hate to lose, as well as . . .' His voice faded and his eyes widened in surprise as he took in Flo's condition. 'I didn't know, luv,' he whispered. 'Jaysus, I didn't know.'

Flo was stumbling up the stairs. Halfway, she turned, 'Don't tell our Martha you've seen me,' she implored. 'Please!'

'Of course not, luv.' He looked stunned. 'Flo!' he called, but by then Flo was in the bedroom and had slammed the door.

She heard him go into the parlour, and a few minutes later Mam returned from the shops. 'Are you all right, girl?' she called.

'I'm just having a little lie-down, Mam.'

'I'll bring a cup of tea up in a minute, then I'm going round to St Theresa's to do the flowers for Sunday.'

Mam was obviously unaware that Albert was in the

parlour and remained unaware for the whole time she was at home. After she'd gone, Albert didn't stir or make even the smallest of sounds. Flo wondered if he was still searching for his wallet. Perhaps he was contemplating handing in a week's notice and finding somewhere more respectable to live.

Another half-hour passed, and still no sound. Then the parlour door opened and heavy footsteps could be heard coming upstairs. There was a tap on the door and a voice said hesitantly, 'Flo?'

'Yes?'

'Would you come downstairs a minute, luv? I'd like to talk to you.'

'What about?' Flo said warily.

'Come down and see.'

A few minutes later she and Albert were sitting stiffly in the living room. She felt over-conscious of her enormous stomach and hoped Albert wasn't intent on giving her a lecture, because she'd tell him it was none of his business. She felt deeply ashamed when, instead of a lecture, Albert mumbled, 'I've missed you, Flo. The house doesn't seem as bright and cheery without you.'

'I've been . . . upstairs,' she said lamely.

He shifted uncomfortably in the chair, then, without looking at her directly, said, 'I hope you don't mind me seeming personal, luv, but what's happened to the feller who . . . ?' Words failed him.

'He's dead,' said Flo.

'I thought he might be in the forces, like, and one day he'd turn up and you'd get married.'

'There's no chance of that, not when he's dead.'

'Of course not.' His face was cherry red, and she could see beads of perspiration glistening on his forehead. That he was sweating so profusely made his uniform pong even more strongly than it normally did. She wondered why on earth he was so embarrassed, when if anyone should be it was her. 'It'll be hard, bringing up a kiddie without a husband,' he said awkwardly.

'I'll manage. I'll have to, won't I?'

'It'll still be hard, and the thing is, I'd like to make it easier if you'll let me.' He paused and his face grew even redder before he plunged on. 'I'd like to marry you, Flo, and provide you and the little 'un with a home. I earn decent money as an inspector on the trams, and it's a good, secure job with prospects of promotion to depot superintendent. We could get a nice little house between us, and I've enough put away to buy the furniture we'd need. What do you say, luv?'

Flo hoped the distaste she felt didn't show on her face: the last thing in the world she wanted was to hurt him, but the idea of sharing a bed with a middle-aged man with a pot belly and a dreadful smell made her feel sick.

'It's kind of you, Albert —' she began, but he interrupted, as if he wanted to get everything off his chest.

'Of course, I wouldn't expect to be a proper husband, luv. We'd have separate rooms, and if you ever wanted to leave, it'd be up to you. There'd be no strings. To make it easier, we could get wed in one of those register-office places. I'd just be getting you out of a temporary hole, as it were. You'd have marriage lines, and if we did it quick enough, the baby'd have a dad, at least on paper.'

He was incredibly unselfish, and Flo was angry with herself for finding his proposal so disagreeable. But she'd once dreamed of sharing her life with Tommy O'Mara, beside whom Albert Colquitt was — well, there wasn't any comparison. On the other hand, she thought, as she leaned back in the chair and stared into the fire, would it really be so disagreeable? It would be getting her out of a hole, as he put it. No one would call the baby names if it had a father, and Flo wouldn't have to take in laundry but would have a nice, newly furnished house in which to live. She wouldn't be taking advantage of him, not in a mean way, because it was his idea. Of course, everyone would kick up hell at the idea of a Clancy getting married in a register office but, under the circumstances, Flo didn't care. And Martha would be livid, claiming Flo had stolen Albert from right under her nose.

She was still wondering how to respond when Albert said wistfully, 'Me wife died in childbirth, you know, along with the baby. It was a girl. We were going to call her Patricia, Patsy, if we had a girl. I've always wanted a kiddie of me own.'

If he hadn't said that she might have agreed to marry him, if only on a temporary basis – he'd made it clear that she could leave whenever she wanted. But she knew she could never be so cruel as to walk out once he'd grown to love the baby he'd always wanted. She would feel trapped. It would be like a second bereavement and he would lose another wife and child. No, best turn him down now.

So Flo told him, very nicely and very gently, that she couldn't possibly marry him but that she would never forget his kind gesture. She never dreamed that this decision would haunt her for the rest of her days.

Much to Martha's disappointment, Albert took himself off to stay with a cousin in Macclesfield over Christmas, though Flo was glad because it meant she could remain downstairs except when the occasional visitor came. She wondered if he'd gone for that very reason, and said a little prayer that he would enjoy himself in Macclesfield and that the scarf she'd knitted him would keep him warm – the weather throughout the country was freezing cold with snow several feet deep. Before Albert went, he gave the girls a present each: a gold-plated chain bracelet with a tiny charm. Martha's charm was a monkey, Sally's a key and Flo's a heart.

'I bet he meant to give me the heart,' Martha said.

'We'll swop if you like,' Flo offered.

'It doesn't matter now.'

On Christmas Eve, a package arrived from Bel containing a card and a pretty tapestry purse. When Flo opened the card, a photograph fell out. 'Bel's married!'

she cried. 'She's married someone called Bob Knox, he's a Scot.'

'I only met her the once, but she seemed a nice young lady,' Mam said, pleased. 'You must pass on our congratulations, Flo, next time you write. Why not send her one of those Irish cotton doilies as a little present?'

'I wanted those doilies for me bottom drawer, Mam,' Martha pouted.

Flo shook her head. 'Thanks all the same, Mam, but she won't want a doily in the Army. She'd prefer a bottle of scent or a nice pair of stockings.'

'And have you got the wherewithal to buy scent and nice stockings?' Martha asked nastily.

'I'll get a present when I'm earning money of me own,' Flo snapped.

Their mother clapped her hands impatiently. 'Now, girls, stop bickering. It's Christmas, the season of goodwill.'

'Sorry, Flo.' Martha smiled for once. 'I love you, really.'

'I love you too, Sis.'

Later, Martha said to Flo, 'How old is Bel?'

'Eighteen.'

'Only eighteen!' Martha removed her glasses and polished them agitatedly. 'I'll be twenty-four next year.'

Flo wished with all her heart that she could buy a husband for her unhappy sister and hang him on the tree. It didn't help when, on Boxing Day, a telegram arrived for Sally. GOT LICENCE STOP GOT LEAVE STOP BOOK CHURCH MONDAY STOP JOCK.

'I'm getting married on Monday,' Sally sang, starry-eyed.

Flo whooped with joy, and Mam began to cry. 'Sally, luv! This is awful sudden.'

'It's wartime, Mam. It's the way things happen nowadays.'

'Does it mean you'll be leaving home, luv?' Mam sobbed.

'Jock doesn't have a regular port. I'll stay with me family till the war's over, then we'll get a house of our own.'

At this, Mam's tears stopped and she became practical. She'd call on Father Haughey that very day and book the church. Monday afternoon would be best, just in case Jock was late. Even trains had a job getting through the snow. At this, Sally blanched: she had forgotten that the entire country was snowbound. 'He's coming from Solway Firth. Is that far?' No one had the faintest idea so Dad's atlas was brought out and Solway Firth was discovered to be two counties away.

'I'll die if he doesn't get here!' Sally looked as if she might die there and then.

'Surely he'll be coming by ship.' Martha hadn't spoken until then. Her face was as white as the snow outside and her eyes were bleak. She was the eldest, she was being left behind, and she couldn't stand it.

'Of course!' Sally breathed a sigh of relief.

Mam continued to be practical. Did Sally want a white wedding? No? Well, in that case, tomorrow she'd meet her outside the butcher's at dinner-time, and they'd tour the dress shops in Smithdown Road for a nice costume, her wedding present to her daughter. 'It's no use getting pots and pans yet. And we'll have to have a taxi on the day. It's impossible to set foot outside the house in ordinary shoes in this weather, and you can't very well get married in Wellies. As for the reception, I wonder if it's too late to book a room?'

'I don't want a reception, Mam. I'd prefer tea in a café afterwards. Jock's mate will be best man. All I want is me family, you, Martha and Flo.'

'Our Flo can't go,' Martha pointed out. 'Not in her condition.'

Everyone turned to look at Flo, who dropped her eyes, shame-faced. 'I hate the idea of missing your wedding, Sal,' she mumbled.

'I'll be thinking of you, Flo,' Sally said affectionately. 'You'll be there in spirit, if not in the flesh.'

Flo summoned up every charitable instinct in her body. 'Albert will be back from Macclesfield by then,' she said. 'Perhaps he could go instead of me. He'd be a partner for our Martha.'

Albert declared himself supremely honoured to be invited to the wedding. 'He likes to feel part of the family,' Sally said. 'I suspect he's lonely.'

On the day of her sister's wedding, Flo sat alone in the quiet house, thinking how much things had changed over the last twelve months. A year ago Mam was ill, and the sisters' lives had been jogging along uneventfully. Now, Mam had bucked up out of all recognition, Flo had found, and lost, Tommy O'Mara, and was carrying his child, and at this very minute Sally, wearing an ugly pinstriped costume and a white felt hat that made her look like an American gangster, was in the process of becoming Mrs Jock Wilson. Martha was the only one for whom everything was still the same.

She laid her hands contentedly on her stomach. It was odd, but nowadays she scarcely thought about Tommy O'Mara, as if all her love had been transferred to the baby, who chose that moment to give her a vicious kick. She felt a spark of fear. It wasn't due for another six weeks, on St Valentine's Day, exactly nine months and one week since the date of her last period – Mam had worked it out – but what if it arrived early while she was in the house by herself? Martha had booked a midwife under a 'vow of confidentiality', as she put it, who would deliver the baby when the time came. Flo couldn't wait for everything to be over, when her life would change even more.

Snow continued to fall throughout January, and February brought no respite from the Arctic weather. By now Flo was huge, although she remained nimble on her feet. As the days crept by, though, she lost her appetite and felt increasingly sick. Martha left instructions that she was to be fetched immediately if the baby started to arrive when she was at work.

'Surely it would be best to fetch the midwife first?' cried Mam. 'If you'll tell me where she lives, I'll get her.'

'I'd sooner get her meself,' Martha said testily. 'There'll be no need to panic. First babies take ages to arrive. Elsa Cameron was twenty-four hours in labour.'

'Jaysus!' Flo screamed. 'Twenty-four whole hours! Did it hurt much?'

Martha looked away. 'Only a bit.'

The phosphorous fingers on the alarm clock showed twenty past two as Flo twisted restlessly in bed – it was such a palaver turning over. St Valentine's Day had been and gone and still the baby showed no sign of arriving. She lifted the curtain and looked outside. More snow, falling silently and relentlessly in lumps as big as golf balls. The roads would be impassable again tomorrow.

Suddenly, without warning, pain tore through her belly, so forcefully, that she gasped aloud. The sound must have disturbed her sisters, because Martha stopped snoring and Sally stirred.

Flo waited, her heart in her mouth, glad that the time had come but praying that she wouldn't have a pain like that again. She screamed when another pain, far worse, gripped her from head to toe.

'What's the matter?' Sally leaped out of bed, followed by Martha. 'Has it started, luv?'

'Oh, Lord, yes!' Flo groaned. 'Fetch the midwife, Martha, quick.'

'Where does she live?' demanded Sally. 'I'll go.'

'There isn't time for a midwife,' Martha said shortly, 'not if the pains are this strong. Wake Mam up, if she's not awake already, and put water on to boil – two big pans and the kettle. Once you've done that, fetch those old sheets off the top shelf of the airing cupboard.'

'I still think I should get the midwife, Martha. You and Mam can see to Flo while I'm gone.'

'I said there isn't time!' Martha slapped her hand over Flo's mouth when another pain began. 'Don't scream, Flo, we don't want the neighbours hearing. It would happen the night Albert's not out fire-watching,' she added irritably.

'I can't help screaming,' Flo gasped, pushing Martha's hand away. 'I've got to scream.'

Mam came into the room in her nightdress. 'Help me pull the bed round a bit so's I can get on the other side,' she commanded. When it had been moved, she knelt beside her daughter. 'I know it hurts, luv,' she whispered, 'but try and keep a bit quiet, like.'

'I'll try, Mam. Oh, God!' Flo flung her arms into the air and grasped the wooden headboard.

'Keep her arms like that,' Martha instructed. 'I read a book about it in the library.'

Sally brought the sheets, and Flo felt herself being lifted, her nightie pulled up, and the old bedding was slipped beneath her.

'You didn't book a midwife, did you, our Martha?' Sally said in a low, accusing voice. 'It was all a lie. God, you make me sick, you do. You're too bloody respectable by a mile. You'd let our poor Flo suffer just to protect your own miserable reputation. I don't give a sod if me sister has a baby out of wedlock. You're not human, you.'

'Is it true about the midwife, Martha?' Mam said, in a shocked voice.

'Yes!' Martha spat. 'There's not a single one I'd trust to keep her lip buttoned. It's all right for Sal, she's married. I bet Jock wouldn't have been so keen if he'd known what her sister had been up to.'

'It so happens, Jock's known about Flo for months, but it was me he wanted to marry, not me family.'

'Stoppit!' Flo screamed. 'Stoppit!'

'Girls! Girls! This isn't the time to have a fight.' Mam stroked Flo's brow distractedly. 'Do try to keep quiet, there's a good girl.'

'I'm trying, Mam, honest, but it don't half hurt.'

'I know, luv, I know, but we've kept it to ourselves all these months, there's only a short while to go.'

'Can I go for a walk once it's over?'

'Yes, luv. As soon as you're fit, we'll go for a walk together.'

In her agony, Flo forgot that by the time she was fit again she would be gone from the house in Burnett Street. She would be living somewhere else with her baby.

Afterwards, she never thought to ask how long the torment lasted: one hour, two hours, three. All she could remember were the agonising spasms that seized her body regularly and which wouldn't have felt quite so bad if only she could have screamed. But every time she opened her mouth, Martha's hand would slam down on her face and Mam would shake her arm and whisper, 'Try not to make a noise, there's a good girl.'

She was only vaguely aware of the argument raging furiously over her head. 'This is cruel,' Sally hissed. 'You're both being dead cruel. It's only what I'd expect from our Martha, but I'm surprised at you, Mam.'

Then Mam replied, in a strange, cold voice, 'I'm sorry about the midwife, naturally, but one of these days, you'll leave this house, girl, all three of you will. I don't want to be known for the rest of me life as the woman who's daughter had an illegitimate baby, because that's how they'll think of me in the street and in the Legion of Mary, and I'd never be able to hold me head up in front of Father Haughey again.'

Later, Sally demanded, 'What happens if she tears? She'll need stitches. For Christ's sake, at least get the doctor to sew her up.'

'Women didn't have stitches in the past,' Martha said tersely. 'Flo's a healthy girl. She'll mend by herself.'

'I want to go to the lavatory,' Flo wailed. 'Fetch the chamber, quick, or I'll do it in the bed.'

'It's coming!' Mam said urgently.

'Push, Flo,' Martha hissed. 'Push hard.'

'I need the chamber!'

'No, you don't, Flo. It's the baby. *Push!*'

Flo felt sure her body was going to burst and the hurt was so tremendous that the room turned black and little stars appeared, dancing on the ceiling. ' "Dancing in the dark," she bellowed. "Dancing in the dark. Dancing . . ." '

'Oh, Lord!' Sally was almost sobbing. 'She's lost her mind. Now see what you've done!'

Which was the last thing Flo heard until she woke up with a peculiar taste in her mouth. She opened her eyes very, very slowly, because the lids felt too heavy to lift. It was broad daylight outside. Every ounce of strength had drained from her body, and she could barely raise her arms. Unbelievably, for several seconds she forgot about the baby. It wasn't until she noticed her almost flat tummy that she remembered. Despite her all-out weariness, she was gripped by shivers of excitement. She forced herself on to her elbows and looked around the room, but the only strange thing there was a bottle of brandy on the dressing-table which accounted for the funny taste in her mouth, though she couldn't remember drinking it. There was no sign of a baby.

'Mam,' she called weakly. 'Martha, Sal.'

Mam came into the room looking exhausted, but relieved. 'How do you feel, luv?'

'Tired, that's all. Where's the baby?'

'Why, luv, he's gone. Martha took him round to the woman who arranged the adoption. Apparently a very nice couple have been waiting anxiously for him to arrive, not that they cared whether it was a boy or a girl, like. They'll have him by now. He'll be one of the best-loved babies in the whole world.'

It was a boy *and he'd been given away!* Flo's heart leaped to her throat and pounded as loudly as a drum. 'I want my baby,' she croaked. 'I want him this very minute.' She struggled out of bed, but her legs gave way and she fell to the floor. 'Tell me where Martha took him, and I'll fetch him back.'

'Flo, luv.' Mam came over and tried to help her to her feet, but Flo pushed her away and crawled towards the door. If necessary, she'd crawl in her nightdress through the snow to find her son, Tommy's lad, their baby.

'Oh, Flo, my dear, sweet girl,' Mam cried, 'can't you see this is the best possible way? It's what we decided ages ago. You're only nineteen, you've got your whole life ahead of you. You don't want to be burdened with a child at your age!'

'He's not a burden. I want him.' Flo collapsed, weeping on to the floor. 'I want my baby.'

Martha came in. 'It's all over, Flo,' she said gently. 'Now's the time to put the whole thing behind you.'

Between them, they picked her up and helped her back to bed. 'C'mon, luv,' Martha said, 'Have another few spoons of brandy, it'll help you sleep and you need to get your strength back. You'll be pleased to know none of the neighbours have been round wanting to know what all the racket was last night, which means we got away with it, didn't we?'

Why, oh, why hadn't she just taken a chance, run away and hoped everything would turn out all right? Why hadn't she made it plain that she wanted to keep the baby? Why hadn't she married Albert Colquitt?

In the fevered, nightmarish days that followed, Flo remained in bed and tortured herself with the same questions over and over again. She cursed her lack of courage: she'd been too frightened to run away, preferring to remain in the comfort of her home with her family around her, letting them think she was agreeable to the adoption to avoid the inevitable rows. She cursed her ignorance in assuming that she'd have the baby, leap out of bed, and carry him off into the unknown. Finally, she cursed her soft heart for turning down Albert's proposal because she didn't want him hurt at some time in the far-distant future.

All the time, her arms ached to hold her little son. The unwanted milk dried up, her breasts turned to concrete, and her insides felt as if they were shrivelling to nothing. She didn't cry, she was beyond tears.

'What did he look like?' she asked Sally one day.

'He was a dear little thing. I'm sure Mam wished we could have kept him. She cried when Martha made her give him up.'

'At least Mam held him, which is more than I did,' Flo said bitterly. 'I never even saw him.'

'That's what happens when women give their babies up for adoption. They're not allowed to see them, let alone hold them, least so Martha says. It's what's called being cruel to be kind.' Sally's eyes were full of sympathy, but even she thought that what had happened was for the best.

'Our Martha seems to know everything.' Flo had refused to speak to Martha until she revealed the where-abouts of her son.

'That's something I'll just have to get used to,' Martha said blithely, 'I couldn't tell you even if I wanted to because the names of adoptive parents are kept confiden-tial. All I've been told is the baby's got a mam and dad who love him. That should make you happy, not sad. They'll be able to give him all the things that you never could.'

Flo gripped her painful breasts and glared contemptu-ously at her sister. 'They can't give him his mother's milk, can they? There'll be no bond between him and some strange woman who didn't carry him in *her* belly for nine whole months.'

'Don't be silly, Flo.' For once, Martha was unable to meet her sister's eyes. She turned away, her face strangely flushed.

March came, and a few days later the weather changed dramatically. The snow that had lain on the ground for months melted swiftly as the temperature soared.

Spring had arrived!

Flo couldn't resist the bright yellow sunshine that poured into the bedroom, caressing her face with its gentle warmth. She threw back the bedclothes, and got up for the first time in a fortnight. Her legs were still weak, her stomach hurt, her head felt as if it had been stuffed with old rags, but she had to go for a walk.

She walked further every day. Gradually, her young body recovered its strength and vigour. When she met people she knew, they remarked on how fit and well she looked. 'You're a picture of health, Flo. No one would guess you'd been so ill.'

But Flo knew that, no matter how well she looked, she would never be the same person again. She would never stop mourning her lost baby, a month old by now. There was an ache in her chest, as if a little piece of her heart had been removed when her son was taken away.

2

Sally had left the butcher's to take up war work at Rootes Securities, an aircraft factory in Speke, for three times the wages. She was coping well in the machine shop in what used to be a man's job. Even Mam was talking about looking for part-time work. 'After all, there's a war on. We've all got to do our bit.' Albert was out most nights fire-watching, though so far there hadn't been a fire for him to watch.

Flo realised it was time she got back to work. Sally suggested she apply to Rootes Securities. 'If we got on the same shift we could go together on the bus. You'll find it peculiar, working nights, but it's the gear there, Sis. All we do the whole time is laugh.'

Laugh! Flo couldn't imagine smiling again, let alone laughing. Sally fetched an application form for her to fill in and took it back next morning. Later, as Flo roamed the streets of Liverpool, she thought wistfully of Fritz's

Laundry. She'd sooner work there than in a factory, even if the pay was a pittance compared to what Sal earned.

Since emerging from her long confinement, she'd passed the laundry numerous times. The side door was always open, but she hadn't had the nerve to peek inside. She felt sure the women, including Mrs Fritz, had guessed the real reason why she'd left.

On her way home the same day, she passed the laundry again. Smoke was pouring from the chimneys, and a cloud of steam floated out the door.

'I'll pop in and say hello,' she decided. 'If they're rude, then I'll never go again. But I'd like to thank Mr Fritz for the lovely necklace he sent at Christmas.'

She crossed the street, wondering what sort of reception she would get. To her astonishment, when she presented herself at the door, the only person there was Mr Fritz, his shirtsleeves rolled up, working away furiously on the big pressing machine that Flo had come to regard as her own.

'Mr Fritz!'

'Flo!' He stopped work and came over to kiss her warmly on the cheek. 'Why, it's good to see you. It's as if the sun has come out twice today. What are you doing here?'

'I just came to say hello, like, and thank you for the necklace. Where is everyone?'

He spread his arms dramatically. 'Gone! Olive was the first, then Josie, then the others. Once they discovered they could earn twice as much in a factory they upped and went. Not that I blame them. I can't compete with those sort of wages, and why should they make sacrifices on behalf of Mr and Mrs Fritz and their eight children when they have families of their own?'

Mrs Fritz came hurrying out of the drying room with a pile of bedding. Her face hardened when she saw Flo. 'Hello,' she said shortly. She scooped clean washing out of a boiler and disappeared again.

Her husband wrinkled his stubby little nose in

embarrassment. 'Don't take any notice of Stella. She's worn out. Her mother is over from Ireland to look after the children, as we work all the hours God sends, including weekends. You see, Flo,' he went on earnestly, 'lots of hotels and restaurants have lost staff to the war and they send us the washing they used to do themselves. Business has soared, and I hate to turn it away, so Stella and I are trying to cope on our own. I've hired a lad, Jimmy Cromer, to collect and deliver on a bike with a sidecart. He's a right scally, but very reliable for a fourteen-year-old.' He managed to chuckle and look gloomy at the same time. 'One of these days, Stella and I will find ourselves buried under a mountain of sheets and pillowcases, and no one will find us again.'

'Would you like a hand?' Flo blurted. 'Permanent, like.'

'Would I!' He beamed, then bit his lip and glanced uneasily towards the drying room. 'Just a minute, Flo.'

He was gone a long time. Flo couldn't hear what was said, but sensed from the sound of the muffled voices that he and Stella were arguing. She supposed she might as well get on with a bit of pressing rather than stand around doing nothing, so folded several tablecloths and was wreathed in a cloud of hissing steam when he returned.

'We'd love to have you, Flo,' he said, rubbing his hands together happily, though she guessed he was putting it on a bit. Mrs Fritz had probably agreed because they were desperate. As if to prove this, he went on, 'You'll have to make allowances for Stella. As I said, she's worn out. The children daren't look at her in case she snaps their heads off. As for me, I'm very much in her bad books. She regards me as personally responsible for the war and our present difficulties.'

As the profit from the laundry had provided the Fritz family with a high standard of living and a big house in William Square, one of the best addresses in Liverpool, Flo thought it unfair of Stella to complain. She said nothing, but offered to go home, change into old clothes and start work that afternoon.

Mr Fritz accepted her suggestion gratefully. 'But are you sure you're up to it, Flo? Your mother said you were very ill each time I called.' He looked into her eyes and she could tell he knew why she'd been 'ill' but, unlike his wife, he didn't care. 'There'll be three of us doing the work of six.'

'Does that mean the wages will be more?' She was glad to be coming back, but it seemed only fair that if she was doing the work of two women, she should get an increase in wages. He might not be able to compete with a factory, but if business was soaring he should be able to manage a few extra bob.

He blinked, as if the thought hadn't entered his head. Just in case it hadn't, Flo said, 'I've applied for a job in Rootes Securities where our Sally works. She's paid time and a half if she works Saturdays.'

Mr Fritz's shoulders shook with laughter. 'Don't worry, my dear. I promise your pocket won't suffer if you work for me. I'll pay you by the hour from now on, including time and a half on Saturdays.'

Flo blushed. 'I didn't mean to sound greedy, like.'

He pecked both her cheeks and chucked her under the chin. 'I haven't seen you smile yet. Come on, Flo, brighten up my day even further and give me one of your lovely smiles.'

And to Flo's never-ending astonishment, she managed to smile.

Stella Fritz had seemed such a sweet, uncomplaining person in the days when Flo hardly knew her, but after they'd worked side by side for a short while, she turned out to be a sour little woman who complained all the time. Perhaps she was worn out and missed being with her children, but there was no need to be quite so nasty to Mr Fritz, who was blamed for every single thing, from exceptionally dirty sheets that needed boiling twice to food rationing, which had just been introduced.

'Bloody hell! She was only a farm girl back in Ireland,'

Martha said indignantly, when Flo brought up the subject at home – Flo's vow never to speak to her eldest sister had been forgotten. 'She's dead lucky to have hooked someone like Mr Fritz. Have you seen their house in William Square?'

'I hope she's not nasty to you,' Mam remarked. 'If she is I'll go round there and give her a piece of me mind.'

'Oh, she just ignores me, thank goodness.' It was a relief to be beneath the woman's contempt. It meant she could get on with things without expecting the wrath of Cain to fall on her because the chain in the lavatory had stopped working or the soap powder hadn't arrived.

Mr Fritz said privately that he'd never felt so pleased about anything in his life as he was to have Flo back. She told him he was exaggerating, but he maintained stoutly that he meant every word. 'I love my wife, Flo, but she was beginning to get me down. The atmosphere has improved enormously since you reappeared on the scene. Things don't seem so bad if you can make a joke of them. Until you came, it all seemed rather tragic.' Every time Stella went into the drying room, or outside for some fresh air, he would make a peculiar face and sing, 'The dragon lady's gone, oh, the dragon lady's gone. What shall we do now the dragon lady's gone?'

When the dragon lady returned, he would cry, 'Ah, there you are, my love!' Stella would throw him a murderous look and Flo would do her best to stifle a giggle. She thought Mr Fritz was incredibly patient. A less kind-hearted person might have dumped Stella in one of the boilers.

She scarcely noticed spring turn into summer because she was working so hard, sometimes till eight or nine o'clock at night, arriving home bone weary, with feet swollen to twice their normal size, ready to fall into bed where she went to sleep immediately. Sally was equally tired and Martha's brewery was short-staffed, which meant she often had to work late. In order to hang on to their remaining staff, the brewery increased the wages, or the pubs might run out of beer, a situation too horrendous even to contemplate. Mam got a part-time job in a greengrocer's in Park Road. The Clancy family had never been so wealthy, but there was nothing to spend the money on. Rationing meant food was strictly limited, and the girls hadn't time to wander round the shops looking at clothes. They all started post-office accounts, and began to save for the day when the war would be over, though that day seemed a long way off.

By now, the war could no longer be described as 'phoney'. Adolf Hitler had conquered most of Europe; in June, he took France, and although thousands of British and French soldiers were rescued in the great evacuation of Dunkirk, thousands more lost their lives or were taken prisoner. The British Isles was separated from the massed German troops by only a narrow strip of water. People shivered in their beds, because invasion seemed inevitable, although the government did all it could to make an invasion as hazardous as possible. Road signs and the names of stations were removed, barricades were erected, aliens were sent to detention camps all over the country, including nice Mr and Mrs Gabrielli who owned the fish-and-chip shop in Earl Road.

One Monday, Flo arrived at work to find Mrs Fritz all on her own, ironing a white shirt with unnecessary force. Her eyes were red, as if she had been weeping. The two women rarely spoke, but Flo felt bound to ask, 'What's the matter? Is Mr Fritz all right?'

'No, he isn't,' Stella said, in a thin voice. 'He's been rounded up like a common criminal and sent to a detention camp on the Isle of Man. Oh, I said he should have taken British nationality years ago but he was proud of being Austrian, the fool. Not only that, we've lost two of our biggest customers. It seems hotels would sooner have dirty sheets than have them washed in a laundry with a foreign name.' Her Irish accent, scarcely noticeable before, had returned in full force with the power of her anger.

'Oh, no!' Flo was sorry about the lost orders, naturally, but devastated at the thought of dear Mr Fritz, who wouldn't have hurt a fly and loathed Hitler every bit as much as she did, being confined behind bars or barbed wire, like a thief or a murderer. 'How long are they keeping him?' she asked.

'For the duration of the bloody war.'

'Oh, no,' Flo said again.

'I suppose I'll just have to close this place down,' Mrs Fritz said bleakly. 'I can't manage on me own. Anyroad, those cancellations could be the start of an avalanche. Soon, there mightn't be any customers left. I suppose we're lucky the building hasn't been attacked. The German pork butcher's in Lodge Lane had all its winders broken.'

'But you can't close down!' Flo cried. 'You've got to keep going for when Mr Fritz comes home. The laundry is his life. And his old customers won't desert him, not the ones who know him personally. We can cope, just the two of us, if there's going to be less work.'

Mrs Fritz attacked the shirt again and didn't answer. Flo took a load of washing into the drying room and was hanging it on the line when Stella Fritz appeared at the door.

'All right, we'll keep the laundry going between us,' she said, in a cold voice, 'but I'd like it made plain from the start, Flo Clancy, that I don't like you. I know full well what you've been up to, and just because I've agreed we should work together, it doesn't mean that I approve.'

Flo tried to look indifferent. 'I don't care if you approve or not. I'm only doing it for Mr Fritz.'

'As long as we know where we stand.'

'Rightio. There's just one thing. What about changing the name from Fritz's Laundry to something else?'

'Such as?'

'Oh, I dunno.' Flo pondered hard. 'What's your maiden name?'

'McGonegal.'

'McGonegal's Laundry is a bit of a mouthful. What about White? White's Laundry. It's got the same number of letters as Fritz, so it'll be easy to change the sign outside. Of course, it won't fool the old customers but it'll certainly fool the new.' It seemed rather traitorous because no one could have been more patriotic than dear Mr Fritz, but if his foreign name was a hindrance to his business, she felt sure he wouldn't mind it being changed.

After a few hiccups – another two big customers withdrew – by August, White's Laundry was back on its feet. More large hotels sent enormous bundles of washing, including one who'd used the laundry before and seemed content to use it again now the name had been changed.

'That was a good idea you had,' Stella Fritz said grudgingly, the day she heard their old customer had returned.

'Ta,' Flo said.

'Though it means we'll be even more snowed under with work than ever,' she muttered, half to herself.

'Hmm,' Flo muttered back. The two women still rarely spoke. There wasn't the time and they had nothing to say to each other. Occasionally Flo asked if Stella had heard from her husband, and was told he'd written and sounded depressed. It was hard to make out whether Stella was upset or angry that Mr Fritz had gone.

Mam had been discussing with her friends at the Legion of Mary the long hours her youngest daughter worked. One night she said, 'There's these two spinsters in the Legion, twins, Jennifer and Joanna Holbrook. They're in their late seventies, but as spry and fit as women half their age. They want to know if you'd like a hand in the laundry.'

'We're desperate. Stella's tried, but there's better jobs around for women these days. I doubt if two old ladies in their seventies would be much good, though, Mam.'

'I told them to pop in sometime and have a word with Mrs Fritz, anyroad.'

Two days later the Holbrook twins presented themselves to an astonished Stella Fritz. They were nearly six feet tall, stick thin, with narrow, animated faces, and identical to each other in every detail, right down to each item of their clothing. Papa had been in shipping, they explained between them, in their breathless, posh voices, and they'd never done a day's work in their lives, apart from in a voluntary capacity in the other great war.

'Of course, we've been knitting squares for the Red Cross . . .' said one – Flo was never able to recognise one twin from the other.

'. . . and rolling bandages . . .'

'. . . and collecting silver paper . . .'

'. . . but we'd far sooner go *out* to work . . .'

'. . . it would be almost as good as joining up.'

Mrs Fritz looked flummoxed. She glanced at Flo, who rolled her eyes helplessly.

'We wrote to the Army and offered our services . . .'

'. . . but they turned us down . . .'

'. . . even though we explained we could speak French and German fluently.'

'I don't know what to say.' Normally blunt, often rude, Mrs Fritz was stuck for words before the two women towering over her.

'What about a week's trial?' Flo suggested.

One twin clapped her hands and cried, 'That would be marvellous!'

'Absolutely wonderful!' cried the other.

'The money isn't important . . .'

'. . . we'd work for peanuts . . .'

'. . . and regard it as our contribution towards the war.'

Stella Fritz offered them peanuts and agreed that they should start tomorrow.

The twins turned up next day in uniforms that had once been worn by their maids: identical white ankle-length pinafores and gathered caps that covered their eyebrows. They were undoubtedly fit, but not quite as spry as Mam had claimed. Every now and then, they required a 'little sit-down', and would produce silver cigarette cases from the pockets of their pinnies and light each other's cigarette with a silver lighter. Then they would take long, deep puffs, as if they had been deprived for months.

'I needed that, Jen.'

'Same here, Jo.'

When their first week was up, there was no suggestion of them leaving, and once again the atmosphere in the laundry improved. Observing the Holbrook twins at close quarters was like having the front seat in a theatre, because they were as good as a top-class variety act. Even Stella Fritz seemed happier, particularly as they didn't have to work so hard and could leave at a civilised hour. It was nice to have a proper break at dinner-time instead of trying to eat a butty and iron a shirt at the same time. Flo didn't bother going home for dinner, and continued to take butties, which she sometimes ate as she wandered along Smithdown Road peering in shop windows. Once or twice, she ventured into the Mystery, but that part of her life no longer seemed real. It was impossible to believe that eighteen months ago she hadn't even met Tommy O'Mara. She felt like a very old woman trying to recall events that had happened more than half a century before. Flo had once had a lover, then she'd had a baby, but now both were gone, she was back at work in the laundry, and it was as if nothing had ever happened. Nothing at all.

Perhaps Hitler felt too daunted by the English Channel, because the threat of invasion faded, to be replaced by a more immediate terror: air raids. Liverpudlians dreaded the ominous wail of the siren warning them that enemy planes were on their way, while the sweetest sound on earth was the single-pitched tone of the all-clear to announce that the raid was over.

Over tea, Mrs Clancy would reel off the places that had been hit: the Customs House, the Dunlop rubber works, Tunnel Road picture house and Central Station. Edge Hill goods station, where Dad had worked, was seriously damaged. Then Albert Colquitt would come home and reel off a different list.

Sally came home from work one morning to report that Rootes Securities had been narrowly missed, and did Flo know that Josie Driver, who used to work in the laundry, had been killed last week when Ullet Road was bombed? 'I thought she'd gone in a convent.'

Flo was wandering along Smithdown Road in her dinner hour, thinking about last night's raid, when she saw the frock and the war was promptly forgotten.

'Oh, it's dead smart!' She stood in front of the window of Elaine's, Ladies' and Children's Fashions, eyeing the frock longingly. It was mauve, with long sleeves, a black velvet collar and velvet buttons down the front. 'It's dead smart, and only two pounds, nine and eleven. I could wear it for church, or to go dancing in. It's ages since I've been to a dance. And I've enough money saved.' She caught sight of her reflection in the window. She looked a fright. It was about time she smartened herself up, did something with her hair, started to wear powder and lipstick again. She couldn't mope for ever. 'If I bought that frock, perhaps Sally would come dancing with me. I bet Jock wouldn't mind.' It was no use asking Martha because she was convinced that no one would ask a girl with glasses to dance, even though Flo assured her there were plenty of men in glasses who didn't hesitate to ask girls up.

'I'll buy it – least, I'll try it on. If it fits, I'll ask them to put it on one side and come back tomorrer with the money.' Excited, she was about to enter the shop when she saw Nancy O'Mara coming towards her pushing a big black pram.

Nancy was dressed less flamboyantly than the last time Flo had seen her, outside the gates of Cammell Laird, in a plain brown coat that looked rather old. Her hair was in the same plump bun on the back of her thin yellow neck. Long earrings with amber-coloured stones dangled from her ears, dragging the lobes so that they looked elongated and deformed. She stopped at the butcher's shop next door, nudged the brake of the pram with her foot, and went inside.

Curious, Flo temporarily put aside her longing for the mauve frock, and walked along to the butcher's. Nancy had joined the small queue inside and her back was to the window. The hood of the pram was half up. Inside, a pretty baby, about seven or eight months old, with fair hair and a dead perfect little face, half sat, half lay against a frilly white pillow, playing sleepily with a rattle. She supposed it was a boy, because he wore blue: blue bonnet and matinée coat, both hand-knitted. Nancy must be minding him for someone. Flo thought of all the baby clothes she'd knitted which had been left behind when her son had been taken away. She'd asked Sally to hide them, because she hadn't wanted ever to see them again. For the first time, she wondered what her little boy had been wearing when Martha took him out into the snow to give to the couple who'd been so anxiously waiting for him to be born.

One of the baby's mittens had come off. 'You've lost a mitt, love,' she said softly.

At the sound of her voice, the baby turned his head. He smiled straight at her, shook the rattle, and uttered a contented little gurgle. As Flo stared into the two huge pools of green that were the baby's eyes, she felt a tingling creep down her spine, and knew that he was hers. *Martha had given her baby to Nancy O'Mara!*

'Aaah!' she breathed. Her arms reached down to pick her son out of the pram, when a scrawny yellow hand appeared from nowhere and gripped her right arm like a vice.

'Stay away from him!' Nancy O'Mara hissed. 'Don't think you'll ever get him back because I'll kill him first. He's mine. D'you hear?' Her voice rose hysterically and became a shriek. *'He's mine!'*

3

Flo's feet scarcely touched the pavement as she flew along the narrow streets, her mind in turmoil. It would always hurt, but she'd more or less got used to the idea that her baby was with someone else, but she would never get used to him being with Nancy O'Mara. She'd get him back, she'd claim him as her own.

Her face was on fire, and there were waves of pain like contractions in her belly. She had no idea where she was going, but when she found herself in Clement Street, where Nancy O'Mara lived, she realised she'd known all along. Without even thinking what she was going to say, she knocked at the house next door. A woman in a flowered overall answered almost immediately. She wore a scarf over a head crammed with metal curlers. A cigarette was poking out of the corner of her mouth.

The words, the lies, seem to come to Flo quite naturally. 'I'm looking for me friend, Nancy O'Mara, but she doesn't seem to be in. I haven't seen her in ages and thought I'd check if she still lived in the same place before I came all the way back.'

'She's out shopping with the baby, luv. I expect she'll be along any minute.'

Flo feigned surprise. 'Baby! I never knew she was expecting.'

The woman seemed amenable to an unexpected gossip on the doorstep. She folded her arms and leaned nonchalantly against the door frame. 'To tell you the truth, luv, it came as a shock to everyone. Did you know her feller died on the *Thetis*?'

'Yes. That was the last time I seen her. We went together on the ferry to Cammell Laird's. She didn't say she was in the club.'

'She wouldn't have known then, would she?' The woman took a puff of her cigarette and narrowed her eyes. 'Let's see, when was Hugh born? – February, Tommy'd been gone a few months before she told me that she'd copped one.'

Hugh! She'd called him Hugh! How can I ask if she actually saw Nancy pregnant? Flo was wondering desperately how she could frame such a question, when the woman gave a rather sardonic smile, 'It's funny,' she said, 'but Nancy O'Mara's always kept herself to herself. Hardly a soul knocks on that door, yet you're the second friend who's turned up out the blue. Actually, she looked a bit like you, 'cept she wore glasses. I don't suppose the two of you are sisters?'

'I haven't got a sister.'

'Mind you, she doesn't come so often since Hugh was born.'

'Doesn't she?' Flo said faintly.

'No. Y'see, Nancy was one of those women who hides out of sight when she's pregnant. I've a sister-in-law in Wallasey like that, me poor brother has to do all the shopping. Nancy not having a feller, like, this friend used to get her ladyship's groceries for her.'

'The friend with the glasses?'

' 'Sright, luv.'

'Did she have the baby at home or in the hospital?'

'No one's sure about that, luv. Typical of Nancy, she just appeared with him in a pram one day. Proud as punch she was, pushing him round in the snow.' She laughed coarsely. 'If she hadn't announced all those months ago that she was in the club, I'd have thought she'd pinched him.'

'You don't say.'

'Know Nancy well, do you, luv?' The woman looked quite prepared to talk all day.

'Not all that well. Me brother worked at Cammell Laird's and Nancy and Tommy came to his wedding,' Flo explained. 'I've only seen her a few times since.' She was wondering how to get away.

'Well, she certainly fell on her feet when Tommy kicked the bucket. A bob a week she used to pay in life insurance — I only know because me friend's husband's the collector and we used to joke she was planning on doing away with him one of these days, randy bugger that he was. Oh, look, here comes Nancy now.'

Nancy O'Mara had just turned the corner. She didn't notice Flo and the neighbour because all her attention was concentrated on the occupant of the pram. She was shaking her head, laughing and clucking. Then she stopped, tipped the pram towards her, and said something to the baby inside. She laughed again. Her face wore an expression Flo had rarely seen on anyone before: a radiance so intense that it was as if every wish she'd ever made had come true.

'She don't half dote on that baby,' the woman in the flowered overall murmured.

To the woman's astonishment, Flo turned on her heel and walked away.

When she returned to work more than half an hour late Stella Fritz threw her a questioning look, but Flo wasn't in the mood to make apologies or excuses. Throughout the afternoon, she worked like a madwoman, well making up for the time she'd been late. She swung wildly between sorrow, rage and loathing for the sister who had so comprehensively betrayed her. But the feeling that towered above all others was jealousy. She kept seeing Nancy's radiantly happy face; happiness caused solely by the fact that she'd been blessed with the gift of Flo's baby. For eight months, Tommy's wife had had him all to herself, nursed him, soothed him, watched him grow; unique, wonderful experiences that had been denied his real mother. There was the oddest

152

feeling deep within Flo, almost akin to making love with Tommy, when she imagined holding her baby to her breast.

'I'll get him back,' she swore, but remembered Nancy's face again and felt uneasy. *'Don't think you'll ever get him back, because I'll kill him first. He's mine!'* the woman had said. The way she'd looked at the baby wasn't quite natural. She loved him too much. Tommy had always claimed she wasn't quite right in the head, and even Martha had called her funny, a Welsh witch, though it hadn't stopped her from handing over her sister's child, Flo thought bitterly. As the afternoon progressed, it became easy to visualise Nancy O'Mara suffocating the tiny boy with that frilly pillow before she'd let Flo have him.

Perhaps she could snatch him from his pram, take him to another town . . . but Flo knew there would never be an opportunity to steal him. She'd like to bet a hundred pounds that the baby would never be left outside a shop again. Now Nancy knew that Flo had recognised him, she would hang on to him like grim death.

When her youngest sister came storming in Martha was setting the table. Flo thought she looked furtive and immediately guessed why: Nancy O'Mara had been waiting outside the brewery to relay what had happened that afternoon.

Now that the moment had come to pour out the rage that had been mounting ever since dinner-time, scream about the terrible injustice that had been done, Flo couldn't be bothered. What was the point?

Mam was humming to herself in the back kitchen. 'Is that you, Flo?' she called.

'Yes, Mam.'

'I was just telling our Martha, I ordered a chicken today for Christmas. I couldn't believe they were taking orders so early but, as the butcher said, it's only eleven weeks off.'

'That'll be nice, won't it, Flo?' Martha said brightly. 'Maybe Albert will stay with us this year. You know, Mam,' she called, 'it might be possible to put Albert's name down for a chicken as well.'

'I suppose it might. I didn't think o' that.'

'I won't be living here by Christmas,' Flo said. The words seemed just to come out without any previous thought.

Martha's jaw dropped and she looked frightened. 'Why not?'

'You know darn well why not. Because I can't bear to live in the same house as you another minute.'

Mam came bustling in with plates of stew. 'Sal!' she yelled. 'Dinner's on the table. It's blind scouse,' she explained. 'There wasn't a scrap of meat to be had in the butcher's.' She wiped her hands on her pinny. 'What was that I heard about someone not living here by Christmas?'

'Ask our Martha,' Flo said abruptly. 'I don't want any tea tonight, Mam. It's been an awful day and I feel like a lie-down.'

Sally burst into the room, full of beans because she'd had a letter from Jock that morning. She kissed her sister's cheek. 'Hello, Flo,' she sang.

Sally's evident happiness only emphasised Flo's all-embracing misery, but she gave her a long, warm hug before going upstairs. To her surprise, she only lay down for a few minutes before she fell asleep.

It was pitch dark when she woke up. Someone must have been in, because the curtains were drawn. She was collecting her thoughts, remembering the events of the day, when she became conscious of a movement in the room. As her eyes became used to the dimness, she saw that her mother was sitting on the edge of the double bed watching her sleep.

Mam must have sensed she was awake. 'I've been thinking about your uncle Seumus,' she said softly.

'I didn't know I had an uncle Seumus,' Flo said dully.

'He died long before you were born, shot by the English on the banks of the Liffey. He was smuggling arms for the IRA.'

'How old was he?' Another time Flo would have been interested to discover she'd had a romantic, if disreputable, uncle. Right now, she didn't care.

'Nineteen. I was only ten when he died, but I remember our Seumus as clearly as if he died yesterday. He was a grand lad, full of ideals, though not many people, particularly the English, would have agreed with them.' Mam sighed softly. 'I still miss him.'

'What made you think of him just now?'

'You remind me of him, that's why – hot-headed, never thinking before you act. Oh, Flo!' Mam's voice rose. 'Did it never enter your head the trouble it could cause by sleeping with a married man? God Almighty, girl, we were such a happy family before. Now everything's ruined.'

Flo didn't answer straight away. She recalled the first time she'd been on her way to meet Tommy O'Mara outside the Mystery, and the strange feeling she'd had, as if nothing would ever be the same again. It had turned out to be true, but not in the way she'd imagined. Mam was right. The Clancy family was about to break up. Flo could no longer live in the same house as Martha. 'I'm sorry, Mam,' she whispered. 'I'll leave home, like I said. Things'll be better if I'm not here.'

'Better!' Mam said hoarsely. 'Better! How will they be better without you, girl?' She reached out and stroked Flo's cheek. 'You're me daughter and I love you, no matter what you've done. I just wish I could feel so charitable about our Martha.'

'Did she tell you – about Nancy O'Mara?'

Mam nodded bleakly. 'That was a terrible thing to do. I wish to God I'd known what she was up to. The thing is, I've relied too much on Martha since your dad died. I thought she was strong, but she's the weakest of us all. The only way she can feel important is by meddling in other people's lives. If anyone's going to leave home, I'd rather it be Martha, but I suppose she needs me more than you and Sal ever will, particularly if she doesn't manage to catch poor Albert.'

'Oh, Mam!' Her mother seemed to accept that she was leaving, and Flo felt the future loom up before her, dark and uncertain.

'Come on, girl.' Mam stood up with a sigh. 'There's scouse left if you feel like it. Albert's fire-watching, Sal's at work, and Martha's gone to see Elsa Cameron – Norman's had another bad fall. The little lad's only two, and every time I see him he's covered in bruises.'

'Mam?'

'Yes, luv?' Her mother paused at the door.

'D'you think I could get him back – my baby?'

'No, luv. According to Martha, the birth certificate has Nancy down as the mother and Tommy O'Mara as the dad. Everyone in the street believed she was pregnant. Legally, he's hers, fair and square.'

'But you know that's a lie, Mam,' Flo cried. 'We could go to court and swear he's mine.'

Mam's entire demeanour changed. 'Court! Don't talk soft, Florence Clancy,' she said sharply. 'I've no intention of setting foot inside a court. For one thing, we haven't got the money, and second, there'd be a terrible scandal. It'd be in all the papers and I'd never be able to hold me head up in Liverpool again.'

The raid that night was short and not too heavy. The Clancys usually stayed in bed until the last minute, then when danger seemed imminent, they would go down and sit under the stairs. That night, the all-clear sounded before anyone had stirred, but Flo remained wide awake long afterwards. Where would she live? Would Mam let her have some sheets and blankets and a few dishes? They hadn't got a suitcase, so how would she carry her few belongings?

'Are you awake, Flo?' Martha whispered.

Flo made no sign she'd heard, but Martha persisted, 'I know you're awake because you're dead restless.'

'So what if I am?' Flo snapped.

'I thought we could talk.'

'I've nothing to say to you, Martha. You're nothing but a bloody liar. All that talk about me little boy going to a nice mam and dad!'

'Just listen to me a minute. What I did was only for the best.'

'You mean giving my baby to a Welsh witch was only for the best?' Flo laughed contemptuously.

'Nancy's always longed for a child, but the good Lord didn't see fit to answer her prayers. No one could love that baby more than she does.'

'*I* could! And the good Lord had nothing to do with it. It was because Tommy hadn't touched her that way in years. He told me.'

'I was only thinking of you, luv,' Martha said piteously. 'I wish you'd change your mind about leaving home. Mam's dead upset, and I feel as if it's my fault.'

'It *is* your fault,' Flo spat. It was all she could do not to leap out of bed and beat her sister to a pulp until every ounce of frustration and anger had been spent. 'And you weren't thinking of me, you were thinking of yourself, about your stupid reputation and what people would say.' Her voice rose shrilly. 'You couldn't even arrange the adoption properly, could you? I bet you enjoyed conspiring with Nancy, doing her shopping, being her best friend.' She imagined her sister bustling round to Clement Street, eyes gleaming behind her round glasses, sounding Nancy out, skirting round the matter of Flo's pregnancy until she had established that the woman would jump at the chance of having Tommy's child. Neither had dreamed Flo would recognise her own baby, because neither had given birth to a child of their own. Flo buried her face in her hands and began to rock to and fro. 'I wish I'd had the nerve to leave once I realised I was expecting, I wish I'd married Albert, I wish —'

Martha sat up. 'What was that about Albert?' she asked tersely.

Flo blinked. She hadn't meant to mention Albert. There was still time to pretend she'd meant something else or used the wrong name, but all of a sudden she saw an opportunity to hurt her sister, not nearly so badly as she'd been hurt herself but enough to wound. Still she hesitated, because she'd never intentionally hurt anyone in her life. A hard voice inside her insisted that Martha needed to be taught a lesson. '*She took your baby and gave him to Nancy O'Mara,*' the voice reminded her.

'I've never mentioned it before,' she said lightly, 'but Albert knew about the baby. He offered to marry me there and then. He told me about his wife dying in childbirth, and his little girl, Patsy, who died at the same time. He was going to use his savings to buy furniture for our house. In view of what's happened, I'm dead sorry I turned him down.'

'I don't believe you!'

'Ask him.' Flo yawned and slid under the bedclothes. She didn't sleep another wink that night as she lay listening to her sister's sobs, unsure whether to feel glad or ashamed.

She had less trouble than she had expected in finding somewhere to live. Next day, after asking the twins if they would keep their eyes open for a room to let, Stella Fritz sidled up. 'Why are you leaving home?'

Flo resisted telling her to mind her own business. The woman was her employer and they'd been getting on much better lately. 'I just want to, that's all,' she said.

'Is it, I mean, are you . . . ?' Stella's face grew red. It was obvious she thought Flo might be in the club again.

'I'm leaving because our Martha's driving me dotty. Now our Sal's married, there's only me left to boss around. I'll be twenty-one next year, and I thought it was time I lived on me own.'

'I see. You can have our cellar, if you want. It's never used.'

'Cellar!' Flo had visions of a little dark space full of coal. 'I'm not living in a cellar, thanks all the same.'

Stella shook her head impatiently. 'I call it the cellar, but it's really a basement. It's where the housekeeper used to live in the days when William Square was full of nobs. There's a few odds and ends of furniture, and I can let you have some stuff from upstairs. The walls will need a coat of distemper. Otherwise, it's very clean.'

William Square was becoming a bit seedy, Flo thought when she went to see the basement. There was nothing you could put a finger on, but the gracious houses weren't being maintained as they used to be.

The living room was very big, only partially furnished and rather dark, but there was a separate bedroom, a kitchen, and, wonder of wonders, a bathroom with a lavatory. There was even electric light. Everywhere smelt strongly of damp, but all in all, the place was much grander than anywhere Flo had hoped to find.

'Fritz had the gas fire installed. He used to turn it on now 'n' again during the winter, case the damp spread through the house.'

Flo gazed in awe at the efficient-looking fire. Imagine not having to fetch in coal every day! Imagine just pressing a switch for the light, and sitting on the lavatory indoors!

'I'm not sure if I can afford the rent for a place like this.'

'I haven't said what the rent will be, have I? You'd make your own meals and pay your own gas and electricity – there's separate meters down here.' Stella pursed her lips. 'Five bob a week'll do.'

'But you could get as much as seven and six!'

'I could ask ten bob in this part of town, but you'd be doing me a favour if you take it.'

'What sort of favour?'

Stella ignored her and went to stand at the rear window, which overlooked a rather grubby little yard. 'Just look at that!' she said tonelessly. 'Walls, bricks, dirt! Back in Ireland all we could see from our winders was green fields, trees and sky, with the lakes of Killarney sparkling in the distance. It's like living in a prison here.' She seemed to have forgotten that Flo was there. 'It was something Fritz could never understand, that there's some things more important than money, like good clean air and a sweet, blowing wind. All that concerned him was his bloody laundry.'

Flo twisted her hands together uncomfortably, not sure what to say. The Fritzes had always seemed such a happy couple.

'Oh, well.' Stella turned away. 'The palliasse for the bed's up in the loft, case it got damp. I'll fetch it down, as well as a mat for in front of the fire and a few other bits and pieces. Those chairs aren't too comfortable, but there's not much I can do about it — Fritz used to come down here sometimes for a bit of peace and quiet. Me mam'll give the place a good clean, though if you want it painting you'll have to do it yourself. There's some tins of distemper in the yard. It should be ready to move in by Monday.'

It was awful leaving Sally, but when it came to saying goodbye to her mother, Flo felt cold. Mam hadn't acted as badly as Martha, but Flo had never dreamed she could be so hard, preferring her daughter to go without her beloved baby rather than risk the faintest whiff of scandal.

When she made her departure directly after tea on Monday Albert Colquitt wasn't home. 'Give him my love, Mam,' she said. 'Tell him he's been the best lodger in the world and I'll never forget him.' She was aware of a white-faced Martha across the room. Her sister still looked stunned from their row the other night. Flo had ignored her ever since.

Mam was close to tears. 'For goodness sake, luv, you'd

think you had no intention of setting foot in Burnett Street again. You can tell Albert that to his face next time you see him.'

'Tara, Mam. Tara, Sal.' Flo slung the pillowcase containing all her worldly possessions over her shoulder like a sailor. She tried to force her lips to say the words, but they refused to obey, so she left the house without speaking to Martha.

The first few months in William Square were thoroughly enjoyable. Perhaps the favour Stella had mentioned was having Flo look after the little Fritzes — not that the two eldest, Ben and Harry, were little any more. Aged thirteen and fourteen, they were almost as tall as Flo. They invaded the basement flat, all eight of them, on her first night there.

'Have you come to live with us?'

'Did you know our dad?'

'Will you read us a book, Flo?'

'Do you know how to play Strip Jack Naked?' Ben demanded.

'The answer to every question is yes,' Flo grinned. 'Yes, yes, yes, yes. Sit on me knee — what's your name? — and I'll read you the book.'

'I'm Aileen.'

'Come on, then, Aileen.'

From that night on, Flo scarcely had time to have her tea before the children would come pouring down the concrete steps. By then Stella's mother, Mrs McGonegal, had seen enough of her lively grandchildren. She was a withdrawn woman, shy, with a tight, unhappy face. According to Stella, she missed Ireland and its wide open spaces even more than her daughter and couldn't wait to get back. 'And she's petrified of the air raids. She won't come with us to the shelter but crawls under the bed and doesn't come out till the all-clear goes.'

On Sunday afternoons, Flo took the children for walks. They formed a crocodile all the way to the Pier

Head and back again. Sometimes, she took the older ones to the pictures, where they saw Will Hay and Tommy Trinder and laughed till they cried. She suspected Harry had a crush on her, so treated him more tenderly than the others, which only made the crush worse.

A week after Flo moved, Sally came to see her and was startled to find the room full of little Fritzes. 'Have you started a school or something?'

'Aren't they lovely?' Flo said blissfully. 'I can't wait for Christmas. I thought I'd be spending it all by meself for the first time in me life, but Stella's invited me upstairs.' She still saw a trace of disapproval in the little Irishwoman's eyes whenever they spoke. 'I'm making decorations for the tree and it's lovely wandering round the shops at dinner-time looking for prezzies for the kids. I'm buying one a week.'

But by the time Christmas arrived, Stella Fritz, her mother, and her eight children had all gone.

After what everyone called 'the raid to end all raids' at the end of November, when for seven and a half long hours the city of Liverpool suffered a murderous attack from the air, a night when 180 people were killed in one single tragic incident, December brought blessed relief. 'I think Mr Hitler is going to let us spend the festive season in peace,' one of the twins remarked.

She spoke too soon. At twenty past six that night, all hell broke loose as wave after wave of enemy bombers unloaded their lethal cargo of incendiary and high-explosive bombs. The city was racked by explosions for nine and a half hours. Fires crackled furiously, the flames transforming the dark sky into an umbrella of crimson. Ambulances and fire engines screamed through the shattered streets.

Would the dreadful night ever end, Flo wondered, as she sat in the public shelter with the two smallest Fritzes on her knee. It hardly seemed possible that William Square could still be standing. As she tried to comfort the children, she was overcome with worry for her family and her little son.

At one point, Stella muttered, 'It's all right for Fritz, isn't it? He's safe and sound on the Isle of Man.'

At last the all-clear sounded at four o'clock in the morning; the long piercing whine had never been so welcome. Stella gathered the children together and made for home. William Square was just round the corner, and in the red glow the houses appeared miraculously intact. A small fire sizzled cheerfully in the central garden area where an incendiary bomb had fallen and several trees and bushes were alight.

'I'll help put the kids to bed,' Flo offered.

'It's all right,' Stella said tiredly, 'you see to yourself, Flo. Forget about opening up on time tomorrer. The twins have got a key — that's if they turn up themselves.' She sighed. 'I wonder how me mammy is?'

When Flo woke it was broad daylight. The birds were singing merrily. She jumped out of bed, intent on getting to work as quickly as possible — not because she was conscientious but she wanted to make sure that Clement and Burnett Streets hadn't been hit. After a cat's lick, she threw on the clothes she'd worn the day before.

Before leaving, she went upstairs to ask after Mrs McGonegal. To her astonishment, Stella Fritz opened the door wearing her best grey coat and an astrakhan hat with a matching grey bow. Her eyes were shining, and she looked happier than Flo had ever seen her, even in the days when she and Mr Fritz had seemed such an ideal married couple. 'I was about to come and see you,' she cried. 'Come in, Flo. We're off to Ireland this afternoon, to me uncle Kieran's farm in County Kerry. Me mam's over the moon. Oh, I know there's no gas or electricity, the privy's in the garden and you have to draw water from a well, but it's better than being blown to pieces in a raid.'

'I'll miss you.' Flo was devastated when she saw the

row of suitcases in the hall. It was the little Fritzes she'd really miss. She looked forward to their regular invasion of her room, the walks, the visits to the pictures. Upstairs, she could hear their excited cries as they ran from room to room and supposed they were collecting their favourite possessions to take to Ireland.

'The children are dead upset you're being left behind,' Stella said, looking anything but upset herself, 'but I said to them, "Flo's going to take care of things back here. She'll look after the house." I'll leave you the keys, luv, and if you'd just take a look round once a week, like, make sure everything's all right.'

So, that was the favour. Flo had been installed downstairs so that Mrs Fritz could up and leave whenever she liked, safe in the knowledge that the house would be cared for in her absence. Flo wasn't too bothered that she'd been used. It still meant she'd got a lovely flat dead cheap. But now it appeared she'd have the flat for nothing in return for 'services'. Would she mind running the water in cold weather, save the pipes from icing up, lighting a fire now and then to keep the place aired, opening the windows occasionally so it wouldn't smell musty?

'What's happening to the laundry?' Flo asked, when Stella had finished reeling off instructions.

'You'll be in charge from now on, luv,' Stella said carelessly. 'Take on more women, if you can. I'll write and tell you how to put the money in the bank each week.'

'Right,' said Flo stoutly, as yet more responsibility was heaped on her young shoulders. 'I'll just go upstairs and say tara to the children.'

She was about to leave the room, when Stella came over and gripped her by the arms. Her good humour had evaporated and her face was hard. 'There's something I'd like cleared up before I go.'

'What's that?' Flo asked nervously.

'I know full well why you left the laundry that time.

Tell me truthfully, was it my Fritz who fathered your child?'

The question was so outlandish that Flo laughed aloud. 'Of course not! What on earth gave you that idea?'

'I just wondered, that's all.' She smiled and squeezed Flo's arms. 'You're a grand girl, Flo. I'm sorry I was horrible in the past, but everything got on top of me. And I always had me suspicions about you and Fritz. Now, say tara to the kids, and tell them to come down and we'll be on our way.'

It didn't seem possible but the raid that night was even heavier than the one the night before. For more than ten hours, an endless stream of fire-bombs and explosives fell on Liverpool. Flo didn't bother with the shelter, but stayed in bed trying to read a novel she'd found upstairs. She did the same the following night when the raid was even longer. The house seemed no less safe than a brick shelter, and at least she was warm and comfortable and could make a cup of tea whenever she liked.

Each morning, she left promptly for work, although she hadn't had a wink of sleep, and on the way made sure that Clement Street and Burnett Street were still standing.

On Christmas Day she went early to Mass, then spent the morning tidying up after the Fritzes. In their excitement, the children had left clothes and toys everywhere, and there were dirty dishes in the back kitchen. Flo moved from room to room, feeling like a ghost in the big silent house, picking things up, putting them away, gathering together the dirty clothes to wash. She helped herself to a few items for downstairs; a tablecloth, a saucepan, a teapot, more books, and supposed she'd better use up the fresh food that had been left behind – the bacon looked like best back – and Mrs McGonegal had walked miles in search of dried fruit for that Christmas cake.

She went into the living room and sat in the huge bay

window beside the tree that she'd helped to decorate. William Square was deserted, though there must be celebrations going on behind the blank windows. As if to confirm that this was so, a motor car drew up a few doors away and a couple with two children got out. The man opened the boot and handed the children several boxes wrapped in red paper. Flo remembered the presents she'd bought for the Fritzes, which were still hidden under her bed, away from their prying eyes. She'd take them to one of them rest centres that looked after people who'd lost everything in the blitz, let some other kids have the benefit.

The house was so quiet, you could almost sense the quietness ticking away like a bomb. They'd just be finishing dinner in Burnett Street and starting on the sherry. Sally had said that Albert would be there, and Jock. No one would be coming to see Flo because they thought she was spending Christmas with the Fritzes. Flo sniffed dejectedly. It would be easy to have a good ould cry, but the situation was entirely of her own making. If she'd turned down Tommy O'Mara when he'd asked her to go for a walk, she'd be part of the group sitting round the table in Burnett Street with Martha rationing out the sherry.

Sherry! There were half a dozen bottles on the top shelf of the larder. She went into the kitchen, collected a bottle, and was about to take everything downstairs when she noticed the wireless in an alcove beside the fireplace. Unlike Albert's battery set, this one had an electric plug. It was also far superior to Albert's. The Bakelite casing had a tortoiseshell pattern, the gold mesh shaped like a fan.

She spent the rest of the day drinking sherry, half reading a book, half listening to the wireless, and told herself she was having a good time. It wasn't until a man with a lovely deep voice began to sing 'Dancing in the Dark', that she had a good ould cry.

★

On Boxing Day Flo moved the furniture into the middle of the room and distempered the basement a nice fresh lemon. It needed two coats and she was exhausted by the time she had finished and stood admiring her handiwork. The room had brightened up considerably, but the blackout curtains looked dead miserable. She raided upstairs and found several sets of bronze cretonne curtains, which she hung over the blackout. The place was beginning to look like home.

Home! Flo sat on one of the lumpy chairs and put her finger thoughtfully to her chin. She had a home, yes, but she hadn't got a life. The idea of spending more nights alone listening to the wireless made her spirits wilt, and she didn't fancy going to dances or the pictures on her own. Having two sisters not much older than herself meant she'd never gone out of her way to make friends. Bel was the closest to a friend she'd ever had, but Bel wasn't much use up in Scotland. Of course, she could always change her job so that she worked with women of her own age, but she felt honour-bound to keep the business going for Mr Fritz.

'I'll take up voluntary work!' she said aloud. It would occupy the evenings, and she'd always wanted to do something towards the war effort. 'I'll join the Women's Voluntary Service, or help at a rest centre. And Albert said there's even women fire-fighters. I'll make up me mind what to do in the new year.'

Next day, Sally and Jock whizzed in and out, but Flo didn't mention that the Fritzes had gone because Sally might have felt obliged to stay – and you could tell that she and Jock couldn't wait to be by themselves. The day after, Mam came into the laundry to see how she was and Flo said she was fine. She didn't want Mam thinking she regretted leaving home, because she didn't. She might have experienced the most wretched Christmas imaginable, but she'd willingly go through the whole thing again rather than live in the same house as Martha. More than anything, she couldn't stand the idea of anyone feeling sorry for her, though by the time New Year's Eve arrived, Flo was feeling very sorry for herself.

A party was going on across the square, a pianist was thumping out all the latest tunes: 'We'll Meet Again', 'You Were Never Lovelier', 'When You Wish Upon a Star . . .' In Upper Parliament Street, people could be heard singing at the tops of their voices. There'd been little in the way of raids since Christmas, and no doubt everyone felt it was safe to roam the streets again. She switched on the wireless, but the disembodied voices emphasised rather than eased her sense of isolation. She contemplated going early to bed with a book and a glass of sherry – there were only two bottles left – but ever since she was a little girl she'd always been up and about when the clocks chimed in the New Year. She remembered sitting on Dad's knee, everybody kissing and hugging and wishing each other a happy new year, then singing 'Auld Lang Syne'.

I could gatecrash that party! She smiled at the thought, and a memory surfaced: Josie Driver, God rest her soul, had once mentioned ending up on St George's Plateau on New Year's Eve. 'Everyone was stewed to the eyeballs, but we had a dead good time.'

Flo threw on a coat. She'd go into town. At least there would be other human beings around, even if she didn't know them, and they could be as drunk as lords for all she cared. She hadn't been a hundred per cent sober herself since finding that sherry.

The sky was beautifully clear, lit by a half-moon and a million dazzling stars, so it was easy to see in the blackout. Music could be heard coming from the Rialto ballroom and from most of the pubs she passed. People seemed to be enjoying themselves more than ever this year, as if they had put the war to the back of their minds for this one special night.

When she arrived in the city centre it was far too early, and her heart sank when there wasn't a soul to be seen on

St George's Plateau. What on earth shall I do with meself till midnight? she wondered. She began to walk slowly towards the Pier Head, aware that she was the only woman alone. The pubs were still open – they must have got an extension because it was New Year's Eve. She paused outside one. She could see nothing, because the windows had been painted black, and there was a curtain over the door, but inside a girl with a voice like an angel was singing, 'Yours Till the Stars Lose Their Glory', as it had never been sung before.

Flo stared into the black window, seeing Tommy O'Mara's reckless, impudent face gazing back at her, his cap perched on the back of his brown curly hair. Their eyes met and her insides glowed hot. She wanted him, oh, how she wanted him! 'Nobody understood how much we loved each other,' she whispered.

'D'you fancy a drink, luv?'

She turned, startled. A young soldier was standing beside her, twisting his cap nervously in his hands. Lord, he was no more than eighteen, and there was an expression on his fresh, childish face that reflected exactly how she felt herself: a look of aching, gut-wrenching loneliness. She'd like to bet he'd never tried to pick up a girl before, that this was his first time away from home, the first New Year's Eve he hadn't spent within the bosom of his family, and that he was desperate for company. She also saw fear in his eyes. Perhaps he was going overseas shortly and was afraid of being killed. Or perhaps he was just afraid she'd turn him down.

The girl inside the pub stopped singing, everyone thumped the tables, burst into enthusiastic applause, and Flo was hit with an idea that took her breath away. She knew exactly what she could do as her contribution towards the war.

'What a nice idea, luv!' she cried gaily. 'I'd love a drink. Shall we go in here?'

Millie

I

'Are you the Tom who gave her the lamp?' I'd always imagined Flo's friend being as old as Flo herself.

' 'Sright. I got it her in Austria.'

I sat in the armchair, resentful that Tom O'Mara was occupying my favourite spot on the settee, his feet back on the table. 'What were you doing in Austria?'

'Skiing,' he said abruptly.

He looked more the type to prefer a Spanish resort full of bars and fish-and-chip shops, I thought. I said, 'I've always wanted to ski.'

'I didn't know Flo had these.' He ignored my observation and picked up the newspaper cuttings. His fingers were long and slender and I imagined . . . Oh, God! I did my best to hide another shiver. 'That's how me grandad died,' he said, 'On the *Thetis*.'

'Do you know much about it?' I asked eagerly. 'I keep meaning to get a book from the library.'

'Me gran used to pin me ear back about the *Thetis*. She had a book. It's at home. You can have it, if you like. I'll send it round sometime.'

'Thanks,' I said. A pulse in my neck was beating crazily, and I covered it with my hand, worried he'd notice. What on earth was happening to me? Usually, I wouldn't give a man like Tom O'Mara the time of day. I glanced at him surreptitiously and saw that he was staring at the lamp, oblivious of me. I almost felt a nuisance for having interrupted his quiet sojourn in the flat. There was little sign that a party was going on upstairs, just a muffled thumping as people danced, and music that sounded as if

170

it came from some distance away. 'How come you knew, Flo?' I asked.

'She was a friend of me dad's. I knew her all me life.'

'Would it be possible to meet your father? I'd love to talk to him about Flo.'

' "Would it be possible to meet your father?" ' he repeated after me, in such a false, exaggerated impersonation of my accent that I felt my face redden with anger and hurt. 'Christ, girl, you don't half talk posh, like you've got a plum in your gob or something. And you can't talk to me dad about anything. He died fourteen years ago.'

'Is there any need to be so rude?' I spluttered.

Our eyes met briefly. Despite my anger, I searched for a sign that he didn't despise me as much as he pretended, but there was none. He turned away contemptuously. 'People like you make me sick. You were born in Liverpool, yet you talk like the fucking Queen. I think it's called "denying your roots".'

'A day never goes by when I don't remember my roots,' I said shortly. 'And there are people around who could have a great deal of fun with the way you speak.' I stared at him coolly, though cool was the opposite of what I felt. 'I came down for some peace and quiet, not to be insulted. I'd be obliged if you'd go.'

Before he could reply, there was a knock on the window and James called, 'Are you there, Millie?' He must have been looking for me, and someone, Charmian or Herbie, had suggested where I might be.

'Coming!' I stood, aware that Tom O'Mara's eyes had flickered over my body, and felt exultant. My ego demanded that he found me as attractive as I found him, not that it mattered. He was an uncouth lout. Anyway, there was no likelihood of us meeting again. He could keep his book on the *Thetis*, I'd get one for myself. In my iciest voice, I said, 'I've got to go. Kindly put the key on the mantelpiece when you leave. Goodnight.'

★

For James's sake, I decided reluctantly to give Flo's flat a miss the next afternoon. I couldn't bring myself to ask him to leave after refusing to see him all the previous week. Bel and Charmian would be expecting me, I thought wistfully, though I really should get down to clearing things out – and I still hadn't found out about the rent. I was anxious to speak to the landlord and pay another month before the flat was let to someone else, if that hadn't happened already. One of these days I might turn up and find the place stripped bare. The rent book was bound to be among Flo's papers, but I hadn't even discovered where her papers were kept.

'This is nice.' James sighed blissfully as we lay in bed in each other's arms after making love for the third time. 'An unexpected treat. I thought I'd be sent on my way ages ago.' It was almost three o'clock.

'Mmm.' I was too exhausted to reply. I felt guilty and ashamed. James wouldn't feel quite so happy if he knew that every time I closed my eyes he turned into Tom O'Mara.

He nuzzled my breasts. 'This is heaven,' he breathed. 'Oh, darling, if only you knew how much I love you.'

I stroked his head and said dutifully, 'I think I do.'

'But you never tell me you love me back!' he said sulkily. He pulled away and threw himself on to the pillow.

'James, please,' I groaned, 'I'm not in the mood for this.'

'You're never in the mood.'

I leaped out of bed and grabbed my dressing gown. 'I wish to God you'd give me some space,' I snapped. 'Why do you keep nagging me to say things I don't want to say, to feel things I don't feel?'

'Will you ever say them? Will you ever feel them?' He stared at me forlornly.

I stormed out of the room, 'I can't stand any more. I'm going to have a shower and I'm locking the door. I expect you to be gone when I come out.'

When I emerged from the bathroom fifteen minutes later there was no sign of a contrite James begging forgiveness. No doubt he would telephone or come back later, in which case he wouldn't find me in. I got dressed quickly in jeans and an old sweatshirt and raced down to the car. It was already growing dark and I couldn't wait to be in Flo's flat where I knew I would find the tranquillity I craved.

It wasn't to be, but I didn't mind. I was unlocking the front door when Bel Eddison appeared in her leopardskin jacket. 'I thought I heard you. I've been helping Charmian clear up after the party. We were expecting you hours ago.'

'I was delayed. Come and have some sherry. Why weren't you at the party? I looked everywhere for you.'

'I had another engagement.' She smirked. 'I wouldn't say no to a glass of sherry, but me and Charmian have been finishing off the bottles left over from last night. I'm not exactly steady on me legs.' She staggered into the basement and made herself comfortable on the settee. 'Charmian can't come. Jay's going back to university in the morning and she's still sorting out his washing.'

I turned on the lamp and poured us both a drink. I noticed Tom O'Mara's key on the mantelpiece. As the lamp began slowly to revolve, I said, 'I met the man who gave her that last night.'

'Did you now.' Bel hiccuped.

'He told me how his grandad died, and you said Flo was in love with someone who was lost on the *Thetis*. I wondered if they were one and the same person.'

'I said no such thing, luv,' Bel remarked huffily. 'I said, "Draw your own conclusions," if I remember right.'

'Well, I've drawn them, and that's the conclusion I've reached.' I felt that I'd got one up on Bel for a change.

To my consternation, the old woman's face seemed to shrivel, her jaw sagged, and she whispered hoarsely, 'Flo said, "I don't know what I'm going to do if Tommy's dead. Me life's over. I'll never love another man the way I loved him." The thing is, he was a right scally, Tommy O'Mara, not fit to lick Flo's boots. It sticks in me craw to think she wasted her life on a chap like him.'

I hoped Bel wouldn't be angry, but I had to ask, 'Last night, Tom talked about his gran. Does that mean this Tommy was married when . . . ?'

Bel nodded vigorously. 'She was the last girl in the world to go out with a married man, but he spun her a tale. He was such a charmer. He told *me* he was single.'

'You mean, you went out with him, too?' I gasped.

'Yeh.' Bel grimaced. 'I never let on to Flo, it would have killed her, but I'd been out with him twice just before the *Thetis* went down. Some men aren't happy unless they've got a string of women hankering after them. Tom O'Mara's another one like that. He was a nice lad once, but he's grown up without his grandad's charm. A woman would be mad to have anything to do with him.'

'I agree about the lack of charm. I found him very rude.' I would have liked to know more about Tom O'Mara, but Bel might have thought I was interested when I definitely wasn't. Well, I told myself I wasn't. 'Would you like some tea or coffee to sober you up?' I asked instead.

'A cup of coffee would be nice, but only if it's the instant stuff. I can't stand them percolator things. Flo's got one somewhere.'

For the next few hours we chatted amiably. I told her about my job and my problems with James, and she told me about her three husbands, describing the second, Ivor, in hilarious detail. Before she left, I asked where Flo had kept her papers.

'In that pull-down section of the sideboard, the old one. Flo called it her bureau. You'll have your work cut out sorting through that lot. I think she kept every single letter she ever got.'

Bel was right. When I opened the bureau I found

hundreds, possibly thousands, of pieces of paper and letters still in their envelopes, crammed in every pigeon-hole and shelf. I felt tempted to close it again and snuggle on the sofa with sherry and a book, but I'd been irresponsible for far too long. I sighed and pulled out a thick wad of gas bills addressed to Miss Florence Clancy, which, to my astonishment, went back as far as 1941, when the quarterly bill was two and sevenpence.

I wondered what the flat had looked like then – and wasted ages envisaging a young Flo, living alone and pining after Tommy O'Mara. Perhaps that's what the row with Gran had been about, Flo going out with a married man. Gran was incredibly straitlaced, though it didn't seem serious enough to make them lifelong enemies.

The cardboard boxes I'd brought were in the bath-room so I fetched one and threw in the bills. Then I almost took them out again. Flo had kept them for more than half a century and it seemed a shame to chuck them away. I pulled myself together, and more than fifty years of electricity bills quickly joined them. I decided I deserved a break, made coffee and helped myself to a packet of Nice biscuits. On my way to the settee, I jumped when something clattered through the letterbox.

It was a book: *The Admiralty Regrets*. I opened the door, but whoever had delivered it had disappeared.

Fiona was leaning against the railings, smoking. 'Hi,' I said awkwardly.

She glared at me malevolently through the railings. 'Sod off,' she snarled.

Shaken, I closed the door, and put the book aside to read later. I returned to the bureau with my coffee and continued to throw out old papers. One thick wedge of receipts was intriguing. From a hotel in the Isle of Man, they were made out to a Mr and Mrs Hoffmansthal, who had stayed there for the weekend almost every month from 1949 until 1975. I decided to ask Bel about them, then changed my mind. Bel had mentioned that Flo went on retreat to a convent in Wales once a month. Perhaps Flo had kept a few secrets from her old friend and I certainly wasn't about to reveal them after all this time. I threw away the receipts with a sigh. How I'd love to know what lay behind them, and especially the identity of Mr Hoffmansthal.

The contents of the bureau were considerably diminished by the time the unimportant papers had been discarded. All that remained were letters, which I had no intention of throwing away until I'd read every one. Some looked official, big fat brown envelopes, the address typed, but most were handwritten. I tugged out a wad of letters held together with an elastic band. The top one bore a foreign stamp. It had been posted in 1942.

It dawned on me that I hadn't found the rent book that had prompted my search, or a pension book. Flo might have had them in her handbag, which, like Gran, she had kept hidden. After a fruitless search through all the cupboards, I found what I was looking for under the bed, where dust was already beginning to collect.

I took the black leather bag into the living room and emptied the contents on to the coffee table. A tapestry purse fell out, very worn and bulging with coins, followed by a set of keys on a Legs of Man keyring, a wallet, shop receipts, bus tickets, cheque book, metal compact, lipstick, comb . . . I removed a silver hair from the comb and ran it between my fingers. It was the most intimate thing belonging to Flo I'd ever touched, actually part of her. The room was very still, and I almost felt as if she was in the room with me. Yet I wasn't scared. Even when I opened the compact to compare the hair with mine in the mirror, half expecting to see Flo's face instead of my own, I didn't feel frightened, more a comfortable sensation of being watched by someone who cared about me. I knew I was being silly because Flo and I had only set eyes on each other once, and then briefly.

'One day my hair will turn that colour,' I murmured,

and wondered where I would be and who I would be with, should I live to be as old as Flo. For the first time in my life, I thought it would be nice to have children, so that a strange woman I hardly knew wouldn't sort through my possessions when I died.

I came back to earth, told myself to be sensible. The cheque book meant that, like Gran since she'd been robbed, Flo's pension had probably been paid straight into the bank. I flicked through the stubs to see if cheques had been made out for rent, but most appeared to be for cash, which was no help. I would have asked Charmian for the landlord's address, but glancing at my watch, I saw it was past midnight.

Good! It was a perfect excuse to sleep in Flo's comfortable bed again.

One by one, I returned the things to the bag, glancing briefly in the wallet, which held only a bus pass, a cheque guarantee card, four five-pound notes, and a card listing a series of dental appointments two years ago. I was putting the bag away in the bureau when there was a knock on the door.

James! He'd been to my flat, waited, and when I didn't arrive he had guessed where I would be. I wouldn't let him in. If I did, he'd never keep away and this was the only place where no one could reach me. It was one of the reasons why I always seemed to forget to bring my mobile phone. I fumed at the idea of him invading what I'd come to regard as my sanctuary.

'Who is it?' I shouted.

'Tom O'Mara.'

I stood, transfixed, in the middle of the room, my stomach churning. I knew I should tell him what I'd intended to tell James, to go away, but common sense seemed to have deserted me, along with any will-power I might have had. Before I knew what I was doing, I'd opened the door.

Oh, Lord! I'd thought this only happened in books — turning weak at the knees at the sight of a man. The jacket of his black suit was hanging open, and the white collarless shirt, buttoned to the neck, gave him a priest-like air. Neither of us spoke as he followed me inside, with that sensually smooth walk I'd noticed the night before, bringing with him an atmosphere charged with electricity. I patted my hair nervously, aware that my hand was shaking. He was carrying a plastic bag that smelt of food. My mouth watered and I realised I was starving.

He held it out. 'Chinese, from the takeaway round the corner. Joe said there was someone in when he came with the book so I thought I'd see if you were still here on me way home.'

'What's this in aid of?' I gulped.

'Peace-offering,' he said abruptly. 'Flo would have slagged me off for behaving the way I did last night. No one can help the way they speak, you and me included.'

'That's charitable of you, I must say.' I'd worked hard to get rid of my accent, and felt annoyed that Tom O'Mara seemed to regard the lack of one as an affliction.

'Shall we forget about last night and start again?' He bagged my favourite spot on the settee and began to unpack the cartons of food. 'You're Millie, I'm Tom, and we're about to have some nice Chinese nosh – I don't know if you want to use these plastic forks, Flo used to fetch proper ones, and she'd warm plates up in the microwave. She didn't like eating out of boxes.'

I hurried to do as I was told, sensing that he was accustomed to giving orders, when he shouted, 'Fetch a corkscrew and some glasses while you're at it. I've got wine.'

'It's red,' he said, when I obediently brought everything in. 'I'm an ignorant bugger and I don't know if that's what you have with this sort of food.'

'Neither do I.' James always knew what sort of wine to order but I'd never taken much notice.

'I thought you'd be one of those superior sort of people who know about such things.' He shared out the food on to the plates.

'And I thought we'd made a fresh start.'

'You're right. Sorry!' His smile took my breath away. His face softened and he looked charmingly boyish. I could understand what the nineteen-year-old Flo must have seen in his grandfather.

'Did you and Flo do this often?' I asked, when he handed me my plate.

'Once a week. Mondays, usually, when I finish work early.'

'Where do you work?'

'Minerva's. It's a club.'

I'd heard of Minerva's, but had never been there. It had a terrible reputation as a hang-out for gangsters and a source of hard drugs. Scarcely a week passed when there wasn't something in the *Echo* or on local TV about the police raiding it in search of a wanted criminal or because a fight had broken out. As I sipped the rich, musky wine, I wondered what Tom O'Mara did there.

'The wine's nice,' I said.

'So it should be. It's twenty-two quid a bottle at the club.'

'Wow!' I gasped. 'All that much to have with a take-away!'

He dismissed this with a wave of the hand. 'It didn't cost me anything, I just helped meself.'

'You mean you stole it?'

He managed to look both amused and indignant. 'I'm past the stage of nicking things, thanks all the same. Minerva's belongs to me. I can take anything I like.'

I felt a chill run through my body. He was almost certainly a criminal – he might have been in prison for all I knew. If he owned Minerva's, it meant he was involved in the drugs trade and other activities that didn't bear thinking about. But the awful thing, the really appalling thing, was that he became even more desirable in my eyes. I was horrified. I'd never dreamed it was in me to be attracted to someone like Tom O'Mara. Perhaps it was something passed down in the blood: Flo had wasted her life on a scally who, according to Bel, wasn't fit to lick her boots, Mum had fallen for my loathsome father. Now I found myself weak at the knees over possibly the most unsuitable man in the whole of Liverpool. I thought about James, who loved me and was worth ten Tom O'Maras, and for a moment wished it really had been him at the door.

I put my plate on the table and Tom said, 'You haven't eaten much.'

'I've eaten half,' I said defensively. 'I haven't a very big appetite.' He'd already finished, the plate scraped clean.

'I tell you what, let's have some music.' He went over to the record player and lifted the lid.

'Flo's only got the one record.'

'She's got a whole pile in the sideboard. Neil Diamond and Tony Bennett were her favourites. I got her this last year when she started humming it non-stop. She'd play it over and over.' The strains of 'Dancing in the Dark' began to fill the room. 'She said something once, she was half asleep, about dancing in the dark with someone in the Mystery years ago.'

'The Mystery?' I wondered if it had ever crossed his mind that the 'someone' might well have been his grandad.

'Otherwise known as Wavertree playground. There's a sports stadium there now.' He removed his jacket, saying, 'It's hot in here,' and I felt my insides quiver at the sight of his long, lean body, his slim waist.

'You were very fond of Flo?'

'I wasn't just fond of her, I loved her,' he said simply. 'I dunno why 'cos she weren't a relative, but she was more like a gran than me real one. Christ knows what I'd have done without Flo when me dad died.'

Surely he couldn't be so bad if he'd thought so much of Flo. Bing Crosby was singing and I had no idea why I should have a feeling that history was repeating itself when Tom held out his hand and said with a grin, 'Wanna dance, girl?'

I knew I should refuse. I knew I should just laugh and shrug and say, 'No, thanks, I'm not in the mood,' because I also knew what would happen when he took me in his arms. And if it did, if it did, the day might come when I would regret it. The trouble was, I had never before wanted anything so much. My body was crying out for him to touch me.

The lamp continued its steady progress, round and round, casting its dark, blurred shadows on the low ceiling of the room, and I stared at the shifting patterns, looking for the girl in the red coat. Tom O'Mara came across the room, put his hands on my waist and lifted me out of the chair. For a moment I resisted, then threw all caution to the wind. I slid my arms around his neck and kissed him. I could feel him, like a rock, pressing against me. My veins seemed to melt when our exploring tongues met, while his hard, eager hands stroked my back, my waist, my hips, burning, as if his fingers were on fire.

Still kissing, swaying together almost imperceptibly to the music, we moved slowly towards the bedroom. Outside the door, in the little cold lobby, our lips parted, and Tom cupped my face in his hands. He stared deep into my eyes, and I knew that he wanted me every bit as much as I wanted him. Then he opened the door, where the bed with its snowy white cover was waiting, and led me inside. By now, I felt weak with longing, yet once again I hesitated. There was still time to back out, to say no. But Tom O'Mara was kissing me again, touching me with those hot fingers, and I couldn't have said no to save my life. He kicked the door shut behind us.

In the living room, 'Dancing in the Dark' played through to a glorious crescendo. When it finished, I imagined, in a little corner of my mind, the needle raising itself automatically and the arm returning to nestle in the metal groove. There was silence in Flo Clancy's flat, though I knew that the lamp continued to cast its restless shadows over the walls.

★

I was woken by Tom O'Mara stroking my hip. 'You should have eaten the rest of that meal,' he whispered. 'You could do with a bit more flesh on you.'

Turning languorously into his arms, I began to touch him, but he caught my hand. 'I've got to go.'

'Is there nothing I can do to keep you?' I said teasingly. 'Nothing.'

He got out of bed and began to get dressed. I could have kept James in bed if the building was on fire. I lay, admiring his will-power and his slim brown limbs. His skin was as slippery as polished marble, the hollow of his neck as smooth as an egg. There was a tattoo on his chest, a heart with an arrow through it, and a woman's name I couldn't make out. I'd always thought tattoos repulsive, though it was a bit late in the day to remember that. 'What's the hurry?' I enquired.

'It's nearly seven o'clock. Me wife doesn't mind me staying out all night, but she likes me home for breakfast.'

'Mightn't it have been a good idea to mention you had a wife last night?' I said mildly. I wasn't the least bit shocked because I didn't care. We had no future to-gether.

He paused while pulling on his trousers. 'Would it have stopped you?'

'No, but it might have stopped some women.'

'Then those sort of women should ask before leaping into bed with a bloke they hardly know.'

I made one of Bel's faces. 'You sound as if you disapprove of women who sleep with strange men.'

'It so happens that I do.'

'But you don't disapprove of men who do the same?' I laughed, pretending outrage.

'Blokes take what's on offer.' He was buttoning his shirt.

I eased myself to a sitting position. 'Do you know?' I said thoughtfully, 'I truly can't remember offering myself last night.'

'You didn't, but it's different with me and you, isn't it?'

'Is it?'

He sat on the bed. 'You know it is.' He held my face in both hands and kissed me soundly on the lips. I put my arms around his neck and kissed him back, greedy for him, and determined to keep him if I could, even if it meant I'd be late for work.

'I said I've got to go.' His voice was steely. He removed my arms none too gently and went over to the door.

'Oh, well,' I sighed exaggeratedly, 'see you around sometime, Mr O'Mara.' I was still teasing, though my heart was in my mouth, dreading he might take me at my word and say, 'See you too, Millie.'

'What the hell do you mean by that?' I was taken aback by the anger in his green eyes. The muscles were taut in his slender neck. 'Is that all it was to you, a night's shag?'

'You know it wasn't.' I blushed, remembering the night, so different from any I'd ever known. I looked at him directly. 'It was magic.'

I could have sworn he breathed a sigh of relief. 'In that case, I'll be round tonight, about twelve.' He left abruptly. A few seconds later, the front door opened and he shouted, 'It was magic for me, too.'

I got out of bed, removed the crucifix, the statues, and holy pictures off the wall, and put them in the drawer of Flo's bedside cabinet.

'You've been raiding your aunt's wardrobe again,' George said, when I arrived at Stock Masterton. 'I can tell.'

'Is it so obvious?' I stared down at the long, straight black skirt and demure white blouse with a pointed collar.

'Only because you don't usually wear those sort of clothes. You look very appealing. I could eat you for lunch.'

I tried to think of a put-down remark in reply, but couldn't.

George went on, 'That young man of yours must have had the same idea. You've got a love bite on your neck.' He sighed dolefully. 'It's called a hicky in America. I can't remember when I last gave a girl one. I must have been in my teens. Those were the days, eh?' He hooted.

Embarrassed, I went over to my desk and switched on the computer. Diana had just arrived. 'How's your father?' I asked.

'He seemed much better over the weekend,' Diana replied. Her face had lost the tense lines of the previous week. 'In fact, we had a lovely time. He told me all about his experiences during the war. I knew he'd been in Egypt in military intelligence, but I never realised he'd been in so many dangerous scrapes. He was very much a James Bond in his day.' She took an envelope from her bag. 'I managed to finish those notes I mentioned. Did George tell you his offer for the shop in Woolton has been accepted? We could be open by the new year.'

My own report was at home but didn't seem all that important any more. Nevertheless, I had to go back to the flat to collect a few things if I was going to stay at Flo's so I'd pick it up then.

'I'll give this to George.' Diana winked conspiratorially and hurried into his office. She seemed rather pathetic, I thought, yet until recently I'd wanted the job in Woolton just as much, which meant I'd been just as pathetic myself. Now, I didn't care.

The realisation surprised me. I stared at my blurred reflection in the computer screen and wondered what had changed. Me, I decided, though I had no idea why. I felt confused but, then, I'd felt confused throughout my life. Perhaps it was Flo who'd made me see things differently. Perhaps. I wish I'd known her, I thought wistfully, remembering the warm, comfortable sensation I'd had in the flat last night, as if she had been there with me. I had a feeling I could have talked to her about stuff I wouldn't dream of telling anyone else.

And there was Tom O'Mara. I cupped my chin in my

hands and my reflection did the same. I'd been a married woman for four years, and there'd been other men before James, yet it was as if I'd made love for the very first time. My body had never felt so alive, so *used* in the most gratifying way. I held my breath and felt my scalp prickle when I thought about the things that Tom O'Mara and I had done to each other.

'Millie! *Millie!*'

Darren thumped my desk, and I became aware that June was shouting, 'Wake up, sleepyhead. There's a call for you.'

It was the Naughtons again. They'd had details of another house, which sounded ideal, this time in Crosby. I arranged to meet them there at noon, though felt sure it would be another waste of time. Crosby was close to Blundellsands, which meant I could call at home afterwards.

It felt strange going into my flat, as if I'd been away for weeks not merely twenty-four hours. It smelt dusty and unused, long empty. I opened the windows of the balcony to air the place, and had a shower. There was a bruise beneath my breast and another on my thigh and I wondered if Tom O'Mara also bore scars of our night together. I covered the bite on my neck with makeup. The red light was flickering on the answering machine.

My mother's tearful voice announced that Declan had lost his job. 'He was sacked ages ago. Your dad only found out by accident off some chap in the pub. Of course he's livid, called poor Declan all the names under the sun. And, Millicent, I'd like to talk to you about Alison . . . Oh, I'll have to ring off now, luv. Your dad's on his way in.'

I waited. There was no message from James. I was glad, but thought about calling him at work to make sure he was all right. In the end, I decided not to. It might encourage him to think I cared, which I did but not nearly enough to satisfy him. I reversed the tape, packed a few clothes and toiletries in a bag, along with the folder containing the report. As I'd gone to the trouble of writing it, it wouldn't hurt to let George take a look.

He was working alone in his glass cubicle when I got back, so I took the folder in. 'You'll never guess what that bloody woman's gone and done,' he barked immediately he saw me.

I pretended to back away, frightened. 'What woman?' I couldn't recall seeing George so angry before.

'That Diana bitch. She's only given me a list of reasons why I should open the new office! I couldn't believe my eyes when I read it. Does she seriously imagine I haven't thought the whole thing through myself? Jesus Christ, Millie, I've been in the estate-agency business for over thirty years. I know it back to front, yet an idiot woman with a stupid degree thinks she knows better than I do.'

'She was only being helpful, George.'

'More likely after the boss's job,' he sneered. 'As if I'd give it her, the pushy little cow. The job's Oliver's. He never makes a decision without referring to me first, which is the way I like it.' He grinned. 'I guess I must be a control freak.'

'Did you say anything to Diana?'

'I bawled her out and she left for lunch in tears.'

'Oh, George!' I shook my head. 'You'll feel sorry about that tomorrow.' A few weeks ago I would have been as pleased as punch at Diana's fall from grace, but now, for some strange reason, I felt nothing but pity for the woman.

'I know.' He sighed. 'I'm a disagreeable sod. I'll apologise later, though it was still a stupid, tactless thing for her to do.' He nodded at the folder in my hand. 'Is that for me?'

'No. I just came to tell you about the Naughtons. Apparently, the draining board was on the wrong side.'

Later that afternoon, I fed my report into the shredder. I'd never stood the remotest chance of getting the manager's job, and it made me feel acutely embarrassed to have thought that I had.

Tom O'Mara didn't arrive at midnight as he'd promised. An hour later he still wasn't there. I lay on the settee, half watching an old film, not sure what to think. Had I been stood up? Maybe he'd had second thoughts. Maybe he'd meant tomorrow night. I tried to work out how I'd feel if I never saw him again. Hurt, I decided, hurt, insulted and angry, but definitely not heartbroken, possibly a little bit relieved. However, right now relief wasn't uppermost in my mind. I wasn't in love with Tom and never would be, yet my body ached for him and I could have sworn he felt the same. It was easy to while away the time imagining his lips touching every part of me. My pulse began to race, and I felt hot at the thought. 'Please come, Tom,' I prayed. 'Please!'

At some time during the night I fell asleep, and was woken when it was barely daylight by a kiss and the touch of a hand stroking me beneath my dressing-gown.

'How did you get in?' I whispered.

'Took me key back off the mantelpiece, didn't I?'

'You're late,' I yawned. 'Hours late.' It was delicious just lying there, feeling sleepy, yet conscious of his exploring hands.

'There was trouble at the club, and I couldn't ring. Flo always flatly refused to have a phone. How do I undo this knot?'

'I'll do it.' I unfastened the belt and he pulled the robe away.

'Anyroad, I'm here now,' he said, 'and that's all that matters.'

He was kneeling beside me, his face hard with desire. He would never say soft, tender things as James did, yet this only made me want him more. I held out my arms. 'Yes, Tom, that's all that matters.'

Time seemed to stand still; it had lost its meaning, all because of Tom O'Mara. I returned to my flat on Sunday morning to collect more clothes and take a shower – bathing at Flo's was like bathing in the Arctic – and found an increasingly frantic series of messages from my mother on the answering-machine. It was the last Sunday in October and it had completely slipped my mind.

'Don't forget, luv, we're expecting you for dinner on Sunday.'

'Why don't you ever ring back, Millicent? I hate these damn machines. It's like talking to the wall.'

'Have you gone away, Millicent?' the voice wailed fretfully. 'You might have told me. I'd ring your office if I didn't think it would get you into trouble.'

As usual, I felt a mixture of guilt and annoyance. I phoned home immediately. 'I'm sorry, Mum,' I said penitently. 'You were right, I've been away.' I hated lying to my mother, but how could I possibly tell her the truth? 'I know I should have called, but it was a spur-of-the-moment thing, and I was so busy when I got there, I forgot about everything. I'm sorry,' I said again, assuming this would be enough to satisfy her, but apparently not.

'When you got where?' she demanded.

I said the first place I could think of. 'Birmingham.'

'What on earth were you doing there?'

'George sent me.'

'Really!' Mum sounded so impressed that I hated myself even more. 'He must think highly of you, sending you all the way to Birmingham.'

To please her, I took particular pains with my appearance. I wore a cherry red suit with a black T-shirt underneath. To assuage my guilt, and make amends for lying, I stopped on the way to Kirkby and bought a bunch of chrysanthemums and a box of Terry's All Gold.

'You shouldn't have, luv,' Mum protested, though she looked gratifyingly pleased.

When we sat down to lunch, Flo's flat immediately became the main topic of conversation.

'I thought you'd have it well sorted by now,' Mum remarked, when I claimed there were still loads of things to do.

'I only have Sundays free, don't I?' I said defensively. 'You wouldn't believe the amount of stuff Flo had. It's taking ages.'

'Your gran keeps asking about it. I said you'd call in and see her on your way home.'

I groaned. 'Oh, Mum, you didn't!'

'She is your gran, luv. She's desperate for a little keepsake, something to remind her of Flo. A piece of jewellery would be nice.'

Flo mightn't be too pleased at the idea of anything of hers going to someone she'd specifically not wanted at her funeral. As for jewellery, I hadn't come across any so far. Everything's becoming incredibly complicated, I thought worriedly.

Things became even more complicated when Declan asked, 'How's James?'

'He's fine,' I said automatically, only then realising it was a whole week since I'd seen him, and he hadn't called once. Perhaps he'd decided being chucked out was the last straw. I dismissed him from my mind – there was already enough to think about – and said to Declan, 'Have you done anything about college?'

My father choked on his steak and kidney pudding. 'College? Him? You must be joking.'

'I think it's a very good idea,' Colin said quietly. 'If he took an engineering course, he could come and work for me. I could do with another pair of hands.'

'He'd prefer something different, wouldn't you, Declan?' I was determined to air the matter of Declan's future because I had a feeling he would never have the courage to do it himself. 'Something artistic.' I thought it wise not to mention fashion design or my father might choke to death before our very eyes.

My mother regarded him warily. 'It wouldn't hurt, would it, Norman, for our Declan to go to college? After all, Millicent went to night school and look where it got her.'

While Trudy and Colin did the dishes, I wandered down to the bottom of the garden with Scotty. The little dog jumped up and down like a yo-yo in front of me. I eased myself through the gap in the hedge that separated the main garden from the compost heap, and sat down on an enormous hump of hard soil, cuddling Scotty. This was the only place we had been allowed to play when we were little: our father wouldn't allow us on the lawn. I remembered the day when five-year-old Trudy had broken a window in the greenhouse with a tennis ball. She'd been so petrified she was literally shaking with fright and couldn't stop crying. 'He'll kill me when he gets home,' she sobbed hysterically.

Then I'd had the brilliant idea of pretending someone from the houses behind had done it. We exchanged the ball, which our father would have recognised, for a stone, and claimed ignorance when the broken pane was discovered. It was one of the few crimes we ever got away with.

'Penny for them!' Trudy murmured, as she squeezed through the hedge and sat beside me. Scotty, fast asleep, stirred and licked my knee.

'I won't say what I was thinking about. It would only depress you.'

'It was me smashing that window, I bet. I always remember when I come down here. Even now I break out in a sweat.'

I put an arm around her shoulder. 'How's things, Sis?'

Trudy shrugged. 'Okay. I'm growing a hair on me chin. See?'

'You've always had that,' I said. 'It appeared when you were about fourteen.'

'Did it? I've never noticed before. It must be the glasses.'

'What glasses?'

'I need glasses for close work, reading and painting. I've had them for months. I thought you knew.'

'No,' I said sadly. 'There was a time when we knew every single little thing about each other, but now . . .' In the darkness of our room, when our father was out, we'd whisper our innermost secrets to each other.

'Sorry, Sis.'

'Don't be.' I squeezed Trudy's shoulder. 'I'm not complaining. There's all sorts of stuff you don't know about me.'

'Such as?'

'That would be telling.' I grinned enigmatically.

Trudy pulled a face. 'Actually, there's things I can't even talk about with Colin.'

'Would you like to talk about them now?'

'No, Sis. It would take much too long.'

I watched a bee, well past its prime, buzz weakly on a dandelion. I was conscious of feeling far less fraught than I usually did on these occasions. Today hadn't been nearly as bad as other Sundays. Instead of constant reminders of the way things used to be, I was preoccupied with how things were now.

Mum appeared in the gap in the hedge, looking flustered, though she rarely looked anything else. 'You'll get your lovely clothes all dirty sitting on that soil.' She pushed her bulky frame through the sharp twigs and, ignoring her own advice, plopped down heavily beside us. Immediately Scotty jumped off my knee and on to hers. 'I wanted to talk to you both about Alison.' She began to pull at a weed. 'I found Oxford on the atlas,' she said hesitantly. 'It's almost as far as London. I was scared enough driving to Skem so I'll never make it that far in the car – that's if your dad would let me

191

have it – and I couldn't afford to go every week by train.'

'I'll pay your fare, Mum,' I offered at the same time as Trudy said, 'Colin and me will take you.'

'No.' She shook her head. 'I don't want to be dependent on other people. Alison's me daughter. I don't love her any better than I do you and our Declan, but she needs me more than you lot ever will.'

It seemed to me that Alison didn't need anyone in particular, but perhaps the faithful figure of her mother appearing every Sunday provided a sense of security, a vague feeling that she was special in at least one person's eyes. On the other hand, perhaps the need was the other way round, and it was Mum who'd miss Alison. One day, Declan was bound to leave home and Alison, detached and indifferent, would be the only one of her children left. But, somewhat cruelly, fate had decreed she'd be miles away in Oxford.

'I want her to stay with the St Osyth Trust,' Mum was saying. 'They know and understand her. I'd have her home like a shot, but that's out the question with your dad. He's ashamed of her, for one thing, and he's no patience with her funny little ways. So I've decided to move to Oxford.'

'What!' Trudy and I cried together. It was the last thing we'd expected to hear.

'Shush!' She glanced nervously through the hedge, but the garden was empty. Her husband was inside playing with his beloved grandchildren, and Colin was on guard.

'You mean you'd actually leave him?' I gasped. Why hadn't she thought of this years ago when we were all being beaten regularly for the least little thing, and sometimes for nothing at all?

Mum said huskily, 'I should have left him a long time ago, I know, but it never crossed me mind. I always thought that if I became a better wife he'd stop hitting us, but the harder I tried, the worse he got. In the end, perhaps I was punch-drunk or something, but it all seemed quite normal.' Her voice broke. Scotty opened his eyes and looked at her curiously. 'I could never imagine things being any other way. I'm sorry, but at least I got Alison out the road, didn't I?'

'Don't rake over the past, Mum,' Trudy said softly. 'About Oxford, I don't know what to say.'

'Nor me,' I said, and then, meaning it with all my heart, 'I'll miss you, Mum.'

She dug me in the ribs with her elbow. 'Don't talk daft, Millicent. I only see you once a month as it is, and you're never there when I phone. I talk to that silly machine more than I do you.'

'I'd miss your messages,' I cried. 'Honest, Mum, I really would.' Suddenly I felt that there would be a dreadful hole in my life.

'I could still ring and leave messages.' She chuckled.

'Yes, but it wouldn't be the same if you weren't around.'

Trudy was frowning, as if she, too, was trying to contemplate a future that had so unexpectedly changed. 'Melanie and Jake would be lost without their gran,' she said, close to tears.

'They'll still have their grandad,' Mum said comfortably. Behind her back, Trudy grimaced at the idea that she'd still bring her children to Kirkby if Mum wasn't there.

'I'll get meself a full-time job,' Mum was saying, 'and look for a bedsit close to the home so's I can see Alison every day.'

'It's a big step, Mum,' Trudy said. 'Getting a job won't be easy at your age, and bedsits might cost the earth in Oxford.'

'Then I'll go on social security or whatever it's called these days,' Mum said serenely. 'I've never claimed a penny in me life, yet I've always paid me stamps.' She beamed at us. 'I feel better now I've talked to you two. Not a word about this to your dad, mind.'

Trudy shuddered. 'I wouldn't like to be in your shoes

when you tell him. Would you like me and Colin to be here, give you moral support, like?'

'I don't need moral support, luv. I'll tell him to his face, and if he doesn't like it, he can lump it. Anyroad, it's months off yet.'

'Grandma,' Melanie piped, from the other side of the hedge.

'I'm here, sweetheart.' Mum scrambled to her feet, dislodging an indignant Scotty.

'Grandad said he wants a cup of tea.'

'Tell Grandad to make his own tea,' Trudy said curtly.

'No, no, don't say that, Melanie, whatever you do.' A stubby branch caught her cheek, drawing blood, as she frantically pushed her way back through the hedge.

Trudy glanced at me meaningfully. 'I wonder if she'll do it?'

I remembered the photo of Flo taken in Blackpool, the still pretty face, the lovely smile, when Gran opened the door. Age hadn't been as kind to Martha Colquitt as it had to her sister. I could never remember her smiling much, or looking anything but old. Her face was creased into a permanent scowl, and behind the severe, black-framed spectacles with their thick lenses, her eyes were unfriendly, disapproving. Her best feature was her hair, thick and silvery, which she kept in neat waves under a fine, almost invisible net.

'Oh, it's you,' she said sourly. 'Come in. I might as well not have grandchildren, I never see them.' I followed her into the spotlessly clean, over-furnished room, which stank of a mixture of cigarettes, disinfectant and the vile-smelling ointment she rubbed on her rheumatic shoulder.

'Well, I'm here now,' I said brightly. I would have come more often, or so I told myself, if the welcome was ever warm, but even my kindhearted mother found visiting Gran an ordeal, fetching her weekly shopping out of a sense of duty.

The television beside the fireplace was on without the sound. Gran turned it off. 'Nothing on nowadays but rubbish.'

I sat down in an overstuffed armchair. 'Mum said to remind you there's an old film on later that you might like. It's a musical with Beryl Grable.'

'Betty Grable,' Gran corrected irritably. Her faculties were sharper than those of most people half her age, her memory for names and faces prodigious. 'I might watch it, I'll see. It depends on how long you stay. Do you want a cup of tea?'

'Yes, please,' I said politely.

Gran disappeared into the kitchen and I went over to the window. I'd lived in this flat until I was three, and the view from the fifth floor was one of the few things I could remember clearly. It couldn't be called magnificent: a shopping precinct, the Protestant church, miles and miles of red-brick houses, with a glimpse of flat fields in the far distance, a few trees, but it seemed to change from day to day. The sky was never the same, and I always seemed to glimpse a tree or a building I hadn't noticed before. It was certainly better than no view at all, but Gran felt the need to block it out with thick lace curtains, although no one could see inside except from a passing helicopter.

The curtains had been drawn back a few inches, as if Gran had been looking out, which, apart from going to Mass on Sundays, was all she had to do: she looked out of the window, watched television and smoked – an ashtray on the sill was full of butts. Each day must seem endless.

I adjusted the curtain and returned to my seat. God, it was depressing. The room seemed much darker than Flo's basement.

'I can't remember if you take sugar.' Gran came in with tea in two fine china cups, a cigarette poking from her mouth. Because she'd been to Mass that morning she wore a neat brown woollen blouse and skirt, though Mum reported that she usually spent the day in her dressing-gown. She had no friends, no one called, so what was the point in getting dressed?

'I don't, thanks.'

'Your mam forgot to get me favourite fig biscuits. All I've got is digestives.' Poor Mum could never get the shopping right.

'I don't want a biscuit, thanks all the same.' I sipped the tea, doing my best to avoid the ash floating on the top.

The wall above the sideboard was full of photographs in identical cheap plastic frames: Grandad Colquitt, long dead, a genial-looking man with erratic facial hair, various weddings, including mine and Trudy's, lots of photos of the Cameron kids taken at school – the happy faces, grinning widely, telling a terrible lie.

'There's a photo in Flo's of my father as a baby with his mother – my other grandma,' I said. At home his parents were rarely mentioned. All I knew was that his father had been a sailor, and his mother had died when he was twenty.

'Is that so? Your other gran, Elsa, used to be me best friend.' The thin yellow lips trembled slightly. 'What's it like in Flo's place?'

'Nice.' I smiled. 'I found gas bills the other day going back to nineteen forty-one.' At least this showed I'd been making an effort to get things done.

'It was nineteen forty when she moved in,' Gran said. 'November.' Her voice was surprisingly soft, considering she was talking about her lifelong enemy. 'Just before Christmas. Mam didn't find out till later that Mrs Fritz had gone to Ireland, leaving her in that big house all by herself.'

The name seemed familiar. 'Fritz?'

'Mr Fritz owned the laundry where she worked. He was sent to an internment camp during the war.'

'There's a snap of Flo outside the laundry.' In a fit of generosity, I said, 'Would you like me to take you?' Flo might turn in her grave if she knew, but Gran looked so wretched.

'To the laundry!' The crumpled jaw fell open. 'They knocked it down years ago, girl.'

'I meant Flo's. I'm on my way there now to try to get a few more things done,' I said virtuously. 'I'll bring you home in the car.'

Gran shook her head adamantly. 'Toxteth's the last place on earth I'd go. A man was murdered there only last week, stabbed to death right on the pavement. Even the town centre isn't safe any more. A woman at church had her gold chain snatched from round her neck when she was walking through St John's precinct. She almost had a heart attack.' She looked at me with frightened eyes. 'It's a terrible world nowadays, Millicent.'

'Flo lived in Toxteth most of her life without coming to any harm.' I vaguely remembered my father saying the same thing a few weeks ago. 'And Bel lives not far away. She comes and goes all the time.'

'Bel?'

'Flo's friend.'

'I know who Bel is,' Gran said bitterly. 'I met her once when she was young. So, even she didn't bother to tell me when our Flo died!'

'Maybe she didn't know your address.'

'There aren't many Mrs M. Colquitts in the Liverpool phone book. And someone knew where to contact me, didn't they? But only when it was too late.'

'I'm sorry, Gran,' I said awkwardly. I put the cup and saucer down; the dregs were grey with ash. 'I'd better be going. Don't forget to watch that film.'

'I wish you hadn't come,' Gran said tonelessly. She fumbled in the packet for another cigarette. 'You've raked up things I'd considered long forgotten.'

'I'm sorry,' I said again. I'd only come because I'd been told she wanted to see me.

'I expect you can see yourself out.'

'Of course. 'Bye, Gran.'

There was no answer. I closed the door and flew down the stone staircase where the walls were scrawled with graffiti. As I drove towards Toxteth, it was difficult to rid myself of the memory of the stiff, unhappy woman smoking her endless cigarettes.

I parked in William Square, and as I walked back towards Flo's, Bel and Charmian must have seen me arrive for they were standing by the basement stairs. Charmian waved a bottle of wine, and my heart lifted.

'Hi!' I called, beginning to hurry. Gran was forgotten and I had the strangest feeling, as if I *was* Flo, coming home to my friends.

It would seem that the banging wasn't part of a dream. Beside me Tom O'Mara was dead to the world. I almost fell out of bed, pulled on Flo's dressing-gown and hurried towards the door before whoever was there demolished it. The noise was even louder in the living room. Any minute now Charmian or Herbie might appear, wanting to know what was going on.

'Who's there?' I shouted crossly. It must be a drunk who'd come to the wrong house. I looked blearily at my watch – ten past two – and wondered if I should have woken Tom.

The banging stopped. 'It's James. Let me in.'

James! I was wide awake in an instant, and leaned against the door. 'Go away, James, please.'

'I've no intention of going away.' He began to hammer on the door again. 'Let me in!'

'I don't want to see you,' I yelled, but he almost certainly couldn't hear me above the noise he was making. A police siren sounded in the distance, and just in case it had been alerted by a neighbour to investigate the disturbance in William Square, I opened the door.

'You're not . . .' I began, as a wild-eyed James, smelling strongly of alcohol, brushed past me into the room, '. . . coming in.' Too late. I switched on the main light. Flo's room looked so different with every corner brightly illuminated.

James stood in the middle of the room. I'd never

thought him capable of such anger. I shrank before it, terrified, my heart racing. His face, his neck, his fists were swollen, as if at any minute he would explode. 'What the hell do you think you're playing at?' he demanded furiously.

'I don't know what you mean.' I kept my voice mild, stifling my own anger, not wanting to provoke him further.

He glared at me, as if I was the stupidest woman on earth. 'I've been outside your flat since five o'clock waiting for you,' he raged. 'When it got to midnight, I decided to come here, but I couldn't remember where the fucking place was. I drove round and round for ages before I found it.'

I didn't know what to say, so remained silent. Once again I thought about rousing Tom, but it seemed weak. I was determined to handle the situation on my own: with Tom there, things might turn ugly. James began to pace the floor, waving his arms, his face scarlet. 'Last week, after you threw me out, I thought, I'll give her till Sunday, then that's it. If she doesn't phone, it's over.' He thrust his red face into mine. 'You didn't phone, did you? You didn't give a fuck how I was.' He mimicked my voice, which seemed to be becoming a habit with all the men I knew. ' "I'm taking a shower and I expect you to be gone when I come out." And I went, like the good little boy I am. Then I waited for you to get in touch, but apparently you were willing to let me just walk out of your life as if I'd never existed.'

'James.' I put my hands on his arms to try to calm him. The police car screamed along the main road, William Square obviously not its destination. 'You're not making sense. You said it would be over if I didn't phone. Perhaps that would be the best thing.'

'But I love you! Can't you get into your stupid head how much I love you?' His eyes narrowed. 'You know, all my life I've had girls throw themselves at me. I've never gone short, as they say. But you, an uppity little bitch from Kirkby, you're the one I fell in love with, wanted to marry. How *dare* you turn me down?'

This wasn't happening! I closed my eyes for a second, then said quietly, 'I don't love you, James.'

At this, his hands and arms began to twitch, his blue eyes glazed. He raised his huge fist, ready to strike.

I felt myself grow dizzy. I was a little girl again, wishing I were invisible, waiting, head bowed, for a blow to fall. It was no use trying to escape, because wherever I went, wherever I hid, my father would find me and then the punishment would be even worse. I wanted to weep because this was the story of my life.

The blow I was expecting never came. The dizziness faded, reality returned. That part of my life was over. I took a step back. James was still standing, arm raised. 'Christ! What's the matter with me?' he gasped, in a horrified voice.

'What the hell's going on in here?' Tom O'Mara came out of the bedroom fastening his trousers and bare to the waist.

James's face turned ashen, his shoulders slumped. 'How could you, Millie?' he whispered.

Tom wasn't quite as tall as James, or so broad, but before I knew what was happening, he had James's right arm bent behind him with one hand, the other on his collar, and was propelling him roughly towards the door. Despite the way James had just behaved, I was shocked at the sheer brutality of it. 'There's no need for that,' I cried.

The door slammed. After a while, I could hear James stumbling up the concrete steps. I switched on the lamp, turned off the central light, and sat in the middle of Flo's settee, trembling and hugging myself tightly with both arms.

'What was that all about?' asked Tom from behind.

'Can't you guess?'

'Hadn't you told him about me?'

'It was nothing to do with you until you appeared,' I sighed.

A few seconds later, Tom sat on the settee beside me and put a glass of sherry on the coffee table. 'Drink that!' he commanded. 'It'll do you good. Flo took sherry for her nerves.'

I was actually able to smile. 'I get the impression Flo took sherry for an awful lot of things.'

He put his arm around me companionably. It was the first time he'd touched me when I didn't automatically melt. 'So, what's the story with the bloke I just chucked out? Is he the one you were with at the party?'

'Yes, and there isn't a story. He loves me and I don't love him, that's all. He'll feel worse now he's seen you.' I swallowed half the sherry in one go. Thank goodness Tom had been there. Even if James had calmed down he would have been difficult to get rid of. I thought about him driving home, drunk as a lord. The whole thing was my fault. I should have made it plain the minute he said he loved me that I didn't love him. But I did! The trouble with James is that he's spoilt, too used to having girls throw themselves at him to grasp that this one wasn't blinded by his fatal attraction. I sipped more sherry, conscious of Tom's arm, heavy on my shoulders. I would have let him hit me! I just stood there. I'd never have dreamed James had such an ugly side. He was always so gentle. I watched the lamp, waiting for the girl in the red coat, hating James for bringing ugliness into the place I loved, where I'd always felt supremely safe. I'll never see him again, I vowed.

'Better?' Tom enquired. 'You've stopped trembling.'

'Much better.' I snuggled my head against his shoulder. 'Were you happy as a child?'

'That's a funny thing to ask.' He thought for a while. 'I suppose I was. Knowing Flo helped a lot.'

'What was your dad like?'

'Me dad? Oh, he was a soft ould thing. Everyone pissed him about something rotten – Gran, me mam and me, I suppose, as well as the firm he worked for.' His voice became hard. 'That's why I swore I'd be me own boss when I grew up.'

'Where's your mother?'

He shrugged carelessly. 'No idea. She did a runner when I was five. Went off with another bloke.'

I patted his knee. 'I'm sorry.'

'Don't be,' he said carelessly. 'It were good riddance as far as I was concerned.' He kissed my ear. 'What about you?'

'What about me?'

'Were you happy – how did you put it? – as a child?'

'Sometimes I wish I could be reborn and start all over.'

'Well, you can't. You're here and that's it, you can't change anything.'

'Are these your wife's initials?' I traced the heart on his chest with my finger.

'No. Clare's always trying to persuade me to get rid of it. You can get it done with a laser.'

'Have you any children?'

'Two girls, Emma and Susanna.' He raised his eyebrows, and I sensed he was annoyed. 'What's this? The third degree?'

'I wanted to know a few things about you, that's all.'

'What's the point?' he said coldly.

Just as coldly, I replied, 'I thought it would be nice to know a little about the man I've been sleeping with for the past week.' I looked at him. 'Is there nothing you'd like to know about me?'

'You're a great fuck, that's all I care.'

I stiffened and pulled away. 'Do you have to be so coarse?'

He dragged me back against him. 'The less we know about each other the better, don't you understand that?' he whispered urgently. 'I may be coarse, but I'm not thick. I've always taken me wedding vows seriously. I love me kids, and I don't want to spoil things between me and Clare.' He twisted me around, so that I was lying on his knee, and undid the belt on my dressing-gown. 'Let's keep things the way they are. Getting to know each other could be dangerous.'

His hands were setting my body on fire. I told myself that I had no intention of falling in love with someone like him. But he aroused feelings in me that no other man had. His lips came down on mine, and we rolled on to the floor. The pleasure we gave each other was sublime, and in the midst of everything, when I was almost out of my head with delight too exquisite to describe, I could have sworn I shouted, 'I love you.'

Or perhaps it was Tom.

At some time in the early hours of the morning, he carried me into the bedroom. I pretended to be asleep when he tucked the bedclothes around me, and remained like that while he got dressed. It wasn't until the front door clicked behind him that I sat up. 'Did you ever get yourself into a mess like this, Flo?' I asked. 'If your bureau is anything to go by, you led a very neat, ordered life.'

It was ages before I had to leave for work but I got up, ran a few inches of water in the bath and splashed myself awake. I made coffee in the microwave and carried it into the living room, where I tried, unsuccessfully, to empty my mind. But as soon as I got rid of Tom O'Mara, James would take his place, followed by Mum, Alison, Declan, Trudy – what were the things my sister couldn't talk about to Colin?

I was back to Tom again when I noticed that the rising sun was shining through the rear window and the walls of the little yard were glowing a rosy pink. I'd never been up this early before, and it looked so pretty.

So far, I hadn't ventured into the yard. I went outside, wondering if Flo had sat here in the summer with her first cup of tea of the day, as I did on my balcony. A black cat regarded me benignly from the wall and graciously allowed me to stroke its back. The wooden bench was full of mould and needed scrubbing, and the pansies in the plant-holders were dead now. I nearly jumped out of my skin when a head covered with untidy black curls appeared over the neighbouring wall.

'Hi,' Peter Maxwell grinned. 'Remember me? We met the other week at Charmian's party.'

'Of course! You said you lived next door. What are you doing up so early?' I could only see him from the shoulders up and he appeared to be wearing a sleeveless T-shirt.

He flexed a bulging muscle in his arm. 'I work out every morning. I'm off for a jog in a minute.' He winked. 'You can come with me, if you like.'

'You must be joking!'

He rested his arms on the wall and said conversationally, 'Are you all right?'

'Don't I look all right?'

'You look great, even without my glasses. It's just that I heard a commotion in your place last night. I contemplated coming round, but the sounds died down.'

'It was a drunk,' I said dismissively. 'I soon got rid of him.'

'By the way, I'd like to apologise for Sharon.'

'Who's Sharon?'

'Me girlfriend – ex-girlfriend. I tore her off a strip for dragging me away when I was dancing with you at the party. She was very rude.'

'I hardly noticed.'

He looked dismayed. 'And I was quite enjoying our little chat. I thought you were, too.'

'Well, yes, I was,' I conceded.

'It means I've got a spare ticket for the school concert in December. I wondered if you'd come.'

I pulled a face. 'I hate schools.'

'So did I, but they're different when you're an adult. No one will test your spelling or demand the date of the battle of Waterloo. Come on,' he coaxed, 'it's Charles Dickens's *A Christmas Carol*. I'd love you to be there.'

'Why?'

'Because you used to know me as Weedy and I want

you to see me as Peter Maxwell, MA, economics teacher, and scriptwriter of genius – I wrote the script for *A
Christmas Carol* and set it in the present day. Tell you
what,' he said eagerly, 'if you come to the concert, I'll let
you show me round a property and we can negotiate.
Then we'll have both proved to each other that we've
made it.'

I smiled. 'How could I possibly refuse?'

Still smiling, I went indoors. Peter Maxwell had
cheered me up. We'd both been through the mill and
emerged unscathed. I paused in the act of pulling down
the front of Flo's bureau, which hadn't been touched
since the night Tom had arrived with a Chinese takeaway.

Unscathed? Was that true? Until that moment, I'd
never thought I'd ever get over the tragedy of my childhood. I'd thought that, along with Trudy and Declan, I'd
been irreparably damaged. But maybe time was fading
the shadow of my father, and perhaps one day it would go
away altogether. One day, the three of us would emerge,
truly unscathed.

I decided not to think about it any more on such a
lovely morning. I fetched a chair up to the bureau and
took out the bundle of letters held together with the
elastic band. It was rotten, and snapped when I pulled it
off.

William Square began to wake up to the new day: cars
drove away, others came to take their place; feet hurried
past the basement window; children shrieked on their
way to school – a football came over the railings and
landed with a loud clang on the dustbin. But I was only
vaguely aware of these activities. I was too engrossed in
Flo's letters. It wasn't until I returned the last letter to its
envelope that I remembered where I was. The letter was
one of several from the same person, a Gerard Davies
from Swansea, in which he implored Flo yet again to
marry him. 'I love you, Flo. I always will. There'll never
be another girl like you.'

Which was more or less what every other letter had said. They were love letters from a score of different men, all to Flo, and from the tone of quite a few, the relationships hadn't been platonic.

And Bel had claimed that Flo had led the life of a saint!

I remembered the mysterious receipts from the hotel in the Isle of Man. 'Oh, I bet you were a divil in your day, Flo Clancy,' I whispered.

Flo

I

1941

'Oh, Flo, you'll never guess!' Sally threw herself on to the sofa. 'Our Martha's captured Albert Colquitt at long last. They're getting married on St Patrick's Day.'

'Only two weeks off!' Flo sank beside her sister and they collapsed into giggles. 'How on earth did she manage that?'

Sally dropped her voice, though the entire house, all five floors of it, was empty and no one could have overheard. 'I think she seduced him,' she whispered dramatically.

'She what!' screamed Flo, giggling even more. 'You're joking.'

'I'm not, Flo, honest,' Sally assured her, round-eyed. 'One night after we'd gone to bed our Martha got up again. I didn't say anything, and she must have thought I was asleep. I thought she was going to the lavvy, but she sat at the dressing-table and started combing her hair. The moon was shining through the winder, so I could see her as clearly as I can see you now.' Sally frowned thoughtfully. 'I wondered why she hadn't put her curlers in or smothered herself with cold cream. Not only that, she was wearing that pink nightdress – you know, the one Elsa Cameron bought her for her twenty-first. Are you with me so far, Flo?'

'Yes, yes, I'm with you.' Flo wanted to throttle her sister for stretching the tale out so long. 'What happened then?'

'She just disappeared.'

'What d'you mean she just disappeared? You mean she vanished before your very eyes?'

'Of course not, soft girl. She left the room and was gone for ages. I was asleep by the time she got back.'

'Is that all?' Flo said, disappointed. 'I don't know how you worked out she seduced Albert. She might have dozed off on the lavvy. I've nearly done it meself in the middle of the night.'

'Why didn't she put her curlers in, then? Why didn't she use her cream? And she was keeping that nightdress for her bottom drawer. Not only that,' Sally finished triumphantly, 'she wasn't wearing her glasses.'

That seemed to provide final proof of Sally's claim. It was no longer a laughing matter. 'If that's how she caught him, then she's been dead devious,' Flo said soberly. 'Not many men could resist if a girl got into bed with them. She's shamed him into getting married.'

Sally nodded knowingly, with the air of a woman of the world, well aware of men's lack of will-power when it came to sex. 'They're very weak,' she agreed. 'Anyroad, Martha and Albert are going to live at home till the war's over. Mam said she's expecting you at the wedding.'

'In that case, Mam's got another think coming.' Even if she wasn't dead set against her sister, she'd feel peculiar, knowing that Albert had asked her first and that Martha was his second choice – that's if he'd had a choice. She would, though, write him a little note. In the time she had remained in Burnett Street after his kind proposal, she'd always made sure they'd never been alone. He didn't know the truth of what had happened to her baby but it would have been a sore reminder that she shouldn't have turned him down. Last week, her son had had his first birthday. She'd sent a card, writing simply, 'To Hugh, from Flo'. But the card had come back by return of post.

Sally sighed. 'She must have been desperate. Poor Martha.'

'Poor Albert,' Flo said cynically.

The young sailor stood before her, agonisingly shy, his face red with embarrassment. She had noticed him watching her all night. 'Would you like to dance, miss?'

'Of course.' Flo lifted her arms and he clasped her awkwardly. It was the first time he'd ventured on to the floor.

'I'm not very good at this,' he stammered, when he stood on her toe.

'Then you must learn,' she chided him. 'All service-men should learn to dance. This is a waltz, the easiest dance of all. You'll find yourself in all sorts of different towns and cities and it's the best way to meet girls.'

He swallowed, and said daringly, 'I won't meet many girls like you. I hope you don't mind me saying, but you're the prettiest one here.'

'Why on earth should I mind you saying a lovely thing like that? What's your name, luv?'

'Gerard Davies. I come from Swansea.'

'Pleased to meet you, Gerard. I'm Flo Clancy.'

'Pleased to meet you, Flo.'

It always started more or less the same. She only picked the shy ones, who were usually, though not always, very young. Gerard looked eighteen or nineteen, which meant he'd not long left home and would be missing his family.

When the waltz was over, she fanned herself with her hand and said, 'Phew! It's hot in here,' knowing that almost certainly he would offer to buy her a drink. He took the opportunity eagerly, and she chose the cheapest, a lemonade. They sat in a corner of the ballroom, and she asked him about his mum and dad, and what he'd done for a living before he was called up.

His dad ran a smallholding, he told her, and his mum worked in the shop where their vegetables were sold. He had two sisters, both older than him, and everyone had been very proud when he'd passed the scholarship and gone to grammar school. Less than three months ago, he'd gone straight from school into the Navy, and he had no idea what he wanted to do when the war was over. Flo noticed that he had the merest trace of a moustache on his upper lip, and his hands were soft and white. It was easy to believe that until recently he'd been just a school-boy. His brown eyes were wide and guileless. He knew nothing about anything much, yet he was about to fight for his country in the worst war the world had ever known. Flo felt her heart contract at the thought.

The drink finished, they returned to the dance floor. Flo could tell that he was gaining confidence because he had a girl on his arm, and it grew as the night progressed.

At half past eleven, she said she had to be getting home. 'I have to be up for work at the crack of dawn.'

'In the laundry?'

'That's right, luv.' She'd told him quite a lot about herself. She gave a little shudder. 'I don't live far away, but I'm terrified of walking home in the blackout.'

'I'll take you home,' he said, with alacrity, which Flo had known he would. She wasn't a bit scared of the blackout.

Outside, she linked his arm in case they lost each other in the dark. 'Have you got long in Liverpool?'

'No, we're sailing tomorrow, I don't know where to. It's a secret.' She felt his thin, boyish arm tighten on her own, and reckoned he was frightened. Who wouldn't be, knowing about all the ships that had been sunk and the lives that had been lost, mainly of young men like him?

When they got to her flat she made him a cup of tea and something to eat – he appeared to be starving the way he downed the two thick cheese sarnies.

'I'd better be getting back to the ship.' He looked at her shyly. 'It's been a lovely evening, Flo. I've really enjoyed myself.'

'So've I, luv.'

By the door, he flushed scarlet and stammered, 'Can I kiss you, Flo?'

She didn't answer, just closed her eyes and willingly offered her lips. His mouth touched hers, softly, and his arms encircled her waist. She slid her own arms around his neck, and murmured, 'Oh, Gerard!' and he kissed her again, more firmly this time. She didn't demur when his hands fumbled awkwardly and hesitantly with her breasts. She had thought this might happen. It nearly always did.

It was another half-hour before Gerard Davies left Flo in her bed. 'Can I write to you?' he pleaded, as he got back into his uniform. 'It'd be nice to have a girl back home.'

'I'd like that very much, Gerard.'

'And can I see you if I'm in Liverpool again?'

'Of course, luv. But don't turn up unannounced, whatever you do.' She worried that more than one of her young lovers might turn up at the same time. 'Me landlady upstairs wouldn't like it a bit. I'll give you the phone number of the laundry so you can let me know beforehand, like.'

'Thanks, Flo.' Then he said, in an awestruck voice, 'This has been the most wonderful night of my life.'

Gerard Davies was the seventh young man she'd slept with. Flo told herself earnestly that it was her contribution towards the war. Tommy O'Mara had taught her that making love was the most glorious experience on earth, and she wanted to share this experience with a few bashful young men who were about to fight for their country. It made her heart swell to think that they would go into battle, perhaps even die, carrying with them the memory of the wonderful time they'd had with Flo, the pretty young woman from Liverpool, who'd made them feel so special.

It was important that she didn't get pregnant. She'd asked Sally, casual, like, what she and Jock used.

'It's something called a French letter, Flo. They're issued by the Navy. I think you can get them in the chemist's, but I'm not sure.' Sally grinned. 'Why on earth d'you want to know?'

'No reason, I just wondered.'

There was no way Flo would even consider entering a chemist's to ask for French letters, so she inserted a sponge soaked in vinegar which she'd once heard the women in the laundry say was the safest way. But Flo had the strongest feeling she would never have another baby. It was as if the productive part of her had withered away to nothing when her little boy was taken away.

Just after Martha's wedding, Bel wrote to say she was expecting. 'I'll be leaving the ATS, naturally. Bob's being posted to North Africa, so I'll be back in Liverpool soon, looking for somewhere to live. Perhaps I can help out in the laundry if there's a sitting-down job I could do.'

Flo wrote back immediately to say she'd love to have Bel stay until she found a place of her own and that, if necessary, she'd invent a sitting-down job in the laundry. She bought two ounces of white baby wool to knit a matinée jacket, but in April another letter arrived: Bel had had a miscarriage. 'You can't imagine what it's like to lose a baby, Flo. I'm staying in the ATS, though I was looking forward to living in William Square and working in this famous laundry.'

The knitting was put away, unfinished. She seemed to waste a lot of time making baby clothes that would never be worn, Flo thought sadly. She wrote to Bel. 'I wouldn't know, of course, but I can imagine how heartbreaking it must be to lose a baby.'

Flo was proud of the way she'd run the laundry since Stella Fritz had returned to Ireland four months ago. As well as the Holbrook twins, she now employed two young mothers, friends, who worked half a day each. Lottie would turn up at midday with several lusty toddlers in a big black pram, and Moira would take them home. There was also Peggy Lewis, a widow, only four and a half feet tall, who worked like a navvy. Peggy had to leave early to prepare a massive meal for her three lads who worked on the docks and arrived home famished and ready to eat the furniture if there was no food ready.

When the delivery-boy, Jimmy Cromer, a cheeky little bugger but reliable, gave in his notice, having been offered a job with a builder at five bob a week more, Flo immediately increased his wages by ten. Jimmy was thrilled. 'If I stay, can I paint "White's Laundry" on me sidecart?'

'Of course, luv. As long as you do it neat and spell it proper.'

Every Friday, Flo sat in the office working out the week's finances, putting the wages to one side, and taking the surplus to the bank. There were usually several cheques in settlement of their big customers' bills. She paid everything into the Fritizes' account, then made out a statement showing exactly what money had come in and what had gone out, to send to Stella Fritz in County Kerry. At the bottom, she usually added a little message: the laundry was doing fine, there were no problems with the house, the window-cleaner still came once a month and she assumed this was all right. She kept all her own personal bills, stamped 'paid' by the gas and electricity companies, just in case there was ever any argument.

Not once did Stella acknowledge the hard work Flo was putting in to keep the business going and looking after the house. I suppose she's too busy breathing in the good clean air and looking out the winder, Flo thought. In the absence of any authority to tell her otherwise, she promoted herself – she'd remembered a white overall in the office cupboard with Manageress embroidered in red on the breast pocket. It had been there for as long as she could remember, together with a few other odds and ends that customers had forgotten to collect.

'You look dead smart, luv,' Mam exclaimed. She often called in on her way to or from work. 'Manageress at twenty! Who'd have thought it, eh?' Flo did her utmost not to preen. 'Which reminds me,' Mam continued, 'we were talking about you the other night. It's only a fortnight off your twenty-first, May the eighth. Martha and Sal both had a party. We can't let yours go without a little celebration, drink your health an' all. What do you say, Flo?'

'Where would the party be?'

'At home, luv, where else?'

Flo shook her head stubbornly. 'I'm not coming home, Mam, not while our Martha's there.'

'Oh, luv!' Mam's face was a mixture of grief and vexation. 'How long are you going to keep up this feud with Martha? After all, the girl's expecting. I can't wait to have me first grandchild,' she added tactlessly, as if Hugh O'Mara had never existed.

'Sal told me about the baby, Mam, and it's not a feud with Martha. I'm not sure what it is.'

'You'll have to speak to her sometime.'

'No, I won't.' Flo thought about Hugh. Then she thought about Nancy O'Mara, and that no one would take Martha's baby away and give it to a Welsh witch. 'I don't have to speak to our Martha again as long as I live,' she said abruptly.

Mam gave up. 'What about your twenty-first then?'

'You and Sal can come to William Square. I'll ask the women from the laundry, get a bottle of sherry and make sarnies. You can drink me health there.'

Sally reported that Albert seemed relatively content now that he was a member of the family he'd grown so fond of. 'He's started calling Mam "Mother" and she's a bit put out – she's two years younger than him! He always asks about you, Flo. He can't understand why you never come to visit.'

'Tell him I can't stand his wife,' Flo suggested. 'How's her ladyship taken to married life, anyroad?'

'All she's ever wanted was a wedding ring and Mrs in

front of her name. She goes round looking like the cat that ate the cream.'

Now that Albert was to become a father, his joy knew no bounds. Flo was pleased for him: he was a nice man who deserved happiness. But when it came to Martha, she felt only bitterness.

Frequently, in the dinner hour or on her way home, she walked down Clement Street, but she never set eyes on Nancy and there was never a pram outside number eighteen. Once, she thought she heard a baby cry as she passed, but that might have been her imagination.

Everyone in the laundry was pleased to be invited to Flo's twenty-first. 'It won't be much,' she warned. 'There won't be any fellers, for one thing.'

'We don't mind,' Jennifer and Joanna Holbrook said together.

'Me husband wouldn't let me go if there were,' remarked Moira.

Lottie's husband was away in the Army. Nevertheless, she would have felt disloyal going to a party where there were fellers.

'I'm not bothered,' Peggy said, from somewhere within a cloud of steam. 'Anyroad, I see enough of fellers at home. You could ask Jimmy Cromer if he'd like to provide some masculine company.'

'I'm not going to a party full of ould married women,' Jimmy said in a scandalised voice.

'I'm not old and I'm not married,' Flo reminded him.

Jimmy leered at her far too maturely for a fifteen-year-old. 'Will you come out with me, then?'

'I'll do no such thing!'

'In that case, I'm not coming to your party.'

The first week of May brought air raids worse than any the city had known before. For a week, it seemed as if the Luftwaffe's intention was to blast Liverpool out of existence. Flo was convinced that her party would never take place. By the eighth no one would be left alive and there wouldn't be a building still standing. At night she stayed indoors, worried that if she went dancing a raid might start and that she really would be too scared to come home alone. In bed, with her head under the covers, she listened to the house grinding on its foundations as the bombs whistled their way down to earth and the ground shook, though it was the parachute mines, drifting silently and menacingly, that caused the greatest carnage. Bells clanged wildly as fire engines raced to put out the hundreds of fires that crackled away, turning the sky blood red.

Next morning, exhausted but still in one piece, Flo would go to work. There was rarely any sign of public transport and she had to make her way carefully along pavements carpeted with splintered glass, passing the sad, broken remains of buildings that had been the landmarks of a lifetime, and the little streets with yawning gaps where houses had been only the day before. The air was full of floating scraps of charred paper, like black confetti at a funeral.

Everyone at the laundry was miraculously still there to exclaim in horror about the events of the previous night: the narrow escapes, the bomb that had dropped in the next street killing a girl they'd gone to school with, or a chap who'd nearly married their sister. Moira lost the godmother of her youngest child. Peggy's brother-in-law, an ARP warden, was killed outright when the building he was in got a direct hit. How long, everyone wondered, would the terror continue?

'It can't go on for ever,' Peggy maintained.

It was that thought that kept them going. It had to stop sometime.

Flo arrived on the Friday of the nightmarish week to find that during the night all the mains had been fractured. There seemed little point in a laundry without electricity, gas or water so she told everyone they might as well go home. 'You'll still get paid,' she promised, not caring if Stella would approve or not. 'It's not your fault you can't work. It's that bloody Hitler's.'

'What are you going to do?' one of the twins enquired.

'I'll stay, just in case things come on again.'

'We'll stay with you.'

'Same here,' echoed Peggy.

'Me, too,' said Moira.

The next few hours always remained one of Flo's most vivid memories, proof that the human spirit obstinately refused to give in, even in the face of the worst adversity. Peggy produced a pack of cards and they played Strip Jack Naked, Rummy and Snap, and shrieked with laughter for no reason at all, though anyone listening would have thought the laughter a mite hysterical and a bit too loud. Every now and then, they'd pause for a sing-song: 'We'll Meet Again', 'Little Sir Echo', 'Run Rabbit Run'. In their quavery soprano voices, the twins entertained them with a variety of old songs, 'If You Were the Only Girl in the World', and 'Only a Bird in a Gilded Cage'.

Mid-morning, when they would normally have stopped for a cup of tea, Moira said wistfully, 'I'd give anything for a cuppa.'

As if in answer to Moira's prayer, Mrs Clancy appeared suddenly at the side door carrying a teapot. 'I expect you're all parched for a drink,' she said cheerfully. 'I always run a bucket of water before I go to bed, just in case, like, and Mrs Plunkett next door's got one of them paraffin stoves.'

There was a mad dash for cups. As usual, the twins had brought milk because they never used all their ration.

'I've got Albert at home,' Mam said to Flo. 'He hurt his leg fire-watching. He's a terrible patient. All he does is complain about people getting away without paying their fares.'

'There's hardly any trams running.'

'That's what I keep telling him. There's lines up everywhere.' She patted Flo's hand. 'I'm off to work now, luv. I'll call in for the teapot on me way home.'

'It's all right, Mam, I'll bring it. I wouldn't mind having a word with Albert. What time will you be back?' She would take the opportunity of Martha's absence to reassure Albert, though not in words, that they would always be friends. She'd prefer him not to be alone, just in case there was a message in his eyes it would be wiser not to see.

'I'll be home about half two. Sal's on mornings, so she'll be back not long afterwards.'

Later that morning the gas supply was reconnected, and just after one o'clock water came gushing out of the tap in the lavatory, which had been left turned on. There was still no electricity, so the steam-presser remained out of use, but the boilers could be loaded with washing and the ironing done. Flo gave a sigh of relief as the laundry began to function almost normally, the women setting to work with a will. Normality seemed precious in an uncertain, dangerous world, though it didn't last for long.

Just as Flo was thinking that it was almost time to nip round to Burnett Street with the teapot, the air-raid siren began its sinister wail. She particularly hated daylight raids. They were rarely heavy and usually brief but, unlike the night raids, were impossible to ignore – or, at least, pretend to. The women groaned, but when Flo suggested they abandon work for the shelter on the corner, they flatly refused.

'The shelter's just as likely to get a direct hit as the laundry,' said Lottie, who'd recently changed shifts with Moira. 'I'd sooner stay.'

There seemed no argument to this, although the laundry was flimsy in comparison. Soon afterwards a solitary plane could be heard buzzing idly overhead. Everyone went outside to take a look. They could see the German crosses on the wings.

'Is that a Messerschmidt, Jo?'

'No, Jen. It's a Heinkel.'

Suddenly the plane went into a dive. It appeared to be coming straight for them. Peggy screamed and they ran inside and slammed the door. Almost immediately, there was a loud explosion, followed by another, then several more. The plane must have dropped a stick of bombs. From somewhere within the building, there was a thud and the crash of breaking glass.

'Jaysus! That was close!' someone gasped.

They stood still, scarcely breathing, as the plane's engine grew fainter. Then the sound disappeared and the all-clear went. The raid was over.

The laundry had suffered superficial damage. At least, Flo assumed that a shattered office window and the door blown off its hinges could be described as superficial. 'The thing is,' she said shakily, 'I'd forgotten today's the day I do the accounts, otherwise I'd have been in here sorting out the wages, or writing the statement for Mrs Fritz.' There was a small crater in the street outside, and the houses opposite had also lost their doors and windows, but thankfully, no one had been hurt.

The twins began calmly to sweep up the broken glass and restore the room to relative order. Flo decided to take the money home and leave the bank till Monday, but it was important that the women were paid. Using the presser as a desk, she counted out the money and wrote each name on a little brown envelope. She felt angry with herself because her hands were trembling and her writing was all over the place. She'd had a close shave, that was all. Some people suffered far worse without going to pieces. Her stomach was squirming. She felt uneasy, full of dread. 'Pull yourself together, Flo Clancy,' she urged.

'Flo, luv,' a voice said softly.

Flo looked up. Sally was standing at the side door and the feeling of dread grew until it almost choked her. She knew why Sally had come. 'Is it Mam?' she breathed.

Her sister nodded slowly. 'And Albert.'

Sally said, 'Promise you'll make things up with Martha.'

'Why should I?' demanded Flo.

It was almost midnight. The sisters were as yet too exhausted to grieve. They paid no heed to the raid going on outside, which was as bad as any experienced so far, decimating the beleaguered city even further. They were in William Square, the only place Sally had to go now that she'd lost her home in Burnett Street. The joint funeral would take place on Monday, the day after Flo's twenty-first birthday. There was room for Albert in his mother-in-law's grave, where she would join her beloved husband. The wreaths had been ordered, a Requiem Mass arranged, and a friend of Mam's had offered to provide refreshments after the service. Father Haughey was trying to track down Albert's cousin in Macclesfield. The address would have been in the parlour, but there was no longer a parlour, no longer a house, nothing left of the place to which Mr and Mrs Clancy had moved when they married, where they'd brought up their three girls. The bomb had gone through the roof and exploded in the living room, demolishing the houses on both sides. Martha had been safe at the brewery but Mam and Albert, sheltering under the stairs, had been killed instantly. Their shattered bodies lay in the mortuary, waiting for the funeral director to collect.

'Oh, Flo,' Sally moaned, 'how can you be so unChristian and unforgiving? Martha's pregnant and she's lost both her mam and her husband.'

Martha had been whisked from the brewery to Elsa Cameron's house. When Sally went to see her, she was fast asleep, the doctor had given her a sedative.

'I can't begin to imagine how I'd feel if I'd lost Jock and Mam at the same time,' Sally shuddered.

'But you're in love with Jock,' Flo pointed out. 'Martha was no more in love with Albert than I was – and all three of us loved Mam.'

'You're awful hard, Sis.'

'I'm only pointing out the obvious. What's hard about that?'

'Oh, I dunno. It's just that you always seemed such a

soft ould thing. I never dreamed you could be so un-sympathetic.'

'I feel sorry for our Martha,' Flo conceded. 'I just don't want anything more to do with her, that's all.' She felt irritated that Sally didn't seem to appreciate the enormity of what Martha had done. Maybe, because Flo's baby was a bastard, she wasn't supposed to love him the way a married mother would.

'Despite our Martha being an ould bossy-boots, she depended on Mam far more than we did.' Sally sighed. 'She'll miss her something awful. We loved Mam, but we didn't need her.' She turned to her sister and said, 'Don't think I've forgotten about Tommy O'Mara and the baby, Flo. But you're a strong person, a survivor. You've got yourself a nice little home, an important job. It's time to forgive and forget.'

'I'll never forgive Martha, and I'll never forget.' Flo's voice was like ice. 'I'll speak to her politely on Monday, but that's as far as I'm willing to go.'

But Martha was too ill to attend the funeral. And Sally had been right: Elsa Cameron reported that it was her mother Martha kept calling for. There was no mention of Albert.

2

The momentous year had flown by. Suddenly, it was Christmas again and Liverpool, though battered and badly bruised after the week-long May blitz, had survived to fight another day. The raids continued fitfully, but it was rare that the siren went nowadays. Life went on, and mid-December, Martha Colquitt gave birth to a daughter, Kate, named after the grandmother she would never know.

'She's the prettiest thing you've ever seen,' Sally told Flo. 'Ever so placid and good-humoured.'

'That's nice.' Flo did her utmost to sound generous.

'But I wish Martha'd find somewhere else to live.' Sally's brow puckered worriedly. 'I wouldn't want that Elsa Cameron anywhere near a baby of mine. She treats Norman like a punch-bag, poor bugger. He's only four, and such a lovely little chap.'

'What's happened to her husband?'

'Eugene used to come home from sea every few months, but last time he told her she was crackers and he's never been back since. I reckon he's done a bunk, permanent, like.'

'Martha said once Elsa had a sort of illness,' Flo remarked. 'She said some women go that way when they have a baby. Afterwards they're never quite right in the head.'

Sally nodded. 'There's summat wrong with the woman. By rights, Norman should be taken off her. She's not fit to be a mother.'

It seemed grotesquely unfair that Elsa Cameron, unfit to have a child, and Nancy O'Mara, unable to have one, should both have become mothers, yet Flo was childless. She changed the subject before she said something she might later regret.

'What d'you think of me decorations?' she asked. The room was festooned with paper chains and tinsel. Clusters of imitation holly hung in both windows.

'It looks like a grotto. I tried everywhere for decorations, but there's none to be had in the shops.' After living for a few months with Flo, Sally had found herself a small flat not far from Rootes Securities in Speke, which meant that she and Jock could be alone together during the precious times he was on leave.

'I got them from upstairs,' Flo said smugly. 'There's plenty more, if you'd like some. It's like having a big shop up there all to meself.'

'I wouldn't mind a few. I'm expecting Jock any minute, and it'd be nice to have the place looking Christmassy. Don't forget you're invited to Christmas dinner, will you?'

'No. And don't you forget me party the Saturday before. I feel as if I owe the girls in the laundry a party. I never had the one that was planned for me twenty-first.'

Sally twisted her lips ruefully. 'Mam was really looking forward to that. She was trying to get the ingredients for a birthday cake.'

'Was she? You've never mentioned that before.'

'I'd forgotten all about it.'

The sisters were silent for a while, thinking about Mam and Albert and how much their little world had changed over the past few years.

'Oh, well.' Sally sighed. 'I'm on early shift tomorrer. I'd better be getting home.'

It was a sad Christmas, full of bitter-sweet memories of Christmases that had gone before, made even sadder when a letter arrived from Bel to say that Bob had been killed in North Africa. 'I only wish you two had met, Flo,' she wrote. 'He was the dearest husband a woman could have. We were only married two years, almost to the day, and weren't together for a lot of that time, but I'll never stop missing him. Never.'

On New Year's Eve, Flo slipped into the Utility frock that she'd bought especially for the Rialto dance, which would go on till past midnight. It was turquoise linen, made with the minimum amount of material, short sleeves and a narrow collar. She adjusted the mirror on the mantelpiece, took a sip of sherry, and began to curl her hair into a roll.

Would she meet anyone tonight? She was glad Christmas was over and it would soon be 1942. She and Sally had both agreed that they would put the past firmly behind them and start afresh. With a wry smile, Flo glanced at the fluffy blue bunny, still in its Cellophane wrapping on the sideboard. She'd bought it for Hugh, but hadn't had the nerve to take it round to Clement Street, knowing that it would be refused. Anyroad, Hugh would be two in February and had probably grown out of fluffy bunnies. She still looked for him, walking up and down Clement Street two or three times a week. Nancy must have deliberately done her shopping when she knew Flo would be at work because there was never any sign of her out with Hugh. For a while, Flo was worried that she'd moved, but Sally said that Martha had taken Kate to see her.

She sipped more sherry, already slightly drunk and the evening hadn't even started. *She didn't even know what her son looked like!* How could she ever put the past behind her when he would still be on her mind if she lived to be a hundred? She hummed 'Auld Lang Syne', and told herself she was strong, a survivor. She wondered why she wanted to weep when she was getting ready for a dance where she was bound to have a good time. 'Because it's not really what I want,' she told herself bleakly.

When someone knocked on the door she turned, startled. Sal was spending New Year's Eve at Elsa Cameron's with Martha. 'If she's come to persuade me to go with her, she's wasting her time.'

A middle-aged man, sunburned, with hollow eyes and hollow cheeks, was standing outside the door holding a suitcase. He wore an ill-fitting tweed suit, and the collar of his frayed shirt was far too big.

'Yes?' Flo said courteously. She didn't recognise him from Adam.

'Oh, Flo! Have I changed so much?' he said tragically.

'Mr Fritz! Oh, Mr Fritz!' She grabbed his arm and pulled him inside. 'Am I pleased to see you!'

'I'm glad someone is.' He looked ready to shed the tears she'd so recently wanted to shed herself. He came into the flat and she pushed him into a chair, then stared at him as if he were a long-lost, dearly loved relative. He was much thinner than she remembered, but despite his gaunt features and the lines of strain around his jaw, he looked fit and well, as if he'd spent a lot of time working outdoors. His once chubby hands were lean and callused, but without his wire-rimmed glasses he seemed much younger. The more she stared, the less he looked like the Mr Fritz she used to know.

'Are you home for good?' she demanded. She wanted to pat him all over, make sure he was real, and had to remind herself he was only her employer.

He said drily, 'After all this time the powers-that-be decided I wasn't a danger to my adopted country. Just before Christmas they let me go.' His brown eyes grew moist. 'I've been to Ireland, Flo. Stella wasn't pleased to see me, and made it obvious she didn't want me to stay. The younger children didn't know who I was. The others were polite, but they're having such a good time on the farm I think they were scared I'd insist they come home.' He sighed. 'They're known locally as the McGonegals. Stella is ashamed of her married name.'

Flo had no idea what to say. She frowned at her hands and mumbled, 'I always thought you and Mrs Fritz were very happy together.'

'So did I!' Mr Fritz looked puzzled. 'I'm not sure what happened, but as soon as the war started Stella became a different person, bad-tempered, blaming me for things I had no control over. I couldn't produce coal or sugar out of thin air as if I were a magician. I wasn't personally responsible for the air raids. When the women left the laundry for higher wages, that was the last straw as far as Stella was concerned. It was a shock, after so many years, to discover she could be so unpleasant.'

'Perhaps,' Flo said hesitantly, 'once the war's over . . .'

'No.' He shook his head wearily. 'No, it's too late, Flo. I spent eighteen months in the camp. The other married men had letters from their families. Some wives travelled hundreds of miles to see their husbands for just a few hours. I had a single letter from Stella the whole time I was there, and that was to tell me she was back in Ireland and she'd left you in charge of the laundry and William Square.' There was a lost expression on his face.

Something had happened with which he would never come to terms. 'You can't be sure of anything in this life, I hadn't realised that,' he murmured. 'I never thought it possible to feel so very alone, as if I'd never had a family. I still feel like that – alone. Do I actually have a wife and eight children? It seems absurd. It's even worse since I went to Ireland. We were like strangers to each other.'

'Oh, Lord!' Flo was horrified. He was such a dear, sweet man, who wouldn't hurt a fly. She said in her kindest voice, which seemed rather thick and emotional all of a sudden, 'You don't seem like a stranger to me.'

For the first time he smiled. 'That means a lot, Flo. It really does.' He glanced around the room and she hoped he wouldn't recognise the decorations and all the other things she'd pinched from upstairs. 'You've made this place very cosy. It's a relief to have somewhere, someone, to come back to.' He smiled again. 'But you're obviously getting ready for a night out on the town. I expect you have a date with a young man. Don't let me keep you.'

'As if I'd let you spend New Year's Eve all on your own,' Flo cried. 'I was only going to the Rialto by meself.'

Despite his protestations, she refused to leave. 'I'll pretend I got all decked up because I was expecting you,' she said, in the hope that it would make him feel less alone, more welcome.

Apparently it did. By the time she'd made a cup of tea and something to eat, he looked almost cheerful. She poured them both a glass of sherry and told him all about the laundry. 'I hope you don't mind but we changed the name to White's after we lost a lot of business.'

He already knew. Stella had given him the statements Flo had sent. 'It's all I have left now, my laundry.' He sighed, but more like the gloomy Mr Fritz of old than the joyless person who'd just landed on her doorstep.

She described the staff. 'You'll love the twins. They can only manage one person's work between them, but they only get one person's wage, so it doesn't matter.' She told him about Peggy, who had to leave early for her lads' tea, and Lottie and Moira who worked half a day each. 'And, of course, you know Jimmy Cromer, he's a treasure.'

'Jimmy will have to go now I'm back,' Mr Fritz said.

'You can't sack him!' Flo gasped. 'He's a good worker, dead reliable.'

'But there'll be nothing for him to do.' He spread his hands, palms upwards, a gesture she remembered well. 'I'll be able to collect and deliver, won't I?'

'Even so, you can't sack Jimmy for no reason,' Flo said stubbornly.

'He'll be superfluous to requirements, Flo. What better reason is there?'

'It seems very cruel.'

'It's necessary to be cruel sometimes if you run a successful business. It's what capitalism is all about. You can't employ superfluous staff and make a profit.'

'And here's me thinking you wouldn't hurt a fly,' Flo said sarcastically. 'I suppose you'll be reducing the wages next, so you make an even bigger profit. Well, you needn't think I'm working me guts out if everyone leaves.'

His eyes twinkled. 'You've changed, Flo. You would never have spoken to me like that before.'

Flo tossed her head. 'I'm not sorry.'

'Why should you be sorry for expressing an opinion? I like you better this way. But let's have more sherry and save the arguments for tomorrow. It's New Year's Eve. We'll talk about only pleasant things. Tell me, how are your family?'

'I'm afraid there's nothing pleasant to tell.' She explained about Mam and Albert being killed in the same raid that had damaged the laundry.

'So many tragedies.' Mr Fritz looked dejected. 'Hitler has a great deal to answer for. I suppose I should consider myself lucky to be alive.'

As midnight approached, he noticed the wireless and suggested they listen to Big Ben chime in the New Year. 'Is that the set from upstairs?'

'I hope you don't mind. I borrowed it,' Flo said uncomfortably, 'You can have it back tomorrer.'

'Keep it, Flo,' he said warmly. 'It will give me a good excuse to come down and listen to the news.'

'You mean I can stay?' She felt relieved. 'I thought you might prefer to have the house all to yourself, like.'

'My dear Flo,' he laughed, 'would I be silly enough to put my one and only friend out on to the street? Of course you can stay. What's more, this furniture's seen better days. There's a nice little settee and chair in Stella's sitting room that you must have. She's not likely to use it again.'

'Shush!' Flo put her finger to her lips. 'It's about to be nineteen forty-two.'

As the great clock in London chimed in the New Year, they shook hands and Mr Fritz kissed her decorously on the cheek. 'I'd expected it would be dreadful, coming back to the house without Stella and the children, Flo, but it's not been nearly as bad as I'd thought.' He squeezed her hand. 'It really is good to be home.'

He was still the same Mr Fritz, after all, who couldn't hurt a fly. Once face to face with Jimmy Cromer, he couldn't bring himself to dismiss the lad. 'I'm a hopeless capitalist,' he confessed. Instead, he gave him a job in the laundry, which Jimmy said disgustedly was women's work and got bored within a week. As a fit, able sixteen-year-old, he had no problem finding employment in war time, and he left quickly of his own accord.

While she'd been in charge Flo had got used to doing things her way. She had quite a task convincing Mr Fritz that her way was best. He got tetchy when proved wrong, she sulked when he was right, but they were always the best of friends again before the day was over.

He maintained that they provided a substitute family for each other.

'Mam would be pleased,' said Flo. 'She always liked you.'

Life assumed a pleasant pattern. On Sundays, he would come to dinner, armed with a bottle of wine. On Saturday afternoons, Flo had tea upstairs, eating the thick, clumsily made sandwiches with every appearance of enjoyment.

During the week, she continued to go dancing, occasionally bringing home a young serviceman. Upstairs would be in darkness, so Mr Fritz remained ignorant of that part of her life. Not that it was any of his business, she told herself, but it was something she'd sooner keep to herself.

In July, Bel came home on five days' leave prior to being posted to Egypt, and preferred to spend the time with her best friend, Flo, rather than with her horrible aunt Mabel.

Like virtually everyone else, Bel had changed. There was an added maturity to her lovely face, and her violet eyes were no longer quite so dazzling. Even so, she swept into the flat like a breath of fresh air, filling it with noise and laughter. She enthused over the brown plush settee and chair that had once belonged to Stella, the tall sideboard, which had so many useful drawers and cupboards, and was particularly taken with the brass bed from Mr Fritz's spare room. 'It's like a little palace, Flo, but I hate the idea of you living in a hole in the ground.'

'Don't be silly,' Flo said mildly. 'I love it.'

The two girls attracted a chorus of wolf-whistles, and many an admiring glance, as they strolled through the sunlit city streets of an evening in their summer frocks: Bel, the young widow, with her striking red hair and rosy cheeks, and green-eyed Flo, as pale and slender as a lily.

Bel and Mr Fritz took to each other straight away and pretended to flirt extravagantly. On the last night of Bel's leave, he took both girls out to dinner. 'I wonder what

Stella would say if she could see me now.' He chuckled. 'Every man in this restaurant is eyeing me enviously, wondering how such an insignificant little chap managed to get the two most beautiful women in Liverpool to dine with him.'

'Insignificant!' Bel screamed. 'You're dead attractive, you. If I was on the look-out for a feller, I'd grab you like a shot.'

Flo smiled. In the past, no one would have dreamed of describing Mr Fritz as attractive, but since returning from the camp he had acquired a gaunt, melancholy charm. The twins claimed he made their old hearts flutter dangerously, and Peggy declared herself bowled over.

That night, Flo and Bel sat up in bed together drinking their final mug of cocoa. 'I won't half miss you.' Flo sighed. 'The place will seem dead quiet after you've gone.'

'I'm ever so glad I came. It's the first time I've enjoyed meself since Bob was killed.'

'Remember the day we met?' said Flo. 'You were dead impatient because I was upset over Tommy O'Mara. Now you know how I felt.'

'There's a big difference.' Bel's voice was unexpectedly tart. 'Bob was worth crying over, not like Tommy O'Mara!'

'Oh, Bel! How can you say that when you never met him?'

Bel didn't answer straight away. 'Sorry, Flo,' she said eventually. 'It was just the impression I got. But you're well over him now, aren't you?'

'I'm not sure if I ever will be. I've never met a man who comes anywhere near him.' Perhaps if Hugh hadn't always been on her mind to remind her of Tommy's existence, she might have put the memory away.

'It's about time you got yourself a proper feller, girl,' Bel snorted, 'and stopped moping over a man who died three years ago. You're twenty-two. You should be married by now, or at least courting.'

'You sound just like our Martha.' Flo laughed.

'Which reminds me,' Bel went on. 'Why haven't I been to see your Martha's little girl?'

'I thought you didn't like babies.'

'I didn't until I lost the one I was expecting.' Bel's lovely face became unbearably sad. 'You've no idea what it feels like, Flo, having this little person growing inside you. When I had the miscarriage, it was like losing part of meself. Still,' she brightened, 'that's all in the past, and as Bob said to me in his lovely Scots accent just before he was posted to North Africa and we knew he might be killed, "I know you won't forget me, girl, but don't let the memory weigh you down, like unwanted baggage. Go light into the future."' Bel sniffed briefly. 'He was ever so clever, my Bob.'

Flo envied her friend's resilience and ability to look ahead. She spent too much time looking back.

'Anyroad,' Bel persisted, 'what's your Martha's baby like?'

'I've no idea. I haven't seen her.'

Bel's reaction was entirely predictable. 'Why ever not?' she screeched.

'Because me and our Martha had a falling out.'

'What over?'

'Mind your own business,' Flo said irritably, and although Bel pressed for ages to know why, she refused to say another word.

Next morning, the two girls left for Lime Street station, Bel trim and smart in her khaki uniform. Mr Fritz had insisted Flo see her on to the train, even though it meant she'd be hours late for work. He bade Bel a mournful farewell. 'Take care of yourself in Egypt, there's a good girl.' He put his hand over his heart. 'I think I can already feel it breaking.'

Bel flung her arms around his neck. '*You*'re the heart-breaker, Fritz, you ould rascal. Us poor girls aren't safe with chaps like you around. I'm surprised those poor women in the laundry get any work done at all.'

The station was packed with servicemen and women returning from leave or *en route* elsewhere in the British Isles. Bel found herself a seat on the London train and leaned out of the window. 'He's a lovely chap, that Fritz,' she said.

'I know.' Flo nodded.

'I think he fancies you.'

Flo was aghast. 'Don't talk daft, Bel Knox! We're friends, that's all. I'm very fond of him, but he's got a wife and eight children in Ireland.'

Bel winked. 'I think he'd sooner be more than friends. Anyroad, it's over between him and Stella. He told me.'

'Yes, but it still makes him a married man. And they'll never get divorced, they're Catholics.'

'For goodness' sake, Flo. There's a war on. Forget he's married and let yourself go for once.'

The guard blew his whistle, the carriage doors were slammed, and the train began slowly to puff out of the station, Bel still hanging out of the window. Flo walked quickly along beside her. 'One of the first things you said to me was that you didn't approve of going out with married men.'

'Under the circumstances I'd make an exception in the case of you and Mr Fritz,' Bel said. By now, the train was going too fast for Flo to keep up. Bel shouted, 'Think about it, Flo!'

'The thing is,' Flo said under her breath, waving to the red-headed figure until the face was just a blur, 'I'm not sure if I fancy *him*, not in the way Bel's on about. I'm not sure if I'll ever fancy anyone again.'

3

1945

She recognised him immediately, a thin child, delicately boned like Flo herself, hair the colour of wheat. His round, innocent eyes were a beautiful dark green flecked with gold. The other children, boys first, had come charging through the school gates whooping like savages. He came alone, separate from the rest. She could guess one reason why he wasn't part of the gang: the other lads wore shabby jerseys and baggy pants but this five-year old was neatly dressed in grey shorts with a firmly pressed crease, pullover, flannel shirt. Hugh O'Mara was the only child wearing a blazer and tie. Nancy was a good mother, but not very sensitive. Flo would never have allowed her son to stand out in such a ridiculous get-up.

Flo watched as he approached, a sensation in her gut akin to the one she'd had the first time she was on her way to meet his father. She thought of all the times when she'd glimpsed a dark-haired woman with a pushchair on the far side of the Mystery, or crossing the street leading a small boy by the hand. Either it had been someone else, or the woman and child had disappeared when she had hurried to catch up.

Now he was here, and in a few seconds he would be close enough to touch. Not that she would dare. Not just yet.

'Hello,' she said.

He looked at her, and she searched in his eyes for recognition, as if it was inevitable he would sense she wasn't a stranger but his mam, his real flesh-and-blood mam. But there was nothing, just a shy glance.

'What's that you've got there?' she asked. Like all the other children, he was carrying a large brown envelope.

'A photo. It's of all the school taken together.'

'Can I see?'

He opened the envelope and took out the photo. 'The infants are at the front. That's me there.' He pointed to the end of the row, where he was sitting, knees crossed, looking serious. 'Mr Carey said I spoilt it 'cos I'm the only one not smiling.'

'Perhaps there wasn't much to smile about that day.' Flo turned the picture over. The photographer's name was stamped on the back, which meant she could buy a copy for herself.

'I didn't like having me photo taken much,' he said as they began to walk in the direction of Smithdown Road. 'Are you a friend of me mam's?'

'No, but I know some people she knows. I knew your dad quite well.'

His eyes lit up. 'Did ya? He died on a big ship under the sea, but the other boys won't believe me when I tell them.'

'*I* believe you,' Flo declared. 'I've got newspapers at home that tell all about it.'

'Can I come and see them?' he said eagerly. 'I can read a bit.'

There was nothing Flo would have liked more, but she said, 'I live too far away. Tell you what, though, I'll come next Friday and bring the papers with me. We can sit on the grass in the Mystery and I'll read them to you.'

'Can't you come before?' The crestfallen look on his thin face was almost too much to bear. Flo wanted to snatch him up and carry him away. He was much too serious for a five-year-old. She'd like to teach him to laugh and sing, be happy. But it would be cruel to take him from the woman he thought was his mother, the woman he loved more than he would ever love Flo.

She said, 'No, luv. I only get away from work on Fridays when I go to the bank. I should have been back ages ago. Me boss'll be wondering where I am.'

'Me mam works in a sweetshop.'

'I know. Someone told me.' Martha and Nancy O'Mara still saw each other occasionally. Through Sally, Flo had learned that Nancy served in the shop till five o'clock, leaving ninety minutes during which Flo could see her son, although she could only be with him for a fraction of that time because of her own job. St Theresa's junior and infants' school was a few minutes away from the laundry.

'She brings me pear drops home sometimes, and dolly

mixtures.' Unexpectedly, he reached up and put his small hand in hers. Flo could barely breathe as she touched her child for the first time. She stroked the back of his fingers with her thumb, wanting to cry as all sorts of emotions tumbled through her head. She said, knowing it sounded stupid, 'I'd like to be your friend.'

He looked at her gravely. 'Me mam doesn't like me having friends.'

'Why not?' she asked in surprise.

'She said they're a bad inf—' He stumbled over the word and rolled his eyes. 'A bad inflex, or something.'

'A bad influence?'

' 'S right,' he said.

'Perhaps I could be your secret friend.'

'Yes, please. I'd like that.'

They arrived at the laundry, where Mr Fritz was standing by the door looking concerned. He hurried towards them. 'We were worried there'd been a hold-up at the bank. Peggy thought you might have been shot.'

'Peggy's seen too many films.'

'And who's this?' He looked at Hugh benignly.

'This is my friend, Hugh O'Mara.' Flo pushed her son forward. 'Hugh, say hello to me boss, Mr Fritz.'

'Hello,' Hugh said politely.

'Pleased to meet you, Hugh, old chap,' Mr Fritz said jovially.

Flo knelt in front of the little boy and said, in a whisper, 'If ever you're in trouble, this is where you can find me. I'm here every day from eight till half past five, and till one on Sat'days.' She stroked his cheek. 'Remember that, won't you, luv?'

He nodded. 'But I don't know your name!'

'It's Flo Clancy.'

'All right, Flo.'

'Tara, now. I'll see you next Friday.'

He trotted off in his smart clothes, clutching the brown envelope. Flo watched till he turned the corner, and still watched even after he'd gone, imagining him passing the shops in Smithdown Road on his way to Clement Street, where he would remain in the house, alone and friendless, until Nancy came.

'What's the matter, Flo?' Mr Fritz said gently.

'Nothing.' Flo returned to work, and it wasn't until she was inside that she became aware of the tears that were streaming down her cheeks.

For years Gerard Davies had been imploring Flo to marry him. After they'd first met in the Rialto, he'd come to Liverpool whenever he could and he wrote to her regularly. As far as he was concerned, Flo was his girl, his sweetheart. 'We'll see once the war's over,' Flo would say, whenever the subject of marriage was raised.

The war had been over for three months, the lights were on again and the celebrations, the parties, the dancing in the streets were just memories. Gerard Davies had been demobbed and was back in Swansea. He wrote to demand that Flo keep her promise.

He wasn't the only one of her young men to propose – she could have had half a dozen husbands by now – but he was the most persistent. Flo turned down the proposals as tactfully as she could. She didn't want to hurt anyone's feelings. They would never know that things hadn't been quite so wonderful for her as they had been for them. She put the lovely letters away to keep for always.

To Gerard Davies she wrote that she'd only said, 'We'll see,' when the war was over. She hadn't promised anything. She said that she liked him very, very much, and felt honoured that he wanted her for his wife, but he deserved to marry a woman who loved him far more than she did.

Perhaps it was unfortunate that she found Gerard's letter waiting on the doormat when she arrived home the day she'd met Hugh outside school for the first time, otherwise she might have given more serious consideration to his proposal. It would be nice to have a husband, children, a proper house. Sally, who was expecting her first baby in January, had got a nice council house in Huyton with gardens front and back. Jock would complete his naval service in two years' time and they would settle down and raise their family. And Bel had got married again in Egypt to a chap called Ivor, who claimed to be descended from the Hungarian royal family. She enclosed a photo of herself dressed in a lavish lace outfit standing next to a haughty young man with an undeniably regal manner. 'Ivor lives in the land of make-believe,' Bel wrote. 'He's no more royal than my big toe, but he makes me laugh. I'll never love another man the way I loved Bob, but me and Ivor are good company for each other. I'll be back in Liverpool very soon and you can see him for yourself.' The letter was signed, 'Bel (Szerb!)' and there was a PS. 'By the way, I think I'm pregnant!'

Why can't *I* make do with second best? Flo asked herself. Why am I haunted by memories of making love with Tommy O'Mara in the Mystery all those years ago? And why am I obsessed with the son I can never have? She knew that if she married Gerard, she would be only half a wife to him and half a mother to their children. It wouldn't be fair on him or them. She stuck the stamp on the envelope containing the letter to him, thumping it angrily with her fist.

When Bel returned, it was with news of another miscarriage. 'The doctor said I'll never carry a baby to full term. I've got a weak cervix,' she said. Flo nodded sympathetically, as if she knew what it meant.

Bel was upset, but determined not to take the doctor's verdict as final. 'Me and Ivor intend to try again. At least the trying's fun.' She winked. 'It's about time you got married and tried it, Flo.'

'Perhaps, one day.'

'I take it nothing came of you and Mr Fritz?'

'You were imagining things. We're just friends.'

Flo couldn't take to Ivor, whose manner was as haughty as his appearance. He expected his wife to wait on him hand and foot. Bel had a third miscarriage, and went to work behind the handbag counter in Owen Owen's department store, while Ivor lolled around in their flat in Upper Parliament Street, refusing so much as to wash a dish.

'He won't get a job,' Bel raged. She came round to Flo's often to complain and calm her nerves with sherry. 'Whenever I point out a suitable vacancy in the *Echo*, he claims it's beneath him.'

'But it's not beneath him to live off his wife?'

'Apparently not.' Bel snorted so loudly that Flo half expected flames to shoot out of her nostrils. 'I think I'll kick him out, get a divorce.'

'You should never have married him,' Flo said, with the benefit of hindsight.

'I know.' Bel uttered an enormous sigh. 'I don't half envy your Sally. Her little girl's a proper bobby-dazzler, and that Jock seems a dead nice feller.'

'Sal's already in the club again. She's making up for lost time now that Jock'll soon be home for good.'

'Have you been seeing Hugh O'Mara, luv?' Sally asked, one stormy December Sunday when Flo went to see her in Huyton.

'How did you find out?' Flo stammered.

'Someone told Nancy and she told our Martha.' Sally's face was misty with happiness as she nursed nine-month-old Grace on her lap.

'I've been meeting him outside school every Friday for more than a year — I suppose you think I'm daft.'

'Oh, no, luv. I might have done once, but not now.' Sally glanced at her daughter. 'I can't imagine how I'd have felt if someone had taken her away before I'd even seen her, or the little one I've got in here.' She patted her bulging stomach. 'Everyone was dead cruel, Flo, me included. I thought keeping the baby would ruin your life.'

Instead, it was the other way round, Flo thought wryly. 'Is Nancy mad at me?'

'Martha couldn't make out if she was or not. She seemed more resigned than anything. I suppose she thinks it can't do much harm now.'

'I don't suppose it can,' said Flo. 'How is our Martha?' She only asked because it would please Sally, who was forever trying to reunite the sisters.

Sally grimaced and said, predictably, 'I wish you'd go and see her, Flo. She's dead miserable. Kate's starting school in January, and she'll be stuck in the house with Elsa Cameron who's completely off her rocker now. The last time I went she was singing hymns the whole time. By rights, Martha should find a place of her own, but although you'll say she only wants to interfere, Flo, she's not prepared to leave Elsa in sole charge of Norman or the woman's quite likely to kill the poor bugger. Anyroad, Norman would be lost without little Kate. They've been brought up together, and he worships the ground she walks on.'

Hugh O'Mara emerged from school wearing a woollen balaclava, a long fringed scarf, and the horrible navy-blue belted mackintosh that Flo thought made him look like a miniature gas man.

It was another terrible winter, bleaker and icier even than the notorious winter of 1940, and the fuel shortages and power cuts made it seem even worse. Food remained rationed, and in such an austere atmosphere it was hard to believe that Great Britain had won the war.

There was a little girl with Hugh, a pretty child, like a fairy, with long fair hair. She wore three-quarter-length socks and patent-leather shoes, and her winter coat was much too big. There was something familiar about her face, though Flo couldn't remember having seen her before.

'I've got another friend,' Hugh beamed happily at Flo. 'She only started last week, but I knew her before school. Me mam goes to their house sometimes. She's nearly two years younger than me, but that doesn't mean we can't be friends.'

'Of course it doesn't, luv.' He would be seven in a month's time and was shooting upwards like a vigorous sapling. Flo had already bought his present, a toy car. If you twisted the steering wheel, the four wheels turned. She was taking the risk that Nancy wouldn't object.

'Can she come with us to the Mystery?' Hugh said eagerly. 'Have you brought the ball?'

Flo was about to say the little girl should ask her mam first, when another boy came up, a dark, handsome lad of about ten, with an ugly purple and yellow bruise on his forehead. She'd noticed him before. He was a bully and most of the children kept well out of his way. He put a possessive hand on the little girl's shoulder. 'I've got to take her home,' he said, scowling. 'We live in the same house together.' He turned to Hugh and spat, 'You leave her alone, Hugh O'Mara.'

'Don't you dare speak to him like that,' Flo said angrily.

The boy ignored her and pulled the child away. 'C'mon, Kate.'

'Is that Kate Colquitt?' Flo enquired, when the children had gone.

'Yes. Do you know her?'

'I'm her auntie.'

'You never are!' Hugh's brow creased in disbelief. 'I don't understand.'

'Her mam and me are sisters,' Flo explained carefully. Then she said, 'The boy with Kate, is that Norman Cameron?'

'Yes.' Hugh wrinkled his thin shoulders. 'He's not very nice. I don't like him. No one does, not even his mam.'

'Perhaps he can't help not being very nice.' She re-

240

called sadly what a beautiful baby Norman had been, so happy – there was a photo somewhere in the flat, taken on his first birthday, that Martha had given her at the time. She hadn't realised the three children would be at the same school – Hugh and Kate were cousins, not that they'd ever know.

Flo took a rubber ball out of her bag and began to bounce it. 'C'mon, I'll race you to the Mystery. Whoever's last has to climb to the top of the tallest tree and shout "Hallelujah" ten times.' She always won, but Hugh's legs were getting longer. As soon as he was likely to get there first, she'd have to think of a less demanding penalty.

1949

Mr Fritz was stepping out with Mrs Winters, a widow who had tightly permed black hair and wore smart, tailored suits with very short skirts, though her legs were much too thick for ankle-strap shoes – or so Bel claimed when she saw them together. 'I don't like the look of her, Flo. Once she's installed upstairs you'll be out on your arse.'

'Oh, don't!' said Flo. She felt hurt and a touch dismayed, as if Mr Fritz was letting her down. Somehow, unreasonably, she'd considered herself the only woman he wanted in his life, though their relationship had always been strictly platonic.

'It's a pity he and Stella can't get divorced,' Bel remarked. It had taken her several years to get rid of Ivor. 'Still, I suppose the poor chap's got to dip his wick somewhere. I'm glad I'm a woman and not panting for it all the time.'

Mrs Winters lasted only two months. 'I couldn't stand the way she stuck her little finger out like a flagpole when she drank her tea,' Mr Fritz confessed to Flo. 'I felt I wanted to hang something on it.' He stared at her gloomily. 'What happened to your chap from the income-tax office?'

'I gave him up. We didn't have much in common.' All Ray Meadows had wanted to talk about was figures. Bel had tried to insist that Flo encourage him. 'He's dead keen, I can tell, and a good prospect. You're not getting any younger – you'll be thirty next year.' But Flo had decided, once and for all, that she would sooner remain single than marry a man she didn't love wholeheartedly. Books and the cinema provided all the romance and excitement she needed, especially as things usually ended happily. She enjoyed the quiet of her flat, buried half under the ground, drinking sherry, and feeling pleasantly cut off from the real world. Her only regret was that she no longer had a family. She missed the love that Mam and Dad had bestowed on her, and since Sally's son, Ian, had developed muscular dystrophy at the age of two, poor little lad, Flo saw her sister rarely now. Whenever she went to Huyton, Sal and Jock seemed so wrapped up in anxiety for their son that Flo felt in the way. Of course, there was always Martha, but if it hadn't been for her, Flo would have had a son of her own for the past nine years.

'I've been invited to the Isle of Man for the weekend in July,' Mr Fritz said, with the air of a man who'd been asked to attend his own funeral. 'Some of the chaps from the camp are having a reunion. Trouble is, they're taking their wives. I've no one to take.'

By now, half of the little Fritzes were in their twenties. The previous year Mr Fritz had been invited to Ben's wedding but had refused to go. 'I'd feel most peculiar,' he said, 'like a stranger at the feast.' A few weeks ago, he'd received a card to say Ben's wife had given birth to a son. He was a grandfather, which made him feel even more peculiar, and also very old, though he was only fifty.

'I'm sure not every chap will be bringing a wife,' Flo said briskly. 'You'll probably have quite a nice time.'

Over the next few weeks, he continued to raise the subject of the reunion, saying miserably, 'I hate the idea of going by myself.' Or, 'It wouldn't have to be a wife. It would be enough to take a friend.'

'If that's the case, why not ask Mrs Winters?' Flo suggested. 'It's only a few days, and you could put up with her little finger for that long, surely.'

'No, no,' he said, distractedly. 'There's someone else I'd far sooner go with.'

Two days before he was due to leave, he came down to the basement, where he sat, sighing continuously and staring moodily into the gas fire, which wasn't even lit. After half an hour of this, Flo said, 'Bel will be round in a minute. We're going to see *The Keys of the Kingdom* at the Odeon. She's mad about Gregory Peck.'

'Gregory Peck's got everything,' he said despondently. 'I bet he wouldn't be stuck for someone to take with him to the Isle of Man.'

Flo burst out laughing. 'If you carry on like this much longer, I'll offer to go with you meself.'

To her astonishment, he jumped to his feet and caught both her hands in his. 'Oh, *would* you, Flo? I've been wanting to ask for weeks.' His brown eyes were shining in a face that had suddenly come alive. 'We'll have separate rooms, of course we will. My intentions are strictly honourable. And we'll have a lovely time. Joe Loss and his orchestra are playing at the Villa Marina. I haven't been dancing in years.'

'But . . .' Flo began.

'But what, my dear girl?' he cried.

Everyone she knew, apart from Bel, would disapprove, despite the separate bedrooms and Bel would ask loads of embarrassing questions. Even so, perhaps it was the same lack of caution that had led her to accept Tommy O'Mara's invitation a decade ago, because all Flo said was, 'Oh, all right. But I don't want Bel and the women in the laundry to know. They'll only get the wrong idea.'

He put a finger to his lips. 'You can count on me not to breathe a word to a soul.'

★

Flo sat on the edge of the double bed and stared out of the hotel window at the choppy, green-brown waves of the Irish Sea. A large black and white ship with a red funnel was approaching Douglas, spewing white foam in its wake. It was the ship on which they would return to Liverpool.

The sky was overcast, the clouds leaden, as if about to unleash another downpour, and the pavements were still wet from the rain that had fallen all night long and the whole of the previous day. Holidaymakers wandered past forlornly in their plastic raincoats, some of the children carrying buckets and spades.

In the *en suite* bathroom, Mr Fritz could be heard humming as he shaved. At the initial gathering of the ex-internees, a man had shouted, 'Fritz Hofmannsthal, you old rascal! How are you?' and she'd been amazed when Mr Fritz went over and shook his hand.

'I didn't realise that was your name,' she whispered.

'I told you it was a mouthful,' he whispered back.

After proudly introducing her all round as 'My dear friend, Miss Florence Clancy,' Mr Fritz seemed to forget he was supposed to be at a reunion. That night, when they should have been at a special dinner, but were tangoing to 'Jealousy' in the Villa Marina, he said, 'Who wants to celebrate a miserable experience like that? It's the sort of thing I'd sooner forget.'

The first night she'd spent alone in the single bedroom he'd booked for her on the floor above. Yesterday, Sunday, they breakfasted together at a table by the window in the dining room with its cream and maroon striped Regency wallpaper. It was raining cats and dogs, and the sky was so dark that the red-shaded wall lamps had been switched on, making the large room cosy and intimate.

'This is nice,' said Mr Fritz. He touched her hand. 'This is lovely.'

They caught a taxi to Mass and back again, then read the newspapers and drank coffee in the hotel lounge until it was time for lunch. Afterwards, they battled their way through the wind and rain to an amusement arcade, then, in the afternoon, they went to the pictures to see *Notorious* with Cary Grant and Ingrid Bergman. 'I must confess,' Mr Fritz said at dinner, 'that I've always nursed a soft spot for Ingrid Bergman.'

They took their time over the meal and it was ten o'clock by the time the wine was finished. They transferred to the bar for a cocktail, and continued to talk about things of mutual interest: the laundry, the little Fritzes, Flo's family, the house in William Square.

It was an unremarkable few days, yet Flo had rarely enjoyed herself more. It was nice to be with someone she knew so much about. There were no awkward silences, no mad scrambling through her mind for what to say next. She'd known Mr Fritz for more than half her life and they were entirely comfortable with each other.

The clock was striking midnight when he offered to escort her upstairs to her room on the third floor. When they reached the second floor, he paused and looked grave. 'Flo, would you, could you . . .' He gestured along the corridor and stuttered, 'Would you consider doing me the honour of – of –'

After their lovely time together, Flo had anticipated that this might happen and was quite prepared. What harm would it do? None, she had decided. Furthermore, she had no intention of making herself out to be a shy virgin and pretending to be coy. If Stella had known she'd had a baby, then so must he. As he looked incapable of saying the words he wanted, she said them for him. 'Of sleeping with you tonight?'

He was an ardent, yet gentle lover. Flo experienced none of the passion there had been with Tommy O'Mara, but as she hadn't expected to she wasn't disappointed. When it was over, she felt cherished and satisfied. Afterwards they sat up in bed like an old married couple. 'We must do this again, Flo,' he said warmly. 'Perhaps next month, August.'

'I'd like that.' She laid her head affectionately on his shoulder.

'In that case, I'll book a double room in a different hotel, and we'll be Mr and Mrs Hofmannsthal.'

'But we'll still be Miss Clancy and Mr Fritz back in Liverpool?'

He looked at her quizzically. 'I think that would be wise, don't you? Friends at home, lovers in the Isle of Man. That way, you're less likely to tire of me. It can be our little monthly treat, our little adventure. You know,' he breathed happily, 'I've always been a tiny bit in love with you ever since the day you came to the laundry for an interview all those years ago.'

So Bel had been right, after all. Flo squeezed his arm. 'I've always been very fond of you.'

'Let's hope Stella didn't notice, eh?'

She couldn't be bothered telling him that Stella had, because it was too late to do anything about it.

'I suppose we should get some sleep,' he suggested. She slid under the covers and he bent and kissed her forehead. 'We have to be up early to catch the boat home.'

He had fallen asleep immediately, but Flo had lain wondering what she'd tell Bel when she went away again in four weeks' time. She wasn't sure why, but she preferred keeping her relationship with Mr Fritz a secret, even from her best friend. Right now, Bel thought she'd gone on retreat to a convent in Wales. I'll say I'm going on another one. It fits in with the image she's got of me. Let her go on thinking I'm as dull at ditchwater . . .

'The boat's just about to dock, Mr Fritz,' she called.

He came out of the bathroom smiling, a towel tucked under his chin, patting his cheeks. His kindly, good-natured face looked young this morning, almost boyish. 'I think we can dispense with the Mr, don't you, Flo?'

As she smiled back, she felt a surge of emotion, not real love but almost. 'I'd sooner not, if you don't mind. I'll always think of you as Mr Fritz.'

Millie

I

I'd been so engrossed in Flo's love letters that I'd forgotten about the time. I'd be late for work if I didn't hurry. I dragged on the red suit and T-shirt I'd worn the day before, and combed my hair in the car when I stopped at traffic lights. The car behind hooted angrily as I was putting on my lipstick.

Halfway through the morning I answered the phone for the umpteenth time, doing my utmost not to sound as harassed as I felt.

'It's me,' James said humbly.

If I followed my instincts and slammed down the receiver, he would only ring back. 'What do you want?' I snapped.

'To see you, to apologise.'

'I'll take the apology for granted. There's no need for us to see each other.'

'Millie, darling, I don't know what came over me. Let's have dinner tonight. Let me explain.' He sounded desperate, but I hadn't forgotten that he'd raised his fist to strike me. I wasn't interested in explanations or apologies. I could never forgive him.

'I'd sooner not.'

'Please, Millie.' He was almost sobbing. 'Please, darling, I have to see you.'

'Look, James, I'm very busy. I don't like to be rude, but I'm going to ring off. Goodbye.'

An hour later, a van drew up outside the office and a girl came in with a bouquet of red roses for Miss Millicent Cameron; two dozen, surrounded by fern, wrapped in gold paper and tied with copious amounts of scarlet ribbon. There was no card, but only one person could have sent them. I thought them ostentatious, but Diana was impressed. I dumped the flowers on her desk. 'In that case, they're yours. Your father might like them.'

'But they must cost the earth!' Diana protested.

'I don't care. I don't want them.' I changed the subject. 'How's your father?'

Diana's face brightened. 'Much improved. We think he might be in remission. It happens sometimes with cancer. Yesterday I took him to Otterspool, and we had a picnic in the car. I can't think why we've never done things like that before.'

'My mother was talking about moving away from Liverpool, and I suddenly realised how much I'd miss her.' I'd never mentioned anything about my family to Diana before, and felt that I'd made the first gesture towards friendship.

We came to the conclusion that most children took their parents too much for granted, and agreed to lunch together if we could get away at the same time. Diana hissed, 'Is George still cross with me over those notes? I suppose I've blown my chances with that job I was after.'

'The job's Oliver's. It always was. As for the notes, I bet George has forgotten all about them.'

'God, I hope so.' Diana pursed her lips. 'I made a terrible cock-up there. I envy you, Millie. You never do anything to rock the boat. You're always so meek and pliable. Men prefer women they think they can control. George doesn't like me because I'm too independent.' It might have been unintentional, but there was a strong note of spite in her voice. She touched a rose. 'No one's ever sent me flowers like this.'

Whether she meant it or not, I still felt affronted. Meek and pliable? Me? I bent my head over my work, and decided to be too busy when Diana suggested it was time for lunch.

★

After work, I drove to Blundellsands to do some washing and take a shower. There was a message from James on the answering-machine, which I refused to listen to. I switched off the machine and rang my mother. 'Is everything okay, Mum?'

'Everything's fine, luv. Why?'

'It's just that my answering-machine's broken, I'll be out most nights this week and I didn't want you to worry.' Nor did I want a repeat of the Birmingham episode. During the week ahead, a minor crisis of one sort or another was bound to occur in the Cameron household and Mum would need someone to talk to. 'Call me at the office if something important crops up,' I told her.

'As long as it won't get you into trouble, luv.'

It wouldn't, I assured her. 'What will you be up to the nights you're out?' she asked.

I imagined telling the truth: that I would be sleeping with the grandson of the man who'd broken Flo Clancy's heart almost sixty years ago. I said, 'I thought it was time I put in a few more hours at Auntie Flo's. I'm getting nowhere at this rate.'

'I'm sorry you were landed with it, Millicent. I never thought it'd turn out to be such a mammoth task.'

'I'm quite enjoying it.'

'Gran said you'd met Bel Szerb.'

'Bel who?'

'Szerb. At least, that's how I knew her. I think she got married again. She was a dead scream, Bel was.'

'She still is.' After impressing on her that she must nag Declan to apply for a college course, I rang off. The washing had finished its cycle so I hung it over the bath, packed a bag and made my way to William Square and Tom O'Mara.

When I got out of the car, Peter Maxwell was going down the steps to his flat with several files under his arm. He wore jeans, a thick check shirt and a donkey jacket. He grinned at me through the railings. 'Hi! Fancy a coffee and a chocolate biccy?'

'I wouldn't mind.' His laid-back, easy-going manner was welcome after James's histrionics.

His flat was completely different from next door: red-tiled floor, red curtains and white walls hung with abstract paintings. It was a man's room. Apart from the paintings and a single white-shaded lamp, there were no other ornaments and the furniture was minimal, mainly of natural wood. Two armchairs were upholstered in black and white check. The effect was cool and airy, tranquil, giving the impression that the occupant was at peace with himself, which I envied.

'This isn't a bit like Flo's,' I remarked. Another difference was that everywhere was warm due to the two large radiators, one at each end of the room.

'I know. I'll just put the kettle on.' He took off his coat, hung it behind the door and disappeared into the kitchen. When he came back, he said, 'I used to see your auntie at least once a week. It was my job to get rid of the bottles.'

'What bottles?'

He grinned. 'The sherry bottles. She didn't want Charmian, the binmen and that aged but gorgeous red-head to know how much she was drinking. Flo was knocking back more than a bottle a day over the last year. She was a nice old girl, though. I liked her.'

'I only saw her once, at another great-aunt's funeral.'

'I wish I'd known you two were related. Flo would have been tickled pink to know we'd been in the same class at school.' He disappeared into the kitchen again, returning with two mugs of coffee and a packet of Jaffa cakes. 'I'm a lousy house-husband. I'm afraid my cupboards are bare. I hope you've eaten.'

'I keep forgetting to eat.'

He ran his fingers through his beard, which already looked like an untidy bird's nest, and said thoughtfully, 'I'm sure there's a tin of corned beef and a packet of instant spuds out there. I'll knock you up a plate of corned-beef hash if you like?'

'No thanks.' I shuddered. 'That's one of my mother's

favourite dishes. It would remind me too much of home.'

'I used to feel like that about *Coronation Street*,' he said. 'Me mam never missed a single episode, and the house had to be dead quiet. You daren't sneeze else you'd get a belt around the ear. For years afterwards if I passed a house and heard the music I got goosebumps.'

We stared at each other and laughed. 'Memories, eh!' he said wryly.

At the end of the room, I noticed there were french windows leading to the tiny yard.

'I had them put in last year.' He looked quite house-proud. 'It's nice to have them open in summer, brightens up the place no end. That's how I met Flo. We used to gab to each other over the garden wall.'

'Does that mean you actually own this flat? It's not rented?' I said, surprised.

'I own about a quarter, the building society has the rest.'

'I can't imagine anyone choosing to live round here if they didn't have to,' I said incredulously.

'How dare you criticise my place of abode, Miss Cameron?' he said mildly. 'I love Toxteth. I've been broken into twice, but that can happen anywhere. The people round here are the salt of the earth, including the girls who hang around the square. Okay, so it's violent, but otherwise it's a good place to live, steeped in atmosphere and history. This is the closest to how Liverpool was when it was the greatest port in the world. And did you know that, centuries ago, Toxteth was a royal park where King John used to hunt deer and wild boar?'

'I'm afraid that piece of information has been denied me until now.'

'If you like, I'll take you on a tour one day, show you precisely where his hunting lodges were situated.'

'I *would* like – it sounds fascinating.'

He looked chuffed. 'Then it's a date.'

I stayed for another cup of coffee before going next

door. A scantily clad Fiona was shivering against the railings. To my surprise, she deigned to speak. 'There's been someone looking for you. She said she'd come back another time. It wasn't Bel or Charmian. It was someone else.'

'Thanks for telling me.'

Fiona yawned. 'Any time.'

As usual the air in Flo's flat smelt damp, and it was freezing cold. I turned the fire on full blast and knelt before the hissing jets, shivering and rubbing my hands, thinking enviously of Peter Maxwell's central heating. When the heat became too much, I retreated to my favourite spot on the settee and promptly fell asleep. It was nearly midnight when I woke up and my legs were covered with red blotches from the fire. Everywhere was still and quiet outside and the flat felt as if it was in a time warp, engulfed in flickering shadows and divorced from anything real.

My life's becoming more and more surreal, I thought. I scarcely ate, slept at the most peculiar times, spent hardly any time at home, and had lost interest in my job, though I still worked hard and hoped George hadn't noticed. Worst of all, I was having an affair with a man who was the epitome of everything I normally loathed about men. Things that had once seemed important, no longer mattered.

I went into the bedroom and changed into a night-dress, Flo's quilted dressing-gown, and her pink slippers, then sprayed myself with perfume ready for Tom, who might arrive at any minute. Until he came, I'd sort out a few more of Flo's papers.

With a sense of anticipation usually reserved for the start of a film or a television programme I was looking forward to, I settled in front of the bureau. The first thing I picked up was a bundle of letters from Bel sent during the war. It didn't seem proper to read them so I put them to one side in case Bel would like them back.

Next, a large, very old brown envelope with 'Wythen-shaw's Photographic Studios – Portraits a Speciality' printed on the top left-hand corner. Predictably, it contained a photograph and, as I pulled it out, I wondered why Flo hadn't put it on the table with the others. It was a school photo: five rows of children, the smallest ones sitting cross-legged at the front. A boy at the end of the front row, the only child not smiling, had been circled with pencil.

What on earth was Flo doing with a photo of our Declan? I looked at the back, but there was only a stamped date, September 1945, a third of a century before Declan was born. There was something else inside the envelope, a piece of yellowing paper folded into four. It was a crude, crayon drawing of a woman with sticks for limbs, yellow hair and gooseberry green eyes. Her mouth was a huge upwards red curve, and she wore a blue dress shaped like a triangle with three buttons as big as Smarties down the front. Underneath was printed, in a careful, childish hand, 'MY FREND FLO'. There was a name at the bottom written in pencil: Hugh O'Mara.

Tom's father must have done the drawing I held in my hand. Despite the stick limbs and the mouth that stretched from ear to ear, there was something undeniably real and alive about the woman, as though the youthful artist had done his utmost to convey the inward radiance of his friend Flo. That both items had been together in the envelope meant that the child in the photograph was almost certainly Hugh O'Mara. I would have loved to have shown it to Tom, but Flo must have had a reason for keeping the photo hidden, and it seemed only right to respect it.

Tom had arrived – I could hear his light footsteps, and forgot about photographs, forgot about everything, as I waited for the sound of his key in the door. He came prowling in, a graceful, charismatic figure, despite the tasteless electric blue suit and white frilly shirt. No words were spoken as we stared at each other across the room. Then I got up and walked into his arms and we began to kiss each other hungrily. It was less than twenty-four hours since we'd parted, yet we kissed as if the gap had been much, much longer.

Another bouquet arrived at the office next morning, this time pink and white carnations. I found a vase and put them in the reception area. 'Diana's late.' June remarked. 'I thought she would have called by now.'

When she still hadn't arrived by midday, George approached me. 'Should I ring to see if she's all right? I'm still annoyed with her, but I suppose she's had it rough lately, and it wouldn't hurt to let her know we're concerned.'

'Would you like me to do it?'

'I was hoping you'd take the hint.' He looked relieved.

When I dialled Diana's home there was no reply. 'Perhaps her father's been taken to hospital again,' I suggested.

George had already lost interest. 'Can I buy you lunch?' He jingled the coins in his pocket. 'I'm desperately in need of a shoulder to cry on. I had a letter from Bill this morning. He and Annabel will stay with me over Christmas but, reading between the lines, I could tell they'd sooner not. They're only coming because their mother's off somewhere exotic with her new husband – his name's Crispin, would you believe?'

'I'm sorry, George, but I'm lunching with my sister, and I've an appointment at the Old Roan with the Naughtons at half past two. Perhaps tonight, after work?'

'You're on,' George said glumly, as he mooched into his office. 'I think I'm about to have a panic attack.'

Trudy had phoned earlier. 'Mum said you'd gone to William Square last night, but you weren't there when I called. That girl draped around the railings, is she what I suspect she is?'

I confirmed that she definitely was.

'Will you be there tonight if I come at the same time? I need to talk to someone and there's only you.'

'I'm not sure when I'll get away,' I said quickly. It was selfish, but I didn't want my sister in Flo's flat, which I regarded as my own property until the place was ready for another tenant – which seemed further away than ever. 'Are you free for lunch?' I enquired. 'My treat.'

'I thought you always worked through lunch?'

'I won't today,' I promised.

We met in Central Precinct under the high domed glass roof, where a woman was playing old familiar tunes on a white grand piano, her fingers rippling languorously up and down the keys. Trudy was already seated at a wrought-iron table, looking very smart in a dark green jacket, long black skirt and lace-up boots. We made a pretty pair, the Cameron sisters, I thought wryly: elegant, with our nice clothes, discreetly made-up faces, and lovely ash blonde hair. No one glancing at us would have guessed at our wretched childhood, though Trudy's face was rather pinched and tight, I thought.

'I've never been here before,' she said, when I sat down. 'I love the pianist.'

'Have you noticed what she's playing?' The strains of 'Moon River' came from the piano. 'Mum's favourite.'

Trudy's laugh was rather strained as she rubbed the scar above her left eyebrow. 'There's no escape, is there?'

When I returned from the counter with prawn salads and two giant cream cakes, she said, 'I've just been thinking about the way Mum used to sing it when us kids had been knocked black and blue, and Dad had probably had a go at her.'

'It was her way of coping, I suppose.' I ate several prawns with my fingers – it was my first proper meal since Sunday. 'What did you want to talk about, Sis?' I was reluctant to rush her, but I had to meet the Naughtons in an hour's time.

Trudy was shoving her food around the plate with her fork. 'I don't know where to begin,' she muttered.

'The beginning?'

'That's too far.'

I raised my eyebrows. 'I don't understand.'

My sister threw her fork on to the plate with a sigh. 'It's Colin,' she said.

A knot of fear formed in my stomach. 'What's he done?'

'Nothing,' Trudy said simply. 'He's a good, decent man. I love him, and he loves me, and he adores Melanie and Jake. He works all the hours God sends for us.'

'Then what's the problem, Trude?'

'I don't trust him.' Trudy put her elbows on the table and regarded me with abject misery.

'You mean you think he's having an affair?'

'Of course not. He wouldn't dream of it.' Trudy shook her head impatiently. 'It's nothing to do with affairs. It's to do with the children. Oh, Lord!' She dabbed her eyes with the paper napkin. 'I'm going to cry. Have I smudged my mascara?'

'A bit.' I reached out and rubbed under her eyes. A woman at the next table was watching with interest, but turned away when she saw I'd noticed.

'It's my painting, you see.' Trudy sighed. 'There must be two hundred bottles, jars, decanters and demijohns in the shed, all finished. I've painted light-bulbs, plates, tumblers, brandy glasses – we get them from car-boot sales. The children think it's great, looking for glassware for Mum to paint. And I love doing it, Millie. I get quite carried away, thinking up new ideas, new patterns, and I can't wait to see how they'll turn out. But what am I supposed to do with the damn things?' she said plaintively.

'Sell them,' I said promptly. I still hadn't grasped what the problem was. 'Didn't Colin suggest you have a stall and he'll look after the kids?'

'Yes. But I don't trust him, Mill. I feel terrible about it, but I don't trust him with me children for an entire day. I'm scared he'll hit them, and if he did I'd have to leave.'

I was beginning to make sense of things. 'Has he ever done anything to make you think he would so much as lay a finger on them?' I asked.

'*No!*'

'In that case, don't you think you're being a bit paranoid?' I said. 'More than a bit, in fact. Over-the-top paranoid, if you ask me.'

'I know I am. But I still can't bring meself to leave them. Colin's nagging me soft to start a stall. There's a church hall in Walton where they have a craft fair every Sunday. He can't understand why I keep putting it off.'

'Neither can I. Our father wrecked our childhood, and now you're letting him wreck your marriage. You've got to trust Colin, Trude. You've *got* to.' Even as I spoke, I recalled James, his fist raised . . . 'I think all of us are capable of violence when the chips are down, but only a very perverted person would hit children the way our father hit us.'

Trudy gnawed her bottom lip. 'I must admit I've smacked Jake's bottom once or twice. He can be a little bugger when he's in the mood.'

'Was Colin there?'

'Yes. He was ever so cross and said I must never do it again.'

'But he didn't leave!' I cried. 'And knowing your history – that children who've been abused often abuse their own children – it's *him* who should be worried about leaving Melanie and Jake with *you*! Think how upset you'd be if you thought he suspected you'd hurt them! He's always trusted you, and he deserves your trust. Start the stall now in case he guesses why you're putting it off. He might never forgive you if he does.'

Trudy began to attack her salad. 'I'm glad I talked to you, Sis. I never looked at it like that before.' She paused, a forkful of prawns halfway to her mouth. 'I wonder if Dad was hit when he was little?'

'That's something we'll never know.'

★

I thought about it later on the way to the Old Roan. The only feelings I'd ever had for my father were fear as a child, and loathing as I grew older. But could there have been a reason for his behaviour? For the first time in my life, I wondered if a badly damaged human being could be lurking inside the monster I'd always known.

The Naughtons found the garden of the property in Old Roan much too big, and I drove back to work irritated by the waste of time.

When I went in, George announced 'Diana's father's dead. She called earlier. He passed away peacefully in his sleep during the night.'

'How did she sound?'

'As hard as nails,' George said indignantly. 'You'd think she was calling to say her car wouldn't start.'

'She's putting it on. I reckon she's devastated.'

'You're an exceedingly charitable person, Ms Millicent Cameron. Anyway, the funeral's Friday afternoon.' He drooped. 'I suppose I'd better put in an appearance, represent the firm, as it were.'

'Do you mind if I come with you?'

'Mind? Of course not. I've rarely had a more welcome offer.'

Later, I called my mother with the news – she was always ghoulishly interested in hearing about a death. 'How old was he?'

'A good eighty,' I replied. 'Diana's parents were middle-aged when she was born.' I decided to change the subject. 'I met our Trudy for lunch.'

'That's nice, luv,' Mum said. 'I like it when you two get together.'

'Perhaps the three of us could have lunch one day, you and me and Trude. You'd love the restaurant, Mum.'

'Oh, I dunno, luv,' she said, flustered. 'I'd never get back in time to do your dad's tea.'

I assured her she'd have bags of time and my father needn't know anything.

'I'll think about it,' she promised.

'You'll have to do more than think, Mum,' I said. 'I'm going to badger you rotten till you say yes.'

There was a pause. 'You sound happy, Millicent. Has something nice happened? Has James proposed?'

'James is history, Mum. Perhaps I'm happy because I've just had lunch with my sister.'

'Whatever it is, luv, I'm glad. You were getting very hard. Not long ago, you wouldn't have dreamed of asking your mam out to lunch. Now, what's all this about James being history?'

Apart from George and me, there were only five other mourners at the funeral: Diana, stiff and unemotional, two women neighbours, and two old men who'd been friends of Diana's father.

It was a bone-chilling November day and a wind flecked with ice blew through the cemetery, whisking in and out of the gravestones, stripping the last few leaves off the trees.

'I didn't think people got buried any more,' George muttered, through chattering teeth. 'I thought they popped 'em in an oven. At least it'd be warmer for the mourners.'

I watched the coffin being lowered into the grave, then the vicar said a few respectful words, and Diana came over and thanked us for coming. I took her hand as we walked towards the cars, George trailing behind.

'I'm sorry about your father. At least he didn't suffer much pain.'

'No, and as everyone keeps saying, he had a good innings.' Diana removed her hand. 'You get over these things. From now on, I'll be able to live my life as I please.'

'If you need someone to talk to,' I said gently, 'then don't hesitate to ring. If I'm not there, I'll be at number one William Square. There's no phone, so you'll just have to turn up.'

'Thank you, Millie, but I'm fine. I can't understand people who go to pieces when somebody dies.'

2

Church bells pealed, nearby and far away, high-pitched and rippling, deep-toned and sonorous. I opened my eyes: a cold sun shimmered through the white curtains, and Tom O'Mara was leaning over me. His brown hair was loose, framing his long face. If it hadn't been for the earrings and the tattoo, he would have resembled one of the saints in the pictures I'd taken down.

'I was just wondering,' he said, 'what is it between us two?'

'I don't know what you're talking about.'

'I mean, the truth is, you're an uppity bitch, full of airs and graces, and your accent gets on me wick.'

My lips quivered as I traced the outline of the heart on his chest. 'I've always steered clear of your sort, and the way you speak sets my teeth on edge.'

He pulled the bedclothes down to my waist and buried his head in my breasts. 'So, what is it between us two?' he asked again. His lips fastened on my left breast, and I squealed in delight when his tongue touched the nipple.

'I haven't a clue,' I gasped truthfully. The deep-down feeling of intimacy was frightening, because I couldn't visualise there ever being an end. The bells were still ringing as we made love, and it wasn't until it was over that I said, 'Why are you still here?' He'd usually gone before sunrise and Flo's alarm clock showed almost half past nine.

'Me wife's taken the girls to see her mam. I thought we'd spend the day together, or at least part of it. I've got to be at the club by five.'

I was thrilled at the notion of spending the day in bed with Tom O'Mara, but he had other ideas. 'C'mon, let's have summat to eat and we'll be off.'

'Off where?' I sat up and blew the hair out of my eyes. Tom was getting dressed.

'Southport.'

'Why Southport?'

'I'll tell you later, after we've had some grub.' He pulled on a blue polo-neck sweater, and went over to the mirror, where he combed his hair and scooped it back into a ponytail with an elastic band. I watched, entranced. It was such a feminine gesture coming from such an overwhelmingly masculine man. 'Me stomach thinks me throat's been cut,' he said. 'I'm starving.'

'There isn't any "grub", as you call it, except for a few old packets of biscuits.'

He groaned. 'In that case, I'll just have a cup of tea and we'll get something to eat on the way. The pubs'll be open by then.'

The sun was as bright as a lemon, and little white clouds were chasing each other across the pale blue sky. The wind was dry and crisp and very cold. I stuffed my hands in the pockets of my tan overcoat, glad that I was wearing boots – after the funeral yesterday I'd gone home for some warm clothes.

Tom's car, a silver-blue Mercedes, was parked round the corner, a suede coat on the back seat. I remarked that he was taking a risk, leaving an expensive coat in full view. 'Someone might steal it.'

'It would be more than their life was worth.' His lips curled. 'Everyone knows whose car this is. They wouldn't dare touch it.'

'You sound like a Mafia godfather!' The words were meant as an insult, but Tom's face was impassive as he replied, 'No one's going to rip me off and get away with it, and the same goes for me friends and family. That's why Flo was always safe in her place. People round here know what's good for them, and that means not mucking around with anything belonging to Tom O'Mara.'

'I see.' The ominous message that lay beyond his words was repellent, yet I didn't hesitate to get into the car with him. I felt very aware of his closeness, the way he held the steering wheel, his long brown hand touching the gear lever.

'What are you looking at?' he asked.

'You. I haven't seen you in daylight before.'

He slid a disc into the CD player and a man with a hard, angry voice began to sing 'The Wild Rover'. 'I love Irish music,' he said. Then he looked at me in a way that made me catch my breath. 'You look great in daylight.' He started up the engine and steered aggressively into the traffic. 'But you're doing me head in, girl. I wish I'd never met you.'

We stopped at a pub in Formby, the first customers of the day. Tom demolished a mixed grill, while I forced myself to eat a slice of toast. As soon as he'd finished, I poured us a second cup of coffee, and said, 'Now will you tell me why we're going to Southport?'

'I thought you'd like to meet me gran.'

I looked at him, startled. 'Your paternal grandmother?'

'What the hell does that mean?' he almost snarled.

'Is it your father's mother?'

He banged the cup down on the saucer. 'Christ! You talk like a fuckin' encyclopaedia. It's me dad's mam, Nancy O'Mara, eighty-six years old, as fit as a fiddle, but completely gaga.'

The nursing-home was a large, detached house in a quiet road full of equally large houses, all set in spacious, well-tended grounds. The décor inside was subdued and expensive, the floors thickly carpeted in beige. The fees must have been horrendous, and I assumed it was Tom who paid.

The smiling woman in Reception toned perfectly with her surroundings: beige suit, beige shoes, beige hair. When she saw Tom, the smile became a simper. The barmaid in the pub had looked at him in the same way.

'How's me gran been?' he enquired abruptly.

'Just the same,' the woman gushed. 'Sometimes she seems very aware of what people say to her, but in the main she lives in a world of her own. We persuade her to do her exercises every day and she's in remarkably good shape for a woman of her age. She's in the garden, which is no place for an old lady on a day like today but there's no arguing with Nancy. We just wrap her up and let her go.'

Tom led the way through to the rear of the house where a door opened on to a vast lawn. On the far side, a woman was sitting ramrod stiff on a wooden bench. She looked tiny beneath the fir trees that towered over the garden on three sides, so thick that not even the faintest glimmer of sunlight could get through.

She watched our approach with interest, ebony eyes flashing brilliantly in her hawk-like, liver-spotted face. Snow-white hair, with streaks of black, was piled in a bun as big as a loaf at the nape of her stringy neck. She wore a crimson coat and fur-trimmed black boots. A black lace stole was draped around her shoulders.

'Have you come to read the meter?' she enquired, in a hoarse, deep voice, when Tom sat down beside her. He motioned to me to sit the other side.

'No, Gran. It's Tom, and I've brought a friend to see you. It's no good introducing you,' he whispered. 'She wouldn't take it in.'

'There's no need to introduce her,' Nancy said unexpectedly. 'I know who she is.' She fixed the glittering eyes in their dry brown sockets on me. 'Oh, yes! I know who she is.'

'Who am I, then?' I felt uncomfortable, slightly afraid, under the woman's piercing gaze.

Nancy cackled. 'That would be telling!' Her long face became fretful. 'The chap hasn't been to read the meter in ages. One of these days, they'll cut the 'leccy off.'

'Stop worrying about the meter, Gran. Everything's all right. It's all been seen to.' Tom's attitude to his grandmother was tolerantly offhand. He hadn't kissed her, and seemed to be there out of a sense of duty, rather than affection.

A woman in a grey cotton frock and a white apron was coming towards us with a tray of tea-things. Nancy grabbed it eagerly, apparently capable of pouring the tea, heaping sugar in all three cups. We were drinking it in silence when I noticed that one of her dangling jet earrings had caught in the stole. I leaned over to unhook it, but was shrugged away with a sharp, 'Don't touch me!'

I made a face at Tom. 'I don't think she likes me.' I was hoping we wouldn't stay long. The garden was a melancholy place, cheerless and dark, the only sound was the dew plopping from the trees on to the thick, wet grass. It was doubtful that the old woman appreciated visitors. I'd hoped to get from her a feeling of the past, of the woman who'd been married to Tommy O'Mara when he'd lost his life on the *Thetis* in 1939, but it was impossible to imagine Nancy being young.

Tom said, 'Gran's never liked anyone much. The only person she ever cared about was me dad.' He glanced at his watch. 'We'll go soon. I don't mind paying the bills, but visiting bores me rigid. I only come once a month to keep the nursing staff on their toes. I don't want them thinking they don't have to look after her proper.'

For the next quarter of an hour, I did my awkward best to engage Nancy in conversation. I admired her coat, asked who did her hair, remarked on the weather, enquired about the food. It was hard to make out whether the old woman was merely being cussed when she didn't answer, or genuinely didn't understand.

'You're wasting your time,' Tom said eventually. 'Sometimes she catches on if you talk about the things she used to know, like the war, or the shops in Smithdown Road.'

'I can't talk about either.' Of course there was the *Thetis*, but under the circumstances that mightn't be a good idea.

'C'mon let's go.' Tom squeezed Nancy's shoulder. 'Tara, Gran. See you next month.'

We were half-way across the lawn, when a hoarse voice called, 'Hey, you.' We turned to see her beckoning.

Tom gave me a little push. 'It's you she wants.'

'Are you sure? Why should she want me?' I went back reluctantly, and got a fright when a hand came out and grabbed me painfully by the arm, pulling me downwards until our faces were almost touching. I could smell the fetid breath. 'I know what you're up to, Flo Clancy,' she said, in a voice that sent shivers of ice down my spine. 'But it won't work. Your Martha gave him to me fair and square. He's mine. You'll not get him back, not ever. I've told you before, I'll kill him first.'

'She's making a hole for her own back,' said Bel.

'A rod,' corrected Charmian. 'She's making a rod for her own back, or she's digging herself into a hole. You've got your sayings mixed up.'

'Tch, tch!' Bel snorted loudly. 'She knows what I mean.'

'Would you mind not talking about me in the third person?' I said mildly. 'Furthermore, it's none of your business who I go out with. I can make a hole for my own back if I like.'

'Rod,' said Charmian

'Rod, hole, whatever.' I waved a dismissive hand. I supposed it was inevitable that Tom O'Mara's regular visits to the basement flat wouldn't go unnoticed. When he had dropped me off after we got back from Southport Bel had been watching from Charmian's window to witness my folly.

'Fiona said he'd been in and out, but I didn't believe her.' Bel made no secret of her disapproval. 'Young 'uns nowadays,' she said disgustedly, 'they hop in and out of bed with each other like rabbits. I've only slept with three men in me life, and I married 'em all first.'

'Yes, but times have changed, Bel,' Charmian reminded her. She gave me a wink as she refilled the glasses, though even Charmian looked worried. 'I hope you don't mind me saying this, Millie, but Tom O'Mara's got a terrible reputation. It's not just women but all sorts of other things – drugs, for one. I wouldn't go near that club of his. It worried me to death when our Jay invited him to his twenty-first. I don't think Flo could have known the things he was up to.'

As the evening wore on, my irritation with the pair diminished in proportion to how much I drank. By the time we'd finished a bottle of sherry and started on another, the last, I didn't give a damn what anybody thought. I lay on the rug in front of the fire staring up at the faces of my friends, feeling extraordinarily happy and without a care in the world. 'He's a scoundrel,' I agreed, 'a villain, a good-for-nothing rogue. But he's also drop-down-dead gorgeous.'

'What's happening with poor James?' Bel demanded.

I thought hard, but couldn't remember. Before I could say anything there was a knock at the door and I said, 'Perhaps that's him now.' I walked unsteadily to the door and for several seconds couldn't recognise either of the small, clearly distressed women standing outside.

'You said it was all right to come,' a familiar voice said.

'Of course.' I blinked, and the two women merged into one: Diana, a different Diana from the one I'd always known, with uncombed hair and no makeup, her face white and shrivelled, like melting wax. I asked her in, trying not to sound too drunkenly effusive, and introduced her to Bel and Charmian, adding, because it was obvious that she was in a terrible state. 'Diana's father died last week. He was only buried the day before yesterday.'

Bel, who was over-effusive even when she was sober, jumped to her feet and took the new arrival in her arms. 'You poor girl! Sit down, luv – here, have my place on the settee. Oh, I bet you're feeling dead awful. Charmian, fetch the girl summat to drink. Millie, plump that cushion up and stick it behind her.'

Diana burst into tears. 'I've felt so alone since he died. The house is like a morgue,' she cried. 'I wanted someone to talk to.'

She was eaten up with guilt and anxious to share it. The words came pouring out in a plaintive, childish voice, nothing like her usual terse, clipped tones.

She'd always blamed her father for the fact that she'd never married, she sobbed. 'He said he was sorry. He took the blame but it wasn't his fault at all. No one's ever asked me to marry them. I was using poor Daddy as an excuse for being single, for having to stay in night after night, when I only stayed in because I had nowhere else to go. I'm a total failure as a human being, and it's nobody's fault but my own.'

'Don't be silly, luv,' Bel soothed. 'You stayed with your dad, didn't you? That was very kind and unselfish.'

But Diana wailed, 'I think he wanted to be rid of me so he could have his friends round for bridge. When I came home from university, he offered to buy me a flat. I refused. I told myself it was my duty to stay but I was terrified of being on my own. Then I complained so much about his friends that he stopped asking them. It was me who ruined his life, not the other way round.'

'You're exaggerating,' I said, in what I hoped was a sober, sensible voice. 'I'm sure it wasn't as bad as that.'

'It was,' Diana insisted tearfully.

'In time, you'll see things more reasonably,' Charmian said gently. 'I felt dead guilty when me own mam died. I wished I'd been to see her more often, that I'd been a better daughter.'

Having exhausted the subject of her relationship with her father, Diana turned to her job. She was worried about losing it. George didn't like her, no one did. She'd never fitted in. 'Daddy's gone, and if my job goes, too, I think I'll kill myself.'

'George sometimes gives the impression of being an

ogre, but he wouldn't dream of firing you,' I assured her, adding, though I wasn't convinced that it was true, 'He regards you as an asset to the firm.'

At ten o'clock, Herbie came down to demand the return of his wife, and Charmian went reluctantly upstairs. Bel muttered that it was time she was making tracks.

'I suppose I'd better go, too,' Diana sighed, 'though I dread the thought of spending another night on my own.'

'Come home with me,' Bel said instantly. 'I've got a spare bedroom. I can make the bed up in a jiffy.'

'Can I? Oh, Bel! You're the nicest person I've ever known.' Diana threw her arms around Bel's neck and looked as if she might easily cry again.

Nancy had said, 'I know who she is. Oh, yes, I know who she is.' She had taken me for Flo. They must have known each other, all those years ago. Was Nancy aware that Flo had been in love with her husband? And what did she mean when she said, 'Your Martha gave him to me fair and square. You're not getting him back. I'll kill him first.'

It didn't make sense, but perhaps that wasn't surprising coming from an elderly woman who'd lost her mind. Even so, Nancy must have had a reason for saying it.

I took the newspaper cuttings describing the last days of the *Thetis* over to the bureau and placed them alongside the school photo with the child who looked so much like Declan. Beside the photo, I put Hugh O'Mara's drawing of 'MY FREND FLO'. I looked thoughtfully from the cuttings to the photo to the drawing, then back again. The *Thetis* had gone down in June 1939, the photo had been taken six years later and the little boy was in the bottom class, which meant he must have been five and born in 1940. 'Your Martha gave him to me fair and square.' Flo had left instructions that Gran wasn't to be invited to her funeral. What had she done to make Flo hate her so much?

'*Your Martha gave him to me fair and square.*'

I felt my heart begin to race as I peered closely at the face of the little boy. He was a Clancy, no doubt about it, the same pale hair, slim build, Declan's sensitive features.

Suddenly, everything fell into place. Tommy O'Mara had been the child's father, but his real mother had been Flo. Somehow, Gran had given the baby to Nancy, against Flo's wishes, or she wouldn't have wanted him back. 'I've told you before, I'll kill him first,' Nancy had said.

It meant that Tom O'Mara and I were distant cousins. Tom had the Clancys' green eyes.

Poor Flo! I glanced around the basement room, at its fussy ordinariness, the flowers, lace cloths, abundant ornaments. When I'd first come, it had seemed typical of a place where a pleasant, but rather dull, unmarried woman had lived out most of her life. But as I'd discovered more about Flo, the atmosphere in the room had changed. There was the Flo who'd received those passionate love letters during the war; the woman who'd stayed in the Isle of Man with a man with a foreign name. The flat no longer seemed ordinary, but touched with an aura of romance and a whiff of mystery. This was where a twenty-year-old Flo had come when she was already a mother, but a mother without a child. Now, tragedy was mingled with the romance.

Yet, despite everything, Flo might have been happy. I would never know.

There was a box of drawing-pins in the bureau. I shook some out and pinned the drawing to the wall over the mantelpiece. Flo might have wanted to put it there herself fifty years ago.

The following Tuesday was unusually quiet at Stock Masterton. George went out at midday and hadn't returned by six. Darren and Elliot took the opportunity to leave early, and shortly afterwards June went home. Only Oliver and I were left.

He stretched his arms and yawned. 'I suppose one of us had better stay till George comes back.'

'Where did he go?' I asked.

'He didn't say. He got a phone call and went rushing off.'

'I'll wait,' I offered. Oliver had a long journey home through the Mersey tunnel to a remote village on the Wirral.

'Thanks, Millie.' He gave me a warm, grateful smile. 'You're a chum.'

Oliver had only been gone a few minutes when the light on the switchboard flashed to indicate there was a call. I was astonished to discover an angry Bel at the other end of the line. 'Is that woman there?' she barked.

I assumed she meant Diana, who'd been staying with her since Sunday. 'No, she hasn't been in since her father died. I thought she was with you?'

'She was until this morning,' Bel said. 'She seemed much better when she got up. I went to get us a nice chicken for tea but when I got back she'd upped and gone. Not a word of thanks, no tara, nothing!' she finished, with a high-pitched flourish.

'Perhaps she's coming back,' I suggested. 'She's gone home to collect something.'

'In that case she should have left a note – and it doesn't take five hours to get to and from Hunts Cross.' A loud indignant snort echoed round the empty office. 'Honest, Millie, me ears are numb from listening to her go on and on about bloody Daddy. I'm an ould softheart, me, and I didn't mind a bit, but I'm dead annoyed to think she's just scarpered. She ate me out of house and home. Me freezer compartment's nearly empty!'

'I'm sorry, Bel. I don't know what to say.' If Diana had been there, I could have easily strangled her for treating Bel so rudely. 'Why not come round to Flo's tonight for dinner?' I offered in an attempt to soothe her feelings.

'It'll be a takeaway, mind, from that Chinese place round the corner.'

'Me favourite's sweet and sour pork, and I really go for those little pancakes with roots in.'

'By the way, I found a bundle of letters in the bureau from you to Flo. I thought you might like them to read.'

'No, ta, luv,' Bel said firmly. 'Flo offered them to me once, but I said no to her too. I'm happy now, but I was happier when I wrote them. I'd sooner not be reminded of the ould days. Just chuck 'em out. See you later, luv.'

It was nearly seven by the time George strode into the office. 'I'd like a word with you, Millie,' he snapped, as he passed my desk and went into his cubicle.

Somewhat bemused by his tone, I followed, and was even more bemused when he nodded towards a chair, 'Sit down.' It seemed very formal. People usually sat down without waiting for an invitation.

George placed his arms on the desk and clasped his hands together, his expression grave and accusing. 'I don't think much of the way you treated Diana when she came to you for help,' he said coldly.

I heard the creak of my dropping jaw. 'I haven't the faintest idea what you're talking about.'

'Apparently she called at William Square, as you had invited her to do, desperate for someone to talk to, urgently in need of a shoulder to cry on . . ,'

'That's right.' My voice shook. I was at a loss to understand what was wrong.

'But instead of help,' George went on, 'all she found was you and two other women all pissed out of your minds. Not only that, you quickly got her in the same drunken state as yourselves. Even worse, the poor girl was virtually kidnapped by a ghastly old woman who wouldn't let her go. She's been stuck in this woman's dismal little house for days. She rang just before lunch and I was forced to go and rescue her. I found her shaking, crying, and in a terrible state.'

I burst out laughing. 'Rescue her! Don't be so bloody

stupid, George. Bel's anything but ghastly. In fact, Diana said she was the nicest person she'd ever met. Also, she's about seventy-five – a bit old to kidnap someone less than half her age, wouldn't you say?' It wasn't worth adding that although I'd never been in Bel's house I imagined it would be anything but dismal.

But George's face grew colder, if that was possible, and he said, 'I've never pulled rank, Millie. I've always treated my employees as equals, friends. I do, however, own this firm, and take exception to being called stupid by someone whose wages I pay.'

But he *was* being stupid! Diana had fooled him completely, putting on an act so outrageous that I marvelled at her nerve. I said nothing, just sat there, stunned, contemplating her treachery. She'd used us – me, Bel, Charmian – to rid herself of the guilt she'd felt over her father's death. Then she'd probably felt ashamed of having told so much and turned against us, possibly worried I'd tell George or the others in the office the things she'd said when she bared her soul.

'Oh, and another thing, Millie, I'd prefer it if you didn't refer to me in public as an ogre.'

'But I didn't . . .' I began, then remembered that I had. 'I didn't mean it in an offensive way.' I wanted to explain why I'd used the word, but it would probably be a waste of time at the moment. Just now George's mind was made up. It would be sensible to wait until he was able to see sense again, then put him right. 'Where is Diana now?' I asked.

'My place,' he said briefly. 'The poor girl's still very tearful. She's been through a lot lately. Her father dying was bad enough, but you and your friends only made it worse.'

'That's not fair, George,' I felt bound to say. 'If you think about it hard enough, you'll know it's not fair. Diana's having you on.'

For the first time, he looked straight at me and there was a trace of comprehension in his eyes. Then he blinked furiously and said, 'I'd better be getting back. I've promised to take her out to dinner.'

He strode out of the office, a knight on a white charger returning to his damsel in distress. I understood what had happened. His wife and children no longer needed him, his mother was dead, he was a man with no call on his emotions. Diana had got through to the part of him that longed for someone to cherish and protect.

When I sat down at my desk my legs were shaking, my mind a whirl. It was all so unreasonable, so unjust. I picked up the telephone, badly in need of someone sympathetic to talk to. Colin answered when I called Trudy and said she was out. 'She's taken Melanie and Jake to see *101 Dalmatians*. By the way, her bottle stall will be up and running on Sunday. She was going to call you.'

'I'll be there,' I promised.

Then I rang Mum. I couldn't explain what had happened, it would only upset her, but at least she would be a friendly voice. To my dismay, when the receiver at the other end was picked up my father reeled off the number. He always sounded mild, rather genial, on the telephone and it was hard to connect the pleasant voice with the man I knew. I didn't waste time with small talk. 'Is Mum there?'

'She's in bed with a touch of flu.'

'Oh!' I was temporarily flummoxed. 'Oh, well, give her my love and say I'll come and see her tomorrow after work. I'd come tonight, but I've promised to meet someone at Flo's.'

'All right, luv. How's things with you?'

'Fine,' I said brusquely. ' 'Bye.'

Bel would be only too willing to provide sympathy in buckets, though I wouldn't mention anything about kidnapping, or she was quite likely to burst a blood vessel.

'It's only me, Mum,' I called, as I ran upstairs. I found her propped up against a heap of pillows looking sleepy, but pleased with herself.

'Hello, Millicent.' She smiled when I went in and planted a kiss on her plump, pasty cheek. 'I'm all on me own. Your dad's gone to the pub and Declan's round at a mate's house.'

'How do you feel? I've been worried about you all day.' Halfway through the morning, I had wondered suddenly if flu was the real reason for her being in bed. Maybe my father had been up to his old tricks again.

'There's no need to worry, luv.' The contented smile was still there, enough to convince me that my suspicions were unwarranted. 'I'm really enjoying lying here and being waited on. Our Declan's been looking after me, and Trudy came this afternoon with some grapes. Now you've brought a lovely bunch of carnations, me favour-ite.' She buried her nose in them. 'They smell dead gorgeous. It's nice to know me children care about their mam. I even got a get-well card from Alison, though I don't suppose it was her idea to send it. I had to ring up on Sunday and say I couldn't go. The bug had already caught up with me by then, and I didn't feel up to the drive.'

'You should have rung, Mum. I would have come before.'

'I didn't want to bother you, Millicent. I know you're always busy.'

'Oh, Mum!' I stroked her brow, which felt rather hot. 'You've got a temperature,' I said, with a frown

'The doctor's given me some tablets. Look what the women in the shop sent.' She pointed to a little wicker basket of dried flowers on the bedside table next to Alison's card. She seemed far less bothered about being ill than that everybody had been so kind. 'Mrs Bradley from next door keeps bringing bowls of home-made soup. The potato's nice and tasty, but Declan ate the onion.' She giggled girlishly. 'I might be sick more often if this is the sort of treatment I can expect. Your dad's even brought a cup of tea up twice. I think he's a reformed character.'

'Don't bank on it, Mum.'

'I won't, luv. Look!' She patted her stomach. 'I've lost weight. This nightie would hardly go round me before but now it's dead loose. I used to be slim as a girl, just like you.'

'I know. Your wedding photo's downstairs.'

'That's right. I'd like to be slim again by the time I move to Oxford.' She giggled again. 'Start a new life with a new figure.'

I stared at her anxiously. Her expression was as innocent as a baby's. She'd lived under the iron hand of her husband for thirty years and had no idea how to cope with the world outside – how to deal with landlords other than the council, for instance, and the social-security people could easily convince her she wasn't entitled to a penny. 'Are you still set on that idea, Mum?'

'Oh, yes, luv.' She smiled radiantly. 'I'm looking forward to it, not just seeing our Alison more often but living on me own. I thought I might go back to nursing. They say the National Health Service is understaffed.'

'Nursing!' I gasped. 'I never knew you'd been a nurse.'

'I was halfway through training to become state registered when I married your dad.' She sighed. 'I was sorry to give it up.'

'You should have finished your training, then got married,' I said indignantly.

'Life doesn't always go the way you want it, Millicent.'

'I suppose not.'

There was a noise downstairs. 'Jaysus!' she gasped, terrified. 'I hope that's not your dad back! I hope he hasn't heard.'

But it was only Scotty, bored with being left alone and

275

looking for company. He came bouncing up the stairs and leaped on to the bed, settling himself comfortably between Mum's legs. He pushed his nose between her knees and looked at her adoringly.

'How's Flo's place coming along?'

'I'm nearly there,' I lied.

Mum laughed. 'Oh, come off it, luv. I don't know what you're up to but I've been to Flo's, remember? You can't kid me it takes six or seven weeks to sort out a one-bedroom flat.'

'Oh, Mum!' I slipped off my shoes and sat in my father's place on the bed. It was time I told her the truth. I took my mother's white hand, threaded with startling blue veins. 'I love it there, and I'm having a great time. I've met all sorts of interesting people. You already know Bel, then there's Charmian and Herbie upstairs, a young man next door who comes from Kirkby and was in my class at school, and . . . well, this other guy who knew Flo.'

'Bel used to be very glamorous.'

'She still is.'

'So you haven't done a thing,' Mum said, smiling.

'We've drunk all Flo's sherry and I've cleared out her bureau – well, almost. Otherwise, the place is no different from the first day I went.'

'Have you been paying the rent?'

'No, Mum.' I'd remembered to ask Charmian when the rent collector called. He came monthly, she said, and had been twice since Flo died but had never mentioned the basement flat. Next time he came Charmian had promised to ask about it. 'Flo must have paid several months in advance,' I told Mum. 'So far, I haven't come across a rent book.'

'I'd love to see the place again,' she said wistfully. 'See if it's changed much.'

'Come next week, Mum.' I couldn't keep the flat to myself for ever. 'Come one evening when I can show you round. The weekend would be even better. There's a takeaway round the corner. I'll buy more sherry and we can have a feast. Bel would love to meet you again, and you'll like Charmian.'

Mum squeezed my hand. 'I'll come as soon as I'm better. Now, I'm in a lovely hazy daze, all them tablets. I hope you won't mind if I go to sleep in front of you.'

'I'll make myself a cup of tea when you do.'

We talked in a desultory way about Declan: he'd had a form from a college, had filled it in and sent it off. Wasn't it smashing Trudy having her own stall? 'I hope I'm well enough to go by Sunday,' Mum said sleepily.

When her head began to droop I released her hand. I stayed where I was for a while, glancing round the dismal room. Years ago, Mum had painted all the furniture cream to make it look like a matching set, but she hadn't rubbed the varnish off underneath and the paint had started to peel. Perhaps she'd like that lovely stuff in Flo's bedroom, which I coveted — except that she was moving to Oxford. Where on earth did she get the courage from even to think of changing the course of her life at fifty-five? I sighed, got off the bed, adjusted the pillows and drew the bedclothes up to her shoulders. There was no heating upstairs and the air smelt cold. Scotty, also asleep by now and snoring gently, gave a little grunt when the eiderdown beneath him was disturbed.

Downstairs, I put the kettle on and stood watching until it boiled. It felt strange being in this house, danger free, able to do anything I wanted. Yet I still felt on edge, scared I might break something or put something down in the wrong place. I poured the water into the pot, stirred it to make the tea strong, then took a cup into the lounge. The fire was dying, the hearth full of ash. I threw on a few more coals and watched them slowly catch alight. On the right-hand side of the fireplace an owl made out of string was hanging from a nail that protruded crookedly from the wall. Dad's best belt had hung there once, the one he wore on Sundays: black leather, two inches wide, the heavy brass buckle with a deadly sharp prong. I touched the owl gingerly: such an innocuous thing to put in its place.

The back door opened and my father came in. I was still fingering the owl. 'This is where you used to keep your belt,' I reminded him.

His face flushed a deep, ugly scarlet, but he didn't speak. How did he feel, I wondered, now that his children had grown up and we could see him for what he was? Was he ashamed? Uncomfortable? Embarrassed? Or perhaps he didn't give a damn.

I looked at him, properly for once, and tried to relate the handsome, shambling, probably drunken figure to the photo of the bright-eyed baby at Flo's, but it was inconceivable to think that they were the same person. My gaze returned to the owl. 'You nearly blinded our Trudy with that belt.'

He'd been lashing out at Trudy, the skirt of her gymslip scrunched in a ball in his hand. When she tried to get away, he dragged her back so violently by the collar of her school blouse, that she'd choked and lost consciousness. He probably hadn't meant the buckle to hit her forehead, narrowly missing her eye, but Trudy had been left with a permanent reminder of the incident every time she glanced in the mirror.

My father looked at me, bleary-eyed and bewildered. He still didn't speak.

'Mum's asleep,' I said. 'Tell her goodbye from me.'

He spoke at last. 'Did she seem all right to you? I've been worried. She's had a terrible temperature.' His voice was gruff and querulous.

'I think she'll live.' Could it be that he actually *loved* my mother? That he loved us all? I took my cup into the back kitchen and washed it, then left by the back door without saying another word.

Mrs Bradley was leaning on next door's gate talking to another woman. 'How's your mam, luv?' she asked. She

278

was smartly dressed in a sequinned frock and the gigantic fur coat that she wore when she went ballroom dancing with Mr Bradley.

'She seems much better.'

'That's good,' Mrs Bradley said comfortably. 'I was just saying to Norma here how much better everywhere looks without that wreck of a car littering the place.'

Not only had the burnt out car gone, but the boarded up house was occupied. There were lace curtains in the windows and a television was on in the lounge.

'We got a petition up and sent it to the Council, didn't we, Norma?' Norma nodded agreement. 'What right have some folks got, spoiling the street for the rest of us? It's a respectable place, Kirkby. I remember us moving from Scotland Road in nineteen fifty-eight. It was like a palace after our little two-up, two-down. Will was tickled pink to have a garden.'

I went over to my car, unlocked the door and paused for a moment. Mrs Bradley and Norma were still talking. Mr Bradley came out, a thick car coat over his old-fashioned evening suit. He waved and I waved back.

Still I waited by the car, the door half-open. For the first time, I noticed the pretty gardens. Some of the original front doors had been replaced with more ornate designs, heavily panelled with lots of brassware. There were coachlamps outside several houses. It dawned on me that there was nothing wrong with Kirkby! It was all in my head, all to do with my childhood, my father, school. I'd centred my loathing on the place when it was my life that was wrong!

'What's up with George?' June demanded, for the umpteenth time. 'He's been like a bear with a sore head this week.'

Elliot swung his well-shod feet on to the desk. 'Perhaps he's going through the male menopause.'

'I reckon he's missing Diana.' Darren grinned.

Everyone except me hooted with derision, and Oliver

said miserably, 'She'll be back on Monday, spreading her usual discord and as moody as hell.'

'Actually,' June hissed, 'I didn't say anything before in case I was hearing things, but Diana rang George this morning and when I put her through I could have sworn he called her darling.'

There was a gasp of disbelief.

'Never!'

'I don't believe it!'

'You must have been hearing things, June.'

It figures, I thought. She's managed to wrap him round her little finger. I was glad no one seemed to have noticed that it was me, more than anyone, on whom George vented his bad temper. One day, I'd tried to explain that I'd done nothing wrong, but he was only interested in Diana's version of the story.

What on earth would it be like when she returned? Awful, I decided. She'd be lording it over everyone, particularly me. I wondered if I should look for another job, but my only qualification was a single A level, along with the time spent working at Stock Masterton. Would another estate agent take me on with such a paltry record? I tried to tell myself that it didn't matter, but in my heart of hearts I knew it did. The time I spent at Flo's, the nights with Tom O'Mara, were bound to end sometime, and I'd have to live in the real world again, where my job mattered very much. I had a mortgage, I had to eat. And if I left this job, I'd have to return the car.

Taking advantage of George's absence, Darren and Elliot went home early, followed shortly by June. I suggested that Oliver make himself scarce and I would stay until six in case there were any phone calls: the office closed an hour earlier on Saturday. Oliver accepted the offer thankfully. 'We're in the middle of decorating. I'd like to get it done by Christmas.'

The door had hardly closed when it opened again. I looked up, thinking Oliver had forgotten something.

'I've been waiting across the road for everyone to go,' said James. 'I was praying you'd be the last.'

Over the past few weeks I had almost forgotten James's existence, and was surprised at how glad I was to see the tall, familiar figure; so glad that, for the moment, I put to the back of my mind what had happened the last time we met. He wore a new suit, grey flannel, and a pale blue shirt, and was leaning against the door regarding me shyly.

'Hi,' I said.

'Phew!' He put his hand on his chest in a gesture of relief. 'I was expecting to have something thrown at me – a computer, a telephone, a notebook, at least.' He came down the room and perched on the edge of Diana's desk. 'How's life?'

'Ninety per cent fine, ten per cent lousy.'

'Tell me about the lousy ten per cent.'

I'd always been able to talk to him about humdrum, day-to-day matters. We spent ages discussing the meaning of a film we'd just seen, what frock I should wear to a party, his job, mine. It would have been a waste of time trying to talk to Tom O'Mara about office politics or Mum being ill, Trudy having a bottle stall or Declan going to college. Perhaps that was why I was so pleased to see James – not as a lover but as a friend.

I told him all about the week's events, and about Diana's treachery. 'Now George is really cross with me and I think I've blown my job.'

'But that's totally unfair!' James expostulated angrily.

It was comforting to hear Diana being called a conniving bitch and that George was a fool to let himself be taken in. I felt better after listening to James's loudly expressed indignation and didn't demur when he offered to buy me dinner.

'Shall we go to the wine bar where we first met?'

'I'd prefer to try that new place by the Cavern.' I didn't want to go somewhere that evoked old memories in case he got the idea that everything was back to normal, which it wasn't. 'I'll just ring home, make sure my mother's all right.'

Declan answered and assured me that mum was fine.

'Say hello to Declan for me.' James mouthed.

'James says hello, Declan.'

'I thought mam said James was history?'

I laughed. 'Bye, love.' I took a mirror out of my handbag, powdered my nose, combed my hair, re-touched my lipstick. When I looked up James was watching me with an expression on his rugged face that I remembered well. Our eyes met, he shook his head slightly, as if remonstrating with himself, then turned away. 'I'm sorry,' he said. 'I'm doing my best not to put a foot wrong. I promise not to say a word out of place until the time feels right.'

I began to regret accepting the dinner invitation because I knew I would never feel the same about James after what had happened, but I hadn't the heart to change my mind when he was being so nice.

The restaurant was filled with memorabilia of the Beatles' era. We ordered salad, baked potatoes and a bottle of wine. While we waited, I asked, 'How's the Socialist Workers' Party?'

He looked faintly embarrassed. 'I never went back – it's not really my scene. They were a decent crowd, but I only joined to please you.'

'To please me! I can't remember ever expressing left-wing opinions,' I exclaimed. 'I'm totally uninterested in politics.'

'So am I, though those dockers got a raw deal and I'm on their side. No, I joined because I got the impression you thought I was shallow. I was trying to prove I had some depth.' He glanced at me curiously. 'Did I suc-ceed?'

'I don't know.' I shrugged. 'I never thought about it much.'

'I doubt if you ever thought about me much,' he said drily.

'You promised not to say things like that,' I admonished.

'I'm not criticising,' he assured me. 'I'm trying to be coolly matter-of-fact. I pressurised you too much. I fell in love with you, deeply, passionately, wholeheartedly, and expected you to love me back in exactly the same way at exactly the same time. I wasn't prepared to wait. I wouldn't let you breathe.' He made a face. 'I'm used to getting everything I want, you see.'

'Including girls throwing themselves at you since you were fifteen!' I reminded him.

'Aw, shit, Millie.' He cringed. 'I'd had too much to drink, and I'd been waiting all week for you to call. I couldn't believe it was over between us.'

I played with my food. 'You nearly hit me, James. You would have, if Tom hadn't appeared.'

His face flickered with pain. 'So that's his name.' He leaned across the table, put his hand on mine, then hastily removed it. 'I would never, never have hit you, darling.'

There, in such civilised surroundings, it was easy to believe that he was a decent, honourable man who'd been driven over the edge. If I could feel about him as he did about me, everything would be perfect. He began to eat, but only because the food was there. 'This Tom,' he said, in a strained voice, 'are you in love with him?'

'No,'

'Is he with you?'

'No.'

'Who is he? How did you meet?'

'He was a friend of Flo's.' I smiled. 'She had an affair with his grandfather.'

'So, history is repeating itself.'

'Something like that.' I sipped the wine, which seemed preferable to the food. 'Look, can we change the subject?' I felt uncomfortable discussing my current lover with my old one.

'Perhaps that wouldn't be a bad idea.' James sighed.

'I'm trying valiantly to be grown-up but I think I'm about to explode with jealousy.'

We left the restaurant, the meal hardly touched but the wine finished, and strolled down Water Street towards the Pier Head. After a while, I linked James's arm. 'I'd like us always to be friends,' I said.

'Only a woman would ask a man who was crazy about her to be her friend,' he said with a dry chuckle.

'What would a man do in the same situation?' I asked.

'Run a mile, change his phone number, move house if necessary. If some woman had been chasing me as vigilantly as I was chasing you, I would have done all three in order to get away. You were very patient, Millie.'

The nearer we got to the river, the colder and more sharply the November wind blew. With my free hand, I tried to turn up the collar of my coat. James stopped, released my arm, and did it for me. 'I was with you when you bought this coat. You couldn't make up your mind whether to buy this colour or black. I said I preferred black, so you bought the other.' Still holding the collar by its corners, he said softly, 'Is that really all that's left for us, Millie, to be friends?'

'James . . .'

He released my collar and tucked my arm back in his. 'Okay, friends it is. Am I allowed to ask if I can see you again within the relatively near future?'

'Perhaps one night next week?'

We dodged through the traffic towards the Pier Head, where we propped our arms on the rail and stared at the lights of Birkenhead, reflected, dazzling, misshapen blobs, in the choppy waters of the Mersey.

'You know,' James said softly, 'we see movies about great love affairs that make us conventional folk seem very run-of-the-mill. We never imagine ourselves having the same passionate feelings as the characters on the screen, yet over the last few weeks, no one could have felt more gutted than I have. I was convinced I'd rather die if I couldn't have you.'

I said nothing, but shuddered as the wind gusted up my skirt.

James stared intently at the lights, as if the words he wanted to say were written there, prompting him. 'I wished I were a philosopher, who could cope with things more . . .' he grinned, '. . . more philosophically. Or a spiritual person, who would look at it with an intellectual sort of fatalism. But I don't go to church, I'm not even sure if I believe in God.'

'Did you come to a conclusion?' I asked gently.

'Yes – that I didn't want to die after all. That life goes on, whatever horrendous things might happen.' He grinned again. 'And that I still love you as much as I ever did, but less frenetically. Even so,' he finished, on a mock-cheerful note, 'I could easily throttle this Tom character.'

It had started to rain, so we walked back quickly to where my car was parked. On the way, he asked what was wrong with my mother.

'Flu. She's almost better.'

'I was always kept well hidden from your family. I only met Declan by accident. Were you ashamed of me or something?'

'Of course not, silly. It's them I was –' I stopped. All of a sudden I didn't care if he knew every single thing there was to know about me. 'Actually, James, my sister's having a stall at a craft market tomorrow. Perhaps you'd like to come if you're free.'

I was back at Flo's, going through the remainder of her papers. For the first time, I felt the urge to hurry things along, to finish with the bureau, get started on the rest of the flat. I emptied out the contents of a large brown envelope. Guarantees, all of which had run out, for a variety of electrical goods. I stuffed them back into the envelope and threw it on the floor. The next item was a plastic folder containing bank statements. I leafed through them, hoping they would give a clue to how the rent was paid. If Flo had set up a standing order, it would explain why the collector hadn't called, and also why there'd been little in the post – no electricity or gas bills, no demand for council tax. I admonished myself for being so negligent. I should have done this long ago, got in touch with the bank, sorted out Flo's financial affairs.

To my surprise, the account was a business one, begun in 1976 according to the first statement. The current balance was – my eyes widened – *twenty-three thousand, seven hundred and fifty pounds, and elevenpence*.

'Flo Clancy!' I gasped. 'What the hell have you been up to?'

I grabbed the next envelope in the rapidly diminishing pile. It was long and narrow and bore the name of a solicitor in Castle Street, a few doors along from Stock Masterton. My hands were shaking as I pulled out the thick sheets of cream paper folded inside, the pages tied together with bright pink tape. It was a Deed of Property, dated March 1965, written in complicated legal jargon that was hard to understand. I had to read the first paragraph three times before it made sense.

Fritz Erik Hofmannsthal hereinafter referred to as the party of the first part of Number One William Square Liverpool hereby transfers the leasehold of the section of Number One William Square hitherto known as the basement to Miss Florence Clancy hereinafter referred to as the party of the second part currently resident in the section of the property which is to be transferred for a period of one hundred years . . .

No wonder no one had called to collect the rent! Flo owned the leasehold of the flat in which she'd spent most of her life. My brain worked overtime. Fritz Erik Hofmannsthal! It was Fritz's laundry where Flo had worked; Mr and Mrs Hofmannsthal had spent a weekend on the Isle of Man every month for over twenty years.

'Oh, Flo!' I whispered. I went over and picked up the snapshot taken outside the laundry nearly sixty years before; Flo, with her wondrous smile, Mr Fritz's arm around her slim waist.

I had no idea why I should want to cry, but I was finding it hard to hold back the tears. I felt as if I knew everything there was to know about Flo Clancy: the lover lost on the *Thetis*, the baby who had gone to another woman, the servicemen she'd made love to in this very flat. Now Mr Fritz . . .

Yet the more I knew, the more mysterious Flo became. I wanted to get under her skin, know how she felt about all the tragedies and romances in her life, but it was too late, far too late. Not even Bel knew the things that I did about her lifelong friend. I'm glad it was me who went through her papers, I thought. I'll never tell another soul about all this.

Of course, I'd have to tell someone about the money and the property. It dawned on me that, under the circumstances, Flo would almost certainly have made a will.

Curious, I was about to go back to the bureau, when the front door opened and Tom O'Mara came in, his face, as usual, sombre and unsmiling, and looking like a dark, sinister angel in a long black mac.

I caught my breath, and half lifted my arms towards him as he stood staring at me from just inside the door. 'I'm neglecting the club because of you,' he said accusingly, 'neglecting me family. You're on me mind every minute of every day.' He removed his coat and threw it on the settee. 'You're driving me fucking crazy.'

'I'll be finished here soon, then I'll be back in Blundellsands. You won't want to come all that way to see me.'

'I'd come the length of the country to be with you.'

I wanted him to stop talking, to take me in his arms so that we could make love. I forgot about James, about Flo, Stock Masterton. All I wanted, more than anything on earth, was for Tom O'Mara to bury himself inside me.

Tom shook himself, gracefully, like a cat. 'I think I'm in love with you, but I don't want to be.' He wiped his wet brow with his hand. 'I feel as if I'm under a spell. I want to keep away from you, but I can't.'

'I know,' I murmured. I didn't like him, I couldn't talk to him, he was hard, unsympathetic, a crook. But I felt drawn to him as I'd been drawn to no man before.

We made love in a frenzy, without tenderness, but with a passion that left us both speechless and exhausted. When I woke up next morning, Tom was still asleep, his arm around my waist. I wanted to slip away, escape, because I was frightened. Instead, I turned over and stroked his face. His green eyes opened and stared into mine and he began to touch me. We were locked into each other. There was no escape.

Flo

I

1962

Sally and Jock's son, Ian, died as he had lived; quietly and bravely and without a fuss. He was sixteen. The funeral took place on a suffocatingly hot day in July and the crematorium chapel was packed. The mourners stood and knelt when they were told, their movements slow and lethargic, a sheen of perspiration on their faces, their clothes damp. There were flowers everywhere, their scent sweet and sickly, overpowering.

Flo was at the back, fanning herself with a hymn book. She hated funerals, but who in their right mind didn't? The last one she'd been to was for Joanna and Jennifer Holbrook. Joanna had passed away peacefully in her sleep, and the following night her sister had joined her. But at least the twins had managed more than four score years on this earth, whereas Ian . . . She averted her eyes from the coffin with its crucifix of red and white roses. The coffin was tiny, because he'd grown no bigger than a ten-year-old and every time she looked at it she wanted to burst into tears.

She wished she'd asked Mr Fritz or Bel to come with her. She knew hardly anyone except Sally and Jock. Grace, their daughter, was a cold, aloof girl, who'd always resented the care and attention bestowed upon her invalid brother. She was in the front pew next to her dad, looking bored and not the least upset. She wasn't even wearing dark clothes, but a pink summer frock with a drawstring neck.

The woman on Grace's other side, who was kneeling,

her head buried in her hands, must be melting in that black, long-sleeved woollen frock, she thought. Then the woman lifted her head and whispered something to the girl.

Martha.

Oh, Lord! She looked like an ould woman, her face all wizened and sour. She might well have achieved the coveted title of Mrs before her name and a lovely daughter but, if her expression was anything to go by, it had done nothing to make her happy. Or the nice new flat in Kirkby that she'd moved into a few years ago when Elsa Cameron had stuck her head in the gas oven and ended her tragic life. Perhaps happiness was in the soul, part of you, and it didn't matter what events took place outside. Some people, Martha was one, were born to be miserable.

'I'm happy,' Flo told herself. 'At least on the surface. I make the best of things. I'm happy with Mr Fritz, and me and Bel still have a dead good time, even though we're both gone forty – but I don't half wish we were twenty years younger. I'd love to go to the Cavern, I really would, and see them Beatles lads in the flesh.'

She was vaguely aware of someone genuflecting at the end of the pew. Then the person knelt beside her and whispered, 'Hello, Flo.'

'Hugh!' She flushed with pleasure and patted his arm. He was twenty-three and, as far as Flo was concerned, the finest-looking young man on the planet: tall, slender, with a gentle face, gentle eyes and the sweetest smile she'd ever seen. His hair had grown darker and was now a dusky brown, only a shade lighter than his father's, though it wasn't curly like Tommy's. He was mad about music and haunted the Cavern; she always listened to the charts on the wireless so she could talk to him on equal terms.

'I thought you couldn't get off work?' she said softly. He'd served an apprenticeship as an electrician and worked for a small firm in Anfield.

'I told them it was a funeral. They couldn't very well

refuse. Ian was me friend, he taught me to play chess. Anyroad, I promised Kate I'd come.' He nodded towards the front of the church, and a girl in the row behind Sally and Jock turned round as if she'd sensed someone was talking about her. She had the Clancys' green eyes and silvery hair, and Flo had the strangest feeling she was looking at her younger self in a mirror.

So, this was Kate Colquitt. She'd been at St Theresa's Junior and Infants' school when Flo last saw her, that hulking great lad, Norman Cameron, never far from her side. Sally was right to say she'd grown into a beautiful young woman. Kate twitched her lips at Hugh, almost, but not quite, in a smile, because this was, after all, a funeral. The man kneeling next to her must have noticed the movement. He twisted round and gave Hugh a look that made Flo's blood curdle, a look of hate, full of threats, as if he resented his companion even acknowledging another man's existence.

Norman Cameron, still watching over Kate like an evil guardian of the night.

Everyone stood to sing a hymn: 'Oh, Mary, we crown thee with blossoms today, Queen of the Angels and Queen of the May.' It wasn't May and wasn't appropriate, but it had been Ian's favourite.

Flo saw Norman Cameron find the page for Kate, as if she was incapable of finding it for herself. She felt concerned for the girl, although she hardly knew her. Sally said Norman wanted them to get married and Martha, anxious as ever to meddle in other people's lives, was all for it. Kate had managed so far to hold out. She was working at Walton hospital as an auxiliary and wanted to become a state registered nurse.

'Norman's had a terrible life,' Sally had said, only a few weeks ago. 'No one could have had a worse mam than Elsa, yet the poor lad was inconsolable when she topped herself. I feel dead sorry for him. But he makes me flesh creep, and he's so much in love with Kate it's unhealthy. You'd think he owned her or something.'

'She should find herself another boyfriend,' Flo said spiritedly. 'Try and break away.'

'I reckon Norman would kill any man who dared lay a finger on her.'

'Lord Almighty!' Flo gasped.

The hymn finished, the priest entered the pulpit and began to speak about Ian. He must have known him well because his words were full of feeling: a bright, happy lad who'd borne his illness with the patience of a saint and had almost made it to adulthood due to the selfless commitment of his parents. The world would be a sadder and emptier place without Ian Wilson. Heaven, though, would be enriched by the presence of such a pure, unsullied soul . . .

Flo switched off. Any minute now, he'd start telling Sally and Jock that they should feel privileged their child was dead and had gone to a better place, where he was, even now, safely in the arms of God.

The priest finished. Flo buried her head in her hands when it was time for them to pray. The soft whisper of the organ came from the grille in the wall, the sound gradually growing louder, but not enough to hide a slight whirring noise. Flo peeped through her fingers and saw the curtains behind the altar open slowly and the coffin slide out of sight. The curtains closed and there was an agonised gasp from Sally as her son disappeared for ever. Jock put an arm around her shoulders, and Flo imagined the little curling red and blue flames licking the coffin, spreading, meeting, then devouring it and its precious contents, until only the ashes remained.

'Don't cry, Flo.' Hugh offered her his hanky.

'I didn't realise I was.' She pushed the hanky away. 'You look as if you might need it yourself.'

The service over, they went outside, where the heat was almost as great as it had been in church. When everyone stood round the display of flowers, which were laid out on the parched grass, the blooms wilting rapidly in the hot sunshine, Flo kept to the back. She could see her own wreath, irises and white roses, and would have liked to look for the flowers that Bel and Mr Fritz had sent, but didn't want to come up against Martha, particularly not today.

Hugh was talking to the bereaved parents. He shook hands with Jock and kissed Sally's cheek, very grown-up, very gentlemanly. Nancy O'Mara had raised him well. If she'd been there, she would have felt as proud as Flo. He came over. 'I have to be getting back to work.'

'I'll be going meself in a minute, after I've had a word with our Sally.'

He looked surprised. 'I thought you'd be going back to the house.'

'You're not the only one who has to be at work.'

'In that case,' he said, trying to sound casual, 'I'll give you a lift part of the way.' He had a car, his pride and joy, a little blue Ford Popular.

'That'd be nice, luv. Ta.'

What was she supposed to say to Sally? 'I'm dead sorry, Sal. I feel terrible for you. He was a lovely lad. I don't know how you'll cope without him.' After a few stumbling phrases, she threw her arms around her sister. 'Oh, Lord, Sal, you know what I mean.'

'I know, girl.' Sally nodded bleakly, then grabbed Flo's arm. 'Sis, I want you to do something for me.'

'I'll do anything, Sal, you know that.'

'Make things up with our Martha.' She shook Flo's arm impatiently. 'There's enough misery in the world without adding to it when there's no need. Martha would be overjoyed if you two were friends again.'

Flo glanced at Martha, who was talking to her daughter, Norman Cameron a dark shadow by her side. They weren't exactly a happy family group, but the mother and daughter relationship was there for all to see. Then she looked at Hugh, waiting, hands in pockets, for his 'friend' Flo, and she felt a sense of loss as vivid and painful as the morning she'd woken up and discovered her son had been taken away. Martha hadn't just stolen her son, she'd stolen her life.

Very gently, she removed her sister's hand. 'Anything but that, Sal,' she said.

'I'll miss Ian,' Hugh said, when they were in the car. He smiled shyly. 'I'll miss Kate, too. She was often there when I went to see him. It was the only place she went without Norman Cameron in tow.'

'D'you fancy her, luv?' They would make a perfect couple, Flo thought excitedly. The Catholic Church forbade relationships between cousins, though marriage might be possible with a dispensation. But as neither Hugh nor Kate were aware that they were related, there would be no need for the Church to become involved.

His pale cheeks went pink. 'She's okay.' He'd had several girlfriends, all of whom Nancy had disliked on sight. 'You'd think I was royalty or something,' he'd grumbled to Flo. 'She doesn't think any girl I bring home is good enough for me.'

Flo was inclined to agree, though where Nancy was concerned she always kept her opinions to herself.

Hugh dropped her off in Lime Street. 'See you soon, Flo, perhaps tomorrer.'

It was too nice a day to sit on a bus and Flo decided to walk home. She was in no hurry. Although she'd told Hugh she should be at work, her shift didn't start until two. A few years ago, when launderettes had sprung up all over the place and White's Laundry saw their work trickle away to almost nothing, Mr Fritz had closed the place down. Then he had opened a chain of launderettes, six in all, and put Flo in charge of the biggest, an ex-chandler's shop in Smithdown Road, less than a mile from William Square.

'Hello, gorgeous!' A man, quite good-looking, was standing in front, blocking her way.

'Hello . . .' She stared at him, frowning, before realising that he was a stranger trying to pick her up. 'I thought I knew you,' she said, exasperated.

'You could, very easily. I'd certainly like to know you.'

'Get lost,' she said, but smiled as she dodged past. It was flattering to think that at forty-two she could still attract men. She caught a glimpse of her reflection in the windows as she walked up Mount Pleasant. She never wore black, apart from skirts, and Bel had loaned her a frock for the funeral; very fine cotton with short sleeves and a sunray-pleated skirt. The wide belt made her already slim waist look tiny. She hadn't put on an ounce of weight with age. When they went on their regular visits to the Isle of Man, Mr Fritz complained that she looked no more than thirty. People would think he was spending a dirty weekend with his secretary.

'We're not married, so it is a dirty weekend.' Flo giggled.

He looked horrified. 'Flo! Our weekends together have been the most beautiful times of my life. Nevertheless,' he grumbled, 'all the other guests probably think they're dirty.'

Flo offered to dye her hair grey and draw wrinkles on her face, but he said that wouldn't do either. 'I rather enjoy getting envious glances from other men.' There was no pleasing him, she said.

She passed the women's hospital where Nancy O'Mara had recently had a hysterectomy. Hugh, the dutiful son, had gone to see her after work every night. On the way home, he sometimes called in at the launderette. He usually popped in at least once a week.

'How's Mrs O'Mara?' she asked. It sounded silly, but she could never bring herself to refer to Nancy as his mam.

'Progressing normally, according to the doctor.'

During the time he'd been at secondary modern school, she'd thought she'd lost him. Until then, he'd got into the habit of sticking his head round the door of the laundry on his way home from St Theresa's, just to say hello. When he changed schools, she had the good sense not to wait for him outside when she went to the bank on Fridays, reckoning an eleven-going-on-twelve-year-old in long trousers wouldn't be seen dead playing ball in the Mystery with a woman almost twenty years his senior.

'Where's your little friend?' Mr Fritz asked, after Hugh hadn't shown his face in months.

'He's at a different school and comes home a different way,' Flo explained, doing her best not to appear as cut up as she felt about it.

'That's a shame. I'd grown quite fond of him.' He gave Flo a look full of sympathy and understanding, as if he'd guessed the truth a long time ago.

The months became years. She saw Hugh once when he was fourteen. He was on his way home with a crowd of lads who were kicking a tin can to each other on the other side of the road. She was glad his collar was undone, his tie crooked, that he looked an untidy mess. She was even glad about the tin can. Nancy might not like it, but he'd found his place, he'd made friends, he was one of the lads. She felt a tug at her heart as she melted into a shop doorway out of sight. If only he was coming home to me!

Although Flo had a great time in the launderette – the customers came in with so many funny stories that her sides still hurt with laughter when she went home – she could never get her son out of her mind. She heard through Sally that he'd left school and begun an apprenticeship as an electrician. It wasn't what she would have chosen for him: she would have liked him to become something grander, perhaps even go to university.

It wasn't until almost five years ago, Christmas 1957, that she had seen Hugh again. The launderette was festooned with decorations, drooping in the damp. All afternoon she'd been pressing home-made mince pies and sherry on her 'ladies', as she called them – a few had even returned with more washing they'd scraped to-gether because they'd had such a good time. The bench was full of women waiting for the machines to finish, and Flo was slightly tipsy, having drunk too many people's health when she wished them merry Christmas. Mr Fritz usually toured his six establishments daily to ensure that the automatic machines were working properly and not in need of his expert attention, but always ended up at Flo's because it had the nicest atmosphere. His brown eyes twinkled as he accused her of being in charge of a launderette while under the influence of alcohol. Just then the door opened for the hundredth time that day and he said, 'Why, look who's here!'

Hugh! A shy, smiling Hugh, in an old army jacket with a small khaki haversack thrown over his shoulder.

My son has grown up! She wanted to weep for all the years she'd missed. She wanted to hug and kiss him, to ask why he'd deserted his mam for so long, but merely smiled back and said, 'Hello, luv.'

'You've grown some,' Mr Fritz said enviously. 'You must be six foot at least.'

'Six foot one,' Hugh said modestly.

He never explained why he hadn't come before, why he'd come now, and Flo never asked. She guessed it was something to do with age, that between eleven and seventeen, he hadn't felt it proper for her to be his friend, but as he'd grown older something had drawn him back. She didn't care what it was. It was enough that he'd come, and continued to come, to tell her about his job, his girlfriends, how he was saving up to buy a car. Once, a few months ago, he had said, 'I wish me mam was a bit more like you, Flo. She thinks I'm crackers to want a car, but you wouldn't mind, would you?'

'I should have caught the bus,' she muttered, halfway home, when the straps of her high-heeled sandals began to dig into her feet. It would be a relief to reach William Square, where she'd have a nice cool bath before she went to work.

Stella Fritz would have a fit if she could see the square now. There was scarcely a house left that hadn't been turned into flats or bedsits and they all looked run down, uncared-for. Even worse, one or two women – Flo refused to believe they were prostitutes – had begun to hang around at night, apparently waiting for men to pick them up. Twice, Flo had been propositioned on her way home in the dark, and Bel had threatened that if anyone else asked how much she charged, she'd thump them. There were frequent fights, which led to the police arriving. Mr Fritz moaned that the place was becoming dead rowdy, and Flo, who loved the square and never wanted to live anywhere else, had to concede that it had deteriorated.

She felt better after the bath and when she had changed into a pale blue cotton frock and canvas shoes. All afternoon, she couldn't get Sally out of her mind. On numerous occasions her ladies wanted to know what was wrong. 'You look as if you've swallowed a quid and shat a sixpence. What's up, Flo?'

If she told them about Ian, she knew what would happen: their great, generous hearts would overflow with sympathy, which would be expressed in flowery, dramatic language a poet would envy. She would only cry, she might possibly howl. She told them she was feeling out of sorts, that the heat was getting her down

Flo loved her ladies. They were coarse, often dirt poor, but they struggled through life with a cheerfulness of spirit that never ceased to amaze her. Through the door they would burst in their shabby clothes, which were usually too big or too small, too long or too short, carrying immense bags of washing. There were black ladies and white ladies, quite often grossly overweight because they existed on a diet of chip butties, but always with a smile on their careworn, prematurely old faces, making a great joke of their bunions and varicose veins, the swollen joints that plagued them, the mysterious lumps that had suddenly appeared on their bodies that they intended to ignore. 'I couldn't go in the ozzie and let them take it away, could I? Not with five kids to look after, and me ould feller propped up in the boozer all day long.'

It could be seven kids, ten kids, twelve. Most of the husbands were unemployed, and more than a few of Flo's ladies went out cleaning early in the morning or late at night. It was their money that paid the rent and put food on the table, but that didn't stop some husbands taking out their frustration with the government and society in general on their wives. Flo often found herself bathing bruises or bandaging cuts, cursing the perpetrators to high heaven.

But the women refused to listen to a word of criticism of their men – 'He couldn't help it, luv. He was stewed rotten. He wouldn't dream of hitting me when he's sober,' which Flo found an unsatisfactory explanation for her ladies' sometimes appalling injuries. She cosseted them, made them tea, laughed at their jokes, admired them. The only thing she refused was to let them do their washing on tick, which Mr Fritz had strictly forbidden. 'Before you can say Jack Robinson, they'll have run up a huge bill and we'll never get paid. No, Flo. They put their own coins in the machine and that's final. And if I find you've been loaning your own money, I'll be very cross indeed. They're a canny lot, and pretty soon you'll be subsidising washing for the whole of Toxteth.'

The thought of Mr Fritz being cross wouldn't have caused a tremor in a rabbit, but Flo was careful to take heed of his advice.

At seven o'clock on the day of Ian's funeral, it was a relief when she could turn the Open sign to Closed. Mr Fritz came and went, promising to have some iced tea ready for when she came home – he was obsessed with his new refrigerator. It would be another hour before all the machines were finished and she could tidy up and leave. The place felt like an oven. Perhaps that was why she had remained so slim: since she was thirteen, she'd spent a high proportion of her waking hours in the equivalent of a Turkish bath.

Bel had been promoted to manageress of ladies' outer-wear in Owen Owens: long coats, short coats, raincoats, furs. She was frequently wined and dined by representatives of clothing firms who wanted her to stock their products. Occasionally, when Flo had nothing better to do, she would go to Owen Owens and listen while Bel dealt with a customer.

'Modom, that coat looks simply divine on you. Of course, Modom has a perfect figure, and red is definitely your colour.' The accent, Bel's idea of 'posh', and the voice, haughty yet obsequious, was stomach–churning. When the customer wasn't looking, Bel would make a hideous face at Flo, and mouth, 'Sod off!'

On her way home from the launderette, Flo let herself into her friend's flat in Upper Parliament Street, where Bel was lying on her luridly patterned settee wearing black satin lounging pyjamas and reading *She*. She looked up and grinned widely, the deeply etched laughter lines around her eyes and mouth adding yet more character to her already animated face. 'You look as if you've just been for a turn in one of your machines,' she said.

'I feel as if I have.' Flo threw herself into an armchair with a sigh. Bel's flat wasn't relaxing, more like a fairground with its bright walls and ceilings, and curtains that could do serious damage to the eyes. Still, it was nice to sit in a comfortable chair at last. 'I want you to promise me something, Bel,' she said.

'What, luv?'

'If I die before you, make sure I'm buried, not cremated. I want a few bits of me left to rise to heaven when the Day of Judgement comes.'

'Rightio, Flo,' Bel said laconically. 'I don't give a stuff what they do with me. Once I'm dead, they can throw me in the Mersey for all I care, or feed me to the lions at Chester Zoo.'

'Another thing, Bel. I've taken out an insurance policy to cover the cost of me funeral. It's in the first-aid box in the cupboard by the fireplace, the right-hand side. I'd put it in the bureau with all me papers, but you'd never find it. I can never find anything meself.'

'That's because you keep every single bit of paper that drops through your letterbox,' Bel snorted.

'It's a legacy from Stella Fritz. I always kept me bills in case she accused me of not paying the 'leccy, or something. Now I can't get out of the habit. Anyroad, when I'm looking for something, it's nice reading through me old letters. I've still got the ones you sent during the war. You can have them back if you like.' She didn't say, because Bel would have been disgusted, that it was quite interesting to look at old bills, see how much prices had gone up.

Bel grimaced. 'Thanks, but no thanks.'

'One more thing. Under no circumstances must our Martha come to me funeral. I'm not having it, d'you hear?'

'I hear, Flo, but why all this morbid talk about death and funerals?'

'I took the policy out years ago. It was this morning at the crematorium that I decided I'd sooner be buried.'

'Flo!' Bel's face was a tragedy. 'I'd completely forgotten about Ian's funeral. Was it awful, luv? How's your Sally taking it? Did the dress fit all right?'

'The dress looked simply divine,' Flo said tiredly. The expression had become a joke between them. 'As for the other, it was awful, yes. Sally's taken it hard, and so's Jock.'

'Shall we do something exciting tomorrer night, Sat'day, like go somewhere dead extravagant for a meal? It might cheer you up.'

'Sorry, Bel, but I'm going on retreat in the morning.'

Bel groaned. 'You're a miserable bugger, Flo Clancy. What do you do on these retreats, anyroad?'

'Pray,' Flo said virtuously.

'They're a waste of time – a waste of life!'

'I don't see you doing anything earth-shattering.'

'I've got an important job.'

'So've I.'

'I get taken out to dinner.'

'Mr Fritz takes me out to dinner sometimes.'

'He takes us both, so that's not counted.' Bel sat on the edge of the settee and rested her chin in her hands. She said, thoughtfully, 'Actually, Flo, it's well past the time you and Fritz got something going together.'

Flo laughed. 'I'm happy as I am, thanks all the same. Anyroad, it's well past the time you found yourself another husband.'

Bel ignored this. 'These damn retreats, I can't think of anything more boring and miserable than praying non-stop for two whole days.'

'Oh, I dunno,' said Flo. 'The thing is, I always come back feeling spiritually uplifted and enriched.'

2

'I can't understand it,' Sally said distractedly. 'It's as if Ian was the glue that kept us together.' She ran her fingers through her short, greying hair. 'But when did me and Jock need anything to keep us together? I love him, and I know he loves me. Remember the day we met him and his mate, Flo, on the New Brighton ferry?'

'I'll never forget that day, luv.' It was the last time she had seen Tommy O'Mara.

Her sister's marriage was falling apart. Grace didn't help. She accused her mam and dad of always having cold-shouldered her, of making her feel second best. 'Then me and Jock have a go at each other,' Sally moaned. 'I tell him it's his fault Grace feels the way she does, and he says it's mine.'

The only good thing to come out of the whole sad business was that the two sisters had become close again.

Sally frequently turned up at the launderette just as Flo was closing, and they would walk back to William Square, arm in arm. Jock went to a social club in Kirkby almost every night – 'As if all he wants is to have a good time with his mates. I think I remind him too much of what we went through with Ian. He won't come with me to church.'

'I don't know what advice to give, Sal,' Flo said truthfully. She thought her sister spent far too much time in church, but preferred not to say so. 'Perhaps it's just a stage he's going through. He needs to let off steam. Jock's a good man at heart.'

'It's not advice I need,' Sally sniffed, 'just someone to talk to. Our Martha's come up with enough advice to write a book, from giving our Grace a good hiding to wiping the floor with Jock.'

'Both of which would do more harm than good.'

'That's what I said. Mind you, her Kate's been a great help. She often comes round to see me.' Suddenly Sally seemed to find a mole on the back of her hand enormously interesting. Without meeting her sister's eyes, she mumbled, 'I can't understand how our Martha ended up with such a lovely daughter, and we were landed with Grace. Oh!' she cried tearfully. 'Forget I said that. I love my girl, but I don't half wish she were different.'

'I wish all sorts of things were different, Sal.' Flo sighed 'You must bring Kate round to see me sometime. I'd like to get to know her.'

She had never intended it to be this way, but it had all started the day she first saw Tommy O'Mara through a mist of steam in Fritz's laundry: Flo's life seemed to be divided into little boxes, each one carefully marked 'Secret'.

Martha and Sally knew this about her, Mr Fritz knew that. Hugh O'Mara thought he was her friend. No one knew about the servicemen during the war. There were her bogus 'retreats'. Bel, who thought she knew everything there was to know, knew virtually nothing, only that for a short time before the war she'd gone out with Tommy O'Mara.

Flo often worried that one day something might be said that would lift the lid off a box, give away one of her secrets, expose one of her lies.

It nearly happened the day Sally came to the flat, bringing Kate Colquitt with her. Bel was there, and they'd just watched *Roman Holiday* on television – Bel still went weak at the knees over Gregory Peck.

'This is Kate Colquitt, our Martha's girl,' Sally said.

Flo could have sworn that Bel's ears twitched. She still longed to know why Flo and Martha never spoke. 'Martha's girl, eh! Pleased to meet you, Kate. How's your mam keeping these days?'

'Very well, thank you.' The girl had a sweet, high-pitched voice.

'Why didn't you bring her with you?' Bel enquired cunningly. Flo threw her a murderous glance. Bel caught the look and winked.

Kate merely replied, 'Me mam doesn't know I've come.' She turned to Flo, green eyes shining in her lovely fresh face. 'I've always wanted to meet you, Auntie Flo. I saw you at Ian's funeral. I was going to introduce meself, but when I looked for you you'd gone.'

'Please call me Flo. "Auntie" makes me feel a bit peculiar.'

'Okay.' She followed her aunt into the kitchen when Flo went to make a pot of tea, chatting volubly. 'I like your flat, it's the gear. I'd love a place of me own, but me mam's dead set against it. She says I'm too young. How old were you when you came here, Flo?'

'Twenty.'

'There! Next month I'll be twenty-two. So I'm not too young, am I?' She looked at Flo, wide-eyed and artless.

'I was a very old twenty,' Flo muttered. An incredibly

old twenty compared to this girl, who was too innocent for this world. She looked as vulnerable and defenceless as a flower by the wayside.

'There are times,' Kate sighed, 'when I'd love to be by meself. Y'know, read a book and stuff, watch the telly.'

Flo imagined her mother, Martha the Manipulator, never allowing her daughter a minute's peace. 'Why do you need a red bow in your hair when you're only going to see Josie Driver?' 'I'd sooner you didn't go out with a Protestant, Sal.' 'You've always got your head buried in a book, Flo Clancy.' And then there was Norman, which meant that Kate had two overbearing people to cope with, wanting her to do things their way. Sally said that he had moved to Kirkby and he was round at the house almost every night.

'Are you having a party on your birthday?' Flo asked brightly, as she arranged the cups and saucers on a tray.

'Just a few friends. You can come if you like.'

'Ta, luv, but I don't think that's such a good idea.' She picked up the tray. 'D'you mind bringing that plate of biscuits with you, save me coming back?'

'What happened between you and me mam, Flo?' Kate enquired earnestly. 'Auntie Sally says I'm not to mention I've been to see you. It must be something awful bad.'

Flo chuckled. 'That's something you need to ask your mam, luv.' One thing she knew for certain was that the girl wouldn't get a truthful answer.

They went into the living room. 'You took your time,' Bel said. 'I'm parched for a cuppa.'

'I remember you used to wait for Hugh O'Mara out-side St Theresa's,' Kate went on, 'though I didn't know you were me auntie then.'

Bel's head jerked upwards and she looked at Flo, her face full of questions.

The very second Sally and Kate left, Bel burst out, 'Hugh O'Mara! Who's Hugh O'Mara? Is he related to Tommy? I didn't know he had a kid.'

'Why should you?'

'I thought you'd have said.'

Flo explained that Hugh had been born after Tommy died. It was hateful giving credit to Nancy for something she'd done herself, but too much time had passed for Bel to know the truth. Flo couldn't have stood the gasps of incredulity, the astounded comments. Bel *would* have crawled through the snow to get back her baby. Bel would have stood on the rooftops screaming to the world that her baby had been stolen, then demolished Nancy's front door with a battering ram once she had discovered where he was. The realisation that another woman wouldn't have taken it as meekly as she had made Flo feel uneasy. It was a bit late to regret what a coward she'd been, too easily influenced by the wishes of her family.

'That's all very well,' Bel hooted, when Flo finished her careful explanation, 'but what the hell were you doing waiting for the lad outside St Theresa's?'

I should have been a spy, Flo thought. I would have been brilliant at lying meself out of the most dangerous situations. She said that a woman at the laundry had had a son in the same class as Hugh. 'They were friends. I used to go by St Theresa's on Fridays on me way from the bank. Peggy asked me to make sure Jimmy was going straight home. That's how I met Hugh. He was a nice lad, quite different from his dad. I still see him,' she added casually. 'If he's passing the launderette, he might drop in.'

'Why didn't you tell me this before?' Bel said, outraged out of all proportion.

'I didn't think you'd be interested.'

'Why, Flo Clancy, you know I'm interested in *everything!*'

'Well, you know now, don't you?' Flo snapped.

It was a whole year before Jock tired of the social club and Sally stopped going quite so often to church. The old harmony was restored. It helped when Grace got engaged to a nice young man called Keith, who worked in a bank, and became absorbed in plans for her wedding eighteen months off at Easter 1966. 'Jock's pulling out all the stops. It's going to be a grand affair,' Sally announced. 'He thinks if we spend all our savings she'll realise we love her just as much as we did Ian.'

Sally continued coming to William Square, sometimes bringing Kate Colquitt with her. Flo and Kate got on like a house on fire. 'You should have had kids, Flo,' said Bel, who usually managed to be there when visitors came. 'You would have made a wonderful mother.'

It was a bitterly cold January afternoon, a month after her twenty-third birthday, when Kate turned up alone at the launderette. 'I hope you don't mind. I finish work at four.' She made a nervous face. 'Norman's off with a terrible cold and he's moved in with us for a while so me mam can look after him. I don't feel like going home just yet. I can't stand it when both of them get on to me.'

'I don't mind a bit, luv.' Flo sat the girl in her cubby-hole and made her some tea. Once she'd warmed up, she'd let her loose among her ladies, who'd soon make her forget her troubles. 'What do they get on to you about?' she asked.

Kate raised her shoulders and heaved a great sigh. 'Norman wants us to get married and me mam thinks it's a grand idea. He's so sweet. I can't remember a time when he hasn't been around, yet . . . oh, I dunno. It's worse now Grace is engaged – she's four years younger than me. Mam keeps saying I'll be left on the shelf, but I'm not sure if I care. I've started training to be a State Registered Nurse, and I'd like to finish before I settle down. In fact, sometimes I think I wouldn't mind staying single like you, Flo.'

She made herself useful, helping to untangle washing that had knotted together in the spin-driers, and getting on famously with the customers. She was still there when Flo was about to turn the Open sign to Closed, and Hugh O'Mara came in wearing the leather coat that had taken three months to save for, and which Nancy strongly disapproved of him wearing for work.

'Hugh!' Kate cried, her face lighting up with pleasure. 'I haven't seen you in ages.'

He appeared equally pleased to find her there. They sat on a bench, heads together, engrossed in conversation, and when the time came for Flo to lock up, the pair wandered off happily, arm in arm. A few days later, Kate turned up again, then Hugh arrived as if it had been prearranged. The same thing happened the next week and the next, until Flo got used to Tuesday and Friday being the days when Kate came to help untangle the washing, was joined by Hugh, and they would go off together into the night. She watched, entranced, as the looks they gave each other became more and more intimate. She realised they were falling in love, and couldn't have approved more. Her son would never find a prettier, nicer, more suitable wife than Kate Colquitt. She felt sure that even Nancy would be pleased when she was told. So far, everyone except Flo was being kept in the dark.

As the months crept by they were still in the dark. It was obvious to everyone in the launderette, including Mr Fritz, that the young couple were mad about each other, but Kate was too scared to tell her mam. 'She never liked Hugh much. She said there was something not quite right about his background.' She asked Flo how people got married in Gretna Green.

'I've no idea, luv,' Flo confessed, exasperated. She badly wanted to interfere, to tell them to get a move on, but held her tongue.

'Martha suspects Kate's got a secret boyfriend,' Sally remarked one day. Apparently there were nights when Kate didn't get home till all hours and refused to say where she'd been. Poor Norman Cameron was doing his nut.

Flo wondered if Kate was more scared of Norman than of her mam. 'He'd kill any man who laid a finger on her,'

Sally had said once. Perhaps she was scared for Hugh. Or maybe she was enjoying the clandestine nature of the affair, just as Flo had enjoyed her illicit meetings with Hugh's father all those years ago.

Secrecy must have run in both families, the O'Maras and the Clancys, because Kate and Hugh continued to see each other for over a year before everyone found out and all hell broke loose.

Flo had been out of bed barely five minutes when there was a pounding on the door. She opened it, still in her dressing-gown, and Sally came storming in, her normally placid face red with rage.

'Why aren't you at work?' Flo said, in surprise. Sally had been working full-time at Peterssen's the confectioner's to help with the wedding expenses, which were turning out to be horrendous. She wondered why her sister was so angry. Had Jock gone off the rails again? Grace was getting married on Saturday – perhaps she'd called it off or, even worse, perhaps Keith had.

Either Sally didn't hear the question or she ignored it. 'You knew, didn't you?' she said, loudly and accusingly.

'Knew what?' Flo stammered.

'About Kate and Hugh, soft girl. Nancy O'Mara passed the launderette on the bus last night and she saw them come out kissing and canoodling, so you must have known.'

'So what if I did?'

'You're a bloody idiot, Flo Clancy, you truly are. They're *cousins*!'

'I know darn well they're cousins. What's wrong with that?'

'They're *Catholic* cousins. The Church forbids that sort of thing between cousins.' Sally was staring at her sister belligerently, as if Flo had committed the worst possible crime. 'I hope they're not planning on getting married or anything daft like that.'

'They are, actually, once Kate plucks up the courage to

309

tell her mam. It's not illegal. As they don't know they're related, under the circumstances it never entered me head that anyone would care.'

'Holy Mary, Mother of God.' Sally groaned. 'Not care! You never heard anything like the commotion that went on in our Martha's last night. 'Stead of going home, Nancy went straight to Kirkby, then Martha sent for me. We had to turn Norman Cameron away as we didn't want him listening to private family business. Me and Nancy had left before Kate came home. Christ knows what Martha said to the girl. And what's Nancy supposed to tell Hugh?' She groaned again. 'Why the hell didn't you do something to stop it, Flo?'

Flo gave a little sarcastic laugh. 'Such as?'

'I don't know, do I?'

'I suppose,' Flo said slowly, conscious of her own anger grating in her voice, 'I could have said "Sorry, Hugh, but you're not to have any romantic notions about Kate Colquitt, because the truth is, I'm your mam, not Nancy, which means you're cousins." That might have stopped it, and I'm sure everyone would have been dead pleased, particularly Martha and Nancy.'

Sally's rage subsided. 'I'm sorry, luv. Our Martha got me all worked up. I hardly slept a wink all night, but I shouldn't have blamed you.' She looked curiously at her sister. 'Did you ever think about telling him when he got older?'

Flo had thought about it a million times. 'Yes, but I decided it wouldn't be fair. It might do the poor lad's head in, knowing the truth after all this time. He'd feel betrayed. All the deceit, all the lies. He might never want to see either me or Nancy again, and he'd be the one who'd suffer most.'

Sally shivered suddenly. 'It's cold in here.'

'I'm used to it. I'll turn the fire on.'

'What are we going to do, Flo, about Kate and Hugh?'

'Leave them alone, do nothing. Let them get wed with everyone's blessing.'

'Come off it, Flo. You must be out of your mind,' Sally said resignedly.

'I've never felt saner.' Flo's voice was cold. 'You, Martha and Nancy are nothing but a bunch of hypocrites. You pride yourselves on being great Catholics, yet you're quite happy to let me son be lied to all his life. Martha and Nancy caused this mess and I don't see why Hugh and Kate should suffer. Anyroad, marriage isn't out of the question. Perhaps they can get a dispensation?' She couldn't understand the need some people had to interfere in other people's lives. The young couple had fallen in love in all innocence, and they were perfect for each other. She was desperate for them to be left alone, not be parted over some silly rule that couldn't even be explained to them. Kate was a nice girl, but she was weak. Once Martha got to work on her, Flo couldn't imagine her holding out.

'I suggested a dispensation,' Sally said tiredly, 'but Martha and Nancy nearly hit the roof. How would they explain the situation for one thing? It's not just the parish priest who gets involved, it can go up as far as the bishop. And it means Hugh and Kate would have to know the truth.'

'But, Sal,' Flo tried to convey her desperation to her sister, 'we're the only ones who know they're cousins. It's not against the law of the land. If all of us kept our traps shut, Hugh and Kate could get married tomorrer.'

To her relief, Sally looked more than half convinced. 'There might be something in what you say,' she conceded. 'I'll go straight to Kirkby and see our Martha.'

Over the next few days, Flo tried to ring Sally several times from the telephone in the launderette, but either there was no reply or Jock said she was out somewhere, busy with arrangements for Grace's wedding. There was no sign, either, of Hugh or Kate. She prayed that Hugh wouldn't be annoyed or get into trouble if she rang him at work, but when she did, she was told he hadn't been in all week. Desperation turned to frustration when she realised there was nothing she could do. She thought of going to Martha's, or to Clement Street to see Nancy, but she didn't trust herself not to blurt out the truth if there was a row.

She had bought a new outfit for Grace's wedding: a pale blue and pink check frock with a white Peter Pan collar, a white silk beret and gloves, and high-heeled linen shoes. On the day, she went through the motions, chatting to the guests, agreeing that the bride looked like a film star in her raw silk dress. She did her best to get Sally on one side and pump her for information, but found it impossible and came to the conclusion that her sister was avoiding her. She wanted to know why Martha wasn't there and what on earth had happened to Kate, who was supposed to be a bridesmaid.

The ceremony had been over for twenty-four hours, the newly wedded couple had already landed safely in Tenerife to start their fortnight's honeymoon when Sally came to William Square to tell Flo that, at the same time as Grace had been joined in holy matrimony to Keith, in another church in another part of Liverpool, Norman Cameron had taken Kate Colquitt to be his wife. It had been a hastily arranged ceremony, with an emergency licence, attended by only a few friends. The bride wore a borrowed dress. They were spending two days in Rhyl for their honeymoon

'Martha made me promise not to tell you,' Sally said. 'She thought you might turn up and make a fuss.'

'Since when did I ever make a fuss?' Flo asked bitterly. 'I let her tread all over me. I let her ruin me life, just as she's ruined Kate's.' She thought of Hugh, who must have felt betrayed when he heard the news.

'You're exaggerating, Flo. Norman has loved Kate all his life. Now his dreams have come true and they're married. He'll make the best husband in the world.'

Perhaps Norman's dreams had been nightmares, because the stories that reached Flo in the months and years that followed scarcely told of a man who loved his wife.

Kate Colquitt, now Cameron, had become pregnant straight away. Late the following November she gave birth to a daughter, Millicent. Flo hadn't set eyes on Kate since the girl had walked out of the launderette on Hugh's arm just before Easter. She felt hurt at first, until a dismayed Sally informed her that Norman hardly let his new wife out of doors. 'She can go to the local shops and to church, but no further. I can't think why, but he doesn't trust her. Perhaps he knows about Hugh O'Mara, but Kate was single then so what does it matter?'

On impulse, Flo decided to go and see her niece at the maternity hospital. Afternoon visiting was from two till three so she arranged for the woman who did the morning shift at the launderette to hang on until she got back. 'I'm off to see me niece in hospital,' she said proudly. 'She's just had a baby, a little girl.'

'Would you like to see the baby first?' the nurse enquired, when Flo asked where she could find Mrs Kathleen Cameron.

'That'd be nice.'

The hospital bustled with visitors, mainly women at this time of day. 'That's her, second row back, second cot from the end.' The nurse's voice dropped to a whisper: 'I wouldn't want anyone else to hear, but she's one of the prettiest babies we've ever had.'

Flo was left alone to stare through the nursery window at the rows of babies. Some were howling furiously, their little faces red and screwed up in rage. A few were awake but quiet, their small bodies squirming against the tightly wrapped blankets. The rest, Millicent Cameron among them, were fast asleep.

'Aah!' Flo breathed. She was perfect, with long lashes quivering on her waxen cheeks, and a little pink rosebud mouth. Hugh had probably looked like that. She wondered if he'd also had such a head of hair: masses of little curls, like delicate ribbons. I never even knew how much he weighed, she thought. She pressed her forehead against the glass in order to see better. 'I wish you all the luck in the world, Millie Cameron,' she whispered. 'And I tell you this much, luv, I don't half wish you were mine.'

She left the nursery and went to the ward, but when she looked through the glass panel in the door, Martha was sitting beside Kate's bed. Flo sighed and turned away. On the way out, she took another long look at her new great-niece. She felt tears running warmly down her cheeks, sighed, wiped them away with her sleeve and went home.

Almost two decades passed before she saw Kate Cameron and her daughter again.

The girl came into the launderette and looked challengingly at Flo. She had jet black wavy hair, wide brown eyes, and enough makeup on her coarse, attractive face to last most women a week. She seemed to be wearing only half a skirt, and a sweater several sizes too small so it strained against her large, bouncing breasts. A cigarette protruded from the corner of her red, greasy mouth, and she spoke out of the other corner like Humphrey Bogart. 'Are you the one who's a friend of Hugh O'Mara?' she demanded in a deep, sultry voice.

Flo blinked. 'Yes.'

'He said I could leave a message with you. If he comes in, tell him I'll meet him outside Yates's Wine Lodge at half past eight.'

'Rightio. What name shall I say?'

'Carmel McNulty.' The girl turned, flicked ash on the floor, and strode out, hips swaying, long legs enticing in their black, fishnet tights.

Flo's ladies were all eyes and ears. 'Was that Carmel McNulty?' one enquired eagerly.

'Apparently so,' Flo conceded.

'I hope that nice Hugh chap isn't going out with her. She's no better than she ought to be, that girl.'

Everyone seemed to know or have heard of Carmel NcNulty.

'Didn't her last feller end up in Walton jail?'

'She was a hard-faced bitch even when she was a little 'un.'

'I'd give my lads the back of me hand if any of 'em dared to look twice at Carmel McNulty.'

Flo listened, appalled. In the year since Kate had got married, Hugh had never mentioned her name, or been seen with another girl. Surely he didn't have designs on Carmel McNulty. Maybe she had designs on him. Hugh was a catch – one of the best-looking men in all Liverpool, with his own car and a good, steady job. Perhaps she was prejudiced, but Flo couldn't understand why there wasn't a whole line of women queuing to snap him up.

Having demolished Carmel McNulty, Flo's ladies began to put her back together again. 'Mind you, Carmel's got her hands full with her mam. How many kids has Tossie got?'

'Twenty?' someone suggested.

'Twenty!' Flo squeaked.

'Nah, I think it was eighteen at the last count.'

'Carmel's the eldest and she's had a babby to look after ever since she wasn't much more than a babby herself.'

'She still looks after 'em. I saw her only the other Sunday pushing a pramload of kids down Brownlow Hill.'

'You can't blame her wanting a good time after all that. How old is she now?'

'Nineteen.'

Six weeks later Hugh O'Mara and Carmel McNulty were married. The bride held her bouquet over her already swelling stomach. Flo went to the church and watched through the railings. It was more like a school outing than a wedding, as hordes of large and small McNultys chased each other around the churchyard.

Nancy O'Mara hadn't changed much: she still wore her black hair in the same enormous bun and the same peculiar clothes, a long flowing red dress and a black velvet bolero. She looked as if at any minute she might produce castanets and start dancing, except that her face was set like yellow concrete in an expression of disgust. According to a rather sullen Hugh, she loathed Carmel and Carmel loathed her. Nancy had only come to the wedding because of what people would say if she didn't.'

'It serves you right,' Flo murmured. 'If it weren't for you and our Martha, Hugh would be married to Kate by now and everyone would be happy, apart from Norman Cameron.' Instead, Kate was stuck with a man who kept her a prisoner, and Hugh was marrying a woman he didn't love. There was nothing wrong with Carmel: once she'd got to know her, Flo liked the girl. She was big-hearted, generous to a fault, and as tough as old boots. But she wasn't Hugh's type. Flo clutched the railings with both hands. Her son was doing his best to look as if he was enjoying his wedding day, but his mam could tell he was as miserable as sin.

Flo went through the backyard of the terraced house in Mulliner Street and let herself into the untidy kitchen. She shouted, 'Is he ready for his walk yet, Carmel?'

Carmel appeared in slacks and one of Hugh's old shirts, a cigarette between her lips. She looked exhausted. 'The little bugger kept us awake half the night laughing! I'll be glad to be shut of him for a few hours, I really will.'

A small boy burst into the kitchen and flung his arms around Flo's legs. 'Can we go to the Mystery? Can we play ball? Can I have a lolly? Can I walk and not sit in me pushchair?'

Smiling, Flo loosened the arms around her legs and picked the child up. 'You're a weight, young man!'

Tom O'Mara was over-active and inordinately precocious for a three-year-old. Even as a baby, he had hardly slept. He didn't cry, but demanded attention with loud noises, which got louder and louder if he was ignored. As he grew older, he would rattle the bars of his cot and fling the bedding on the floor. Lately, he'd begun to sit up in bed in the early hours of the morning chanting nursery rhymes or singing, and now, apparently, laughing. He could already read a little, count up to a hundred and tell the time. Carmel said she'd never come across a child quite like him. 'I feel like knocking bloody hell out of the little bugger, but you can't very well hit a kid for being happy!'

When relations between Carmel and her mother-in-law broke down completely and Nancy was barred from Mulliner Street, Flo grasped the opportunity and offered to take her grandson out in the mornings.

'Would you, Flo?' Carmel said gratefully. 'Honest, I don't know where Hugh found a friend like you. I wish you were me mother-in-law, I really do.'

It was June, not exactly hot, but quite warm. Flo played football with Tom until her limbs could no longer move. She lay on the grass and declared herself a goal post. 'You can kick the ball at me, but don't expect to have it kicked back. I'm worn out.'

Tom sat on her stomach. He was a handsome little chap with the same devil-may-care expression on his face as his grandad. 'Are you old?'

'Is fifty-one old? I'm not sure.'

'Dad's old.'

'No, he's not, luv. He's nineteen years younger than me.'

'Mam says he's old.'

Things were not well with the O'Maras. In the evenings, after being stuck in the house all day with a child who would crack the patience of a saint, Carmel was anxious for a break, a bit of excitement. Hugh, who worked hard and was rarely home before seven, preferred to stay in and watch television. Flo had offered to babysit and did occasionally at weekends, but in the main the couple stayed put, much to Carmel's chagrin. She declared loudly and aggressively that she was bored out of

317

her skull and might as well be married to an old-age pensioner.

Flo couldn't help but sympathise. Hugh was growing old before his time. He already had a stoop, his hair was thinning, his gentle face was that of a man weighed down by the cares of the world. He was unhappy. Flo could see it in his dead, green eyes. He didn't seem to care when Carmel started going out alone. She was going clubbing, she announced. Hugh was welcome to come with her if he wanted, otherwise he would just have to like it or lump it.

After the launderette had closed, Flo often went to Mulliner Street to sit with her son. She had never thought she would have the freedom to be alone with Hugh, Nancy out of the picture. Even so, she would have preferred the circumstances to be different. They didn't talk much. He sat with his eyes fixed on the television, but she could tell he wasn't really watching.

'Do you see much of Kate nowadays?' he asked one night.

'No, luv. I haven't seen her in years.'

'I wonder how she is.'

She didn't dare repeat the things Sally told her – Hugh was miserable enough. 'She's had another baby, a little girl called Trudy,' was all she said.

Another night he said, 'Why did you wait for me outside St Theresa's that day, Flo? I've often wondered.'

'I wanted to meet you. I knew your dad, remember?'

'That's right. What was he like? Mam never talked about him much, except that he died on that submarine.'

'The *Thetis*. He was an ould divil, your dad. Full of himself, dead conceited. Women were after him like flies.' Perhaps she should have come up with a more positive, more flattering description, but at least she hadn't told him his dad had lied through his teeth.

Hugh allowed himself the glimmer of a smile. 'Not like me.'

'No, I'm pleased to say.' She didn't like the way he

318

always talked about the past, as if he'd given up on the future. Usually, Tom could be heard upstairs, where he'd been put to bed hours ago, making aeroplane or car noises, but Hugh seemed unaware of his delightful son and his attractive wife – who might be as common as muck but was basically a good girl, anxious to be a good wife. Carmel was only twenty-three: she needed a husband who did more than just bring home a regular wage. If only Hugh would take her out now and then, she'd be happy, but he didn't seem to care.

In the Mystery, Tom bounced several times on her stomach. 'Strewth, luv,' Flo gasped. 'Are you out to kill me?'

'Can we go to your house for a cuppa tea?'

'There isn't time, Tom. It'd make me late for work.' Sometimes when it was raining she took him to William Square and read him books, which he adored. 'I'll get you an ice lolly, then take you back to your mam.'

He gave her stomach a final, painful bounce. 'Rightio, Flo.'

When she returned the kitchen was still in a state. It was unlike Carmel not to tidy up – she usually kept the house spotless. Flo went into the living room and could hear voices upstairs, one a man's. 'Carmel,' she shouted.

It was several minutes before Carmel came running down. She'd changed into a mini-skirted Crimplene frock. Her lipstick was smudged.

Flo frowned. 'Is Hugh home?'

The girl looked at her boldly. 'No.'

'I see.'

'I doubt if you do, Flo. If you were married to that drip Hugh O'Mara you might see then.'

'It's none of me business, is it, girl?' Flo considered herself the last person on earth entitled to criticise another woman's morals, but her heart ached for her unhappy, lacklustre son.

Tom had turned five and been at school only a matter of weeks when Carmel walked out for good. 'She's gone

to live in Brighton with some chap she met in a club,'
Hugh said wearily. 'She said she would have taken Tom
but her new feller doesn't want to be landed with a kid.
"Flo will look after him," she said.'

'I'll be happy to.' It would never have come to this if
I'd been allowed to keep me baby, Flo thought sadly.

'There won't be any need,' Hugh said, in his expressionless voice. 'I'm moving back in with me mam. She'll
take care of Tom. She's not seen much of him 'cept when
I took him round.'

Flo turned away, her lips twisted bitterly. She supposed
that that was the last she would see of her grandson, but on
the day that the family moved to Clement Street to live
with Nancy, Tom O'Mara burst into the launderette after
school. He was everything his father had never been:
untidy, uninhibited, full of beans. 'Hiya, Flo,' he sang.

'What are you doing here?' she gasped. He'd come half
a mile out of his way to get there. She noticed he had a
skull and crossbones drawn upside down on both knees.
'Mrs O'Mara will be worried stiff wondering where
you've got to.'

'You mean me gran? Don't like her. Me mam always
said she was an ould cow. Can I have a cuppa tea, Flo?'
He settled on a bench and allowed himself to be made a
fuss of by Flo's ladies.

'How on earth could Carmel McNulty bring herself to
walk out on such a little angel?'

'He's the spitting image of Hugh.'

'He's the spitting image of Carmel.'

From then on, Tom never failed to turn up for a cup of
tea after school. Nancy couldn't control him and Flo
didn't even try.

3

Mr Fritz was seventy-five, the same age as the century,
and becoming frail. His limbs were swollen and twisted

with arthritis, and it was heartbreaking to see him strug-gle up and down the basement steps with his stick. Even worse, more important parts of his body had ceased to work. He and Flo went to the Isle of Man rarely nowa-days, and then only to lie in each other's arms.

'I'm sorry, Flo,' he would say mournfully, 'I'm like one of my old washing-machines. I need reconditioning. A new motor wouldn't do me any harm.'

'Don't be silly, luv. I'm not exactly in tip-top condi-tion meself,' Flo would answer. In fact, she was as fit as a fiddle and missed making love.

Increasingly his family came over from Ireland to see him. Flo found it difficult to recognise the hard-eyed middle-aged men and women as the children she'd once played with, taken for walks and to the pictures. Their attitude towards her was unfriendly and suspicious. She sensed that they were worried she might have undue influence over the man with whom she'd shared a house for so long, a house that was now worth many thousands of pounds, added to which there were the six launder-ettes. All of a sudden, the little Fritzes seemed to regard their father's welfare of great importance.

'Harry would like me to live with him in Dublin,' Mr Fritz said, the night after Ben and Harry had been to stay for the weekend. 'And I had a letter from Aileen the other day. She never married, you know, and she wants me to live with her!' He chuckled happily. 'It's nice to know my children want to look after me in my old age, don't you think, Flo?'

'Yes, luv,' Flo said warmly. She felt frightened, con-vinced that it was their inheritance his children were concerned with.

'I told Harry that, if I went, I'd want nothing to do with Stella.' Flo went cold. He was actually considering Harry's offer. 'He said they hardly see her nowadays. She's still on the same farm and the toilet facilities are barely civilised, which is why none of them go to visit.'

It turned out he just wanted to spend a long holiday in

Dublin, to get to know his children properly again. 'I would never leave you, Flo,' he said. 'Not for good.'

While he was away, the launderettes could virtually run themselves, but for the second time in her life, Flo was left in charge of Mr Fritz's business. This time though, an agent would collect the money each day and bank it. Flo would be sent a cheque to pay the staff, with the power to hire and fire should the need arise. Herbie Smith, a reliable plumber, had promised to be on call in case any of the machines broke down.

Harry came over from Ireland to fetch his father, and Flo longed to remind this cold, unpleasant man that he'd once had a crush on her. Mr Fritz made his painful way down the steps towards the taxi that would take them to the Irish boat. He gave Flo a chaste kiss on the cheek. 'I'll be back in three months. Keep an eye on upstairs for me.'

'Of course, luv. I've done it before, haven't I?' Flo had no idea why she should want to cry, but cry she did.

'So you have, my dear Flo.' There were tears in his own rheumy eyes. 'The day I came home from the camp and found you here will always remain one of my fondest memories, though not as precious as our weekends together.' He grasped both her hands in his. 'You'll write, won't you? Has Harry given you the address in Dublin?'

'I'll write every week,' Flo vowed. Harry was looking at them darkly, as if all the family's suspicions had been confirmed. 'C'mon, Dad,' he said, making no attempt to keep the impatience out of his voice. Flo felt even more frightened for Mr Fritz, the man she had loved since she was thirteen, not romantically, not passionately, but as the dearest of friends. 'I'll miss you,' she sobbed. 'The place won't seem the same.'

'It's not for long, Flo. The three months will go by in a flash.'

He'd been gone less than a fortnight when Flo heard noises coming from upstairs as if furniture was being moved around. She ran outside. The front door was open and two men were struggling down the steps with the big pine dresser from the kitchen. A removal van was parked further along the square.

'What's happening?' she cried.

'We're taking the good stuff to auction and leaving the rubbish behind,' she was told brusquely.

Flo returned to the basement, knowing that her worst fears had been realised. Mr Fritz would never again live in William Square.

Soon afterwards, a gang of workmen descended on the house. Each floor was being converted into a separate flat, and Flo feared for herself. She'd always insisted on paying rent, but it was a nominal sum. What if the little Fritzes put up the rent so that it was beyond her means? What if they threw her out? She couldn't imagine living anywhere else, where she might have to share a kitchen and lavatory with other tenants. Flo had grown used to her subterranean existence, where she happily ignored the real world. The years were marked for her not by the election of various governments, Labour or Conservatives, the Cuban crisis or the assassination of an American president, but by films and music, *Gone with the Wind, Singing in the Rain, The Sound of Music*: Paul Newman, Marlon Brando, the Beatles . . .

'Mr Fritz would never throw you out!' Bel scoffed.

'I'm not sure if he's got much say in things any more,' said Flo.

'You can always live with me.'

'That's very kind of you, Bel, but I couldn't stand you bellowing down me ear all day long. And it's not just the flat I'm worried about, what about me job?' Each week, she sent her rent, along with a little report: a woman had left and she'd had to take on someone new, a machine had needed servicing and she enclosed Herbie Smith's bill. The address Harry had given her turned out to be a firm of accountants, and although she frequently enclosed a letter for Mr Fritz, there'd been no reply so far, and she wondered if her letters were being passed on.

Four families moved in upstairs, but Flo heard nothing about her own situation. 'Perhaps the little Fritzes are playing games with me,' she said to Bel. 'Lulling me into a sense of false security, like.' She might come home one day to find the locks changed and her furniture dumped on the pavement.

Bel made one of her famous faces. 'Don't talk daft. Y'know, what you need is to get away for a while, leave all your troubles behind. I've been thinking, why don't we go on holiday? A woman at work is going to Spain for two whole weeks on a charter flight, I think it's called. It's ever so cheap and she said there's still a few places left.'

'Spain! I've never been abroad.'

'Neither have I since I left the forces, but that's no reason not to go now. We might cop a couple of fellers out there.'

The small swimming pool shone like a dazzling sapphire in the light of the huge amber moon, and the navy sky was powdered lavishly with glittering stars. Less than fifty feet away, the waters of the Mediterranean shimmered and rustled softly and couples were clearly visible lying clasped in each other's arms on the narrow strip of Costa Brava sand. Somewhere a guitarist was strumming a vaguely familiar tune, and people were still in the pool, although it was past midnight. There was laughter, voices, the clink of glasses from the outside bar.

Flo, on the balcony of their room on the second floor of the hotel, refilled her glass from the jug of sangria and wondered if you could buy it in Liverpool. Wine was so cheap that she and Bel were convinced they would never be sober if they lived in Spain.

They'd been lucky to get a room with a view like this. The guests on the other side of the building could see only more and more of the hotels that cluttered the entire length of coast.

Someone opened a door by the pool and a blast of music filled the air: The Who, singing, 'I can See For Miles . . .' 'Miles and miles and miles,' Flo sang, until the door closed and all she could hear was the guitarist again. Every night at the Old Tyme Dance while she was being led sedately around the floor to the strains of 'When Irish Eyes Are Smiling', or 'Goodnight, Eileen', she thought enviously of the youngsters in the other ballroom leaping around madly to the sound of Dire Straits or ABBA.

Bel hadn't bothered to inform her that the group they were travelling with were old-age pensioners. Flo had been horrified when they got on the plane and she found herself surrounded by people with hearing aids and walking sticks and not a single head of hair in sight that wasn't grey.

To her further consternation, there were actually a few wolf-whistles – in this company, two women in their mid-fifties must seem like teenagers: Bel still managed to look incredibly glamorous, though her lovely red hair was in reality lovely grey hair that had required a tint for years.

There were still five more days of the holiday to go, and Flo supposed she'd had quite a good time. During the day, they wandered round Lloret del Mar, admiring the palm trees and the sparkling blue sea. They bought little trinkets in the gift shops. She got Bel a pretty mosaic bracelet, and Bel bought her a set of three little brass plaques that had taken Flo's fancy. Then they had found a bar that stocked every liqueur in existence and were sampling them one by one. Flo had sent cards to every- one she could think of, including Mr Fritz, though she had no faith that he would get it. Why had he never written as he'd promised? It was six months since he'd left William Square and she worried about him all the time. If she didn't hear soon, she resolved to go over to Ireland in search of him, even though she didn't have a proper address.

Evenings, they went dancing. Flo wrinkled her nose: she hated being taken in a pair of gnarled, sunburnt arms for the Gay Gordons or the Military Two-step or, somewhat daringly, a rumba, played to a slow, plodding beat in case it overtaxed a few dicky hearts. Mr Fritz was old, but in her eyes he had always remained the same lovely little man with brown fuzzy hair and twinkling eyes she'd first met in the laundry. The other night one sly old bugger in fancy shorts had had the nerve to get fresh during the last waltz.

'You're no spring chicken yourself,' Bel snorted, when Flo complained.

'I wouldn't mind dancing with fellers me own age,' Flo said haughtily. Bel had taken up with Eddie Eddison, a widower in his seventies, who came from Maynard Street, though it seemed daft to come all the way to Spain to click with a feller who lived only two streets away in Liverpool.

Most nights when Bel wasn't looking, Flo slipped away. She enjoyed sitting on the balcony, staring at the sky, listening to the sounds by the pool, drinking wine. When she got home, she might do something with her backyard, paint the walls a nice colour, buy some plants and a table and chairs, turn it into one of them patio things. It would be pleasant to sit outside in the good weather. The flat could get stuffy when it was hot.

That's if the flat remained hers. Oh, Lord, Bel would be cross if she knew she was worrying about the flat again. Flo rested her arms on the balcony and stared down at the pool. Even at this hour children were still up. Two little boys, one about Tom O'Mara's age, were splashing water at each other in the shallow end. If only she could have brought Tom with her. He would have had the time of his life. Instead of dancing with men old enough to be her father, or sitting alone on a balcony, she could have been down at the pool with Tom. It seemed a normal, everyday thing to do, to bring your grandson on holiday, but the things that normal, everyday people did seemed to have passed her by.

Flo sat back in her chair and sighed. Another few days and they could go home. She couldn't wait, though she wouldn't let Bel know she was homesick. She would laugh and smile, and look cheerful, pretend to be having a great time, make the best of things as she always had.

Out of the corner of her eye, she glimpsed a star shoot across the sky. It disappeared into the infinite darkness – or was it just her imagination that she could see the faintest, barely discernible burst of yellow, which meant that millions and millions of miles away there'd been an almighty explosion?

The idea made her shudder, and she remembered being told as a child that God had created the world in seven days. 'But did He create the universe as well, Dad? Did He create the sun and the moon and the stars at the same time?' She couldn't remember what his answer had been.

It was ages since she'd thought about Dad. Living in Burnett Street had been perfect when he was alive and Martha had yet to assume the role of Being In Charge. Flo had never planned on getting married, but had just known that one day she would and that she would have children, two at least. Then, as if the shooting star had struck its target, Flo felt as if every muscle in her body had instantly wasted, as if every bone had turned to jelly. All that was left was her heart, which pounded like a hammer in her cavernous chest.

She'd spent her entire adult life in the way she was spending this holiday! Making the best of things, pretending to enjoy herself. *Waiting for it to end!*

'Oh, Lord!' The awful feeling passed as quickly as it had come, but in the mad scramble of thoughts that followed she knew that she should have made the best of things in a more practical way, by marrying Gerard Davies, for instance, or almost any one of those other young servicemen. It was no use blaming Martha. It was Flo's own fault that she'd wasted her life.

The basement flat felt unusually chilly when she arrived home from Spain to find three letters waiting for her on the mat. She went through them on her way to the kitchen to put the kettle on, aching for a cup of tea made with ordinary leaves instead of those silly teabags. Two were bills, but she stopped in her tracks when she saw the name and address of a solicitor in Castle Street on the third. She'd never had a letter from a solicitor before, and her hands were trembling as she tore it open, convinced that the little Fritzes were demanding formally that she quit the flat.

The heading was enough to make her burst into tears. 'Re: Fritz Erik Hofmannsthal (deceased).'

He was dead! *Mr Fritz was dead* – and not one of his children had bothered to let her know. Flo forgot the tea and poured a glass of sherry instead. Her imagination ran riot as she thought of all the different ways he might have died, none of them pleasant. She'd like to bet he'd wanted to return to William Square and be with her, but his children hadn't let him. Lovely, long-cherished memories flicked through her brain: the laundry on Tuesdays when he'd brought cream cakes, the day Stella had taken the photograph of him and his girls outside – the family had just come back from Anglesey and seemed so happy. How strange and cruel life could be that it should all have turned so sour. She recalled their first weekend in the Isle of Man, two old friends comfortably together at last.

It was a long time before she could bring herself to read the letter, to learn that dear Mr Fritz had bequeathed her the leasehold of the basement flat, as well as the launderette in Smithdown Road. The letter finished, 'We would be obliged if you would telephone for an appointment so that arrangements can be made for various papers to be signed.'

'Mr Hofmannsthal's children are seeking to question the validity of his will,' the solicitor informed her. He was younger than expected, not the least bit pompous, and from his build and his broken nose, looked like a rugby player or a boxer. 'But as same was dictated in my presence ten years ago while my client was in full possession of his senses, there is no question of it not being valid.'

'I don't think the little Fritzes liked me very much,' Flo said, in a small voice. 'Least, not since they stopped being little.'

'They like you even less now, which isn't surprising. You're very much the fly in the ointment. They want the house in William Square put on the market, but it won't fetch anything like it would have done had the basement been included.' The solicitor smiled, as if this pleased him enormously.

'I'm sorry,' Flo said weakly.

'Good heavens, Miss Clancy!' he exploded. 'Sorry is the very last thing you should be. It's what my client, Fritz Hofmannsthal, wanted, and I'm sure he had the best reason in the world for doing so.'

Flo felt herself go pink, wondering what Mr Fritz might have told him. 'Do I still have to look after the other launderettes?' she enquired.

The solicitor was so outraged to discover that she'd been 'acting as manager', as he put it, for six whole months without even so much as a thank-you from the little Fritzes, that he suggested putting in a claim against the estate for 'services rendered'. 'We'll demand ten pounds a week for the period involved, and probably end up with five. Will that suit you?'

Flo was about to say she didn't want a penny, but changed her mind. Even if she gave away the money, it was better than the little Fritzes having it. 'Five pounds a week would be fine,' she said.

The whole thing went into another of Flo's invisible

boxes marked 'Secret'. If people found out, they would wonder why Mr Fritz had remembered her so generously. She owned her own property. She owned her own business. But no one would ever know.

In his day Edward Eddison had been a professional magician and had appeared halfway down the bill in theatres all over the country. When he married Bel Szerb in a register office two months after their holiday in Spain, he produced two white doves from his sleeve, which fluttered around the room, much to the annoyance of the registrar who disapproved of confetti, let alone live birds.

Bel, gorgeous in lavender tulle and a feathered hat, screamed with laughter when a bird settled happily on her head.

Flo, still shaken by the strange, unsettling thoughts she'd had in Spain and the loss of Mr Fritz, felt depressed when the ceremony was over, and Bel and Eddie departed to Bournemouth on their honeymoon. The newly-weds intended to live in Eddie's house in Maynard Street, and Bel planned on doing the place up from top to bottom. Flo tried to cheer herself up by decorating her own flat. She painted the walls white and the big wooden beams across the middle of the room black. The plaques Bel had bought her in Spain went well against the glossy surface, and when she mentioned this to her ladies, they presented her with several more. She painted the little yard a pretty rose pink, bought garden furniture and plant-holders, but when it came to new furniture for inside, she couldn't bring herself to part with a thing. After all, Mr Fritz and Jimmy Cromer had struggled downstairs with the settee and chair out of Stella's sitting room, as well as the big sideboard, which was probably an antique – if the little Fritzes had known it would probably have gone for auction, along with the lovely oak wardrobe and chest-of-drawers in the bedroom. As for the brass bed, she'd no intention of changing it for one of those padded-base things like they'd had in Spain – it had been like sleeping on wooden planks. She even felt quite fond of the little rag rug in front of the fire, which had been there when she arrived. She made do with buying pictures for the walls and armfuls of silk flowers to arrange in vases, and a nest of round tables to put the vases on. The big table she folded against the wall because she rarely used it. Nowadays, she ate on the settee in front of the television. Last Christmas, Bel had bought her a coffee table for this very purpose, an ugly thing, Flo thought secretly, with legs like clumps of giant onions.

The only light that glimmered through this dark period was her grandson Tom, seven years old and a continual thorn in the side of Nancy O'Mara, just like his grandad. Tom came and went as he pleased, no matter what Nancy told him. Hugh, of whom Flo saw little these days, appeared to have given up on his son and took no interest. On Sundays, Flo would return from Mass to find Tom sitting on the steps outside her flat, ready to spend the day with her. She took him to matinée performances at the cinema. Once she got used to the idea that she was her own boss and could take time off whenever she pleased, she and Tom sometimes went to football matches to see Everton or Liverpool play.

Tom was at Flo's place too often to be kept hidden in one of her secret boxes, so Bel got used to finding him there, though she thought it most peculiar. 'You're obsessed with the O'Maras, Flo,' she hissed. 'Tommy, Hugh, now little Tom.'

Gradually the dark period passed. It was a relief when the unpleasant middle-aged couple on the ground floor moved out, and a beautiful black girl, still a teenager, with two small children, moved in. But Flo was shocked to the core when she discovered that Charmian was one of the women who took up position along the railings of the square each night. Even so, it was hard not to say, 'Good morning,' or 'Isn't it a lovely day?' or 'We could do with some rain, couldn't we?' when they came face to face. The two became rather wary friends, although Charmian continually felt the need to defend her doubtful and precarious lifestyle. 'Me husband walked out on me. No one'll give me a job with two kids under school age. How else am I supposed to feed 'em and pay the rent?' she demanded aggressively, the first time she came down to the basement flat.

'Don't go on at me, luv,' Flo said mildly. 'It's your life. I haven't uttered a word of criticism, have I?'

'I can see it in your eyes. You're disgusted.'

'No, I'm not, luv. The disgust is in your own eyes. I think you're ashamed, else you wouldn't go on about it so much.'

Charmian stormed out, but returned the following night to say, 'You're right, but I don't know another way to keep me head above water.'

Flo said nothing. As the months rolled by, she listened patiently while Charmian struggled loudly and vocally with her conscience. When the woman who worked the morning shift in the launderette gave in her notice, Flo casually mentioned it to her upstairs neighbour. 'There'll be a job going the Monday after next, eight till two. The pay isn't bad, enough for the rent and to keep two kids without too much of a struggle.'

Charmian glared at her. 'Is that a hint?'

'No, luv, it's an offer.' Flo shrugged. 'It's up to you if you take it.'

'What about the owner? He mightn't want an ex-pro working in his bloody launderette.'

The girl scowled, but she hated what she was doing and Flo could tell that she was tempted. 'The owner will go on my recommendation.'

'And you'd recommend me when you know . . .' Two large tears rolled down the satiny cheeks. 'Oh, Flo!'

Eddie Eddison didn't last long. He died a happy man in the arms of his glamorous wife only eighteen months after their wedding. Bel was left with a hefty weekly pension, a gold Cortina saloon, and immediately began to take driving lessons.

Charmian gave up her job when she married the emergency plumber, Herbie Smith, who moved into the ground-floor flat with his ready-made family. Unlike his dad, Tom O'Mara didn't desert his friend Flo when he started comprehensive school. He was a cocky little bugger, full of confidence and sure of his place in the world. It didn't bother him being seen going to the pictures on Sunday afternoons with a middle-aged woman, or two middle-aged women if Bel decided to come. Bel had transferred her affections from Gregory Peck to Sean Connery.

1983

When his dad died Tom was fifteen, and the cockiness, the confidence, turned out to be nothing but a sham.

The firm in Anfield swore that the accident had been caused by negligence on the part of their workman, Hugh O'Mara. The house he was rewiring was dripping with damp: he'd been a fool to try fitting a plug in a socket that was hanging off the wall, the existing wiring having been installed half a century before. Knowing O'Mara, he'd probably had only half his mind on the job. His heart hadn't been in it for years. He was usually in either a trance or a daydream, the boss was never sure. Anyroad, the stupid sod had been thrown across the room, killed instantly.

Flo didn't go to the funeral. She couldn't have stood it if Nancy, the Welsh witch, had behaved as she had outside the gates of Cammell Laird's, weeping and wailing and making an exhibition of herself. At least she'd had a claim on Tommy, but she'd none on Hugh.

It was as if Hugh had already been dead a long time, Flo thought, strangely unmoved, as if she had already mourned his loss. Tom, though, was distraught. He came into the launderette after the funeral, his face red and swollen as if he'd been crying for days. Flo took him into her cubicle out of the way of her ladies' curious eyes.

'No one wants me, Flo,' he wept. 'Me mam walked out, me dad went and died on me, and Gran doesn't like me.'

He was almost as tall as her. Flo's heart ached as she stroked his bleak, tearstained face. If only her own history could have been rewritten, how would things have turned out then? 'I like you, luv,' she whispered.

'Promise not to die, Flo. Promise not to go away like everybody else.' He buried his face in her shoulder.

'We've all got to die sometime, luv. But I won't go away, I promise that much. I'll always be here for you.'

Tom took a long time to recover from the loss of his dad. When he did, there was a callousness about him that saddened Flo, a chill in his green eyes that hadn't been there before. He left school before he could sit his O levels and moved out of his gran's house to doss down in the homes of various friends, sleeping occasionally on Flo's settee if he was desperate. He got a job helping out at St John's market. 'I'm going to start a stall meself one day,' he boasted. 'There's no way I'm working for someone else all me life, not like me dad.'

He brought her presents sometimes: a portable wireless for the kitchen, expensive perfume, a lovely leather handbag. She accepted them with a show of gratitude, although she was worried sick that they were stolen. He even offered to get her a colour telly at half the list price.

'No ta, luv.' She would have loved a colour telly, but felt it might encourage the criminal tendencies she was convinced he had.

★

Bel was doing her utmost to persuade her friend to retire in May, when she turned sixty-five. 'You've worked non-stop since you were thirteen, Flo,' she said coaxingly. 'That's fifty-two long years now. It's time to put your feet up, like me.'

Tact had never been one of Bel's stronger virtues: the reason behind her solicitude for Flo's welfare was obvious. 'You only want me to retire so you'll have company during the day.'

'True,' Bel conceded. 'But that doesn't mean it's not a good idea.'

The launderette provided a good, steady income, and Flo had no intention of giving up, not while she remained fit and well, though she got tired if she was on her feet for too long. Her ladies had changed over the years, but they were still the irrepressible, good-humoured Scousers she loved. Nowadays not all were poor: they went on holiday to places like Majorca and Torremolinos and brought brasses back for Flo's walls.

When the letter came from the property firm in London offering to buy her out for twenty-five thousand pounds, her first instinct was to refuse. The firm was acting for a client who wished to turn the entire block into a supermarket. But the offer had come as a boon to Flo's neighbours. Hardly anyone ordered coal at a coal office, these days, when they could phone from home. Who'd buy wallpaper and paint from a little shop that had to charge the full price when it could be got for much less from a big do-it-yourself store? The watch-repairer, the picture-framer, the cobbler all reported that business was at an all-time low. Flo couldn't bring herself to turn down the offer and spoil things for those who were desperate to take it.

There were thousands of pounds in the bank now and not much to spend it on. Flo went to see the solicitor in Castle Street and made a will. She'd never thought she'd have property and money to leave behind, but she knew who she wanted to have it. She put the copy at the bottom of the papers in the bureau – one of these days, she must clear everything out. There was stuff in there she'd sooner people didn't know about when she died.

She bought the coveted colour television, a micro-wave oven, because they seemed useful, and a nice modern music centre, hoping that the man in Rush-worth and Draper's didn't think a woman of her age foolish when she chose a dozen or so records: the Beatles, Neil Diamond, Tony Bennett. She didn't *feel* old, but later the same day, when she was wandering around Lewis's department store, she saw an elderly woman, who looked familiar with rather nice silver hair, coming towards her. As they got closer, she realised she was walking towards a mirror and that the woman was herself. She *was* old! What's more, she looked it.

When Bel was told she laughed. 'Of course you're old, girl. We all grow old if we don't die young. The thing is to get the best you can out of life till it's time to draw your last breath. Let's do something dead exciting this week-end, like drive to Blackpool. Or how about London for a change?' She was fearless in the car and would have driven as far as the moon if there'd been a road.

'Oh, Bel,' Flo said shakily, always grateful for her friend's unfailing cheerfulness and good humour. 'I'm ever so glad I went to Birkenhead that morning and met you.'

Bel squeezed her hand affectionately. 'Me too, girl. At least one good thing came out of that business with Tommy O'Mara, eh?'

'Where did we go wrong, Flo?' Sally cried. She asked Flo the same question every time they met.

Flo always gave the same reply. 'Don't ask me, luv.'

Ten years before, Grace, Keith and their two sons had upped roots and gone to live in Australia. Sally and Jock only occasionally received a letter from their daughter, and Grace ignored their pleas to come and visit. Jock was becoming surlier in his old age, Sally more and more unhappy. One of these days, she said bitterly, she was convinced she would die of a broken heart.

'I could easily have done the same when me little boy was taken,' Flo said. She thought of Bel with her three husbands and three lost babies. In her opinion, Sally was giving up far too easily. 'You and Jock have still got each other, as well as your health and strength. You should go out more, go on holiday. It's never too late to have a good time.'

'It is for some people. You're different, Flo. You're made of iron. You keep smiling no matter what.'

Flo couldn't remember when she'd last seen her sister smile. It was impossible to connect this listless, elderly woman with the happy, brown-haired girl from Burnett Street.

Sally went on, 'I remember when we were at school, everyone used to remark on me sister with the lovely smile.'

'Why don't you come to the pictures with me and Bel one night?' Flo urged. 'Or round to William Square one Sunday when Charmian usually pops down for a sherry and a natter.'

'What's the use?'

Grace didn't bother to cross the world to be with her father when her mother died. Sally's heart gave up one night when she was asleep in bed, but perhaps it really had broken.

Bel went with Flo to the funeral on a dreary day in March. It was windy, dry, sunless. Grey clouds chased each other across a paler grey sky. Jock held up remarkably well throughout the Requiem Mass. When Flo had gone to see him, he said that he intended moving to Aberdeen to live with his brother, and she could tell that he was looking forward to returning to the city of his birth. It was as if he and Sally had dragged each other down in their misery, frozen in their grief, unable to come to terms with the loss of Ian, and Grace's indifference. Flo had expected that Sally's death would be the last straw for Jock; instead, it seemed to have released him from a state of perpetual mourning.

It was obvious that Martha, stiff with self-importance, was relishing her role of Being in Charge. Jock, a bit put out, said that she'd taken over the funeral arrangements, had ordered the coffin, the flowers, seen the priest. In the cemetery, in the wind, beneath the racing clouds, Flo saw the gleam in her sister's eyes behind the thick-lensed glasses that she remembered well, as if this was a military operation and she'd like to tell everyone where to stand. When the coffin was lowered into the grave, Jock suddenly put up his hand to shield his eyes and Martha poked him sharply in the ribs. It wasn't done for a man to cry, not even at his wife's funeral. That gesture put paid to the vague thoughts Flo had had of exchanging a few polite words with her sister.

The Camerons were there; Norman handsome and scowling – but, oh, Kate had changed so much, her lovely hair chopped short, her once slim figure swollen and shapeless. There was a battered look on her anxious face, no bruises, bumps or scars, but the same look some of Flo's ladies had, which told of a hard life with many crosses to bear. Yet her eyes remained bright, as if she retained a hope that things would get better one day – or perhaps the light in her eyes was for her children, who would have made any mother proud. Millicent, whom Flo had last glimpsed in the hospital, only a few days' old, had grown into a graceful, slender young woman, with none of her mother's vulnerability apparent in her lovely, strong-willed face. She was with her husband, as was Trudy, whose wedding had been only a few weeks before. Trudy was pretty, but she lacked her sister's grace and air of determination. However, it was the son, Declan, who took Flo's breath away. A slight, delicate lad of ten, it could have been her own little boy she was staring at across the open grave. The Clancys might well be pale-skinned, pale-haired and thin-boned, but they had

338

powerful genes that thrust their way forcefully through each generation. There was no sign of Albert Colquitt in Kate, no indication that Norman Cameron was the father of these three fragile, will o'-the-wisp children. There was another girl, Flo knew, Alison, who had something wrong with her and was in a home in Skem.

'Aren't we going for refreshments?' Bel was disappointed when the mourners turned to leave and Flo made her way towards the gold Cortina.

'I'm not prepared to eat a bite that's been prepared by our Martha,' Flo snapped. 'And don't look at me like that, Bel Eddison, because there's not a chance in hell I'll tell you why. If you're hungry, we'll stop at a pub. I wouldn't mind a good stiff drink meself.'

Sally had gone, to become a memory like Mam and Dad, Mr Fritz and Hugh. Each time someone close to her died, it was as if a chapter in her life had come to an end. One day, Flo too would die and the book would close for ever. She sighed. She definitely needed that drink.

September, 1996

Flo pressed her fingers against her throbbing temples, but the pressure seemed only to emphasise the nagging pain. She knew she should have been to the doctor long ago with these awful headaches but, as she said to Bel, 'If there's summat seriously wrong, I'd sooner not know.' There were times when the pain became unbearable, and all she wanted to do was scream: it felt as if an iron band was being screwed tighter and tighter around her scalp. A glass of sherry made it worse, two glasses made it better, and with three she felt so light-headed that the pain disappeared. Getting drunk seemed preferable to having her head cut open and someone poking around inside, turning her into a vegetable. Peter, the nice young lad from next door who reminded her so much of Mr Fritz, got rid of the bottles for her because she felt too embarrassed to put them out for the binmen.

A concerned Bel had persuaded her to have her eyes tested, but the optician said she had excellent sight for a woman of her age, though he prescribed glasses for reading.

Mam, Flo remembered, had been terrified of letting a doctor near her with a knife. The girls used to get upset, worried that she'd die. But Mam had only been in her forties. Flo was seventy-six, nobody's wife, nobody's daughter, with no children to care if she lived or died. Bel would miss her terribly, Charmian less so, what with a husband, two kids and three grandchildren to look after since Minola had gone back to school. Tom O'Mara didn't need her so much now that he was married with a family, two lovely little girls, though he still came to William Square regularly, at least once a week, often bearing food from the Chinese takeaway around the corner and a bottle of wine. She never asked how he made the money he was so obviously flush with. After years spent living on his wits, involved in ventures that were barely this side of legal, he was now something to do with a club that he adamantly refused to talk about. Flo suspected she was probably the only person on earth who knew the real Tom O'Mara, the man who loved and fussed over her tenderly, and brought her little presents. Outside the four walls of her flat, she'd like to bet that Tom was an entirely different person – even his wife and children might not know how soft and gentle he could be. Bel, who couldn't stand him, had to concede it was decent of him to put Nancy in a posh nursing-home in Southport when her mind went haywire and she could remember nothing since the war.

Music filled the basement flat, reaching every nook and corner, wrapping around her like a magic blanket woven from the dearest of memories. And shadows from the lamp Tom had brought from abroad passed slowly over the walls, the figures lifesize. When Flo felt especially dizzy, the figures seemed real, alive. He had brought the record, too, not long ago. 'Close your eyes,' he said teasingly, when he came in. 'I've got you a prezzie, a surprise.'

So Flo had closed her eyes, and suddenly the strains of 'Dancing in the Dark' came from the speakers at each end of the room. Her eyes had snapped open and for several seconds she felt muddled. She'd told no one that this was the tune she and Tommy had danced to in the Mystery more than half a century ago. 'What made you buy that, luv?' she asked querulously.

'You've been humming it non-stop for months. I thought you'd like to hear it sung by an expert. That's Bing Crosby, that is, the one who sings "White Christmas."'

'I know who Bing Crosby is. It's lovely, Tom. Ta very much.'

At first she didn't play the record much, scared of raking up the painful past, but lately, as her head got worse and she couldn't read, not even with her new glasses, she played it more and more often. It was soothing, better than a book, to remember her own romantic affair, more passionate and tragic than anything she'd ever read. She saw herself dancing under the trees with her lost lover, making love, whispering what was to be their final goodbye.

Bel had told her she should exercise more, not sit like a lump in front of the telly getting sozzled every day. 'I ride for miles every morning on me bike in the bathroom,' she hooted loudly, through her ghastly new dentures, which were much too big and made her look like an elderly Esther Rantzen.

'I'm seventy-six, Bel,' Flo said indignantly. 'I'm entitled to be a sozzled lump at my age.' What would she have done without Bel? Without Charmian and Tom, Mr Fritz, Sally, even Hugh, her son, for a while? She'd been lucky to have so many people to love and love her back.

'What time is it?' She looked at the clock. Just gone six. But was that night or morning? What month was it?

What year? It was frightening when she couldn't remember things, when she forgot to go to bed, forgot to eat, forgot to watch one of her favourite programmes on the telly. Once she'd nearly gone out in her nightie. One of these days she'd forget who she was. It wasn't that she was losing her mind like Nancy. She smiled. No, the trouble was, she was either in terrible pain or as drunk as a lord.

She went over to the window and lifted the curtain, but still couldn't tell if it was dawn or dusk. A thick mist hung in the air, suspended a few feet from the pavement. There were noises in the square, but there always were, no matter what the time; a car drove away, she could hear people talking, someone walked past and she could see less of them than usual because their knees were shrouded in mist. She heard the clink of milk bottles. It must be morning, which meant she'd been sitting up all night.

The record, which she'd played countless times, came to an end yet again. Oddly, the ensuing silence felt louder than the music. It was a buzz, as if she was surrounded by a million bees. As she listened to the silence, Flo's mind drained of everything and became completely blank. She sat on the chest in front of the window and wondered what was she doing in this strange room full of shadows. There was too much furniture, too many ornaments, too many flowers. She didn't like it. A memory returned, crawling like a worm into her head: she lived in Burnett Street with Mam and Dad.

'But what am I doing here?' she asked of the strange room and the shadowy figures passing overhead. There was no answer. Had she been visiting someone? Whose house was this?

'Is anyone there?' Still no answer. Flo pressed her hands together distractedly, trying to make up her mind what was the best thing to do. Get away from this place, obviously, go home. Even better, go into work early, get on with the pressing left over from yesterday. It would give Mr Fritz a nice surprise when he came in.

She saw a coat hanging behind the door that looked

faintly familiar. She put it on and went outside. A man was running towards her dressed in a funny red outfit, just like Father Christmas. 'Mr Fritz!' She smiled.

The man reached her. 'It's Peter Maxwell, Flo, from next door. I've been for a run. But what are you doing out so early, luv? It's awful damp. You'll get a chill.'

'I've got to go somewhere,' she said vaguely.

'Would you like me to come with you?' The man was looking at her worriedly.

'No, ta,' she told him pleasantly.

She set off into the wet mist at a fast pace, along Upper Parliament Street and into Smithdown Road, passing closed shops and empty shops, new buildings and old, Clement Street and Mulliner Street, names that seemed familiar, though she couldn't remember why. She looked for the dress shop, which had that lovely lilac frock in the window — she'd seen it only yesterday and intended to buy it. Later, in the dinner hour, she might well come back and get it. But she couldn't see the shop anywhere. The fog didn't help — perhaps that was why no trams were running — she could scarcely see across the road. Worse, when she turned into Gainsborough Road, there was no sign of the laundry. A brick building stood in the place where the old wooden shed should be, a clinic, with notices in the window advertising a playgroup, ante-natal classes, a mother and toddler group.

'Oh, Lord!' Flo groaned. The fog seemed to have entered her head. It lifted briefly when she read the notices and wondered how she had got to Gainsborough Road. Why was her heart racing? Why did her legs feel so weak? She didn't realise she'd walked for miles with the energy of a young girl. The fog drifted in again, smothering the pain and everything that was real.

'I'll go and see Mam and Dad.' She made her way towards Burnett Street. The fog in her head cleared for a second when she stood outside the three terraced proper-ties at the end of the street and remembered that they'd been built on the spot where the Clancys' and two neighbouring houses used to be. She stood for a moment, staring up at the tiled roofs, the small windows. The door of the middle house opened and a man in a donkey jacket and greasy overalls came out.

'Are you after something, missus?' he demanded irritably, when he found an elderly woman standing virtually on his doorstep.

'I used to live here,' said Flo.

'You couldn't have.' He scowled. 'Me and the missus were the first to move in when the place was built forty years ago.'

The fog had descended again, enveloping her brain. 'There used to be a bay window and steps up to the door.' She put a trembling hand to her forehead. 'Did it get bombed? Is that what happened?'

'Look, luv,' the man's gruff voice became kind, 'you seem a bit confused, like. Would you like to come inside and me missus'll make you a cup of tea, then take you home? You live round here, do you?'

'I thought I lived here.' Flo wanted to cry. She said fretfully, 'Is the Mystery still there?'

'Of course it is, luv, but this isn't a good time to go walking in the park.'

But Flo was already on her way, nineteen years old, with a red ribbon in her hair, about to meet Tommy O'Mara outside the gates for the first time. She felt as if she was walking towards her destiny, and that afterwards nothing would be the same again.

He wasn't there. He was probably inside waiting under one of the trees, which were shrouded in a veil of mist. The wet grass quickly soaked through her shoes as she made her way towards them. A whiff of reality returned when she noticed the road leading from gate to gate, and the sports arena glimmering palely through the haze, things that hadn't been there before.

It was 1996, not 1939. 'Flo Clancy,' she breathed, 'you're making a right fool of yourself this morning.' She'd better catch the bus home while she had the sense to do it. But she hadn't brought a handbag, she had no money. She wept aloud. 'I feel too weary to walk all that way back.'

She plodded back towards the gates. It wouldn't be a bad idea to take the red ribbon out of her hair. It must look dead stupid on an ould woman. She blinked when she found there was no ribbon there. Martha must have snatched it off before she left the house.

Poor Martha! Flo had never before had such a feeling of sympathy for the sister who'd never had much happiness in her life, if any. 'It's time to forgive and forget, luv.' Sally must have said that a hundred times over the years.

'I'll go and see her tomorrer,' Flo vowed. 'I'll take her a bunch of flowers.' At that moment, she couldn't precisely remember where Martha lived, but it would come. The fog inside her head kept lifting and falling, she kept drifting backwards and forwards in time, and the present was becoming confused with the past. She was leaving through the gates when she heard a shout. 'Flo!'

Flo turned. Her face melted into a smile, the dimples deepened in her wrinkled face, she could feel the brightness shining from her eyes as she watched Tommy O'Mara emerge from the white mist that swirled and floated in and around the Mystery and come towards her. She stood stock-still, waiting for him, waiting for him to take her in his arms

She waved. Oh, he was a divil of a man, with his swaggering walk, a red hanky tied carelessly around his neck, an old tweed cap perched jauntily on the back of his brown curls. She had never stopped loving him. She never would.

'Flo, girl,' he called again.

'Tommy!' Flo held out her arms to welcome her handsome lover, who had never told a lie, had meant everything he'd said, who would have married her one day if he hadn't gone down with the *Thetis*. They would have lived happily ever after with their child. Then, from somewhere within the hazy clouds, she heard the orchestra of her dream a lifetime ago, playing 'Dancing in the Dark'. Her tired old body was swaying, this way and that, to the music that swelled and quivered in the smoky, dew-spangled morning.

She didn't hear the lorry backing slowly through the fog and the gates of the Mystery. It hit her full square, flinging her forward, and the phantom figure of Tommy O'Mara was the last thing Flo saw before she died.

The lorry drove away, the driver unaware that he'd hit anyone.

It was a young lad on his way home from his paper round who found the body. He stared at the old woman lying face down on the path. Was she dead, or had she just fainted?

He knelt down and gingerly turned the old girl over by the shoulder. She was dead all right, he could tell, but, Jaysus, never in all his life before had he seen such a brilliant smile.

Millie

I

The church hall was an Aladdin's cave of treasures; stalls with handmade jewellery, tie-dyed T-shirts, embroidered waistcoats, patchwork cushions, pottery, paintings, intricately moulded candles far too elegant to burn. But I'm sure I wasn't prejudiced in thinking our Trudy's stall was the most outstanding of all – and the cheapest.

Colin had added a shelf to the back of a pasting table so that the glassware could be exhibited on two levels. Nightlights flickered in painted wineglasses and tumblers that had been placed between the taller bottles so that the flames glittered through the jewel-coloured glass, the patterns outlined lavishly in gold or silver. The stall was alive with every imaginable hue – 'Like a rainbow on fire,' I said, and sighed with satisfaction when everything was done. I'd come early to help Trudy set up.

Trudy was shaking, as if she was about to take the starring role in her first play. 'What if I don't sell a single thing?'

'Don't be daft. I've got my eye on at least five bottles for Christmas presents.'

'I can't take money off me sister.'

'What nonsense! There's no room for sentiment now you're a businesswoman, Trude.'

'Oh, Mill!' Trudy glanced left and right at the other stallholders, most of whom had finished setting up and were waiting impatiently for the doors to open at eleven o'clock. 'I feel dead conspicuous.'

'You look perfectly okay to me. Would you like a cup of tea?'

'I'd love one. But don't stay away long, Sis,' she called nervously, as I went towards the room behind the stage where tea and coffee were being served. 'I can't do this on me own.'

It turned out to be a day when the Camerons came of age, I thought afterwards, when we appeared to be just like any other family. James came at exactly half past eleven, as promised. Declan was already there, deeply interested in the process of tie-dying. Mum arrived at midday, her face red and bothered. Beads of perspiration glistened on her brow, although the November day was cold. I went to meet her. 'Your dad turned dead nasty when he realised I was going out,' she panted. 'He insisted I made his dinner first. I've put it in a low oven for when he comes home from the pub, but I daren't think what it'll be like by then.' She dropped her handbag, bent to retrieve it, then dropped the car keys and her gloves. 'How's our Trudy getting on?'

'Her bottles are selling like hot cakes. Half have already gone. She's not asking nearly enough.' Trudy hadn't even noticed I was no longer there. Flushed with confidence, she was coping with her busy stall on her own. I clutched my mother's arm. 'Mum, could you come back to Flo's with me when this is over? There's something I want to show you.'

'What on earth can that be, luv?'

'You won't know till you've seen it, will you?'

She shook her head. 'I couldn't possibly, Millicent. Your dad was in a terrible mood. It'd be best if I went straight home.'

'In that case I'll come over tonight and fetch you,' I said firmly. 'There's something you've got to see.'

James had already been introduced to Trudy. It was time he met my mother. How could I ever have felt ashamed, I wondered, with a lump in my throat, of this warm-hearted, kind woman, whose face shone with pleasure as she said, 'I'm ever so pleased to meet you, James, luv. Does your mam call you Jim or Jimmy?'

When Colin arrived with Melanie and Jake after dinner, Trudy's stall was almost empty. Starry-eyed and triumphant, she'd taken over two hundred pounds. 'I can't believe people are actually willing to pay for me bottles. Just imagine, they'll be on window-sills all over Liverpool.' She promised to paint more for me over the next few days. Mum was in her element. She wandered around, saying, 'I see you've bought one of me daughter's bottles. Aren't they lovely?' If people were inclined to stop and chat, she'd tell them about her other daughter. 'That's her over there,' I heard her say more than once. 'That's our Millicent. She works for an estate agent in Liverpool town centre. And that's me son, the lad in the brown jersey. He's going to college next year.'

To everyone's astonishment, Gran turned up and bought the last of Trudy's bottles. 'I couldn't very well not come, could I?' she grunted sourly. 'Someone gave me a lift. I hope our Kate came in the car so she can take me home.'

I studied my grandmother carefully. This was the woman who'd given Flo's baby to Nancy O'Mara. Oh, how I'd love to find out exactly what had happened. But this wasn't the right time – would there ever be a right time to raise such an emotive subject?

We all went into the room behind the stage for a cup of tea. Trudy folded up her stall and joined us, which meant that there were three Camerons, four Daleys, Martha Colquitt and James – who were, inexplicably, having an animated conversation about football. The only person missing was my father, which probably accounted for the jubilant atmosphere.

'I never thought I'd witness this,' Colin whispered to me.

'Witness what?'

'Well, it's almost a case of Happy Families, isn't it? It's the way you'd expect any normal family to behave. Everyone's had a great day, including the kids.'

When it was time to leave, I arranged to pick up Mum

at seven o'clock and take her to Flo's flat. My father would have gone out again by then.

'I wish you'd tell me what it's all about,' she said.

'What is it all about?' James asked later. We'd driven into town in our separate cars and met up in a restaurant for a meal. 'I'd hoped we'd spend the rest of the day together.'

I ignored the last comment. 'It's something truly amazing and wonderful,' I said happily. 'Auntie Flo's left her flat and all her money, nearly twenty-four thousand pounds, to Mum. I only found a copy of the will last night. I want her to be at Flo's when she reads it for herself.'

When I drew up outside, the house in Kirkby was in darkness. Surprised, I went round to the back. The kitchen door was unlocked, which meant that someone must be in. 'Mum?' I shouted. 'Declan? Is anybody home? It's me.'

A faint noise came from upstairs, a whimper. Alarmed, I switched on the light on the stairs and went up. 'Mum?' I called.

'In here, luv.' The voice, little more than a whisper, came from the front bedroom. I pushed open the door and reached for the light switch.

'Don't turn the light on, Millicent.'

I ignored her. In the dim glow of the low wattage bulb, I saw my mother half sitting, half lying in bed. Her right eye was swollen, her lip split and bleeding. She had bruises on both arms. She looked utterly wretched, but despite everything, there was still that indefatigable look in her eyes, as though she was the most resilient victim in the world, who would survive whatever came her way. I was convinced that if a tank rolled over her, she would pick herself up and carry on as if nothing had happened.

'Mum! Oh, Mum, what's he done to you?' Rage enveloped me like a cloak and I could scarcely speak. If

350

my father had been there, I think I could easily have killed him.

'Close the curtains, luv. I don't want people seeing in.'

I drew them with an angry flourish, and sat on the bed. Mum winced. 'It's not as bad as it looks,' she said. 'I tried to ring you, stop you coming, but all I got was your machine.'

'I've been in town with James.' I forced myself to speak calmly.

'Mrs Bradley dabbed some TCP on it, and she bathed me eye an' all. I'm just a tiny bit tipsy too. She gave me this great big glass of brandy. She wanted to call the police, but I wouldn't let her.' Over the years, Mrs Bradley had frequently threatened to report Norman Cameron, but Mum had always stopped her. 'I told her this was the first time he'd hit me in years, which is the God's honest truth.'

'What brought it on, Mum?'

She shrugged, then winced again. 'His dinner was ruined. I knew it would be, stuck in the oven all that time.'

'You mean this . . .' I gestured towards the black eye, the split lip, the bruises – '. . . is solely due to a ruined dinner?'

'Only partly. I was out an awful long time, Millicent, nearly four hours. And, oh, it was a lovely afternoon.' Her eyes brightened when she thought about the day that had gone. 'I really enjoyed meself, what with our Trudy doing so well, Colin and the kids being there, your gran turning up, you and Declan. James is ever such a nice chap, I really liked him.' She managed a laugh. 'I even bought meself a pair of earrings to wear at your wedding – little red flowered ones to go with me best coat.'

'Oh, Mum!' I lightly touched her fading hair.

She sighed. 'He could never stand me being happy. I daren't ever come in with a smile on me face that I got from somewhere else, it always riled him. It makes him feel shut out, and he hates that. Today I just didn't think.

I suppose I expected him to be pleased about Trudy and everything. 'Stead, he just lashed out at me. He'd been getting more and more worked up the longer I stayed out.'

'He's always been a miserable bugger,' I said acidly.

There was a long silence. Mum seemed to have drifted off into a world of her own. A motorbike growled to a halt outside. I got up and looked through the curtains. A girl from a house opposite came out, got on to the pillion, and the bike shot away. I stayed at the window, though there was no longer anything to see apart from the orange street lights, the still houses, the occasional car driving by. A group of boys wandered past, kicking a football to each other. Then my mother spoke in a soft, far-away voice: 'I remember once, I was only a titch, two or three. We'd been out for the day, your gran and me. It was late when we got back. Did I ever tell you we lived with Elsa Cameron for a long time? Anyroad, Elsa was out, and we heard noises coming from the cupboard under the stairs, terrible sobs. The poor little lad had been shut in there in the dark for hours. You never saw anything like his eyes, all feverish and bright, as if he'd have gone mad if he'd been left there much longer. He was only six.'

'Who are you talking about, Mum?' I asked perplexed.

'Why, your dad, luv. After that, your gran never left him alone with Elsa again. She had that illness, they call it purple depression or something now. She should never have been allowed to keep a child.'

I felt myself grow cold. I recalled the photo in Flo's flat of the grim-looking woman with the beautiful baby on her knee, the baby that had become my father. I tried to visualise the monster who had conducted a reign of terror throughout our childhood as a terrified little boy of six. It was hard. 'Why have you never told us this before, Mum?' I asked shakily.

'Your dad made me swear never to breathe a word to another soul. I suppose he felt ashamed. I'd be obliged if you didn't mention to him that I'd told you.'

'It might have helped us to understand.' It only might have.

'I suppose things would have been different if I hadn't let him down,' she said, half to herself.

'In what way, Mum?'

Her face went blank, as if she'd said too much. 'Oh, it doesn't matter, luv. It's a long time ago now. Do you fancy a cup of tea? I'm dying for one meself. I haven't had one since I came home.'

'I'll make one straight away. Where's Declan?'

'He's not back yet. He went off with the couple who made them funny-coloured T-shirts.'

While I made the tea my mind was in a whirl. I had no idea what to think. No matter what had happened to my father, it was impossible to excuse the things he'd done. It wasn't Mum's fault, or his children's, that his own mother had suffered from puerperal depression. Why take it out on us?

When I returned to the bedroom with the tea, Mum said, 'What's the big surprise for me at Flo's? Or are you still not prepared to tell me unless I'm actually there?'

'I'd forgotten all about it!' I took hold of both Mum's hands. 'Prepare yourself for a shock. Flo's left you her flat and all her worldly wealth. Twenty-three thousand, seven hundred and fifty-two pounds and elevenpence to be precise.'

I didn't leave until my father came home. The back door opened, I kissed Mum goodbye, and went downstairs. He was coming through the kitchen, unsteady on his feet, eyes blurred.

'If you lay a finger on my mother again,' I said, in a grating voice that made my ears tingle, 'so help me, I'll kill you.' He looked at me vacantly, as if he wasn't sure where the strange voice had come from. 'Do you understand?' I persisted.

He nodded. I paused, my hand on the front door, feeling oddly perturbed by the look of naked misery on

353

his face, which I probably wouldn't have noticed before. Then he said something that didn't make sense, but nevertheless made my stomach curl.

'It's all your fault.'

I was scratching through my mind, trying to think of a response, when I realised he was drunk, talking rubbish. I shook myself and left.

I'd tried to talk Mum into leaving there and then. Flo's flat was ready to move into. Wasn't it fortunate I hadn't touched a thing? The place was exactly as Flo had left it.

'There's no hurry, luv,' she said. 'Your poor dad'll be feeling dead sorry about things for a week or two. I'd sooner tell him, face to face, when I'm ready to go. I owe him that much, and I won't be scared, not now I've got money and somewhere to live. It makes me feel strong.' She still looked stunned, as if she couldn't get over the news of her good fortune. 'I remember saying to Flo how much I liked her flat when I first went there. I can't believe it's mine,' had been her initial reaction.

'Don't tell Dad about the money yet,' I warned. 'If he got his hands on it, every penny would go in no time on the lottery and the horses.'

'I may look a fool, Millicent, I've probably been a fool for most of me life, but I'm not that stupid.'

'Come and have a proper look round in the morning,' I said excitedly. 'I'll take the day off work. I've still got two days' holiday left, I was leaving them till Christmas.' My mind was working overtime, sorting out my mother's life. 'You need only stay at Flo's for a few months, then you can sell it and buy a similar place in Oxford.'

'Mmm, I suppose I could,' Mum said, in a dreamy, rather vague way that made me wonder if she could ever bring herself to leave Kirkby when it came right down to it.

'Do you still love him?' I demanded sharply.

'No, Millicent. I never loved him. The trouble is, you

might find this hard to believe, but he loves me, he always has. I'm not sure how he'll manage with me not here.' She laughed girlishly when she saw me frown 'Don't worry, I'm going. I'd already planned to, hadn't I? It's thirty years last Easter since we were married, so I've done me stint. You and Trudy have got your own lives, Declan will be off soon. Now, Alison comes first.'

'And you? What about you?' I was doing my best to hide my impatience. 'Isn't it time you put yourself first?'

'I'll be doing that when there's just me and Alison.'

Later, when I parked the car in William Square, I thought sadly that this would be one of the last nights I would spend there. But the place was staying in the family, at least for a while. Even if that hadn't been the case, I could still come back to see Bel and Charmian. As I went down the steps to the basement room, I saw that the light was on and my heart lifted eagerly. I opened the door. Tom O'Mara was sitting on the settee watching television, his feet resting on the coffee table. Everything that had been good or bad about the day that would shortly end was forgotten.

'Hi,' he said. Our eyes met. 'You're late.'

'No, you're early.'

'Whatever.' He stood up and took me in his arms and we locked together in a long, lingering kiss. I couldn't wait for us to make love, I couldn't wait a minute longer. Neither could he. He picked me up and, still kissing, carried me into the bedroom.

Later, when it was over, Tom fell asleep, but I had never felt more wide awake, as if little electric currents were passing endlessly around my head. The affair had to end some time. He would never get divorced, and I didn't want him to. Perhaps, now that I was moving back to Blundellsands, it was time to call a halt. But could I bring myself to turn him away? Would he let me? Had I the will to resist if he flatly refused to be turned away?

My restless brain refused to stop working. Would

Mum be safe in Toxteth, even if it wasn't going to be for ever? It hadn't crossed my mind till now. I thought of the few people I knew who already lived here: Charmian and Herbie and their children, Bel, Peter Maxwell, nice, respectable, honest people, like Flo. Anyway, Mum would be safer anywhere in the world, including Toxteth, than with her husband.

When I got up in the morning, I must clear the bureau of the things that gave away Flo's secrets. I'd keep the love letters, the photo of the little boy who looked so much like Declan, and the drawing he'd done of 'MY FREND FLO'. No wonder Tom had felt so drawn towards her. He was her grandson. I recalled how indifferent he'd been with Nancy.

'Don't worry, Flo,' I whispered. 'Everything's safe with me.'

At half past nine next morning, I asked Charmian if I could use her phone – I never remembered to bring my mobile to William Square – and called Stock Masterton to say I wasn't coming in. Oliver answered. 'Diana's back,' he hissed. 'She's ruling the roost already.'

I groaned. 'I'm not looking forward to tomorrow.'

Next, I called the solicitor in Castle Street who'd dealt with Flo's affairs and made an appointment for late that afternoon.

Downstairs again, the bureau looked pathetically empty, the papers I wanted to keep already stowed in the boot of the car, the rest thrown away. I dusted everywhere, swept the yard, pulled the last few dead leaves off the plants, had a word with the same black cat that had watched me before. Then I cleaned the kitchen and the bathroom, although they'd scarcely been used, but I wanted everywhere to look perfect for when Mum came. The flat looked different today, not just cleaner but more impersonal. I didn't feel quite so much at home.

I'd barely finished when there was a knock on the door. It was too early for Mum. Perhaps it was Charmian inviting me upstairs for a coffee. I rather hoped so. Charmian had been thrilled to learn that my mother was moving in below. I was sure they'd get on well together.

'Gran!' I remarked in astonishment, when I opened the door. 'Come in.'

'Your mam phoned with the news this morning,' Martha Colquitt said grumpily, as she crunched into the living room in the crêpe-soled, fur-lined boots that were almost as old as I was. She wore a camel coat, and a jersey hat shaped like a turban with a pearl brooch in the middle. The room instantly began to reek of mothballs and liniment. 'I had an appointment at the women's hospital, so I thought I'd come and look the place over.'

'What's wrong? I mean, why did you have to go to hospital?' None of us Cameron children had much affection for our grandmother, but it was impossible to imagine life without her bad-tempered presence.

Gran was predictably bad-tempered with her reply. 'I dunno what's wrong, do I?' she barked. 'They took X-rays and did tests. I have to wait for the results till I know what's wrong.' Her voice softened. 'So this is where she lived, our Flo. I always wondered what it looked like.' She walked into the room. 'This is her all over. She liked things to be pretty.'

I watched her closely. I'd never seen her face so gentle, almost tender, as she surveyed her sister's room. 'Take your coat off, Gran,' I said. 'Would you like a coffee?'

'I never touch coffee, you should know that by now. I'll have tea. And I'll not take me coat off, thanks all the same. I'm not stopping long.'

'I'm afraid there's only powdered milk.'

Gran shrugged. 'I suppose that'll have to do, won't it?' Her head was cocked on one side, she was almost smiling as she watched Flo's lamp turn round. 'I'm dying for a ciggie and it tastes better with a cup of tea.'

When I came back, she was examining the drawing on the wall over the mantelpiece, which I'd meant to take down.

'What does this say?' She peered at it closely, her nose almost touching the wall. 'I can't see in these glasses, and I left me reading ones at home. I could never get along with them bi-focals.'

'It says, "MY FREND FLO". It was done by someone called Hugh O'Mara.'

Gran took a step back, but continued to stare at the drawing. I would have given anything to know what was going on inside her head. A faint hum came from upstairs, Charmian was vacuuming the carpets. One of Minola's children gave a little shriek. Gran was still looking at the drawing, as if she'd forgotten I was there. I licked my lips, which suddenly felt dry. I didn't want to upset her, but I *had* to know.

'He was Flo's son, wasn't he, Gran? She had him by a man called Tommy O'Mara who died on the *Thetis*. He probably never knew she was pregnant.' I licked my lips again before plunging on. 'You gave him away to Tommy's wife, Nancy.'

'What in God's name are you talking about, girl?' She spun round, wobbling slightly when her clumsy boots became tangled with each other. I felt myself shrivel before the angry eyes behind the thick lenses. 'What the hell do you know about it?'

'I know because Nancy told me.'

'Nancy!' The yellow lips split in a hoarse, unbelieving laugh. 'Don't talk rubbish, girl. Nancy's dead.'

'No, she isn't, Gran. I met her the other week. She's in a nursing-home in Southport. She said . . .' I screwed up my eyes and tried to remember word for word what Nancy had said. I visualised the old liver-spotted face, the hot dark eyes, the long fingers clawing at my arm. 'She said, "Your Martha gave him to me fair and square. You're not getting him back. I'll kill him first." Her's mind's gone,' I finished. 'She thought I was Flo.'

Gran's face crumpled and she started to cry, an alarming and uncomfortable sight. She stumbled back into a chair and lit a cigarette with shaking hands.

'Gran!' I put the tea down, ran across the room and knelt at her feet. 'I didn't mean to upset you.' I was angry with myself for being too curious, too uncaring, yet I knew I wouldn't have hesitated to do the same thing again.

'It's all right, Millicent. Where's that tea?' There was a loud sniff, a quick removal of spectacles to wipe her eyes, a conscious effort to pull herself together. She looked embarrassed, unused to revealing any emotion except anger. Her hands were still shaking as she took the tea, though she'd recovered enough to grimace disapprovingly at the mug. She said, 'I never regretted what I did. It's hard for you young 'uns to realise the disgrace it was in those days for a baby to be born on the wrong side of the blanket. The whole family would have suffered.' Her face was hard again, her tone fierce. This was the grandmother I had known all my life. 'Nancy kept her head down and Hugh well hidden for a good six months. We never dreamed Flo would recognise the baby after all that time.'

She wasn't sorry! Despite everything that had happened, losing her sister for a lifetime, she still wasn't sorry. Frowning, she jabbed the air with her cigarette. 'I can't understand this business with you and Nancy. Who told you about her? Who took you to see her in Southport?'

I sank back until I was sitting cross-legged on the floor, the heat from the gas-fire hot on my shoulders. 'Tom O'Mara did. He's Nancy's grandson – or Flo's grandson. I'm not sure how to describe him.'

'Tom O'Mara!' Gran's eyes narrowed. She stared, her gaze so penetrating, so intensely suspicious, that I knew straight away she'd guessed what was going on. I felt my cheeks burn.

At the same time, to my surprise, her face turned parchment white. Her bottom lip quivered. She looked a hundred years old. She put the half-full mug on the floor, the cigarette fell in, sizzled briefly and floated on the top, but she didn't seem to notice. She Immediately lit another. 'I reckon there's a curse on the Clancys and the O'Maras,' she said. Her voice was dull, listless, almost funereal. It scared me.

'What do you mean?'

'Well, first there was Flo and Tommy.' She took a long, hard drag on the cigarette, and the end glowed bright red. 'Then our Kate and Hugh. Would you believe they actually wanted to get married?' She gave a little strained laugh, and nodded at me incredulously.

'Why couldn't they get married?' I ventured. *I'd nearly had Hugh O'Mara for a father!*

'Because they were cousins, of course,' Gran explained, as if to a child. 'It's not allowed – least, it wasn't then. Fortunately, Norman stepped in like the good lad he always was, even though he knew he was accepting soiled goods. Poor Norman . . . Until then, he'd worshipped the ground your mam walked on. He would have made the best husband in the world if she hadn't spoiled things.'

'I don't know what you're talking about, Gran.'

'I'm talking about your mam being up the stick when she married Norman Cameron.' She still spoke in the same flat, dull voice, which seemed at odds with the rather coarse expression. 'We told her Hugh O'Mara had done a bunk once he knew she was pregnant, else we'd never have got her up the aisle.'

'Who's we?' I said weakly.

'Me and Nancy. As if we could have asked for a dispensation, like our Sally suggested. Imagine telling the Church authorities about our Flo's dirty little secret.' She almost choked on the last words.

Upstairs the vacuuming had stopped. I heard the front door open and Charmian come out with the children. I felt totally mixed up. My brain, which had been working so well the night before, could no longer take anything in. What was this leading up to?

'If Mum was pregnant when she married my father,' I said slowly, 'then what happened to the baby?'

'I'm looking at her.'

'Me?'

'Yes, Millicent, you.' Gran's eyes had shrunk, skull-like, deep into their sockets. She took another long puff on her cigarette, and blew the smoke out in an equally long sigh. 'You know what that means, don't you?'

I felt myself tingle all over. 'Hugh O'Mara was my father?'

'That's right. It means something else an' all. Jesus, Mary and Joseph!' She groaned. 'It was bad enough with our Kate! I bet the devil's laughing up his sleeve at the moment.' She leaned forward, her eyes boring into mine. 'Think, Millicent, think what it means.'

So I thought very hard and eventually came up with the answer. 'It means that Tom is my brother, my half-brother,' I breathed.

2

'Millie,' Diana said importantly, 'Will you come here a minute, please?'

'Yes, miss.' I abandoned the photocopier and stood in front of Diana's desk, my hands clasped meekly behind my back. June grinned and Elliot stifled a giggle.

Diana looked at my suspiciously, not sure if she was being made fun of. She flourished a sheet of paper. 'This property you went to see last week, the one in Banks. On the particulars you describe the upstairs as having a recess with a window. You quite clearly don't know that this is what's called an oriel window. Would you change it, please, before we run the details off?'

The first thing I'd done when I was promoted was buy a book on architecture so that I could accurately describe any unusual aspects of a building. 'I'm afraid you've got it wrong, Diana,' I said sweetly. 'An oriel is a recess in the projection of a building. There's no projection on the house in Banks, just a recess.'

Diana waved the paper again. 'I beg to differ. I think I know what an oriel window is by now.'

'Millie's right,' Oliver said, from across the room. 'I doubt if I could have described it better myself.' The man sitting next to him at the same desk, nodded. Barry Green had only started the day before. He was taking over as assistant manager when Oliver transferred to Woolton on 1 January. 'I second that,' Barry said, with a charming smile.

'Even I knew that,' June chortled.

'Oh!' Diana got up and flounced into George's office. She slammed the door, and everyone glanced at each other in patient resignation when we heard the sound of her raised, complaining voice.

'Actually,' June said, 'I've never heard of an oriel window. I just wanted to get up Madam's nose.'

'I must say,' Barry Green remarked, 'that I'm glad the horrendous Miss Riddick won't be here much longer. I don't know what's got into George but he's well and truly smitten.' Barry Green had given George his first job thirty years ago, and they had remained friends ever since. His vast experience as an estate agent hadn't prevented him from being made redundant when the chain he worked for had been taken over by a building society. He reminded me of actors in the old black-and-white British films I sometimes watched on television. In his sixties, with bountiful silver hair, perfectly coiffured, he wore a light grey suit with a slight sheen, and an eggshell blue bow-tie. His diction, like his hair, was perfect, as was his moustache, two neat, silvery fish. He looked the embodiment of a 1930s ladies' man, but appearances were deceptive. Barry had a wife, Tess, four children and eight grandchildren, whose various achievements he let slip into the conversation whenever he found the opportunity. One son was an architect, his two daughters had given up dazzling careers when they started their families, several grandchildren were already at university, including the one who could walk at eight months and play the piano when she was three. He rarely mentioned his youngest son, who was abroad, but no one asked what he was up to in case Barry launched into another long, adulatory explanation.

There was nothing subtle about the change of atmosphere in Stock Masterton since Diana had returned yesterday. I wondered if it was just my imagination that I was being picked on more than the others. If I hadn't been so preoccupied with my own life, it might have mattered more. Diana wasn't rude, merely loudly and forcefully officious. She kept telling people what to do when they already knew, offering advice when it wasn't needed. She was having an affair with the boss and wanted everyone to know how much her stock had risen.

'What did you mean,' I said to Barry, 'about Diana not being here much longer?' Maybe she was leaving to marry George.

'Because she's coming to Woolton with me.' Oliver sighed. 'George only told me yesterday. She's got a title, assistant manager. I'm not sure if I can stand it.'

'Your bad luck is our good fortune,' I said cheerfully. With Diana out of the way, perhaps I could get back on good terms with George.

This seemed unlikely when Diana appeared, saying, 'George would like a word with you, Millie.'

'I'd be obliged,' George said coldly, when I went in, 'if in future you'd refrain from upsetting Diana in front of the entire office. Everyone makes mistakes from time to time. It doesn't help to have them exposed in public.'

I made one of the faces I'd caught off Bel. 'Isn't this all a bit juvenile, George, like telling tales at school?'

'It's not long since the poor girl's father died. She's feeling very vulnerable at the moment.'

'So am I,' I said curtly. I'd scarcely slept for two nights in a row and was already sick to death of the situation at work. I knew I was only sinking to Diana's level when I said, 'It was Diana who pointed out my mistake first –

what she thought was a mistake. I put her right, that's all. As she did it in front of the entire office, Oliver and Barry merely backed me up.'

'Oh, is that what really happened?' George looked nonplussed.

'Yes, George, it is.'

'I'm sorry, I must have got the wrong end of the stick.' He became quite friendly and asked how I was getting on with the flat in William Square.

'It's a long story, George. Perhaps I could tell it to you one day over lunch?' I'd only tell him the least important bits.

'Great idea, Millie. We'll do that, eh?'

Diana was scowling at me through the glass partition. I resisted the urge to stick out my tongue, and reckoned there was no chance of having lunch with George once she got back to work on him. She seemed to be pursuing a private vendetta against me.

When I came out, June shouted, 'There's just been a phone call, Millie. Some woman particularly asked for you. She says her boss, a Mr Thomas, has a property to sell as soon as poss in Clement Street off Smithdown Road, number eighteen. It belonged to a relative. He wants a valuation. I looked in the diary and told her you'd be there at two o'clock.'

'I think I'll go,' Diana stretched her arms. 'I feel like some fresh air.'

'They asked for Millie,' June said pointedly.

'This is an estate agent's, not a hairdresser's,' Diana snapped. 'It doesn't matter who goes.'

Oliver said sweetly, ''Yes, it does, Diana. It might be a former client who would prefer Millie rather than another member of staff.' He winked at me. 'Will you be all right on your own? Take Darren, if you'd feel safer.'

'I doubt if I'll come to any harm in Clement Street, it's too built-up.' Female staff weren't usually sent to deal with properties if a man on his own was involved.

It felt odd to drive past William Square and think of

Flo's flat, as familiar now as the back of my hand, waiting for my mother to move in on Friday. Yesterday, she'd astounded me by announcing that when the time came for Alison to leave Skelmersdale, she'd have her in William Square instead of going to Oxford.

'Is that wise, Mum?' I said worriedly. 'You realise it's a red-light area. That girl outside is a prostitute. And it can be very violent.'

'I don't know what's wise or not, luv. Our Alison's always had plenty of care and attention, but she's never had much love. The change is bound to upset her, whether she goes to Oxford or comes to me, so I'd like to give it a chance.' Kate's eyes glistened. 'We'll sleep together in the same bed and I'll hold her in me arms if she'll let me. As to the prostitutes, they're only working girls who've fallen on hard times. They won't harm our Alison. The violence I'll just have to take a chance on. After all, I can always move, can't I?'

I regarded her doubtfully. 'I hope you're not making a terrible mistake. What will you live on?'

'I'll eke out the money Flo left so it lasts as long as possible. In a few years, I'll be due for me pension. I might get a carer's allowance for looking after Alison. Don't worry, luv,' she said serenely, 'I'll be all right. I haven't felt so happy in ages.'

Perhaps the last time she'd been happy was with Hugh O'Mara. Even now, the next day, I found it difficult to grasp what Gran had told me.

I turned into Clement Street, found a place to park, took a photograph of number eighteen, then knocked at the door. The street was comprised of small terraced properties, the front doors opening on to the pavement. The house in question had been relatively well maintained, though the downstairs window-sill could have done with a fresh coat of paint. I noticed the step hadn't been cleaned in a while.

The door opened, 'Hello, Millie,' said Tom O'Mara.

Yesterday, I'd written to him, then fled back to

Blundellsands when I came out of the solicitor's with my mother, so there would have been no one in when he turned up at Flo's last night. I'd thought long and hard about what to write. In the end, I'd merely stated the facts baldly, without embellishment or comment. I didn't put 'Dear Tom', or who the letter was from, just a few necessary words that explained everything. He would know who'd sent it. I'd posted it to the club because I didn't know his address.

Tom turned and went down the narrow hallway into a room at the rear of the house. He was dressed in all black: leather jacket, jeans, T-shirt. I took a deep breath and followed, closing the door behind me. The room was furnished sixties style, with a lime green carpet, orange curtains, a melamine table, two grey plastic easy chairs, one each side of the elaborate tiled fireplace, which had little insets for knick-knacks. Everything was shabby and well used, and there were no ornaments, or other signs that the place was inhabited.

'This is where me gran used to live,' Tom said. His jacket creaked silkily as he sat in one of the chairs and stretched out his long legs. He wore expensive boots with a zip in the side, and looked out of place in the small dark room with its cheap furniture. I sat in the other chair. 'I bought it years ago as an investment. I got tenants in when Nancy went to Southport. Now they've moved I thought I'd sell. They say the price of property has started to go up.'

'When did you decide to sell?'

'This morning, when I heard from you. It made a good excuse. I got a woman from the club to ring the place you work. I had to see you again.'

'Why?'

'I dunno.' He shrugged elegantly. 'To see what it felt like, maybe, knowing you were me sister, knowing it was over.' He looked at me curiously. 'Didn't you want to see me?'

'Oh, I don't know, Tom. I've no idea what to think.' I

felt slightly uncomfortable, but not embarrassed or ashamed. I'd pooh-poohed Gran's gruesome claim that the family was cursed, that the devil was involved, and the world was about to end because a half-sister and brother who'd known nothing about their relationship had slept with each other. 'We didn't know, Gran. It wasn't our fault. If it hadn't been for all the secrets . . .' It was irritating to know that I was now accumulating secrets of my own, things I couldn't tell my mother or Trudy or Declan. 'Don't repeat a word of this to your mam,' Gran pleaded. 'I'd be obliged if you wouldn't mention to your dad that I told you,' Mum had said the other night, about something or other I couldn't remember right now.

'You can go back to that boyfriend of yours,' Tom remarked drily. 'What's his name?'

'James.'

He looked amused. 'James and Millie. They go well together. What's Millie short for, anyroad? I always meant to ask.'

'Millicent.'

There was silence. Then Tom said something that made my stomach lurch. 'Will you come upstairs with me?' He nodded at the door. 'There's a bed.'

'*No!*' Despite my vehemently expressed horror, somewhere within the furthest reaches of my mind, I remembered what we'd been to each other and did my best not to imagine what it would be like now.

'I just wondered,' Tom said lightly. 'It's not that I want to, bloody hell, no. The whole idea makes me feel dead peculiar. I'm just trying to get things sorted in me head.'

'It's all over, Tom.' I could hardly speak.

'Christ, Millie, I know that. I'm not suggesting otherwise.' He smiled. Over the short time I'd known him, he'd rarely smiled. Whenever he did, I'd always thought him even more extraordinarily attractive than he already was, more desirable. I had that same feeling again, and it made me slightly nauseous. He went on, 'I wish we'd found out we were related before we . . .' he stopped, unwilling to say the words. 'It would have been great, knowing I had a sister.'

'And knowing Flo was your gran.' And my gran, I realised with a shock.

'Aye.' He nodded. 'That would have been great an' all.'

I refused to meet his eyes, worried about what I might see there. It seemed sensible to get away as quickly as possible. I took my notebook out of my bag and said briskly, 'Is it really your intention to put the house on the market?'

'I'd like to get rid of it, yes.'

'Then I'd better take some details.' I stood, smoothed my skirt, conscious of Tom watching my every move. I didn't look at him. 'I'll start upstairs.'

Quickly, I measured the rooms, made a note of the cupboards, the state of decoration, the small modern bathroom at the rear. Downstairs again, I took a quick look in the lounge, which was the same size as the front bedroom and had a black iron fireplace with a flower-painted tile surround, which could be sold for a bomb if it was taken out. There was an ugly brocade three-piece with brass pillars supporting the arms – I must tell Tom to get rid of the furniture.

In the hall, I paused for a moment. Tommy O'Mara had lived here, walked in and out of the same rooms, up and down the same stairs, sat in the same spot where I'd sat only a few minutes ago when I talked to his grandson. One day, a long time ago, Martha Colquitt, my other gran, had probably come to this house bringing Flo's baby with her, the baby who'd turned out to be my father. I stood very still, and in my mind's eye, I could actually see the things happening like in an old, faded film, as if they were genuine memories, as if I'd lived through them, taken part. It was an eerie feeling, but not unpleasant

When I went into the living room, Tom O'Mara had

gone. He'd left the key to Flo's flat on top of my handbag. He must have slipped out of the back when I was upstairs, and I was glad that my main emotion was relief, mixed with all sorts of other feelings that I preferred not to delve into. A car started up some way down the street and I didn't even consider looking through the net curtains to see if it was him. In one sense, I felt numb. In another, I felt entirely the opposite. I knew I would never make love with another man the way I had with Tommy O'Mara – Tom! The thing that had drawn us together was a crime, yet it would be impossible to forget.

When I returned to the office, Diana was cock-a-hoop. She'd just shown the Naughtons round a property in Childwall, and they were anxious to buy.

'How many places did you show them, Millie – ten, a dozen? I only took them once and they fell in love with it straight away,' she crowed.

'I'm sure they were more influenced by the house than the agent,' I said mildly. Right now, I couldn't give a damn about the Naughtons, or Diana.

After my parents' thirty brutal, wretched years of marriage, I expected there would be something equally brutal about its end: a fight, a huge scene, lots of screaming and yelling. I even visualised my father physically refusing to let Mum go. In other words, I was dreading Friday. Several times during the week, I asked Mum, 'What time are you leaving?'

'For goodness sake, Millicent, I don't know. It's not high noon or anything. I'll pack me suitcase during the day, and once I've had me tea I'll tell him I'm off before he has time to brood over it.'

'It can't possibly be that simple, Mum.'

'He can't stop me, can he? He can't guard over me for ever.' She bit her lip thoughtfully. 'I'll leave him a casserole in the fridge for the weekend.' She smiled at me radiantly. Over the last few days, the anxious lines around her eyes and mouth had smoothed away. I had never known her look so happy.

'I'll come straight from work and give you a lift,' I offered.

'There's no need, Millicent. I'll catch the bus. I won't have much to carry — a suitcase, that's all.'

I didn't argue, but on Friday, as soon as I finished work, I drove straight to Kirkby. Trudy had obviously had the same idea. When I drew up the Cortina was parked outside the house.

My mother was kneeling on the kitchen floor playing with Scotty, who was lying on his back, wriggling in ecstasy as his tummy was tickled. 'I'll really miss this little chap,' she said tearfully, when I went in. 'I'd take him with me if there was a garden. But never mind, he'll be company for your dad.'

'Where is he?' I asked.

'In the front room.'

'Does he know?'

'Yes. He's taken it hard, I knew he would. He pleaded with me to stay. He promised to turn over a new leaf.'

'Really!' I said sarcastically.

Mum laughed. 'Yes, really.'

'Do you believe him?'

'Not for a minute, luv. I don't think he could, no matter how much he might want to.'

Trudy came into the room with a plastic bag. 'You'd forgotten your toothbrush, Mum.' She grinned at me. 'Hi, Sis. She's hardly taking a thing, just a few clothes, that's all.'

'I don't want to leave your dad with the house all bare. It'll be nice to start afresh with Flo's stuff. I must say,' Mum nodded at the ancient stove, 'I'll be glad to see the back of that ould thing.'

'Flo's is even older,' I said.

'Yes, but she's got a microwave, hasn't she? I've always wanted a microwave. Now, Trudy,' she turned to my sister, 'I want you to promise that you'll bring Melanie and Jake to see their grandad from time to time. He loves them kids, and it would be cruel to deprive him of their company.'

Trudy rubbed the scar on her left eyebrow and muttered, 'I'm not promising anything, Mum. We'll just have to see.'

'Well,' Mum said cheerfully, 'it's time I was off.'

The moment had come. Trudy and I looked at each other, and I saw my own incredulous excitement reflected in her green eyes as we followed Mum into the hall, where she paused at the door of the lounge. The television was on, a travel programme showing an exotic location with palm trees, sun and sand. To my surprise, Declan was sitting on the settee reading a newspaper. My father – the man I'd always thought was my father – was smoking, apparently quite calm, but there was something tight about his shoulders, and he seemed to hold the smoke in for too long before he blew it out again.

'I'm going now, Norman,' Mum said. She spoke as casually as if she were going to the shops. I sensed a subtle shifting of power.

Her husband shrugged. 'Please yerself,' he said.

'Your clean shirts are in the airing cupboard, and there's a meat casserole in the fridge. It should last at least two days.'

Declan got up. 'I'll come out and say tara, Mam.'

'Heavens, lad! I'll be seeing you tomorrer. You promised to come to dinner, didn't you? There's no need for taras.'

'Yes, there is, Mam. Today's special.'

Trudy picked up the suitcase and we trooped outside. Dry-eyed and slightly breathless, Mum paused under the orange street lights, looking back, her brow furrowed in bewilderment, at the house of silent screams and hidden tears, as if either that, or the future she was about to embark on, was nothing but a dream. Trudy put the case into the boot of the Cortina, Mum gave a queenly wave, and the car drove away.

It was as easy as that.

Declan and I were left standing at the gate, with me feeling inordinately deflated by this turn of events. I'd expected to take my mother to William Square, help her settle in, show her where everything was, gradually hand the place over. But now I felt excluded, unnecessary. All of a sudden it hurt badly, imagining other people going through Flo's things, sitting in Flo's place, watching her lamp swirl round, playing her favourite record.

Scotty came out and licked my shoe. I picked him up and buried my face in his rough, curly coat to hide the tears that trickled down my cheeks. I'd never felt so much at home anywhere as I'd done at Flo's. From the very first time I'd gone there, the flat had seemed mine. I knew I was being stupid, but it was almost as if I'd entered my aunt's body, become Flo, experienced the various highs and lows of her life. I'd discovered something about myself during the short time I'd spent there, though I wasn't sure what it was. I only knew I felt differently about things, as if Flo had somehow got through to me that I would survive. Never once, in all the nights I'd slept there, had I dreamed the old dream, heard the slithering footsteps on the stairs, wished I were invisible.

I sighed. I could follow the Cortina, still help Mum settle in, but I knew I was being daft, feeling so possessive about a basement flat that had belonged to a woman I'd never even spoken to.

'What's the matter, Sis?' Declan said softly.

'I feel a bit sad, that's all.'

Declan misunderstood. 'Mam will be all right, you'll see.'

'I know she will, Dec.' I put Scotty down and gave his beard a final rub, wondering if I would ever see the little dog again. 'Will he be all right?'

'Scotty's the only member of the family Dad's never laid a finger on.' Declan grinned.

'And what about you? You can always sleep on the sofa in my place until you find somewhere of your own.' I'd

372

welcome his company at the moment. The thought of returning, alone, to Blundellsands and the flat I'd been so proud of was infinitely depressing.

'Thanks, Millie, but I think I'll stay with me dad.'

I stared at him, open-mouthed. 'But I thought you couldn't wait to get away?'

'Yes, but he needs me, least he needs someone, and I suppose I'll do.'

'Oh, Dec!' I touched his thin face. My heart felt troubled at the idea of my gentle brother staying in Kirkby with Norman Cameron.

'He can't be all bad,' Declan said, with such kind reasonableness, considering all that had happened, that I felt even worse. 'I know he loves us. Something must have happened to make him the way he is.'

I thought of the little boy locked in a cupboard. 'Perhaps something did.' I watched Scotty sniffing the rose bushes in the front garden. One day, I might come back. Perhaps we could talk. Perhaps.

A taxi drew up outside the house next door and hooted its horn. The Bradleys came out, dressed in their ball-room-dancing gear.

'Has your mam gone?' Mrs Bradley shouted.

'A few minutes ago,' I replied.

'About time, too. I'm going to see her next week.' Mr Bradley helped to scoop the layers of net skirt into the taxi. As it drove away, I said, 'I suppose I'd better go, it's cold out here.' I kissed Declan's cheek. 'Take care, Dec. I won't stop worrying about you, I know I won't.'

'There's no need to worry, Mill. Nowadays, me and Dad understand each other in our own peculiar way. He accepts me for what I am.'

I paused in the act of unlocking the car. 'And what's that, Dec?'

Beneath the glare of the street lights, Declan flushed. 'I reckon you already know, Sis.' He closed the gate. 'Do you mind?'

'Christ Almighty, Dec!' I exploded. 'Of course I don't

mind. It would only make me love you more, except I love you to death already.'

'Ta, Sis.' He picked Scotty up and waved a shaggy paw. 'See you, Mill.'

I started up the car and watched through the mirror as my brother, still hugging Scotty, went back into the house. A door had opened for my mother, at the same time as one had closed for Declan.

3

Every morning, I woke up with the feeling that I'd lost something infinitely precious. I had no idea what it was that I'd lost, only that it had left a chasm in my life that would never be refilled. There was an ache in my heart, and the sense of loss remained with me for hours.

My flat, my home, seemed unfamiliar, like that of a stranger. I stared, mystified, at various objects: the shell-shaped soap dish in the bathroom, a gaudy tea-towel, the yellow filing basket on the desk, and had no idea where they'd come from. Were they mine? I couldn't remember buying them. Nor could I remember where particular things were kept. It was as if I'd been away for years, having to open cupboards and drawers to search for the bread knife or a duster. There was food in the fridge that was weeks old: wilted lettuce, soggy apples, a carton of potato salad that I was scared to take the lid off. The cheese was covered in mould.

The only place where I felt comfortable and at ease was the balcony. Most nights I sat outside wearing my warmest coat, watching the branches of the bare trees as they waved, like the long nails of a witch, against the dark sky. I listened to the creatures of the night rustling in and out of the bushes below. There were hedgehogs, two, never seen during the day. The light from the living room was cast sharply across the untidy grass and straggly plants – no one tended the garden in winter – and under the light I read the book that Tom O'Mara had given me about the *Thetis*. I read about the bungling and ineptitude of those at the top, the heroism and desperation of the ordinary seamen as they tried to rescue the men who were trapped, so near and yet so far.

How would it have been, I wondered, if Tommy O'Mara hadn't died? How differently would things have turned out for Flo?

I felt very old, like someone who knew that the best years of their life were over and was patiently sitting out the rest. Having a birthday didn't help. I turned thirty, and became obsessed with wondering how the next ten years would turn out. What would I be doing when I was forty? Would I be married, have children? Where would I be living? Where would I be working? Would Mum still be living in William Square with Alison?

Which was stupid. I told myself how stupid I was being a hundred times a day, and made sure no one guessed how dispirited I felt. When I went with James to the theatre one night, I sat in the bar in the interval while he went to fetch the drinks. He came back, saying, 'Are you all right, darling? I looked across and your face was terribly sad.'

'I'm fine,' I said confidently.

'Are you sure? Is it over between you and that Tom chap? I've kept longing to ask. Is that why you're sad?'

'I said I wasn't sad, James, though it is over between me and Tom.'

He looked relieved. 'I'm glad there's no one else.'

'I never said that!' His face collapsed in hurt. I knew I was being horrid, but the last thing I wanted was to offer him encouragement. The strangest thing had happened with James, and I didn't know how to deal with it.

He'd promised not to pressurise me and he hadn't, but in the few times I'd seen him since we'd broken up, then come together again, he wanted to know every little thing about me, every detail. It was as if now that he could no longer have my body he was determined to

375

possess my mind. Perhaps some people were willing to divulge their every thought, their every wish, but I wasn't one of them.

It was hard to escape from such overpowering, almost suffocating love, his tremendous need, which some women might have envied. It was also hard to reject, as if I was giving away something uniquely precious by refusing him. Such love might never come my way again. He appeared to worship the ground I walked on.

Where had I heard those words said before only recently? The bell rang once to indicate that the interval was nearly over and I finished off my drink. Back in the theatre I remembered. They were the words Gran had used to describe how Norman Cameron had felt about my mother . . .

The curtain rose, but as far as I was concerned the actors' efforts were wasted. I had no idea what had happened in the first act. Perhaps you could love someone too much, so much that you resented all the things they did without you, resented them even being happy if you weren't the reason why they smiled.

It wasn't strictly true to hint that there was someone else, but tomorrow night I was meeting Peter Maxwell. He was going to show me where the tall, wild forests had once been in Toxteth, which King John had turned into a royal park and where he had hunted deer and wild boar.

'It's incredible!' I breathed, the following evening, as we strolled through the icy drizzle along Upper Parliament Street and into Smithdown Road. I closed my eyes and tried to imagine I was stepping through a thick forest and the drizzle was the dew dripping from the trees at dawn.

'The area's mentioned in the Domesday Book,' he said proudly.

I forgot how cold the night was as he explained, with mounting enthusiasm, that Lodge Lane was called after one of the King's hunting lodges, that the ancient manor of Smethedon was where the name Smithdown came from. The descriptions, the words he used seemed incongruous, as we passed the narrow built-up streets and endless shops. Traffic fizzed by in the wet; cars, buses, lorries, headlights fixed on the noxious fumes spewing out from the vehicles in front, and reflected in the watery surface. We seemed to be walking through a toxic yellow fog, as Peter talked about Dingle Dell, Knot's Hole, sandstone-cliff creeks, glens, farms, a game reserve. He even quoted a poem – 'The Nymph of the Dingle'.

'It's fascinating, Peter,' I said, when he paused for breath. His black bushy hair and beard glistened in the damp, as if they'd been touched with frost.

'I've not nearly finished, but this isn't a good night. Perhaps we could come one Sunday. I can show you other places. Did you know that less than two centuries ago Bootle was a spa? There used to be watermills, springs, sandhills and fields of flowers?'

I confessed I'd had no idea. He asked if I'd like a drink, and when I said yes he steered me into the nearest pub. 'Will it be safe in here?' I asked nervously.

'I doubt it,' he said soberly, though I noticed his eyes were twinkling. 'We're probably taking our lives in our hands.'

The pub was old-fashioned, Victorian, with sparkling brasses and a gold-tinted mirror behind the bar. The few customers looked very ordinary and not in the least threatening.

'Well, we seemed to have survived so far,' Peter said, apparently amazed. 'What would you like to drink?'

I poked him in the ribs with my elbow. 'Stop making fun of me. I'd like half a cider, please.'

A few minutes later he returned with the drinks. 'Sorry I was so long, but the barman offered me five thousand quid to carry out a contract-killing. See those old girls over there?' He pointed to two elderly women sitting in a corner. 'One's a Mafia godfather in disguise, the other is the chief importer of heroin in the northwest. The cops have been after her for years. She's the one he wanted me to kill.' He took his donkey jacket off and threw it on a vacant chair. Underneath, he wore a polo-necked jersey, which had several loose threads. He regarded me solemnly. 'I refused, of course, so I doubt if we'll get out of here alive.'

By now, I was doubled up with laughter. 'I'm sorry, but I always feel a bit fearful around here.'

'It sounds priggish, but the worst thing to fear is fear itself. Taking the worst possible scenario, no one's safe anywhere.'

'I like being with you, it's rather soothing.' I smiled, feeling unusually contented.

He stroked his beard and looked thoughtful. 'To be "soothing" is not my ultimate aim when I'm with a beautiful young woman, but it'll do.'

I welcomed the fact that he was so easy to be with, relaxing, particularly after the intensity of James, and the total preoccupation Tom O'Mara and I had had with each other. There was a hint of flirtatiousness between us, which meant nothing. He reminded me about the Christmas concert at his school next week. 'You promised you'd come.'

'I hadn't forgotten.' It would soon be Christmas and I hadn't bought a single present. I must remind Trudy about the bottles she'd promised to paint, and remembered that one had been for Diana. After the way things had gone, I wasn't sure whether to give it to her or not.

For the next half-hour, we chatted about nothing in particular. We'd been in the same year at school, which meant that Peter had also recently had his thirtieth birthday, and we discussed how incredibly old we felt. 'It's quite different from turning twenty. Twenty's exciting, like the start of a big adventure. Come thirty, the excitement's over,' he remarked, with a grin.

'Don't say that. You make thirty sound very dull.'

'I didn't mean it to sound dull, just less exciting. By thirty you more or less know where you are. Would you like another drink?'

'No thanks. I thought I'd pop in and see my mother. I left my car in William Square.'

'I've already met your mum. She seems exceptionally nice.' He reached for his jacket. 'Come on. If we make a sudden rush for the exit, we might get out of here all in one piece.'

It was only natural that Mum should have the keys to Flo's flat. Even so, I felt slightly miffed at having to knock to be let in. Fiona, who was draped outside in her usual spot, condescended to give me a curt nod.

'Hello, luv!' Mum's face split into a delighted smile when she opened the door. 'You're out late. It's gone ten.'

Peter Maxwell leaned over the railings. 'Hi, there, Kate. 'Night, Millie. See you next week.'

'Goodnight, Peter.'

'Have you been out with him?' Mum sounded slightly shocked as she closed the door.

'He's very nice.'

'Oh, he's a lovely young feller. I knew his mam in Kirkby. She's a horrible woman, not a bit like Peter. No, I just thought you and James were back together for good, like.'

'We're back together. I doubt very much if it's for good.'

Mum shook her head in despair. 'I can't keep up with you, Millicent.' Then, eyes shining, she demanded, 'What do you think of me new carpet?'

In the two weeks since I had left and my mother had taken over, much in the flat had changed. Too much, I thought darkly, but kept my opinion to myself. It was none of my business, but as far as I was concerned Flo's flat had been perfect. I wouldn't have altered it one iota. But now the silk flowers had gone because they gathered dust, as well as the little round tables and the brasses on the beams. Colin had fitted deadlocks on the windows, a heater on the bathroom ceiling and, with Declan's help, was going to wallpaper the place throughout. 'Something

379

fitting,' Mum announced excitedly, 'little rosebuds, violets, sprigs of flowers.' She would have liked a new three-piece, but needed to conserve the money and was buying stretch covers instead. 'I don't like that dark velour stuff. It's dead miserable.' Next week, British Telecom were coming to install a phone.

I regarded the maroon fitted carpet. 'It looks smart.' I far preferred the faded old linoleum. 'What's happened to the rag rug?'

'I chucked it, luv. It was only a homemade thing.'

Trudy came out of the bedroom, struggling with a cardboard box full of clothes. 'Hello, Sis. I didn't know you were here. I'm just sorting out the wardrobe. Phew!' She plonked the box down and wiped her forehead with the back of her hand. 'I'll take this lot to Oxfam tomorrow, Mum. Hey, Mill, what do you think of this? I thought I'd keep it. It's not at all old-fashioned.' She held up the pink and blue check frock with a Peter Pan collar. 'I'm sure it'll fit.'

'It's lovely, Trude.' It had fitted me perfectly. George had said it made me look sweet and demure.

'Help yourself to anything that takes your fancy, Millicent,' Mum said generously.

'There's nothing I want, Mum.' I felt all choked up. It was horrible to see Flo's things being thrown away, given to Oxfam. I didn't even want Trudy to have the check frock. Then I thought of something I did want – wanted desperately. 'Actually, Mum, I'd like that lamp, the swirly one.' I looked at the television, but the lamp wasn't there, and I felt a thrust of pure, cold anger. If it had been chucked away I'd track it down, buy it back from Oxfam . . .

'I'm afraid your gran's already nabbed it,' Mum said apologetically. 'I wish I'd known, luv. You should have said before.'

If I'd known she was going to tear the place apart, I would have. I knew I was being unreasonable, and felt even more unreasonable when I refused a cup of tea. 'I only came for a minute to say hello. I think I'll have an early night.'

I'd never felt less like an early night. Outside, I thought about calling on Charmian, but the ground-floor flat was in darkness – Herbie had to get up at the crack of dawn for work. Peter Maxwell's light was on, but did I know him well enough to call at this hour? He might think I was being presumptuous, a bit pushy.

Fiona, in a short fur coat, thigh-length boots, and no other visible sign of clothing, was staring at me suspiciously, as if I'd set myself up in competition. I got into the car and drove round to Maynard Street. It was weeks since I'd seen Bel, though she'd been to William Square to renew her acquaintance with Mum.

'She'll probably think me an idiot.' I didn't even switch the engine off when I parked as near as I could to Bel's house, but drove off immediately. On my way to Blundellsands, I slipped a tape into the deck and turned up Freddie Mercury's powerful voice as loud as it would go to drown my brain and stop me from thinking how much I would have liked someone to talk to. It didn't work, so I turned it down and talked to myself instead. 'I must pull myself together, keep telling myself there is Life After Flo. Tomorrow I'll take a proper lunch break, buy some Christmas presents. I'll get jewellery for Mum, gold earrings or a chain.' By the time I got home I was still musing on what to get Declan, feeling more cheerful. My flat was slowly beginning to feel my own again, though it still seemed oddly empty when I went in.

Mum's decorating splurge was catching. I didn't want to change the colour of my own living-room walls, but a wide frieze would look nice, or stencilled flowers. I decided I'd take a look at patterns at the weekend.

Next day after lunch, I was showing June the gold chain with a K for Kate that I'd bought for Mum, and the red-velvet knee-length dress with short sleeves I'd got as a

Christmas present for myself, when George called, 'Can I have a word with you, Millie?'

'Sit down,' he said shortly, when I entered his office. This was always a bad sign, and I wondered what I'd done wrong now. He cleared his throat. 'I've been having a long talk with . . . with someone about your position in the firm. It was pointed out that you have no qualifications for the job you do. Darren and Elliot both have degrees, and even June has three A levels.' He regarded me sternly, as if all this was new to him and he'd been misled.

'You knew that when you took me on, George. You knew it when you promoted me.' I tried to keep my voice steady. 'I've always carried out my work satisfactorily. No one has ever complained.'

George acknowledged this with a cursory nod. 'That's true, Millie, but it was also pointed out that there are a lot of people around, highly qualified people, who might do the work even better. Yet by employing you, I am, in effect, denying one of these people a position with Stock Masterton.' He leaned forward, frowning earnestly. 'Look at that business with the Naughtons, for example. You must have shown them around a dozen properties, but Diana had only to take them once and a deal was clinched on the spot.'

I clenched my fists, feeling the nails digging painfully into my palms. My heart thumped crazily. 'Are you giving me the sack, George?' I'd never find another equivalent job if I was sacked.

He looked slightly uncomfortable. 'No, no, of course not. We, that is, I, thought it would be a good idea if you went to Woolton with Oliver and Diana.'

'I don't understand,' I stammered. 'If I'm useless here, I'll be just as useless in Woolton.'

'No one's said you're useless, Millie. Oh dear!' He put his hand to his chest. 'I feel a panic attack coming. Lately, I've been having them quite frequently. No, we . . . I think you should be our receptionist. After all, that's what you were originally taken on as.'

It was so unfair. I'd never asked to be promoted, it had been all his idea. I blinked back hot tears of anger. No way would I let him see me cry. I knew I'd be burning my boats, but didn't care. I said, 'I'm afraid that isn't acceptable, George. I'd sooner leave. I'll finish at the end of the month.'

It hadn't gone quite the way he wanted – the way he knew Diana wanted. He rubbed his chest, frowning. 'Then you'd be breaking your contract. One month's notice is required, dated the first of the month.'

'In that case,' I said coolly, though I felt anything but cool, 'I'll leave at the end of January.' I got up and went to the door. 'I'll let you have my resignation in writing this afternoon.'

It was worse, far more shocking, than having discovered all those closely kept family secrets. I'd been dumbfounded to learn that my father wasn't who I'd thought he was. But I'd rejected Norman Cameron a long time ago, and the news didn't matter now – in fact, it was welcome. As for Tom O'Mara, I had thought I would never forget, but already it was hard to remember the way we'd felt about each other. There was just relief that it was all over, though I knew I would worry about him, watch for his name and any mention of Minerva's in the paper, hope that he wouldn't come to harm in the vicious world he lived in. After all, he was my brother.

But the business with my job – trivial in comparison to the rest – was different, directed against me personally. I felt as if someone had just delivered a mammoth blow, knocking all the stuffing out of me. I realised that my job had given me a sense of identity, a feeling of achievement, and without it I was nothing. I hadn't, after all, done better than the other girls in my class, the ones who'd seemed so much smarter than me. I was the backward child again, the girl who could hardly read, so hopeless that I hadn't been entered for a single O level.

Later, when I tried to type a letter of resignation, my fingers no longer seemed capable of accepting messages from my brain. I'd thought George was my friend. I'd tried to help Diana. Why had they turned against me? I felt betrayed.

In the window, through the glass around the boards showing the houses Stock Masterton had for sale, I watched the people passing, their bodies crouched protectively as they fought their way through the gale that howled up Castle Street from the Mersey. I longed to go down to the Pier Head, hold on to the railings, let the wind blow me any way it wanted.

There was a photo of Nancy's house on one of the boards in the window, between the house in Banks which didn't have an oriel window, and a manor house with ten acres of grounds priced at half a million, which George dealt with exclusively. I'd asked Oliver if he would please send someone else to Clement Street if a prospective purchaser wanted to view. 'I know the chap who's selling it slightly. I'd sooner not go,' I said. I still felt the same when the keys for the property arrived through the post, which meant that no one would be there. Unlike Flo's flat, Nancy's house, the place where she'd lived with Tommy O'Mara, where the father I'd never known had been raised, would go to strangers, who would know nothing about the drama that had taken place. People rarely thought about previous owners when they bought a house, no matter how old it was. As far as they were concerned, its history began when they themselves moved in.

Across the office, Darren and Elliot were having a deskbound lunch, eating sandwiches and giggling over something in *Viz*. I felt envious of their gloriously trouble-free lives. June was on the telephone, Barry's carefully combed silver head was bent over a heap of files. Oliver was out with a client. In his office, George, who usually made his presence loudly felt, was strangely quiet. At the next desk, Diana was singing a little tune as she typed into her computer. Was there a note of triumph in her voice? She must know why George had called me in, be aware of my humiliation. Was it worth making a fuss, I wondered, causing a row, telling Diana exactly what I thought in front of everyone? No, it wasn't, I decided. George seemed slightly ashamed of what he'd done. If I left quietly, at least I'd get a good reference, possibly a glowing one if he felt contrite enough.

Oliver returned, his face flushed by the wind. He hung up the keys. 'Whew!' he exclaimed. 'That was a proper shambles. Mum and Dad insisted on viewing the loft, so I went up with them, then one of the kids pushed the ladder up and the damn thing got stuck halfway. I thought I'd be there all afternoon. I managed to do a Tarzan and swing myself down.'

Diana said, 'I was beginning to wonder why you were taking so long.'

'Were you now! I didn't realise you kept an eye on my movements.' Oliver took his coat off, then put it on again. 'I think a beer and a snack in the Wig and Pen is called for after that misadventure. Come on, Millie, I'll treat you.'

I looked up, surprised. Oliver had never made such an offer before. 'I've already been to lunch.'

At the same time, Diana said quickly, 'She's already had lunch, Oliver.'

Oliver poked his head inside George's office. 'I'm off for a quick bevy, George, and taking Millie with me. Okay?'

George didn't look up. 'Okay,' he mumbled.

'Okay, Diana?' Oliver raised his eyebrows questioningly.

'It's none of my business, is it?'

'Too right it isn't.'

'What was all that about?' I asked, when we were outside. The wind gripped me immediately, powerfully, blowing my hair up into a fan around my head. The air was sharp and clean and refreshingly salty. I twisted my face to and fro, trying to breathe in as much as I could, until I felt almost light-headed.

Oliver's usually good-natured face twisted into a scowl. 'I loathe that bloody woman. I can't abide the thought of working with her. I want her to know that when we move I'm the one in charge. She thinks I'm a wimp who can't take decisions, but she doesn't realise how much George regards Stock Masterton as his baby. Take a major decision over his head and he goes ballistic. She'll find that out for herself soon enough if she starts throwing her weight around.'

When we turned into Dale Street the wind lessened fractionally. Oliver's scowl disappeared and he said kindly, 'Enough of my hang-ups. It's you I'm worried about. You look as if you've been crying, which is why I asked you out.'

I clapped my hands to my cheeks, which felt both hot and cold. 'I haven't been crying, but I'm dead upset. Is it so obvious?'

'Yes. I don't want to pry. Don't tell me if it's something private.'

We arrived at the Wig and Pen, where the midday rush was over and only a few tables were occupied. Oliver brought me a whisky and a chicken sandwich, and I told him what had happened. 'I feel gutted,' I finished. I could have said more, much more, but kept myself to a few short words.

Oliver shook his head unbelievingly. 'Darren and Elliot may well have degrees, but neither has an ounce of charm. As for Diana, she positively alienates the clients. She's in completely the wrong profession, which George knows only too well. He's talked about letting her go more than once.' He shook his head again. 'I don't understand the sudden turnaround. Mind you, the poor man has been an emotional wreck since his wife walked out with the children. He's easy prey for any woman who sets her cap at him.'

'But why does Diana hate me so much?' I wailed.

'That's easy to explain.' Oliver smiled and patted my hand. 'George was smitten with you right from the start.

386

I think I can safely say that your promotion had more to do with your legs than your capabilities, not that you didn't make a good fist of the job once you had it,' he added hastily, when he saw my dismayed expression. 'I wasn't the only one to notice, Diana did, too. She's jealous of you, Millie. She wants you out of George's way.'

'I knew George liked me, that's all,' I muttered. 'You see an awful lot, Oliver.' I felt a bit better. I'd been demoted because of another person's weakness, not my own, though it didn't change the fact I was about to give up my job.

On the way back to the office, Oliver said, 'By the way, you mentioned the Naughtons. Mr Naughton rang this morning to say they've withdrawn from the house in Childwall. They parked outside for several nights. Apparently, there's several teenagers next door, belting music out till all hours, which they find totally unacceptable – it would seem the neighbours they have now are darn near perfect.'

Despite everything, I couldn't help laughing. The talk with Oliver had done me good. I even felt a tiny bit flattered. Diana might well have had the upper hand at the moment but, incredibly, it was me who had the power. If I wanted I could ruin everything. I was no good at flirting, but I knew how it was done, I could learn. I didn't know I'd ever had George, but I could easily get him back. It was a challenge I might once have welcomed but, thinking about it now, it seemed rather demeaning.

'About the Naughtons,' I remarked, 'it's time someone suggested they stay put. They're already in their ideal house, and they'll never find another like it.'

'Someone already has – me. Mr Naughton said he'd never wanted to move, it was all his wife's idea. He's going to try to talk her out of it. If he's successful, every estate agent on Merseyside will breathe a big sigh of relief.'

There was no tortuous Christmas dinner in Kirkby this year to bring back memories of the bleak dinners that had gone before. Norman Cameron had always nursed a decidedly unfestive spirit throughout the holiday, grim and bitter, his dark eyes searching for any signs of unwelcome gaiety from his children, rationing our time spent in front of the television or with our presents. For the first time, with a glimmer of understanding, I wondered if his own childhood Christmases had been so dark that he could see no other way, though I wasn't convinced I would ever have the Christian charity to forgive.

This year, we had dinner at Flo's without Norman. The dining table was pulled out as far as it would go, so big that only a sheet would cover it. It was set for eight, and there was already a trifle laid out, mince pies, an iced cake from Charmian, the plates intertwined with tinsel. Night-lights in delicately painted wine glasses were waiting to be lit when the meal began. Mum asked Trudy if she would bring her cutlery because there wasn't enough, so Trudy bought her a set for Christmas. It wasn't an expensive set, the handles were bright red plastic, but they looked perfect on the table with the red paper napkins.

There was a real tree in the window, the coloured lights shaped like pears, and new decorations strung from wall to wall. The flat – no longer Flo's with its carpet, new curtains and pink-and-white-flowered wallpaper – was warm with the smell of roasting turkey and Christmas pudding. Melanie and Jake were persuaded that it was too cold to eat on the wooden table in the yard. 'You can have a drink out there afterwards,' Trudy told them, 'as long as you get well wrapped up first.'

Bel was there. She'd always had dinner with Flo on Christmas Day, ever since she'd come out of the forces, she'd hinted, and she wasn't looking forward to eating alone for the first time in her life. 'Mr Fritz always came. Later I used to bring Edward, and Charmian would come down with her little ones. When she married Herbie, me and Flo used to have our dinner upstairs.' She turned up on the day in her leopardskin fur coat, a silver lamé suit and high-heeled silver boots, her hair a magnificent halo of russet waves and curls, and her lovely old face as shrivelled as one of the nuts in the bowl on the sideboard. The first thing she did was grab my hand. 'I've not seen much of you lately, girl. I thought we were friends.'

'I nearly called one night, but it was awfully late,' I explained. 'I wanted someone to talk to, but I was worried you'd think I was stupid.'

'Jaysus, Millie. You're talking to the stupidest woman in the world. I always welcome company, no matter what the hour. What was it you wanted to talk about?'

'I can't remember now. I think I was missing Flo.'

'You never met her, but you miss her. Now, that really is stupid.' Bel's beautiful eyes were wise. 'Mind you, luv, I understand, I'll never stop missing Flo.' The violet eyes searched the room. 'Where's your gran, by the way? There's something I've always wanted to ask Martha Colquitt.'

'She's at an old-age pensioners' do in Kirkby.' Gran needed an operation, only minor, but her own prognosis was gloomy – she was convinced she'd die: 'Me mam swore she'd never let a surgeon near her with a knife,' she'd said. 'I don't trust them doctors.'

I gave Bel her present, an unusual oval-shaped bottle that Trudy had painted various shades of blue and green. Bel gave me an intricately patterned mosaic bracelet. 'It's not new, Flo bought it me in Spain. I thought you'd like it as a memento.'

'Oh, thank you,' I breathed. I fastened the bracelet on to my wrist. 'I'll treasure it all my life.'

Mum presided over the table. I could scarcely take my eyes off my new mother, and every now and then noticed the others glancing at her curiously, as if they, too, found it hard to believe that this Kate Cameron had been lurking behind the old one for so many years. She already looked thinner. Charmian had trimmed and silver-tinted her hair the day before, and the thick, straight fringe and feathery cut took years off her. For the first time in ages, she was wearing makeup, and had bought a new dress – the last new one had been for Trudy's wedding ten years ago. It was plain dark green, emphasising the colour of her sparkling eyes. She already had my present, the gold chain with K for Kate, around her neck. Mum was reborn, confident, relaxed, with her children all around her, except for Alison who was coming to tea that afternoon. 'As an experiment, like, to see how she gets on. See if she takes to the place.' It would be best if not too many people were around in case it frightened her. I was going to Southport to have tea with James's family, the Daleys to Colin's parents in Norris Green. Bel had been invited upstairs. Only Declan would be there to see if his sister felt at home in William Square.

Declan seemed perfectly content living in Kirkby with his father. They saw little of each other, Norman either at work or in the pub, and Declan deeply involved with helping the couple he'd met at the craft fair with their tie-dyed T-shirts. His own first attempts had been highly professional, and Melanie and Jake had been given one each as a present. Next September, he was starting a course in fabric design.

'What about that young feller from next door?' Bel said suddenly. 'Flo always had him in for a drink on Christmas Day.'

I offered to fetch Peter Maxwell. It was a still, windless day, without a patch of blue in the sombre grey sky. The leathery leaves on the trees in the central garden shone dully, still wet with dew. Cars lined the square, but otherwise it was empty, no sign of Fiona or the other girls, who must be having a rare day off. Gran had once mentioned that Flo had spent her first Christmas in the flat entirely alone: Mrs Fritz had gone to Ireland. I wondered what it had looked like then, with only a few cars and a single family living in each house.

Peter was getting ready to have Christmas dinner with a colleague from school. There was just time for a drink with the Camerons.

'Did you enjoy the play?' he asked, as he walked around the plain room with its clean-cut furniture, so different from next door, turning off lights and testing locks.

'It was very cleverly written and well acted,' I said tactfully. It had been awful and I hoped he hadn't any ambition to become a playwright. 'I found it hard to talk to the other teachers, though. I kept expecting to get marks out of ten whenever I answered a question.'

'They liked you. Quite a few said next day what a cracking girl you were.' He took his coat off the rack, and dark eyes glinted at me mischievously. 'They wanted to know when we were getting married.'

'What did you say?'

'What do you think I said?'

I stuck my finger under my chin and thought hard. 'Never?'

Peter laughed. 'Precisely! There's no spark, is there, Millie? I wish there were because I like you very much. We know things about each other that would be hard to tell other people.' He looked at me quizzically 'Could you pretend I'm a woman so we could be best friends?'

'Oh, Peter!' He was right, there was no spark. If we went out together for long enough we might get married because it seemed the comfortable thing to do, but it wasn't what I wanted – and neither did he. 'You'd need to do something about your beard before I could remotely regard you as a woman, but there's nothing wrong with having a man for a best friend.'

He kissed my forehead, as if to seal our friendship. 'Friends it is, then. Now, where's that drink? Has your mum got beer? I'm not a wine person.'

★

I was convinced that nowhere on earth could a family have enjoyed their Christmas dinner more than the Camerons. It was nothing to do with the food, though for the first time in months I ate a proper, three-course meal, and the skirt of my red-velvet dress felt tight when I'd finished. It was to do with a shared sense that the nightmare had ended. It had already faded, a little, for Trudy and me, but now it was well and truly over for Mum. As for Declan, he was coping. The only awkward moment came when Melanie, pulling a cracker with her father, said in surprise, 'Where's Grandad?'

'He couldn't come, luv,' Mum said firmly. She looked anxiously at Declan 'He's all right, isn't he?'

'Fine, Mam. He'll have found a pub that's open all day. That's where he'd have been, anyroad.'

'I suppose so.' A shadow almost cast itself over Mum's face, but she blinked it away. 'I'll go round in a day or so, give the house a bit of a clean, like, take him some rations.'

Later, when Trudy and I were washing the dishes, Trudy said, a touch bitterly, 'What a pity she couldn't have brought herself to do this years ago. Think of all the misery it would have saved.'

'It was the money and the flat that gave her the courage, Trude.'

'I'd never have stood it for a minute. I'd have been off the first time he laid a finger on me, and once he'd touched me kids . . .' Trudy shook her head. It was beyond her comprehension.

I reached for a fresh tea-towel – the one I was using was sopping wet. 'We're a different generation, but there's an even newer generation of kids roaming the streets of London and other cities who've run away from violent homes. Why didn't we run away, Trude? He nearly killed you once, but you still stayed. You waited for Colin to rescue you, like I waited for Gary.'

Trudy stared at me blankly. 'I think I felt paralysed,' she whispered.

'Maybe Mum did, too.' One day soon, despite my promise, I resolved to tell Trudy and Declan about the little boy locked in the cupboard. They had a right to know, and could be left to make their own judgement.

Melanie and Jake were aching to sit in the yard. Colin put their coats on, Kate supplied a glass of lemonade and a plate of mince pies and, giggling, they perched themselves on the bench in front of the wooden table. I watched through the window, bemused. It seemed such an uncomfortable thing to do on a cold day in December, and I marvelled at the children's ability to turn it into a great adventure. Colin and Trudy came indoors, shivering. 'Perhaps we could get some garden furniture?' Trudy suggested. They began to discuss the best sort to buy, wood or plastic. They would have preferred wrought-iron, but it was too expensive.

It was just such mundane, ordinary decisions that made the world go round, I thought wryly. Freed from the tensions and the dreary atmosphere of our old house, I became aware of the easy-going intimacy between Colin and my sister, the way they smiled at each other for no reason in particular, as if they were passing on an unspoken message or reading one another's thoughts. I noticed the way they seemed to form a unit with their children, a little world of their own. I thought how satisfying it must be to have little human beings completely dependent upon you, loving you without question, the most important person in their lives. To my surprise, I felt envious of my sister.

Though I could have what she had, I thought later at the Athertons', I could have it easily, straight away. I could be a wife, possibly a mother, by next Christmas. All I had to do was say yes to James. I'd no longer have to worry about my job. I could share in some of this . . .

The difference between my mother's Christmas table and the Athertons' couldn't have been greater. Cut-glass decanters, crystal glasses, heavy silver cutlery with embossed handles, beautifully laundered napkins in silver rings were laid with geometrical precision on a vast expanse of rich, gleaming mahogany, with a rather formal display of upright chrysanthemums in the centre. The dining room was about half as big again as Flo's entire flat, with only a fraction of the furniture. The curtains were ivory satin, drawn carefully to hang in smooth, symmetrical folds.

Mrs Atherton had kissed me coolly on the cheek. 'It's ages since we've seen you, dear. What have you been doing to my son?'

'Nothing that I know of,' I replied, startled. Had James told her about our problems? Or Mrs Atherton might have guessed. After all, she was his mother.

Anna, James's sister, was up from London with her husband and two children. I'd never met her before and found it hard to believe that she'd been an anarchist at university. Her husband, Jonathan, was a dealer in the City, a hearty, fresh-faced man with neat brown hair and designer spectacles. The children, boys, were equally neat, in white shirts, grey pullovers and shorts. They were well behaved and said little, even when their parents encouraged them to talk. I found myself yearning for Melanie and Jake's bright faces, their inability to keep quiet no matter how many times they were told. I longed to discuss garden furniture and tie-dyed T-shirts. Instead, I was forced to listen to Jonathan's talk of bull markets and bear markets, shorts, longs and mediums, stocks and shares. He'd recently netted a cool hundred thou profit on a highly risky venture in Indonesia that everyone else had been too afraid to touch. Anna, blonde hair swinging, pretty face glowing with admiration, leaned over and stroked his chin. 'You're so clever, darling!' she cooed.

Throughout the meal, James kept his eyes glued on me so firmly that I felt uncomfortable. Afterwards we went into the vast, chintzy living room, where he sat on the arm of my chair, towering over me. I felt as if I'd been stamped with his personal seal of ownership.

Jonathan gave his rather unfortunate high-pitched giggle and said to James, 'Understand you've given up flirting with left-wing politics, brother-in-law. Are you still marching with those wretched dockers?'

'I haven't for some time,' James admitted.

So far, Mr Atherton hadn't opened his mouth except to eat; his eyes were always far away, thinking of other things, probably business. He spoke now, with contempt in his voice: 'Lazy buggers, don't know which side their bread's buttered. It's about time they got back to work.'

I had no idea if I was pro-establishment or anti, or if my politics were left or right, I only knew it made my blood boil to hear the dockers being called 'lazy buggers' by a man smoking a fat cigar who owned three garages. I wished I knew some hard facts and figures that I could quote in the dockers' defence, but I knew nothing about the dispute other than it was happening. I jumped up. 'Excuse me.'

In the eau-di-Nil tiled bathroom with its matching carpet and fittings, I stared unseeingly at my reflection in the mirror and realised, with a sense of overwhelming relief, that I was wasting James's time. I felt alien from his family. If I loved him, I would have taken them on and done my best, but I didn't love him and never would. 'I'm glad I came,' I whispered. 'It's helped me make up my mind once and for all.'

When I came out, James was hovering on the landing, and I felt a stab of anger. I wanted to say something coarse and brutal: 'Would you like to have come in to watch me pee?'

He stared at me and I felt repelled by the abject adoration in his eyes. 'You look lovely in that dress,' he said huskily. 'You suit red.' He tried to take me in his arms, nuzzle my hair, but I pushed him away. He patted his pocket, 'I've a present for you, a ring.'

'I don't want it!'

'But, Millie . . .' His lips twisted in an arc of misery. 'Is it this other chap you've been seeing?'

'I haven't been seeing another chap – least I have, but he's just a friend. There's no one, James. No one!' I emphasised the last word, my voice unnaturally shrill, to impress upon him that I was announcing I was free – and he was free to forget me and find someone else.

We began to argue. He refused to believe I meant what I said. Anna must have heard the raised voices. She came out into the hall downstairs. 'Are you two all right?' Her laugh tinkled up the stairs. 'Oh, you're just having a little domestic.' She made a show of pretending to creep back into the room.

James's eyes were glassy, his face was swollen, red. I didn't know this man. Falling in love with me had changed him for the worse. 'It can't be over,' he insisted doggedly.

'It is, James.' I was worried that he was about to hit me. His fists were clenching and unclenching, as if he was itching to use them and it could only be on me. Then I did something that surprised me later when I thought about it. I flung my arms around his neck and hugged him tightly. 'James, I'm bad for you,' I whispered urgently. 'Can't you see? There's something not quite right about the way you love me.' I stroked his neck. 'One of these days, you'll meet someone else who you'll love in a quite different way, and everything will be wonderful for you both.' I pulled away. 'Goodbye, darling,' I said softly.

He remained silent, his eyes no longer glassy, but full of misery and shock. I thought, I wasn't sure, that there was also a trace of comprehension that I could be right.

I flew down the stairs, opened the door of the living room, and said breathlessly, 'I'm awfully sorry, I have to go. Thank you so much for the meal. It was lovely. No, no, please don't get up,' I implored, when Mrs Atherton began to get to her feet. 'I'll see myself out.'

It was past nine when I got back to Blundellsands. The first thing I did was ring my mother. Alison had been very quiet but not too disturbed by the strange surroundings. 'She didn't flick her fingers, the way she does when she's upset,' Mum said gratefully.

Relieved, I hung up my red dress carefully and ran a bath. Afterwards I watched a Woody Allen film on television, then went to bed with a book and a glass of warm milk, feeling contented and relaxed.

Just after midnight the telephone rang. I prayed it wouldn't be James, pleading for a second chance or a third, or whatever it would be by now, but when I picked up the extension by the bed, Peter Maxwell said cheerfully, 'Hi! I've just got in and thought I'd give you a ring. Did you have a nice day?'

'Nice and not so nice. I finished with a boyfriend. It wasn't very pleasant.'

'The hunk from the party?'

'That's right.'

'I didn't realise you were still seeing him. He's definitely not your type.'

'Are you going to be the arbiter of who's my type from now on?' I smiled at the receiver.

'It's what friends are for. I shall always ask for your opinion on any future girlfriends.'

'It shall be given with pleasure,' I said graciously. We chatted idly, and he was about to ring off when I remembered something. 'By the way, knowing it won't be taken the wrong way and you'll think I'm after your body or your money, would you like to come to a drinks party tomorrow afternoon?'

'Sorry, but I'm taking a group of first-years to a pantomime. Will you be at Charmian's on New Year's Eve?'

I said I would, and we promised each other the first dance.

The drinks party was being held at Barry Green's. He had casually offered an invitation to the whole office. 'We've been having one on Boxing Day for more than thirty years. The world and his wife usually come. Any time between noon and four, you're all welcome.'

Elliot and Darren had wrinkled their noses: a drinks party sounded much too tame. June would be away. Oliver welcomed the idea of escaping from his kids for a few hours. 'I love them, but it's usually hell on earth at home over Christmas.' George, who always went anyway, would be there with Diana, bringing his children who were over from France. I had intended taking James, but now I would have to go alone.

The Greens' house in Waterloo, only a mile from my flat, was semi-detached and spacious, the furniture and carpets shabby and worn. The Christmas decorations looked well used, as if the same things were hung in the same place year after year. Everywhere had a comfortable, lived-in look, very different from the Athertons' Ideal Home. By the time I got there it was already crowded. Barry's wife, Tess, let me in. She was a pretty woman with a tumble of grey curls and a wide, smiling mouth, wearing an emerald-green jumpsuit. She took my coat and ordered me to mingle. 'I'll do the hostess bit later and we'll have a proper talk. Right now, I'm busy with the food.'

I found Oliver and his alarmingly aggressive wife, Jennifer, waved to George, who was standing in a corner with two rather sullen teenagers, clutching his chest as if in the throes of a panic attack. There was no sign of Diana. Barry came up with a tray of drinks. 'Food's in the kitchen, help yourselves, won't you?' He'd abandoned the usual bow-tie for a Paisley cravat under a canary-yellow pullover.

Over the holiday, Jennifer had been pressing Oliver remorselessly to start his own estate agency. 'Then he won't get pissed around rotten by whoever George happens to be screwing at the moment. I told him, "Millie will go in with you."' She gave me a painful but encouraging dig. 'You would, wouldn't you, Millie? You could be his assistant.'

'Willingly,' I said, with a smile. Oliver groaned.

Over the next few hours, I well and truly mingled.

Several guests were estate agents, and we gravely discussed the state of the market. Was it up or down? One man gave me his card. 'If you should ever think of changing your job . . .' Barry introduced me to his children: Roger, the architect, an earnest man in jeans and an Arran sweater, Emma and Sadie, who would take the world by storm for a second time as soon as their children were old enough and they could resume their careers.

'Where's your other son?' I asked. 'Is he still abroad?'

Barry's perfectly groomed moustache quivered slightly. 'According to his mother, Sam won't be gracing us with his presence until New Year's Eve.'

Later, I forced myself to approach George. He eyed me appreciatively in my red dress before introducing me to his children, Annabel and Bill. 'Have you had a nice holiday?' I asked them.

They both shrugged. 'Okay.'

'I haven't a clue what teenagers get up to nowadays.' George sighed and looked harassed. 'I think they've been rather bored.' Bill rolled his eyes to confirm that this was definitely the case.

'Why don't you take them to the Cavern?' I suggested.

'Oh, Dad, would you?' Annabel pleaded. 'The girls at school will turn green if I tell them I've been to the Cavern.'

'Aren't I a bit old?' George said plaintively.

'You can just hover in the background,' I said. 'By the way, where's Diana? I thought she'd be here.'

George shrugged vaguely. 'She spent Christmas at her place. I haven't seen her in a few days.'

'Diana's horrible!' Bill burst out. 'You'll never guess what she did. She actually drew up a timetable of things for us to do – the pantomime, McDonald's, card games, charades, and idiotic films to watch on telly. She seemed to think we were children!'

Tactfully I wandered off. People had begun to leave. For the first time, I was aware of being the only youngish woman without a partner, and felt conspicuous as the crowd thinned, though I told myself I shouldn't care. I went upstairs to look for my coat. It was with a pile of others in what appeared to be Barry and Tess's untidy bedroom. I was putting it on when Tess came in, wearing her rather impish smile. 'Ah, there you are, Millie! I've been so rude. I always like to have a little chat with guests who've come for the first time, get to know them, as it were.' She sat on the bed and patted the space next to her. 'Sit down a minute.'

Under Tess's friendly questioning, I revealed all sorts of things about myself I wouldn't normally: about Diana, being demoted, James, and the awful tea at the Athertons' the day before.

'Never mind, love,' Tess said comfortingly. 'Things always turn out for the best in the long run, or so I've always found. Oh, well,' she levered herself off the bed, 'I'd better go downstairs and be the good hostess. I always feel a sense of relief when it's over, but sad too that it will be another year before I see some of our friends again. The children always found them a bit of a giggle, but they wouldn't miss their mum and dad's Boxing Day party.'

'Except Sam,' I reminded her.

'Ah, yes, Sam. He's in Mexico.' I was surprised when Tess looked at me rather speculatively, then said, 'Let me show you our Sam.' She opened the drawer in a bedside cupboard and took out a sheaf of newspaper cuttings. 'Barry doesn't know I've kept these. He's rather ashamed of Sam.' She handed me a cutting. 'That's him, in the *Daily Express*.'

A wiry young man with crew-cut hair was standing on a wall, baring his chest defiantly to the world. He held a banner aloft proclaiming, AXE THE TAX. Several policemen were reaching up in a vain attempt to grab his feet. 'He was sentenced to three months in prison or a thousand-pound fine for that,' Tess said proudly. 'Barry paid the fine and he was released, much to Sam's disgust. They rub one another up the wrong way, yet secretly they think the world of each other.'

There was a photo of Sam at the gates of Greenham Common with his then girlfriend, several of him protesting during the miners' strike. 'He hasn't been in court for years,' Tess said, slightly disappointed. 'Our three elder children are very conformist, but Sam takes after me. I used to go on CND marches when I was a girl – Barry disapproved of that, too.'

'What's he doing in Mexico? Has he gone to start a war?' I wasn't sure if I approved of Sam or not, but I admired his independent spirit.

'Oh, no. He's a record producer. He spends three or four months of the year travelling the world, taping folk songs, tribal music, that sort of thing. Then he comes home and turns them into proper recordings. He's got a studio in the attic. Much to his dad's amazement he's doing very well.' Suddenly she changed the subject, rather drastically, I thought. 'I expect your mum worries about you, still single at your age?'

'She does, yes.'

Tess hadn't changed the subject, after all. 'I worry terribly about Sam. He's thirty-three and I wish he'd establish some roots, start a family, have something more worthwhile to come home to than boring old Mum and Dad.'

A woman came in to collect her coat and Tess put the cuttings away. I thanked her for a lovely time and went home.

Over the final days of the year, I felt like two different people. There was only a skeleton staff at work and I had several half-days off, during which time I stencilled flowers on the corners of the living room and cleaned the flat from top to bottom, whistling tunelessly, happy. But when I stopped for a break, my mood would darken and I would feel restless, haunted by a sense of failure and hopelessness. There'd been a time, not long ago, when

I'd considered myself the only Cameron with an aim in life and any hope of a bright, successful future, but now I was the one with nothing to look forward to. Empty years loomed ahead, a vast, yawning abyss.

Mum had got a job in an office and would start the following week. 'Only making the tea, running a few errands.' She'd giggled merrily. 'I'll be the office junior. It's just temporary, till Alison comes.'

Trudy was gearing up for when Melanie started school in January or painting bottles for the stall she intended having every week. Should I get a hobby? I wondered. I rang Declan several times, worried that Norman would answer and whether I should engage him in conversation if he did, but there was never any reply. I badly missed Flo's flat, where I'd been quite happy to do nothing but watch the swirling lamp and listen to music. For want of something to do, on Sunday morning, I went to Mass at the Cathedral with my mother. I felt no spiritual reawakening or miraculous re-conversion in the remarkable circular building with its brilliant blue stained-glass windows, but on the way back to Flo's, I thought I might go again. Then something happened that I'd always dreaded.

Two boys were coming towards us. I hardly took them in, aware only that they were about fourteen and relatively well dressed. As they passed, one leaped at Mum and snatched the chain with K for Kate from around her neck.

Mum screamed, the boys ran only a short distance, then turned. The one who'd snatched the chain dangled it at us tauntingly, before they skipped away, laughing, almost dancing in their triumph.

'It could have happened anywhere,' Mum said later, when we were back at Flo's and she'd calmed down after I'd made us tea. 'It's not just Liverpool. It could have happened anywhere in the world.'

Something funny was going on between George and

Diana — or perhaps there was nothing going on at all. Everyone managed to glean little pieces of information and put them together to make a whole. It appeared that George had suggested Diana return home when it became obvious that she and the children weren't getting on, but had made no suggestion that she come back now that the children had gone. She'd spent Christmas alone in the house where she'd lived with her father. Even Oliver had to concede he felt sorry for the haggard little woman who stumbled round the office as if she were drunk, ignored by George. It wasn't that George was being deliberately cruel, he was taken up with the new office, which was opening in a few days' time. He appeared to have forgotten that Diana existed.

Like Oliver, I was sorry for Diana. If I'd been gutted by my demotion, she must have been feeling as if the bottom had dropped out of her world. But I was terrified that I was seeing myself in another five or ten years' time. Might I one day find myself waiting for a kind word from a man I'd been hoping would rescue me from a life of loneliness?

'Is this the girl who's just dumped a guy who runs an Aston Martin speaking?' Peter Maxwell chuckled when I phoned him. 'Men are terrified of loneliness, not just women. Sit back, have a good time, and see what happens. Don't wait for things, don't expect them, they won't come any sooner. It's like that song Flo used to play all the time. We're all dancing in the dark.'

'You're very clever,' I said admiringly. We rang off, deciding that if we were still single at forty we would live next door to each other.

I thought of James, who was going through the same experience as Diana, and wondered if I'd been too cruel, too abrupt. If he hadn't followed me to the bathroom, I would have told him tactfully in a more appropriate place. I recalled the way he'd been outside the nightclub — it seemed like years ago, but it was only a few months — when he'd said he was sick of selling cars to idiots like himself. He wanted to do something more worthwhile with his life. And the time by the Pier Head when he told me how much he loved me. He'd joined the Socialist Workers' Party to prove he wasn't shallow. We'd got on well until he decided he was in love with me; from then on, he began to fall apart. I felt sure that one day James would marry someone who didn't play such havoc with his emotions. They would have several children, and he would be back in the Conservative Party, still running his father's garage – perhaps all three – having forgotten he'd ever wanted to do anything else.

On New Year's Eve, I woke up with that aching feeling of loss again, a haunting sensation that something was missing from my life. I'd never been able to identify what it was, but in the darkness of my bedroom on the final day of the year, the knowledge came washing over me so forcefully that my body froze.

I was mourning the father I'd never known!

After a while, I made myself get up, convinced I might freeze altogether, die, if I stayed in bed any longer. I felt heavy and lethargic as I made myself a cup of tea. After I'd drunk it, I fetched the photo of my father, the one I'd found at Flo's, and stared at the sober little five-year-old, the only child not smiling. How would it have been if he'd married Mum? Would there have been a Trudy, a Declan, an Alison? If so, they would be different from the ones I knew now, and Tom O'Mara would never have existed. I remembered reading that if a time traveller went back to the beginning of time and destroyed a blade of grass, it could change the entire course of history.

It was all becoming too deep for me. Anyway, if I thought about it long enough it would be easy to cry and never stop. I took a long shower, made myself a decent breakfast for a change, then went to work, feeling only slightly better.

Stock Masterton was in turmoil. The Woolton office

had been decorated and furnished; it was ready to move into the following day. To celebrate the opening, clients would be offered refreshments and a glass of wine. There were adverts in the local press, though no mention of the food and drink, otherwise there would be a deluge of people who had no intention of buying or selling a house.

Every file had been copied, duplicates made of the wall charts. The contents of Oliver and Diana's desks were transferred. People kept rushing in, collecting papers and rushing out again. I sat behind my desk, feeling dazed. I hadn't the faintest idea what was happening to me. Should I transfer my things to Woolton or not? George seemed to have forgotten that I was to have been the receptionist, just as he'd forgotten that Diana lived and breathed. I'd typed out my notice weeks ago and put it on his desk, but it had never been acknowledged. Yesterday he'd asked me to make an appointment early in January with a firm who were erecting a small estate in Seaforth and wanted Stock Masterton to handle the sales side.

'An appointment for you?' I enquired.

'No, for yourself, of course,' George replied testily. There was mention of someone called Sandra in the new office, but no one seemed sure what job she was to do.

Oliver was no help. He complained that he was being kept in the dark and was at loggerheads with George, though George hadn't noticed, and Jennifer, Oliver's wife, was touring commercial property agents, presenting him with sheafs of offices to rent when he got home. 'She's approached her father for a loan,' he said soon after I arrived. 'I told her that Diana's like a pricked balloon, but she said, "You never know, the whole thing might start up again." Would you come in with me, Millie?' he said plaintively. 'I don't think I could do it on my own.'

'I'd be glad to,' I told him, for the umpteenth time. Even if my job turned out to be safe, after all, I didn't think I could bring myself to trust George again.

To add further to my confusion Barry Green came up

later in the morning and looked at me searchingly, as if he'd never seen me before, then gave a little 'Humph' of what sounded like approval. 'Tess has suggested I invite you round to dinner one night next week,' he said jovially. 'She said to please give her a ring if you'd like to come.'

I said I would, and meant it. I'd liked Tess enormously, and everything else about the Green household. I was thrilled to be asked to dinner.

Oliver took off again for Woolton. George was in his office, noisily slamming drawers and talking to himself. Everyone else was either at lunch or in Woolton, except for Darren, who had taken a client to view Nancy O'Mara's old house in Clement Street. I'd seriously thought of buying the place myself, cutting my mortgage by a third. After about half a minute, I realised it would be wrong, like going back instead of forward.

I leaned on my desk and thought about Flo, who would always remain a mystery, even though I knew so much about her. Had she been happy in the flat in William Square with her memories of Tommy O'Mara? Flo, with her secret lover, her secret child, the weekends spent with Mr Fritz on the Isle of Man.

George appeared, clutching his forehead dramatically, and announced that he was off to the Wig and Pen to have a pint and a panic attack. June had already left for lunch.

There'd been numerous times in the past when I'd been in the office alone, but when George slammed the door, it was like being shut in a place I'd never been before. I looked around uneasily, as if adjusting to strange new surroundings. There were decorations, very tasteful: a silver tree with 'presents' – a dozen empty boxes wrapped in red and green foil – and silver bells pinned to the walls. The fluorescent lights seemed to be humming much too loudly. Outside, people hurried past, loaded with carrier bags, and I remembered that the sales were on. The sound of the endless traffic was oddly muted, and I had a sensation of being in a different dimension, and while I could see the people, they couldn't see me. The light, bouncing off one of the silver bells on the wall behind, was reflected in turn on to the screen of the computer, and all I could see was the dark shadow of my head surrounded by a bright, blurred halo. I stared at the screen, hypnotised, and the shadows seemed to shift and change until I thought I could see a face, but it wasn't mine. The eyes were very old, set in deep, black hollows, the mouth was . . .

The phone on my desk rang stridently. I jumped and grabbed the receiver, glad to escape from the face on the screen. It was Declan.

'Could you come to Mam's early tonight?' he said eagerly. The Camerons and the Daleys had been invited to Charmian and Herbie's New Year's Eve party.

'Why?'

'You'll never guess what our Trudy's bought!' Declan paused for effect. 'Champagne! I've never had champagne before. We're going to drink to the future, before we go upstairs. Oh, and there'll be a special guest – Scotty!'

I laughed, delighted, and promised to be there by eight. When I rang off, there was no longer a face on the computer, merely the dazzling reflection of a silver bell, and the office appeared quite normal. A man tapped on the window and made the thumbs-up sign. He could see me, I was real. I smiled at him and he opened the door.

'You should bottle that smile and sell it, luv,' he said. 'You'd make a fortune.'

I knew then that I'd come through. My mind cleared, and I was myself again, but better than the self I'd been before. The future no longer seemed bleak and hopeless, but bright and full of promise. Never again would I dream about slithering footsteps on the stairs or wake up with a feeling that something was missing from my life. I stretched my arms as wide as they would go, scarcely able to contain the sensation of total happiness.

There was wine on Elliot's desk. I went over and

poured myself a glass just as the door opened and a boy came in, not very tall, with an engaging face burned dark brown by the sun. He looked so ridiculous I had to smile. A long mac swirled around his muddy, wrinkled boots, but the comical thing about him was his hat: a brown felt beehive with a wide turned-up brim and a brightly patterned band.

'Hi!' He grinned, and lines of merriment crinkled beneath his eyes and around his mouth. I realised that this wasn't a boy but a man. I recognised the young rebel in the photographs Tess Green had showed me on Boxing Day, as well as her impish smile.

I returned to my desk. 'If you're looking for your father, I'm afraid he's out, I'm not sure where.'

'Shit,' he said amiably. 'Will he be long?'

'I'm not sure about that, either.'

'How come you know who I am?'

'Your mum showed me your photograph.'

He grinned again. 'Did she now?'

The atmosphere in the office had changed yet again. There was a tingling in the air, a crackle of excitement.

'So, you're just back from Mexico,' I said.

'That's right, early this morning. Dad had left for work by then, and Mum suggested I come and make my peace. I'd promised to be home for Christmas, you see, but got delayed. Dad gets worked up about these things, not like Mum. I had to borrow his matinée-idol mac. I mislaid my coat somewhere on the journey.' He gestured vaguely. 'He'll be annoyed.'

I could feel my lips twitching and longed to laugh. 'It's a pity you didn't mislay your hat instead.'

He removed the beehive and regarded it dispassionately. His hair was yellow, like wild straw. 'All the men wear them in Mexico.'

'This is Liverpool,' I reminded him.

'So it is.' He threw the hat to me like a frisbee. I caught it and put it on. 'It suits you. Keep it, not to wear, to hang on the wall.'

'Thanks. Help yourself to a drink while you're wait-ing.'

He poured a glass of wine and perched on the edge of his father's desk. I noticed his eyes were very blue, his face neither ugly nor handsome. It was an interesting face, open and expressive, and I could tell he had a great sense of humour. 'You obviously know loads about me,' he said, 'but I bet you'll be astounded to learn I also know a lot about you. You're Millie Cameron, you live in Blundellsands, have just dumped a boyfriend called James, and are in a bit of a tizzy over your job.'

'What on earth possessed your mum to tell you that?' I wasn't sure whether to be annoyed or not.

'Because – you'll be horrified to hear this – she really fancies you for a daughter-in-law. She started pinning my ear back about it the minute I arrived home. That's the real reason she asked me to come, not to see Dad but to see you.'

I released the laughter I'd been trying to contain ever since he came in. 'That's a mad idea.'

'I just thought I'd warn you, because I understand you've been invited to dinner next week, when Mum will really get to work on you.'

'Will you be there?'

'She'll handcuff me to the chair if I refuse. What about you? Will you come?'

'Under the circumstances,' I said gravely, 'I'll have to give the matter some thought.'

I removed the Mexican hat, which suddenly felt too heavy, and laid it carefully on the desk. The door opened and Oliver came in, followed by a sullen Diana.

'Do you fancy lunch?' Sam Green said. 'We can laugh ourselves silly over my mother.' Our eyes met fleetingly and I felt something pass between us. I had no idea if it meant something or not.

I reached for my bag. 'Why not?'

And why not go to dinner at the Greens' next week. If the truth be known, I quite liked Sam Green, and fancied

Tess for a mother-in-law. Nothing might come of it, but so what? As Peter Maxwell said, we were all dancing in the dark.

All Orion/Phoenix titles are available at your local bookshop or from the following address:

Mail Order Department
Littlehampton Book Services
FREEPOST BR535
Worthing, West Sussex, BN13 3BR
telephone 01903 828503, *facsimile* 01903 828802
e-mail MailOrders@lbsltd.co.uk
(Please ensure that you include full postal address details)

Payment can be made either by credit/debit card (Visa, Mastercard, Access and Switch accepted) or by sending a £ Sterling cheque or postal order made payable to *Littlehampton Book Services*.
DO NOT SEND CASH OR CURRENCY.

Please add the following to cover postage and packing

UK and BFPO:
£1.50 for the first book, and 50p for each additional book to a maximum of £3.50

Overseas and Eire:
£2.50 for the first book plus £1.00 for the second book and 50p for each additional book ordered

---

BLOCK CAPITALS PLEASE

name of cardholder ....

address of cardholder ....

....

....

....

postcode ....

delivery address
(if different from cardholder)

....

....

....

....

postcode ....

☐ I enclose my remittance for £..

☐ please debit my Mastercard/Visa/Access/Switch (delete as appropriate)

card number [ ][ ][ ][ ][ ][ ][ ][ ][ ][ ][ ][ ][ ][ ][ ][ ][ ]

expiry date [ ][ ][ ][ ]   Switch issue no. [ ][ ]

signature ....

prices and availability are subject to change without notice